The first romance stories Stephanie Laurens read were set against the backdrop of Regency England, and these continue to exert a special attraction for her. As an escape from the dry world of professional science, Stephanie started writing Regency romances, eight of which were published in the UK. Subsequently, she turned her hand to longer historical romances set in the Regency period. The first, *Captain Jack's Woman*, was published in the US by Avon Books in 1997. *A Secret Love* and *All About Love*, the titles featured in *Love at Last*, were among the first books she wrote about the masterful, arrogant Cynster clan. The other Cynster novels are: *Devil's Bride*, *A Rake's Vow*, *Scandal's Bride*, *A Rogue's Proposal*, *All About Passion*, *The Promise in a Kiss*, *On a Wild Night*, *On a Wicked Dawn*, *The Perfect Lover*, *The Ideal Bride* and *What Price Love?*. She has also written five books about the seven dashing bachelors of the Bastion Club: *The Lady Chosen*, *A Gentleman's Honour*, *A Lady of His Own*, *A Fine Passion* and *To Distraction*.

Stephanie's last seventeen releases have been *New York Times*, *USA Today* and *Publishers Weekly* bestsellers. Stephanie lives in a leafy suburb of Melbourne with her husband and two daughters, along with two cats, Shakespeare and Marlowe.

Visit Stephanie's website at
www.stephanielaurens.com

STEPHANIE LAURENS

Love at Last

TWO CLASSIC CYNSTER NOVELS

A SECRET LOVE

&

ALL ABOUT LOVE

AVON BOOKS

An imprint of HarperCollins*Publishers*

AVON BOOKS
An imprint of HarperCollins*Publishers*

A Secret Love first published in the USA in 2000
and *All About Love* first published in the USA in 2001
by Avon Books, an imprint of HarperCollins*Publishers*, Inc.
This combined edition first published in Australia in 2006
by HarperCollins*Publishers* Australia Pty Limited
ABN 36 009 913 517
www.harpercollins.com.au

Published by arrangement with HarperCollins*Publishers*, Inc.,
New York, NY, USA. All rights reserved.

HarperCollins*Publishers*
25 Ryde Road, Pymble, Sydney, NSW 2073, Australia
31 View Road, Glenfield, Auckland 10, New Zealand
77–85 Fulham Palace Road, London, W6 8JB, United Kingdom
2 Bloor Street East, 20th floor, Toronto, Ontario M4W 1A8, Canada
10 East 53rd Street, New York NY 10022, USA

Laurens, Stephanie.
  Love at last: two classic Cynster novels.
  ISBN 13: 978 0 7322 8325 4.
  ISBN 10: 0 7322 8325 6.
  1. Cynster family (Fictitious characters).
  I. Title. II. Title: Secret love. III. Title: All about love.
A823.3

Cover photograph by Mary Javorek
Stephanie Laurens lettering on cover by Patricia Barrow
Cover design adapted by Katy Wright, HarperCollins Design Studio
Author photograph by James Flaagan
Typeset in 10/12 Times by Kirby Jones
Printed and bound in Australia by Griffin Press on 70gsm Bulky Book Ivory

5 4 3 2 1   06 07 08 09

Love at Last

A Secret Love

The Bar Cynster Family Tree

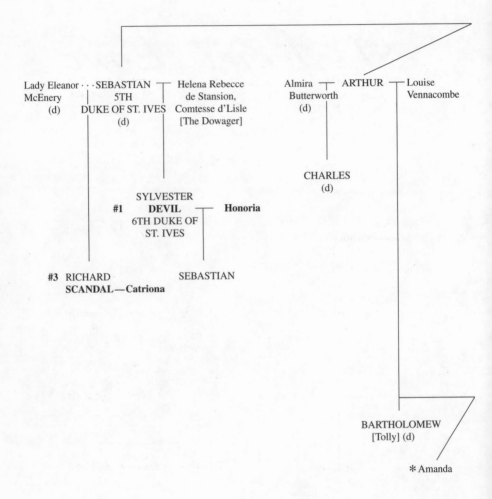

Lady Eleanor · · ·SEBASTIAN ⊤ Helena Rebecce
McEnery | 5TH | de Stansion,
(d) DUKE OF ST. IVES Comtesse d'Lisle
(d) [The Dowager]

Almira ⊤ ARTHUR ⊤ Louise
Butterworth | Vennacombe
(d)

CHARLES
(d)

SYLVESTER
#1 DEVIL ⊤ Honoria
6TH DUKE OF
ST. IVES

SEBASTIAN

#3 RICHARD
SCANDAL—Catriona

BARTHOLOMEW
[Tolly] (d)

* Amanda

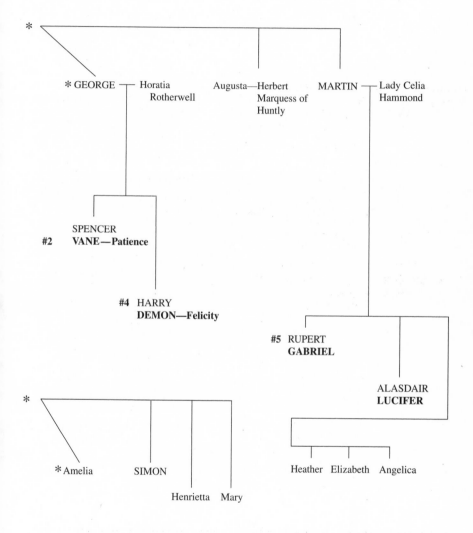

MALE CYNSTERS named in capitals   *** denotes twins**

PROLOGUE

April 17, 1820
Morwellan Park, Somerset

D isaster stared her in the face.
    Again.

Seated at her desk in the library of Morwellan Park, Alathea Morwellan gazed at the letter she held, barely seeing the precise script of her family's agent. The substance of the missive was burned into her brain. Its last paragraph read:

I fear, my dear, that my sentiments concur with yours. I can see no evidence that we have made any mistake.

No mistake. She'd suspected, virtually expected that that would be the case, yet …

Exhaling, Alathea laid the letter down. Her hand shook. A youthful cheer reached her, borne on the breeze wafting through the long windows. She hesitated, then stood and glided to the French windows standing open to the south lawn.

On the rolling expanse separating the terrace from the ornamental lake, her stepbrothers and stepsisters played an exuberant game of catch. Sunlight flashed on one fair head—Alathea's eldest stepbrother, Charlie, leaped high and snatched the ball from the air, denying Jeremy, only ten but always game. Despite his emerging elegance, Charlie, nineteen, was good-naturedly caught up in the game, indulging his juniors, Jeremy and Augusta, just six. Their older sisters, Mary, eighteen, and Alice, seventeen, had also joined in.

The entire household was currently in the throes of preparing to remove to London so Mary and Alice could be introduced to the ton. Nevertheless, both girls threw themselves into the game, ringlets framing innocently happy faces, the serious business of their come-outs in no way dampening their joy in simple pleasures.

A whoop from Charlie signaled a wild throw—the ball flew over all three girls and bounced toward the house. It struck the flags of the path and bounced even higher, clearing the shallow steps to land on the terrace. Two more diminishing bounces, and it tumbled over the library threshold and rolled along the polished boards. Raising her skirt, Alathea placed one foot on the ball, stilling it. She considered it, then looked out to see Mary and Alice racing, laughing and gasping, toward the terrace. Stooping, Alathea scooped up the ball; balancing it on one palm, she strolled out onto the terrace.

Mary and Alice skidded to a halt before the steps, laughing and grinning.

"Me, Allie, *me!*"

"No! Al-a-the-a! *Sweet* Allie—me!"

Alathea waited as if weighing her choice while little Augusta, left far in the rear, panted up. She stopped some yards behind the older girls and raised her angel's face to Alathea.

With a grin, Alathea lobbed the ball over the older girls' heads. Open-mouthed, they watched it soar past. With a gurgling laugh, Augusta pounced, grabbed the ball, and raced away down the slope.

Flashing Alathea conspiratorial grins, Mary called after Augusta, Alice cheered, and both set out in pursuit.

Alathea remained on the terrace, the warmth suffusing her owing nothing to the bright sunshine. A movement beneath a large oak caught her eye. Her stepmother, Serena, and her father, the earl, waved from the bench where they sat indulgently watching their children.

Smiling, Alathea returned the wave. Looking back at her stepsiblings, now headed in a wild melee toward the lake, she drew in a long breath, then, lips firming, turned back into the library.

Crossing to the desk, she let her gaze dwell on the tapestries gracing the walls, the paintings in their gilded frames, the leather-bound, gilt-encrusted spines lining the shelves. The long library was one of the features of Morwellan Park, principal seat of the earls of Meredith. Morwellans had occupied the Park for centuries, from long before the earldom's creation in the fourteenth. The present gracious house had been built by her great-grandfather, the grounds expertly landscaped under her grandfather's exacting eye.

Regaining the large carved desk, hers for the last eleven years, Alathea looked at the letter lying on the blotter. Any chance that she would crumple in the face of such adversity as the letter portended was past. Nothing—*no one*— was going to steal the simple peace she'd sacrificed the last eleven years of her life to secure for her family.

Gazing at Wiggs's letter, she considered the enormity of what she faced, too practical not to recognize the difficulties and dangers. But it wasn't the first time she'd stood on the lip of the abyss and stared ruin—financial and social—in the face.

Picking up the letter, she sat and reread it. It had arrived in reply to an urgent missive from her dispatched post haste to London three days before. Three days before, when her world had, for the second time in her life, been rocked to its foundations.

While dusting her father's room, a maid had discovered a legal document stuffed inside a large vase. Luckily, the girl had had the wit to take the paper to the housekeeper and cook, Mrs. Figgs, who had immediately bustled into the library to lay it before her.

Satisfied she'd missed nothing in Wiggs's reply, Alathea set his letter aside. Her glance strayed to the left desk drawer where the wretched document at the heart of the matter lay. A promissory note. She didn't need to read it again— every last detail was etched in her brain. The note committed the earl of Meredith to pay upon call a sum that exceeded the present total worth of the earldom. In return, the earl would receive a handsome percentage of the profits realized by the Central East Africa Gold Company.

There was, of course, no guarantee such profits would ever materialize, and neither she, nor Wiggs, nor any of his peers, had so much as heard of the Central East Africa Gold Company.

If any good would have come of burning the note, she would happily have built a bonfire on the Aubusson rug, but it was only a copy. Her dear, vague, hopelessly impractical father had, entirely without understanding what he was about, signed away his family's future. Wiggs had confirmed that the note was legally sound and executable, so if the call was made for the amount stipulated, the family would be bankrupt. They would lose not only the minor properties and Morwellan House in London, all still mortgaged to the hilt, but also Morwellan Park, and everything that went with it.

If she wished to ensure that Morwellans remained at Morwellan Park, that Charlie and his sons had their ancestral home intact to inherit, that her stepsisters had their come-outs and the chance to make the marriages they deserved, she was going to have to find some way out of this.

Just as she had before.

Absentmindedly tapping a pencil on the blotter, Alathea gazed unseeing at the portrait of her great-grandfather, facing her down the long length of the room.

This wasn't the first time her father had brought the earldom to the brink of ruin; she'd faced the prospect of abject poverty before. For a gentlewoman reared within the elite circle of the haut ton, the prospect had been—and still was—frightening, all the more so for being somewhat beyond her ken. Abject poverty she had no more than a hazy notion of—she had no wish for either herself or, more importantly, her innocent siblings, to gain any closer acquaintance with the state.

At least, this time, she was more mature, more knowlegeable—better able to deal with the threat. The first time ...

Her thoughts flowed back to that afternoon eleven years before when, as she was poised to make her come-out, fate had forced her to stop, draw breath, and change direction. From that day, she'd carried the burden of managing the family's finances, working tirelessly to rebuild the family's fortunes, all the while maintaining an outward show of affluence. She'd insisted the boys go to Eton, and then to Oxford; Charlie would go up for the autumn term in September. She'd scrimped and saved to take Mary and Alice to town for their come-outs, and to have sufficient funds to puff them off in style.

The household was eagerly anticipating removing to London in just a few days. For herself, she'd anticipated savoring a subtle victory over fate when her stepsisters made their curtsies to the ton.

For long moments, Alathea stared down the room, considering, assessing—rejecting. This time, frugality would not serve her cause—no amount of scrimping could amass the amount needed to meet the obligation stipulated in the note. Turning, she pulled open the left drawer. Retrieving the note, she perused it again, carefully evaluating. Considering the very real possibility that the Central East Africa Gold Company was a fraud.

The company had that feel to it—no legitimate enterprise would have cozened her father, patently unversed in business dealings, into committing such a huge sum to a speculative venture, certainly not without some discreet assessment of whether he could meet the obligation. The more she considered, the more she was convinced that neither she nor Wiggs had made any mistake—the Central East Africa Gold Company was a swindle.

She was not at all inclined to meekly surrender all she'd fought for, all she'd spent the last eleven years securing—all her family's future—to feather the nest of a pack of dastardly rogues.

There had to be a way out—it was up to her to find it.

CHAPTER

One

May 6, 1820
London

Swirls of mist wreathed Gabriel Cynster's shoulders as he prowled the porch of St. Georges' Church, just off Hanover Square. The air was chill, the gloom within the porch smudged here and there by weak shafts of light thrown by the street lamps.

It was three o'clock; fashionable London lay sleeping. The coaches ferrying late-night revelers home had ceased to rumble—an intense but watchful quiet had settled over the town.

Reaching the end of the porch, Gabriel swung around. Eyes narrowed, he scanned the stone tunnel formed by the front of the church and the tall columns supporting its facade. The mist eddied and swirled, obscuring his view. He'd stood in the same place a week before, watching Demon, one of his cousins, drive off with his new wife. He'd felt a sudden chill—a premonition, a presentiment; perhaps it had been of this.

Three o'clock in the porch of St. Georges—that was what the note had said. He'd been half inclined to set it aside, a poor joke assuredly, but something in the words had tweaked an impulse more powerful than curiosity. The note had been penned in desperation, although, despite close analysis, he couldn't see why he was so sure of that. The mysterious countess, whoever she was, had written simply and directly requesting this meeting so she could explain her need for his aid.

So he was here—where was she?

On the thought, the city's bells tolled, the reverberations stirring the heavy blanket of the night. Not all the belltowers tolled the night watches; enough did to set up a strange cadence, a pattern of sound repeated in different registers. The muted notes faded, then died. Silence, again, descended.

Gabriel stirred. Impatient, he started back along the porch, his stride slow, easy.

And she appeared, stepping from the deep shadows about the church door. Mist clung to her skirts as she turned, slowly, regally, to face him. She was cloaked and veiled, as impenetrable, secret, and mysterious as the night.

Gabriel narrowed his eyes. Had she been there all along? Had he walked past her without seeing or sensing her presence? His stride unfaltering, he continued toward her. She lifted her head as he neared, but only slightly.

She was very tall. Halting with only a foot between them, Gabriel discovered he couldn't see over her head, which was amazing. He stood well over six feet tall; the countess had to be six feet tall herself. Despite the heavy cloak, one glance had been enough to assure him all her six feet were in perfect proportion.

"Good morning, Mr. Cynster. Thank you for coming."

He inclined his head, jettisoning any wild thought that this was some witless prank—a youth dressed as a woman. The few steps she'd taken, the way she'd turned—to his experienced senses, her movements defined her as female. And her tone was soft and low, the very essence of woman.

A mature woman—she was definitely not young.

"Your note said you needed my help."

"I do." After a moment, she added, "My family does."

"Your family?" In the gloom, her veil was impenetrable; he couldn't see even a hint of her chin or her lips.

"My stepfamily, I should say."

Her perfume reached him, exotic, alluring. "Perhaps we'd better define just what your problem is, and why you think I can help."

"You can help. I would never have asked to meet you—would never reveal what I'm about to tell you—if I didn't know you could help." She paused, then drew breath. "My problem concerns a promissory note signed by my late husband."

"*Late* husband?"

She inclined her head. "I'm a widow."

"How long ago did your husband die?"

"Over a year ago."

"So his estate has been probated."

"Yes. The title and entailed estate are now with my stepson, Charles."

"Stepson?"

"I was my husband's second wife. We were married some years ago—for him, it was a very late second marriage. He was ill for some time before his death. All his children were by his first wife."

He hesitated, then asked, "Am I to understand that you've taken your late husband's children under your wing?"

"Yes. I consider their welfare my responsibility. It's because of that—them—that I'm seeking your aid." Gabriel studied her veiled countenance, knowing she was watching his. "You mentioned a promissory note."

"I should explain that my husband had a weakness for engaging in speculative ventures. Over his last years, the family's agent and I endeavored to keep his investments in such schemes to a minimum, in which endeavors we were largely successful. However, three weeks ago, a maid stumbled on a legal paper, tucked away and clearly forgotten. It was a promissory note."

"To which company?"

"The Central East Africa Gold Company. Have you heard of it?" He shook his head. "Not a whisper."

"Neither has our agent, nor any of his colleagues."

"The company's address should be on the note."

"It's not—just the name of the firm of solicitors who drew up the document."

Gabriel juggled the pieces of the jigsaw she was handing him, aware each piece had been carefully vetted first. "This note—do you have it?"

From beneath her cloak, she drew out a rolled parchment.

Taking it, Gabriel inwardly raised his brows—she'd certainly come prepared. Despite straining his eyes, he'd caught not a glimpse of the gown beneath her voluminous cloak. Her hands, too, were covered, encased in leather gloves long enough to reach the cuffs of her sleeves. Unrolling the parchment, he turned so the light from the street lamps fell on the single page.

The promissor's signature—the first thing he looked at—was covered by a piece of thick paper fixed in place with sealing wax. He looked at the countess.

Calmly, she stated, "You don't need to know the family's name."

"Why not?"

"That will become evident when you read the note."

Squinting in the poor light, he did so. "This appears to be legal." He read it again, then looked up. "The investment is certainly large and, given it is speculative, therefore constitutes a very great risk. If the company had not been fully investigated and appropriately vouched for, then the investment was certainly unwise. I do not, however, see your problem."

"The problem lies in the fact that the amount promised is considerably more than the present total worth of the earldom."

Gabriel looked again at the amount written on the note and swiftly recalculated, but he hadn't misread. "If this sum will clean out the earldom's coffers, then …"

"Precisely," the countess said with the decisiveness that seemed characteristic. "I mentioned that my husband was fond of speculating. The family has for more than a decade existed on the very brink of financial ruin, from before I married into it. After our marriage, I discovered the truth. After that, I oversaw all financial matters. Between us, my husband's agent and I were able to hold things together and keep the family's head above water."

Her voice hardened in a vain attempt to hide her vulnerability. "That note, however, would be the end. Our problem in a nutshell is that the note does indeed appear legal, in which case, if it is executed and the money called in, the family will be bankrupt."

"Which is why you don't wish me to know your name."

"You know the haut ton—we move in the same circles. If any hint of our financial straits, even leaving aside the threat of the note, was to become common knowledge, the family would be socially ruined. The children would never be able to take their rightful places in our world."

The call to arms was a physical tug. Gabriel shifted. "Children. You mentioned Charles, the youthful earl. What others?"

She hesitated, then said, "There are two girls, Maria and Alicia—we're in town now because they're to be presented. I've saved for years so they could have their come-outs …" Her voice suspended. After a moment, she continued, "And there are two others still in the schoolroom, and an older cousin, Seraphina; she's part of the family, too."

Gabriel listened, more to her tone than her words. Her devotion sounded clearly—the caring, the commitment. The anxiety. Whatever else the countess was concealing, she couldn't hide that.

Raising the note, he studied the signature of the company's chairman. Composed of bold, harsh strokes, the signature was illegible, certainly not one he knew. "You didn't say why you thought I could help."

His tone was vague—he'd already guessed the answer.

She straightened her shoulders. "We—our agent and I—believe the company is a fraud, a venture undertaken purely to milk funds from gullible investors. The note itself is suspicious in that neither the company's address nor its principals are noted, and there's also the fact that a legitimate speculative company accepting a promissory note for such an amount would have sought some verification that the amount could indeed be paid."

"No check was made?"

"It would have been referred to our agent. As you might imagine, our bank has been in close touch with him for years. We've checked as far as we can without raising suspicions and found nothing to change our view. The Central East Africa Gold Company looks like a fraud." She drew in a tight breath. "And if that's so, then if we can gather enough evidence to prove it and present such evidence in the Chancery Court, the promissory note could be declared invalid. But we must succeed before the note is executed, and it's already over a year since it was signed."

Rerolling the note, Gabriel considered her; despite the veil and cloak, he felt he knew a great deal of her. "Why me?"

He handed her the note; she took it, slipping it once more under her cloak. "You've built something of a reputation for exposing fraudulent schemes, and"—lifting her head, she studied him—"you're a Cynster."

He almost laughed. "Why does that matter?"

"Because Cynsters like challenges."

He looked at her veiled face. "True," he purred.

Her chin rose another notch. "And because I know I can entrust the family's secret to a Cynster."

He raised a brow, inviting explanation.

She hesitated, then stated, "If you agree to help us, I must ask you to swear that you will not at any time seek to identify me or my family." She halted, then went on, "And if you don't agree to help, I know I can trust you not to mention this meeting, or anything you deduce from it, to anyone."

Gabriel raised both brows; he regarded her with veiled amusement, and a certain respect. She had a boldness rarely found in women—only that could account for this charade, well thought out, well executed. The countess had all her wits about her; she'd studied her mark and had laid her plans—her enticements—well.

She was deliberately offering him a challenge.

Did she imagine, he wondered, that he would focus solely on the company? Was the other challenge she was flaunting before him intentional, or ...?

Did it matter?

"If I agree to help you, where do you imagine we would start?" The question was out before he'd considered—once he had, he inwardly raised his brows at the "we."

"The company's solicitors. Or at least the ones who drew up the note—Thurlow and Brown. Their name's on the note."

"But not their address."

"No, but if they're a legitimate firm—and they must be, don't you think?—then they should be easy to trace. I could have done that myself, but ..."

"But you didn't think your agent would approve of what you have in mind once you discover the address, so you didn't want to ask him?"

Despite her veil, he could imagine the look she cast him, the narrowing of her eyes, the firming of her lips. She nodded, again that definite affirmation. "Precisely. I imagine some form of search will be required. I doubt a legitimate firm of solicitors will volunteer information on one of their clients."

Gabriel wasn't so sure—he'd know once he located Thurlow and Brown.

"We'll need to learn who the principals of the company are, and then learn the details of the company's business."

"Prospective business." He shot her a look, wishing he could see through her veil. "You do realize that any investigating risks alerting the company's principals? If the company is the sham you think it, then any hint of too close interest from anyone, particularly and especially me, will activate the call on promised funds. That's how swindlers will react—they'll grab what they've got and disappear before anyone can learn too much."

They'd been standing for more than half an hour in the mausoleumlike porch. The temperature was dropping as dawn approached; the chill of the mists was deepening. Gabriel was aware of it, but in his cloak he wasn't cold. Beneath her heavy cloak the countess was tense, almost shivering.

Lips tightening, he suppressed the urge to draw her closer and ruthlessly, relentlessly stated, "By investigating the company, you risk the note being called in and your family being made bankrupt." If she was determined to brave the fire, she needed to understand she could get burned.

Her head rose; her spine stiffened. "If I don't investigate the company and prove it's a fraud, my family will *definitely* be bankrupt."

He listened but could detect no hint of wavering, of anything less than informed but unshakable resolution. He nodded. "Very well. If you've made the decision to investigate the company, then yes, I'll help you."

If he'd expected gushing thanks, he'd have been disappointed—luckily, he'd had no such expectation. She stood still, studying him. "And you'll swear …?"

Stifling a sigh, he raised his right hand. "Before God, I swear—"

"On your name as a Cynster."

He blinked at her, then continued, "On my name as a Cynster, that I will not seek to identify you or your family. All right?"

Her sigh fell like silk in the night. "Yes." She relaxed, losing much of her stiff tension.

His increased proportionately. "When gentlemen reach an agreement, they usually shake hands."

She hesitated, then extended one hand.

He grasped it, then changed his hold, fingers sliding about hers until his thumb rested in her palm. Then he drew her to him.

He heard her indrawn breath, felt the sudden leaping of her pulse, sensed the shock that seared her. With his other hand, he tipped up her chin, angling her lips to his.

"I thought we were going to shake hands." Her words were a breathless whisper.

"You're no gentleman." He studied her face; the glint of her eyes was all he could see through the fine black veil, but with her head tipped up, he could discern the outline of her lips. "When a gentleman and a lady seal a pact, they do it like this." Lowering his head, he touched his lips to hers.

Beneath the silk, they were soft, resilient, lush—pure temptation. They barely moved under his, yet their inherent promise was easy to sense, very easy for him to read. That kiss should have registered as the most chaste of his career—instead, it was a spark set to tinder, prelude to a conflagration. The knowledge—absolute and definite—shook him. He lifted his head, looked down on her veiled face, and wondered if she knew.

Her fingers, still locked in his, trembled. Through his fingers under her chin, he felt the fragile tension that had gripped her. His gaze on her face, he raised her hand and brushed a kiss on her gloved fingers, then, reluctantly, he released her. "I'll find out where Thurlow and Brown hang their plaque and see what I can learn. I assume you'll want to be kept informed. How will I contact you?"

She stepped back. "I'll contact you."

He felt her gaze scan his face, then, still brittlely tense, she gathered herself and inclined her head. "Thank you. Good night."

The mists parted then reformed behind her as she descended the porch steps. And then she was gone, leaving him alone in the shadows.

Gabriel drew in a deep breath. The fog carried the sounds of her departure to his ears. Her shoes tapped along the pavement, then harness clinked. Heavier feet thumped and a latch clicked, then, after a pause, clicked again. Seconds later came the slap of reins on a horse's rump, then carriage wheels rattled, fading into the night.

It was half past three in the morning, and he was wide awake.

Lips lifting self-deprecatingly, Gabriel stepped down from the porch. Drawing his cloak about him, he set out to walk the short distance to his house.

He felt energized, ready to take on the world. The previous morning, before the countess's note arrived, he'd been sitting morosely over his coffee wondering how to extract himself from the mire of disaffected boredom into which he'd sunk. He'd considered every enterprise, every possible endeavor, every entertainment—none had awakened the smallest spark of interest.

The countess's note had stirred not just interest but curiosity and speculation. His curiosity had largely been satisfied; his speculation, however ...

Here was a courageous, defiant widow staunchly determined to defend her family—stepfamily, no less—against the threat of dire poverty, against the certainty of becoming poor relations, if not outcasts. Her enemies were the nebulous backers of a company thought to be fraudulent. The situation called for decisive action tempered by caution, with all investigations and inquiries needing to remain covert and clandestine. That much, she'd told him.

So what did he know?

She was an Englishwoman, unquestionably gently bred—her accent, her bearing and her smooth declaration that they moved in similar circles had settled that. And she knew her Cynsters well. Not only had she stated it, her whole presentation had been artfully designed to appeal to his Cynster instincts.

Gabriel swung into Brook Street. One thing the countess didn't know was that he rarely reacted impulsively these days. He'd learned to keep his instincts in check—his business dealings demanded it. He also had a definite dislike of being manipulated—in any field. In this case, however, he'd decided to play along.

The countess was, after all, an intriguing challenge in her own right. All close to six feet of her. And a lot of that six feet was leg, a consideration guaranteed to fix his rakish interest. As for her lips and the delights they promised ... he'd already decided they'd be his.

Occasionally, liaisons happened like that—one look, one touch, and he'd know. He couldn't, however, recall being affected quite so forcefully before, nor committing so decisively and definitely to the chase. And its ultimate outcome.

Again, energy surged through him. This—the countess and her problem—was precisely what he needed to fill the present lack in his life: a challenge and a conquest combined.

Reaching his house, he climbed the steps and let himself in. He shut and bolted the door, then glanced toward the parlor. In the bookcase by the fireplace resided a copy of *Burke's Peerage*.

Lips quirking, he strode for the stairs. If he hadn't promised not to seek out her identity, he would have made straight for the bookcase and, despite the hour, ascertained just which earl had recently died to be succeeded by a son called Charles. There couldn't be that many. Instead, feeling decidedly virtuous, not something that often occurred, he headed for his bed, all manner of plans revolving in his head.

He'd promised he wouldn't seek out her identity—he hadn't promised he wouldn't persuade her to reveal all to him.

Her name. Her face. Those long legs. And more.

"*Well?* How did it go?"

Raising her veil, Alathea stared at the group of eager faces clustered about the bottom of the stairs. She had only that instant crossed the threshold of Morwellan House in Mount Street; behind her, Crisp, the butler, slid the bolts home and turned, eager not to miss any of her tale.

The question had come from Nellie, Alathea's maid, presently wrapped in an old paisley bedrobe. Surrounding Nellie in various stages of deshabille stood other members of Alathea's most stalwart band of supporters—the household's senior servants.

"Come now, m'lady, don't keep us in suspense."

That from Figgs, the cook-housekeeper. The others all nodded—Folwell, Alathea's groom, his forelock bobbing, Crisp, joining them, carrying the rolled promissory note she had handed him for safekeeping.

Alathea inwardly sighed. In what other tonnish establishment would a lady of the house, returning from an illicit rendezvous at four in the morning, meet with such a reception? Quelling her skittish nerves, telling herself that the fact he'd kissed her didn't show, she set her veil back. "He agreed."

"Well—there now!" Thin as a rake, Miss Helm, the governess, nervously clutched her pink wrapper. "I'm sure Mr. Cynster will take care of it all and expose these *dreadful* men."

"Praise be," intoned Connor, Serena's severe dresser.

"Indeed"—Alathea walked forward into the light thrown by the candles Nellie, Figgs, and Miss Helm were holding—"but you should all be in bed. He's agreed to help—there's nothing more to hear." She caught Nellie's eye.

Nellie sniffed, but buttoned her lip.

Alathea shooed the others off, then headed up the stairs, Nellie on her heels, lighting her way.

"So what happened?" Nellie hissed as they reached the gallery.

"Shh!" Alathea gestured down the corridor. Nellie grumbled but held her tongue as they passed Alathea's parents' rooms, then Mary's and Alice's, eventually reaching her room at the corridor's end.

Nellie shut the door behind them. Alathea untied her cloak, then let it fall— Nellie caught it as she stepped away.

"So now, my fine miss—you're not going to tell me he didn't see through your disguise?"

"Of course he didn't—I told you he wouldn't." He wouldn't have kissed her if he had. Sinking onto her dressing table stool, Alathea pulled pins from her hair, freeing the thick mass from the unaccustomed chignon. She normally wore her hair in a knot on the top of her head with the strands about her face puffed to form a living frame. It was an old-fashioned style but it suited her. The chignon had suited her, too, but the unusual style had pulled her hair in different directions—her scalp hurt.

Nellie came to help, frowning as she searched out pins in the silky soft mass. "I can't believe after all the years you two spent rollin' about the fields that he wouldn't simply look at you, veil and cloak or no, and instantly know you."

"You forget—despite the years we spent 'rollin' about the fields,' Rupert has barely seen me for over a decade. Just the odd meeting here and there."

"He didn't recognize your voice?"

"No. My tone was quite different." She'd spoken as she would to Augusta, her tone warm and low, not tart and waspish as when she normally spoke with him. Except for those few breathless moments ... but she didn't think he'd ever heard her breathless before. She couldn't recall ever feeling so nervous and skittish before. With a sigh, she let her head tip back as her hair finally fell loose. "You're not giving me sufficient credit. I'm a very good actress, after all."

Nellie humphed but didn't argue. She started to brush Alathea's long hair.

Closing her eyes, Alathea relaxed. She excelled at charades; she could think herself into a part very well, as long as she understood the character. In this case, that was easy. "I kept to the truth as far as possible—he truly thinks I'm a countess."

Nellie humphed. "I still can't see why you couldn't simply write him a nice letter, asking him to look into this company for you."

"Because I would have had to sign it 'Alathea Morwellan.' "

"He would have done it, I'm sure."

"Oh, he wouldn't have *refused*, but what he would have done was refer it to his agent—that Mr. Montague. Without telling Rupert *why* it's so desperately needful to prove this company a fraud, it wouldn't have seemed important— important enough to stir him personally to action."

"I can't see why you don't just tell him—"

"No!" Eyes opening, Alathea straightened. For an instant, the lines between mistress and maid were clear—there in the matriarchal light in Alathea's eyes, in her stern expression, and in the suddenly wary look in Nellie's face.

Alathea let her expression ease; she hesitated, but Nellie was the only one with whom she dared discuss her plans, the only one who knew them all. The only one she trusted with them all. While she suspected that meant she was trusting the entire little band downstairs, as the others never presumed to mention it, she could live with that. She had to talk to someone. Drawing in a breath, she settled on the stool. "Believe it or not, Nellie, I still have my pride." She shut her eyes as Nellie resumed her brushing. "Sometimes, I think it's all I truly have left. I won't risk it by telling even him all. No one knows just how close to ruin we came—what depth of ruin we now face."

"He'd be sympathetic, I should think. He wouldn't noise it abroad."

"That's not the point. Not with him. I don't think you can imagine, Nellie, just how rich the Cynsters are. Even I have trouble assimilating the sums I know he regularly deals with."

"Can't see why it matters, meself."

Alathea felt the familiar tugs as Nellie started braiding her hair. "Let's just say that while I can cope with fraudulent companies and imminent disaster, the one thing I really don't think I could face is pity."

His pity.

Nellie sighed. "Ah, well, if that's the way it must be …" Alathea sensed her fatalistic shrug. After a moment, Nellie asked, "But how'd you get him to agree to help if'n you didn't tell him about the family all but being rolled up if that wretched company asks for their money?"

"*That*"—Alathea opened her eyes—"was the main point of my masquerade. I did tell him. All of it. I could hardly expect him to help without knowing the details, and he certainly wouldn't have helped if there hadn't been a real family and a real threat. He's never been easy to stir to action, but he is a Cynster and they always respond to certain prods. He had to be convinced of both the family and the threat, but the way I told it, it's the countess's family. I cast my father as my dead husband, with me as the countess, his second wife, and all the children as my stepchildren, instead of my stepbrothers and stepsisters. Serena I made into a cousin."

She paused, remembering.

"What happened?"

Alathea looked up to see Nellie regarding her in concern.

"It's no use telling me something didn't go wrong—I can always tell when you look like that."

"Nothing went *wrong*." She wasn't about to tell Nellie about that kiss. "I just hadn't thought of names for all the children. I used Charles for Charlie— it's a common enough name after all—but I hadn't expected Rupert to ask me about the others. When he did … well, I was so deep in being the countess, I couldn't really think. I called them to mind and had to put names to them instantly or he would have grown suspicious."

Dropping her completed braid, Nellie stared at her. "You didn't go and call them by their real names?"

Rising, Alathea stepped away from the table. "Not exactly."

Nellie started unlacing her gown. "So what did you call them?"

"Maria, Alicia, and Seraphina. I skipped the others."

"So what happens the first time he finds himself in a room with one of those books that list the lot of you? All he'll have to do will be to look up the earls—you being a countess—and it'll jump off the page at him. And he'll know who you are then, too." Straightening, Nellie helped her out of her gown. "Wouldn't want to be in your shoes then, miss—not when he finds out. He won't be pleased."

"I know." Alathea shivered, and prayed Nellie thought it was because she was cold. She knew exactly what would happen if luck dealt against her and Rupert Melrose Cynster discovered *she* was his mysterious countess—that she was the woman he'd kissed in the porch of St. Georges.

All hell would break lose.

He didn't have a temper, any more than she did.

Which meant he didn't appear to have one, until he lost it.

"That's why," she continued, head emerging from the nightgown Nellie had thrown over her, "I made him swear not to try and identify me. The way I have it planned, he need never learn the truth."

She knew he wouldn't appreciate having the wool pulled over his eyes. He had a deep, very real dislike of any form of deception. That, she suspected, was what lay behind his growing reputation for unmasking business frauds. "For now, everything's perfect—he's met the countess, heard her story, and agreed to help. He actually wants to help—wants to expose these men and their company. That's important." Whether she was reassuring Nellie or herself she wasn't sure; her stomach hadn't relaxed since he'd kissed her. "Lady Celia's forever complaining about him being too indolent, too bored with life. The countess's problem will give him something to work on, something that interests him."

Nellie snorted. "Next you'll be saying being gulled will be good for him."

Alathea had the grace to blush. "It won't hurt him. And I'll be careful, so there's no reason to think he ever will know that he's been 'gulled,' as you put it. I'll make sure he never meets the countess in daylight, or in any decent illumination. I'll always wear a veil. With heels to make me even taller"—she gestured to the high-heeled shoes she'd discarded by the dressing table—"and that perfume"—another wave indicated the Venetian glass flacon standing before her mirror—"which is nothing like anything Alathea Morwellan has ever worn, I really do not see that there's any danger of him knowing me."

Alathea glided to the bed; Nellie bustled ahead, turning down the covers and removing the copper warming pan. Slipping between the sheets, Alathea sighed. "So all is well. And when the company's exposed and her family saved, the countess will simply"—she waved gracefully—"disappear in a drift of mist."

Nellie humphed. She shuffled about, tidying things away, hanging up Alathea's clothes. From the wardrobe, she looked back at Alathea. "I still don't see why you couldn't simply go and see him, and tell him to his face what this is all about. Pride's all very well, but this is serious."

"It's not only pride." Lying back, Alathea gazed at the canopy. "I didn't ask him to his face because he very likely would not have helped me, not personally. He'd have directed me to Montague as fast as he politely could, and that simply won't do. I—we—need *his* help, not the assistance of his henchman. I need the knight on his charger, not his squire."

"I don't see that—he'd have helped, why wouldn't he? It's not as if you two don't go back near to all your lives. He's known you since you was in your cradle. You played as babies and all through the years, right up until you was fifteen and ready to be a lady." Her tidying done, candle in hand, Nellie approached the big bed. "If you was just to go to him and explain it all, I'm sure he'd help."

"Believe me, Nellie, that wouldn't work. While he'll extend himself to help the mysterious countess, he would never do the same for me." Turning onto her side, Alathea closed her eyes and ignored Nellie's disbelieving sniff. "Good night."

After a moment, a soft, grumbling "Good night" reached her. The candlelight playing on her eyelids faded, then the door clicked as Nellie let herself out.

Alathea sighed, sinking deeper into the mattress, trying to relax the muscles that had tensed when he'd kisssed her. That was the one development she hadn't foreseen but it was hardly serious, presumably the sort of sophisticated dalliance he practiced on all likely ladies. If she could start her charade again, she'd think twice about making herself a widow, one already out of mourning, but it was done—the masquerade had begun. And while she might not be able to fully explain it to Nellie, her charade was absolutely essential.

Rupert Melrose Cynster, her childhood playmate, was the one, perfectly armed knight she'd had to win to her side. She knew his true mettle—what he could accomplish, would accomplish, once he was fully committed to a cause. With him as her champion, they would have a real chance of triumphing over the Central East Africa Gold Company. Without his aid, that feat had appeared close to impossible.

Knowing him of old—so well, so thoroughly—she'd known that to secure his commitment, she would need to fully engage his ofttimes fickle interest. She needed him to *focus* on her problem, willingly bringing his considerable abilities to bear. So she'd invented the countess and, cloaked in beguiling mystery, had set about recruiting him, body and soul, to her cause.

She'd won her first battle—he was ready to fight beside her. For the first time since Figgs had placed the wretched promissory note before her, she allowed herself to believe in ultimate victory.

As far as the ton would see, the Morwellans were in town as expected to allow the younger daughters to make their curtsies to society and for Charlie to make his bow. She, the eldest daughter, now an ape-leader, would hug the shadows, assisting with her stepsisters' come-outs, in her spare moments donning cloak and veil to masquerade as the countess and remove the sword presently poised over her family's future.

She smiled at such melodramatic thoughts. They came easily to mind—she knew precisely what she was doing. She also knew precisely why Rupert wouldn't have helped her as he would the countess, although it wasn't something she was eager to explain, even to Nellie.

They disliked being in the same room, certainly not within ten feet of each other. Any closer proximity was like wearing a hair shirt. The peculiarity had afflicted them from the age of eleven and twelve; since then, it had been a constant in their lives. What caused it remained a mystery. As their younger selves, they'd tried to ignore it, pretend it wasn't there, but the relief they'd both felt when her impending ladyhood had spelled an end to their all but daily association had been too real to ignore.

Of course they'd never discussed it, but his reaction was there in the sharpening of his hazel gaze, the sudden tensing of his muscles, in the difficulty he had remaining near her for more than a few minutes. Uncomfortable wasn't an adequate description—the affliction was far worse than that.

She'd never been able to decide if she reacted to him as he did to her, or if her aggravation arose in response to his. Whatever the truth, their mutual affliction was something they'd learned to live with, learned to hide, and ultimately, learned to avoid. Neither would unnecessarily precipitate a prolonged encounter.

That was why, despite growing up as they had, despite their families being such close neighbors, he and she had never waltzed. They had danced—one country dance. Even that had left her breathless, waspish and thoroughly out of temper. Like him, she wasn't given to displays of temper—the only one able to provoke her, all but instantly, was he.

And that—all of that—explained why the countess had walked the porch of St. Georges. While she could not, absolutely, know his mind and thus be certain he would not have personally helped her, she imagined his instincts would have prompted him to help, but his reaction to her would have mitigated against it. Dealing with the company for her would mean seeing her frequently, often alone, which usually made the affliction worse. They'd met briefly only a few months ago—their affliction was stronger than ever. They'd reduced each other to quivering rage in under three minutes. She couldn't believe, if she asked for his help, that he'd break the habit of years and readily spend hours in her company—or, if he did, that it wouldn't drive them both demented.

More to the point, she hadn't been able to risk finding out. If she'd presented her problem to him as herself, only to have him send her to Montague, she couldn't then have appeared as the countess.

No choice.

He would never forgive her if he ever found out—ever learned *she* was the countess. He would probably do worse than that. But she'd had no choice— her conscience wasn't troubling her, not really. If there'd been any other sure way of getting him to help her without deceiving him, she would have taken it, but …

She was halfway asleep, drifting in the mists, her mind revisiting bits and pieces of their rendezvous, revolving more and more about that unnerving kiss, when she started awake. Blinking, eyes wide, she stared up at the canopy—and considered the fact that their decades-old mutual affliction had not reared its head that night.

CHAPTER
Two

" A la-*the*-aaa. Whoo-hoo! Allie! Can you pass the butter, please?"
Alathea focused—Alice was pointing across the luncheon table.
Bemusedly glancing in that direction, her brain belatedly caught up with
reality; lifting the butter dish, she passed it across.

"You're in a brown study today." Serena was sitting next to her, at the end
of the table.

Alathea waved dismissively. "I didn't sleep all that well last night." She'd
been so keyed up, primed to play the countess, desperate to secure Rupert's
aid, that she'd rested not at all before her three o'clock appointment. And
afterwards ... after her success, after that kiss, after realizing ... she shook
aside the distraction. "I'm still not used to all the street sounds."

"Perhaps you should move to another room?"

Glancing at Serena's sweet face, brow furrowed with concern, Alathea
clasped her stepmother's hand. "Don't worry. I'm perfectly happy with my
room. It faces the back gardens as it is."

Serena's face eased. "Well ...if you're sure. But now Alice has woken you
up"—her eyes twinkled—"I wanted to check how much we can afford to
spend on the girls' walking dresses."

Alathea gladly gave Serena her attention. Short, plump, and fashionably
matronly, Serena was gentle and retiring, yet in the matter of her daughters'
come-outs, she'd proved both shrewd and well up to snuff. With real relief,
Alathea had consigned all the details of their social lives, including their
wardrobes, to Serena, more than content to play a supporting role in that
sphere. They'd been in town for just over a week and all was on track for a
pleasant Season all around.

All she had to do was prove the Central East Africa Gold Company a fraud,
and all would be well.

The thought returned her mind to its preoccupation—and to the man she'd
recruited last night. She glanced around the table, viewing her family as if
through his eyes. She and Serena discussed materials, trimmings, and bonnets,
with Mary and Alice hanging on every word. At the table's other end, her

father, Charlie, and Jeremy discussed the more masculine entertainments on offer. Alathea heard her father muse on the attractions of Gentleman Jackson's Boxing Saloon, a prospect guaranteed to divert both Charlie as well as his precocious younger brother.

Leaving Serena, Mary, and Alice debating colors, Alathea turned to the youngest member of the family, sitting quietly beside her, a large doll on her lap. "And how are you and Rose today, poppet?"

Lady Augusta Morwellan raised huge brown eyes to Alathea's face and smiled trustingly. "I had a lovely time in the garden this morning, but Rose here"—she turned the doll so Alathea could inspect her—"has been *fractious*. Miss Helm and I think we should take her for a walk this afternoon."

"A walk? Oh, yes! That's a lovely idea—just what we need." Having settled her sartorial requirements, Mary, all bouncing brown ringlets and glowing eyes, was ready for the next excitement.

"I'm starting to feel hemmed in with all these houses and streets." With fair hair and doelike eyes, Alice was more serious and contained. She smiled at Augusta. "And Augusta won't want us disturbing Rose with our chatter."

Augusta returned the smile sweetly. "No. Rose needs quiet." Too young to share in the excitement that had infected the rest of the family, Augusta was content to stroll the nearby square, her hand in Miss Helm's, and stare, wide-eyed, at all the new and different sights.

"Is there somewhere else we can go—other than the park, I mean?" Alice looked from Alathea to Serena. "We won't have our new dresses until next week, so it's probably better we don't go there too often."

"I would prefer that you didn't haunt the park anyway," Serena said. "Better to appear only a few times a week, and we were there yesterday."

"So where shall we go? It has to be somewhere with trees and lawns." Mary fixed her glowing gaze on Alathea's face.

"Actually …" Alathea considered—just because she'd successfully recruited her knight didn't mean she had to sit on her hands and leave all the investigating to him. She refocused on her stepsisters' faces. "There's a particular park I know of, quiet and pleasant, cut off from all the noise. It's very like the country—you can almost forget you're in London."

"That sounds perfect," Alice declared. "Let's go there."

"We're going to Bond Street!" Jeremy pushed back his chair.

Charlie and the earl did the same. The earl smiled at his womenfolk. "I'll take these two off for the afternoon."

"I'm going to learn to box!" Jeremy danced around the table, thrusting his fists through the air, dealing summarily with invisible opponents. Laughing, Charlie caught Jeremy's fists, then half-waltzed, half-wrestled him out of the room. Jeremy's piping protests and Charlie's deeper amused taunts faded as they progressed in the direction of the front door.

Mary and Alice rose to follow. "We'll get our bonnets." Mary looked at Alathea. "Shall I fetch yours?"

"Please." Alathea rose, too.

The earl stopped by her side, his fingers light on her arm. "Is everything all right?" he asked quietly.

Alathea looked up. Despite his age and the troubles resting heavily on his shoulders, her father, two inches taller than she, remained a strikingly handsome man. Glimpsing shadows of pain and regret in his eyes, she smiled reassuringly; she caught his hand and squeezed. "Everything's going well."

He'd been devastated when he'd learned about the promissory note. He'd thought the sum pledged was much smaller—the wording of the note was such that arithmetic was required to determine the total sum. All he'd intended was to gain a few extra guineas to spend on the girls' weddings. She'd spent some time comforting him, assuring him that although the situation was bad, it was not the final end.

It had been hard for him to carry on as if nothing had happened so the children wouldn't suspect. Only the three of them—he, she and Serena—knew of the latest threat or, indeed, of the perilous state of the earldom's finances. From the first, they'd agreed that the children were never to know that their future hung by such a slender thread.

Despite the fact she had spent all her adult life putting right the problems her father had caused, Alathea had never been able to hold it against him. He was the most lovable, and loving, man—he was simply incapable when it came to money.

Now he smiled, a sad, forlorn smile. "Is there anything I can do?"

She hugged his arm. "Just keep doing what you've been doing, Papa—keep Jeremy entertained and out of mischief." She drew back. "You're so good with them—they're both a real credit to you."

"Indeed," Serena agreed. "And if Alathea says there's nothing to worry about, then there's no sense worrying. She'll keep us informed—you know she always does."

The earl seemed about to speak, then muffled cries and thumps came from the front hall.

The earl's lips twitched. "I'd better get out there before Crisp hands in his notice." He touched his lips to Alathea's temple, stooped to kiss Serena's cheek, then he strode out to the hall, squaring his shoulders and lifting his head as he crossed the threshold.

With Serena, Alathea followed more slowly. From the dining room doorway, they watched the melee in the hall resolve itself under the earl's direction. "He's really a wonderful father," Serena said as the earl ushered his sons out of the front door.

"I know." Alathea smiled at his departing back. "I'm really very impressed with Charlie." She glanced at Serena. "The next earl of Morwellan will hold a candle to all comers. He's an amazing amalgam of you both."

Pleased, Serena inclined her head. "But he's also got a very large dose of *your* commonsense. Thanks to you, my dear, the next earl of Morwellan will know how to manage his brass!"

They both laughed, yet it was true. Not only was Charlie handsome, unruffleably good-natured, never high in the instep, and always game for a lark, but he was, largely due to Serena, thoughtful, considerate and openly caring. Thanks to the earl's influence, he was a gentleman to his toes and, as he also spent at least one session a week with Alathea in the estate office, and had for some years, he was at nineteen in a fair way to understanding how to successfully manage the estate. While he still did not know the level to which the earldom's coffers had sunk, Charlie now knew at least the basics of how to keep them filling up.

"He'll make an excellent earl." Alathea looked up as Mary and Alice came clattering down the stairs, bonnets on, ribbons streaming, her own bonnet dangling from Mary's hand. Augusta had slipped out earlier; Alathea glimpsed her littlest stepsister heading out to the garden, her hand in Miss Helm's.

Charlie, Jeremy, Mary, Alice, and Augusta—they were the ultimate reasons she'd invented the countess. Even if he discovered her deception, Alathea couldn't believe her knight would disapprove of her motives.

"Come on!" Alice waved her parasol at the door. "The afternoon's winging—we've already ordered the carriage."

Accepting her bonnet, Alathea turned to the mirror to settle it over her topknot.

Casting a critical eye over her daughters, Serena straightened a ribbon here, tweaked a curl there. "Where do you intend going?"

Alathea turned from the mirror as the clop of hooves heralded the carriage. "I'd thought to go to Lincoln's Inn Fields. The trees are tall, the grass green and well tended, and it's never crowded."

Serena nodded. "Yes, you're right—but what an odd place to think of."

Alathea merely smiled and followed Mary and Alice down the steps.

Gabriel discovered the bronze plaque identifying the offices of Thurlow and Brown along the south face of Lincoln's Inn. Surrounding a rectangular cobbled courtyard, the Inn housed nothing but legal chambers. Its inner walls were punctuated with regularly spaced open archways, each giving access to a shadowy stairwell. On the wall beside each archway, bronze plaques bore witness to the legal firms housed off the stairway within.

After consulting a book listing the solicitors of the Inns of Court, Montague had directed Gabriel to Lincoln's Inn, describing the firm as small, old, but undistinguished, with no known association with any matter remotely illegal. As he climbed the stairs, Gabriel reflected that, if he'd been behind the sort of swindle it seemed likely the Central East Africa Gold Company was, then the first step he'd take to lull gullible investors would be to retain such a firm as Thurlow and Brown. A firm stultifyingly correct and all but moribund, unlikely to boast the talents or connections that might give rise to unanswerable questions.

Thurlow and Brown's rooms were on the second level, to the rear of the building. Gabriel reached for the knob of the heavy oak door, noting the large lock beneath the knob. Sauntering in, he scanned the small reception area. Behind a low railing, an old clerk worked at a raised desk, guarding access to a short corridor leading to one room at the rear, and to a second room off the reception area.

"Yes? Can I help you?" The clerk clutched at the angled desktop. Frowning, he flipped through a diary. "You don't have an appointment." He made it sound like an offense.

His expression one of affable boredom, Gabriel shut the door, noting that there were no bolts or extra latches, only that large and cumbersome lock.

"Thurlow," he murmured, turning back to the clerk. "There was a Thurlow at Eton when I was there. I wonder if it's the same one?"

"Couldn't be. His nibs"—the clerk waved an ink-stained hand at the half open door giving off the reception area—"is old enough to be your dad."

"That so?" Gabriel sounded disappointed. Clearly "his nibs" was out. "Ah, well. It was really Mr. Browne I came to see."

Again the clerk frowned; again he checked his book. "You're not down for this afternoon ..."

"I'm not? How odd. I was sure the pater said two."

The clerk shook his head. "Mr. Brown's out. I'm not expecting him back until later."

Letting annoyance flash across his features, Gabriel thumped the reception railing with his cane. "If that isn't just like Theo Browne! Never could keep his engagements straight!"

"*Theo* Brown?"

Gabriel looked at the clerk. "Yes—Mr. Browne."

"But that's not *our* Mr. Brown."

"It isn't?" Gabriel stared at the clerk. "Is your Browne spelled with an 'e'?"

The clerk shook his head.

"Damn!" Gabriel swung away. "I was sure it was Thurlow and Browne." He frowned. "Maybe it's Thirston and Browne. Thrapston and Browne. Something like that." He looked questioningly at the clerk.

Who shook his head. "I'm sorry I can't help you, sir. Don't know of any firms with names like that. Mind you, there is Browne, Browne and Tillson in the other quad—might they be the ones you're after?"

"Browne, Browne and Tillson." Gabriel repeated the name twice with different inflections, then shrugged. "Who knows. Could be." He swung to the door. "The other quad, you say?"

"Aye, sir—across the carriage road through the Inn."

Waving his cane in farewell, Gabriel went out, closing the door behind him. Then he grinned and strolled down the stairs.

Regaining the sunshine, he strode across the cobbles. He'd seen enough to confirm Thurlow and Brown's standing—precisely as Montague had said, stuffily, dustily dull. He'd learned which room was whose, and through the open doors he'd seen the locked client boxes lining the walls of both partners' rooms. They didn't lock the boxes away somewhere else. They were there, within easy reach, and the only lock between the landing and the boxes was the old wrist-breaker on the main door.

There had also been no sign of any junior clerk. There'd been only one desk, and little space outside the partners' rooms—no area for a clerk or office boy to spend the night.

Entirely satisfied with his afternoon's work, Gabriel saluted the gatekeeper with his cane and strode through the secondary gateway into the adjoining Fields.

Before him, a small army of old trees, like ancient sentinels, spread their branches protectively over gravel walks and swaths of lawn. Sunlight streamed down. The breeze ruffled leaves, shedding shifting shadows over the green carpets on which gentlemen and ladies strolled while waiting for others consulting in the surrounding chambers.

Gabriel paused in the cobbled forecourt beyond the gate, gazing unseeing at the trees.

Would the countess be impatient enough to contact him that evening? The possibility tantalized, even more so as the realization sank in that her impatience could not possibly match his. While with her, he'd felt he knew her, knew the sort of woman she was; away from her, he'd realized how little he knew of the real woman behind the veil. Learning more, quickly, seemed imperative—he especially needed to learn how to put his hand on a woman who thus far had been a phantom in the night.

Unfortunately, he couldn't learn more until she contacted him—at least now, when she did, he'd have something to report.

Shrugging off his distraction, he settled on Aldwych as his best bet for a hackney and set out along the south side of the Fields. Halfway along, he heard himself hailed.

"*Gabriel!*"

"Over here!"

The voices coming from the Fields were assuredly feminine, equally assuredly young. Halting, Gabriel scanned the shaded lawns; two sweet young things, their parasols tilted at crazy angles, were bobbing up and down and waving madly. Squinting against the sunlight, he recognized Mary and Alice Morwellan. Raising his cane in reply, he waited until a dowager's black carriage rolled soberly past, then started across the narrow street.

Alathea saw him coming, and had to fight down an urge to screech at her sisters—what had they *done*? She'd seen him walk through the gates of the Inn and pause. Her attention locked on him, she'd assured herself that he wouldn't notice her in the shadows, that there was no reason for her heart to gallop, for her nerves to twitch.

He'd remained safely ignorant of her presence—she'd been surprised he'd acted so swiftly on the countess's behalf. That was, she presumed, why he was here—if she'd known, she would never have risked coming. Having him find her anywhere near any location he would associate with the countess had formed no part of her careful plans. She needed to keep her two personas completely distinct, especially near him.

As he'd walked along the street, cane swinging, broad shoulders square, sunlight had gleamed on his chestnut hair, gilding the lightly curling locks. Her thoughts had slowed, halted—she'd completely forgotten Mary and Alice were with her.

They'd seen him and called—now there was no escape. As he crossed the grass toward them, she drew in a breath, lifted her chin, tightened her fists about her parasol's handle—and tried to quell her panic.

He couldn't recognize lips he'd kissed but not seen, could he?

Smiling easily, Gabriel strode into the trees' shadows. As he neared, Mary and Alice stopped jigging and contented themselves with beaming; only then, with his eyes adjusting and with their dancing parasols no longer distracting him, did he see the lady standing behind them.

Alathea.

His stride almost faltered.

She stood straight and tall, silently contained, her parasol held at precisely the correct angle to protect her fine skin from the sun. Not, of course, waving at him.

Masking his reaction—the powerful jolt that shook him whenever he saw her unexpectedly and the prickling sensation that followed—he continued his advance. She watched him with her usual cool regard, her customary challenge—a haughty watchfulness that never failed to get his goat.

Forcing his gaze from her, he smiled and greeted Mary and Alice, veritable pictures in mull muslin. He made them laugh by bowing extravagantly over their hands.

"We were utterly amazed to see you!" Mary said.

"We've been to the park twice," Alice confided, "but that was earlier than this. You probably weren't about."

Refraining from replying that he rarely inhabited the park, at least not during the fashionable hours, he fought to keep his gaze on them. "I knew you were coming to town, but I hadn't realized you were here." He'd last met them in January, at a party given by his mother at his family home, Quiverstone Manor in Somerset. Morwellan Park and the Manor shared a long boundary; the combined lands and the nearby Quantock Hills had been his childhood stamping ground—his, his brother Lucifer's, and Alathea's.

With easy familiarity, he complimented both girls, fielding their questions, displaying his suave London persona to their evident delight. Yet while he distracted them with trivialities, his attention remained riveted on the cool presence a few feet away. Why that should be so was an abiding mystery—Mary and Alice were effervescent delights. Alathea in contrast was cool, composed, still—in some peculiar way, a lodestone for his senses. The girls were as bubbling, tumbling streams, while Alathea was a deep pool of peace, calm, and something else he'd never succeeded in defining. He was intensely aware of her, as she was of him; he was acutely conscious they had not exchanged greetings.

They never did. Not really.

Steeling himself, he lifted his gaze from Mary's and Alice's faces and looked at Alathea. At her hair. But she was wearing a bonnet—he couldn't tell whether she was also wearing one of her ridiculous caps, or one of those foolish scraps of lace she'd started placing about her topknot. She probably was concealing some such frippery nonsense, but he couldn't comment unless he saw it. Lips thinning, he lowered his gaze until his eyes met hers. "I hadn't realized you were in London."

He was speaking directly to her, specifically of her, his tone quite different from when he'd spoken to the girls.

Her lashes flickered; her grip on her parasol tightened. "Good afternoon, Rupert. It is a lovely day. We came up to town a week ago."

He stiffened.

Alathea sensed it. Her stomach knotted with panic, she looked at Mary and Alice and forced herself to smile serenely. "The girls will be making their come-outs shortly."

After a fractional hesitation, he followed her lead. "Indeed?" Turning back to Mary and Alice, he quizzed them on their plans.

Alathea tried to breathe evenly, tried to hold her sudden lightheadedness at bay. She refused to let her gaze slide his way. She knew his face as well as her own—the large, heavily hooded eyes, the mobile lips given to wry quirks, the classic planes of nose and forehead, the uncompromisingly square chin. He was tall enough to see over her head—one of the few who could do so. He was strong enough to subdue her if he wished, and ruthless enough to do it. There was nothing about him physically that she didn't already know, nothing to set such a sharp edge to her usual tension.

Nothing beyond the fact that she'd seen him last night in the porch of St. Georges, while he hadn't seen her.

The memory of his lips covering hers, of the beguiling touch of his fingers beneath her chin, locked her lungs, tightened her nerves, set her senses leaping. Her lips tingled.

"Our ball will be in three weeks," Mary was telling him. "You'll be invited, of course."

"Will you come?" Alice asked.

"I wouldn't miss it for the world." His gaze flicked to Alathea's face, then he looked back at the girls.

Gabriel knew exactly how a cat with its fur rubbed the wrong way felt—precisely how he always felt near Alathea. How she did it he did not know; he didn't even know if she had to do anything—it simply seemed his inevitable reaction to her. He'd react, and she'd snap back. The air between them would crackle. It had started when they were children and had grown more intense with the years.

He kept his gaze on the girls, ruthlessly stifling the urge to turn to Alathea. "But what are you doing here?"

"It was Allie's idea."

Blithely, they turned to her; gritting his teeth, he had to do the same.

Coolly, she shrugged. "I'd heard of it as a quiet place to stroll—one where ladies would be unlikely to encounter any of the more rakish elements."

Like him.

She'd chosen to live her life buried in the country—why she thought that gave her the right to disapprove of his lifestyle he did not know; he only knew she did. "Indeed?"

He debated pressing her—both for her real reason for being in the Fields and also over her impertinence in disapproving of him. Even with the girls all ears and bright eyes before them, he could easily lift the conversation to a level where they wouldn't understand. This, however, was Alathea. She was intractably stubborn—he would learn nothing she didn't wish him to know. She was also possessed of a wit quite the equal of his; the last time they'd crossed verbal swords—in January, over the stupid Alexandrine cap she'd worn to his mother's party—they'd both bled. If, eyes flashing, cheeks flushed with temper, she hadn't stuck her nose in the air and walked—stalked—away from him, he would quite possibly have strangled her.

Lips compressed, he shot her a glance—she met it fearlessly. She was watching, waiting, as aware of the direction of his thoughts as he. She was ready and willing to engage in one of their customary duels.

No true gentleman ever disappointed a lady.

"I take it you'll be accompanying Mary and Alice about town?"

She went to nod, stopped, and haughtily lifted her head. "Of course."

"In that case"—he smiled disarmingly at Mary and Alice—"I'll have to see what amusements I can steer your way."

"There's no need to put yourself out—unlike some I could mention, I don't require to be constantly amused."

"I think you'll discover that unless one is constantly amused, life in the ton can be hellishly boring. What, other than boredom, could possibly have brought you here?"

"A wish to avoid impertinent gentlemen."

"How fortunate, then, that I chanced upon you. If avoiding impertinent gentlemen is your aim, a lady within the ton can never be too careful. There's no telling precisely where or when she'll encounter the most shocking impertinence."

Mary and Alice smiled trustingly up at him; all they heard was his fashionable drawl. Alathea, he knew, detected the steel beneath it; he could sense her increasing tension.

"You forget—I'm perfectly capable of dealing with outrageous impertinence, however unamusing I might find such encounters."

"Strange to say, most ladies don't find such encounters unamusing at all."

"I am not '*most ladies*.' I do not find the particular distractions to which you are devoted at all amusing."

"That's because you've yet to experience them. Besides," he glibly added, "you're used to riding every day. You'll need some activity to … keep you exercised."

He raised eyes filled with limpid innocence to hers, expecting to meet a narrow-eyed glance brimming with aggravation. Instead, her eyes were wide, not shocked but ... it took him a moment to place their expression.

Defensive. He'd made her defensive.

Guilt rose within him.

Hell! Even when he won a round with her, he still lost.

Stifling a sigh—over what he did not know—he looked away, trying to dampen what he thought of as his bristling fur—that odd aggression she always evoked—and act normally. Reasonably.

He shrugged lightly. "I must be on my way."

"I dare say."

To his relief, she contented herself with that small barb. She watched as he bowed to the girls, setting them laughing again. Then he straightened and deliberately caught her gaze.

It was like looking into a mirror—they both had hazel eyes. When he looked into hers, he usually saw his own thoughts and feelings, reflected over and again, into infinity.

Not today. Today all he saw was a definite defensiveness—a shield shutting her off from him. Protecting her from him.

He blinked, breaking the contact. With a curt nod, which she returned, he swung on his heel and strode off.

Slowing as he neared the edge of the lawn, he wondered what he would have done if she'd offered her hand. That unanswerable question led to the thought of when last he'd touched her in any way. He couldn't remember, but it was certainly not in the last decade.

He crossed the street, wriggling his shoulders as his peculiar tension drained; he called it relief at being out of her presence, but it wasn't that. It was the reaction—the one he'd never understood but which she evoked so strongly—subsiding again.

Until next they met.

Alathea watched him go; only when his boots struck the cobbles did she breathe freely again. Her nerves easing, she looked around. Beside her, Mary and Alice blithely chatted, serenely unaware. It always amazed her that their nearest and dearest never saw anything odd in their fraught encounters—other than themselves, only Lucifer saw, presumably because he'd grown up side by side with them and knew them both so well.

As her pulse slowed, elation bloomed within her.

He hadn't recognized her.

Indeed, after the total absence of his typical reaction to her when he'd met the countess last night, combined with the strong resurgence of it in the last hour, she doubted he'd ever make the connection.

This morning, she'd woken to the certain knowledge that it wasn't her physical self that he found so provoking. If he didn't know she was Alathea

Morwellan, nothing happened. No suppressed irritation, no sparks, no clashes. Blissful nothing. Cloaked and veiled, she was just another woman.

She didn't want to dwell on why that made her feel so happy, as if a weight had suddenly lifted from her heart. It was clearly her identity that caused his problem—and it was, she now knew, *his* problem, something that arose first in him, to which she then reacted.

Knowing didn't make the outcome any easier to endure, but …

She focused on the wrought iron gates through which he had emerged. They were open to admit coaches to the courtyard of the Inn. She could see the Inn's archways and the glint of bronze plaques—it wasn't hard to guess the purpose of the plaques.

He'd seemed satisfied and confident when he'd strolled away from the gates.

Drawing in a determined, fully recovered breath, Alathea smiled at Mary and Alice. "Come, girls. Let's stroll about the Inn."

Evening came, and with it a strange restlessness.

Gabriel prowled the parlor of his house in Brook Street. He'd dined and was dressed to go out, to grace the ballroom of whichever tonnish hostess he chose to favor with his presence. There were four invitations from which to choose; none, however, enticed.

He wondered where the countess would spend her evening. He wondered where Alathea would spend hers.

The door opened; he paused in his pacing. His gentleman's gentleman, Chance, pale hair gleaming, immaculately turned out in regulation black, entered with the replenished brandy decanter and fresh glasses on a tray.

"Pour me one, will you?" Gabriel swung away as Chance, short and slight, headed for the sideboard. He felt peculiarly distracted; he hoped a stiff brandy would clear his mind.

He'd left Lincoln's Inn buoyed by his small success, focused on the countess and the sensual game unfolding between them. Then he'd met Alathea. Ten minutes in her company had left him feeling like the earth had shifted beneath his feet.

She'd been part of his life for as long as he could remember; never before had she shut him out of her thoughts. Never before had she been anything but utterly free with her opinions, even when he'd wished otherwise. When they'd met in January, she'd been her usual open, sharp-tongued self. This afternoon, she'd shut him out, kept him at a distance.

Something had changed. He couldn't believe his comments had made her defensive; it had to be something else. Had something happened to her that he hadn't heard about?

The prospect unsettled him. He wanted to focus on the countess, but his thoughts kept drifting to Alathea.

Reaching the room's end, he swung around—and nearly mowed Chance down.

Chance staggered back—Gabriel caught his arm, simultaneously rescuing the brimming tumbler from the wildly tipping salver.

"Hoo!" Chance waved the salver before his unprepossessing visage. "That was a close one."

Gabriel caught his eye, paused, then said, "That will be all."

"Aye, aye, sir!" With cheery insouciance, Chance headed for the door.

Gabriel sighed. "Not 'Aye, aye'—a simple 'Yes, sir' will do."

"Oh." Chance paused at the door. "Right-oh, then. 'Yessir,' it is!"

He opened the door, and saw Lucifer about to enter—Chance stepped back, bowing and waving. "Come you right in, sir. I was just a-leaving."

"Thank you, Chance." Grinning, Lucifer strolled in. With unimpaired serenity, Chance bounced out—then remembered and returned to shut the door.

Closing his eyes, Gabriel took a large swallow of brandy.

Lucifer chuckled. "I told you it wouldn't simply be a matter of a suit of clothes."

"I don't care." Opening his eyes, Gabriel regarded the exceedingly large quantity of brandy in the tumbler, then sighed, turned, and sank into a well-stuffed armchair to one side of the hearth. "He'll become something employable if it kills him."

"Judging by his progress to date, it might kill you first."

"Quite possibly." Gabriel took another fortifying swallow. "I'll risk it."

Standing before the mantelpiece checking his own stack of invitations, Lucifer shot him a look. "I thought you were going to say you'd 'chance' it."

"That would be redundant—I *am* 'chancing' it. Precisely why I named him that."

Chance was not Chance's real name—no one, including Chance, knew what that was. As for his age, they'd settled on twenty-five. Chance was a product of the London slums; his elevation to the house in Brook Street had come about through his own merit. Caught up in the stews while helping a friend, Gabriel might not have made it out again but for Chance's aid, given not for any promise of reward, but simply in the way of helping another man with the scales weighted heavily and unfairly against him. Chance had, in a way, rescued Gabriel—Gabriel, in turn, had rescued Chance.

"Which have you chosen?" Lucifer looked from his invitations to the four lined up on Gabriel's side of the mantelpiece.

"I haven't. They all seem similarly boring."

"*Boring?*" Lucifer glanced at him. "You want to be careful of using that word, and even more of giving way to the feeling. Just look where it got Richard. And Devil. And Vane, too, come to think of it."

"But not Demon—he wasn't bored."

"He was running, and that didn't work, either." After a moment, Lucifer added, "And anyway, I'm sure he *is* bored now. He's not even sure they'll come up for any of the Season." His tone labeled such behavior incomprehensible.

"Give him time—they've only been married a week."

A week ago, Demon Harry Cynster, their cousin and a member of the group of six popularly known as the Bar Cynster, had said the fateful words and taken a bride, one who shared his interest in horse-racing. Demon and Felicity were presently making a prolonged tour of the major racecourses.

Nursing his brandy, Gabriel mused, "After a few weeks, or months, I dare say the novelty will wear off."

Lucifer threw him a cynical look. They were both well aware that when Cynsters married, the novelty did not, strange as it seemed, wear off at all. Quite the opposite. To them both, it was an inexplicable conundrum, however, as the last unmarried members of the group, they were exceedingly wary of having it explained to them.

How on earth men like them—like Devil, Vane, Richard, and Demon—could suddenly turn their backs on all the feminine delights so freely on offer within the ton, and happily—and to all appearances contentedly—settle to wedded bliss and the charms of just one woman, was a mystery that confounded their male minds and defied their imaginations.

Both sincerely hoped it never happened to them.

Resettling his cloak, Lucifer selected one gilt-edged card from his stack. "I'm going to Molly Hardwick's." He glanced at Gabriel. "Coming?"

Gabriel studied his brother's face; anticipation glinted in the dark blue eyes. "Who'll be at Molly Hardwick's?"

Lucifer's quick smile flashed. "A certain young matron whose husband finds the bills before Parliament more enticing than she."

That was Lucifer's speciality—convincing ladies of insufficiently serviced passions that permitting him to service them was in their best interests. Considering his brother's long, lean frame and rakishly disheveled black locks, Gabriel raised a brow. "What's the odds?"

"None at all." Lucifer strolled to the door. "She'll surrender—not tonight, but soon." Pausing at the door, he nodded at the glass of brandy. "I take it you're going to see that to the end, in which case, I'll leave you to it." With a wave, he opened the door; an instant later it clicked shut behind him.

Gabriel studied the dark panels, then raised his glass and took another sip. Transferring his gaze to the fire burning in the grate, he stretched out his legs, crossed his ankles, and settled down for the evening.

It was, he felt, a telling fact that he would rather wait out the hours until midnight here, safe and comfortable before his own hearth, than risk his freedom in a tonnish ballroom, no matter how tempting the ladies filling it. Ever since Demon's engagement had been announced nearly a month ago, every matron with a daughter suitable in any degree had set her sights on him, as if marriage was some poisoned chalice the Bar Cynster was handing around, member to member, and he was the next in line.

They could live in hope, but he wasn't about to drink.

Turning his head, he studied the pile of journals stacked on a side table. The latest issue of the *Gentlemen's Magazine* was there, yet ... he'd rather consider the countess—all six feet of her. It was rare to meet a lady so tall ...

Alathea was nearly as tall.

Three minutes later, he shook aside the thoughts that, unbidden, had crowded into his mind. Confusing thoughts, unsettling thoughts, thoughts that left him more distracted than he could ever remember feeling. Clearing his mind, he focused on the countess.

He enjoyed helping people—not in the general sense but specifically. Individual people. Like Chance. Like the countess.

The countess needed his help—even more, she had asked for it. Alathea didn't, and hadn't. Given how he felt, that was probably just as well. His gaze fixed on the flames, he kept his mind on the countess—on plotting the next phase in their investigation, and planning the next stage in her seduction.

CHAPTER
Three

At twenty minutes past midnight, Gabriel stood outside the oak door guarding the offices of Thurlow and Brown and studied the old lock. He'd seen no one while crossing the quiet courtyard. Light had shone from a few windows, where clerks were presumably laboring through the night; the rooms directly below were occupied, but no one had heard him slip past on the stair.

He felt in his pocket for the lockpick he'd brought, one capable of dealing with such a large lock. Simultaneously, without thought, he tested the door, turning the knob—The door eased open.

Gabriel stared at the door, at the lock that had been unlocked, and tried to imagine the old clerk shutting up and going home without locking up.

That scenario wasn't convincing.

He could see no light through the crack between door and jamb. He eased the door further open. As earlier in the day, it opened noiselessly. The reception area and the room off it were in darkness. In the room at the end of the corridor, however, faint light gleamed.

Shutting the door, Gabriel eased the bolt home. Leaning his cane beside the door, he paused, letting his eyes adjust to the denser gloom, noting again the position of the wooden gate in the railing of the reception area through which clients were admitted to the chambers beyond.

That, too, opened noiselessly.

His footfalls muffled by the runner, he made his way silently along the corridor and wondered if it was remotely possible that Mr. Brown without an "e" was working late. The occasionally pulsing light presumably came from a lamp turned very low; the lamp was also partially screened, the light thrown back into the room, away from the windows, presumably toward Brown's desk. Pausing at the threshold, Gabriel listened—and heard the steady flick of pages being turned. Then came the soft thump of a book being closed, then papers were shuffled. That was followed by a different sound—he eventually placed it as papers and books being placed into a tin box, and the box shut.

Another box was opened. A second later came more flicking—steady, even, purposeful.

It didn't sound like Mr. Brown.

Beyond curious, Gabriel stepped over the threshold into the shadowed gap created by the half-open door and looked around its edge.

A tall cloaked and hooded figure stood before the large desk, rifling the papers she'd lifted from one of the boxes stacked on the desktop. Her gloved hands gave her away, as did the curve of her jaw, fleetingly revealed when she tilted her head, angling a document so that the light fell more definitely on it. The lamp stood on the desk to her left, a tall ledger propped around it to act as a screen.

Conscious of the tension leaving muscles he hadn't been aware he'd tensed, Gabriel leaned against the bookshelves and considered.

He waited until she'd methodically searched the contents of the now open box and restacked the papers. Then he reached out and pushed the door.

It squeaked.

She gasped. Papers scattered. In a furious flurry she flicked down her veil and whirled, so quickly that, despite watching closely, he failed to catch even a glimpse of her face. One hand at her breast, the other clutching the edge of the desk against which she'd backed, the countess stared at him, as deeply incognito as she'd been in Hanover Square.

"*Oh!*" Her voice wavered as if uncertain of its register, then, with an obvious effort, she caught her breath and said in the same low tone he recalled, "It's you."

He bowed. "As you see."

She continued to stare at him. "You ... gave me quite a start."

"I would apologize, but"—he pushed away from the bookshelves and advanced upon her—"I hadn't expected to find you here." Halting before her, he studied the glint of eyes behind her veil, and wished the veil were thinner. "I thought *I* was supposed to locate Messrs. Thurlow and Brown. How did you know they were here?"

She was breathing rapidly, her gaze locked on his face, then she looked away. With a sliding step, she slipped out of the trap between him and the desk, smoothly turning so she faced the desk again. "I chanced upon them." Her voice was very low; it strengthened as, collecting the scattered papers, she went on, "I had to visit our family solicitor in Chancery Lane and on impulse I strolled into the Inn. I saw the plaques, so I wandered about—and found them."

"You *should* have left it to me. Sent a note and stayed safely at home while I did this." Why he was so annoyed, he couldn't have said. She was, after all, a free agent—except that she'd asked for his help.

She shrugged. "I thought, as I'd found them, I'd see what I could discover. The sooner we locate the company, the better. All we need is their address."

Gabriel inwardly frowned. Had his kissing her made her regret approaching him? If so, too late—she had. Her breathless skittishness reached him clearly, but he knew women too well to confuse resistance with rejection. If she wasn't seriously tempted, she wouldn't be skittish. "How did you get in? The door was unlocked ..." Only then did he notice that the boxes she'd been searching were padlocked. Only one was presently open, but ... "You can pick locks."

She shifted. "Well—yes." She gestured briefly. "It's a small talent I have."

He wondered what other talents she was concealing. "As it happens, it's a talent I share." He reached for one of the boxes she'd yet to search. Each was labeled but only with a surname. The one he held was labeled "Mitcham." He looked at the small lock.

"Here."

He glanced up. One delicate hand, gloved in the finest Cordovan leather, offered a hairpin.

"It's just the right size."

His hand surrounded hers as he plucked it from her fingers. He had the box open in a trice; setting back the lid, he picked up the mass of papers within. "Have you stumbled on any details yet—names or other references to the company?"

"No. Nothing. There's no box here or in the other room with the company's name on it, but there must be a box for them, surely? If they're a client, they would have a box, don't you think?"

"So one would imagine." Gabriel glanced around the room. It confirmed his impression of the firm's incumbents. "Messrs. Thurlow and Brown appear staunchly conservative—if the company's a client, they'll have a box."

Side by side, they searched swiftly but thoroughly. An hour ticked by. Eventually, the countess sighed. Setting the papers back in the last box, she closed it, and pushed the box to Gabriel to relock. "Nothing."

"We've still got Thurlow's room. This will only have been half the practice." Replacing the locked box on the top of the last shelf, Gabriel returned, picked up the lamp, and waved her on.

She'd already closed and replaced the ledger she'd used as a screen; now she gave the desk one last, comprehensive glance, checking all was as it had been, then she preceded him out of the door.

"Was this ajar?"

"Yes." She glanced back and nodded at how he'd left the door. "Like that."

In Thurlow's room, they arranged their workplace—the desk cleared, the lamp set and screened as before—then set to. It was slow, demanding work, scanning document after document, looking for any mention of the Central East Africa Gold Company. If anything, Thurlow's room held more boxes than Brown's; the bookshelves were taller.

Gabriel was halfway through yet another box, when he heard a strangled "*Oh!*" He looked up—just in time to drop the papers he held, cross the room in two strides, and catch the stack of boxes teetering over the countess's head.

She was tall enough to reach the top shelf but, in this room, she hadn't been able to grip the boxes, only touch them. At full stretch, she'd coaxed a stack of boxes to the edge of the shelf; they'd tipped, then started to slide ...

He reached over her head and grabbed them, his arms outside hers, his shoulders enclosing hers. They both froze, gripping the tin boxes, desperate not to let them clatter to the floor.

There was less than an inch between them.

Her perfume rose, wreathing his senses; her womanly warmth, clothed in soft, sensual flesh, teased them. The urge to close that small gap, to feel her lean against him, waxed strong.

He sensed the leap of her pulse, the sudden fluster that gripped her. He heard her indrawn breath, sensed her uncertainty—Tilting his head, he touched his lips to her veiled temple. She stilled—the tension that gripped her changed in a flash from physical to sensual; from clinging to a physical pose, she was now teetering on a sensual precipice. He shifted, closing the gap between them until she stood stretched upward against him, touching but not pressing. Sliding his lips from her temple, caressing the line exposed by her backswept hair, he dipped his head and traced the whorl of her ear, then slid his lips lower to tease and tantalize the sensitive spot below her lobe.

Skillfully he tempted her to ease her locked muscles and lean against him. The silk veil shifted beneath his lips, a secondary caress. She caught her breath on a shaky sob and held it; he bent his head and traced the long line of her throat until, at last, she exhaled. Tentatively, ready to take flight at the slightest sign, she let her shoulders ease against his upper chest.

Inwardly smiling in triumph, he angled his head upward, pressing gentle kisses into the hollow of her throat, encouraging her to raise her chin until finally her head tipped back against his shoulder. The warm curves of her back sank more definitely against him.

He wanted much more, but their hands were locked on the boxes still held high and he didn't dare break the spell. She was sweetly responsive but oh-so-skittish, like a mare never gentled to a man's hand. So he kept each caress simple, direct, unthreatening, and as each moment passed, she sank more definitely against him. The subtle warmth of her flowed over his hardness; he was aroused but held the pain at bay. It flashed into his mind that she was a castle he intended storming; his present victory was much like watching her drawbridge come down.

Eventually, she was leaning fully back against him. A fine tension still gripped her, but that derived more from fascinated anticipation than resistance. He pressed a firmer kiss in the hollow beneath her ear, and heard her shivery breath. A tremor shook her, followed by a shaky gasp.

"I'm going to drop these boxes."

He raised his head and looked, and stifled a sigh. Her arms were quivering. He straightened—instantly, she did, too. She drew in a breath and held it. He eased back. Very carefully, she shifted her hands and gripped the lower two boxes, allowing him to lift the upper three away.

Lowering her arms, she stepped sideways, then turned and, spine poker straight, unmistakable resolution in every line, carried the two boxes back to the desk.

Leaving him with three tin boxes and a definite ache.

Jaw setting, Gabriel carried the boxes to the desk, stacking them atop hers. She'd already opened one box. Without glancing at him, she lifted the papers from it and started flicking through them. Eyes narrowing, he considered simply hauling her into his arms; the stiff, abrupt way in which she was turning pages argued against it.

Gritting his teeth, he picked up the pile of papers he'd been searching. He sent her a hard-edged glance. If she saw it, she gave no sign.

They continued to search in silence.

Just as he was wondering if, perhaps, he'd been wrong, and the Central East Africa Gold Company for some unknown reason had not merited a box, the countess straightened.

"This is it."

Gabriel glanced at the box; it was labeled "Swales."

Holding a stack of papers to the lamplight, the countess swiftly studied each in turn. He shifted to stand behind her so he could read over her shoulder. "Those are documents the company would need for registration to conduct business in the City of London." He scanned the sheet she held. "And the company is a formal client of Thurlow and Brown."

"Because all these list Thurlow and Brown as the contact?"

"Yes. The firm must have been hired when the company first entered the City. That means there'll be very few pieces of legal paper listing the company's address."

"There must be one, surely?" She looked up at him over her shoulder; her lips were outlined by her veil. His gaze locked on them and she froze, then a fragile shiver shook her. She looked away and breathlessly asked, "Or will we need to search some government office to find it?"

She didn't see the subtle smile that curved his lips. "There should be at least two documents listing the company's address. One is the main registration of the company, but that will in all likelihood be with the company. The other, however, is a document all solicitors prepare, but which many clients don't know about."

Reaching out, he tugged at the last sheet in the stack; she let him draw it free. He held it up, and smiled. "Here we are—the internal instructions for the firm on how to make contact with the client."

"Mr. Joshua Swales," she read. "Agent of the Central East Africa Gold Company, in the care of Mr. Henry Feaggins, 142 Fulham Road."

They reread the names and address, then Gabriel returned the sheet to the box. Taking the sheaf from the countess's hands, he rifled through it.

"What are you looking for?"

"I wondered if we'd be lucky enough to find a list of investors ... or a list of promissory notes the firm's prepared ... but no." Frowning, he restacked the papers. "Whoever they are, the company are certainly careful."

She held the box as he set the papers back in, then he closed and relocked it. Carrying the other boxes, she followed him back to the shelf. He restacked the boxes in the right order, then turned to discover her already back at the desk, setting it to rights, straightening the blotter, realigning the inkstand.

Completing a last visual scan of the room, he lifted the lamp. "Where did this come from?"

"The little table out here."

She led the way. Gabriel set the lamp down on the side table she indicated, then waited until she passed through the gate in the railings before turning the wick down. The light died. "Let's hope," he murmured, moving around the clerk's desk to the gate, "that the clerk is not the sort to keep a careful eye on the level of his lamp oil."

She returned no comment, but waited by the door.

Retrieving his cane, he opened it. She stepped through. He followed, shutting the door, then crouching down to turn the heavy tumblers of the lock. Not a simple task. They finally fell into place. "How on earth did you manage it?" he asked as he straightened.

"With difficulty."

Certainly not with a hairpin. Stifling his curiosity, he followed her down the stairs. Her heels clicked on the stone. Crossing the cobbles silently would be impossible. At the bottom of the stairs, he took her hand and placed it on his sleeve. She looked up at him—he assumed in surprise. "I presume your carriage is waiting?"

"At the far corner of the Fields."

"I'll escort you to it." In the circumstances, she could hardly argue, yet he knew she considered it. If she'd tried, he would have informed her that, courtesy of five tin boxes, she now had more chance of flying to her carriage than of dismissing him with nothing more than words.

There were rules to all engagements, in seduction as in war; he knew them all and was a past master at exploiting them for his own good. After the first clashes, every lady he'd ever engaged with had decided his exploitation had been for her good, too. Ultimately, the countess would not complain.

They set off, openly crossing the courtyard. He felt her fingers on his sleeve flutter nervously, then settle. He glanced at her veiled face, then let his gaze skate down her cloaked form. "You appear to be a recently bereaved widow who could thus have good reason for visiting the Inn late."

She glanced at him, then gave a slight nod and lifted her head.

Approving the imperious tilt to her chin, Gabriel looked ahead. She was no mean actress—there was now not a hint of trepidation to be seen. If he had to have a female partner, he was glad it was she. She could think, pick locks, and carry off a charade—all definite positives. Despite his irritation on first finding her here, he now felt in considerable charity with her role.

He would, of course, put his foot down and ensure she engaged in no more midnight searches, but that would have to wait until after they got past the porter nodding in his box by the gate. Head up, spine straight, the countess walked past as if the porter didn't exist. The man touched his fingers respectfully to his cap, then yawned and slouched back on his stool.

They walked on. In the shadows cast by the huge trees of the Fields, a small black carriage waited, the horses' heads hanging. As they neared, the coachman glanced around, then hunched over his reins.

Halting by the carriage, Gabriel opened the door.

The countess put out her hand. "Thank you—"

"In a moment." Taking her hand, he urged her into the carriage. He felt her puzzled glance as she complied. As she settled on the seat, he glanced at her coachman. "Brook Street—just past South Molton." With that, he followed the countess into the carriage and shut the door.

She stared at him, then scooted further over as he turned and sat beside her. The carriage rocked into motion.

After an instant's fraught silence, she said, "I wasn't aware I had offered you a ride."

Gabriel considered her veiled face. "No doubt you would have—I thought I'd save you the trouble."

He heard a small spurt of laughter, instantly suppressed. Lips curving, he faced forward. "After all, we need to consider our next move." He'd already mapped out several; all could be attempted in a closed carriage rolling through the night.

"Indeed." Her tone was equable.

"But first, a point I should have made plain at the outset. You asked for my help and I agreed to give it. You also asked for my promise not to seek out your identity."

She stiffened. "Have you?"

His lightheartedness evaporated. "I promised. So no. I haven't." Each word was clipped, each sentence definite. "But if you want me to play your game any further—if we're to continue our alliance and save your stepfamily from ruin—*you'll* have to promise to abide by *my* rules."

Her silence lasted for a good fifty yards. Then, "Your rules?"

He could feel her gaze on the side of his face; he continued to look forward.

"And what are they? These rules of yours."

"Rule number one—you must promise never again to act without my knowledge."

She stirred slightly. "Your *knowledge*?"

Gabriel hid a cynical smile; he'd dealt with women long enough not to label it "permission."

"If you and I act independently, especially in such a delicate affair as this, there's a good chance we'll cross tracks to disastrous effect. If that happens, and we reveal our interest to the company too early, then all you've worked for will go for nought. And you are not sufficiently *au fait* with how matters are dealt with in the City to appreciate all the ramifications of what we might learn, which is, after all, why you sought my help in the first place."

She had none of her sex's usual wariness of silence; again, she claimed it to calculate, to consider. As they swayed around a corner, she asked, "These rules—what are the others?"

"There are only two—I've told you one."

"And the second?"

He turned his head and looked at her. "For each piece of information we gather, I get to claim a reward."

"A reward?" Wariness had crept into her tone.

He suppressed a wolfish smile. "Reward—a customary token of gratitude given in return for services rendered."

She knew precisely what he meant, her knowledge clear in the fine tension that gripped her. After a moment, she cleared her throat. "What reward do you want?"

"For locating Thurlow and Brown—a kiss."

She went still—so still he wondered if he'd shocked her. But she could hardly be surprised—she knew very well who and what he was. From behind her veil, she stared at him, but if she was flustered, there was no sign of it— her hands, folded in her lap, remained still. "A kiss?"

"Hmm." This time, he couldn't stop his lips curving, couldn't suppress the seductive purr that entered his voice. "Without the veil. Take it off."

"No." Calm—absolute.

Arrogantly, he raised his brows.

She shifted on the seat. "No. The veil ... I ..."

He sighed resignedly. "Very well." Before she could think of some pretext on which to refuse the kiss altogether, he framed her face with one hand, his thumb under the edge of her veil, lifting it from her lips as he covered them with his.

Her lips had parted on a startled exclamation—as he caught them, she stilled. She didn't freeze, didn't panic—she simply sat, warm and alive, and let him fashion his lips to hers. He tilted her chin slightly; her face moved easily—she wasn't stiff. But there was no response as he pressed the caress upon her.

He wasn't having that, but he knew when to be patient.

He kissed her lightly, gently shifting his lips on hers, artfully dallying, waiting ...

Her first surrender was a shiver—piercingly sweet, a ripple of pure sensation. He sensed the hitch in her breathing, the increasing tension in her spine.

Then her lips moved, firming under his, still not giving, but alive. It was as if she was a statue coming to life, cool marble slowly heating, stone carapace melting, giving way to flesh, blood, and life.

He held her face steady and increased the pressure of the kiss. Acutely focused on her, he knew when she lifted one gloved hand from her lap, raising it to where his hand cupped her face. Her fingers hovered, an inch from his hand, then, very gently, almost as if she wasn't sure he—his hand—was real, she touched her fingertips to the backs of his.

The hesitant touch rocked him—it held a wondering innocence that captivated and held him.

Her leather-encased fingertips trailed, tracing the back of his hand; they hesitated for one quivering instant, then settled.

Like a butterfly on the back of his hand.

Her fingers didn't grip, didn't tug—they simply touched. He drew breath—drew her perfume deep—and deepened the caress. Asking—for once in his life, not demanding.

And she gave. Of her own accord, she tipped her face further, swaying toward him as she offered her lips.

He swooped like a conqueror and took, claimed—but immediately reined back when he sensed her sudden skitter. She was unused to being kissed. Strange as that seemed, he knew it for fact—he didn't ponder the cause but set himself to ease her, tease her, encourage her.

She was a quick study—soon she was kissing him back, gently but without reserve. He longed to draw her into his arms, but experience warned against it. Her nervousness was now explained—for whatever reason, she wasn't used to this. His lips on hers, his hand about her face, seemed, at this moment, all she could assimilate, so he set himself to work with that.

Set himself to cajole and tease, to lead her to yield more, to seek more. When she hesitantly parted her lips, he felt he'd won a siege, but he was careful, this time, of taking advantage too quickly—which meant he savored every sweet moment of her surrender, the whole extended like a necklace of precious, individual gems of sensation.

When she tentatively touched his tongue with hers, then slowly, sinuously, caressed him in return, his head very nearly spun.

She was like fine wine—best savored slowly.

He finally drew back as the carriage rumbled around a corner. Chest swelling, he studied her lips, briefly illuminated by a street flare. They were full, deeply rosy, slightly swollen. "Now, for learning Swales's address ..."

Her lips parted—whether in protest or invitation he didn't wait to learn. He covered them again; they molded easily, this time, to his, and parted fully the instant he touched them with his tongue.

Brook Street couldn't be much farther. The thought spurred him to drink more deeply, to take all she offered—then seek, search, and tempt her further.

She gave—not so much easily as willingly, taking hesitant steps along a path he instinctively knew she'd never trod. She'd never before been passionately kissed, never been awakened in this way. He had to wonder about her late husband, and whether she'd been awakened at all.

He held her steady, urging her on, his lips ruthless, just this side of hard. He would have taken her further, much further, but tonight they'd run out of time.

The carriage slowed, then rocked to a halt.

Reluctantly, he released her lips. For one instant, as their breaths mingled, he was tempted ... then he drew away his hand and let her veil fall. She would reveal herself to him of her own accord. That was one moment he intended to fully savor.

He straightened. She sank against the seat. She tried to speak and almost choked; clearing her throat, she tried again. "Mr. Cynster ..."

"My name is Gabriel."

Despite her veil, their gazes locked. She stared at him, her breasts rising and falling beneath her cloak. "I thought you had to consider our next move."

His gaze didn't waver. "Believe me, I am."

He waited; when she made no reply but continued to stare at him, he inclined his head. "Until our next meeting." He reached for the door. "Incidentally, when will that be?"

After a moment, she managed, "I'll contact you in a day or two."

She was still breathless; he hid a triumphant smile. "Very well." Deliberately, he let his gaze harden, pinning her where she sat. "But you will remember what I said. Leave Swales to me."

Although it was no question, he waited. Eventually, she nodded—one of her usual crisp nods. "Yes. All right."

Satisfied, he opened the door and stepped down to the pavement. Shutting the door, he signaled to the coachman. The reins flicked; the coach rumbled on.

He watched it roll away, then turned and climbed his steps, a great deal more than merely satisfied with the achievements of the night.

CHAPTER
Four

S he'd never felt so *breathless* in her life.

One elbow propped on the dining table, Alathea toyed with her toast and struggled to bring some order to the chaos of her mind. Not a simple task with her senses still reeling.

How naive she'd been to ignore the portent of that first, oh-so-innocent kiss. Sealing a pact, indeed! It hadn't occurred to her that, with no prickly reaction to stop him, he would most assuredly kiss her again. So now here she was, in a totally unexpected, never-before-experienced fluster. Just the thought of last night's kiss—*series* of kisses—was enough to addle her brain. One conclusion, however, was horrifyingly clear. Her errant knight believed she was a married woman—an *experienced* married woman—one with whom he could freely dally. But she wasn't. Thus far, he hadn't suspected that fact, but how far could she travel his road of rewards without giving herself away?

Without *having* to give herself away?

All that was bad enough, but to top it all, he'd filched the reins from her grasp. God alone knew where her carefully laid plans were now headed.

She should have foreseen his move to take control; he'd always been the leader in their childhood games. But they were no longer children, and for the last ten years she'd been accustomed to command; being summarily relegated to the rank of follower was a little hard to take.

About her, the rest of her family talked, ate, laughed; sunk in her thoughts, she barely heard them. Picking up her toast, she crunched, and decided she'd have to allow at least the appearance of him being in charge. His Cynster self would settle for nothing less; it was pointless beating her head against that wall. That didn't mean she had to meekly let him make all the decisions, only let him think he was. Which led to the question of how she could ensure that he didn't forge on and simply leave her in ignorance.

She would have to meet with him regularly, a prospect that made her edgy. Organizing their next meeting was logically her next step, but she'd yet to recover from their last. She'd counted on his deep vein of chivalry in enticing him to her aid—not in her wildest dreams had she imagined he'd extrapolate so fiendishly as to claim a reward.

Even that word was now forever altered in her mind. Now it instantly evoked something illicit. Something exciting, thrilling, tempting—Seductive.

Her thoughts whirled; her lungs seized. Simply recalling that moment in the carriage when, with typical highhandedness, he'd set his lips to hers still made her dizzy. Remembering what had followed sent color rushing to her cheeks.

Instantly, she banished the mental visions, and the remembered sensations as well. If anything, the latter were worse. Lifting her teacup, she sipped and prayed no one had noticed her blush. She hadn't blushed in the last five years, possibly not in the last ten. If she suddenly started coloring up over nothing, questions would be asked—speculation would be born. Quite the last thing she needed.

Ruthlessly burying all memories of the drive to his house, she told herself she had no reason to berate herself; she couldn't have avoided it—any of it— without raising his suspicions. There was no point considering it further, beyond sending heartfelt thanks to her guardian angel—she'd very nearly blurted out his name when he'd released her. "Rupert" had hovered on the tip of her tongue; she'd only just managed to swallow the word. Uttering it would have spelled an immediate end to her charade; she was the only female younger than his mother who persisted in calling him by his given name. He'd told her so himself.

Why she was so stubborn about it she didn't know—it was like clinging to a simpler time long gone. She'd always thought of him as Rupert.

My name is Gabriel.

His words rang in her mind. Gazing at the windows, she pondered; he was right—he was Gabriel now, not Rupert. Gabriel contained the boy, the youth, the man she'd known as Rupert, but also encompassed more. A greater depth, a greater spectrum of experience—a deeper reserve.

After a moment, she mentally shook herself and finished her tea. As the countess, she would have to remember to call him Gabriel, while Alathea still dubbed him Rupert.

And she would have to find a way to limit the rewards Gabriel would, without doubt, attempt to claim.

"I think we should call on Lady Hertford this morning." Checking the day's invitations, Serena looked consideringly at Mary and Alice. "She's giving an at-home, and I *think*, if you wear those gowns that were delivered yesterday, it would be a useful venue at which to be seen."

"Oh, yes!" Mary exclaimed. "Do let's start going about."

"Will there be other young ladies there?" Alice asked.

"Naturally." Serena turned to Alathea. "And you must come, too, my dear, or else I'll have to spend all my time explaining your absence."

That was said with a sweet but determined smile; Alathea smiled back. "Of course, I'll come, if nothing else to lend support."

Mary and Alice brightened even more. Amid serious discussion of ribbons, bonnets and reticules, they all retired upstairs to prepare for the projected excursion.

It was, indeed, very like a military sortie. An hour later, standing at the side of Lady Hertford's drawing room, Alathea hid a grin. Serena had led the metaphorical charge into her ladyship's arena, positioning her troops with keen eye and shrewd judgment. Mary and Alice were engaged with a group of similarly young and inexperienced damsels, chattering animatedly, all initial shyness forgotten. Serena was sitting with Lady Chelmsford and the Duchess of Lewes, both of whom also had under their wings young ladies making their come-outs. Alathea would have wagered a tidy sum that the talk had already veered to which gentlemen might be expected to unearth handkerchiefs to drop this Season.

For herself, she stood quietly at the side of the room, although she knew she'd been noted by all. As Serena had remarked, if she hadn't appeared, her whereabouts would have been questioned, but now that the matrons present had confirmed that the earl's eldest daughter—unmarried, which was a mystery, but quite an ape-leader now—was in no way out of the ordinary and was quite comfortable with her stepsisters and stepmother—well, with no grist for the gossip mill to be found, she'd been dismissed from their collective consciousness.

That suited her very well.

Finishing her tea, she glanced around for a table on which to set her cup. Spying one beyond the *chaise* on which her hostess sat chatting to one of her bosom-bows, Alathea glided along the wall, passing behind the *chaise* to set her cup down. She was about to retreat when the words "Central East Africa Gold Company" froze her where she stood.

She stared at the back of Lady Hertford's frizzy red head.

"An absolutely *certain* return, my cousin said, so naturally I told Geoffrey. I gave him the name of the man in charge, but Geoffrey's been hemming and hawing, dragging his feet." Leaning closer to her friend, Lady Hertford lowered her voice. "You may be sure I pointed out that what with the *unexpected costs* his heir has incurred at Oxford, he should be eager to better his current standing—I told him plainly that this year, Jane would need not just better gowns but more in her portion as well. But would he be moved?"

Lady Hertford sat poker straight, disapproval for her errant spouse in every line. "I'm convinced," she hissed, "that it's only because my dearest cousin Ernest suggested it, and Geoffrey's never liked Ernest."

Her friend murmured sympathetically, then turned the conversation to their offspring. Alathea moved away. Clearly, Lord Hertford shared her reaction to the Central East Africa Gold Company—in his case, if her ladyship was to be believed, because of who was "in charge."

From across the room, a turbaned dowager beckoned; Alathea obeyed the summons. With a serene smile firmly in place, she withstood an intensive inquisition on her obsession for the country and her spinster state. Not, of course, that the words "unfashionable recluse" or "husband" ever featured in the conversation.

Invincible serenity and an adamant refusal to be drawn finally won her her release from Lady Merricks, who snorted and waved her away. "Unconscionable—that's what it is, miss! Your grandmama would have been the first to say so."

With that observation ringing in her ears, Alathea gravitated back to the side of the room, and wondered if she dared broach the subject of the Central East Africa Gold Company with her hostess. One glance at Lady Hertford's round and ruddy countenance put paid to that idea. Her ladyship was unlikely to have any information beyond what she'd already divulged. More to the point, she would be amazed by Alathea's inquiry. Ladies of her ilk, young or otherwise, should have no interest in such matters—ladies of her ilk were not supposed to know such matters existed.

Which was a definite hurdle, for she could not, on the same count, beard his lordship, either.

Alathea glanced at the door. Did she dare slip out and search Lord Hertford's study? She debated the likelihood of finding anything helpful; if learning the name of the man behind the company had been enough to cool his lordship's interest, it seemed unlikely he would have needed to write it down.

The probable return did not seem worth the risk of getting caught searching Lord Hertford's study. She could just imagine the scandal *that* would provoke, especially if her reasons for searching ever came out.

And what if Gabriel learned of it?

No. She'd have to be patient. The very word chafed—she trenchantly repeated it. In the matter of the Central East Africa Gold Company, she was the countess and the countess had put her trust in Gabriel.

Patience and trust were all very well, but such virtues did nothing to ease her curiosity or allay the conviction that, if she left him too much to his own devices, Gabriel would either solve the entire matter and then present himself before her expecting to claim some impossible reward, or he'd become mired in some distracting detail and lose the thread entirely. Either was possible. If *he* had always been the leader, *she* had always been his *eminence grise*. It was time to reclaim that position.

They were attending an evening party at Osbaldestone House. Standing by the *chaise* on which Serena sat conversing with Lady Chadwick, Alathea scanned the crowd gathered to celebrate Lady Osbaldestone's sixtieth birthday. For her purpose, the setting was perfect.

Two days had passed since their unplanned meeting at Lincoln's Inn, two days in which Gabriel should have investigated the company's agent and his place of business. It was time for the countess to ask for a report.

Before her, the flower of the ton mingled and met. There was no dancing, just a string quartet installed in an alcove, vainly striving to be heard over the din. Talk—gossip and repartee—were the primary occupations of the evening, activities at which the guest of honor excelled.

Lady Osbaldestone was sitting on a *chaise* facing the room's center. Alathea glanced her way. The old lady thumped her cane on the floor, then pointed it at Vane Cynster, currently standing before her. Vane stepped back as if taking refuge behind the willowy figure of his wife. Alathea had met Patience Cynster in the park a few days before. Patience curtsied with unruffleable calm before her ladyship.

Alathea wished *she* had a little more patience—her eyes strayed to the clock for the third time in ten minutes. It was not yet ten o'clock; the party had barely begun. Guests were still arriving. Gabriel was already here, but it was too early for the countess to materialize.

The Cynsters were here *en masse*, Lady Osbaldestone being a connection. Alathea was watching two beauties presently holding court under Gabriel's oddly unimpressed eye when long fingers wrapped about her elbow.

"Welcome to town, my dear."

The fingers slid down to tangle with hers and briefly squeeze. Alathea turned, a smile lighting her face. "I wondered where you were." She ran an appreciative glance over the tall, dark-haired, dark-garbed figure beside her. "Now what am I supposed to call you—Alasdair? Or Lucifer?"

His smile flashed, the pirate beneath the fashionable facade showing briefly. "Either will do."

Alathea raised a brow. "Both accurate?"

"I do my poor best."

"I'm sure you do." She looked across the room. "But what's he doing?"

Lucifer followed her gaze to his brother. "Guard duty. We take turns."

Alathea studied the girls and caught the resemblance. "They're your cousins?"

"Hmm. They don't have an older brother to watch over them, so we do. Devil's in charge, of course, but he's not often in town these days. Very busy taking care of the ducal acres, the ducal purse, and the ducal succession."

Alathea's gaze shifted to the tall, striking figure of the Duke of St. Ives. "I see." Devil was paying amazingly close attention to a haughtily commanding lady standing by his side. "The lady with him ...?"

"Honoria, his duchess."

"Ah!" Alathea nodded; Devil's intent gaze was now explained. She'd met all Gabriel's and Lucifer's male cousins occasionally over the years; she had no difficulty picking them out from the crowd. The family resemblance was definite, their general handsomeness a byword, although they were all identifiably distinct, from Devil's striking, piratical looks, to Vane's cool grace, to Gabriel's classical features and Lucifer's dark beauty. "I can't see the other two." She scanned the crowd again.

"They're not here. Richard and his witch are resident in Scotland."

"His witch?"

"Well, his wife, but she truly is a witch of sorts. She's known as the Lady of the Vale in those parts."

"Indeed?"

"Mmm. And Demon's busy escorting his new wife on a prolonged tour of the racetracks."

"Racetracks?"

"They have a shared interest in racing Thoroughbreds."

"Oh." Alathea checked her mental list. "That leaves only you two still unwed."

Lucifer narrowed his eyes at her. *"Et tu, Brute?"*

Alathea smiled. "Merely an observation."

"Just as well, or I might be tempted to point out that those who live in glass houses shouldn't throw stones."

Alathea's smile didn't waver. "You know I've decided marriage isn't for me."

"I know you've told me so—what I've never understood is why."

Shaking her head, she looked away. "Never mind." Her gaze returned to the two blond beauties chatting gaily, studiously ignoring Gabriel's lounging, deliberately intimidating presence mere yards away. "Your young cousins—are they twins?"

"Yes. This is their second Season, but they are only eighteen."

"Eighteen?" Alathea glanced at Lucifer, then back at the girls, confirming the modish gowns a touch more elegant than permissable for a girl in her first Season, the more sophisticated hairstyles, the assurance in the girls' gestures. Considering Gabriel watching over them like a potentially lethal avenging angel, Alathea shook her head. "What on earth does he—you—think you're doing? If they're eighteen … why"—she swung to look at Mary and Alice talking in a group nearby—"Alice is only seventeen."

"She is?" Lucifer turned to stare at Mary and Alice. "Good Lord—I didn't notice they were here." He frowned, then glanced across the room at his cousins. "If you'll excuse me?"

Without waiting for an answer, he swooped on Mary and Alice. With effortless charm, he detached them from their circle. One on each arm, he bore them across the room. Alathea watched, the question of what he was doing fading from her mind as the answer presented itself. He introduced her sisters to his cousins—a moment later, he slipped away from the enlarged circle now containing all four young ladies surrounded by a bevy of exceedingly safe, exceedingly careful young gentlemen.

The pleased-with-himself look on Lucifer's face as he slid into the crowd had Alathea shaking her head, not in wonder so much as resignation. She'd been the recipient of the protectiveness of Cynster males often enough to recognize the impulse. Knowing she was supposed to approve, although she wasn't at all sure she did, she smiled in reply to Lucifer's questioning glance.

Lucifer headed for Gabriel. Smoothly, Alathea joined the circle about Serena's *chaise*. From the corner of her eye, she watched Lucifer explain his new arrangement; Gabriel nodded and passed the watch to Lucifer. Lucifer pulled a face but acquiesced, taking Gabriel's place by the wall.

Alathea darted a glance at the clock. Perfect. Lucifer's maneuvers were going to prove unexpectedly helpful; for the next hour she felt sure she could rely on him and his fair cousins to keep Mary and Alice happily occupied. And any minute now ...

Majestic, yet blending into the glittering scene, Lady Osbaldestone's butler cleaved through the crowd. He stopped before Gabriel and presented a silver salver. Gabriel lifted a note from the salver, dismissing the butler with a nod. Opening the folded sheet, he scanned it, then refolded it and slipped it into his pocket.

The entire proceedings had taken no more than a minute—unless one had been watching Gabriel specifically, in the crush, nothing would have been seen. Not a flicker of expression betrayed his thoughts—on anything.

Trusting he'd respond to the instructions in the note, Alathea looked away, giving her attention to Serena and her neighbors until it was time for her next move.

She reached the gazebo five minutes early, already slightly breathless. She told herself it was because she'd hurried, because she'd kept trying to watch in every direction at once to make sure no one saw her slip away. The vise locked about her lungs owed nothing to the fact that she was soon to meet Gabriel—not Rupert, but his far more dangerous alter ego—once more in the dark of night.

Folwell had been waiting as instructed in the thick bushes lining the carriage drive. He'd brought her cloak, veil and high-heeled shoes, and her special perfume. Drawing in a deep breath—steeling herself—Alathea let the exotic scent wreathe through her brain. She *was* the countess.

In her disguise, she actually felt like someone else—not Lady Alathea Morwellan, spinster, ape-leader. It was as if her anonimity and the seductive perfume brought out another side of her—she had little difficulty sliding into her role.

The gazebo stood tucked away at the end of the shrubbery—she'd remembered it from years ago. It was far enough from the house to be safe from the risk of others chancing by, and so overhung by trees and rampant shrubs that she need not fear any stray beam of light, a pertinent consideration as she'd been unable to change her gown.

Outside, gravel crunched. A sudden thrill shot through her; tingles of excitement raced over her skin. Facing the archway, she drew herself up, head erect, hands clasped before her. Anticipation slid, insidiously compelling, through her veins. Ruthlessly quelling a reactive shiver, she drew in a tight breath. Tonight, she was determined to hold her own.

He appeared, a black silhouette filling the doorway, her sworn knight come to report. He was a dark presence, intensely masculine, achingly familiar yet so unnervingly unknown. Pausing on the threshold, he located her in the dark; he hesitated—she felt his gaze rake her, felt an inexplicable urge to turn and flee. Instead, she stood still, silent and challenging.

He strolled forward.

"Good evening, my dear."

She was a creature of night and shadow, discernible only as a darker shape in the dense gloom within the gazebo. Her height, her veil and cloak— Gabriel could see nothing beyond that, but his senses had abruptly focused; he was sure it was she. Halting directly before her, he studied her, very conscious of the alluring perfume that rose from her flesh. "You didn't sign your note."

Despite not being able to see it, he knew she raised a haughty brow. "How many ladies send you messages to meet them in dark gazebos?"

"More than you'd care to count."

She stilled. "Were you expecting someone else?"

"No." He paused, then added, "I was expecting you." Not here at Osbaldestone House, under his very nose, but he hadn't imagined she'd calmly sit in her drawing room and wait for a week before contacting him again. "I expect you'd like to know what I've learned?"

He heard the purr in his voice, and sensed her wariness.

"Indeed." She lifted her chin; he could feel the challenge in her gaze.

"Swales doesn't live at that address on the Fulham Road—it's a public house called the Onslow Arms. Henry Feaggins is the proprietor. He holds the mail for Swales."

"Does Feaggins know where Swales lives?"

"No—Swales simply stops by every few days. There was no mail to be collected, so I sent a letter—a blank sheet. Swales came in this morning and picked it up. My man followed him—Swales went to a mansion in Egerton Gardens. It seems he lives there."

"Who owns the mansion?"

"Lord Archibald Douglas."

"Lord Douglas?"

He looked sharply at her. "Do you know him?"

She shook her head. "Could Lord Douglas be the chairman of the company?"

Her question effectively answered his. "Unlikely—Archie Douglas cares for nothing beyond wine, women, and cards. Spending money is his forte, not making it. However ..." He paused, considering how much to reveal. Looking at her veiled face, upturned to his, he inwardly admitted that it was her investigation as much, if not more, than his. "If Swales is the company agent and he's using Archie's home as his base, then there's a very good chance— better than even money—that a good friend of Archie's, who also happens to be in residence at this time, is the real power behind the Central East Africa Gold Company."

"And who is this friend?"

"Mr. Ranald Crowley." The name hung heavy on the air, laden with dislike.

"You know him." It wasn't a question.

"We've never met. We have, however, crossed swords, financially speaking, and I know a great deal of his reputation."

"Which is?"

"Not good. He's a black-hearted scoundrel. He's been thought to have been involved in a number of less-than-straightforward dealings, but whenever the authorities show any interest, the venture simply evaporates. There's never been any proof against him, but in the … shall we say, underworld of business, he's well known." He hesitated, then added, "And well feared. He's said to be cunning and dangerous—few doubt he would balk at murder if the gain was sufficient."

She shivered and wrapped her arms about her. "So he's a *clever*, black-hearted scoundrel." A moment later, she said, "I overheard that Lord Hertford declined to invest in the company purely because of 'the man in charge.' "

Focused on her, Gabriel waved dismissively. "Don't worry about Crowley—I'll look into the situation."

He reached for her—she was in his arms before she knew it. Amazed to find her hands resting on his chest, she looked up. "What—?"

He heard the fluster in her voice, sensed the anticipation that flashed through her. Inwardly, he grinned. "My reward for locating Swales."

She hauled in a rushed breath. "I never said anything about rewards."

"I know." Tightening his arm about her, he brushed her veil aside and lowered his lips to hers, touching them lingeringly once, twice … she quivered, then surrendered. He caught his breath as her supple, womanly warmth sank against his much harder frame—a tentative, evocative caress. His lips a mere whisker from hers, he murmured, "You'll need to pay nevertheless."

She made no effort to deny him—he claimed his due, his lips firming, then hardening on hers. She met him, not proactive but ready to follow his lead, her reactions a mirror reflecting his desire, her giving a reflection of his need. Inch by unconscious inch, her hands stole upward, eventually sliding over his shoulders. She angled her head, inviting him to deepen the kiss.

He did. She sank into his embrace and he tightened his arms, and his hold, on her. Her perfume sank into his brain.

All he asked for, she gave, not just willingly but with an openhearted generosity that was an invitation to plunder. So he plundered, but with no sense of seizing anything that wasn't freely given. If he wanted, she gave—readily, easily, as if she delighted in the giving. Which only made him want more.

He pushed her veil back; with her head tipped up, there was no need to hold it. Sliding his hand down, he found the opening of her cloak. With her arms over his shoulders, he couldn't flick the cloak up and over hers. Instead, he parted it, sliding his palm over the silk of her gown, around to the back of her waist. Supporting her there, he transferred his other hand beneath the heavy cloak; closing both hands about her hips, he drew her nearer.

She obliged without a murmur of dissent—she was so tall, they were nearly hip to hip, her thighs against his, the hollow at their apex a cradle for his erection. If she was aware of it, she gave no sign, not that he gave her time to think. His lips remained on hers, commanding her senses while his sought wilder pleasures.

When he closed his hand about her breast, he wondered if he'd gone too far—the shock that lanced through her was very real. He instinctively soothed, distracting her with his lips, his tongue, with increasingly explicit kisses, but he didn't remove his hand. Moments later, she drew in a shaky breath. Beneath his hand, her breast swelled; against his palm, he felt the furling of her nipple. Only then did he caress the soft flesh, feeling it heat and firm. She was wearing nothing more than two layers of fine silk; the temptation to do away with them, to lower his head and set his mouth to her sweet flesh, grew with every second, with every shared breath.

He let the compulsion grow, caressing, teasing, taunting, kneading, stroking until he knew her breasts were aching, longing for more. Only then did he slip the tiny buttons closing her bodice free. Sliding his fingers across her silken shoulder, he searched, and found the ribbons of her chemise.

She knew what he was doing. Her awareness, focused, heightened, followed his fingers; the fine tension investing the supple muscles along her spine tightened—then locked as he tugged. The tiny bow unraveled; the ribbons slid free. He paused, deliberately easing back from their kiss, giving her a chance to stop him if she would. He knew very well she wouldn't. He searched, found, and tugged again. Her breath shivered against his lips. Smoothly, he drew her chemise down, deliberately dragging the silk over her sensitized flesh.

Then, deliberately, he pressed aside the heavier silk of her bodice and closed his hand, skin to petal-soft skin, about her breast.

Her breathing fractured. His fingers firmed and she gasped.

He took her lips again, too hungry, too needy, even while his senses feasted. She'd never been touched, not as he was touching her, caressing her until she whimpered and clung. Her flesh was warm, her nipples tight buds as she gave herself up to his touch. She was a sensual innocent, as generous with her body as she had been with her lips, every bit as instinctively giving. The hot mounds of her breasts were a sensual delight far too tempting to ignore.

She murmured incoherently when he drew his lips from hers, nudging her head back so he could trace the line of her throat, remembering just in time not to mark her. The sweet flesh filling his hand beckoned; he lowered his head and heard her stifled cry.

It was a warning, one he was too experienced not to heed. He was driving too fast, pushing her relentlessly along a path she'd never trod. So he slowed, introducing her to each sensation, letting her assimilate the glory of each before moving on to the next. Only when she was fully prepared did he draw one aching peak into his mouth. Her fingers sank into his shoulders; she arched in his arms, but not to pull away. She was hot and malleable under his hands, the very essence of sensual woman in the night.

She was fascinating, a houri, a woman of endless temptation—he basked in her warmth, feasted on her bounty, secure in the knowledge that she would eventually be his. Not tonight, but soon. Very soon.

When, at last, he lifted his head, she pressed herself to him, her body afire, helpless in her need. He took the lips she offered, glorying in her eagerness. He sent his hands roaming over her hips, over the smooth swells of her derriere, tracing the hemispheres, then artfully caressing until she shifted her hips sensuously against his, searching instinctively for ease.

He gave her none—not tonight. She might be wondrously responsive, gloriously giving, but tonight would be too far, too fast. She was sensually naive, definitely untutored, even if she could not be precisely innocent. Having known only a much older husband who had clearly failed to appreciate her, that was obviously the case. She was following his lead blind; he knew it. He, however, knew precisely what they were about, knew very well how the timing went, how the play should pan out. And even though he'd restructured the script and advanced her lessons to the point where her ultimate surrender was imminent, that time was not yet.

Thus spake the coldly calculating mind of a highly experienced rake. His body, unfortunately, was far from cold and didn't want to listen; most of his mind was similarly enthralled with the wonder in his arms.

It took iron will and every ounce of his determination even to think of letting her go, to accept that this interlude filled with burgeoning sensuality and such gloriously heady promise had to come to a close. An unfulfilled close. Even when his mind was finally won over, convincing his lips, tongue, arms and hands to comply was a battle.

He finally succeeded in lifting his head. Drawing in a huge breath, feeling her breasts hot and firm against his expanding chest, he stole just one more minute to revel in the feel of her against him, in the trusting way she leaned into him, the soft huff of her breath against his jaw, the heady temptation of her perfume. And her.

She sighed—a shivery exhalation laden with arousal, her breath caressed his cheek.

His arms, about to relax, tightened instead; he turned his head, his lips seeking hers, his script forgotten—She stopped him with a hand on his cheek. "Enough."

For an instant, he teetered on the brink, her injunction at odds with the way she lay, supple and enticing in his arms.

As if she sensed the clash of will and desire, she repeated, "You've had reward enough."

He caught her hand, held it—unsure even in his own mind what he would do next. Then he drew breath, turned her hand, and placed a kiss in her palm. "For now."

He straightened, setting her on her feet, supporting her until she was steady.

Her first movement was to raise her hand and—weakly—flip down her veil. He could now see her outline clearly; transparently dazed, she looked down at her gaping bodice. He reached for her. "Here—let me."

She did. He drew her chemise up, tied the ribbons loosely, then closed her bodice. Her nervousness grew. The instant the last button was secured, she resettled her cloak, then glanced around. "Ah ..." She was clearly having trouble reassembling her wits. Drawing in another breath, she waved—weakly still—to the house. "You go back first."

Despite having found her here, he wasn't about to leave her here, alone in the dark. "I'll walk you to the edge of the shrubbery, then I'll go on ahead."

For one instant, he thought she'd argue, but then she nodded. "Very well."

He offered his arm and she took it; pacing slowly, he led her out of the gazebo.

She said nothing as they strolled the winding walks, leaving him to reflect on how at ease in her company he felt, and how, despite the sensual flickering of her nerves, she was confident enough, reassured enough, not to invoke conversation's protective screen. Now he thought of it, she'd yet to make an aimless remark. Meaningless patter was not the countess's style.

They reached the last hedge and she stopped. He scanned her veiled face, then inclined his head. "Until next time."

Turning, he strode across the lawn.

Her pulse still galloping, her head still whirling, Alathea watched her broad-shouldered knight cross to the house, saw him silhouetted by its blazing windows. He went up the terrace steps and in through the open doors without once looking back.

Shrinking back into the darkness, she waited for long minutes while her fevered skin cooled, while her heartbeat steadied, while the exhilaration that had gripped her—the daring, the compulsion, and that frighteningly wild and wanton desire—waned. She tried to think but couldn't. Finally, hugging the shadows, she made her way around to the carriage drive.

Folwell was waiting; she handed him her cloak and veil, and changed her shoes. He slipped away, taking her disguise back to the carriage. Once more herself—at least in appearance—she reentered the house by a side door, then made her way to the withdrawing room.

Luckily, the event wasn't a major ball; the withdrawing room was quiet. Sitting before a table provided with a mirror, she ordered warm water and towel and set about bathing her wrists, temples, and throat, removing all trace of the countess's exotic scent. Then she asked for cold water, dipped in a corner of the towel, and when no other lady was looking, held the cold compress to her swollen lips.

She didn't dare peek, but she was sure he must have marked her. Scalded her, or so it had felt. Thank God nothing showed above her neckline. Just the thought of his mouth on her breasts sent heat rushing to them. She could feel his hands caressing her—she wished they still were.

In the mirror, she met her own eyes. She looked deep for long minutes, then grimaced. Looking down, she dipped the towel into the cold water; after a surreptitious glance around, she reapplied it to her still rosy lips.

She wasn't in the habit of deceiving herself—there was no point pretending that she hadn't known he would claim a reward if he'd uncovered any new facts, and that the likelihood of his having done so had been high. She'd gone to the gazebo knowing her protests would very likely prove too weak to stop him claiming all he wished.

She'd been right about that, but it was too late for regrets. In truth, she wasn't sure she harbored any.

That, however, did not alter the fact that she was now in deep trouble.

He thought they were playing a game—one at which he was an acknowledged expert but which she had never played before. She knew some of the rules, but not all of them; she knew some of the moves, but not enough of them. She'd initiated the charade, but now he'd taken control and was rescripting her role to suit his own needs.

To suit his own desires.

She tried to summon a suitable degree of annoyance; the thought that he desired her wouldn't let annoyance form. The very concept intrigued her, lured her. No serpent had ever been so persuasive; no apple so tempting.

No knight so invincibly demanding.

That last made her sigh—changing direction was impossible. She'd started the charade; she'd have to play her part. Her options were severely limited.

She studied her reflection, then, with her usual deliberation, decided: While alone with him, she wasn't Lady Alathea Morwellan but his mysterious countess. It was the countess he'd kissed and the countess who'd responded.

Not her.

There'd been no harm done; none would be done.

She lowered the towel. He'd seemed to find her kisses—and the rest of her—quite satisfactory as a reward. She'd sensed his hunger—his appetite; she was certain that was not something he would fabricate. Their interaction was in no way harming him, and while it might be unsettling—even eye-opening—it wasn't hurting her.

And the fact that her kisses were enough to satisfy one of the ton's most exacting lovers was an invisible feather she'd proudly wear in her spinster cap—the cap she'd wear for the rest of her life.

Refocusing on the mirror, she critically surveyed her face and lips. Almost normal.

Her lips twisted wryly. Impossible to play the hypocrite and pretend that she hadn't enjoyed it—that she hadn't felt a thrill, an excitement beyond anything she'd previously known. In those long minutes when he'd held her in her arms, claiming her, she'd felt a woman whole for the first time in her life.

Indeed, he made her feel like a woman other than herself—or did he simply make her feel things she shouldn't, compulsions she'd had no idea she could experience. She was twenty-nine, on the shelf, very definitely an old maid. In his arms, she hadn't felt old at all—she'd felt alive.

Driven by necessity, she'd set aside all hope of ever knowing what it was to be a woman with a man. She'd had her longings, but she'd locked them away, telling herself they could never be fulfilled. And they never could be—not all of them, not now. But if, in protecting her family again as she was, the chance was offered to experience just a little of what she'd had to forgo, wasn't that merely justice?

And if she knew she was playing with fire? Tempting fate beyond the bounds of all sanity?

Setting down the towel, she stared into her eyes, then she stood and turned toward the door.

She couldn't turn her back on her family, which meant she couldn't walk away from Gabriel.

Whether she wished it or not, she was trapped in her charade.

CHAPTER

Five

Heathcote Montague's office looked down on a small courtyard tucked away behind buildings a stone's throw from the Bank of England. Standing before the window, Gabriel stared down at the cobbles, his mind fixed on the countess.

Who *was* she? Had she been a guest at Osbaldestone House, lips curving with secret laughter as she waltzed past him? Or, knowing he, together with all the Cynsters, would be there, had she slipped in uninvited, waited in the garden until their meeting, then slipped away through the shadows again? If so, she'd taken a considerable risk—who knows whom she might inadvertently have met. He didn't like her taking risks—that was one point he fully intended to make clear.

But only after he'd made love to her—after he'd had his fill of her feminine delights and pleasured her into oblivion.

He had a strong suspicion she didn't even know what sexual oblivion was. But she would—just as soon as he had her alone again. After last night, that much was certain—he'd already had his fill of restless nights.

"Hmm. Nothing here."

It took him a moment to return to the present, then he turned.

Heathcote Montague, perennially neat, precise but self-effacing, set the three notes he'd just received to one side of his desk and looked up. "I've heard back from nearly everyone. None of us, nor any of our clients, have been approached. Precisely what one would expect if the Central East Africa Gold Company is another of Crowley's crooked schemes."

"Us" referred to the select band of "men of business" who handled the financial affairs and investments of the wealthiest families in England.

"I think"—deserting the window, Gabriel started to pace—"given it is Crowley behind it and he's avoiding all knowledgeable investors, then we can reasonably conclude the scheme's a fraud. Furthermore, if the amounts involved are comparable to that on the promissory note I saw, this scheme's going to cause considerable financial distress if it runs its course."

"Indeed." Montague leaned back. "But you know the law's view as well as I. The authorities won't step in until fraud is apparent—"

"By which time it's always too late." Gabriel faced Montague. "I want to shut this scheme down, quickly and cleanly."

"That's going to be difficult with promissory notes." Montague held his gaze. "I assume you don't want this note you saw executed."

"No."

Montague grimaced. "After last time, Crowley's not going to explain his plans to you."

"Not that he explained them to me last time." Gabriel returned to the window. He and Ranald Crowley had a short but not sweet past history. One of Crowley's first ventures, floated in the City, had sounded very neat, looked very tempting. It had been poised to draw in a large number of the ton, until he had been asked for his opinion. He'd considered the proposal, asked a few pertinent but not obvious questions, to which there were no good answers, and the pigeons had taken flight. The incident had closed many doors for Crowley.

"You're probably," Montague observed, "one of Crowley's least favorite people."

"Which means I can't appear or show my hand in any way in this case. And nor can you."

"The mere mention of the name Cynster will be enough to raise his hackles."

"And his suspicions. If he's as cunning as his reputation paints him, he'll know all about me by now."

"True, but we're going need details of the specific proposal made to investors to secure their promissory notes in order to prove fraud."

"So we need a trustworthy sheep."

Montague blinked. "A sheep?"

Gabriel met his gaze. "Someone who can believably line up to be fleeced."

"Serena!"

Together with Serena, seated beside her, Alathea turned to see Lady Celia Cynster waving from her barouche drawn up beside the carriageway.

Waving in reply, Serena spoke to their coachman. "Here, Jacobs—as close as you can."

Spine poker straight, Jacobs angled their carriage onto the verge three carriages from Celia's. By the time Alathea, Mary, and Alice had stepped down to the grass, Celia and her girls were upon them.

"Wonderful!" Celia watched her daughters, Heather, sixteen, and Eliza, fifteen, greet Mary and Alice. The air was instantly abuzz with chatter and innocent queries. The four girls had the years of their shared childhoods to bind them in much the same way as Alathea, Lucifer, and Gabriel. Celia gestured at her offspring. "They insist on coming for a drive, only to become bored after the first five minutes."

"They have yet to learn that social chatter is the … *comme ca va?*—oil that makes the ton's wheels go around?"

"Oil that greases the ton's wheels." Celia turned to the speaker, a strikingly beautiful older lady who had strolled up in her wake.

Alathea curtsied deeply. "Your Grace."

Serena, still seated in the carriage, bowed and echoed the words.

Smiling, Helena, Dowager Duchess of St. Ives, put out a gloved hand to tip up Alathea's face. "You grow more attractive with the years, *ma petite*."

Through her frequent visits to Quiverstone Manor, the Dowager was well known to the Morwellans. Alathea smiled and rose; the Dowager's brows rose, too. "Not so petite." Catching Alathea's eye, she lifted one brow even higher. "Which makes it even more of a mystery why you are not wed, *hein*?"

The words were uttered softly; Alathea smiled and refused to be drawn. While she was used to such queries, the intelligence behind the Dowager's pale green eyes always left her with the uncomfortable feeling that here was one who suspected the truth.

The carriage rocked as Serena rose, clearly intending to join them. Helena waved her back. "No, no. I will ascend and we can chat in comfort." She gestured at Celia and Alathea. "These two must stretch their legs in the service of propriety."

Alathea and Celia looked in the direction of Helena's nod; the four girls, heads together, arms linked, were already strolling the lawn.

Celia sighed resignedly. "At least we can stroll together and chat."

Leaving Helena settling in beside Serena, Alathea and Celia followed the four girls, but with no intention of joining them. They only needed to keep the girls in sight, leaving them free to talk without reserve.

Celia immediately availed herself of that freedom. "Have you spoken to Rupert since coming up to town?"

"Yes." Alathea mentally scrambled to recall the meeting—the one with Rupert, not Gabriel. "We met briefly while the girls and I were out walking."

"Well, then. You'll have seen. What *am* I to do with him?"

Alathea swallowed the observation that no one had ever been able to "do" anything with Rupert Melrose Cynster.

He was as malleable as granite and always on guard against manipulation. As for Gabriel ..."I saw nothing unusual. What worries you so?"

"Him! *He!*" Celia's fists clenched on the handle of her parasol. "He's even more infuriating than his father. At least, by his age, Martin had had the good sense to marry me. But will Rupert turn his mind to the same task?"

"He's only thirty."

"Which is more than old enough. Demon has married, and Richard, too—Richard's only a bare year older than Rupert." A minute later, Celia sighed. "It's not so much the marrying as his frame of mind. He doesn't even *look* at ladies properly, at least not with a view to any legitimate connection. And even the other sort of connection—well, the reports are hardly encouraging."

Alathea tried to keep her lips shut, but ... "Encouraging?"

Ahead, the four girls burst out laughing; glancing their way, Celia explained, "It is apparently common knowledge that Rupert is cold—even with his mistresses he remains distant and aloof."

"He always was ..." About to say "reserved," Alathea reconsidered. "Guarded." That was much closer to the mark. "He always keeps his feelings under very close control."

"Control is one thing—true disinterest is another." Celia's concern shadowed her eyes. "If he can't catch fire even in that arena, what chance is there for any acceptable lady to set tinder to his wick?"

Alathea fought to keep her lips straight. By any standard, their conversation was exceedingly improper, but she and Celia had a decade-long habit of discussing her sons—Alathea's childhood companions—with a frankness that would have made their subjects' ears burn. But Rupert cold? It wasn't an adjective she'd ever associated with him, not as Alathea Morwellan and even less as the countess. "Are you sure you're getting the true picture? Mightn't you be hearing solely from those ladies he hasn't been ..."—she gestured—"'interested in?'"

"Would that that were so. But my information has frequently come from disgruntled ladies he *has* been 'interested in.' One and all, they've despaired of making any serious impression on him. If half the tales told are true, he barely remembers their names!"

Alathea's brows rose. Rupert being vague over a name was a sure sign he was not paying attention, which meant he was not truly "interested" at all. "Perhaps," she said, steering the conversation away from her nemesis, "Alasdair will marry first."

"Hah! Don't be fooled by all that easygoing charm. He's even worse than Rupert. Oh, not that he's cold—quite the opposite. But he's feckless, footloose, and overindulged. He's busy enjoying himself without any long-term ties—he's developed a deep-seated conviction he doesn't need any shackles on his freedom." Celia's humph was the definition of disapproving. "All I can do is pray some lady has what it takes to bring him to his knees." She looked up, checking the girls still strolling ahead. After a moment, she murmured, "But it's really Rupert who worries me. He's so detached. Uninvolved."

Alathea frowned. Gabriel hadn't treated the countess as if he were detached or uninvolved. Far from it, but she could hardly reassure Celia with that news. It seemed odd that the portrait Celia was painting was so different from the man she knew, let alone the man she was discovering, the man who had held her in his arms last night.

Celia sighed. "Put it down to a mother's concern for her firstborn if you will, but I can't see how any lady is going to break through Rupert's defenses."

It was possible if one had known him for years and knew where the chinks were. Nevertheless, Alathea inwardly admitted that she could easily see him steadfastly refusing to let any lady close, not in the emotional sense. He didn't like close—he didn't like emotional. He and she had been emotionally close all their lives, and look how he reacted to that. If Celia was correct, she was the only female he had ever allowed within his guard ...

Everything within her stilled. Had his experience with her, of her, hardened him against all women?

Then she remembered the countess. With the countess, he was intent, attentive, certainly not distant and cold. Perhaps distant and cold came later? After …?

Inwardly frowning, she shook aside her thoughts. Looking ahead, she saw the four girls nearing a group of budding dandies. "Perhaps we'd better catch up."

Celia looked; her gaze sharpened. "Indeed."

Where in London was he to find a suitable sheep?

Leaving Lucifer and the friends with whom they'd lunched in the smoking room of White's, Gabriel scanned the occupants of the rooms through which he passed. None fitted his bill. It had to be someone with no obvious connection to the Cynsters, yet someone he could trust. Someone sharp enough to play a part but appear vacuous. Someone willing to take orders from him. Someone reliable.

Someone with money to invest and some hope of appearing gullible.

While he had contacts aplenty who would qualify on most counts, that last criterion excused them all. Where was he supposed to find such a someone?

Pausing on the steps of White's, he considered, then strolled down and headed for Bond Street.

It was the height of the Season and the sun was shining—as he'd expected, all the ton and their relatives were strolling the fashionable street. The crowd was considerable, the traffic snarled. He ambled, scanning the faces, noting those he knew, assessing, rejecting, considering alternatives—trying to ignore the female half of the population. He needed a sheep, not a tall lady.

Even if he saw the countess, he doubted he'd know her. Other than her height and her perfume, he knew so little of her. If he kissed her, he'd know, but he could hardly kiss every possible lady on the off-chance she was his houri. Besides, he'd already determined that the fastest way to get the countess precisely where he wanted her was to learn more about the company—and that necessitated finding a sheep.

He was halfway along the street when, immediately ahead, four ladies stepped out of a milliner's shop and congregated on the pavement. In the instant he recognized the Morwellans, Alathea raised her head and looked directly at him. Serena, Mary, and Alice followed her gaze—their faces promptly lit with smiles.

There was nothing for it but to do the pretty. Sliding into his fashionable persona, he shook Serena's hand, exchanged nods with Mary and Alice, and lastly, more stiffly, with Alathea. As all four ladies stepped free of the throng by the shop windows, closer to the curb so they could converse more easily, Alathea hung back, then took up a position a good yard away from him, so that they both had their backs to the congested carriageway with Serena, Mary, and Alice strung between, facing them.

"We met your mother and your sisters only this morning," Serena informed him.

"In the park," Mary added. "We strolled—it was such fun."

"There were some silly gentlemen about," Alice said. "They had *monstrous* cravats—nothing like yours or Lucifer's."

He responded easily, in truth without thought. Even though Serena, Mary, and Alice ranked high on his list of people to be kind to, with Alathea three feet away, his senses, as always, slewed to her.

And prickled, and itched.

Even though he'd barely glanced at her, he knew she was wearing a lavender walking dress and a chip bonnet that covered her haloed hair. Under the bonnet, he was certain, would lurk one of those scraps of lace he found so offensive. He couldn't comment, not even elliptically, not with Serena before him … on the other hand, if he caught Alathea's eye, she would know what he was thinking.

With that in mind, he glanced her way.

The carriage horse behind her reared, kicking over the traces—He grabbed Alathea and hauled her to him, swinging around, instinctively shielding her. A hoof whizzed past their heads. The horse screamed, dragged the carriage, then tried to kick again—the rising knee caught him in the back.

He jerked, but stayed upright.

Pandemonium ensued. Everybody yelled. Men ran from all over to help. Others called instructions. One lady had hysterics—another swooned. In seconds, they were surrounded by a noisy crowd; the driver of the green horse was the center of attention.

Gabriel stood motionless on the curb, Alathea locked in his arms. His senses were reeling, his wits no less so. At the edge of his awareness, he heard Serena, Mary, and Alice shrilly scolding the driver—they were incensed but not hysterical. Everyone around them was watching the melee in the road, temporarily ignoring him and Alathea.

He tried to catch his breath, and couldn't. A host of emotions poured through him, relief that she was unhurt not the least. He hadn't been gentle— he'd slammed her against him, then held tight; she was plastered to him from shoulder to knee. She'd gasped, then gasped again as his body had jolted with the horse's kick.

Her gaze was fixed over his shoulder, but from her fractured breathing, he suspected she saw nothing. A light, flowery fragrance rose from her breasts, crushed to his chest; soft whorls of hair peeked from under her bonnet, mere inches from his face.

He felt her catch her breath; a slight shiver went through her. She gathered herself—he could feel steel infuse the fine muscles in her back—then she turned her head and looked into his face.

Their gazes met and held—hazel drowning in hazel. Hers were clouded, so many emotions chasing each other across her eyes that he couldn't identify any of them. Then, abruptly, the clouds cleared and one emotion shone through.

He recognized it instantly, even though it had been years since last he'd seen it. Concern poured from her eyes and warmed him—he'd forgotten how it always had.

"Are you all right?" Her hands, trapped between them, fisted in his coat. "The horse kicked you."

When he didn't immediately reply she tried to shake him. Her body shifted against his. He caught his breath. "Yes, I'm all right." But he wasn't. "Only the knee connected—not the hoof."

She stilled in his arms, open concern for him filling her face. "It must hurt."

All of him hurt—he was so aroused he was in agony.

He knew the instant she realized. Flush against him, she couldn't help but know. Her gaze flickered, then her lashes lowered—her gaze fell to his lips, then to his cravat. An instant later, she sucked in a small breath and wriggled—just a little. It was a long ago sign between them; she wasn't attempting to break free—she knew she couldn't—she was asking to be let go.

Forcing his arms to unlock, then setting her back from him was the hardest physical labor he'd ever performed. She immediately fussed with her skirts and didn't look at him.

He felt flustered, awkward, embarrassed … he swung on his heel to view the disaster in the road, praying she hadn't noticed the color in his cheeks.

Alathea knew the instant his gaze left her. She couldn't breathe; her wits were reeling so crazily she felt disorientated as well as dizzy. Straightening, she pretended to watch as the fracas was resolved, grateful when it required Gabriel's intervention. Rigid, she waited on the pavement, stiffly inclining her head when the gentleman who'd been in charge of the young horse approached with profuse apologies.

In her mind, she repeated a single refrain: Gabriel hadn't realized.

Not yet.

The question of whether he would suddenly see the light kept her stiff as a poker.

Then Serena bustled up, all matronly concern, both for her and her protector.

"Are you *sure* you're all right?" Uninhibited by age or elegance, Serena grabbed Gabriel's arm and made him swing around.

Alathea allowed herself a fleeting glance at his face as Serena brushed off his coat.

He frowned and all but squirmed. "No harm done." Freeing himself from Serena's grasp, he gathered Mary and Alice with a glance. "It would be wise to retreat." He hesitated, then asked Serena, "Is your carriage close?"

"Jacobs is waiting just around the corner." Serena waved back along the street.

For the first time since he'd let her go, Gabriel looked directly at her; Alathea immediately waved Mary and Alice before her, then turned in the direction of the carriage. The last thing she needed was to stroll on his arm.

He offered his arm to Serena; she was very ready to lean on his strength. She filled the distance back to the carriage with sincere and copious thanks for his prompt and efficient action. Safely separated from him by Mary and Alice, Alathea murmured her agreement, allowing her stepmother's praise to stand in place of her own.

She was grateful—she knew she should thank him. But she wasn't game to get too close to him, not when she'd so recently been in his arms. She had no idea what might trigger a fateful convergence of memories; holding her head high, she walked to the carriage, apprehension crawling along her spine.

By lengthening her stride, she reached the carriage first and climbed in without waiting for his assistance. He shot her a hard glance, then handed the others up. He stepped back and saluted; Jacobs flicked his reins.

At the very last, Alathea turned her head—their gazes met, held ... she inclined her head and looked forward.

Gabriel watched the carriage rattle away down the side street, his gaze locked on Alathea's chip bonnet, on her shoulders encased in lavender twill. He watched until the carriage disappeared around a corner, then, his expression turning grim, he headed back to Bond Street.

Rejoining the bustling throng, he walked along, his gaze fixed ahead, unseeing. He still felt stunned—poleaxed to be precise. To be so aroused by Alathea. He couldn't understand why it had happened, but he could hardly pretend it hadn't—he was still feeling the definite effects.

He was also feeling rocked, off balance, and hideously uncomfortable. He'd never felt that way about her—they'd always been such close friends, *that* had never raised its head.

He walked on; gradually, his mind cleared.

And the obvious answer presented itself, much to his intense relief.

Not Alathea—the countess. He'd spent all last night plotting the how and where of her ultimate seduction, teasing himself with all the details; this morning, he'd set out to implement his plan. Then fate in the guise of a horse had flung Alathea into his arms. Obvious.

It was hardly surprising that his body had confused the two women—both were tall, although the countess was definitely taller. They were both slender, willowy—very similar in build. They both had the same fine, supple muscles in their backs, but that, he assumed, was to be expected of any very tall, slender woman—an architectural necessity.

The physically obvious, however, was the limit of their similarity. If he dared kiss her, Alathea would tear a verbal strip off him—she certainly wouldn't melt into his arms with that gloriously seductive sensual generosity the countess displayed.

The thought made him smile. His next thought—of what Alathea would make of his reaction once she'd had time to consider it—eradicated all inclination to levity. Then he recalled her long-standing opinion of him and his rakish lifestyle; once again, he smiled. She would doubtless put his reaction down to unbridled lust—and she wouldn't be wrong. But it was the countess he lusted after, his houri of the night.

He wanted her intensely. Somewhat to his surprise, that want went further than the physical. He actually wanted to know her—who she was, what she enjoyed, what she thought, what made her laugh. She was mysterious and intriguing, yet, oddly, he felt very close to her.

She was a puzzle he intended solving—taking apart at every level.

To do that, he needed to press on with his plan ... Lifting his head, he refocused on his surroundings. He'd nearly reached the end of Bond Street. Crossing the road, he started back, once again scanning the crowds. He still needed a sheep. There had to be *someone*—"Gracious! And what's got into you?"

The query and the cane levelled at his navel jerked him to attention.

"Going about with your nose in the air in Bond Street! Why, you don't even know who you're cutting."

Looking into a pair of bird-bright eyes in an old, soft face, Gabriel smiled. "Minnie." Brushing aside her cane, he dropped a quick kiss on her cheek.

"Humph." Minnie's tone was unmollified but her eyes twinkled. "Remind me to tell Celia about this, Timms."

"Indeed." The tall lady beside Minnie lost her fight to keep her lips straight. "Quite unconscionable, going about Bond Street without due regard."

Gabriel bowed extravagantly. "Am I forgiven?" he asked as he straightened.

"We'll consider it." Minnie looked around. "Ah! Here's Gerrard."

Gabriel watched as Minnie's nephew, Gerrard Debbington, brother to Patience, Vane's wife, crossed the street, the bag of nuts he'd clearly been dispatched to fetch in one hand.

"Here you are." Handing the bag to Minnie, Gerrard smiled easily.

Gabriel returned the smile. "Still keeping watch on Minnie's pearls?"

"No more threat, thank goodness. I'm staying with Vane and Patience, but I stop by to take a stroll with Minnie now and then."

Although just eighteen, Gerrard appeared older, his assurance in part due to his brother-in-law's influence; it was Vane's elegant hand Gabriel detected behind Gerrard's fashionable town rig. At close to six feet, Gerrard had the height and breadth of shoulder to carry the austere lines. The rest of his appearance, his easygoing demeanor, his directness and self-confidence, could largely be laid at his sister's door; Patience Cynster was the very epitome of directness.

Gabriel opened his mouth, then quickly shut it. He needed to think. Gerrard was, after all, only eighteen, and there were risks involved. And he was Patience's brother.

"We're going to look in at Asprey's." Minnie fixed him with an innocent look. "Perhaps there's some little thing you need from there?"

Gabriel returned the look with one equally innocent. "Not at present." The image of the countess drifted through his mind. Perhaps, after she'd rewarded him, he would reward her. Diamonds would look well on such a tall woman. Filing the thought away, he bowed. "I won't keep you."

With a humph softened by a smile, Minnie nodded. Timms took her arm and they moved on. With a grin and a nod, Gerrard turned to follow.

Gabriel hesitated, then called, "Gerrard?"

Gerrard turned back. "Yes?"

"Do you know where Vane is at present?"

"If you want him, try Manton's. I know he was going to meet Devil there sometime this afternoon." With a brisk salute, Gabriel headed for Manton's.

"It'll have to be August." Devil extended his arm and pulled the trigger. His shot was an inch off the center of the target.

Vane squinted down the alley. "That seems awfully close. Is Richard sure?"

"As I understood it, it's Catriona who's sure. Richard, at this stage, isn't sure of anything."

Moving past Devil to take his shot, Vane grimaced. "I know the feeling."

"What's this?" Lounging against the partition wall, Gabriel fixed them with a look of mock dismay. "A lesson for expectant fathers?"

Devil grinned. "Come to learn?"

"Thank you, no."

Grimly, Vane sighted down the long barrel of his pistol. "You'll come to this, too."

Gabriel grimaced. "Someday perhaps, but spare me my innocence. No details, please."

Both Honoria, Devil's duchess, and Patience were pregnant. While Devil was displaying the detachment of one who'd been through the wringer before, Vane was already edgy. He pulled the trigger. As the smoke cleared, they saw his bullet had barely nicked the target.

Devil sent the attendant to get another pistol, then turned to Gabriel. "I assume you've heard that our mothers have determined on a special family gathering to welcome Catriona into the family?"

"She's definitely coming down, then?"

Devil nodded. "Mama had a letter from her yesterday. Catriona's decreed she can travel until the end of August. What with Honoria due early July and Patience later that month, it'll have to be August for this celebration of theirs."

Gabriel blinked, replaying Devil's words. "Don't tell me Richard's joined your club."

"He has indeed." Vane grinned evilly. "Now all it needs is for Demon and Flick to get back from their wanderings with Flick blooming, so to speak, and just think where that'll leave you come August."

Gabriel swore. "I'd better warn Lucifer. Mama is going to be impossible."

"You could, of course, cheer her up."

The look Gabriel leveled at Devil was that of a man betrayed. "That is a truly horrible thought."

Devil laughed. "Strange to say one gets used to the state." One black brow arched suggestively. "There are compensations."

"There'd have to be," Gabriel muttered.

"But if you didn't come to discuss our impending paternity, what brings you here?" Vane, too, settled his shoulders against the wall.

"A swindle." Briefly, Gabriel outlined Crowley's scheme, avoiding all mention of the countess.

"Crowley." Devil cocked a brow at Gabriel. "Wasn't he the one with the investment in some diamond mine?"

Gabriel nodded.

"You exposed that one, too, didn't you?" Vane asked.

Again Gabriel nodded. "Which is why I need help this time, and not from you or the others." He looked at Vane. "I need someone not obviously connected."

Vane looked puzzled; Gabriel quickly explained the necessity of learning the precise details of the offer made to investors.

"And …?" Vane prompted.

"What do you think about using Gerrard Debbington?"

Vane blinked. "As your sheep?"

"I haven't been seen about with him, and if he gives Minnie's address rather than yours, then there's no reason anyone will immediately connect him with any Cynsters. I know Crowley's not *au fait* with the ton—he uses Archie Douglas as his source in that arena, and Archie wouldn't know Gerrard from Adam."

"True."

"And even if Archie did ask around, checking Gerrard's background, all he'd hear is that Gerrard is reasonably wealthy and owns a nice manor in Derbyshire. He wouldn't think to ask after Gerrard's connections, or Gerrard's sister."

"Or Gerrard's guardians."

"Precisely. Gerrard appears distinctly older than he is."

Vane considered. "I can't see any reason why Gerrard couldn't develop an interest in gold mining." He looked at Gabriel. "Provided, of course, that we don't tell Patience."

"I hadn't imagined doing so."

"Well, then." Vane straightened away from the wall as the attendant slipped back into the alley. "I'll explain the matter to Gerrard, if you like, and see what he thinks. If he's agreeable, I'll send him to see you."

Gabriel nodded. "Do." Picking up the extra pistol the attendant had brought, he hefted it. "So what's the score?"

They fired ten rounds. Gabriel beat the others easily, a fact that made him frown. "Marriage," he observed, "has dulled your edges."

Vane shrugged. "It's just a game—hardly important. Marriage has a way of rescripting your priorities."

Gabriel stared at him, then looked at Devil, who merely looked back, making no attempt to correct Vane's strange thinking.

Reading his thoughts in his eyes, Devil grinned. "Start thinking about it, for as sure as August follows July, your time will come."

The words froze Gabriel, just as they had at Demon's wedding; again, a tingle of presentiment glissaded down his spine. He managed to suppress his reactive shiver. Adopting an easy expression and his usual debonair manner, he accompanied the other two outside.

* * *

At five o'clock, Gabriel was idly scanning the *Gentleman's Magazine* when someone knocked on his door. Listening, he heard Chance's footsteps all but dance up the hall; smiling, he returned to the magazine.

A minute later, the parlor door opened. Chance stood in the doorway. "A Mr. Debbington to see you, m'lord."

Gabriel inwardly sighed. "Thank you, Chance, but I'm not a lord."

Chance's brow furrowed. "I thought as how all the Quality was lords."

"No."

"Oh." Catching a glimpse of Gerrard, waiting at his elbow to get past, Chance stepped aside, and all but shooed Gerrard over the threshold. "Well, here you are. Do you want me to pour you some brandy?'

"No. That will be all."

"Very good, sir." With commendable aplomb, Chance bowed himself out, and remembered to shut the door.

Gerrard stared at the closed door, then looked questioningly at Gabriel.

"He's in training." Gabriel waved Gerrard to a chair. "Would you like some brandy?"

Gerrard grinned. "No. Patience would be sure to notice." Once at ease in the chair, he met Gabriel's gaze. "Vane told me about this swindle you're trying to expose. I'd be happy to help. What do you need me to do?"

Omitting all mention of the countess, Gabriel outlined his plan.

CHAPTER
Six

At noon the next day, Gabriel descended the steps of the Burlington Hotel, well satisfied with the arrangements he'd made. His plan was in motion and developing nicely. Soon the countess would be his.

Turning into Bond Street, he looked ahead. His steps slowed.

Alathea stood on the corner of Bruton Street, hanging back by the shop facade, her gaze on the crowd surrounding a nut vendor.

She'd always been particularly partial to nuts—and she was clearly debating pushing into the crowd to secure a bag. At this hour, the rowdy crew about the vendor's stall was composed of young sprigs and boisterous bucks.

Lips setting, Gabriel had crossed the street before he'd even thought of what he was doing—or going to do. The memory of his last encounter with Alathea flashed—too hotly—into his mind. His jaw set more firmly. Perhaps a bag of nuts would go some small way toward mending his fences with her.

He could hardly excuse his reaction to her by explaining he'd confused her with another lady.

Alathea eyed the circle of male backs between her and the source of the wonderful smell of roasting nuts. That succulent smell had lured her from the doorway of the modiste's where Serena, Mary, and Alice were engaged in making last-minute adjustments to their ballgowns. The salon had been airless and cramped, so she'd come down to the street, intending to simply wait.

That smell had made her stomach growl. Pushing into the crowd, however, would very likely expose her to a score of impertinent remarks. Still … her mouth was watering. Deciding she could not exist a minute longer without a bag of nuts, she stepped forward—

"Here."

A strong hand closed about her elbow and drew her back—her heart nearly leaped free of her chest!

Without meeting her eyes, Gabriel moved past her. "Let me."

She did, for the simple reason that she dared not move—her legs had turned to jelly. Her latest plan for survival dictated she avoid him at all costs— she'd intended to do just that. She'd been *doing* just that—she was in *Bruton*

Street at *noon*, for heaven's sake! What was *he* doing here? She'd never have left the safety of the salon if she'd known he was about.

She clung to her irritation—undoubtedly wiser than surrendering to her panic.

Gabriel turned back to her, a brown paper bag in his hand. "Here."

She took the bag and busied herself opening it. "Thank you." She popped a nut into her mouth, then offered the nuts to him.

He took a handful, his gaze on her face. "What are you doing here?"

She met his eyes fleetingly. "I'm waiting for Serena and the girls." She gestured down Bruton Street. "They're at a fitting."

Looking down, she took her time selecting another nut. If she gave him absolutely no encouragement, perhaps he would go away. She was acutely aware that the longer she was alone with him as herself, the greater the danger of his recognizing his countess.

Then her conscience prodded—hard. *Damn!* She didn't want to, but ... Lifting her head, she fixed her gaze on his right ear. "I have to thank you for yesterday. I would have been kicked if you hadn't ..."

Grabbed her, held her—been aroused by her.

She quickly ended her sentence with a gesture, but her consciousness must have shown in her eyes. To her amazement, from under her lashes, she saw color trace his cheekbones. He was embarrassed? Good lord!

"It was nothing." His accents were clipped. After a moment, he added in a low voice, "I'd rather you forgot the incident entirely."

She shrugged and turned to stroll back to the modiste's. "If you wish." Dare she suggest he do the same?

He fell into step beside her—there seemed little point suggesting he leave her to walk the street alone. Luckily, the bag of nuts gave her a perfect reason for not taking his arm; touching him again would be inviting disaster. As it was, she could stroll with a good two feet separating them—reasonably safe. She flourished the bag of nuts between them, inviting him to help himself as they strolled. It felt like feeding tidbits to a potentially lethal leopard to keep him distracted while she strolled to the cage door.

Thankfully, the door of the modiste's wasn't far. She stopped beside it, contemplating handing him the almost empty bag in lieu of her hand. "Thank you for the nuts." She met his gaze and realized he was frowning.

She froze—apprehension locked her lungs. Had she said something? Done something?

"You don't happen to know ..." His tone was diffident. He glanced away. "Have you met a countess, one recently widowed—?"

Gabriel broke off. What was he *doing*? One glance at Alathea's face confirmed he'd said enough. Her expression was deadpan, her eyes blank.

"No."

He mentally kicked himself. She knew him well enough to guess why he'd asked. A spurt of resentment surfaced; she'd always turned aside any reference to Lucifer's conquests with an amused glance, but she'd never extended the same leniency to him.

He frowned. "Forget I asked."

She looked at him, blank still. "I will."

Her voice sounded odd.

He was about to step back, make his excuses, and leave, when the rowdy crew from the nut vendor's stall came barrelling past. One jostled his shoulder. He turned, stepping closer to the shop front, closer to Alathea, instinctively shielding her once more. The group streamed past, then were gone. Turning back to Alathea, his farewells froze on his tongue. "What's the matter?"

She'd paled—she was breathing quickly and leaning against the doorframe. Her eyes had been shut—now they flew open.

"Nothing. Here!" Alathea thrust the nut bag at him, then whirled and opened the modiste's door. "Serena will be wondering where I've got to."

With that, she fled—there was no other word for it. She dashed into the small foyer, grabbed up her skirts and flew up the stairs to the salon. She didn't care what he thought of her departure—she simply couldn't bear to be so near him—not anymore. Not as Alathea Morwellan.

Two days later, Alathea stood at the window of her office, sunk in thought. Wiggs had just left. In light of his worry over the promissory note, she'd felt compelled to reveal that she'd engaged the services of Gabriel Cynster. Wiggs had been impressed—and hugely relieved. He'd recalled that the Cynsters were their neighbors in Somerset. Luckily, she'd remembered to suggest that, given the necessary secrecy surrounding their investigations, Wiggs should not communicate with Mr. Cynster other than through her.

The rotund man of business had gone off much happier than when he'd arrived. She'd asked him to clarify the procedure for approaching the Chancery Court to have the promissory note declared invalid once they'd secured proof of fraud. She hoped the matter could be dealt with via a petition direct to the bench, avoiding any mention of the family name in open court and the added expense of a barrister.

In the matter of their investigations, all was proceeding smoothly; she wished she could feel as comfortable over the way matters were proceeding between her and Gabriel.

For the past two days, she'd done all she could to avoid meeting him. Not seeing him, however, didn't ease the guilt she felt over his embarrassment. It was doubtless irrational but the feeling was there.

Lurking in her mind was the recognition that he always stepped forward whenever she needed him; incidents like the horse in Bond Street, the crowd about the street vendor—those were not unusual, not for him and her. Despite their difficulty—indeed, in the teeth of it—he'd always helped her whenever he'd known she needed help. He was helping her now, even if, this time, he didn't know it was her he was helping.

He deserved better from her than deceit, but what could she do?

She sighed and concentrated, forcing herself to deal with the latest twist in her charade. For a start, she would make an effort to reinstitute their old relationship and behave normally toward him so he'd forget his embarrassment. As herself, beyond that moment in Bond Street, she'd barely touched his sleeve over the past decade—surely she could get through the next weeks without touching him more than that?

And secondly, regardless of all else, no matter the struggle, she would not allow—*could not* allow—the susceptibility that had overcome her in Bruton Street to surface again. If he came close, she would suffer in stoic silence. That much, she owed him.

She frowned, realizing she now thought of him by his preferred name. Then she shrugged. Better to think of him as Gabriel—Gabriel was the man she had to deal with now. Perhaps, if she bore that in mind, the hurdles she kept encountering might not be quite so surprising.

Gazing at the shifting greens beyond the window, she set aside her resolutions and turned to her next problem: how to learn of his plans. That he had plans, she didn't doubt. He'd told her to leave Crowley to him; it was tempting to simply do so. Unfortunately, as he didn't know her family's identity, that course was too risky. And she needed some control over his capacity to claim rewards.

That was another hurdle. While she desperately wanted to arrange another meeting to ask what he'd learned, what he was doing, what he had planned, justifying the likely indiscretion was not easy. It was perfectly possible he'd discovered something new, some significant fact—what reward would he claim if he had?

Her experience was insufficient to provide an answer. And she wasn't sure she trusted herself—not while in his arms.

That was the part she understood least. While with him as the countess, she seemed to occupy a position in relation to him that had never been available to Alathea Morwellan, despite the fact she knew him so well. It wasn't only the illicit nature of their interaction, but some different, deeper linkage, a sharing more profound. A sharing she coveted but knew she couldn't have.

She'd never been the sort to throw her cap over the windmill; she'd never been the least bit wild. Yet while she was the countess and he treated her as someone different, she'd started thinking and feeling differently, too.

Her charade had taken on new and dangerous dimensions.

A knock fell on the door. She turned. Folwell, her groom, looked in. He saluted respectfully; she smiled and waved him forward, returning to the desk. "Anything to report?"

"Nothing today, m'lady"—Folwell halted before the desk—"but that Chance … he's a right talker, he is. With due respect, m'lady, I had to put him right—tip him the wink. He talks far too free about Mr. Rupert. That's not how it's done, m'lady, as you know."

"Indeed, but in this case, Chance's talkativeness has been useful."

"Oh, he still chatters to me and Dodswell, of course. But we don't want him chattering to no one else."

"Quite so." Alathea restrained a smile at Folwell's instructing Gabriel's odd new gentlemen's gentleman. She'd already received a highly colored account of how Chance had come into his position; all she'd subsequently heard had made her quite keen to meet him. The eccentricity Gabriel had displayed over Chance was both familiar and endearing. As she'd told Celia, Gabriel wasn't cold, but rather, controlled. She was prepared to wager Celia didn't know about Chance.

"Mr. Rupert's not met with Mr. Debbington again?"

"No, m'lady. Just that one meeting like I mentioned. Mr. Debbington hasn't been back."

"No notes or letters?"

"There was one note last night, m'lady, but Chance doesn't know who it was from. Mr. Rupert read it and seemed pleased, but he didn't say anything to Chance, of course."

"Hmm." Celia's complaints wafted through Alathea's brain; she considered Folwell. "What about ladies? Have there been any women visiting? Or has he gone out …?" With her back to the window, Folwell couldn't see her blush.

"No, m'lady. No one. Dodswell says there's been no females in the house for an age—weeks, at least. He says Mr. Alasdair's hunting a new one"—it was Folwell's turn to blush—"but Mr. Rupert's been staying quiet at home, except for going to family gatherings and to meet some mysterious person. That'd be you, m'lady."

"Yes—thank you Folwell." Alathea nodded. "Keep stopping by every day, but try to avoid Mr. Rupert's notice."

"I'll do that, m'lady." Folwell ducked his head. "You can count on me."

After he'd gone, Alathea considered the picture that was emerging of Gabriel's life. Celia had always given the definite impression that there was a constant stream of ladies going through the Brook Street house. Admittedly, there were two of them, Lucifer as well as Gabriel, but it certainly seemed that at present, Gabriel was not pulling his weight. Not, at least, in that arena.

Pencil tapping absentmindedly, she pondered that fact.

Augusta, Marchioness of Huntly, held a *grande balle* two nights later. What distinguished it from other balls, Alathea could not have said; it was just as crowded, just as boring. She'd never had much time for balls; the Hunt Ball and one or two others through the year were quite enough for her. To be forced to endure a major ball every night was fast becoming her personal definition of torture. However, the Marchioness was the Dowager's sister-in-law, a Cynster by birth; there'd been no question of declining her invitation.

At least the ball gave her an opportunity to keep an eye on her nemesis; it was possible his plans included meetings at balls. From the side of the ballroom, to which she doggedly clung, she watched him prowl. She was tall enough to see him easily, but she was careful not to fix her gaze. In her mind, she repeated her latest resolution: She would avoid him if possible, but if they were to meet, she would behave as she always had, as if she'd never stood locked in his arms in Bond Street—or anywhere else.

Thankfully, he was heading away from her, broad shoulders shifting under a coat of walnut-black. The brown tint in the material turned his hair to burnished brown; the stark simplicity of the cut only emphasized his stature and intensified the predatory aura he exuded.

After a moment, she unfocused her gaze and shifted it to the crowd between them. Then she glanced at the walls. Their crepe decorations caught her eye. She fell to considering how to reduce the cost of decorating the huge ballroom at Morwellan House while still achieving a satisfactory result. The ball at which Mary and Alice would make their formal curtsies to the ton was all too rapidly nearing.

"Why the *devil* can't you leave those wretched things at home? Or better yet, fling them in the fire."

Alathea whirled; her heart leaped to her throat. She'd been so absorbed, he'd been able to walk right up to her. Her eyes searched his—he was watching her, waiting ... her resolution rang in her ears. "I'm twenty-nine, for heaven's sake!"

"I know precisely how old you are."

She lifted her chin. "People expect me to wear a cap."

"There's no more than ten people in this room who can even *see* the horrendous thing."

"It is *not* horrendous—it's the very latest style!"

"There's a style in horror? Amazing. Nevertheless, it doesn't suit you."

"Indeed? And why is that?" Heat flooded her cheeks. "Its color, perhaps?"

The cap was the exact same shade as her gown of pomona green silk, an exceedingly fashionable hue that suited her to perfection. Eyes narrowed, she dared him to suggest otherwise; they were right back to normal, no doubt about that.

His gaze swept her face, then returned to his aversion. "It could be solid gold, and it would still be tawdry."

"Tawdry?"

Up to then, their conversation had been conducted in muted tones; Alathea nearly choked trying to preserve her outward calm. Her gaze on his face, she drew in another breath and in tones of unswerving defiance stated, "As I so choose, I will wear a cap for the rest of my life, and there's not one thing you can do about it. I therefore suggest you either grow accustomed to the fact or, if that's too much to ask, keep your opinions to yourself."

His jaw clenched; his gaze swung down to lock with hers. Eyes hard, lips compressed—all but toe to toe—they stood by the side of the Huntlys' ballroom, each waiting for the other to back down first.

"Oh, *Allie!*"

The anguished tone had them both turning. Alice materialized from the crowd. *"Look."* Woebegone, she lifted her skirt to show the trailing flounce. "That stupid Lord Melton trod on it during the last dance, and now my lovely new gown is ruined!"

"No, no." Alathea put her arm around Alice and hugged her. "It's no great problem. I've pins in my reticule. We'll just go to the withdrawing room and I'll pin it up so you won't miss the rest of the dances, and then Nellie can mend it as good as new when we get home."

"Oh." Alice looked at Gabriel, blinked and gave him a watery smile. Then she looked at Alathea. "Can we go now?"

"Yes." Alathea threw a haughtily dismissive glance at Gabriel. "We've concluded our conversation."

There was heat in his eyes when they met hers, but by the time his gaze reached Alice, his expression was mild. "Flounces rip all the time—just ask the twins. They rip one every second ball."

Alice smiled sweetly and glanced expectantly at Alathea.

"Come along. The withdrawing room will be just along the corridor." As she led the way, Alathea could feel Gabriel's gaze on her back. He'd been carping about her caps for the last three years, ever since she'd first started wearing them. The cause of his vehement dislike was a mystery, to him, she suspected, as much as to her—and nothing had changed, thank God.

They were back to what passed for normal for them.

As Alathea walked out of the ballroom, Gabriel heaved an inward sigh of relief and turned away. Good! Everything was back as it used to be—the concern that had nagged at him for the past few days literally evaporated. After his blunder in Bruton Street, the need to set matters straight with Alathea and reestablish their habitual interaction had distracted him, even impinging on his concentration on his plans for the countess.

But all was now settled. Alathea had clearly harbored a similar wish—she'd been ready to revert to their customary behavior as soon as he'd offered the opportunity; he'd seen that consideration flash through her eyes before she'd first snapped at him.

The sense of release he felt was very real—now he could turn his attention fully to the matter that, increasingly, called to his warrior's soul. The countess and her seduction—now all his energies could be focused on that.

The torn flounce took five minutes to fix. In no rush to return, Alathea called for a glass of water and sipped; the exchange with Gabriel had shaken her more than she cared to admit. She was finding it increasingly hard to rip up at him, to keep her voice sharp and shrewish, and not let it soften to the countess's tone—the tone she used privately to those she loved.

Yet another difficulty when she had difficulties enough.

Ten minutes later, she reentered the ballroom in Alice's wake. Gabriel was nowhere in sight.

Alice returned to her circle of very young ladies and equally youthful gentlemen. Alathea strolled; scanning the crowd, she located Gabriel. Unobtrusively, she took up a position beside the wall opposite him, this time near a protective pillar. Not, it seemed, that anything could protect her from the attentions of Cynsters—Lucifer strolled up almost immediately.

"Torn flounce?"

Alathea blinked. "Yes. How did you know?"

"The twins try that all the time."

"*Try* it?"

"Try to use the excuse to slip away. Mind you, the flounce or ruffle or whatever usually *is* torn, but if one was to accept that the plethora of injuries their wardrobes sustain was due to the clumsiness of their partners, you'd expect the entire male half of the ton to be clod-footed."

Alathea didn't smile. "But why do the twins try to slip away?"

"Because they have fantasies of meeting with unsuitable gentlemen if only they could escape from our sight."

Alathea checked; Lucifer's expression was perfectly serious. He scanned the crowd, then glanced her way. "But you know what it's like—I saw you keeping watch over young Alice."

"I wasn't keeping watch over her—she'd never ripped a flounce before and didn't have pins, or know how to pin it up. I was simply helping her."

"Maybe so, but you know the ropes—you were watching over her as well."

Alathea had had a surfeit of male Cynsters that evening. Drawing in a breath, she held it for a moment, then turned to her companion. "Alasdair."

That got his attention. He glanced her way, one brow rising.

"You and your equally misguided brother have got to put an end to this ridiculous obsession. The twins are eighteen. I've met them; I've conversed with them. They are sensible and level-headed young ladies, perfectly capable of managing their own lives, at least to the extent of interacting with suitable gentlemen and selecting their own consorts."

Lucifer frowned. He opened his mouth—

"No! Be quiet and hear me out. I've had quite enough of arguing with Cynsters this evening, and you may tell your brother that, too!" She flashed him a darkling glance. "You must both understand that your constant surveillance is driving the twins demented. If you don't give them the space to find their stride, they'll kick over the traces, and then you'll be left trying to make a poor fist out of some unholy mess. How would you feel if you were cabin'd, cribb'd and confin'd every time you set foot in a ballroom?"

"That's different. We can take care of ourselves." Lucifer searched her face, then he sighed. "I'd forgotten you haven't spent much time in London." His smile flashed, the essence of brotherly condescension. "There are all sorts of bounders drifting through the ton—we couldn't possibly leave the twins unwatched. It would be like staking out two lambs and then walking away and letting the wolves have at them. That's why we watch. And you needn't worry about Mary and Alice—it's as easy to watch four as it is to watch two."

He was in earnest. Alathea considered a heartfelt groan. "Has it ever occurred to you that the twins just possibly might be able to take care of themselves?"

"In this arena?" Glancing at the subjects of their discussion, Lucifer shook his head. "How could they possibly? And you must admit, when it comes to sweeping ladies off their feet, we are the reigning experts."

Alathea resisted rolling her eyes to the skies. She was determined to puncture, or at least dent, their Cynster egos. Scanning the ballroom, she searched for inspiration.

And saw Gerrard Debbington stroll up to Gabriel, who was chatting with an acquaintance. Gerrard nodded easily. Gabriel nodded back. Even from across the room, Alathea could sense the sudden focusing of his awareness.

"You see," Lucifer said, shifting closer, "take the case of Lord Chantry, currently sniffing around Amelia's skirts."

"Chantry?" Alathea's gaze was fixed across the room. The gentleman who'd been conversing with Gabriel departed, leaving him alone with Gerrard. Instantly, the tenor of the conversation changed. Gerrard shifted; she could no longer see his face.

"Hmm. He's supposed to have a nice little estate in Dorset and is a thoroughly charming fellow, as far as the ladies can see."

"Really?" Alathea could tell from the intensity of Gabriel's expression that whatever Gerrard was saying was extremely important.

"However, there's another side to Chantry."

She had to get closer so she could overhear; they were obviously discussing something vital.

"He's in dun territory. All but rolled up."

About to move, Alathea focused nearer to hand—and found herself face to face with Lucifer. "What?"

"He's under the hatches and looking for a quick wedding with a nice bit of brass tied to the bouquet."

"Who?"

"Lord Chantry." Lucifer frowned at her. "I've been telling you about him so you'll understand why we watch over the twins. Haven't you been listening?"

Alathea blinked. Pushing past Lucifer, hurrying across the crowded ballroom, and somehow getting close enough to Gabriel to overhear what was being said was impossible. Aside from anything else, Lucifer would be at her heels. "Umm ... yes. Tell me more."

She shifted so she could keep Gabriel in view.

Lucifer eased back. "So that's Chantry. And of course Amelia's been smiling sweetly at him for the last week. Silly puss. I tried to tell her but would she listen? Oh, no. Stuck her nose in the air and insisted Chantry was amusing."

Alathea considered telling him Amelia was probably encouraging Chantry simply to tease him and Gabriel.

Gabriel looked up. As if summoned, Devil, the object of Gabriel's glance, detached himself from Honoria's circle and made his way to join the conference.

Something major was being planned. "Another perfect example of a bounder is Hendricks—there—to Amanda's right. He's even worse than Chantry." Letting Lucifer's monologue roll past her, Alathea watched the meeting taking place across the room. Vane strolled up as if just passing by;

he, too, joined the discussion. Ideas—arrangements?—were batted back and forth; that much was clear from the shifting glances, the occasional gestures. At last, a decision was made. Whatever it was, it involved Gerrard Debbington. Gerrard and Gabriel. Devil and Vane appeared to be advisers, less involved in the details of whatever was planned.

She had to learn the plan.

"So, you see, that's why we watch over them. Do you understand now?"

She refocused on Lucifer. What was the right answer? Yes? No? She sighed. "Never mind." The twins would have to fight their own battles. Putting a hand on his arm, she eased him back. "There's a waltz starting—come and dance. I need distraction."

"I can't—I'm on watch."

"Gabriel's free—signal to him. He can take over."

Lucifer did, and Gabriel did, and she got her distraction.

Much good did it do her.

By the time she was in the carriage rolling home through the deserted streets, she'd accepted the fact that she would have to meet with her knight again. Cudgeling her brains, she tried to devise some way for the countess to meet him in safety. Somewhere that would inhibit him from claiming any further reward.

He'd had reward enough.

She couldn't, in all conscience, allow him to claim anything more, not even if he'd learned further facts. He'd taken liberties enough as it was.

But how to prevent his taking more?

CHAPTER

Seven

"Good morning, Mr. Cynster." Gabriel halted and turned; the countess was walking toward him. Along the pavement of Brook Street in broad daylight. She was, as usual, fully cloaked and veiled. Gabriel arched a brow. The hunter in him recognized her strategy, but if she thought to deny him all reward, she'd yield something else, instead.

No veil was impenetrable in daylight.

Then she stopped before him, her face high, and he saw the black mask she wore under the veil. He wondered if she played chess. "Good morning ..." He let his greeting die away for want of a name or specific title; as he straightened from his bow, he amended, "Madam."

He sensed her smile, concealed beneath the mask, then she gestured in the direction he'd been heading. "May I walk with you?"

"By all means." He offered his arm and she laid her gloved hand on his sleeve. As they strolled in the direction of Bond Street, he was intensely aware of her height. He could see over the heads of most ladies; it was consequently easy to largely ignore them even when they were on his arm. Ignoring the countess was impossible; she impinged on his awareness in so many ways.

It was just past midday and the ton was slowly stirring, gentlemen emerging from their doors as he had to seek refuge or congenial company in the clubs around St. James.

"I assume," his companion said, her voice, as ever, soft and low, "that you're proceeding with the matter of the Central East Africa Gold Company?"

"Indeed." Swiftly considering, he continued, "In order to prove fraud, it's imperative we have witnesses to and evidence of the precise details of the proposal the company representatives present to prospective investors. My man of business has made discreet inquiries, but none of the more wealthy, experienced investors, nor their men of business, have been approached by the company. That being so, we'll need to send the company a potential investor."

She looked down. They crossed South Molton Street before she asked, "Who do you have in mind for the role?"

"A young friend by the name of Gerrard Debbington. He has the presence to pass as over twenty-one, although in fact he's a minor. That, of course, gives him a perfect and valid reason to not, after the company's presentation, sign any promissory note himself."

"His guardians would have to sign."

"Quite. But he's not going to mention them until the end of the interview."

She looked up. "What interview?"

His expression impassive, Gabriel considered the bright glint that was all he could see of her eyes. He didn't know their color, yet he suspected they wouldn't be blue. Brown? Green? "Gerrard has spent the last few days ambling about in all the right places, making vague noises about finding something better to do with his brass than buy up more fields."

"And?"

"Yesterday, Archie Douglas just happened to bump into him."

"And?"

The repeated word held a note of impatience; Gabriel kept his lips straight. "Archie chatted about the Central East Africa Gold Company. When Gerrard showed the right sort of interest, a meeting with the company's representatives was mooted."

"When?"

"Archie had to confirm the details with his friends, but Gerrard, as per instructions, suggested tomorrow evening at the Burlington Hotel."

"Do you think the company representatives, by which I assume you mean Crowley, will agree?"

"I'm quite sure they'll agree. Archie wouldn't have approached Gerrard if Crowley hadn't already singled out his mark."

"But ..." Anxiety colored the word. "I believe Gerrard Debbington is a connection of yours. Of the Cynsters. Is that wise?"

Gabriel inwardly frowned. Who was she? "He is, but the connection isn't obvious, at least not in this sense. Archie Douglas is not highly regarded by the ton's hostesses; he won't know of the connection. Crowley's scrutiny will focus on Gerrard's background, which shows he's a wealthy young gentleman from the shires. If the company was in the habit of more prudently checking their marks, they wouldn't have bothered with your late husband."

"Hmm."

His fair companion sounded less than convinced. "Put it this way, if Crowley had any inkling that Gerrard Debbington was in any way associated with me, Gerrard would never have been approached."

Her head lifted. She gave one of her distinctive nods. "Yes, that's true. So ... you think Gerrard Debbington can effectively pass himself off as a gullible investor?"

"I'm sure of it. I'll drill him in what we need to know, and give him pointers—a primer, if you will—so he'll know the most useful questions to ask, all couched in language appropriate for a young gentleman fancying himself the next Golden Ball."

"Yes, but do you think he'll be able to carry off the"—she waved—"characterization, as it were? If he's only eighteen ..."

"He does a very good job of appearing less intelligent than he is. He simply stares vaguely—vacuously—at whoever's talking. He has an innocent-looking face with large eyes and one of those charmingly youthful smiles. He appears as open as a book at all times—that doesn't necessarily mean he is." Gabriel glanced at the countess. "I don't know if you're aware, but he's a budding painter, so even in the most social of settings he's usually considering the line of people's faces, their clothing, coloring, and so on, even while he's supposedly engaged in conversation."

The countess looked him in the eye. "I see."

So she did play chess, but he was a master. "So Gerrard will meet with the company's representatives tomorrow evening. I've chosen the Burlington as it's the sort of place at which someone like Gerrard's supposed self would stay. He'll have a suite, and while he speaks with whoever arrives to make the presentation in the sitting room, I'll be listening from the adjoining bedchamber."

"Do you expect Crowley to appear?"

"Impossible to be sure. There's no reason he needs to show himself but, based on how he's behaved in the past, I suspect he'll be there. He seems to take delight in personally gloating over those he swindles."

"I want to attend—to listen in on this meeting."

Gabriel frowned. "There's no need for you to be there."

"Nevertheless. I'd like to hear for myself what the Company offers and, ultimately, it means we'll have an extra witness to the presentation if need arises."

Gabriel frowned harder. "What about Gerrard? If you want to preserve your anonymity, surely you won't want him to know of your existence. While I might respect your request not to discover your identity, Gerrard is, after all, only eighteen and possesses an artist's eye."

She stopped. "He doesn't know that you're investigating the company at my behest?"

"As I've investigated other companies purely through my own inclination, there was no need to advance any reason for my interest in the Central East Africa Gold Company. Particularly not with Crowley at its helm."

She fell silent; he could almost hear her mind working. Then she looked up. "Will Mr. Debbington actually be staying at the Burlington?"

"No. He'll arrive about half an hour before the meeting's due to start."

"Very well—I'll arrive before him. I assume you'll be there?"

Gabriel set his lips. "Yes, but—"

"There'll be no danger to me personally, or to my anonymity, if I secret myself in the bedchamber before Mr. Debbington arrives, hear the presentation, and then wait until after he's left to do the same."

Gabriel held her veiled gaze. "I cannot fathom why you should be so set on senselessly exposing yourself—"

"I insist."

Chin angled imperiously, she held his gaze. Lips thinning, he let the moment stretch, and stretch, then grudgingly gave way. "Very well. You'll need to arrive at the Burlington no later than nine."

He sensed the triumph that flooded her—she thought she'd won a round. Under her mask, she was no doubt beaming. He kept his lips compressed, his frowning gaze on her veiled face.

"I'll leave you now." Withdrawing her hand, she looked back up the street.

He glanced around and saw a small black carriage, presumably the one that had driven him home from Lincoln's Inn, drawn up by the curb behind them. "I'll walk you to your carriage." Before she could blink, he recaptured her hand and trapped it on his sleeve. She hesitated, then acquiesced, somewhat stiffly.

Gabriel raked the carriage as they neared, but it was an anonymous affair— small, black and unadorned—identical to the second carriage most large households maintained in the capital. Used to ferry their owners about discreetly, such carriages carried no insignia blazoned on the door, or identifying detail worked into the body. No hint of the countess's identity there.

The horses were nondescript. He glanced at the coachman; he was hunched over the reins, his head sunk between his shoulders. The man wore a heavy coat and plain breeches—no livery.

The countess had thought of everything.

He opened the carriage door and handed her in. Pausing on the step, she looked back at him. "Until tomorrow evening at nine."

"Indeed." He held her gaze for an instant, then let her go. "I'll leave a message with the porter to conduct you to the suite." Stepping back, he shut the door, then stood and watched the carriage drive away.

Only when it had rumbled around the corner did he allow his victorious smile to show.

He was waiting in the best suite at the Burlington when, at five minutes to nine o'clock the next evening, she knocked on the door. He opened it and stood back, careful not to smile too intently as, inevitably veiled and cloaked, she swept past him.

Shutting the door, he watched as she scanned the room, taking in the two lamps on side tables flanking the hearth, spilling their light over the scene. Two armchairs and a sofa were drawn up in a comfortable arrangement around a low table before the hearth. Heavy curtains screened the windows; the fire dancing in the grate turned the scene cozy. A well-stocked tantalus stood within reach of one of the armchairs.

When she turned to face him, he got the distinct impression she approved of his stagecraft. "When will Mr. Debbington arrive?"

Gabriel glanced at the clock on the mantelpiece. "Soon." He nodded at the door opposite the hearth. "Perhaps you'd care to inspect our vantage point?"

Her skirts swirled as she turned; he followed as she crossed the room.

Pausing beyond the threshold, she looked around. "Oh, yes. This is perfect."

Gabriel thought so, too. In the cavelike gloom created by the heavy curtains, a huge four-poster bed sat in stately splendor. It possessed a goodly number of plump pillows and the mattress was thick. He'd already confirmed it met his standards; the countess would have no reason to cavil.

She, of course, paid no attention to the bed; her comment was occasioned by the convenient gap between the half-closed door and its jamb, a gap that gave anyone standing behind the door a perfect view of the seats before the sitting room fireplace.

She was squinting at them when another knock fell on the door.

Gabriel met her questioning glance. "Gerrard. I'll need to rehearse his lines—he won't know you're here."

He spoke in a whisper. She nodded. Leaving her, he crossed to the door.

Gerrard stood in the corridor looking sleekly debonair, his youth revealed only by the expectant light in his eyes. "All ready?"

"I was about to ask you the same question." Waving him to the seats by the fire, Gabriel shut the door. "We should go over your lessons."

"Oh, yes." Gerrard made himself comfortable in what was clearly the host's chair. "I hadn't realized how much there was to learn about giving people money."

"Many don't, which is precisely what men like Crowley count on." Gabriel walked to the other armchair, then hesitated. Then he walked to the wall, picked up a straight-backed chair, and carried it over to face Gerrard. "Better to play safe ..." Sitting, he fixed Gerrard with a keen glance. "Now ..."

He led Gerrard through a catechism of terms and conditions, couched in popular investing cant. At the end of twenty minutes, he nodded. "You'll do." He glanced at the clock. "We'd better speak in whispers from now on."

Gerrard nodded. His gaze drifted to the tantalus; he rose and poured himself a small amount of brandy, swirling it around the glass to make it appear there'd been more originally. He met Gabriel's gaze as he resat, cradling the balloon in his fingers. "I'll offer them a drink, don't you think?"

"Good idea." Gabriel nodded at the glass in Gerrard's hand.

Gerrard grinned.

An aggressive knock fell on the door.

Rising, Gabriel held up a hand to stay Gerrard, then picked up his chair and silently returned it to its place against the wall. After one last glance about the scene, he crossed to the darkened bedchamber and stepped behind the door.

Gerrard set down his glass, then stood, straightened his sleeves, and strolled to the door. Opening it, he looked out. "Yes?"

"I believe you're expecting us." The deep booming voice carried clearly to the two behind the bedchamber door. "We represent the Central East Africa Gold Company."

* * *

Gabriel took up his position behind the countess. In the darkened bedchamber, she was no more than a dense shadow, her veiled face lit by the weak light shafting between door and jamb. Slightly to one side of her, Gabriel watched Gerrard greet his visitors with earnest affability.

After shaking hands, Gerrard waved the two men to the sofa. "Please be seated, gentlemen."

Gabriel struggled to block out the countess's perfume and concentrate; this was his first view of Crowley. Although he'd only been able to hear the names exchanged, he had no doubt which of the two was he. He was a bull of a man; comparing his height with Gerrard's, Gabriel pegged him at just on six feet. Six feet of muscled bulk; Crowley would easily have made two of Gerrard. Heavy black brows, thick and strong, slashed across his face, overhanging deep-set eyes. His face was fleshy, his features as coarse as the black hair that curled thickly over his large head.

That head appeared sunk directly into hulking shoulders; his arms were heavily thewed, as were his legs. He was wide and barrel-chested; he looked as strong as an ox and probably was. The only weakness Gabriel could discern was that he moved heavily, with no suppleness to his frame; when Gerrard offered a drink just as Crowley was about to sit, he had to turn his entire body toward Gerrard to answer, not just his head.

He was a distinctly unlovely specimen, but not specifically ugly. His thick lips were presently curved in an easy smile, softening the pugnacious line of his jaw and lending his otherwise unprepossessing countenance a certain charm. Indeed, there was raw energy—an animal magnetism—conveyed in the brilliance of his gaze and in the sheer strength of his movements.

Some women would find that attractive.

Gabriel glanced at the countess. Her attention was riveted on the scene in the sitting room. He looked back to see Crowley lean back on the sofa, completely at ease now he'd seen Gerrard. The expression on his face reminded Gabriel of a cat about to start playing with a mouse—anticipation of the kill oozed from Crowley's pores.

A soft sound reached Gabriel. He glanced at the countess, and realized he'd heard her swiftly indrawn breath. She'd tensed; as he watched, she almost imperceptibly shuddered.

Looking back at the scene playing out before them, Gabriel could understand. At his vacuous best, Gerrard was chatting amiably with the other man; he wasn't looking at Crowley's face. Yet Gerrard, sensitive and observant, wouldn't be—couldn't be—unaware of Crowely's potent menace. Gabriel's respect for the younger man grew as, with every evidence of artless innocence, Gerrard turned to Crowley.

While Gerrard engaged Crowley in banal preliminaries, asking about the basic nature of the company's business, Gabriel studied the other man, Swales, the company's agent.

He was average in almost every way—average height, average build, common in his coloring. His features were indistinguishable from those of countless others, his clothing likewise anonymous. The only thing that set Swales apart was that while his face with its bland expression seemed like a mask, his eyes were never still. Even now, although there was no one in the room bar Gerrard and Crowley, Swales's gaze darted constantly, now here, now there.

Crowley was the predator, Swales the scavenger.

"I see." Gerrard nodded. "And these gold deposits are in the south of Africa, you say?"

"Not the south." Crowley smiled patronizingly. "They're in the central part of the continent. That's where the 'Central East' in the company's name comes from."

"Oh!" Gerrard's face lit. "I see now, yes. What's the country's name?"

"There's more than one country involved."

Gabriel listened, occasionally tensing as Gerrard artfully probed, but Patience's brother possessed a real knack for pressing just so far, then sliding away into patent and unthreatening ignorance one word before Crowley tensed. Gerrard played his part to perfection, and played Crowley just as well.

The countess was equally on edge, equally concerned; she tensed at precisely the same moments he did, then relaxed as Gerrard once again played out Crowley's line. Crowley was the one hooked on the lure, being artfully reeled in, not the other way about.

By the end of an hour, when Gerrard finally allowed Swales to show him the promissory note, they had heard all they could hope to hear, and that from Crowley's lips. He'd named the locations of three of the company's mining claims, and also cited towns where he said the company had a workforce and buildings established. He'd dropped a host of names supposedly of African officials backing the company, and of African authorities from whom permissions had been received. Under subtle prompting, he'd revealed figures aplenty, enough to keep Montague busy for a week. He'd also twice mentioned that the company was close to commencing the next phase of development.

They'd learned what they needed to know, and Gabriel was exhausted by the constant ebb and flow of helpless tension. The countess was sagging, too. Gerrard, on the other hand, was positively glowing. Crowley and Swales saw it as enthusiasm; Gabriel knew it was suppressed excitement at his triumph.

"So you see"—Swales leaned closer to Gerrard, pointing to the lower portion of the promissory note, now unrolled on Gerrard's knees—"if you just sign here, we'll be all right and tight."

"Oh, yes. Right-ho!" Gerrard started rerolling the note. "I'll get it signed right and tight, and then we'll all be happy, what?" He grinned at Crowley and Swales.

There was an instant of silence, then Crowley said, "*Get* it signed? Why can't you sign it now?"

Gerrard looked at him as if he'd admitted to lunacy. "But ... my dear man, *I* can't sign. I'm a minor." Having dropped his bombshell, Gerrard looked from Crowley to Swales and back again. "Didn't you know?"

Crowley's face darkened. "No. We didn't know." Shifting forward, he held out a hand for the note.

Gerrard grinned and held onto it. "Well, there's no need to worry, y'know. M'sister's my main guardian and she'll sign whatever I tell her to. Well, why wouldn't she? She's got no head for business—she leaves that to me."

Crowley hesitated, his gaze fixed unwaveringly on Gerrard's innocent countenance. Then he asked, "Who's your other guardian? Do they have to sign, too?"

"Well, yes—that's how things usually are if there's a female involved, don't y'know. But my other guardian's an old stick—bumbling old fool—my late pater's old solicitor. He lives buried in the country. Once m'sister signs, then he will, too, and all will be right as a trivet."

Crowley glanced at Swales, who shrugged. Crowley looked back at Gerrard, then nodded. "Very well." He stood, slowly bringing his bulk up off the sofa.

Gerrard unfolded his long limbs with the effortless grace of the young and held out his hand. "Right then. I'll get the deed done, the note signed, and get it back to you forthwith."

He shook hands with Crowley, and then with Swales, then accompanied them to the door. As they reached it, Crowley paused. Gabriel and the countess shifted, craning to keep them in sight.

"So when can we expect to get the note back?"

Gerrard grinned, the epitome of foolish vacuity. "Oh, a few weeks should do it."

"Weeks!" Crowley's face darkened again.

Gerrard blinked at him. "Why, yes—didn't I say? The pater's old solicitor lives in Derbyshire." When Crowley continued to glower, Gerrard's brows rose, his expression degenerating to that of a child fearing denial of a promised treat. "Why? There's no tearing rush, is there?"

Crowley studied Gerrard's face, then, very gradually, drew back. "As I said, the company's close to commencing the next phase of operations. Once we reach that point, we won't be accepting any more promissory notes. If you want a share in our profits, you'll need to get the note signed and returned to us—you can send it to Thurlow and Brown, of Lincoln's Inn."

"But if you don't get it to us soon," Swales put in, "you'll miss out."

"Oh, no chance of that! I'll get m'sister to sign and get it off tomorrow. If I send it by rider, it'll be back before we know it, what?"

"Just make sure it is." With one last intimidating glance, Crowley hauled open the door.

Swales followed him into the corridor. Gerrard stopped on the threshold. "Well, thank you, and good-bye."

Crowley's growled farewell rumbled back to them, drowning out Swales's reply.

Gerrard stood at the door, watching them depart, his silly smile still in place, then he stepped back, closed the door, and let his mask fall.

Gabriel closed his hands about the countess's shoulders. She sagged back against him—for one blissful moment, from shoulder to hip, she caressed him—then she remembered herself and stiffly straightened. Smiling in the dark, Gabriel squeezed her shoulders, then released her. Leaving her behind the door, he went out to Gerrard.

He put a finger to his lips as Gerrard faced him. Gerrard dutifully held silent. They both waited, listening, then Gabriel signaled Gerrard to open the door and look out.

Gerrard did, then stepped back and closed the door. "They're gone."

Gabriel nodded, scanning Gerrard's face. "Well done."

Gerrard smiled. "It was the longest performance I've ever given, but he didn't seem to suspect."

"I'm sure he didn't. If he had, he wouldn't have been anywhere near as accommodating." Crossing to the escritoire by the windows, Gabriel drew out paper and pen. "Now to the last act. We need to write down everything we heard, and sign and date it."

Gerrard drew up a chair. Together, they recounted the conversation, noting down names, locations and amounts. With his sharp visual memory, Gerrard was able to review the conversation, verifying Gabriel's recollections and adding further snippets. An hour had passed before they were satisfied.

Gabriel pushed back from the escritoire. "That gives us a lot to check, a lot to verify—more than enough chance to prove fraud." He glanced at Gerrard, just as Gerrard yawned. "Now it's time you were off home."

Gerrard grinned and rose. "Tiring work, acting, and I'm driving to Brighton with friends tomorrow, so I'd best turn in."

Gabriel followed Gerrard to the door. Gerrard stopped by the sofa. "Here— you'd better take this, too."

"Indeed." Gabriel accepted the rolled promissory note. "It's absolute evidence that this meeting took place."

Reaching the door, Gerrard looked back. "Are you coming?"

Stowing the note and their account of the meeting in the inside pocket of his coat, Gabriel shook his head. "Not just yet. We shouldn't be seen together. You go ahead—I'll follow later. Duggan is waiting for you, isn't he?" Duggan was Vane's groom.

Gerrard nodded. "He'll drive me back to Curzon Street. Let me know how it goes." With a salute, he went out of the door, shutting it softly behind him.

Gabriel considered the closed door, then walked across and snibbed the lock. He surveyed the room, then strolled to the lamp beside the fireplace, turning it, then its mate, very low, shrouding the room in shadows. Satisfied, he headed for the bedchamber, for the epilogue to the evening's performance.

CHAPTER

Eight

The countess was waiting, no longer behind the door but seated on the end of the bed. A dark shadow, she rose as he neared.

"Do you really think there are mining claims in those places—Kafia, Fangak, and Lodwar?"

"I'd be greatly surprised if there's anything there at all. Towns or villages, maybe, but no mining. We'll check." He couldn't see her other than as a denser figure in the gloom; the already dark room had darkened even further with the dimming of the light from the sitting room. So he had to rely on his other senses—they told him she was still absorbed with Crowley's revelations. "He gave us more than enough facts, not only names and places but also figures and projections. I've got it all down. To get the company's notes declared invalid all we need do is prove *some* of those claims false, not all of them."

"Still"—he heard the frown in her voice—"it won't be easy to prove what really is happening in deepest Africa. Did you recognize any of the places he mentioned?"

"No, but there must be someone in London who will."

"He also stated that they were close to commencing the next stage of development—surely that's his way of saying that they plan to call in the promissory notes soon."

"He's not at that stage yet. Unless something triggers the call, he'll wait to see how many more gullible gentlemen up from the shires for the Season he can lure into his net."

Silence ensued. Her gnawing anxiety reached him clearly. He stepped closer. "It's a significant victory to have got that much detail from him."

"Oh, indeed!" She looked up. "Mr. Debbington was quite splendid."

"And what about the *eminence grise* behind the scenes?"

He knew precisely when she realized—realized she was alone with him in a very dark bedchamber with a very large bed a mere foot away. Her spine straightened, her chin tilted higher; a fine tension gripped her.

"You've been very ... inventive."

He slid one arm about her waist. "I intend being a great deal more inventive yet."

He drew her against him. After only the slightest resistance, she permitted it, settling breast to chest, hip to hip, thigh to thigh, as if she belonged there.

"You've been very successful." Her tone was slightly breathless.

His lips curved. "I've been brilliant." He found the edge of her veil. Slowly, he lifted it. All the way up. She caught her breath, one hand rising, hovering … but she allowed it. The room was so dark he couldn't possibly distinguish her features. Then he bent his head and set his lips—to the lips that were waiting for him.

Waiting, yearning, ready to pay his price—he knew she had no idea how precious, how heady, he found her lack of guile, her open generosity, the way she yielded her mouth at his demand, the way she sank against him, into him. The way she gave without restraint.

There was power in her giving. As before, it caught him, captured him, and held him in thrall. He had to have more—know more—of her. His fingers found the ties of her cloak; a minute later, it slid from her shoulders to pool on the floor at their feet. A curved clip across the crown of her head anchored her veil; he slid one hand under the veil, past her throat, and encountered the heavy weight of her hair, coiled at her nape. Soft as silk, it caressed the backs of his fingers; without conscious direction, they searched. Her pins pattered on the floor; her hair spilled over his hands, both the one at her throat and the one at her waist. Her hair was long and so soft; he caught strands between his fingers and played, enthralled by the texture.

He sensed the hitch in her breathing. Closing his fist in her hair, he drew her head back, exposing the column of her throat. Blind in the dense darkness, he slid his lips from hers to trace the supple line and find the spot where her pulse beat hotly. He laved it, then sucked—her breath hitched again. Her fingers had speared through his hair; they spread over his skull as he shifted his hold and closed his hands over her breasts.

Already firm, they swelled and filled his palms, heated flesh begging for his attention. Straightening, dragging in a swift breath, he caught her lips again. She kissed him back—avidly, greedily, as ravenous as he. When he rotated his thumbs about her already ruched nipples, she gasped. Without thought, he backed her until she came up against the wall. Inwardly, he tried to shake his head to clear it of the miasma of lust fogging it. He'd just moved her away from the bed, a patently silly move. Now he'd have to move her back again.

Later.

Trapping her lips with his, he pinned her to the wall and set his fingers to her laces.

He couldn't think—he hadn't planned, although he'd tried to. He rarely embarked on a seduction these days, especially not one he was particularly intent on, without some idea of what would work best, what possibilities were most likely, what avenues held most promise of fulfillment. In thinking of how he would have the countess, he hadn't been able to get past the need to touch her, to know her.

A surprisingly simple need for such an experienced lover as he, and one surprisingly compelling.

He had her laces free, her gown loose, in the space of a heated minute. Using his weight to immobilize her, he reached up and dislodged her hands from his hair. Drawing her hands and arms down, he leaned into their kiss— she drew him deep, then played havoc with his senses. For one definable instant, he lost his will entirely and simply existed, utterly in thrall, then the hot pressure of her breasts against his chest recalled him to his urgent need.

He had to touch her, caress her—feel her. If she wouldn't allow him to see her, he would have to learn her by touch, by having her against him, skin to bare skin, heat to heat.

Without any veils, any cloaks, any barriers between them.

He needed to know her.

Releasing her hands, he reached for her shoulders and swiftly drew her gown down, pushing the sleeves down her arms, deftly freeing her breasts. He sensed her hesitation, the tremor of uncertainty that shook her; capturing her lips, her attention, in a searing kiss, he left her gown in folds about her hips and cupped her breasts, now covered only by the thin silk of her chemise.

Her hesitation evaporated. She gripped his face with both hands and kissed him back, every bit as urgent as he. Through the silk, her skin burned; the ripe swells tipped by nipples hard as pebbles beckoned. Her chemise was fastened by a row of tiny buttons. He ravaged her mouth as he swiftly undid them. He was already aching, rigid with need, but more than anything he wanted to savor each moment, each revelation. Each bit of her as he uncovered it.

Her breasts were a delight. Firm and full, they filled his hands, generous, hot and heavy. Pushing the open halves of her chemise wide, he kneaded and heard her moan. The evocative sound sent another, unnecessary rush of blood to his loins. Dragging his lips from hers, he ducked his head, trailing open-mouthed kisses over her throat, her collarbone, to where her flesh mounded in his hands.

Then he feasted.

She moaned, and panted, and even sighed his name as he tasted, licked, and suckled. He had to be marking her; although he couldn't see, the thought sent a surge of sheer possessiveness through him. He drew one peak deep into his mouth; she cried out. Her knees buckled. He leaned into her, holding her up, his erection hard against her lower belly, his balls cradled between her thighs.

Her softness flowed around him as she slid her arms about his shoulders and clung; her perfume, evocative as sin, wrapped about them.

He lifted his head and found her lips again, swollen and hot and needy. She drew him in, tongue tangling with his, boldly inciting. He slid his hands down to her hips, then further, tracing the smooth lines of her flanks. Her nipples, hard and tight, were twin points of flame surrounded by the fire of her breasts, crushed against his chest as he pressed her to the wall. Her hips tilted into his.

He wasn't even thinking when he grasped the folds of her gown in both hands and pushed them from her hips. His senses didn't register the sibilant "swoosh" as he shifted and the silk slithered to the floor. His senses had seized.

She was like hot, supple silk, alive, enchanted, all his. Her limbs, all but naked, shifted sensuously against him, not to push him away but to enclose him more sweetly. If he'd ever dreamed of a houri, then she was here, in his arms, nubile, nearly naked, ready to fulfill his every want, ready to kill him with pleasure. He couldn't catch his breath, mentally or physically; lust closed like a fist about his gut and shut off his brain. His hands dove beneath the hem of her chemise to close possessively about the globes of her bottom.

Her kiss only grew hotter, sweeter, headier. She tasted like the elixir of the gods.

She levered herself up, tightening her arms about his shoulders. His legs had been outside hers, trapping hers; now he supported her and shifted, pressing one long thigh between hers. She murmured, an incoherent sound lost between their lips. He set her down; she balanced on her toes, held high by her hold on him and pinned by his chest. Shifting, he released her luscious derriere and slid both hands forward, caressing the sweet indentation where hip met thigh before moving on to the front of her naked thighs. With his thumbs, he found the crease at the top of each thigh; pressing lightly, he slid both thumbs slowly inward.

Her breathing fragmented; their kiss turned desperate as his thumbs tangled in her silky curls. He played, teasing, being tantalized, then, skillfully plundering her mouth, he sent one hand upward, fingers splaying over the delicate skin of her stomach, caressing, then kneading evocatively. In almost the same breath, he let the fingers of his other hand drift down, gently pressing in, searching through her heated softness to find her.

If he hadn't been kissing her, he sensed she would have gasped. She was slick, swollen, and so hot. Her breasts strained against his chest; he held her steady and gently probed, then stroked, soothed, only to take further liberties.

The intimacy was new to her—he knew that in his bones. Her late husband must have been a clod. Yet she was flowering sweetly for him; her nectar burned his fingers as he circled her entrance, then drew back to caress the nubbin of flesh now tight and throbbing with need.

She quivered, her fingers digging into his upper arms as she arched her head away. He allowed her to break the kiss and catch a shattered breath, then he deliberately reached deeper and circled her entrance again …

She shivered. He was asking and she understood—after a fractional hesitation, she bent one knee, sliding her slender calf around his leg. Opening herself for him.

The only thing he managed to remember after that was that she hadn't been pleasured like this before. So he penetrated her slowly, letting her feel every tiny increment as he slid one finger into her sheath. She was scalding hot; he wasn't surprised to discover she was tight as well. Her experience of intimacy appeared miniscule. She clamped firmly about his finger, her breath shivering in his ear. He turned his head, found her lips, and soothed her with a long, slow kiss. As he withdrew his finger, her hips instinctively tilted, her body begging for more. He gave it to her, clinging to the reins of his impulses, howling to have her, urgent and ravenous. He was too experienced a lover not to know what would be best for her; with his lips on hers, reassuring, distracting, and inciting in turn, he set himself to show her what could be.

And when her fingers bit deep and she pulled back from their kiss as her body shattered in glory, he felt like a conqueror, victorious, triumphant, with the spoils of his conquest in his arms. Her released passion washed over him in waves, surge after surge of heat and fierce delight. The soft moan that escaped her, one of fulfillment laced with residual need, the waft of her ragged breaths against his cheek, the thundering of her heart pressed close to his, the evocative muskiness that rose from where his fingers filled her to combine with her perfume and drive him mad—all urged him on.

She was ready, so gloriously tall, and he was desperate.

It was the work of seconds to release his straining staff, to lift the leg she'd crooked about his knee to his hip. To draw his fingers from her hot wetness and set the head of his erection to her entrance. Gripping her hips, he caught her lips and plunged into her mouth, and into her heat.

She screamed.

The sound, trapped between their lips, reverberated through his head. Then she tensed, like a vise, about him.

He gasped, breaking their kiss, grimly fighting for control. It couldn't be— yet it was. Had been. The shock shook at least a few of his wits into place. After a fraught second in which he tettered on the brink of madness, he managed to block out the physical long enough to ask, "How?"

He had barely enough air in his lungs to form the word, but with her face close by his, she heard.

"I ..."

Her voice quavered; she was, it seemed, as shocked as he, if not for the same reason. That, he could understand. If this was her first time ... he was buried to the hilt inside her.

She gulped in air. Her words came in a shaky whisper by his ear. "I was a child bride. My husband ... he was much older. And ill. He wasn't able to ..." She released her grip on his arm to gesture. The movement caused her to shift upon him—she caught her breath on a fractured gasp.

"Shh. Gently." He found her lips and soothed her with a kiss while he struggled to take it in. A child bride left virginal by her aging husband? No doubt it did happen, although it had never before happened to him. Her unexpected innocence, however, raised a most pertinent question. Had she known he would ...?

It took all his effort, and the last shreds of his will, to force himself to ask, "Do you want me to stop?"

Hardly elegant phrasing, but it was all he could manage with her clamped, the tightest, hottest, wettest dream he'd ever had, about him.

Her answer was a long time coming. His teeth were gritted, every muscle straining against the driving need to have her. With what little wit he still possessed he fought to ignore the warmth of the lush body in his arms, the constantly fluctuating pressure against his chest as she breathed rapidly, raggedly. He was so aware of her breathing, he knew when she reached her decision and drew in a deeper breath to deliver it.

He steeled himself to accept it—and prayed.

She shook her head. "No."

He exhaled. "Thank God."

"What—?"

He kissed her deeply, reassuringly, then lifted his head. "Don't think, just do as I say." He hesitated, wishing for the hundredth time that he could see, then added, "It'll feel a lot better very soon." He could only guess what she was feeling—he couldn't remember the last virgin he'd had. But she was still very tense; every muscle below her waist was locked tight. She was certainly not comfortable; she might even be in pain.

Withdrawing from her and repairing to the bed would have been the simple option. Unfortunately, with her tensed as she was, withdrawing from her would probably cause her more pain. But the bed was a must. "Raise your other leg—wrap it about my waist. I'll hold you." When she hesitated, he brushed her lips with his. "Trust me. I'll carry you to the bed."

She drew in a breath, and lifted her other leg, moving more confidently when she felt his hands shift and he took her weight. Locking her legs about him, sliding her arms about his shoulders for balance, she levered herself up a little, easing herself from him.

He gripped her hips. "That's enough." Grimly denying the impulse to surge back into her, he turned and carried her the few feet to the bed. Carefully, he laid her down with her hips close to the edge. As he'd expected, she relaxed just a little on finding the bed beneath her. Just enough for him to ease out of her a fraction more as he straightened, not fully but so he leaned over her, his weight on his locked arms.

Keeping his hips still, he found her face and brushed back the strands of gossamer soft hair that had fallen across her cheek. Her veil was still in place, still brushed back—he left it as it was. That, one day, she would remove for him, when she was ready to trust him with her name. Tonight, she was trusting him with her body—for tonight, that was enough.

Framing her jaw, he leaned forward and kissed her. For a moment, she lay passive, then responded. Once she was kissing him back freely, he flexed his hips and pressed into her again, filling her, stretching her even more than before. She sucked in a breath and tensed, but then eased. He drew back and pressed in again, then repeated the movement, his action steady and even. He kept the tempo slow until her muscles relaxed, until her legs were loose about his hips, her hands lax, fingers trailing on his sleeves, her body open and accepting and starting to stir, starting to lift and surge with his rhythm.

Mildly triumphant, he drew back. "Don't move. Just wait." Then he straightened completely. Reaching around, he felt for her shoes, and removed them. Tracing her long legs upward until he encountered her garters, he stripped them and her stockings off. Her chemise was the merest wisp of fine silk—he decided to ignore it for the moment. Shrugging out of his coat, he heard the crackle of the promissory note and their lists; he tossed the coat toward where he'd seen a chair. His waistcoat and shirt followed in short order, then he toed off his shoes and stripped off his trousers.

The lamps in the sitting room had gone out; the darkness was intense. He couldn't see her—only feel her, hear her, sense her. And she couldn't see him.

"What ...?"

He reached for her, sliding his hands along her flanks, up over her sides. "Just trust me." He joined her on the bed, rolling and lifting her as he did, moving them back so their long legs weren't hanging over the edge.

She gasped as he rose over her again, her hands clutching wildly as, palms flat on either side of her, he braced his arms and held himself above her. Wedging his hips between her widespread thighs, he surged and filled her until she was full. Then he lowered his head, searching for her lips. Her fluttering hands found his face, then her lips joined with his. She offered them, and her mouth, willingly, lovingly. He took both as he rocked her, rocked into her, until she was once again easy, accepting the smooth slide of his staff into her sheath with gratifying eagerness.

Pulling back from the kiss, he held himself above her and changed the tenor of their joining. He kept the rhythm slow, but rolled his hips as he entered her, encouraging her to spread her thighs wider, raise her knees higher.

Then her fingertips hesitantly touched his chest, another of her butterfly caresses. He bit his lip and concentrated on keeping to his slow beat. His muscles flickered and twitched as her fingers delicately traced over his chest, his waist, his flanks. Stifling a gasp, he thrust deeper. "Wrap your legs around me like before."

She obeyed instantly, locking her legs about his hips. "Now what?"

She couldn't see his smile. "Now we ride."

They did. Together.

He'd purposely darkened the room to ease her fear of revealing herself, her identity, to him. In doing so, he'd unwittingly created a sensual situation beyond even his ken. Making love in total darkness emphasized the tactile sensations and amplified the soft, intensely sensual sounds. It was a new and very different experience, loving a woman blind.

He was aware of every square inch where they touched, aware of the screening quality of her silk chemise, nowhere near as fine as the skin beneath it. He heard every little hitch in her breathing, every soft sound she made; he was attuned to every moan, every gasped, incoherent entreaty. He knew her perfume, but it was another scent that wreathed his brain, that of her and her alone. In his arms, in the dark, she became the epitome of woman, in truth the houri he'd labelled her. She was the essence of joy and the essence of madness; she was the ultimate challenge.

His senses were full of her, focused most completely on where they joined. The heightened sensations left him reeling.

He'd never before had a woman to equal her. That was borne in on him as they rode on, through their sensual landscape, scaling higher and ever higher peaks. She matched him—not just physically, although that was wonder enough; she clung, gasped, shattered, then rose again to ride on. But she was there, with him, urging him on, daring and challenging, joyously inviting him to dive into the sensual whirlpool her body had become. A whirlpool of giving.

He demanded and she gave—not just generously but with a wild abandon that shattered his control. He couldn't get enough of her; he drank greedily, yet her well was never dry.

She gave him joy and delight and pleasure unimaginable, and in the giving received the same. When the end finally came and their ride ended in soul-shattering glory, he was, for the first time in his life, utterly beyond this world.

One thought drifted past: He'd been the first to have her.

A second later, that deeply buried part of him he rarely let loose growled a correction: The *only* one to have her.

Holding her close, feeling her soften beneath him, he shut his eyes and drifted into pleasured bliss.

She woke slowly, her senses gradually returning, her scattered wits reassembling in fits and starts. The first thing she was aware of was that there were tears in her eyes. They weren't tears of regret but of joy—a joy too deep, too intense to find expression in word or thought.

So *that* was what lay between a woman and a man. The thought brought a surge of giddy delight, followed immediately by a rush of gratitude—to him who had demonstrated so well.

Her lips kicked up at the ends. She'd heard for years that he was an expert in that sphere—she could now attest to the fact. He'd been gentle and tender, at least once he'd realized she was a novice, but later ... she didn't think he'd held back.

She was glad—glad of the experience, glad it had happened. Especially glad it had happened with him. That last made her frown.

Even though it was dark and had been throughout, so that he'd been no more than a phantom, kissing her, caressing her, she'd always known it was he.

Him. Her senses focused on the heavy body lying upon her, the heaviness within her, filling her, stretching her ...

The realization jolted her fully awake.

Her immediate thought was that this wasn't she—or not the same she. She had a naked man in her arms and they were joined; she was changed forever physically. And emotionally; she couldn't forget how she'd writhed beneath him, wanton and wanting. She was incontrovertibly altered—she could never go back to who she'd been.

She waited for the recriminations to start, the dire prophecies, the hysterical outpourings. Nothing came. Instead, she remained at peace, filled with a warm glow she'd never known, never even imagined existed. And she couldn't regret it.

It had been no one's fault; she hadn't imagined it could happen against a wall, not with them both upright. Her feet had been firmly on the floor. Her head, of course, had been wholly in the clouds, her wits swept away on a tide of pure desire.

The thought brought the experience back to her—the burgeoning excitement, the scintillating thrill, the pure, unadulterated joy. This, here, with him, would be the only chance she'd ever have of experiencing it—the true magnificence of being a woman, a woman joined with a man. There was no one she was hurting; no one in her life to care. No one who would ever know. She'd been condemned by circumstance to die an old maid; what harm could there be in this, her one taste of glory? It would have to last her the rest of her life.

Although he'd been inside her before she'd realized his intention, she'd known precisely what she was doing when she'd told him not to stop. She'd had plenty of experience in making decisions; she knew how it felt when she'd decided right. It felt like this.

In the same way she'd never looked back, never regretted turning her back on London and her Season all those years ago, she would not regret this. No matter what complications arose, she'd experienced and enjoyed—and lusted.

A gurgle of inner laughter welled up inside her. Sternly quelling it, she tried to shift, only to find it impossible. The movement once more focused her senses on the hard male body pressing hers into the bed. He was heavy, yet oddly, she rather liked the feeling of his weighted limbs pressing her into the mattress. She wasn't uncomfortable, indeed, quite the opposite, strange though that seemed. Her legs had relaxed from about his waist but were still tangled with his. One of her arms was draped over his shoulder; her other hand lay against his side.

Him. She couldn't take it in; her mind kept shying from the thought, from allowing his image to form. In the dark, he'd simply been a magnificent male, one she trusted so deeply the thought that he might physically hurt her had simply not occurred. She'd given herself to him and he'd taken her, swept her up in his arms and introduced her to delights she could still only barely comprehend.

Yet she knew who he was.

Didn't she?

Frowning, she slipped her hand from his side and, very gently, touched his shoulder. When his breathing continued deep and even, she let her fingers wander, tracing the wide bone, the sleek muscle bands. Spreading her fingers, she explored the side of his chest, then his back, sensing the power in the steely muscles beneath the smooth skin.

She'd seen his naked chest years before; even then, it had fascinated her, although she'd told herself she was merely curious. Now she could indulge; letting her hands wander, she filled her senses with him.

Her skin came alive, all over. The sudden rush of sensation made her breath hitch; he was so warm, so male, so vibrantly real. A tide of heady feeling welled and surged through her. The wave reared and crashed—and rocked her, tore her from her moorings and tossed her into a turbulent swell. She caught her breath, quivering, helplessly adrift on an emotional sea whipped by sudden turmoil.

Rupert?

No—Gabriel.

The reality struck to her bones. He was deeply familiar in so many ways, yet in truth he was a man she'd only recently met. She could feel his hands on her, still holding her even in sleep. Those strong, clever hands had loved her, caressed her, brought her untold joy and delight. Their touch was burned into her memory, as was the empty ache that had swept her, the ache only he evoked and only he could ease.

Shifting her head, she peered at his face, but the darkness defeated her. All she knew was his warm weight, the touch of his hands, and the stream of feeling that welled and poured through her, from her, leaving her shaking inside.

It took a minute to catch her breath, to steady herself, to reground herself in reality and let the fantasy—and that exultation that left her so vulnerable—fade away.

He'd be horrified if he knew, if he realized it was she. So why was every instinct she possessed screaming that this was right, so right, when she knew, logically, it was all wrong?

As she stared into darkness, confusion reigning in her mind, he stirred.

Then he shifted; she realized he was turning toward her, then the pressure on her chest eased. His warmth was still close, her lower body still pressed heavily into the bed. It took her a moment to realize that he was resting his weight on his elbows.

She remembered her veil. Propelled by sudden panic, she started to reach ... then realized he was as blind as she. The darkness was so intense, even though she knew his face was mere inches from hers, she couldn't see it.

"That was quite a ride, countess."

The lazy, gravelly words drifted down; his breath wafted across her cheek. His lips followed, searching and finding hers, then settling for a long, slow, exceedingly thorough kiss. When he finally brought it to an end and released her lips, she could tell his were curved.

"How do you feel?"

Stretched. Still full of him. "Alive." How true. Her skin was heating again. How could that be?

As if he could read her thoughts, his lips returned to hers, and he was smiling even more definitely. Another lengthy kiss left her close to conflagration; ending it, he murmured, "Are you game for another gallop?"

He pressed inward, and she realized that he definitely was. Her hips tilted, inviting him deeper; she concluded she must be, too. She tightened her arms about him, wordlessly urging him closer. He settled upon her, settled his lips on hers, and sank deeply into her—into her mouth, into her body.

This time, he was in no hurry. Before, he'd been reined, restrained; this time, he savored her, rocking her deeply, pleasuring her well. The heat inside her grew until her bones melted. She drew back from their kiss to drag in a breath. His lips slid down her throat, then, to her surprise, she felt him shift, pull back. He withdrew from her, leaving her suddenly, achingly empty. Sliding lower, he fastened his mouth leisurely over one nipple.

The scalding heat was a shock; she gasped, then relaxed, then tensed again as he artfully played. The sound she made when he rasped her nipple with his tongue reminded her of a cat; when he grazed the tortured bud with his teeth, she nearly died.

"Gently."

The word was a soothing sigh feathering over her heated flesh as he turned his attention to her other breast, to the neglected peak that was already aching for his touch. When it came, she arched like a puppet whose strings were in his hands. His warm chuckle rewarded her.

"How old are you?"

His lips drifted lower, skating over her midriff.

"Umm ... late twenties."

"Hmm." He slid lower, his lips trailing a hot path to her navel. "You've got a lot of catching up to do."

"I have?"

He reached one hand up to fondle her breasts; the other slid down and around, stroking over her bottom and along the backs of her thighs. "Oh, yes."

He sounded very sure.

"You may as well start now."

She didn't argue. She was sensing him, seeing him anew—and it was a fascinating insight. This tenderly passionate seducer set a completely new dimension to this male she'd never, it now seemed, completely known. She'd never met him as the sensual adult male—in that guise, he was an enticing creature, cloaked in darkness, maybe, but oh so tempting.

The world slid away; reality faded as his hands wove their magic.

"What should I do?"

He lifted his head from where he was nibbling his way across her stomach, the skin taut and flickering. Her nerves were similarly afflicted.

"Just lie back." She could hear a certain male smugness in his voice. "Lie back, relax, and let the pleasure take you."

She had no strength, no motivation to do otherwise, so she did. If she'd had any inkling of what he had in mind, she would have summoned strength from somewhere. But she didn't. So she indulged her senses, and indulged herself with the indescribable pleasure of indulging him.

The warm, vibrant body arching beneath him held Gabriel's attention more completely, more effectively, than any woman before. Than anything in his life before.

Nothing had ever been this compelling. Never before had he experienced such total and abject surrender to the moment, to the worship of shared pleasure. There was something more here, something deeper, more powerful, more fascinating. The connoisseur was enthralled; the man was captivated.

Whatever new caress, whatever outrageous delight he pressed on her, she accepted—eagerly, gratefully—and, in return, she ravished him with her body, lavished upon him an unrestricted, unrestrained invitation to take, to plunder, to enjoy.

To search, to plumb, to discover—to know. Completely, absolutely, without barriers or guile. There was no part of her she hid from him, no part of her she denied him. He only had to reach, to wordlessly ask, to be invited to take, to touch, to sate his hunger in her.

Her generosity was not limited to the physical. He sensed no reticence, no emotional distance, no private core of feeling she kept screened. Even as he steered her toward the culminating climax, he could sense the vulnerability she didn't try to hide.

It was that that ensnared him, focused his attention so completely. He'd opened sensual doors for her; in return, she'd opened a door he'd never imagined existed, a door into a realm of deeper intimacy, far more explicit, more dangerous, more exciting. An abject innocent, she'd shown him how much more there could be in this sphere—a sphere in which he'd thought he'd known it all.

He'd never known this—this all-consuming passion. She was open, honest, and soul-shatteringly courageous in her giving. Without conditions, she offered the ultimate satiation—something deep inside him shook as, driven, he reached to claim it.

And then it was his, and they were caught in the tide, buffeted by the glory. The intense release swelled, rose, then washed through them, and he was drowning in the bottomless well of her giving, in the ultimate ecstasy.

His last thought as he slid beneath the wave was that she was his. Tonight— and forever.

He woke in the depths of the night. For one instant, he savored the fluid stillness that held them, then reluctantly he disengaged, lifting from her and untangling their limbs, then sinking down beside her and gathering her to him. He would have liked to simply lie there, sharing the contentment, the aftermath of pleasure still warm in their veins, but she woke, too, and turned skittish. Not with any false modesty but with anxiety.

"I must go." A reluctance to match his resonated in her words, colored her determination. That last, however, was strong.

She pushed away and he let her go, shaken by the spike of need that drove him to pull her back. He'd never been possessive; it was, he told himself, simply that he'd enjoyed her so well, that the experience of her was so new to him.

He listened as she slipped from the bed, tracking her by sound as she rounded the bed to grope by the wall for her gown.

Rising, he found his trousers, pulled them on, then padded into the sitting room. He returned a moment later, having relighted both lamps. She was in her gown, her veil already down; she was struggling to redo her laces.

"Here." Strolling up, he caught her about the waist and turned her. "Let me."

Expertly, he did them up, noting the fine tension that had gripped her the instant he'd touched her. He left her drawing on her stockings in the semi-darkness, and quickly finished dressing. By the time he shrugged into his coat, she was fully cloaked and veiled. He wasn't surprised by her sudden bolt back into secrecy, but he was very tired of that veil.

She glanced at him. "I'll see myself out." The words were slightly breathless.

"No." Strolling forward, he stopped by her side. "I'll see you to your carriage."

She considered arguing; he could sense it in her stance. But then she acquiesced with an inclination of her head. Not haughty, but careful.

Without another word, he escorted her from the room, down the stairs, and through the foyer. The sleepy doorman let them out with barely a glance, too busy stifling a yawn.

Her black carriage was waiting just along the street. He handed her in, then she turned back to him. He felt her gaze search his face, lit by a nearby street flare, then she inclined her head again.

"Thank you."

The soft words feathered his senses, leaving him very sure that it was not his efforts regarding the company for which she was thanking him.

She settled into the dark of the carriage; he shut the door and nodded at her coachman. "Drive on."

The coach rattled away. Filling his chest with a slow, deep breath, he watched it turn the corner, then he exhaled and headed home. The sense of achievement that suffused him was profound and intensely satisfying. Intensely gratifying.

Everything—*everything*—was going very well.

CHAPTER
Nine

"Well, miss, and what's got into you?"

Alathea snapped to attention. Reflected in the dressing table mirror before her, she saw Nellie shaking out her pillows and airing her bed.

Nellie caught her eye. "You've been staring at that mirror for the past five minutes, and seeing nothing is my guess."

Alathea gestured, brushing the query aside, praying she wouldn't blush, that her face showed no evidence of her thoughts. Heaven forbid.

"That meeting of yours last night must have been a long one—four o'clock again before you got in. Jacobs said you was in there for all those hours."

Alathea picked up her brush. "We had to discuss what we'd learned."

"So you've found something out about this wretched company—you and Mr. Rupert?"

"Indeed." Setting the brush to her hair, Alathea forced her mind to that aspect of the night. "We've learned enough to frame our case. All we need do now is assemble the right proofs, and we'll be free."

Easier said than done, no doubt, but she was convinced last night had set their feet on the road to success. Despite her careful words to Gabriel, she'd felt buoyed by their first real gain, the first scent of ultimate victory.

She'd been careful to hide her elation, aware he'd sense it and take advantage.

He'd taken advantage anyway.

So had she.

"Here, let me." Nellie lifted the brush from her slack grasp. "Good for nothing, this morning, you are."

Alathea blinked. "I was just … thinking."

Nellie shot her a shrewd look. "Well, I dare say there are lots of facts from this meeting you need chew on."

"Hmm." Facts. Sensations, emotions—revelations. She had a lot to think about.

Throughout the day, her mind wandered, considering, pondering, reliving the golden moments, carefully fixing each in her memory, storing them away against the cold years ahead. Again and again, she was jerked back to the present—by Charlie asking after one of their tenants, by Alice wanting her opinion on a particular shade of ribbon, by Jeremy frowning over a piece of arithmetic.

Finally, in the quiet of the afternoon when, after luncheon, all the females of the family repaired to the back parlor for a quiet hour before driving in the park or attending an afternoon tea, Augusta climbed into Alathea's lap, sitting astride her knees. Placing her soft hands on Alathea's cheeks, Augusta stared into her eyes. "You keep going away—far away."

Alathea looked into Augusta's large brown eyes.

Augusta searched hers. "Where is it you go?"

To another world, one of darkness, sensation, and indescribable wonder.

Alathea smiled. "Sorry, poppet, I've got lots on my mind just now." Rose had been dumped in her lap between them; Alathea lifted the doll and studied her. "How is Rose finding London?"

The distraction worked, not for her but for Augusta. Fifteen minutes later, when Augusta slipped from her lap and went to play with Rose in a splash of sunlight, Alathea exchanged a fond and, she hoped, undisturbingly mild glance with Serena, then quietly left the room.

She sought refuge in her office.

Standing arms crossed before the window, she forced herself to concentrate on the company's plans, all that Crowley had disclosed the previous evening. Despite her senses' preoccupation, there was nothing requiring thought in all the rest. It had happened—she'd seized and enjoyed the experience, but that was all there was to it. She wouldn't rescue her family from destitution by dwelling on such matters—on the substance of dreams. Her only major worry arising from her interlude with Gabriel was the difficulty she would experience in facing him as Alathea Morwellan. Knowing him in the biblical sense, and knowing he knew her in the same way but didn't know it was she, wasn't going to make her life any easier.

Despite her charade, she was not a naturally deceitful person; she'd never imagined having to deceive him in this way.

If he ever found out ...

Dragging in a breath, she turned from the window. Sensibility was not her strong suit—whatever leanings she'd had in that direction had been eradicated eleven years ago. Determinedly, she focused on the company and Crowley. It took mere minutes to concede that she could not, no matter how much she wished it, proceed without Gabriel. Quite aside from the fact that dismissing him would probably be more difficult than summoning him in the first place, she could see no way forward without him.

She couldn't break in, or even organize to have someone else break in, to Douglas's mansion. She'd had Jacobs drive her around Egerton Gardens; Folwell had chatted to a street sweeper and discovered which of the large, new houses belonged to Douglas, but breaking in was too risky. Although they might find some of the proofs they needed, the chances of Crowley or Swales realizing their records had been searched and, as Charlie would phrase it, getting the wind up, was high. Then they'd call in the promissory notes and she'd be too busy beating off creditors to press any claim in court.

And she didn't like Crowley. The thought of meeting him at night alone and cut off from help was the substance of nightmares. He was evil. She'd sensed it very clearly, watching him as he'd watched Gerrard Debbington, seeing the cruel gleam in his eyes. Gabriel had said Crowley liked to gloat over his potential victims, but it was more than that. He viewed people as prey. There was viciousness and real cruelty beneath his semicivilized veneer.

She wanted him as far away from her family as possible.

All things considered—and she did mean all—the only sensible way forward was to find the needed proofs without delay. Then Crowley would no longer be a threat, and the countess could fade into the mists.

"Fangak. Lodwar. What was the other one?" Sitting at her desk, she drew a sheet of paper onto the blotter and reached for a pen. "Kafia—that was it."

She wrote the names down, then settled to list all the names and locations she could recall Crowley mentioning.

"Mary? Alice?" Alathea peeked into Mary's bedchamber, where her elder stepsisters often repaired when they were supposed to be resting. Sure enough, both were lolling on the bed wearing identical expressions of disgusted boredom. They both lifted their heads to look at her.

Alathea grinned. "I'm going to Hatchard's. Serena said you could come if you wished."

Mary sat bolt upright. "They have a lending library, don't they?"

Alice was already rolling from the bed. "I'll come."

Alathea watched them scramble into shoes, struggle into spencers, grab bonnets, casting only the most perfunctory of glances at their reflections. "There is a lending library, but before you go looking for Mrs. Radcliffe's latest, I want you to help me find some books."

"On what?" Alice asked as she joined her at the door.

"On Africa."

"That was *boring*." On a long-drawn yawn, Jeremy sank deeper into the seat of the hackney and leaned against Alathea's shoulder. "I thought they would have known about digging up gold. All they wanted to talk about was melting it."

"Hmm." Alathea grimaced. She'd thought the gentlemen at the Metallurgical Institute would have known about mining, too. Unfortunately, the academy, whose sign she'd glimpsed when walking with Mary and Alice, had proved to focus solely on refining metals and the subsequent workings. The good gentlemen had known less than she about gold mining in Central East Africa. Despite reading late into the night, she knew virtually nothing about the subject.

Alathea glanced at Augusta, snuggled on her other side with Rose propped on her lap. At least Augusta was happy, unconcerned with mining gold. "How's Rose?"

"Rose is good." Augusta looked at Rose's face, then turned her once more to the window. "She's seeing more of the city—it's crowded and noisy, but she feels safe in here with me and you."

Alathea smiled, closing her hand around the small fingers snuggled trustingly into hers. "That's good. Rose is growing up—she'll be a big girl soon."

"But not yet." Augusta looked into her face. "Do you think Miss Helm will be all better when we get back?"

Miss Helm had developed the sniffles, which was why Alathea had Augusta with her. "I'm sure Miss Helm will be recovered by tomorrow, but you and Rose must be very good with her this evening."

"Oh, we will." Augusta turned Rose's face to hers. "We'll be specially good. We won't even say she has to read to us before bed."

"I'll come and read to you, poppet."

"But you have to go to the ball."

Alathea stroked Augusta's hair. "I'll come and read to you first—I can go on later in the other carriage."

"I say!" Jeremy jerked upright, staring out of the window. "Look at *that*!"

Alathea did—it took a moment before she realized what she was looking at. "It's a pedestrian curricle—at least, I suppose that's what it is."

She'd heard of the contraptions. Both she and Jeremy leaned close to the window, with Augusta pressing between; they all watched the gentleman in a natty checkered coat balanced precariously above the large wheel weave in and out of the traffic until he disappeared from view.

"Well!" Eyes alight, Jeremy sank back.

Alathea looked at his face. "No."

Her tone was absolute; Jeremy's face fell. "But, Allie—just think—"

"I am—I'm thinking of your mother."

"I wouldn't fall off—I'd be extra specially careful." Alathea met his eye. "Just like you were extra specially careful when I allowed you to drive the gig?"

"I only got tipped in the river—and anyway, that was old Dobbins's fault."

Alathea held her tongue. The hackney rolled on, taking them back into the fashionable district. As they turned into Mount Street, she glanced again at Jeremy's face. He was still dreaming of the dangerous contraption; she knew he wouldn't let go of his dream until he'd experienced it, or something worse. He was adventurous, the sort who simply had to try things out. It was a compulsion she understood.

"Pedestrian curricles have been around for some years." Her musing comment had Jeremy turning, his eyes lighting. She met his bright gaze. "I'll ask your mama. Perhaps Folwell can find one—"

"Whoopee!"

"*On* one condition."

Jeremy stopped bouncing on the seat, but his eyes still glowed. "What condition?"

"That you promise not to use it in town at all, but only once we're back at Morwellan Park." Where the lawns were thick and cushioning.

Jeremy considered for only a moment. "All right. I promise."

Alathea nodded as the carriage rocked to a stop before Morwellan House. "Very well. I'll speak with your mama."

Propping up the wall at yet another ball, Alathea stifled a yawn. She blinked her eyes wide, struggling to keep them open; she'd spent the past two nights reading into the small hours after the rest of the household was abed. It was the only time she had to herself to wade through the tomes she'd found on Africa.

Central East Africa, however, continued to elude her. What little she could find on the region was largely speculative, and exceedingly scant on detail.

A familiar head of burnished chestnut hove into sight above the masses. The most peculiar thrill shot through her; she immediately looked for cover. There was not a palm or shadowy alcove anywhere near. Besides, that might not be wise. Getting trapped with him in the shadows was likely to scramble her wits.

Beneath her skirts, she bent her knees and sank just enough so that she was no longer so readily detected by her height. Through gaps in the horrendous crush, she caught glimpses of Gabriel as he prowled the room.

For some peculiar reason, at least viewing him from a distance, he seemed like a different man. She could see, appreciate, aspects of him she hadn't truly noticed before, like the perfection of his restrained elegance, and the subtle aura of leashed power that cloaked his tall frame. And his reserve, that distance, apparently unbreachable, that he maintained between himself and the world.

He was bored—truly bored. She could see why Celia and the ladies of the ton despaired. They were right in thinking he didn't see them at all; from the way his face was set, the steadiness of his gaze, she would have wagered Morwellan Park that he was thinking more of Central East Africa than of a glittering ballroom in Mayfair.

One lady braved his detachment and put her hand on his sleeve. He smiled, urbanely charming; gracefully, he lifted her hand and bowed over it. Straightening, he exchanged a light word, some quip to set the lady laughing, hoping ... only to be disappointed as with no more than that superficiality, he smoothly moved on.

He was a master at sliding through a crowd, refusing to be anchored, ineffably polite, arrogantly assured, and utterly impossible.

"Alathea! Good gracious, my dear—what peculiar fetish do you have with walls?"

Abruptly straightening, Alathea looked around—into Celia Cynster's startled eyes. "I was ... just easing my legs."

Celia gave her a hard, inherently maternal stare, but was distracted by a glimpse of her firstborn through the crowd. "*There* he is! I made him promise to attend—he's been to hardly any balls this entire Season—well, only family affairs. How on earth does he expect to find a wife?"

"I don't think securing a wife is uppermost in his mind."

Celia nearly pouted. "Well, he had better get started on the matter—he's not getting any younger."

Alathea kept her lips sealed.

"Lady Hendricks has been dropping hints that her daughter Emily might suit."

An image of the lovely Miss Hendricks popped into Alathea's mind. The young lady was sweet, modest, and excessively quiet. "Don't you think she's a little too timid?"

"Of course she's too timid! Rupert wouldn't know what to do with her—and she certainly wouldn't know what to do with *him*."

Alathea hid a smile. "Are you really entertaining any hope that some lady will be able to influence Rupert? He's the least easy to influence person I know."

Celia sighed. "Believe me, my dear, the *right* lady could do a great deal with Rupert, because, you see, he'd let her."

"Lady Alathea!"

Blinking, Alathea refocused on Mary and Alice, strolling with Heather and Eliza ahead of her on the lawns. It was clearly not they who had called. Looking around, she discovered two blond beauties rushing to catch her up. Both held on to elegant bonnets, ribbons streaming in the breeze; profusions of golden ringlets danced on their shoulders.

Recognizing the twins, Alathea halted. She'd been introduced to them at a ball, but they hadn't had a chance for any lengthy chat.

Gaining her side, the twins waved at their cousins, then turned beaming smiles upon her as they flanked her. Alathea got the distinct impression she'd been captured.

"We wondered if we might speak with you," one began.

Alathea smiled, a shrewd suspicion of what was to come dawning in her mind. "You'll have to take pity on me—I can't remember which of you is which."

"I'm Amelia," the one who'd spoken testified.

"And I'm Amanda," the other said, making it sound like a confession. "We wondered if you'd mind giving us your opinion."

"On what subject?"

"Well, you've known Gabriel and Lucifer since they were young. We've decided that the only way we'll be able to escape them and find our own husbands is for them to get married, so we wanted to ask if you could give us any pointers."

"Any hints as to who might be suitable—"

"Or characteristics to avoid, like being hen-brained."

"Although that does narrow the candidates."

Alathea looked from one bright face to the other—they were earnest, eager, and totally serious. She stifled a gurgle of laughter. "You want to marry them off so they'll no longer be in your way?"

"So they'll no longer guard us like the crown jewels!"

"We've heard," Amelia said darkly, "that some gentlemen won't even come near us, simply because of the ructions that might ensue."

"They actually cross us off their lists, right from the first, all because of those two!" Amanda all but shook her fist at her absent cousins. "How on earth can we reasonably assess all the possibilities—"

"And make sure they've assessed us properly, too—"

"If our watchdogs are forever snarling—"

"And they always snarl loudest at the most *interesting* gentlemen!"

"Well," Amanda went on, "you know what gentlemen are like. If there's the least hurdle, then they simply won't bother exerting themselves."

"Well, they don't need to, do they? There's always so many other ladies about for whom they need exert themselves not at all."

"So you see, when it comes to eligibility, we're laboring under an unfair disadvantage."

"Oh, dear." Alathea fought to straighten her lips. "You know, I really don't think Gabriel and Lucifer would like you to think of them as an 'unfair disadvantage.' " She suspected they'd be hurt, their male egos bruised.

Amanda kicked at the grass. "Well, we don't plan on telling them, but that doesn't excuse the fact. They *are* a disadvantage."

"And they are unfair, too."

Alathea didn't argue—she thought the same. They *were* being pigheadedly unfair, refusing to see that Amanda and Amelia had any modicum of sense and, regardless of all else, had every right to choose their own husbands. The way Gabriel and Lucifer had always treated her—as an equal companion—stood in stark contrast to how they treated the twins. Although they'd always interposed themselves between her and any threat, they hadn't tried to stop her from encountering those threats.

Looking up, she checked her charges ambling ahead; all four girls were engrossed in some avid discussion. Alathea glanced at the twins—at Amanda, scowling at the grass as she walked, then at Amelia, softer of face but with the same determined set to her chin. "Why do you think their marrying will help?"

Amanda looked up. "Well, it has with all the others. They're no longer a problem."

"All you have to do is look, and you'll see it. Why, Devil was the worst, but he's so much easier now."

"Once they marry, it's as if all their attention is focused on the lady they wed."

"And their families."

Alathea pondered that.

"We think we should concentrate on Gabriel first."

"Simply because he's the elder." Amelia glanced at Alathea. "Do you think that's the right tack?"

Alathea considered the picture of Gabriel trying to maintain his repressive watch over the twins while simultaneously fending off ladies the twins themselves introduced. He wouldn't have time to cause her any problems. "I think … that your aunt Celia could give you some names."

Amanda brightened. "That's a thought."

"There would be no need," Alathea mused, elaborating on the picture in her mind, "to be overly subtle. The ladies won't care as long as they gain some time by his side, and he'll know what you're up to from the first, so there's no need to be careful on that count."

Amelia stopped dead. "He'll be trapped." She swung to face Alathea and Amanda, her eyes alight. "He won't be able to escape—"

"Except"—Amanda concluded with great relish—"by leaving us alone."

Hookhams Lending Library in Bond Street was Alathea's port of call the next morning. Unfortunately, their section on Africa was almost nonexistent. Nevertheless, she borrowed all four books; old and rather tattered, they held out little promise. Juggling them under her arm, she stepped down to the pavement. The biggest book slipped—her shoe skidded off the last step—

"Careful!"

Hard hands gripped her arms and righted her. Jerking her head up, Alathea stared—into Lucifer's face. She swallowed her sigh of relief, and struggled to calm her thudding heart. For one moment, with the sun behind him, she'd thought him his brother. "Ah …"

"Here—give me those."

He didn't, of course, give her any choice. "Oh—yes!" Alathea drew in a quick breath. "Have you been riding this morning?"

He looked at her. "In the park? No. Why?"

She shrugged. "I just wondered … I'd love to go for a ride, but it's so impossible here—only being allowed to amble in the park."

"If you want to ride"—he tucked her books under one arm and fell in beside her—"you'll need to organize an excursion to the country."

Alathea grimaced. "I may as well wait until we return home." Her only hope was to keep him talking, to hold his attention so he didn't glance at the books. Africa was an unusual topic, certainly an odd one for her to be studying in depth. Given that Lucifer shared Gabriel's house, and she knew how they tossed tidbits and observations back and forth … she drew in a breath. "But the Season's still got weeks and weeks to go."

"Indeed, and those weeks are crammed with more balls than ever." Lucifer frowned at the pavement. "And now here's Gabriel threatening to eschew all but compulsory family events."

"Oh? Why?"

"The damned twins have gone on the offensive."

"Offensive? What do you mean?"

"Last night, they swanned up to Gabriel on three separate occasions with a different lady each time, and cornered him."

Alathea wished she'd seen it. "Couldn't he get away?"

"Not easy with one of the twins hanging on his arm and refusing to let go."

"Oh, dear."

"Oh, dear, indeed. You know what will happen, don't you?"

She looked at him questioningly.

"He'll wash his hands of the hussies."

"Leaving you in the firing line."

Lucifer stopped dead. "Good God."

She managed to keep him grumbling about the twins all the way to where her carriage waited. Deftly dropping a kiss on his cheek, she snagged her books from under his arm.

He frowned at her. "What was that for?"

"Just for being you." Safe in the carriage, the books on the seat beside her, she smiled gloriously. He humphed, shut the carriage door, and waved her away. She was still smiling when she crossed the threshold of Morwellan House; she nodded brightly to Crisp as he held the door. Stacking her books on the table beneath the mirror, she reached up to remove her bonnet.

"There you are, dear."

Serena stood in the drawing room doorway. Placing her hat on top of the books, Alathea crossed the hall. "Do we have guests?" she whispered.

"No, no. I just wanted to speak with you." Serena stepped back into the drawing room. "It's about your father."

"Oh." Following her and shutting the door, Alathea raised her brows.

"He's in one of his states." Serena raised her hands helplessly. "You know—under the weather but not ill."

"Has anything happened?"

"Not today. He was a little quiet when he came in yesterday, but he didn't say anything. You know he would normally be at White's by now, but instead he's sitting in the library."

They looked at each other, concern mirrored in their faces. Then Alathea nodded. "I'll go and speak with him."

Serena smiled. "Thank you—he always listens to you."

Alathea hugged her stepmother. "He always listens to you, too, but we talk about different things."

Her smile strengthening, Serena returned the hug. "Have you learned anything more about this promissory note?"

Alathea nodded. "I think we've found a way—a legal way—to have the note declared invalid, but I don't want to get anyone's hopes up yet."

"That's probably wise. Just tell us when we're free."

They exchanged quick smiles, then Alathea headed for the library.

The door opened noiselessly; she slipped in, noting that the curtains were open, the room bright, not shrouded in gloom. A good sign. While her father did not make a habit of succumbing to the blue devils, he had, she knew, been inwardly berating himself over the wretched promissory note. He'd put on a brave face for her sake and Serena's, but he would feel the sense of failure, of self-reproach, deeply.

Sitting in his favorite armchair, the earl was looking out over the back lawn. Mary and Alice were cutting roses, each girl as delicately beautiful as the blooms they laid in their baskets. Beyond them, Charlie was teaching Jeremy the rudiments of cricket while Augusta and Miss Helm were seated on a rug in the sunshine, reading a book. The garden was enclosed by stone walls, visible here and there between trees and thick bushes. The scene could have been a painting depicting fashionable family life, but it wasn't a figment of anyone's imagination—it was real, and it was theirs.

Empowering certainty filling her, Alathea touched her father's shoulder. "Papa?"

So engrossed had he been, he hadn't known she was there. He looked up, then his lips curved ruefully. "Good morning, my dear."

Catching her hand, he squeezed it; he continued to hold it as she sat on the arm of his chair. Alathea leaned her shoulder against his, comforted by the solidity beneath his coat. "What is it?"

He sighed, the sound deep and defeated. "I really hoped you'd be wrong about that company—that the Central East Africa Gold Company would ultimately turn out to be legitimate. That I hadn't made yet another mistake."

He paused; Alathea held his hand firmly and waited.

"But you and Wiggs were right. It was all a hum. Chappie I met at White's yesterday told me so. He was from those parts—Central East Africa. He knew the company. Condemned it as a racket set up to gull simpletons into parting with their brass." He grimaced. "I could hardly disagree."

"You couldn't have known …" Alathea blinked. "This man, who was he?"

"Sailor fellow—a Captain something. Didn't catch his last name."

"What did he look like?"

At the sudden tension in her voice, the earl turned to meet her gaze. "He was of middle height, rather portly. Had great grizzled whiskers down both cheeks. His clothes marked him as a seaman, senior rank—there's always a nautical air to such men." He searched Alathea's face. "Why? Is he important?"

Alathea reined in her excitement. "He could be. Wiggs and I think there's a legal way of overturning the promissory note, but we need to learn more about the company's business. A man like this captain could be very helpful." She gripped her father's hand. "Was he with anyone you knew?"

Her father shook his head. "No. But if it's important, I can ask around."

"Do, Papa—it could be *very* important. And if you should stumble across him again, promise me you'll bring him home."

Her father's brows quirked, but he nodded. "Right, then. I suppose I'd better get on to White's and see if I can track him down."

"Oh, yes!" Alathea bounced to her feet as he rose. "This could help us *enormously*, Papa. Thank you!" She swooped at him and kissed him on the cheek.

Catching her within one arm, he hugged her. "Thank *you*, my dear." He looked into her face, then placed a gentle kiss on her forehead. "Don't ever think I don't appreciate all you've done—I don't know what I did right to deserve you. I can only be glad you're mine."

Alathea blinked rapidly. "Oh, Papa!" She hugged him quickly, then broke away, glancing through the window. "I must get Jeremy off to his lessons or he'll play cricket all day."

Still blinking, she hurried out.

CHAPTER

Ten

That evening at Lady Castlereagh's ball, Alathea found herself plagued by gentlemen. With but little help from her, the number of mature bachelors who considered her an agreeable dance partner had been steadily growing as the Season progressed. Despite Celia's conviction that she hugged the walls, she was too astute to do so constantly. True anonymity meant doing nothing to make herself remarkable; she therefore duly danced and waltzed, not every dance but enough to ensure no one saw need to comment on her abstention.

Indeed, she enjoyed waltzing, although there were few men tall enough to meet her requirements. Yet despite the hurdle of her unusual height, the ranks of her admirers, as Serena insisted on terming them, had somehow swollen to the legion.

Which made life exceedingly awkward when, after two dances, she wanted to slink into the shadows, the better to consider her current difficulties. The principal one was present, garbed in severe walnut-black, his locks burnished, his manner ineffably urbane. He'd extended himself to dance the same two dances she had, but was now ambling, deliberately aimlessly, through the crowd. If he could dispense with the need to do the pretty and converse, she felt it only fair that she could, too.

"I'm afraid, dear sirs"—she beamed a smile at the gentlemen surrounding her—"that I must leave you for the present. One of my stepsisters ..." With an airy wave, she led them to believe she'd been summoned across the room. As joining Mary and Alice meant braving a gaggle of youthful damsels, none of the gentlemen offered to accompany her. They bowed and begged for promises of her return; she smiled and glided away from them.

The crush was unbelievable. Lady Castlereagh was one of the senior hostesses—her invitations could not be declined. That, Alathea suspected, accounted for the presence of most of the Cynsters, Gabriel included. Using the crowd to her advantage, she made her way to a narrow embrasure occupied by a pedestal topped by a bust of Wellington. She took refuge in the lee of the pedestal, screened from at least half the room.

Thankfully also screened from some of the noise—it was hard to hear her own thoughts. Across the room, she saw Gabriel, with obvious reluctance, relieve Lucifer of his watch on the twins. Taking up a position almost directly opposite her, Gabriel looked wary.

Alathea grinned. She searched the throng for the twins. Even using Gabriel's gaze for direction, she still couldn't see them. With an expectant sigh, she settled back, almost against the wall but not quite. Anyone seeing her would assume she was waiting for some gentleman or a youthful charge to return to her side.

Thus concealed, she settled to ponder how to tell her knight on a white charger where he should look for their relief. She'd issued the summons; he'd come galloping to her aid—now she was stuck with him and his notion of rewards. Dealing with him further was going to prove difficult, but she couldn't proceed without him.

Coming up with the captain, stumbling upon him in the crowd on a dance floor, was beyond unlikely—his sort stuck to the clubs, not the park or the ton's entertainments. The captain was effectively out of her reach. She didn't dare pin all her hopes on her father appearing one day for luncheon with the captain in tow.

She had to tell Gabriel about the captain, and as soon as possible. Who knew how long a seagoing captain would remain ashore? He might already have sailed, but she refused to consider the possibility. Fate couldn't be that cruel. But how to tell Gabriel in safety?

A letter had seemed possible until she'd drafted one. Even though she'd included her father's description of the captain verbatim, the letter lacked life, and reeked of cowardice. She couldn't even sign it other than as "The Countess." Instead of sending it off, she'd torn it up and resumed her pondering.

If she didn't see Gabriel face to face, she would have no way of knowing how he reacted to her news, nor could she question him over what he'd learned—she was quite sure he wouldn't have been idle in the five days since they'd last met.

At the Burlington Hotel.

The mere name sent a wave of uncertainty through her; she immediately blocked it off. She couldn't afford to let her emotions rule her, or dictate her moves. What had Gabriel learned? Had Crowley done anything more? These were questions to which she needed answers; she would get answers only if she met Gabriel face to face, of that she was absolutely sure.

But the thought of being private, alone with him in the dark, made her shiver—and not with dread. The fact only increased her wariness and made her question her arguments. Were they merely rationalizations?

Standing in the pedestal's shadow, she examined, dissected, and reassembled her thoughts—and got nowhere. The situation irked; her inability to make up her mind rasped her temper.

Then he moved. She'd been watching him from the corner of her eye. As he forcefully handed the twins' watch back to Lucifer, then stepped into the crowd, she straightened. A clamp slowly closed about her lungs. There was, she told herself, no reason he should stroll her way, no reason he even knew she was there.

She'd underestimated the power of her cap.

It drew him like a lodestone. He cleaved through the crowd so efficiently that, once she realized she was indeed his target, she didn't have time to beat a retreat. He halted beside her.

Trapped, she raised her chin and fixed him with a glare. "Don't say a word."

His eyes held hers for a pregnant moment; she inwardly quivered, and told herself he couldn't see through her disguise. That he'd never see the woman who'd lain naked in his arms in the lady who now stood before him.

Lips thinning, Gabriel nodded curtly. "There's obviously no need, although I can't see why you bother—your hair will go gray soon enough."

Alathea's eyes flashed, but instead of ripping up at him, she smiled. Acidly. "I'm quite sure you'll have gray hairs aplenty if you persist in acting like a dog with a bone over your young cousins."

"You know nothing about the matter, so don't start."

"I know the twins are perfectly capable of taking care of themselves."

He snorted derisively. "Which shows how much you know."

"I would have thought"—her tone had him tensing—"that any females capable of routing one of the Cynsters, capable of detecting the chink in his armor and plotting and acting to press their advantage, and succeeding, would be thought capable of managing even the ton's most notorious rakes." Her gaze slid around to his face. "Don't you?"

Gabriel felt his eyes narrow; his temper surged. He would infinitely have preferred impassivity, but with her, that always seemed beyond him. He transfixed her with a glittering glance. "*You* told them."

He didn't need the artful lift of her brows to tell him that was the truth.

"They approached me with their problem—I merely made an observation."

"*You* are the cause of their current obsession with finding me a suitable bride."

"Now, now"—she wagged a finger at him—"you know perfectly well I couldn't be responsible for that. You're the one who's yet to marry. You're the one in need of a wife. The twins are merely trying to be helpful."

What he muttered in response was far from polite; Alathea merely smiled. "They're trying to be helpful in exactly the same way you're trying to help them."

"And what way is that?"

She looked him in the eye. "Misguidedly."

He blinked.

When he didn't immediately respond, she looked away. "I rather wondered how you'd react if the shoe was on the other foot."

"You knew damned well how I'd react." He gritted his teeth. "You only suggested it to plague me." Her lips quirked, very briefly but enough to set his temper soaring. "I know Lucifer attempted to explain the need for our watch on the twins—he clearly didn't succeed. So perhaps a demonstration's in order"—he lifted his gaze to the cap covering her soft hair—"to drive the point through your demonstrably thick skull."

Her head whipped around. She was frowning. He shifted closer, crowding her into the nook between the pedestal and the alcove wall. Clamping one hand on the pedestal's top, he caged her into the small space.

Meeting her gaze, fell intent in his, he was surprised to see her eyes flare—surprised to see how far into the gap between the pedestal and the wall she'd backed herself.

Her gaze falling to his chest, mere inches from hers, Alathea swallowed and wrenched her gaze back up to his face. She fought against the urge to press one hand to her breast in a vain effort to calm her leaping heart. *Oh, God!* In situations like this, she would customarily slap a hand to his chest and shove—she wouldn't hesitate, wouldn't stop to consider any possible impropriety. And although her strength couldn't possibly shift him, if she shoved, he'd move.

But she didn't dare touch him.

Couldn't guarantee what her hands would do if she did.

Gracious heavens! What on earth was she to do? She could already see puzzlement dawning in his eyes.

Senses reeling—he was far too close!—she stiffened her spine, drew herself up to her full height, and made a passable attempt at looking down her nose at him. "I do wish you'd *think*!" Her gaze locked with his, she did—frantically. "Protecting them from real threats—threats that actually materialize—is all very well, but in this case, your"—she gestured, using her wave to make him lean back—"constant *hovering* is actually limiting their opportunities. It's not fair."

"Fair?" He snorted. To her immense relief, he eased back, letting go of the pedestal and turning to glance to where she imagined the twins must be. "I can't see where fairness comes into it."

"Can't you?" Able to breathe again, she dragged in a breath. "Just think. You never used to stop me from ... oh, riding neck or nothing with you and Alasdair—you wouldn't stop me doing it now."

"You ride like the devil. There's no need to stop you—you'd be in no danger."

"Ah, but if there was something dangerous in my path—if, for instance, I'd jumped a fence into a field with an enraged bull. Wouldn't you come racing to save me?"

The look he shot her was disgusted—disgusted she'd even asked. "Of course I would." After a moment, he added more softly, "You know I would."

She inclined her head, a very odd knot of emotion in her stomach; as children, he'd always been the first to interpose himself between her and any danger. "Yes—and that's precisely what I mean about the way you're suffocating the twins."

Deliberately, she fell silent. She sensed his reluctance; it poured from him in waves. He didn't want to hear her theory, didn't want to canvass the possibility that he, his brother, and his cousins might be wrong, might be overreacting. Because if he did, he'd have to rein in his Cynster protectiveness, and that, she well knew, was very hard to do.

Eventually, he shot her a far from encouraging glance. "Why suffocating?"

She looked away, across the sea of heads. "Because you won't let them spread their wings. Rather than letting them ride wild, stepping in only if they're threatened, you're making sure they're not threatened in the first place by ensuring they never ride at all." He opened his mouth; she held up a placating hand. "A perfectly valid approach in other contexts, but in this arena, it means you're blocking off all chance of their learning to ride—all chance of their succeeding. Well"—she gestured across the room—"just look at them." She couldn't see them, but he could. "They may be surrounded by ten gentlemen—"

"Twenty."

"How ever many!" Her terse tone had him meeting her gaze. "Can't you see they're the *wrong* men?"

Gabriel looked at the teeming masses around the twins, and tried to tell himself he couldn't see it at all.

"Can you seriously imagine any of those innocuous gentlemen married to the twins? Or is it more accurate to say you—all of you—have been carefully avoiding imagining the twins married at all?"

She was like his conscience, whispering in his ear. Like his conscience, he couldn't ignore her. "I'll think about it," he growled, unwilling to even meet her eyes. All he would see was the truth, his own truth reflected back at him.

He dragged in a breath, chest swelling against the usual constriction, the constriction he always felt when around her. Lord, she made him uncomfortable. Even now, when they weren't tearing strips off each other but having what was, for them, a rational discussion, his insides felt scored, like claws had dragged down from his throat over his chest, then locked about his heart, his gut.

She'd shaken him, too. Again. Why the devil had she looked at him like that—eyes wide with *what*?—when he'd backed her against the wall? The sight had rocked him; even now, his skin was prickling just because she was close.

His impulse, as always, was to verbally lash at her, to drive her away even though, if she was in the same room, he would compulsively head for her side. Stupid. He wished he could tell himself that he disliked her, but he didn't. He never had. Keeping his gaze from her ridiculous cap—the sight would assuredly set him off—he drew in another breath, scanning the nearer guests, about to bow and excuse himself—

He narrowed his eyes. "What the devil ...?"

The muttered question went unanswered as Lord Coleburn, Mr. Henry Simpkins and Lord Falworth, all smiling easily, strolled up.

"There you are, my dear lady." Falworth swept Alathea an elegant bow.

"We thought you might need rescuing," Henry Simpkins stated, his gaze sweeping over Gabriel before coming to rest on Alathea's face. "From the crush, don't you know?"

"It is indeed horrendous," Alathea smoothly returned. She waited for Gabriel to excuse himself and move on; instead, he remained planted like an oak at her side. With Wellington immediately to her left, she couldn't escape; her would-be cavaliers were forced to deploy themselves in a semicircle before her and Gabriel. As if they were on trial. Heaving an inward sigh, she introduced him, quite sure the others would know him at least by reputation.

That last became rapidly apparent. By dint of various subtle quips, Coleburn, Simpkins, and Falworth all made it plain they thought Gabriel would find better entertainment elsewhere. Alathea was not at all surprised when he shrugged their suggestions aside, looking for all the world as if he was fighting a yawn. He probably was. She certainly was. If she'd wanted to stand by the wall and converse with a gaggle of gentlemen, Coleburn, Simpkins, and Falworth would not have been her choice. She would rather converse with the Devil himself, presently on her right; at least, with him, she was never in danger of mentally drifting away and losing track of the conversation.

Despite the lack of stimulation, she was distinctly relieved that Gabriel did not decide to enliven proceedings by surgically dissecting Simpkins, who seemed intent on putting himself first in line with his studied and not-quite-nonchalant quips. Lady Castlereagh would not appreciate blood on her ballroom floor.

"And so Mrs. Dalrymple insisted we ride on, but the oxer at the end of the fourth field forced her to retire. Well"—Falworth spread his hands—"what could I do? We had to do a Brummel and take refuge in a nearby farmhouse."

The other gentlemen seemed mildly intrigued by Falworth's description of his aborted outing with the Cottesmore. All except Gabriel, who was doing a remarkable imitation of a marble statue. An utterly meaningless smile on her lips, Alathea inwardly sighed and let Falworth's words flow past her.

Beyond their little circle, a tall gentleman, as tall as Gabriel, strolled nonchalantly by. His idle gaze passed over them, then halted. He stopped, noting Gabriel, then his gaze slid back to her.

The gentleman smiled; Alathea nearly blinked. Charming did as charming was, but this was something rather more. Her lips had curved in reply before she'd even thought. The gentleman's smile deepened; he inclined his head. His gaze on her face, he approached with the same easy, loose-limbed prowl that characterized the Cynsters and, Alathea surmised, certain of their peers.

Gabriel's reaction was immediate and intense. Alathea barely had time to consider the why before the wherefore was bowing before her.

"Chillingworth, my dear. I don't believe we've met." Gracefully straightening, he flicked a glance at Gabriel. "But I'm sure I can prevail upon Cynster here to do the honors."

Gabriel let his silence stretch until it was just this side of insulting before grudgingly saying, "Lady Alathea Morwellan—Chillingworth, earl of."

Arching a warning brow at him, Alathea gave Chillingworth her hand. "A pleasure, my lord. Are you enjoying her ladyship's offerings?" There was a string quartet laboring somewhere, and a busy cardroom.

"To be honest, I've found the evening a mite dull." Releasing her hand, Chillingworth smiled. "A little too tame for my liking."

Alathea raised a brow. "Indeed?"

"Hmm. I count myself lucky to have spotted you in this crowd." His gaze was filled with appreciation, especially of her height. His lips curved. "Fortunate, indeed."

Alathea stifled a gurgle of laughter; beside her, Gabriel stiffened. Eyes dancing, she essayed, "I'm engaged in planning a ball for my stepmother. Tell me, what entertainments would best entice gentlemen such as yourself?"

The look Gabriel shot her was unmitigatingly censorious; Alathea ignored it.

So did Chillingworth. "Your fair presence would greatly entice me."

She met his gaze with a blank look. "Yes, but beyond that?"

He nearly choked trying to swallow his laugh. "Ah ... *beyond* that?"

"Come now, Chillingworth. I'm sure, if you concentrate, you'll remember what it is that brings you to these affairs." Gabriel's languid drawl deflected the earl's attention.

Chillingworth's brows rose. Leaning one arm on the pedestal's top, he frowned. "Let me think."

Gabriel snorted softly.

"Not hordes." Catching Alathea's eye, Chillingworth continued, "I can't think why the cachet of exclusivity isn't more widely appreciated."

His gaze on the guests shifting and shuffling before them, causing the three other gentlemen, now relegated to the outer ranks, to have to constantly give way, then struggle back, Gabriel humphed in agreement. "God knows why they imagine literally rubbing shoulders all evening to be fun."

"Because no hostess is game to call the ton's bluff, so we're all left to suffer." Alathea swept the gathering with a resigned eye.

"At least," Gabriel muttered, "we can see reasonably well. It must be worse for those who can't."

"I'm sure it is," Alathea returned. "Mary, Alice, and Serena seem to spend half their time trying to find their way about."

Chillingworth had been watching them, taking in this exchange. "Hmm. As to other requirements, while gentlemen such as I—and Cynster here—might be partial to sonatas and airs in their place, having a set of screeching violins set up in a corner merely constitutes unwarranted distraction."

"Distraction?" Alathea glanced at him. "Distraction from what?"

The direct question made Chillingworth blink. He slid a glance at Gabriel.

Alathea's lips quirked. "From your customary pursuits?"

Chillingworth straightened; Gabriel merely threw her a resigned glance. "Don't mind her," he advised Chillingworth. "Although perhaps I should warn you it only gets worse."

Alathea favored him with a haughty look. "You can't talk."

Glancing from one to the other, Chillingworth stated, "You know each other."

Alathea waved dismissively. "From birth—our association was decided for us, not by us."

Gabriel's brows rose. "Nicely put."

The puzzled look in Chillingworth's eyes didn't entirely evaporate, but he settled beside Alathea again. "Where were we?"

"The amenities you prefer for your customary pursuits."

Alathea was enjoying herself; both Chillingworth and Gabriel sent repressive glances her way.

"Very well." Chillingworth accepted the challenge. "Not a dance schedule that includes only two waltzes. Apropos of that, my dear, I believe the orchestra is about to make itself useful and indulge us with a waltz." Straightening, he smiled, both charming and challenging. "Can I tempt you to brave the floor with me?"

Alathea returned the smile, perfectly ready to take up his challenge, equally ready to give Gabriel a chance to slope off. They'd been in each other's company without descending into cutting sarcasm for nearly half an hour; there was no sense in stretching their luck.

She held out her hand. "Indeed, my lord—I'd be delighted."

Gabriel gritted his teeth, held his breath, and willed himself to stillness. God knew, he didn't want to waltz with Alathea—the mere thought sent itching heat washing over his skin like a rash. But … he didn't want her waltzing with Chillingworth. Or anyone else, but Chillingworth was, typically, the worst choice she could have made of all the gentlemen in the room. Not that she hadn't chosen quite deliberately; she might be twenty-nine but she still possessed a healthy vein of minxlike tendencies, victim to a strain of considered recklessness.

He watched as Chillingworth led her to the floor, then took her lightly in his arms. She laughed at some quip and they began to revolve; as they whirled down the room, Gabriel inwardly snorted. There she went, tempting fate with her eyes wide open.

Shifting his gaze, he saw Lucifer, still on guard but chatting with two friends while the twins danced. Gabriel located them, each in the arms of a suitably innocuous gentleman.

Alathea's words rang in his head; he inwardly humphed. He'd think about it. His gaze drifted over the dancers, and settled again.

The waltz was nearly over before Alathea identified the peculiar sensation afflicting her. It had started not when Chillingworth first took her into his arms but later, as they'd commenced their second revolution around the room.

She'd enjoyed the waltz. Despite his predilections, Chillingworth was charming, witty, and a gentleman to his toes. He was very like Lucifer and his

Cynster cousins; she'd treated him as she would them—he'd responded in like vein, with a bantering air. She'd relaxed.

That was when the other sensation had made itself felt, like an intent gaze fixed directly between her shoulder blades. Its very intensity was what finally identified its source.

When Chillingworth gallantly returned her to the spot beside Wellington's bust, she was smiling and quietly simmering.

One look at Gabriel's face, into his hard hazel eyes, and her temper surged. She'd successfully reached through his armor to prick him about the twins; he was paying her back by watching her instead, simply to discompose her. Sliding into the space beside him, she muttered, "Don't you have anything better to do?"

He looked at her blankly. "No."

It was impossible to shift him, so there he stayed; by the end of the evening, she was ready to commit murder. But in the carriage home, she had to bottle up her spleen and listen encouragingly to Mary and Alice prattle happily of their doings. To her considerable satisfaction, both had found their feet and were attracting the right sort of attention. As they left the carriage and climbed the steps to the front door, Alathea exchanged a speculative glance with Serena. Their campaign was progressing well.

She was doing less well. By the time she gained her room and Nellie had shut the door behind her, she felt like a human volcano.

"One of these days," she informed Nellie through clenched teeth, "he's going to come up to me when I have a dangerous weapon in my hands, and then I'll end in the Tower, and it'll all be his fault!"

"The Tower?" Nellie was totally confused.

"Imprisoned for *murdering* him!" Alathea let the reins of her temper fly free. "You should have seen him! You can't imagine!" She fell to pacing before the hearth. "He was more impossible than even I would have believed, even for him. Just because I told him—and convinced him, too—that he was wrong to so suffocate the twins, he left off suffocating them, and suffocated me, instead!"

"Suffocated ...?"

"Watched over me as if I was his sister! Tried to menace and chase away any entertaining gentleman." She swung about, her skirts shushing furiously. "At least he didn't succeed with Chillingworth, thank God! But all through supper—!" Words failed her; she threw a rapier-edged glance at the door. "I have never felt so much like a bone with a large dog, teeth-bared, standing over me. And you should have seen his performance over the second waltz! I'd already danced the first with Chillingworth, and saw no reason why I shouldn't indulge him with the second as well—he is nicely tall, which is such a blessing in a waltz—but Gabriel behaved like a ... a bloody archbishop! You'd have thought he'd never waltzed with a lady himself in his life!"

Arms folded, she paced on. "It wasn't as if he wanted to waltz with me himself—oh, no! He's never waltzed with me in his life! He just wanted to be difficult! And he's so hard to counter! I sincerely commiserate with the twins, and can only be glad if I've shaken him to his senses over them."

She scowled. "Except that he now seems focused on me." She pondered that, then shrugged. "Presumably he was only doing it for tonight, just to pay me back. Whatever, I've had quite enough of the arrogant ways of Mr. Gabriel Cynster."

"Who?"

Alathea plonked herself down on the stool before her dressing table. "Rupert. Gabriel's his nickname."

Nellie let down her hair and started brushing it. Alathea let the familiar, rhythmic tug-and-release soothe her. Her mind reverted to the problem that had earlier consumed her, the problem she'd largely forgotten in the heat engendered by Gabriel's behavior in the ballroom.

When she'd been Alathea Morwellan.

That had been bad enough. His behavior when she was the countess seemed even further beyond her control.

"This has gone on long enough—I need to take charge."

"You do?"

"Hmm. All very well for him to take the reins, but that's clearly too dangerous. It's *my* problem—he's *my* knight—*I* summoned him. He's going to have to learn to do my bidding, not the other way about. I'm going to have to make that point plain."

She—the countess—was going to have to see him again.

Alathea frowned. "I need to tell him about the captain."

What happened at the Burlington would *not* happen again. That had simply been an opportunistic event, a combination of location, opportunity, and elation—and her weakness—that he'd sensed, seen, and seized.

She'd let him seize. She wouldn't, she swore, be so weak this time. Be so easily swept off her feet and onto a bed.

No. But it was senseless to take any chances.

"I can't risk another meeting in daylight."

"Why not? He can't see your face even then, not if you wear that mask under your veil."

"True. But he'll look more closely, and there'll be enough of my face showing ..."

He might guess. He'd seen her at close quarters frequently enough in the past weeks. His powers of observation were acute when he concentrated, and after their last meeting at the Burlington, she was quite sure he'd be concentrating on the countess. Especially if she proved intent on keeping him at a polite distance.

Yet distance, polite or otherwise, was imperative.

"I've got to meet with him again." Frowning, she drummed her fingers on the dressing table. If she could devise a meeting where opportunity was lacking, so he got no chance to seize anything at all, she'd be safe.

* * *

"A letter for you, m'lord—er, sir." With a flourish, Chance placed the silver salver he'd taken to wielding at every opportunity on the breakfast table at Gabriel's right.

"Thank you, Chance." Setting aside his coffee mug, Gabriel picked up the folded sheet of heavy white parchment and looked for the letter knife.

"Oh—ah!" Chance jigged and searched his pockets. "Here." He brandished a small rusty knife. "I'll do it."

"No, Chance, that's quite all right." Gabriel held on to the note. "I can manage."

"Right-ho." Swiping up the salver, Chance departed.

Gabriel broke the seal with his thumbnail. Lips thinning, he opened the note.

He'd been expecting it for the last four days. He was more than a trifle aggrieved that the countess had taken so long to summon him to another meeting. The delay lay like a blot on his record, an adverse reflection on his skill. At least the note had finally come.

He scanned the few lines within, then rolled his eyes to the ceiling. A *carriage*?

He sighed. Well, she had been a virgin, so what could he expect? She was plainly a novice at arranging lovers' trysts.

CHAPTER
Eleven

It was a moonless night. The wind soughed and sighed in the trees lining the carriage drive close by the Stanhope Gate. Waiting impatiently in the shadows, Gabriel resisted the urge to shake his head.

Midnight at the Stanhope Gate was only a marginal improvement on three o'clock in the porch of St. Georges. The countess had been reading too many gothic novels. In this case, she'd either forgotten that the park gates were locked at sunset, or was counting on him exercising his peculiar talents on the padlock that had secured the wrought iron gates. He'd done so and left the gates wide. It wasn't unheard of for an open gate to be forgotten.

At least there wasn't any mist, only layers of shadows spreading over the parkland, shifting and drifting with the wind. There was just enough light to see by, to make out shapes but not their detail.

In the distance, a bell tolled, the first note in the midnight chorus. He listened as the other belltowers joined in, then the count was done, and the last note died into the brooding night. Silence returned, and settled.

The rattle of a carriage wheel was his first intimation that his wait was at an end. There were carriages aplenty rolling around Mayfair, but they were far enough away to ignore. The steady rattle continued, punctuated by the clop of hooves, then the small black carriage, lamps unlit, rolled between the gate posts into the gloom of the park.

Gabriel stepped onto the verge. The coachman redirected his horses; the carriage slowed and halted. Gabriel opened the door and climbed into a darkness even denser than had prevailed in the bedchamber at the Burlington.

He sat and felt leather beneath him, and sensed a warm presence beside him.

"Mr. Cynster."

Gabriel grinned into the dark. "Countess."

She gasped as she landed in his lap. It took only an instant for his fingers to find her veil, and then his lips were on hers.

It was a searing kiss—he made sure of that. A kiss to steal her wits, to make her senses reel. A kiss to light her fires, and his.

Her lips softened the instant his firmed; they parted the second he traced their contours. She melted in his arms as he grew more rigid; he didn't lift his head until she was dazed and dizzy, too breathless to utter the words her whirling mind couldn't begin to form.

He hesitated only a moment, their heated breaths mingling in the dark, the rhythm of their breathing already fragmented. He sensed her yearning, sensed the swollen, parted, hungry lips less than an inch from his.

Closing the distance, he sealed her fate. And his.

This time, however, he was determined to remain in control, to orchestrate their play until the very end. He'd plotted and planned and fantasized. After he'd had his wicked way with her and treated her to the full spectrum of sensations an experienced lover could evoke, he would wager his hard-won reputation that she wouldn't wait days to return to him.

His lips on hers, he quickly dispensed with her cloak and set her veil fully back. Drawing back from their kiss, he let his fingertips linger over the delicate skin of her forehead, the arch of her brows, the sweep of her cheeks. Her jaw was firm and finely wrought, her throat long, slender ... elegant.

At the base of her throat, her pulse beat hotly. The scooped neckline of her gown revealed the upper swells of her full breasts. His fingers traced; his memories strengthened. Need burgeoned.

Her breath shivered on his lips; she quivered in his arms.

"Your coachman. What instructions did you give?"

She drew in a shaky breath; he sensed her struggle to think. "I told him to drive slowly around the avenue ... until we'd finished our meeting."

"Perfect." Reaching up, he rapped on the carriage roof. A second later, the carriage lurched, then ponderously rolled forward.

She straightened. "I—"

Her breath caught on a hitch as, lowering his arm, he closed his hand possessively about one breast. He kneaded and she shuddered. Nudging her head up, he took her lips again, and set himself to cast her wits to the wind.

It wasn't difficult; she put up no resistance to speak of. She seemed a natural in this sphere, a deeply sensual woman, her consciousness surrendering willingly to the moment, to the physical thrill, the sexual excitement, the indescribable delight of give and take.

At first, it was he who took and she who gave, then he mentally drew back, inwardly reasserted control, then deliberately embarked on his script, his carefully plotted plan to bind her to him with sensual chains.

His lips on hers, he reached for her laces.

Divesting her of her gown was no great feat, not to one of his extensive experience. But he accomplished the deed slowly, savoring every inch of her curves as he exposed them, much to her shivering delight.

Not that she was cold. Thick curtains sealed the carriage windows. With their heated bodies enclosed within the small space, she would be in no danger of taking a chill despite the totality of his plans. That was just as well as, with her warm weight across his thighs, her luscious curves filling his arms and her hungry lips under his, he was in no state to rework them. Tonight, fate was on his side.

Lifting her, he eased the soft gown past her hips, then set her down, the bare backs of her thighs, exposed beneath her short chemise, in direct contact with his trousers. Through their kiss, he sensed the heightening of her tension. He set out to heighten it some more.

Deepening the kiss, he held her steady, one arm about her. Closing his hand on her bare thigh, he brushed her gown down by caressing her long limbs, first down one leg, then the other. Swiping up the gown, he tossed it on the seat beside him, and caught her foot. He slipped her shoe off, surprised to note its weight. As he dispensed with the other, he realized the heels were high. Skimming his hand up one leg, he located her garter, a few inches above her knee.

He toyed with the band. On? Or off? He reviewed his plan. Her lips shifted under his; she struggled to draw breath, to surface from the fog of desire in which he was deliberately shrouding her. He stilled her with a searching, ravishing kiss, and quickly rolled her stockings down and off, sending them to join her gown.

Leaving her clad only in her silk chemise.

He drew her to him, deeper into his embrace; tipping her head back, he plundered her mouth. She responded ardently, caught up in the hot tangle of their tongues, the melding of their lips.

His quick fingers slipped the tiny buttons closing her chemise free, all the way to her navel. The instant the last slipped its mooring, he closed his fist in the fine garment; pulling back from the kiss, he drew the chemise up and over her head in one movement.

"Oh!" She grasped, not the chemise, but her veil.

His steadying hand now on bare skin, he grinned into the dark. Discarding the chemise, he reached for her face, touching gently, then framing her jaw. "Your veil's still there." That was part of his plan, having her totally naked except for that damned veil.

Her hands fluttered; the fingers of one touched the back of his hand as he drew her face nearer. He touched her lips with his tongue and they parted; he surged in, then retreated, settling to nibble, tantalize, tease … until she shifted on his thighs, trying to press her own demands, unsure what those demands should be.

He knew. Urging her hands, her arms, over his shoulders, he drew her around. Clasping one bare calf, savoring the smooth skin, he drew the limb up, lifting that leg over his thighs as he turned her, then released her, leaving her, blissfully naked but for her veil, sitting astride his long thighs.

Oh, yes. Before she had time to even try to think, he reached for her face with both hands, holding her steady for an incendiary kiss, one that left them both gasping, chests heaving, bodies heated and urgent. Hers had softened; his had hardened. Their panting breaths mingled. He slid his fingers under the back of her veil, finding the pins that anchored her hair. As they rained on the floor, their lips met again. Heat welled, swelled, grew.

Her hair cascaded down her back, long strands curling on her shoulders. He kissed her long and hard, then drew back.

She tried to lean closer, to follow his lips with hers, but he closed his hands about her shoulders. "No." Even though he couldn't see, could only feel with his senses at full stretch, he knew she was dazed, wanting but not yet frantic, her wits disengaged but her senses still aware. "Not yet."

They'd only just begun.

"Sit still, and concentrate on what you feel."

She shuddered lightly, but did as he asked. He hadn't expected an argument—she was far beyond that—yet he went slowly; he had no intention of overwhelming her—not yet.

Curving his hands about her shoulders, he trailed his fingers lightly down, over the long sweeps of her arms, over her elbows and forearms, down to her wrists, then slid his fingertips along her palms, drawing them out across her fingers. Fingertip to fingertip, he held her arms out from her sides, then let them fall.

She was mesmerized; he knew that as he reached out again, and touched her breasts. They were already swollen, the peaks hard, begging for his attention. For long, heated moments he touched only with the pads of his fingers, listening as her breathing grew increasingly ragged. Then, leaning forward, he cupped one warm mound in his hand and took the peak into his mouth.

A cry died in her throat; her body arched convulsively. He suckled, one hand closing on her knee, the other lifting her flesh to his lips. When that nipple was aching and throbbing, he changed hands and tortured the other.

Her head fell back, her hair a gossamer curtain, its end brushing her hips, her bare bottom and his knees. Her spine bowed, every nerve drew taut; like the master he was, he let them tighten, and tighten, until she couldn't breathe, until she quivered, as fragile as spun glass, then he released her breast and leaned back.

He sensed the huge, shaky breath she drew in. Leaving his hand on her knee, more to reassure than to hold her, he gave her only a moment of surcease, then lifted his hand again.

To her ribs, tracing the fine skin over the smooth bones, then trailing his fingertips down to her waist. Releasing her knee, he closed both hands about her waist, circling her almost completely. Splaying his fingers over the supple muscles in her back, he touched, stroked, caressed.

She eased a little; his lips curving in a smile she couldn't see, he let his hands slide to caress her derriere, then sent them smoothly gliding over her flanks. And away.

For one instant, he left her there, posed on his knees in her naked glory. Then he reached out and touched her again.

He splayed his hand over her taut stomach. She shuddered, but her spine was so rigid she only swayed slightly, then tensed even more as he gently kneaded. She caught her breath on a sob. "I—"

"Don't talk." He waited a heartbeat, then added, "Just feel."

He waited until her senses refocused, then removed his hand. Clasping her knees, he slid his hands up, fingers gliding over the long, taut muscles of her outer thighs, his thumbs grazing the quivering inner faces. At the tops of her thighs, he ran his thumbs over and up, following the creases between thigh and torso outward. Then he removed his hands again.

Again he waited, leaving her quivering expectantly in the dark. Then, with one hand, he reached out again.

And touched her between her widespread thighs.

Her breath shook; she quaked.

"Shh."

He traced the swollen folds, exposed and open to him. He suspected she hadn't realized, modestly shrouded by the dark.

She realized now; she reached out—he felt her fingers brush his sleeve.

"No. Leave your hands at your sides."

She didn't immediately obey, but as he continued to caress her, the slow, steady stroking reassured her, and she let her arms fall.

Her breathing was shallow, racing with her heart. He didn't want to speak again, to risk breaking the spell. She was hot and wet, his fingers slick with her dew. He found the tight nubbin concealed between her folds and circled it, but that wasn't his target. He waited until she'd steadied, until she'd stabilized on a narrow ledge one step away from the peak, then zeroed in.

The long slide of his finger entering her, spearing in, inexorably penetrating and filling her softness, sent her into spasm. Every muscle locked, so tight she was shivering, every fragment of awareness focused, waiting for the final touch that would shatter her.

He didn't administer it; the time was not yet. His finger buried in her sheath he held still, blocking all awareness of the heated softness that gripped him, the supple strength of her inner muscles, the hot honey that dampened his hand, the evocative scent that wreathed his brain.

Then she stabilized again, and the peak had moved away, one step further on. He knew, but doubted she did. He started to caress her again.

How long he prolonged the delicious torture, how many times he brought her almost to the peak, then let it shift away, he didn't know, but she was wild, sobbing in her need, her fingers clenched on his arms, her lips burning his, when he finally thrust deep and let her fly.

She came apart in his arms.

Cursing the darkness that stopped him from seeing it, from reaping the reward of his expertise, he gathered her to him, letting her cling, then cradling her as she collapsed completely.

He drew her closer, sensing her heartbeat, feeling it thunder, then slow. Then she stirred.

"I want you."

His lips curved against her hair. "I know."

Her breath was a soft huff against his neck as she shifted, and reached, and found him. "How?"

Her fist closed, and he shook. "Ah ..."

Fingers as quick as his slipped the buttons on his waistband, brushed aside his shirt. Slim digits dipped, then stroked, caressed ...

Words were superfluous. He drew her hips nearer, sliding his own to the edge of the seat. They met—it was she who sank down, a long-drawn sigh shattering in her throat. It was all he could do to stifle his groan as she closed hotly about him. After that, he lost touch with the world as she became his reality, the hot, wet, generous woman who loved him in the dark.

She was everything he craved, mysterious, giving, intensely feminine; in some sensual way, she held a mirror to his soul. She filled his senses until he recalled no other, until he knew nothing beyond her luscious heat and the primal need that gripped him.

He sank into her and she wrapped herself about him; at his urging, she shifted her legs, awkward for a moment as she repositioned them, locking them around his hips. When she sank fully onto him again, she gasped. Gripping her hips, he lifted her, thrusting upward as he lowered her.

She sobbed, then found his lips. They clung, and loved, gave and took and gave again. The horses plodded slowly on.

The gloom inside the carriage became a heated cave, filled with lust, desire, and so much more. Hunger, greed, joy, and delirium all spun, a kaleidoscope in the dark. Then she flew high and he followed, soaring beyond the stars. The end left them shattered, broken and destroyed, reborn in each other's arms.

The gentle swaying of the carriage slowly drew them back to earth, yet they lay still, letting the long, achingly sweet moments wash over them, neither ready to lose the soul-deep communion.

His lips at her temple, her hair silk against his cheek, Gabriel dragged in a breath. His chest swelled, shifting her warm weight. He locked his arms around her; he didn't want to let go. Didn't want to lose the peace she'd brought him—she and she alone.

Never had he reached this state, this depth of feeling. Beyond sensation, beyond the world, a sea of unnameable emotion still lapped him. He wanted to deny it, shrug it aside. It frightened him. But it was a drug—he feared he was already addicted.

She stirred, first again. Sitting up, she sighed and shook back her hair. "I meant to tell you ..."

He got the distinct impression she'd intended to say, "before you started this," and, what's more, in a censorious tone. He was too sated to do more than smirk in the dark. He was still buried to the hilt inside her. "What?" Reaching for her, he drew her back into his arms.

She acquiesced, then relaxed; despite her resolution, she was still dazed. "My stepson ... he overheard a conversation at White's—between a Captain Something and another man. The captain was dismissing the Central East Africa Gold Company."

He frowned. "I thought your stepson was too young for White's."

"Oh, he is. This was on the steps—he was walking in St. James Street."

"Who was the captain talking to?"

"Charles didn't know."

"Hmm." It was difficult to think with her warm weight snuggled against him, with her body intimately clasping his. That last, and his resurging vigor, prompted him to say, "A captain recently returned from Africa shouldn't be impossible to trace. The shipping lists, the Port Authority, the major merchant lines. He'll be known somewhere."

"If we have a witness like that, we'd be able to petition the court immediately."

But then there'd be no reason for them to meet, and he'd yet to learn her name. He frowned, grateful for the dark. "Perhaps. It depends on how much he knows." Turning his head, he squinted down at her, but still could see nothing. "I'll look into it."

"Have you heard anything else?"

"I have contacts in Whitehall sounding out the African authorities over the company's mining claims, and there are others I'm hunting up who might know of the company's presence in those particular towns." Shuffling higher on the seat, he glanced upward. "Now—tell your coachman to roll back, slowly, to Brook Street."

She sat up, still clutching his coat, and cleared her throat. "Jones?"

The carriage slowed, then halted. "Ma'am?"

"Brook Street, please—you know where."

"Aye, ma'am."

Taking advantage of her uptilted head, Gabriel pressed his lips to her throat. She fought to stifle a giggle, then sighed.

Then her breath caught. A moment later, she asked, slightly dazed, "Again?"

"I'm hungry."

So was she. They devoured each other at speed, reckless and driven, reaching the bright pinnacle before the carriage even left the park.

It wasn't, unfortunately, all that far to Brook Street. Wrapping her in her cloak, Gabriel shifted her to the seat beside him. He righted his clothes, then leaned over her to press a long kiss to her swollen lips.

The carriage halted; he drew back. From over his shoulder a street flare shone in, laying a narrow swath of light across her face. She was exhausted, her eyes shut—he could just see the edge of a crescent of dark lashes lying on one pale cheek. The strip of light illuminated only that cheek, her earlobe framed by a strand of soft brown hair, the edge of her jaw and the corner of her lips.

Not enough to identify her.

Gabriel hesitated, then he shifted and his shoulder cut off the light. "Sweet dreams, my dear."

Her murmured "Good-bye" was soft and low, a lover's farewell.

Descending to the street, Gabriel watched her carriage roll away; it was all he could do not to call it back. Turning, he climbed his steps, frowning as he reached for his latchkey.

He'd seen her face before. The line of her jaw was familiar.

She was one of his circle.

Who?

Letting himself in, he went up to bed.

Sniff.

Alathea battled to lift her heavy lids, and lost.

Sniff.

Stifling a sigh, she tried again and managed to see through a slit. "Nellie?"

Sniff. "Yes, m'lady," came in dolorous tones. *Sniff.*

Alathea struggled onto her back and raised her head. And saw Nellie, red-nosed with watering red eyes, shaking out her cloak. Alathea dragged in a breath. "Nellie Macarthur! You go straight back to bed. I do not want to see you, or hear of you being about on your feet, not until you're better." Fixing her old maid with a pointed glare, Alathea summoned strength enough to deliver the words "Do you hear?" in appropriately intimidating tones.

Nellie sniffed again. "But who'll see to you? You've got to go to all these balls and parties, and your stepmama rightly says—"

"The tweeny will do for me for the nonce—I'm not entirely helpless."

"But—"

"Doing my hair in a simpler style for a few nights will be a relief. No one will think anything of it." Alathea glared again. "Now go! And don't you dare sneak about downstairs—I'll be speaking with Figgs immediately I get up."

"All right," Nellie grumbled, but Alathea could see from her lethargic movements that she was seriously under the weather.

"I'll tell Figgs to make you some of her broth." Alathea watched Nellie open the door. "Oh—and don't bother to send up the tweeny. I'll ring for her when I'm ready." With barely a nod, Nellie shuffled out. The instant the door closed, Alathea dropped back on her pillows, closed her eyes, and *groaned.* Feelingly. Her thighs would never be the same again.

CHAPTER

Twelve

"Allie?"

Blinking, Alathea refocused. Concern in her eyes, Alice peered at her across the breakfast table.

"Are you coming out into the garden with us?" Mary, beside Alice, looked equally worried.

Alathea summoned a quick smile. "Just wool-gathering. I'll get my hat—you go on ahead."

She rose with them and parted from them in the hall to go up to her room to fetch her gardening hat. Nevertheless, it was half an hour later before she reached the garden.

Mary and Alice hadn't waited for her but had started weeding the long border. Although they looked up when she neared and smiled welcomingly, it was plain they'd been exchanging confidences, whispered comments on their hopes, their dreams. Returning their smiles, Alathea surveyed their endeavors, then looked around. "I'll start on the central bed."

Leaving them to their dreams, she went off to contend with hers.

The central bed circled a small fountain, a water sprite caught in the act of springing free showering droplets back into a wide bowl. Spreading her raffia mat by the bed, presently filled with pansies, Alathea knelt, tugged on her cotton gloves, and set to.

About her, her family went happily about their morning routines. Jeremy and Charlie appeared from around the house, dragging dead limbs cut from overgrown bushes. In half an hour, Jeremy's tutor would arrive, and Charlie would change into his town rig and go out to spend the day with his Eton chums. Miss Helm and Augusta, clutching the ever-present Rose, came out and sat on a wrought iron seat; from what Alathea could hear, they were engaged in a simple botany lesson. After an hour or so, she, Mary, and Alice would retire to wash, change, and prepare for their morning's excursion—whatever Serena had organized. Inside, Serena would be sifting through the invitations, sending notes, plotting their best course through the shoals of the Season. Alathea was content to leave the strategies to her; it was bad enough that she had to weed.

The fiction they'd concocted to hide the fact that they could not afford a second gardener, one to take care of the beds and borders at the Park and the garden of the London house, was that Alathea enjoyed planting and weeding and Serena felt it right that her daughters, too, became knowledgeable in the art of creating a stunning border. And, of course, all gentlemen should have some understanding of landscaping. Luckily, landscaping, borders, and beds were all the rage, although ladies and gentlemen generally only oversaw such projects, a fine distinction the earl, Serena, and Alathea had omitted to mention.

As she reached for a blade of grass cheekily poking up between clumps of pansies, Alathea inwardly sighed. She would much rather never see a weed again, but ... With a yank, she uprooted the interloper and dropped it on the grass beside her. Parting the pansy leaves, she searched for more.

Of course, as soon as her hands were mindlessly busy, her thoughts drifted ...

She could never meet with him privately again. Not ever. The countess was going to have to retreat; she couldn't yet disappear. Despite the fact she'd enjoyed last night hugely, she couldn't possibly risk such a *meeting* again.

In a carriage. She still couldn't quite believe it. If she hadn't been there ...Was there *anywhere* he couldn't ... wouldn't ...

Minutes later, she shook her head. Struggling to hide a smile, she looked down.

Thankfully, no one knew. She'd gathered enough strength to instruct Jacobs to drive around Grosvenor Square while she'd scrambled into her chemise, stockings, shoes, and gown. Her hair she'd had to leave down. Goodness knows what Jacobs had made of the pins he would by now have discovered on the carriage floor. Concealed beneath her veil and cloak, she'd been safe from Crisp's eyes. Other than Jacobs, who'd been busy with his team, only Crisp had been awake when she'd returned. She'd given strict instructions that not even Nellie was to wait up for her on pain of her considerable displeasure. She'd done the same the night she'd gone to the Burlington; she could only thank her stars she had.

So no one knew of her fall from grace. Her lips kicked upward. It had, to her, felt more like an elevation. A revelation certainly, an induction into a realm of earthly bliss. She was not of a mind to wallow in senseless regrets—she'd lived, all but died, and exulted last night, and for that she could only be glad.

Even now, she wasn't free of the lingering spell. She hadn't imagined that the activities theoretically restricted to the marriage bed could result in such an interaction—a voyage into another dimension of feeling where the world fell away and emotion reigned. She'd had her first inkling of that joyous state during their night at the Burlington. Last night, they'd journeyed much further, through landscapes of unutterable delight.

And it had been they, not just she. He'd been there, with her—had it been her inexperience, or had he been as stunned by the glory as she? Whatever, they'd shared it all—the journey, the discovery, the overwhelming satiation, followed by their plunge into that well of deep peace.

It had been the most glorious night of her life.

Her lips quirked. She had to wonder what he'd thought he'd been about, holding her naked on his knees. She assumed it had been part of some plan—he was always planning. She strongly suspected he'd intended her to feel in his power. She had to smile. He couldn't know that she'd sat there, naked before him, and gloried in the power she'd wielded over him.

For power there'd been—those dark, illicit moments had been charged with it—but for every tithe of power he'd held over her, she'd held the same measure over him.

She'd startled him with her statement that she wanted him. Other ladies would not have been so bold. But he hadn't been at all reluctant—oh, no. If she hadn't taken him, he'd have taken her.

Warm memories washed over her, through her—kneeling in the sunlight, she drifted away.

A conspiratorial giggle from Alice drew her back; she blinked—and saw the pansy plant she was holding, roots dangling, in one hand.

With a muttered curse, Alathea plunged it back into the hole from which she'd pulled it and quickly tamped it down. Then she checked her pile of "weeds." Two more pansies were rapidly returned to the soil. She could only hope that if they died, they wouldn't leave a hole in her border.

Inwardly sighing, she sat back on her heels, ignoring the twinges in her thighs. She had to stop thinking of last night. She had to determine how on earth she was going to proceed *after* last night. It seemed she would be safe only on a crowded street in broad daylight, and she'd have to wear a mask under her veil as well.

It would be easy for her to communicate with him by letter, but she couldn't see any way he could reply. And she knew him too well to beard the tiger; if she cut off all contact entirely, he'd come after her. Not trying to discover her identity, but trying to discover her. He'd be very intent, very focused; in such a state, he'd be unstoppable.

And where would that leave her?

She didn't like to think.

No. Folwell would keep her informed of Gabriel's movements. She would send him notes if necessary until they discovered something more, then she'd meet him in Grosvenor Square.

That brought her to the question of what more she could do to further their investigations. A vague recollection of Lady Hester Stanhope's diaries had her turning to scan the long border.

Rising, she dusted her gloves, then stripped them from her hands. Strolling to the long border, she made a show of evaluating the progress made, then nodded. "We've done enough for today." She met Mary's and Alice's bright eyes. "I want to visit Hookhams again. Would you like to come?"

"Oh, yes!"

"Now?"

Alathea turned to the house. "Just a quick visit—I'm sure your mama won't mind."

She found what she was after in the biography of an explorer—a bona fide map of Central East Africa showing more than the major towns. The map told her Fangak, Lodwar and Kingi—Kafia Kingi, to be precise—were indeed towns, albeit small ones.

Leaning back in the chair behind the desk in her office, Alathea pondered her discovery. Was it good? Or discouraging?

About her, the house was peaceful and still. The lamp on her desk shed light onto the open book. In the grate, embers gleamed, warming the night. She'd stolen every moment she could throughout the day to wade through the stack of biographies and diaries she'd borrowed from Hookhams. At last, she'd uncovered something—something real.

The information was good, she decided—at least it gave them something to check. Surely they'd be able to find someone other than the mysterious captain who knew the area, now she knew where the area was.

On the stairs, the long-case clock chimed the hour. Three o'clock, the beginning of a new day. Stifling a yawn, Alathea closed the book and rose. It was definitely time for bed.

The next day, she spent the afternoon within the hallowed halls of the Royal Society.

"Unfortunately," the secretary informed her, peering at her through a thick pair of *pince-nez*, "there are no lectures presently scheduled on Central East Africa."

"Oh. Can the society recommend any expert on the area with whom I could consult?"

The man pursed his lips, stared at her, then nodded. "If you'll take a seat, I'll check the records."

Retreating to a wooden bench along the wall, Alathea waited for fifteen minutes, only to have the man return, shaking his head and looking rather peeved.

"We do not," he informed her, "have any expert on East Africa listed. Three who could speak with authority on West Africa, but not the East."

Alathea thanked him and left. Pausing on the steps, she considered, then headed for her carriage. "Where can we find the city's map makers, Jacobs?"

Along the Strand, was the answer. She inquired at three separate establishments, and got the same answer at all three. For their maps on Central East Africa, they relied on explorers' notes. Yes, their present maps of the area were extremely short on detail, but they were awaiting confirmation.

"It wouldn't do, miss," one rigidly correct gentleman lectured her, "for us to publish a map on which we showed towns we weren't absolutely positive were there."

"Yes, I see." Alathea turned to leave, then turned back. "The explorers whose notes you're waiting to confirm—are they in London?"

"Regretfully no, miss. They are all, at present, in Africa. Exploring."

There was nothing to be done but smile, and leave. Defeated.

Alathea returned to Mount Street feeling unaccustomedly weary.

"Thank you, Crisp." She handed the butler her bonnet. "I think I'll just sit in the library for a while."

"Indeed, miss. Do you wish for tea?"

"Please."

The tea arrived but did little to alleviate the feeling of helplessness that dragged at her. Every time she thought she was on the brink of substantiating some solid fact, the proof evaporated. Her hopes would soar, only to be dashed. Meanwhile, the days were passing. The day Crowley would call in his promissory notes was inexorably approaching.

Doom leered at her through Crowley's eyes.

Alathea sighed. Setting aside her empty cup, she flopped back in the armchair and closed her eyes. Perhaps, if she rested just for a few minutes ...

"Are you asleep?"

Realizing she had been, Alathea blinked her eyes wide, then smiled—a spontaneous smile of real joy—at Augusta's little face. "Hello, sweetling. Where have you been today?"

Taking the question for the invitation it was, Augusta climbed into Alathea's lap and settled herself so she could see Alathea's face. Wedging Rose between them, she proceeded to distract Alathea with a detailed account of her day. Alathea listened, putting a question here and there, making understanding or sympathetic comments as required.

"So, you see," Augusta concluded, hugging Rose to her chest and snuggling closer, pressing her head to Alathea's breast, "it's been a *frightfully* busy day."

Alathea chuckled; raising a hand, she smoothed Augusta's hair. Small arms, small body tucked close to her side, she felt a warm, emotional tug; Augusta was the daughter she wished she could have had. She banished the thought immediately; she was obviously overtired. Too much investigating.

Too many meetings.

Then Augusta wriggled and sat up. "Hmm-mmm." She sniffed at Alathea's throat. "You smell extra nice today."

Alathea's answering smile froze on her face as she realized the significance of Augusta's remark.

She was wearing the countess's scent.

Good God! She closed her eyes. What would have happened if she'd run into Gabriel? She'd been in the city and, earlier, not far from St. James, his habitual haunts.

Drawing in a breath, she opened her eyes. "Come along, poppet. I need to go upstairs and wash before dinner." Before anyone else noticed she was not quite the same woman she had been.

Two evenings later, Alathea was sitting with Jeremy in the schoolroom, Augusta in her lap, a detailed atlas from Hookhams open on the table, when the little tweeny appeared, breathless, at the door.

"If you please, Lady Alathea," she piped, "but it's time for you to get dressed, m'lady."

Noting the way the little maid was wringing her hands and at a loss to account for it, Alathea looked at the mantel clock.

Then she understood the agitation.

"Indeed." Lifting Augusta and settling her on the seat with a fond kiss, Alathea met Jeremy's eyes. "We'll continue this tomorrow."

Only too glad to escape the shackles of African geography, Jeremy grinned and turned to Augusta. "Come on, Gussie. We can play catch before dinner."

"I'm not *Gussie*." The tone of Augusta's objection boded ill for the peace of the evening.

"Jeremy …" From the door, Alathea fixed him with a matriarchal eye.

"Oh, very well. *Augusta* then. Anyway, do you want to play or not?"

Leaving them in reasonable harmony, Alathea hurried to her room. By the time she reached it, she was even more agitated than the tweeny. They were to dine with the Arbuthnots, then attend the ball their old friends were giving to formally introduce their granddaughter to the ton. It was a major function; all the senior hostesses would be there. Being late for such a dinner without some cataclysmic excuse would sink one beyond reproach.

But the tweeny, who had thus far only helped her get ready for balls without dinners preceeding them, had not realized the earlier hour involved. Not until she'd noticed Serena, Mary, and Alice were all busy dressing.

Oh, God! Alathea stilled the panic that gripped her as her gaze swept her room and found no evidence of any chemise or stockings, let alone her gown, gloves, reticule … Nellie always had everything ready, but with the tweeny she had to specify every item.

For one instant, Alathea considered developing a horrendous headache, but that would leave old Lady Arbuthnot with an odd number about her table. Stifling a sigh, she waved the maid forward. "Quickly. Help me with these laces." At least her hot water was ready and waiting.

As she stripped off her gown and quickly washed, she issued a steady stream of orders for all the items she required to appear presentable. From the corner of her eye, she kept watch on the little maid, making sure each item was correct before asking for the next.

Getting dressed in a scramble was one of her worst nightmares—she hated being rushed, especially for such a major event where she could count on her appearance being scrutinzed by the sharpest eyes in the ton.

Blotting her face with the towel, Alathea shook her head. "No—not those. My dance slippers. The ones with no heel."

Hurrying to the bed, she stripped off her linen chemise, then slipped into the welcoming coolness of silk. At least with the present fashions, she didn't have to bother with petticoats. Throwing her gown of amber silk crepe over her head, she tugged it down, settled it, then whirled and let the tweeny tie the laces. The instant the last was secured, she rushed to her dressing table, plunked herself on the stool, and plunged her hands into her hair.

Pins flew. "Quickly—we'll have to braid it." There was no time for a more sophisticated style.

It was only as the maid reached the end of the long braid that Alathea realized she needed two plaits to make a coronet. "Oh." For one moment, she simply stared, then she waved the tweeny aside and grabbed the braid. "Here—if we do it like this, it should pass muster."

Under-rolling half the thick braid, she bunched it at her nape, then used the long end to circle and bind it. Pushing pins in right and left, up and down, she frantically secured what would pass for a braided chignon.

"There!" Moving her head, she confirmed the mass was anchored, then quickly eased the strands pulled back from her face so they formed a softer frame. One more quick check, then she nodded. "Now ..."

Opening a drawer in the table, she rummaged through her caps. Freeing a fine net heavily encrusted with gold beads, she grimaced. "This will have to do." Setting it over her hair so the lower edge curved about the braided bun, she pinned it in place.

Beyond her door, Mary's and Alice's voices rang, then their quick footsteps hurried for the stairs. Alathea quelled an impulse to look at the clock—she didn't have time. "Jewelry." Flinging open her jewelry box, she blinked. "Oh." Her hand hovered over the contents, all neatly arranged.

"I took the liberty of tidying, miss. Nellie said as how I had to dust and tidy every day."

After one stunned glance at the tweeny's hopeful face, Alathea looked back at the box. "Yes—well. That's all right."

Except that now she hadn't a clue where her pearl earrings were, let alone the matching pendant. Spearing her fingers into the piles, scattering and disarranging as she went, Alathea unearthed the earrings. Standing, she leaned closer to the mirror and quickly fitted them.

"Allie? Are you ready?"

"Open the door," Alathea instructed the maid. As soon as the door swung wide, she called, "I'm coming!" And fell to ransacking her jewelry box again.

In one corner, she noted the Venetian glass flacon that contained the countess's perfume. After her recent mistake, she'd decided to take no further chances—the flacon was one of an identical pair. The other bottle contained her customary perfume; she'd left that out on the table. Her searching fingers finally touched the gold chain she sought; drawing the gold and pearl pendant free, she held the chain around her neck. "Hurry."

The tweeny's fingers were sure; the clasp closed as Mary came rushing to the door.

"The carriage is pulling up! Mama says we have to go *now*!"

"I'm coming." Grabbing the flacon on her table, Alathea liberally sprinkled, then whirled—"Oh, no! Not that reticule—the small gold one!"

The tweeny dived for her armoire; shawls and reticules went flying. "This one?"

Grabbing her shawl from the bed, Alathea headed for the door. "Yes!"

Waving the reticule, the tweeny chased her down the corridor. Settling her shawl over her elbows, Alathea grabbed the reticule, checked it contained a handkerchief and pins, then lengthened her stride, took the stairs two at a time, raced through the tiled foyer, out the door Crisp held wide, pattered down the steps and dove into the carriage.

Folwell shut the door behind her, and the carriage lurched into motion.

The crowd in Lady Arbuthnot's ballroom was unbearably dense. Having arrived as late as he dared, Gabriel inwardly girded his loins, then stepped off the stairs and plunged in. Prevented from propping his shoulders against the wall—there was no spare wall left—he circulated through the crowd, keeping an eagle eye out for those who most wished to see him, intent on seeing them first, and avoiding them.

High on his list of people to be missed were ladies such as Agatha Herries. He didn't see her early enough; she placed herself directly in his path. With no alternative offering, he halted before her. She smiled archly up at him and laid a hand on his sleeve.

"Gabriel, darling."

He nodded. "Agatha."

His tone was the very essence of unencouraging. Despite that, Lady Herries's smile deepened. Calculation gleamed in her eyes. "I wonder if, perhaps, we might find a quiet spot."

"For what?"

She studied him, then let her lids veil her eyes and slowly stroked her hand down his arm. "Just a little proposition I'd like to put to you. A personal matter."

"You can tell me here. In this din, it's unlikely anyone will overhear."

The idea didn't suit, but she knew him too well to push.

"Very well." She glanced around, then looked up at him. "It seems you're destined to choose a wife soon. I wanted to make sure you were fully acquainted with all your options."

"Indeed?"

"My daughter, Clara—I dare say you might remember her. She's been well trained to be an *accommodating* wife, and while our estate and lineage might not measure up to that of the Cynsters, there would, of course, be compensations."

The purr in her voice, the lascivious gleam in her eyes, left no doubt as to what those "compensations" might be.

Gabriel looked at her coldly, then he let his mask slip, let his contempt and revulsion show. Lady Herries paled and stepped back—then had to apologize to the lady she'd backed into.

When she looked back at Gabriel, his expression was impassive once more. "You were misinformed. I am not presently searching for a wife." He inclined his head. "If you'll excuse me."

Stepping around Lady Herries, Gabriel continued on his way, searching, not for a wife, but for a widow. When he found her, after he'd wrung her neck and administered a few other physical torments, he'd turn his mind to marrying her.

First, he had to find her.

She ought to be here. Almost everyone of note was. She was of his circle—that he did not doubt—so where was she?

Behind his elegantly aloof facade, he felt decidedly grim. He'd been sure he'd get one of her countessly summonses the evening following their midnight drive. But he hadn't. He'd spent the whole evening with Chance popping in and out of the parlor like a Jack-in-the-box, wondering why he'd stayed in. Reining in his impatience—not easy after that midnight interlude and the tempest of emotions she'd unleashed—he'd waited at home the following night, with no greater success.

Now he was hungry—ravenous—not just for her, but even more to know she was his, to know where she was, to know he could put his hand on her whenever he wished. He was tense, wound tight with a need to possess far greater than any he'd previously experienced in all the years of his rakish career. He had to find out who she was, where she lived, where she was.

His copy of *Burke's Peerage* had started to exert a hypnotic tug. He'd caught himself considering the leather bound tome on a number of occasions. But he'd promised ... given his word ... the word of a Cynster.

He'd spent all last night, alone again, trying to devise some way around that promise. His Aunt Helena would know who the countess was—she always knew who was whose son, who had recently died, who married a young bride. Unfortunately, Helena would immediately inform his mother of his inquiry, and that he could do without. For hours he'd toyed with the notion of throwing himself on Honoria's mercy and asking for her aid. She'd give it, but it would come at a price; nothing was more certain. The present duchess of St. Ives was not one to pass up a never-to-be-repeated advantage. It was a measure of his desperation that he even contemplated asking her.

In the end, he'd concluded that his promise—the promise the countess had so artfully phrased—bound him too tightly and left him no room to manuever. Thrown back on his own devices, he had come here tonight for the sole purpose of tracking her down.

Her—his houri—the woman who had captured his soul.

Raising his head, he scanned the room. The one feature she could not conceal was her height. There were a number of tall ladies present, but he knew them all—not one was an elusive countess. Alathea, he noted, was presently on the dance floor, partnered by Chillingworth. He looked away. At least the dance was only a cotillion, not a waltz.

"There you are. At last!"

Lucifer struggled free of the crowd. Gabriel raised a questioning brow.

His brother stared at him. "Well, the twins, of course!"

Gabriel looked around, and spotted his fair cousins on the dance floor. "They're dancing."

"I know that," Lucifer stated through his teeth. "But it's more than time for you to take the watch."

Gabriel studied the twins for one second more, then looked back at Lucifer. "Not anymore. They don't need watching. Just as long as we're here if they need us."

Lucifer's jaw nearly dropped. "*What?* You can't be serious."

"Perfectly. They're halfway through their second Season. They know the ropes. They're not ninnyhammers."

"I know that—God knows, they're sharp as tacks. But they're female."

"I'd noticed. I've also noticed that they don't appreciate our endeavors." Gabriel paused, then added, "And they might have reasonable cause to accuse us of excessive interference in their lives."

"Alathea's spoken to you, hasn't she?"

"She's spoken to you, too."

"Well, yes ..." Lucifer turned and surveyed the twins. After a minute, he asked, "Do you really think it's safe?"

Gabriel considered the two bright heads spinning in the dance. "Safe or not, I think we must." After a moment, he glanced at Lucifer. "I don't know about you, but I have other fish to fry."

"Indeed?" One of Lucifer's black brows quirked. "And here I thought your exceedingly unmellow mood was due to enforced abstinence and an overfamiliarity with your own hearth."

"Don't start," Gabriel all but snarled. His exceedingly thin facade threatened to crack.

Lucifer sobered. "Who is she?"

With a definite snarl, Gabriel swung away, moving into the crowd, leaving Lucifer with his brows riding high and real concern in his eyes.

Whoever she was, she had to be here somewhere. Clinging to that conviction, Gabriel started to quarter the room.

Alathea was taking the long way back from the withdrawing room whence she'd retreated to escape her increasingly persistent cavaliers, when she came upon Gabriel in the crowd. As making any headway through the throng required constant tacking, despite being so tall, neither had any warning of the other's approach.

Suddenly, they were face to face—and very close.

They both jumped, tensed, Gabriel with his habitual reaction to her, instantly masked. Alathea saw it and prayed that he thought her reaction merely simple surprise, not the ground-shaking shock it had been. Her breathing had seized; her eyes had flown wide. She kept them locked on his. They were so close, she could sense his strength through every pore, could almost feel the shocking heat of that large body against hers. Wrapped intimately about hers, sunk deep into hers. She swayed slightly toward him, then caught herself. *Heaven help her!* Would it always be like this from now on?

His eyes narrowed. Dragging in a desperate breath, she stiffened her spine and lifted her head. His gaze rose to her beaded hairnet; she tilted her chin even higher and clung to her customary haughtiness.

"It might be gold, but ..."

Temper came to her rescue. "It is *not* tawdry. If you *dare* say it is ..." She held his gaze for an instant longer—long enough to realize that she had to get away. "I have nothing to say to you—I doubt you have anything civil to say to me. I have better things to do than stand here crossing swords with you."

"Indeed?"

That was accompanied by an infuriating lift of one brow.

"Indeed—and I don't wish to hear your opinion of anyone else, either."

"Because it might be true?"

"Regardless of their accuracy, to me, your opinions are neither here nor there." With that, she tried to step around him but the crowd was so tight-packed she couldn't get past unless he gave way.

He didn't immediately. His gaze skimmed her face, searching—she prayed not seeing. Then he inclined his head and shifted. "You will, as always, go to the devil in your own way."

She bestowed a look of regal indifference upon him, then pushed past. Her breast brushed his arm, one thigh touched his. The tremor that rocked her nearly buckled her knees. Lungs locked, she held her spine rigid and forged on and away. She didn't dare look back.

Inwardly shaking his head, Gabriel waited for the muscles that had seized at her touch to relax. They'd touched little over the years but her effect on him hadn't waned. As his chest eased, he dragged in a huge breath—

She was close.

Instantly, he scanned the surrounding crowd. Not one woman in sight was tall enough, but he couldn't mistake that perfume. It was the essence of her, the scent that wreathed his dreams. He breathed in again. The perfume was still strong, but dispersing. She'd been very ... close ...

His muscles locked like stone. Slowly, he turned, and stared at the slender back of the exceptionally tall woman who had, just a moment before, stood very close to him.

It couldn't be.

For one finite moment, his mind flatly rejected what his senses were screaming.

Then reality fractured.

Alathea felt Gabriel's gaze on her back, like a knife between her shoulder blades. Her lungs seized; panic clutching her stomach she shot a glance behind.

He was tacking through the crowd in her wake. His eyes met hers, their expression primitive. For an instant, the sight paralyzed her. Then she whirled and tried to go faster, to slip through the crowd and escape.

The crowd only got denser. Lady Hendricks called and waved—Alathea had to stop, smile, touch fingers. Then she was on her way again, breathlessly dodging, weaving, desperately seeking an easier path through the crush—

Hard fingers locked around her elbow.

She froze. In the instant her panicked wits reengaged, he bent his head and murmured, "Don't bother."

His lips brushed her ear. Suppressing a shiver, she stiffened. He stood at her right shoulder, her elbow in a viselike grip; even without his warning, she knew that grip would be unbreakable. And he was furious. Past furious. The anger pouring from him scorched her. What had given her away?

"This way."

He'd been looking over the sea of heads; now he steered her toward one side of the room. She forced her feet to move. She could not cause a scene, not here. In his present mood he was capable of anything, even picking her up, tossing her over his shoulder, and stalking off with her. His temper once aroused was a force to contend with; challenging it now would be foolhardy. As they moved toward one wall, she struggled to marshal her wits, her arguments, her denials, bracing herself for what was to come.

She didn't see the door until they stood before it; he opened it and marched her into an unlit and thankfully uninhabited gallery. He didn't stop until they were at the end where a long window, curtains wide, poured moonlight into the narrow room.

Placing her directly in the silver beam, he swung to face her.

His gaze raked her face, devoured her features as if he'd never seen them before. His face was chiseled, harder than stone, every edge sharp. Lips compressed, his jaw set, his heavy lids too low for her to see his eyes, he studied her. His gaze lingered on her jaw, then he lifted his lids and looked into her eyes. For a long moment, he held her gaze, hazel to hazel. Tense beyond bearing, her nerves stretched tight, she wondered what he could see.

"It was you."

Although laced with wonder, his tone brooked no argument. She raised her brows. "What on earth are you on about?"

His brows rose but his expression didn't waver. "Denial? Surely you can do better than that?"

"I dare say if I knew what misbegotten notion you've taken into your fevered brain I could more specifically address it, but as I don't, denial seems the safest option." She looked away, too afraid that if she continued to meet his eyes she would see his knowledge of her—his physical knowledge of her—blazoned in the hazel. Then she'd remember, too, and vulnerability would sweep her—and he'd pounce.

The touch of long fingers curving about her face nearly brought her to her knees. His grip firmed; deliberately, he turned her head until her eyes met his again.

"Oh, you *know*—there's no point denying it." His words were clipped; fury raged beneath them. He hesitated, then added, "Your perfume gave you away."

Her perfume?

The tweeny. Tidying. Emptying her jewelry box onto the table. Then putting everything back in. Two identical flacons, one in, one out.

Her expression had blanked; her lips started to form an "Oh." Alathea caught herself and glared. "What about my perfume?"

He smiled, not with amusement. "Too late."

"Nonsense!" She lifted her chin from his fingers. "It's simply a particular blend—I dare say many ladies use it."

"Perhaps, but none so tall. So ... accomplished."

When she merely raised a weary brow, he supplied, "So capable of picking locks."

Alathea frowned. "Am I to understand that you're searching for some woman—a tall woman—who wears the same perfume as I and can pick locks?"

"No—you're to understand that I've found her."

His ringing certainty had her looking up—he trapped her gaze. His eyes narrowed, then his gaze dropped to her lips. Insidious, mesmeric attraction flared between them ...

He stepped closer. Alathea's breath caught in her throat. Eyes widening, her gaze fixed on his hard face, she quivered—

The door from the ballroom opened; other guests ambled in.

Gabriel glanced around.

Alathea sucked in a breath. "You're completely and absolutely mistaken."

His head snapped back, but she'd already stepped around him. She swept past the other guests with a regal nod. Head high, in a glide just short of a run, she escaped back into the ballroom.

CHAPTER
Thirteen

A waltz was just starting. Alathea's mad dash nearly sent her into the dancers. She teetered on the edge of the dance floor—

A hard arm collected her, sliding about her waist, swinging her forward, then expertly steadying her. She swallowed a shriek, then fought to catch her breath—and her balance, and her scattered wits, only to lose all three as Gabriel locked his arm around her, trapping her from breast to thigh against him. One hand held fast, he whirled her down the room.

Her body instantly came alive. Her breasts swelled. She fought to hold herself stiffly, but her body molded to his, thighs brushing evocatively at every turn. Their hips swayed together; memories churned.

Within seconds, she'd softened. She refused to meet his eyes, too busy struggling to master her whirling wits, to gather her resolution, to find some way forward. Her composure was all she had left; desperately, she clung to it.

He was holding her very close. As her head continued to whirl, as her body continued to heat with every revolution, she fixed her gaze over his shoulder, and hissed, "You're holding me too close."

Gabriel looked at her face, so achingly familiar yet … had he ever truly seen it before? His temper was up and running, his emotions rioting; he had no idea what he thought or felt. He could barely believe the truth in his arms. His hold on his impulses was tenuous as he let his gaze roam the long slender lines of her throat, the creamy expanse of skin above her neckline, over the rounded swells, now firm, hot and tight, pressed against his chest. "I've held you closer, if you recall."

The gravelly rasp of his words affected them both; she shot him a shocked, breathless, scandalized glance, then looked away.

She said nothing more; her feet followed his, her body flowing with his, fitting so neatly, so totally attuned they could both have waltzed for hours without thought. Gabriel grabbed the moments to bring some order to the chaos in his brain. He frowned as he noticed the difference in her height, then recalled the high heels he'd dropped to the carriage floor three nights before.

Glancing down as they whirled through the next turn, he confirmed his guess. "You never normally wear heels."

Her breasts swelled as she drew in a tight breath. "What *are* you talking about? You're making less sense than poor Skiffy Skeffington!"

His hold on his temper snapped. "Indeed? In that case, I suppose there's no point in asking how long you'd thought to carry on your charade, or in inquiring as to its purpose. You can understand, however, that that last exercises me greatly." He spoke through clenched teeth, his voice sharpened steel. He let his gaze rake her face; he saw only red. "Did you think to trap me into marriage? Is that what this is about? Surely not—" He tightened his hold as she tried to free her hand until he knew he was crushing her fingers. "You know I'd make your life a living hell, so why? Was it the challenge?" Already stiff, she went rigid. He glanced at her set face. "That sounds nearer the mark."

He looked up as they circled, then laughed mirthlessly.

"*God*, when I think of it!—Lincoln's Inn Fields, Bond Street, Bruton Street." He paused, then demanded, "Tell me, in Bruton Street, did you flee into the modiste's because you couldn't contain your laughter?"

She reacted—her hand, crushed in his, jerked, the fine tendons in her neck tensed—but she kept her gaze fixed over his shoulder and her lips pressed stubbornly tight.

"Why did you do it?"

She gave him no answer.

"As the cat's caught your tongue, let me see if I can guess … you missed your chance with your own Season, but given you had to come to London to give Mary and Alice their turn, you thought to enliven your stay by taking a shot at me. Thanks to my fond mama, I'm sure you know my reputation." His tone lashed. "Is that what you thought? That bringing me to my knees as the mysterious countess would be just the thing to enliven your stay?"

Pale, her expression stony, she refused to look at him, to meet his eyes, refused to assure him that he'd got it all wrong, that she'd never betray him like that.

Betrayed was what he felt—not just by her but by her alter ego, too. No matter his devotion, no matter his patience and skill, no matter how deeply he'd come to worship her, the countess would never have revealed her identity to him. As for his dreams …

Bitterness welled, then swelled even higher. She'd struck much deeper than mere dreams. She'd struck straight to his core, just as she always had; she'd stripped away his armor, found his most vulnerable spot and laid it bare. He hadn't even known he possessed such a weakness until she'd uncovered it. He could only curse her for it—she was the very last woman on earth he would willingly reveal any vulnerability to.

But even that was not the worst. The most vital wound, the one that left him bleeding inside, was that, despite knowing him so well, she hadn't trusted him.

That, of it all, hurt the most.

"I always wondered when you'd get tired of your life in the country. Tell me, now I've opened your eyes to the pleasures to be experienced in the capital, are you thinking of—" He didn't even hear what he said, as, element by element, he dismembered her character. Many considered his tongue too sharp for safety; he used it like a surgeon's knife to cut at her, to make her bleed, too. Just as she knew where to strike at him, he knew all her most sensitive spots. Like her height, like the fact she believed herself plain. And too old. He touched on each vulnerable point, savagely rejoicing when she stiffened, when her jaw locked.

He'd salvaged a tiny portion of his pride by the time the music slowed, and the red mist that had clouded his brain and his vision lifted enough for him to see the tears that stood in her eyes.

The music ended. They halted. She stood silent and still in his arms, her expression unyielding yet her whole being vibrating with suppressed emotion.

She met his gaze unflinchingly. Beyond the sheen of her tears, he saw his fury and hurt reflected back at him, over and over again.

"You do not have the first idea what you are talking about."

Each word was distinct, carefully enunciated, underscored with emotion. Before he could react, she pulled roughly from his arms, caught her breath, turned, and swept away.

Leaving him alone in the middle of the dance floor.

Still furious. Still hurt.

Still aroused.

Alathea sat at the breakfast table the next morning in a state of deadened panic. She knew the axe would soon fall, but she couldn't summon the strength to run. She felt physically drained; she'd barely slept a wink. Maintaining an outward show of calm was imperative, yet it was all she could do to smile at her family and pretend to nibble her toast.

Her stomach felt hollow but she couldn't eat. She could only just manage to sip her weak tea. Her head felt steady enough, yet at the same time strangely vacant, as if blocking out all Gabriel's hurtful words had blocked off her own thoughts as well.

She knew she couldn't think—she'd tried for hours last night, but every attempt had ended in tears. She couldn't think of what had happened, much less of what might.

Picking at her toast, she let her family's cheery talk wash over her and drew a little comfort from its warmth.

Then Crisp paused beside her and cleared his throat. "Mr. Cynster is here, m'lady, and wishes to speak with you."

Alathea looked up. *Here*? No—he wouldn't. "Wh—" She stopped and cleared her throat. "Which Mr. Cynster, Crisp?"

"Mr. Rupert, miss."

He would.

Serena waved a plump hand. "Do ask him if he's breakfasted yet, Crisp."

"No!—I mean, I'm sure he would have." Rising, Alathea placed her napkin by her plate. "I'm sure he's not thinking of ham and sausages."

"Well, if you're sure ..." Serena frowned. "But it seems an odd time to call."

Alathea caught her eye. "It's just a little business matter we need to discuss."

"Oh." Serena mouthed the word, and immediately turned back to her family.

Slipping out of the breakfast parlor, Alathea reflected that her last words were no deception. All that Rupert—Gabriel—wished to speak about had occurred because of their "little business matter."

That wasn't going to make the coming interview any easier.

Crisp had shown Gabriel into the back parlor, a quiet room overlooking the rear gardens. On sunny days, the girls liked to gather there, but today, with the clouds closing in and drizzle threatening, it would be a quiet, and private, haven.

It was unlikely they would be disturbed.

Alathea considered that and grimaced. She'd dismissed Crisp and come alone. Hand on the doorknob, she drew in a breath, gathered her wilting strength, and refused to think of what she would face on the other side of the door.

Outwardly calm, she turned the knob and walked in.

His head turned instantly; their gazes locked. He'd been standing by the windows looking out. He considered her unblinkingly, then, in a low voice said, "Close the door. Lock it."

She hesitated.

"We don't need any interruptions."

She hesitated a moment more, then turned, shut the door, and snibbed the lock. Facing him again, she lifted her head, straightened her spine, and clasped her hands before her.

He continued to study her, his face unreadable.

"Come here."

Alathea considered, but she felt the tug, the compulsion. The threat. She forced her feet to carry her forward.

It was the most difficult thing she'd done in her life—crossing the wide parlor under his eye. She kept her head up, her spine rigid, but by the time she reached his side and the light fell full on her face, she was inwardly shaking, her reserves of strength, of resolution, seriously depleted. As she stopped beside him and met his hard gaze, she realized that was precisely as he'd intended.

He searched her face, his gaze sharp, acute, his features warrior-hard. "Now," he said, *"what the devil's going on?"*

Barely leashed anger vibrated behind the words. Drawing her gaze from his, she fixed it on the lawn and the enclosing trees. "You know most of it."

She drew in a breath, to gain time, to gain control. "All that I told you as the countess is true, except—"

"That your supposed late husband is in fact your father, that the youthful Charles is Charlie, Maria is Mary, Alicia is Alice, and Seraphina is Serena. That much I'd guessed."

"Well, then." She shrugged. "That's it."

When he said nothing more, she risked a quick glance. He was waiting—he caught her gaze and held it.

A moment passed.

"Try again."

His temper reached her clearly. There would be no escape. "What do you want to know?" If she could cling to the straightforward, the matter-of-fact, she might just survive his inquisition.

"Is the earldom in as dire straits as you portrayed?"

"Yes."

"Why did you create the countess?"

Straightforward. Matter-of-fact. She returned her gaze to the vista outside. "If I'd written to you or visited you with the story of a suspect note *without* telling you of the family's financial plight, would you have undertaken the investigation yourself or handed it to Montague?"

"If you'd told me the whole story—"

"Put yourself in my shoes. Would you have told you the whole story? How close to ruin we stood? Still stand."

After a moment, he inclined his head. "Very well—I accept that you would have avoided telling me that. But the countess ...?"

She lifted her chin. "It worked."

He waited, but she was too used to silence, to being silent with him, for the ploy to have any effect. His realization rang in his tone. "I take it your father and Serena are not aware of your masquerade."

"No."

"Who does know?"

"No one—well, only the senior servants."

"Your coachman ... that was *Jacobs*?"

She nodded.

"Who of the others?"

"Nellie. Figgs. Miss Helm. Connor. Crisp, of course. And Folwell." She paused, then nodded. "That's all."

He swore under his breath. "*All?*"

She shot him a frown. "They're devoted to me. There's no need to imagine anything will come of it. They always do precisely as I say."

He looked at her, then one brow quirked higher. "Oh?" His tone had dropped to a whisper. Signaling her to silence, he crossed to the door, then flipped the lock and hauled it open in one movement, revealing Nellie, Crisp, Figgs, Miss Helm ...

Alathea simply stared. Then she stiffened and glared. "Go *away!*"

"Well, m'lady." Nellie cast a wary glance at Gabriel. "We were just wondering—"

"I'm perfectly all right. Now *go!*"

They shuffled off. Gabriel closed the door, relocked it, then returned to the window.

"All right. So much for your masquerade." He stopped beside her; shoulder to shoulder, they looked out at the trees cloaked in dull shadow. "You can now tell me why you took it upon yourself to rescue your family."

"Well—" Alathea stopped, seeing the trap. "It seemed most sensible."

"Indeed? Let's see. A maid found the promissory note, which your father signed but somehow forgot about, and then you, your father, and Serena put your heads together, and they decided and agreed to let you pursue the matter—a matter that might destroy their lives—by yourself. Is that how it went?"

She regarded the trees stonily. "No."

"Well?"

The word hung in the air, insistent, persistent ..."I usually handle all the business affairs."

"Why?"

She hesitated. "Papa ... isn't very good with money. You know how ... well, *gentle* he is. He really has no idea—none at all." She met his gaze. "My mother managed the estate until her death. My grandmother managed it before her."

He frowned. After a moment, he asked, "And so you now handle all the estate business?"

"Yes."

His eyes narrowed. "Since when?"

When she looked back at the trees and didn't answer, he stepped between her and the window, leaving them all but nose to nose. His eyes bored into hers. "When did your father cede his authority to you?"

Still she said nothing. He searched her eyes. "Would you rather I asked him?"

If it had been any other man, she'd have called his bluff. "Years ago."

"Eleven years ago?"

She didn't reply.

"That's what it was, wasn't it? That was the reason you left town. Not chicken pox—I never did believe that—but money. Your father had brought the earldom to *point non plus;* somehow, you found out and took up the reins. You cut short your first Season before it had begun and went home." He paused. "Is that what happened?"

Her expression set, she shifted her gaze, staring out over his shoulder.

"Tell me the details. I want to know."

He wouldn't rest until he knew. She drew in a tight breath. "Wiggs came to the house one afternoon. He looked ... desperate. Papa saw him in the library. I went to ask if Papa wanted tea brought in. The library door was ajar. I overheard Wiggs pleading with Papa, explaining how deeply in debt the estate was, and how the expense of giving me my Season would quite literally run us aground. Papa didn't understand. He kept insisting that all would be well, that far from ruining us, my Season would be the earldom's salvation."

"He was counting on you making a good marriage?"

"Yes. Foolishly so."

"It might have worked."

She shook her head. "You haven't considered. I would have had no dowry—quite the opposite. Any successful suitor would have had to rescue the earldom, and the debts were mountainous. I had nothing at all to recommend me except my lineage."

"There are more than a few who would disagree."

She glanced at him, then looked back at the trees. "You forget—this was eleven years ago. Do you remember what I looked like at eighteen? I was painfully thin, even gawky. There was absolutely no chance I would make the sort of match required to save my family."

When she said nothing more, he prompted, "So?"

"When Wiggs left in despair, I went in and talked to Papa. I spent the night going over the estate records Wiggs had brought." She paused, then added, "The next morning, we packed and left London."

"You've been protecting your family—saving them—ever since?"

"Yes."

"Even though it cost you your life—the life you should have had."

"Don't be melodramatic."

"*Me?*" He laughed harshly. "That's the pot calling the kettle black. But if the shoe fits ..." He caught her eye. "And it fits you." He stood directly before her, his gaze locked on her face. "You knew what it would mean from the very first—eleven years ago. If you'd shut your ears to your family's plight and seen out your Season, it's more than likely you would have married well—not, I grant you, well enough to save the earldom, but well enough to save yourself. You would have had a home, a title, a position—a chance to have your own family. All the things you'd been raised to expect. Your own future was there for the taking. You knew that, yet you chose to return to the country and struggle to resurrect the family fortunes, even if it meant you'd become an old maid. After your aborted Season, your family couldn't afford to have you come up again—couldn't afford to let anyone even guess. They certainly couldn't afford a respectable dowry, a point in itself too revealing, but you knew how it would be. So it all fell to you. You sacrificed your life—all of it—for them."

He sounded angry. Alathea set her chin. "You're making too much of it."

He held her gaze mercilessly. "Am I?"

She couldn't avoid his eyes, the understanding lighting the hazel depths. The sacrifice of the years swept over her, the loneliness, the pain borne alone in the depths of the country. The mourning for a life she'd never had a chance to live. Dragging in a too-shallow breath, she fought to keep her gaze steady.

When she was sure she had her voice under control, she said, "Don't you *dare* pity me."

His brow quirked in that way that was quintessentially his. "It hadn't occurred to me. I'm sure you made the decision yourself—you set out to do precisely what you've done. I see nothing to pity in that."

The dry comment gave her sensitivity, her vulnerability, the shield she needed. After a moment, she looked away. "So now you know it all."

Gabriel studied her face and wished that were true. In the hours since he'd learned the truth, he'd been buffeted, shaken, rocked to his soul by a tempest of emotions. Anger, raw fury, a desperate hurt, quenched pride; those were easily identified. Other passions, darker, more turbulent, much harder to define, had swelled the tumult to an ungovernable tide that had scored and ripped its way through him.

Now, in the aftermath, he felt, not empty, but cleared, as if the inner temple he'd built to house his soul had been smashed by the torrent, swept from its foundations and the bricks left scattered by the subsiding flood. Now he faced the task of building his inner house again. He could choose a simpler structure, one without the posturing, the false glamor, the boredom of which he'd grown so tired in recent months. Which bricks he chose to fashion his future was up to him, but the fact that he had a choice to make was due to her.

Only she could have caused such an upheaval.

His life from now on depended on what he did next, what he chose next. He'd come here, his anger still raging, fully intending to ring a peal over her. Now that he'd learned the whole story and finally understood what she'd been doing all along, his anger had resolved into something quite different, something intensely protective.

"What's the current state of the earldom's finances?"

She shot him a glance, then grudgingly offered a figure. "That's the underlying security. The income from the farms adds to that."

"What's that amount to per year?"

Bit by bit he drew the details from her, enough to confirm that not even his genius, not even Devil's touch with management, Vane and Richard's experience, not even Catriona's power could have done more to bail out the Morwellans.

I wish you had come to me earlier—all those years ago.

Thus spake his heart; he knew better than to utter the words.

"So there's nothing more that can be done there. Your family's as secure as it can be in the circumstances." He ignored her offended stare. "What about this man of yours—Wiggs? Is he reliable?"

"I've always found him so." Stiffly, she added, "If it hadn't been for his intercession with the banks, we would have sunk long ago."

That had to be true. "What's he think of your masquerade—or haven't you told him?"

She didn't meet his eye. "He was very relieved when I told him I'd consulted you."

"So he doesn't know you've been consulting in disguise." He caught the look she threw him. "I need to know—I'm bound to meet the man sometime over this."

She blinked, arrested; at first, he didn't understand, then he did.

His jaw set. He felt like throttling her. "I am not going to walk away and leave you to deal with this alone."

Her relief was obvious, even though, sensing his reaction, she tried to hide it. The look in her eyes as they searched his made it clear she didn't understand his response.

Neither did he—not entirely. It was one of the long, vital list of things he didn't yet know, along with what he felt for her. Even now, standing no more than a foot from her, he had no idea what his feelings truly were. He had no intention of touching her—not yet. He couldn't yet contemplate dealing with the force that he knew would be unleashed when next he did, when next he took her in his arms. The time would come, but not yet, not until he'd realigned his mind and his senses to the new reality. The reality where he could stand so close to her and sense nothing beyond her warmth, a sensual, womanly, highly tempting warmth. No overtense, flickering nerves, no prickling uncomfortableness disturbed him. Their decades-old affliction had died last night when he'd hauled her into his arms and waltzed her down Lady Arbuthnot's ballroom.

While he hadn't yet got a firm hold on what he felt, he had even less idea of what she felt about it all.

Some hint of what was in his mind must have shown in his eyes. Hers widened; sudden uncertainty flared.

He held her gaze ruthlessly; he made no attempt to hide his thoughts. She'd given herself to him, albeit in disguise. She was going to have to cope with the outcome.

"What are you thinking?"

Deliberately, he raised a brow.

She actually blushed. Her eyes widened even more, frantically searching his.

"I suggest," he said, the words clipped and precise, "that given the seriousness of the threat the Central East Africa Gold Company poses we set aside further discussion of the ramifications of your masquerade until we've successfully dealt with the company."

He could almost see her feathers subside. A moment later, she nodded. "Agreed." She turned away. "Not that there'll be any ramifications."

He shot out a hand and shackled her wrist. She froze. The eyes that met his when he turned his head were wide. "*Don't* pretend." After a moment, he continued, his tone less forceful, "I said we'd defer discussion of the matter, not that we'd ignore it."

"There's nothing to ignore." Her tone was breathless; her other hand rose to her breast.

Turbulent emotion swelled, threatening to sweep him away. Jaw set, he held it back, but allowed it to infuse his eyes. "*Don't tempt me.*"

The words, dark and low, vibrated with a power Alathea could sense; it gripped her, shook her, then held her, but lightly. If she tried to fight, the grip would tighten, would seize and pin her. For now, he was content to simply hold. Dragging in a shaky breath, she forced herself to look away.

She was immeasurably grateful when, an instant later, his fingers slid from her wrist.

"Have you learned anything since last we discussed the matter?"

The question gave her something to cling to, to respond to sensibly. "Wiggs." Dragging in another breath, she lifted her head. "I asked him to find out the legal procedure involved in getting the note declared invalid. He sent a message yesterday saying he had an appointment with one of the Chancery Court judges tomorrow morning to discuss the possibilities."

"Good. Anything else?"

She grew calmer. "I've been looking for maps of the area to check the locations Crowley mentioned."

"Detailed maps of that area are hard to find."

"True, but I finally found one in a biography. It shows those three towns Crowley mentioned—Fangak, Lodwar, and Kafia. They're small, but there."

"What did the biographer say about them?"

She hesitated. "I don't know. I didn't read the text."

He sighed through his teeth.

"I will! I only found it two days ago. Anyway, what have you been doing? Have you located the captain?"

"No." Gabriel frowned. "It's not that simple. He's definitely not with any of the major shipping lines. There are scores of others to check, so we're checking. I've nosed about White's but no one remembers him. Incidentally, who saw him—Charlie?"

"No, Papa. But he doesn't remember anything beyond what I've told you. And I've made him promise to bring the captain home if he sees him again."

"Hmm. I've got people searching, but it's possible he's no longer in London. Most of the senior seamen come ashore, then head off to visit family, often out of London, returning only a day or so before they're due to sail again."

"So we might not see the captain again."

"Not if we simply wait to see him. There are other possibilities I'm following up." He glanced at the mantelpiece clock. "Speaking of which, I have to be elsewhere." He met Alathea's gaze. "Are we agreed that we'll pool all information so we can settle this business as expeditiously as possible?"

Alathea nodded.

"Good." He held her gaze for an instant, then he raised his hand.

Alathea's breath suspended; lost in the hazel depths of his eyes, she inwardly quivered as his fingers traced, then cradled her jaw. The pad of his thumb brushed slowly over her lips. She felt her eyes flare, her lips soften. Her wits whirled.

"And then," he stated, "we'll settle the rest."

She was tempted to raise a brow; caution stepped in and prevented it. When she simply held his gaze, he nodded.

"I'll call on you tomorrow."

She'd never been afraid of Gabriel; after careful consideration, Alathea concluded she still wasn't. It wasn't fear that tightened her nerves when she caught sight of him while strolling in the park; it was anticipation, but of what she wasn't sure.

Together with Mary, Alice, Heather, and Eliza, she'd been strolling for twenty minutes. Lord Esher and his friend Mr. Carstairs, of the Finchley-Carstairs, young gentlemen of impeccable credentials, had joined the group, his lordship to chat with Mary, while Mr. Carstairs manfully engaged the others, although his gaze strayed frequently to Alice's face.

Ambling in the rear, Alathea had watched the budding romances with an approving eye, until she saw Gabriel approaching. After that, she saw nothing beyond him, severely elegant in morning coat, buckskin breeches, and Hessians, the breeze ruffling his chestnut locks. His expression easy, he greeted her sisters and his with brotherly familiarity, appraised the suddenly tense young men, and nodded his approval. Then his gaze slid to her. Deserting the younger crew, he strolled to her side.

Alathea locked both hands on her parasol handle and prayed he wouldn't commandeer one.

His eyes met hers, then his brow quirked. "I don't bite," he murmured, as he halted beside her. "At least," he amended, voice deepening, "not in public."

Awareness swept her; she felt her blush rise. He viewed the sight, his brow quirked again, then he turned and surveyed the group moving far ahead of them. "I suppose we'd better keep them in sight."

"Indeed." Alathea stepped out; he fell in beside her.

"Have you heard from Wiggs yet?"

"No—his appointment was scheduled for eleven." It was only just past noon.

"Will you be at the Clares' ball tonight?"

"Yes."

"Good—I'll meet you there."

Alathea nodded. That was one benefit of the countess's unmasking; they could now easily meet to exchange information. "I read that explorer's book, at least the relevant parts."

As she jiggled her parasol and dug into her reticule, she felt Gabriel's gaze on her face.

"Burning the midnight oil?"

She flicked him a glance. She didn't need him to tell her she had rings under her eyes. "When else would I get time to read?"

The tartness of the reply had no discernible effect. "Running yourself ragged isn't going to help. What's this?" He took the sheet she thrust at him.

"That's the description the explorer gave of those three towns."

He perused it as they strolled; his brows gradually rose. "How very interesting. When was this explorer in these parts?"

"Only early last year. The book's just been published." Alathea leaned closer, peering at the sheet. She tapped one paragraph. "As I recall, Crowley said the company had purchased a large building in Fangak from some French government agency to house the workers involved in the construction of the company's mines. According to the explorer, Fangak is 'a collection of flimsy wooden huts far from civilization.'"

"Crowley also said Lodwar was on a major road. Instead, it appears to be a tiny settlement halfway up a rugged mountainside, 'well away from the beaten track.'"

Alathea glanced at his face. "It's evidence, isn't it?"

He looked at her, then nodded. Folding the note, he slipped it into his pocket. "But we'll need more." He looked at the group ahead of them. "How's that shaping?"

"Promisingly. Esher becomes more definite by the day, while Carstairs ..." Tilting her head, Alathea considered the young gentleman. "I think he's trying to screw his courage to the sticking point, but is having a hard time believing that it's actually happened to him."

Gabriel snorted. "Poor bugger."

Alathea pretended not to hear.

They strolled on, following the others, then Gabriel halted. "I'll leave you here."

Alathea turned to him, only to feel his fingers close about hers. He raised her hand and considered it, slim fingers trapped by his. Then he lifted his gaze to her eyes.

She couldn't breathe, couldn't think. He was close; because of her height, her parasol shaded them both, creating an illusion of privacy in the middle of the park. They never exchanged the routine pleasantries, touching hands, bowing, but now he held her hand, and her, too; she wondered what he meant to do.

His lips twisted, wry and taunting both. "I'll see you tonight."

He pressed her hand briefly, then released it. With a nod, he left her.

Alathea stood still, breathing evenly, and watched him stride away. Part of her mind noted that he'd left just before their ambling stroll would have brought them into view of the carriage drive, presently lined with the carriages of the ton's matrons, including those of his mother and aunt. The rest of her mind was engrossed with the burning question of what he thought he was about, what tack he intended to take with her.

The situation between them had changed, yet he still wanted her, even though he now knew who she was. He still intended to have her, to continue their illicit liaison; amazing though that seemed, that much was clear.

Very little else was.

With the countess's unmasking, all control of their interaction had passed to him. She was completely in his power, a power she knew better than to imagine he wouldn't, if provoked, wield.

The little group she was watching were drawing ahead. Straightening her parasol, she set out in their wake.

What he had in mind she couldn't begin to guess, any more than she could be sure of his motives. Given their encounters in Bond Street and Bruton Street, let alone the rest, he might well wish to punish her. His present conduct might be a facade, adopted to ease their way while they pursued the company. He was more than honorable enough to put aside his own feelings until they'd dealt with the threat. *Then* he might consider retribution.

Luckily, he rarely held a grudge. By the time their investigations were complete, it was possible, even likely, that his interest in her would have waned, that he would have grown bored and shifted his sights to his next conquest.

A frown in her eyes, Alathea climbed the slope to the carriage drive, and wondered why the prospect of him growing bored with her and thus abandoning any notion of retribution did not bring her any sense of ease.

CHAPTER
Fourteen

L ady Clare's ball was yet another unrelenting crush. The Season was in full swing and everyone simply had to be seen at all the major events. Finally gaining Alathea's side, Gabriel cast a malevolent glance over the jostling throng. "Manic," he muttered.

Lord Montgomery, presently holding Alathea's attention, thought the jibe aimed at him. He bristled. Smiling serenely, Alathea pretended she hadn't heard. "Have your mama and sister come up to town this year?"

Faced with such unequivocal interest, his lordship's hackles subsided. With a disdainful glance at Gabriel, he intoned, "Indeed, indeed! They are, naturally, concerned as to the future of the estate. Why—"

Recently afflicted with a conviction that she would be just the wife for him, his lordship droned on. Alathea let her smile glide over the other eager faces, but did not linger long enough to encourage any to interrupt with his own tale. Completing her circuit brought her glance to Gabriel; he caught it, irritation behind his hazel eyes. He hesitated, then, to her surprise, reached out and took the hand she hadn't thought to offer him. He held it, waiting with studied patience until Lord Montgomery's monologue rolled to a close, then he bowed. As he straightened, Alathea, off-balance and mystified, saw concern color his expression.

"My dear, you're rather pale."

My dear? She nearly goggled.

Gabriel anchored her hand on his sleeve, drawing her within his protective orbit. "Perhaps a stroll outside ... before you faint from the stuffiness."

She'd never fainted in her life. Her gaze trapped in his, Alathea waved a hand weakly before her face. "It is rather hot in here."

His brow quirked; one corner of his lips did, too. "The doors to the terrace are open ..."

The suggestion was greeted with numerous offers to accompany them; obedient to the fingers squeezing hers, Alathea smiled wanly. "The noise ..." She gestured limply. "A few moments of absolute quiet would help, and then I'll be able to return to you."

With that, they had to be content. Gabriel excised her from the circle and steered her down the room. Alathea hoped it appeared that he was dragging her off in brotherly fashion—for her own good—but the speculative frowns in too many eyes made her itch to box his ears. Next, he'd have the scandalmongers watching them avidly, and God only knew what they might see.

They gained the flagged terrace along which a number of couples were strolling. She tried to slide her hand from his sleeve to put greater distance between them. His fingers tightened; she knew better than to tug. "You'll start people talking," she hissed as, acquiescing, she continued to glide close beside him.

"No more than they're talking already of you and the aspirants to your charms. Why on earth do you surround yourself with them?"

"I assure you it's not by choice!" After a moment, she added, "I suspect Serena's been busy on my behalf, *despite* the fact I made it plain that this was Mary's and Alice's Season and I have no interest in attracting a husband. Well"—she gestured to her braided cap—"how much clearer can I make it? Can't they *see*?"

Eyeing the cap with savage dislike, Gabriel bit back the words "Probably not." Her caps offended him at some elemental level. There was, now he thought of it, one sure way of getting rid of them once and for all. Considering the prospect of never seeing another cap covering her hair, he guided her toward the shadowy end of the terrace, presently deserted. "Did Wiggs report on his meeting with the judge?"

Reaching the balustrade at the end of the flags, they surveyed the thick bushes beyond the stone barrier, then turned and leaned against it, hip to hip, shoulder to shoulder, in oddly companionable comfort.

"Yes. It seems we can ask for a decision declaring the note invalid through a petition directly to the bench, without evidence or deliberations being heard in open court."

"Good. That'll make things easier."

"The judge said the speed at which a decision would be given will depend on the quality of our evidence. The more detailed and complete the evidence, the quicker the judgment. If the case was cut and dried, a decision could be formalized in a matter of days."

Gabriel nodded. "When we're ready, I'll alert Devil. He'll make sure it gets immediate attention." Alathea's sudden grin caught his eye. "What?"

She glanced at him. "Just the way you operate." She waved. "Just like that—throw a duke into the equation."

He shrugged. "If one has a duke to throw …"

Her grin fading, Alathea asked, "Have your people learned anything more?"

"No grand revelations, but Montague is making headway with all those figures and projections Crowley spouted. Needless to say, they don't add up. My contacts in Whitehall are still checking the claims he made about various foreign government departments and officials, and the permissions he said the company had already received. The more things that are false, the wider the front on which the company's claims are disproved, the easier it will be to convince the court."

"But a witness—an eyewitness as it were—would be the definitive proof. Have you heard anything more about the captain?"

"Yes and no. Mostly no. There are so many shipping lines, and at too many I have no contact from whom I can discreetly inquire. We can't risk any overt search, not even for the captain. Crowley's too powerful. He may well have contacts who'll report any unusual queries in all shipping lines dealing with his present area of interest."

"Is he that omnipotent?"

"Yes. Don't underestimate him. He may not have attended any recognized school, but he knows how to play his connections well. Witness Archie Douglas." After a moment, Gabriel stated, "Whatever we do, we must never forget Crowley."

The words disturbed Alathea. Frowning, she shook them aside. "There must be some register of the ships and their captains, surely?"

"There is—it's kept by the Port Authority. There are two registers we need to look at—the log which lists all the ships as they enter the Pool of London along with their captain, and the main register of vessels, which shows which shipping line a particular ship sails for. Unfortunately, there was a scandal involving the last port registrar. Consequently, his successor is exceedingly resistant to the idea of allowing anyone access to either the log or the register."

"Exceedingly resistant?"

"Short of an order from the Admirality or the Revenue, there's no way to view those books."

"Hmm."

Gabriel glanced at Alathea. "Don't even *think* of breaking in."

She focused on him. "Why? Because you've already considered it?"

"Yes." His lips twisted. He looked back along the terrace, then straightened. "The office is manned around the clock. At present, searching the log and register is impossible."

Following his gaze to Lucifer, strolling through the shadows toward them, Alathea murmured, "Nothing's impossible when you're twelve years old."

Gabriel shot her a look as Lucifer, brows high, joined them.

"What are you two doing out here?"

What do you think? burned Gabriel's tongue. He hadn't yet had time to steer their interaction into the arena he'd intended.

Alathea waved at him. "He's looking into something for me. An investment."

Turning his head, Gabriel looked at her; her gaze fixed on Lucifer's face, she ignored him.

Lucifer was looking at him. "I think the twins have noticed. They're bubbling and fizzing and exchanging glances like fury. God knows what they'll do once they realize it's true."

"Once they realize what's true?" Alathea asked.

Lucifer turned his dark gaze on her. "When they realize *he's* not watching them anymore."

"He's not?" Alathea looked at Gabriel. He'd developed a consuming interest in his manicured fingernails.

The damned man had listened to her. Listened, and allowed her to influence his direction. She felt slightly giddy.

"He's not. And, at the moment, *I'm* not, either." Belligerently disapproving, Lucifer looked from her to Gabriel and back again. "I just hope you know what you're doing. That bounder Carsworth's sniffing about their skirts."

Gabriel looked up. "Has he approached either of them?"

The question was mild, the underlying tone anything but.

"Well, no," Lucifer admitted.

"Have either of the twins encouraged him?" Alathea put in.

Lucifer's expression turned mulish. "No. He intercepted Amelia—not overtly approaching her, just happening to come upon her in the crowd."

"And?"

His reluctance was palpable, but eventually he conceded, "She put on an act like Aunt Helena. Looked him down, then up, then stuck her nose in the air and swanned past without a word."

"Well, there you are." Straightening, Alathea slipped an arm through his. "They've been very well trained. They're perfectly capable of managing, if you'll only let them."

"Humph!" Lucifer let her turn him up the terrace. Arm in arm, they strolled back toward the open doors spilling light and noise across the flags. Although she spared him not a glance, Alathea was intensely aware that Gabriel prowled very close on her other side.

"Carsworth's a worm—no real threat." Over her head, Lucifer exchanged a glance with Gabriel. "But what happens when they try that trick with someone with a bit more"—he gestured—"*savoir faire?*"

Gabriel shrugged. "So they'll learn."

"Learn what?" Alathea asked as they stepped back into the ballroom.

"Learn what would happen if a lady tried such a ploy on, say, one of us," Lucifer replied.

Alathea raised a brow at Gabriel.

He considered her, then flicked a glance at Lucifer. Confirming his brother's attention had wandered, he looked back, into her eyes. "Try it—and you'll see."

There was something in his eyes that reminded her forcefully of a tiger; the purr in his voice underscored the connection. Recalling what had happened the last time she'd tried, nose in the air, to brush past him, Alathea stiffened her spine and lifted her head. "The twins will manage perfectly well."

Lucifer, scanning the crowd, humphed again. "Well, if you refuse to watch, then I may as well put my time to better use." One black brow arching, he glanced at Gabriel, then, with an elegant nod to Alathea, he shouldered his way into the crowd.

If anything, the crush had worsened. Alathea felt Gabriel's fingers close about hers, then her hand was on his sleeve as he steered her out of the ebb and flow before the doors. The tack he took was in the opposite direction to where they'd left her cavaliers.

"Can you see Mary and Alice?" Why she felt so breathless she couldn't understand.

"No." His lips were close to her ear, his breath a warm caress. "But, like the twins, they'll manage."

So would she, she vowed, as he found them a few square feet of space in which to stand comfortably. Although they were surrounded, they might as well have been alone for all the notice their neighbors took, too caught up in their own conversations.

"Now tell me, what did you mean about being twelve years old?" Gabriel trapped her gaze as she glanced up at him. "In case it's escaped your notice, neither you nor I are."

The meaning in his eyes was quite different from the subject of their discussion. Alathea reined in her skittering wits. "I wasn't referring to us."

"Good."

The subtle easing of his lips did quite peculiar things to her nerves. She dragged in a breath. "I meant—"

"My dear Lady Alathea."

Alathea turned to see the earl of Chillingworth emerging from the crowd. He swept her a necessarily abbreviated bow. "Such solace to discover a divine delight in this unholy crush." He sent a measuring glance Gabriel's way. "So nice to know one's evening won't be a complete waste of time."

Gabriel didn't respond.

Ignoring the burgeoning menace at her elbow, Alathea smiled and gave Chillingworth her hand. "I believe the musicians her ladyship has hired are quite exceptional."

"If only one could hear them," Chillingworth replied. "Are your sisters enjoying their Season?"

"Indeed. Our ball will be held next week—dare we hope you'll attend?"

"No other hostess," Chillingworth avowed, "will have any hope of enticing me elsewhere." His gray gaze roved Alathea's face, then settled on her eyes. "Tell me, have you seen the latest production at the Opera House?"

"Why, no. I had heard—" Alathea broke off as the sea of guests suddenly wavered, then parted. As the clamor of voices dimmed, the opening strains of a waltz filtered through.

"Ah." Chillingworth turned to her. "I wonder, my dear, if you would do me the honor—"

"I'm afraid, dear boy, that this waltz is mine."

Gabriel's languid drawl did nothing to conceal the steel beneath his words. Chillingworth looked up; over Alathea's head, gray eyes clashed with hazel.

Turning, Alathea stared at Gabriel's face, noting the hard edge fell determination lent his features. Relinquishing Chillingworth's gaze, he met hers. "Shall we?"

He gestured to the rapidly clearing dance floor, then his arm shifted beneath her fingers and his hand closed about hers. His gaze flicked to Chillingworth. "His lordship will excuse us."

Giddy, slightly stunned by what she'd glimpsed in his hooded eyes, Alathea smiled apologetically at Chillingworth. The earl bowed easily. Without more ado, Gabriel led her forward. A second later she was in his arms, whirling down the floor.

It took a full circuit before she caught her breath. He was holding her too close again, but she wasn't going to waste what breath she had protesting that point. "I don't suppose there's any sense in pointing out that this waltz wasn't, in fact, yours to claim."

He met her gaze. "Not the slightest."

The look in his eyes stole her breath. She mustered her wilting temper for protection. "Indeed? So whenever you feel like waltzing, I'm to expect—"

"You misunderstand. Henceforth, *all* your waltzes are mine."

"*All?*"

"Every last one." He expertly twirled her around the end of the room; as they joined the long line going back up the ballroom, he continued, "You may dance any other dance with whomever you please, but you'll waltz only with me."

All inclination to argue, to protest, evaporated. *Don't tempt me.* He'd warned her once—the words were again in his eyes. They rang in her head. When she finally managed to draw in another breath, Alathea looked over his shoulder and tried to gather her wits and focus on his motives.

Only to fall victim to her senses, to the seductive shift and sway of their bodies, their long limbs twining, sliding, separating, then coming together again. He waltzed as he did all physical things—effortlessly, expertly, with an inherent grace that only emphasized the leashed power behind every move. He held her easily, his strength palpable, surrounding her, guiding her, protecting her.

She'd waltzed with others but none with his matchless authority, founded as it was in his knowledge, physical and sensual, of her. He knew she couldn't resist, that while in his arms she was helpless. That her heart beat unevenly, that her skin heated, that she would go wherever he led. He had her trapped in a web, one she had helped fashion, of passion, of yearning, of desire slaked by sensual reward. She was his and he knew it. What he meant to do with the knowledge, with her, remained an unsettling unknown.

The music ended and they slowed, then halted. She studied his face, the hard planes unyielding, uninformative, and inwardly sighed. "I should find Serena."

Releasing her, he placed her hand on his sleeve, and protectively steered her through the crowd.

* * *

The following evening, Alathea left her bedchamber once again in a tearing rush. Heading for her office, she flung the door wide and dashed for her desk. Sitting, she pulled a sheet of paper free, settling it on the blotter as she flicked open the inkwell.

"You wanted me, m'lady?"

"Yes, Folwell." Alathea didn't look up. Dipping a pen in the ink, she industriously scribbled. "I want you to deliver this note to Brook Street."

"To Mr. Cynster, m'lady?"

"Yes."

"Now, m'lady?"

"As soon as you get back from driving us to Almacks."

A minute passed, the only sound in the room the scritch-scratch of the pen. Then Alathea blotted her missive, folded it, and scrawled Gabriel's name on the front. She dropped the pen and stood. Waving the note, she crossed the room to Folwell. "There won't be an answer."

Folwell slipped the note into his coat pocket. "I'll drop it off on the way back from King Street."

Alathea nodded. Lips compressed, she strode for the front hall where Serena, Mary, and Alice were waiting.

A minute later, she was in the carriage, rolling across the cobbles to the holy portals of the patronesses' dreary rooms. Almacks! She hadn't liked the place the first time she'd seen it, when she'd been a gawky eighteen. She sincerely doubted she'd enjoy her evening, but ... her sweetly loving stepmother had turned stubborn.

She'd expected to remain home that evening and arrange some discreet rendezvous to discuss her urgent news with Gabriel. Instead, over dinner, Serena had announced that Emily Cowper had made special mention of hoping to see her that evening, having missed her in the park that afternoon. That afternoon, when she'd been off on an excursion to see just how much a twelve-year-old could pry from the otherwise impregnable Port Authority.

Jeremy's success had left her giddy. She desperately wanted to see Gabriel. She'd marshaled all her arguments against Almacks and spent the half hour after dinner laying them out, but Serena had stood firm. That happened so rarely, she'd been forced to acquiesce, which had left her little time to dress. Thankfully, Nellie was fully recovered; despite the rush, her hair was elegantly coiffed, her gloves, reticule, and shawl the correct accessories for her gown of pale green silk.

Not that she cared. Given Gabriel wouldn't be there, her evening would be a complete waste of time. Still, tomorrow morning was, logistically speaking, no different from tonight.

That conclusion rang in her mind the next morning—mockingly. Scrambling to her feet, dusting earth from her cotton gardening gloves and quickly stripping them off, she told herself it didn't matter what he thought, how much he saw.

She looked up as he reached her. "I didn't expect you this side of eleven."

His brow quirked as he calmly took possession of one of her hands. "You said as early as possible."

One long finger stroked her palm. Alathea tried to stiffen. "I thought, for you, as early as possible would be close to noon."

"Did you? Why? I didn't go out last night, remember?"

"Didn't you?"

"No." After a moment, he added, "There was nowhere I wanted to go."

Her gaze locked with his, Alathea felt unaccountably giddy. He couldn't possibly mean ...Was he flirting with her? Abruptly, she cleared her throat and waved vaguely at her stepsiblings. "We like to spend a little time in the garden every morning. Exercise."

"Indeed?" His shrewd gaze swept the garden. He responded to Mary's and Alice's cheery greetings with an easy smile, to Charlie's familiar "Hoi!" with a wave. Jeremy, helping Charlie lug a branch to the bottom of the garden, bobbed his head. Gabriel grinned, his gaze moving on to Miss Helm, who colored when he bowed. Beside the little governess, Augusta sat, Rose clutched in her arms, her wide-eyed gaze riveted on Gabriel.

"I can't recall seeing Jeremy since he was a babe in arms," he murmured. "And I don't believe I've met your youngest sister at all. What's her name?"

"Augusta. She's six."

"Six?" He looked back at her. "When you were six you gave me chicken pox."

"I'd hoped you'd forgotten. You promptly gave it to Lucifer."

"We three were always good at sharing." A moment passed, then he said, "Speaking of which ..."

She waved at the house. "If you'd like—"

"No need to interrupt your endeavors." He looked down. "The grass is dry." So saying, he sat beside her mat, her hand still in his. Looking up at her, he tugged. "You can tell me your news here."

Alathea only just managed not to glare. She subsided with passable grace, settling once more on her knees, tugging her gloves back on. "You know I hate gardening."

His brows rose; from the corner of her eye, she could see him recalling. "So you do. How very devoted of you, to keep your sisters company." A moment passed, then he asked, "Is that why you do it?"

"Yes. No." Her gaze on the pansies, Alathea could feel her cheeks heating. Drawing in a breath, she reminded herself that he already knew more than enough to guess the truth. "They think *I* love gardening, and Serena insists that they should understand the basics of borders and beds from the ground up, so to speak."

She felt his gaze sweep her face, then he looked out over the lawns. "I see. And Charlie and Jeremy are the pruning specialists?"

"More or less."

He said nothing for a moment, one long leg stretched out, the other bent, one arm draped over his raised knee. Then he turned again to her. "So what have you learned?"

Alathea yanked out a clump of grass. "I've learned that being twelve years old can open the register at the Port Authority."

His gaze switched to Jeremy. "It can?"

"I took Jeremy on an excursion to learn about how ships are managed in and out of the Pool of London. The harbor master was extremely accommodating—he has a young boy of his own. Of course, being the son and daughter of a belted earl helped."

"I dare say. But all we had was the captain's description. How on earth did you manage to learn more discreetly? I take it you have."

"Indeed! I primed Jeremy—he has an excellent memory. I described the captain as Papa had seen him, and explained what we needed to find out. We decided it would be best to ask about the information in the log and register, and then ask what it might be useful for. That allowed us to suggest that it could be used to find out which shipping lines carried goods to different parts of the world. At that point, I suitably vaguely remembered a friend of ours, a Mr. Higgenbotham, who—"

"Wait! Who's Higgenbotham? Does he exist?"

"No." Alathea frowned. "He's just part of our tale." She yanked up another weed. "Where was I? Oh, yes—this Mr. Higgenbotham had dropped by with a friend of his, a captain whose ship recently docked from Central East Africa. That, of course, was Jeremy's cue to challenge the harbor master to see if his log and register would tell us who the captain sailed for."

"And the harbor master obliged?"

"Of course! Men always like to demonstrate their abilities before an appreciative audience, especially one composed of a female and a youthful pup. It took him twenty minutes—there were quite a few ships to cross-check—but we think the captain must be one Aloysius Struthers who sails for Bentinck and Company. Their office is in East Smithfield Street. The harbor master recognized the description and is certain Struthers is our man."

Gabriel resisted the urge to shake his head. "Amazing."

"Jeremy," Alathea decreed, plonking another weed onto her pile, "was simply magnificent. Even had you been the harbor master, you would have happily searched the log for him. He played his hand *just* right."

Gabriel raised a brow. "He's obviously like you—he must have inherited the same thespian tendencies."

He waited, but Alathea pointedly ignored the comment, reaching instead for another weed. After a moment, she asked, "So what's next?"

Gabriel looked across the lawns to where her stepbrothers were wrestling with a thick branch. "I'll visit Bentinck and Company this afternoon."

Alathea frowned at him. "I thought you said any open inquiry was too dangerous?"

Completing his scan of the garden, Gabriel returned his gaze to her face. "Surely you don't think you're the only one who can assume a disguise?"

Her lips twitched. "What will you be? A merchant from Hull looking for a fast ship to carry his whitebait to Africa?"

"*Hull?* Good God, no. I'll be an importer of wooden artifacts looking for a reliable line to transport my wares, bought throughout Africa, to St. Katherine's Docks."

"And?"

"And I'll have received a recommendation for Struthers and the line for which he sails but, being an exceedingly fussy client, I'll insist on speaking directly to Struthers before making any decision. That should encourage the company to give me Struthers's direction with all possible dispatch."

Alathea nodded approvingly. "Very good. We'll make a thespian of you yet."

She looked up, expecting some light retort—he was studying her, his hazel gaze steady and keen. He held her trapped, searching, considering ... the sounds of the others, their chatter, their laughter, the bright calls of the birds and the distant rumble of carriage wheels, faded away, leaving just the two of them on the grass in the sunshine.

Then his gaze shifted, dropping to her lips, briefly sweeping lower before returning to her eyes. "The trick," he murmured, his voice very low, "is not in assuming the role, but in knowing when the charade ends and reality starts."

In his eyes, so like hers, lay living reminders of all they'd shared—the childhood triumphs, the youthful adventures, their recent intimacy. Deep in their gaze, Alathea simply existed. Reaching out, he caught a wayward lock of her hair lying loose along her cheek. Taming it, he tucked it back behind her ear. As he withdrew his hand, with the backs of his fingers he caressed the whorl of her ear, then lightly traced the line of her jaw.

His hand dropped.

Their gazes held, then Alathea drew a shaky breath and looked down. He looked away. "I'll see what I can learn."

Gathering his long limbs, he rose. Alathea kept her gaze on her pansies.

"I'll let you know if I'm successful."

She inclined her head. "Yes. Do."

With no "Good-bye," he moved off, waving to the others, stopping to exchange a polite word with Miss Helm. Alathea hesitated, then gave in to the urge to turn her head and watch him as he strode away.

Twelve hours later, Alathea stood by the side of Lady Hendricks's overcrowded music room, enraptured by the composition faultlessly rendered by the capital's most sought-after string quartet. The first segment of the performance was drawing to a close when long fingers curled around her wrist, then slid down to tangle with hers.

Her head whipped around. Her eyes widened. "What on earth are you doing here?"

Gabriel looked at her, an incipient frown in his eyes. "I wanted to see you."

He eased in beside her; she was forced to make room. The last thing she wanted was to draw more eyes their way. "How did you know I was here?" They both spoke in whispers.

"Folwell told me where you were headed."

"Fol—? Oh." She caught his eye. "You know about Folwell."

"Hmm. Has he mentioned my new man?"

"Chance?"

Gabriel nodded. "His tongue runs on wheels, out of my presence or in it. I knew Folwell was haunting my kitchen from the first. I didn't, however, connect his presence with you. I thought he was there to see Dodswell. I know better now, but Folwell does have his uses."

With a sniff, Alathea returned her gaze to the musicians. "I can't believe Lady Hendricks sent you a card for this—not even she could be that naively hopeful."

"She didn't." Gabriel settled close beside her. "I simply walked in, secure in the knowledge she won't show me the door." He studied Alathea's profile, watching it soften as the music drew her back. The line of her jaw fascinated him, a subtle melding of feminine strength and vulnerability. She had always struck him that way—as much a partner as one to be protected. He'd recognized that quality in the countess; he'd known it in Alathea all his life.

Following her gaze to the players, he waited until they concluded their piece on an uplifting crescendo before murmuring, "The captain is presently uncontactable."

The outburst of applause distracted the crowd so none but he saw her disappointment. It filled her eyes as well as her expression. He moved across her, lifting her hand to his sleeve. "Come to the window—we can speak more freely there."

The narrow windows were open, a balcony, barely a ledge, beyond them. A cool breeze wafted the filmy curtains. Pressing them aside, they stood on the threshold, facing each other, hardly private but sufficiently apart from other guests to talk without being overheard.

Alathea leaned back against the window frame. "What did you learn?"

"Aloysius Struthers is our man—the clerks at the shipping line confirmed the description, and also that he's something of an expert on East Africa, having sailed those coasts for the last decade and more. Unfortunately, the captain is presently away visiting friends—the company has no idea where. He has no family and no fixed abode in this country. However, he does call in now and then to check there's no change in his sailing schedule. He's not due to sail again for a month. I left a message guaranteed to bring him to Brook Street the instant he reads it, but he may not get it for a week or more."

Alathea grimaced.

Gabriel hesitated, then continued, "There's also the possibility that he might not be willing to help. The clerks painted a picture of an irascible old gent more concerned with his ships and Africa than anything else. I gather he doesn't have much time for nonsailors."

"Do we have enough proof to mount a case without his testimony?"

Gabriel paused, then said, "Montague's figures are strongly suggestive of deliberate fraud, but are not conclusive. A good barrister could argue his way around them. What else we have on the three towns—Fangak, Lodwar and Kingi—relies on the reports of explorers who are not themselves available to vouch for the details. As for information from the African authorities, my contacts in Whitehall are finding it exceedingly difficult to get any straight answers, which in itself is highly suspicious. For any serious investor, what we have would be more than enough to pass judgment on Crowley's scheme. For a court of law, we need more."

"How much more?"

"I'll keep pressing Whitehall. Without more definitive proof, lodging a petition at this stage would be unwise."

"Essentially, we need the captain."

"Yes, but at the moment, there's nothing more we can do on that front."

"And even if we do find him, he may not help."

Gabriel made no reply. A moment later, the musicians laid bow to string. They both turned toward the dais as the crowd resettled for the next piece. A lilting air, it filled the room with a hauntingly sweet melody. Alathea watched the musicians, letting their art sweep her away, temporarily soothing her fears. Gabriel watched her. The short piece ended; applause rolled through the room. Alathea contributed her share, then sighed and turned to him.

"I'd forgotten you like music."

Her expression turned wry. "To my mind, it's one of the few charms of the capital—to be able to hear the most talented musicians."

Gabriel merely nodded. His gaze went past her, and abruptly sharpened. "Damn! That harpy's actually going to throw her daughter at me."

Looking around, Alathea beheld their hostess bearing down on them, a beaming smile on her face, her pale, clearly reticent daughter in tow. "Well, you are here, after all. She probably sees it as encouragement."

The sound Gabriel made was derisive.

Alathea arched a brow at him. "Shall I leave you to your fate?"

"Don't you dare. That poor girl always loses her tongue about me. God knows why. Conversing with her is worse than pulling teeth."

Alathea smiled as she turned to greet Lady Hendricks. Gabriel appropriated her hand and placed it on his sleeve, thereby denying her ladyship any chance of whisking her off and leaving him alone with her daughter. Lady Hendricks accepted the situation with a puzzled look, settling for gushing over his presence before retreating, leaving her daughter with them. Alathea, who was acquainted with Miss Hendricks, took pity on all concerned and kept the conversation rolling, never straying from any but the most mundane subjects.

After one warning glance from her, Gabriel behaved himself, consenting to chat with debonair charm. When the musicians next took to the dais and, under Gabriel's direction, they parted from Miss Hendricks, the young lady was actually smiling. Gliding through the room on Gabriel's arm, Alathea felt sure Lady Hendricks would be pleased enough to forget her earlier puzzlement.

"Esher and Carstairs are sitting with your sisters." Gabriel shot her a look as they passed out of the music room. "How's that coming along?"

"Very well." Halting in the foyer, Alathea drew her hand from his sleeve and turned to look back into the room. "Inside two weeks, I should think." Then she glanced at Gabriel, her expression growing serious. "Have you … heard anything about either of them?"

"No." He scanned her face. "I've already checked—they're exactly as they appear. Both are wealthy enough to marry as they choose, and in both cases their respective families should be more than content with their securing an earl's daughters as their brides."

"Thank heavens. I'd started to wonder if it was all too good to be true. I never imagined they'd both go off so easily." She looked back at her sisters. "This Season has proved far more felicitous than anyone could have expected."

His gaze on her face, on the delicate line of her jaw, Gabriel slowly nodded. He hesitated, then touched her arm. "Au revoir." Stepping past her, he left the house.

He found her in the park the following afternoon, a willowy vision in pale green. The fine fabric of her gown clung to her hips, swaying evocatively as she trailed in the wake of her sisters and, unfortunately, his. Esher and Carstairs were once more in attendance; Gabriel resigned himself to speaking to both in the next few days regarding their intentions. A subtle prod wouldn't hurt.

His gaze fastened on Alathea. Lengthening his stride, he closed the distance between them. She whirled as he caught up with her. Surprise and awareness flared in her eyes, then she caught herself and inclined her head graciously. "Have you heard anything?"

Taking her hand, an action that now seemed normal, even called for, Gabriel anchored it on his sleeve and drew her to stroll beside him. "No. Nothing more."

"Oh."

He felt her questioning glance. She wanted to know what had brought him here. "I thought you might be interested in the details Montague has put together."

The distraction served; she not only followed his account, but posed a few shrewd questions on the Company's projected costs. He nodded. "I'll get Montague to check—"

"Alathea! Such a pleasant surprise!"

The exclamation brought them up short; absorbed in their discussion, they had not been looking about them. Gabriel muttered a curse as his gaze fell on the countess of Lewes, approaching with her brother, Lord Montgomery.

Alathea smiled. "Cecile! How lovely to see you."

Suppressing a frown, Gabriel exchanged a terse nod with Montgomery. They both waited with feigned patience while the ladies exchanged far more detailed greetings. From references the countess made, Gabriel gathered she and Alathea were contemporaries; their acquaintance dated from Alathea's aborted Season eleven years before. From Montgomery's smug expression, Gabriel surmised his lordship imagined his sister's connection would put him on a closer, more personal footing with Alathea.

"And Mr. Cynster!" The countess turned to him with an arch smile.

"Madam." Gabriel accepted the hand she offered him, bowed easily, and released her. Alathea's fingers slid from his sleeve. Without looking, he caught her hand, enclosing it within his grasp. She stilled. He could all but hear her wondering what he was about.

"Perhaps," the countess continued, ignoring the byplay, "we could stroll together?"

Alathea smiled. "Indeed—why not?"

Gabriel pinched her fingers, then made a great show of tucking her hand into the crook of his elbow. She shot him a sharp glance, then turned to Lord Montgomery. "Is your mother well?"

Feeling distinctly unsocial, Gabriel turned to the countess. "How's Helmsley these days?"

The countess colored and slid around his wicked question. She paid him back by describing her offspring and their illnesses, a subject guaranteed to send any sane gentleman fleeing. Gabriel mentally gritted his teeth and refused to yield. As they strolled on, he noticed that Alathea kept her gaze fixed on Lord Montgomery, paying no attention whatever to all the gory details about the countess's three children. Knowing her as he did, knowing how closely she'd been involved with the care of her stepsiblings, he at first found that odd. Then they reached the Serpentine and he glanced at her face.

She kept it averted; he couldn't see her eyes. He could see the underlying stiffness in her features. Smoothly, he turned to the countess. "Do you plan to attend Lady Richmond's gala?"

The abruptness of the question made the countess pause, but she took to the new topic with alacrity. With a query here and there, he kept her engrossed in the social whirl, well away from the subject of children. His awareness centered on Alathea, he sensed the gradual easing of her tension. She had, indeed, given up a lot to save her stepfamily, far more than she would willingly let anyone know.

"I say! Lady Alathea!"

"My dear lady!"

"Countess, do introduce me."

A bevy of five gentlemen, including Lord Coleburn, Mr. Simpkins and Lord Falworth, swept up to them from behind; if Gabriel had been able to see them, they wouldn't have managed it, but now he and Alathea were caught.

Alathea sensed his increasing irritation. She glanced at him; he was regarding Lord Falworth with an impassive expression and a dangerous glint in his eye.

"Don't you think so, Lady Alathea?"

"Oh—yes." Recalling Falworth's question, she quickly amended, "But only in the company of close friends."

Dealing with her would-be suitors while knowing Gabriel was considering annihilating one or all of them played havoc with her normally unassailable nerves. Her relief was quite genuine when he closed his hand over hers, still tucked in his elbow, and halted.

"I'm afraid," he purred, at his most urbane, "that we must shepherd Lady Alathea's sisters and mine back to our mothers' carriages. You'll have to excuse us."

That last was said with enough underlying command to convince even Lord Montgomery that bowing and making extravagant adieus was the better part of valor.

Gabriel drew her ruthlessly away. He caught his sister Heather's eye and with one brotherly gesture redirected the group now well ahead of them back toward the avenue.

Side by side, strolling easily, their long legs a match for each other, they brought up the rear. Alathea sighed with relief.

Gabriel shot her a dark glance. "You could try to discourage them."

"I haven't encouraged them in the first place!"

They walked on in silence. As they neared the point where Serena's and Celia's carriages would come into view, Alathea slowed, expecting Gabriel to make his excuses and leave her. He tightened his hold on her hand and drew her on.

She looked at him in amazement. He cast her an irritated glance. "I'm not escorting them." His nod indicated the four girls and Esher and Carstairs ahead of them. "I'm escorting *you*."

"I don't *need* escorting."

"Let me be the judge of that."

His expression grimly resolute, that was all he deigned to say. Alathea was too surprised that he'd risk alerting his mother to any particularity between them to marshal any argument, and then they were within sight of the carriages.

With an inward sigh, she kept pace beside him. "This is not going to make things any easier, you know."

She thought he wasn't going to reply, but just before they reached his mother's carriage where Serena and Celia sat in matronly splendor, he murmured, "We left 'easy' behind long ago."

Then they were at the carriage, joining with the girls and Esher and Carstairs. Over the heads, Gabriel fielded a glance from Celia; Alathea, watching closely, could interpret with ease—Celia wanted to know why he was there. Gabriel returned her gaze impassively with a slight lifting of his shoulders, giving Celia to understand he'd simply come upon them and walked them back. Nothing particular at all. His performance was so smooth, if she hadn't known better, Alathea would have believed that, too. Gabriel nodded and Celia smiled, waving him away.

He turned to her—their gazes met. In the folds of her gown their fingers brushed. With a brief nod, he turned and strode away.

Alathea watched him go, a frown in her eyes, an increasingly insistent question revolving in her mind.

CHAPTER
Fifteen

That question was answered two nights later. The Duchess of Richmond's gala was one of the highlights of the Season. The Richmonds' house on the river was thrown open; everyone who was anyone attended. Alathea arrived relatively early with Serena, Mary, and Alice. Her father, out to dinner with friends, would look in later. Leaving Serena on a *chaise* with Lady Arbuthnot and Celia Cynster, Alathea hovered until the circle about Mary and Alice was established, Esher and Carstairs to the fore, then headed for a quiet nook by the wall.

Her attempt at self-effacement was frustrated by Lord Falworth, who spotted her in the crowd. Seconds later, her "court" closed in.

To Alathea's relief, not five minutes passed before Chillingworth joined them. After exchanging the usual pleasantries, the earl settled by her side, displacing Falworth, who sulkily shifted back. As large as Gabriel, Chillingworth had a similar effect on her admirers; challenged, they exerted themselves to converse intelligently.

By the time the orchestra struck up for the first dance, Alathea was feeling in considerable charity with the earl, very ready to grant him her hand. He did not, however, solicit it, calmly standing back while Lord Montgomery begged the honor. With no excuse ready, Alathea was forced to accede to his lordship's fervent plea but as the dance was a cotillion, she was spared most of his pompous declarations.

When at the end of the dance Lord Montgomery returned her to her circle, she was somewhat surprised to discover Chillingworth patiently waiting. Her gratitude bloomed anew as under his direction, the conversation remained lighthearted and general. Then the musicians struck up a waltz, and she realized why the earl was waiting.

The look in his eyes as he bowed before her was flatteringly intent. "If you would do me the honor, my dear?"

Alathea hesitated, another large gentlemen very clear in her mind. She looked up—and found him watching her, waiting to see what she would do, ready to step in and claim her if she didn't fall in with his decree. His intent reached her clearly as the circle of her admirers, noticing him, parted like the Red Sea.

Tamping down a spurt of rebelliousness, accepting she dared not bait Gabriel in his present mood, she glanced at Chillingworth. "I'm afraid, my lord, that I'm already promised. To Mr. Cynster."

That last was redundant; Chillingworth's gaze had fastened on Gabriel's face. Primitive challenge flashed between them, then Chillingworth bowed. "My loss, my dear, but only a temporary one. There'll be many more waltzes tonight." Even more than his words, his tone signalled his intention.

With a grace to match Chillingworth's, Gabriel bowed and held out his hand. Alathea placed her fingers in his, conscious to her toes of the restrained strength in his grasp. He drew her to him, turning as she joined him, effectively cutting off her court. The dance floor was only a step away, and then she was whirling in his arms.

Alathea inwardly frowned. She was aware the outcome of that little scene had pleased him. It hadn't, however, pleased her. "You're drawing too much attention to us."

"In the circumstances, it's inevitable."

"Then *change* the circumstances."

"How?"

"Your insistence that I waltz only with you is ridiculous. It's going to cause comment. It's hardly something one can explain on the grounds of long-standing acquaintance."

"You want me to let you waltz with other men."

"Yes."

"No."

He whirled her through the turn. Alathea gritted her teeth. Why did he imagine he could dictate such things? Because of the hours she'd spent with him in the dark. She bundled the recollections aside. "It isn't wise to attract the attention of the gabblemongers. People are starting to wonder."

"So? They're not wondering anything that will reflect adversely on you."

Yes, they were—if he kept on as he was, the whole ton would soon believe that he and she would marry, but that wasn't going to happen. By the time they'd dealt with Crowley and his company, Gabriel's attraction to her would have waned and he'd be off laying seige to his next conquest. Raising expectations destined never to be fulfilled was not a good idea. Worse, these were the sorts of expectations guaranteed to fuel the gossips' fires. She was too old—far too old—to be eligible.

Alathea seethed through the rest of the waltz, her temper not improved by the speculative glances thrown their way, or by his continuing—and she was quite sure deliberate—rasping of her senses.

By the end of the dance, she was ready to be returned to the safety of her court. He, it transpired, had other ideas. The reception rooms opened one into the other; on his arm, he paraded her through them. Only the increasing crush prevented them from being the focus of far too many eyes.

"Where are we going?"

"Somewhere less crowded."

She could hardly argue with the wisdom of that; tall though she was, she was feeling hemmed in. The small salon to which he took her had palms and statues breaking up the space. Consequently, it boasted areas in which one could converse, not private but protected. Gabriel led her to a nook created by a trio of potted palms and an ornamental arch.

A footman passed with a tray. Gabriel collected two glasses of champagne. "Here—it's only going to get hotter."

Accepting the glass, Alathea sipped, relaxing as the bubbles fizzed down her throat. She scanned the room, then she sensed Gabriel stiffen. When she turned, her gaze collided with Chillingworth's as he joined them in their retreat.

"I count myself fortunate to have found you again, my dear."

Gabriel snorted derisively. "You followed us."

"Actually, no." Chillingworth snared a glass as the footman hove within reach. He sipped, his gaze on Alathea's face. "I assumed, after that little display in the ballroom, that Cynster would retreat to some area more conducive to his purpose."

"A tactic you would know all about."

Chillingworth looked at Gabriel. "That point has been puzzling me. You are, after all, a friend of the family. Your present tack is one I would never have expected."

"That's because you have no idea what my present tack is."

Chillingworth smiled tauntingly. "Oh, no, dear boy. I assure you I'm far from being *that* unimaginative."

"Perhaps," Gabriel returned, sharpened steel beneath the words, "it would be wiser if you were."

"What? And leave the field to you?"

"Hardly the first time you've owned to defeat."

Chillingworth snorted.

Glancing from one to the other, Alathea felt giddy. Despite her height, they were talking over her head, arguing over her as if she wasn't there.

"It would be more to the point," Chillingworth opined, "if, given the circumstances, you'd cease your present act and get out of my way."

"Which act is that?"

"Dog in the manger."

"*Excuse me!*" Eyes flashing, Alathea silenced first Gabriel, who'd opened his lips on a retort, doubtless equally graceless, then she rounded on Chillingworth. "You will pardon me if I find this exchange somewhat less than gratifying."

They both looked at her. She doubted either blushed readily, but slight color now graced their cheeks. The crude nature of their remarks was out of character for both, far from their usual unfailingly elegant poses.

"I am appalled." Glancing from one to the other, she held them silent. "It appears you believe I'm not only *unimaginative*, but deaf as well! For your information, I'm perfectly well aware of both your 'acts'—permit me to tell you I approve of neither. Like any lady of my age and experience, *I* will be the arbiter of my actions; I have no intention of succumbing to the practiced blandishments of either of you. What, however, I find *unforgivable* is your propensity to single-mindedly pursue your own agendas, oblivious to the fact that your attentions are focusing unwanted and unwarranted attention on me!"

She ended glaring at Chillingworth. He had the grace to look contrite. "My apologies, my dear."

Alathea humphed, nodded, and turned to Gabriel. He looked at her for two heartbeats, then his fingers closed about her elbow. He handed his glass to Chillingworth, then took hers and handed that across, too. "If you'll excuse us, there are a few pertinent details we need to clarify."

"By all means," Chillingworth returned. "Once you've clarified the nonexistent nature of your claim, I'll be able to clarify my position." He bowed to Alathea.

Gabriel frowned. "Believe me, in this case, you don't have one."

Before Chillingworth could reply, before Alathea could even see how he reacted, Gabriel drew her forward. Alathea fumed but didn't try to break free; a steel manacle would have been easier to break than Gabriel's hold on her arm. He marched her across the room to where a door stood ajar, giving access to a corridor.

"Where now?" she asked as they stepped through the door.

"Somewhere private. I want to talk to you."

"Indeed? I have a few words to say to you, too."

He led her up a flight of stairs, then back along a quiet wing. The door at the end stood open; beyond lay a small parlor, curtains drawn against the night. A fire burned in the grate. Three candelabra shed golden light on satin and polished wood. The room was empty. Drawing her hand from his arm, Alathea swept across the threshold. He followed. Reaching the fireplace, she swung to face him, and heard the lock fall home.

"This ridiculous situation has got to end." She fixed him with an irate glance. "The countess is no more. She has faded into the mists, never to return."

"*You,* however, are here."

"Yes, *me.* Alathea-who-you've-known-all-your-life. I'm not some delectable courtesan that you have any real interest in seducing. You're annoyed because as the countess you thought I was—you now know better. And you know perfectly well that once you get over being annoyed, you'll be off after some other lady, one more suited to your tastes."

He'd remained by the door; head tilted, he regarded her. "So my interest in you is fueled by annoyance?"

"That, and perversity. A response to Chillingworth and the others. It's almost as if, having relinquished your silly watch on the twins, you've transferred your attention to me!"

"And what's wrong with that?"

"You're obsessively protective! If you'll only stop and think, you'll realize there's no *need*. I need to be protected even less than the twins. Worse, hovering over me is exceedingly unwise. It calls attention to us—you know what people will make of it. Before you know where you are, the ton will have imagined into existence something that simply isn't."

A moment passed, then he asked, "This something that isn't—this illusion you claim the ton will think it sees. What, precisely, is that?"

Alathea huffed out a breath. Across the room, she met his eyes. "They'll imagine we have an understanding, that in the near future they'll read an engagement notice in *The Gazette*. As Chillingworth so sapiently stated, it's widely known that our families are close, that you and I have known each other for years. No one will imagine any illicit connection—they'll imagine we'll wed. Once that idea gains credence, there'll be hell to pay."

"Hmm." He started to walk toward her. "And that's the bee that's buzzing in your bonnet?"

"I have absolutely no desire to spend the rest of the Season explaining to the interested why we aren't about to marry."

"I can guarantee that won't occur."

"Indeed?" She bridled at his patronizing tone. "And how can you be so sure?"

"Because we *are* going to marry."

Gabriel halted directly before her. A full minute passed while she stared at him, speechless. Then her eyes clouded.

"W-*what?*"

"I agreed to defer discussion of the matter until after we'd dealt with the company—that, however, is clearly not to be. So it may as well be now. As far as I'm concerned, we're getting married, and the sooner the better."

"But you never had it in mind to marry me. Not when we spoke after Lady Arbuthnot's ball."

"Thankfully, you never did learn to read my mind. I decided to marry you when I knew you as the countess. The morning after Lady Arbuthnot's ball, I was still adjusting to the startling discovery that it was *you* I'd decided to make my wife. As you might imagine, that was something of a shock."

"But ... you *must* have changed your mind. You don't want to marry me."

"Not only do I *want* to marry you, I am *going* to marry you, a fact that makes my attitude toward you and other gentlemen perfectly understandable. I might be obsessively protective, but only about those of whom I'm obsessively possessive, such as the lady who will be my wife. The ultimate ramification of your masquerade as the countess will be marriage to me. There is, therefore, no false illusion for the ton to see—the only conclusion society will leap to will be the truth."

"As you deem it."

"As it will be." He stepped closer; physical awareness flashed in her eyes. She lifted her chin; he captured her gaze. "This is *real*. I'm not going to grow out of it, or lose interest and become distracted. Marriage to me is your immediate and irrevocable future. If you hadn't realized, you'll need time to adjust, but don't imagine there'll be any other outcome."

"But ..." She shook her head dazedly. "I'm *not* the countess. It was the countess who fascinated you—a lady of mystery and illusion. *I* don't fascinate you—you know everything there is to know about me—"

He kissed her, closed his lips over hers, then closed his arms about her. It was easy to do with her being so tall. Her resistance lasted a heartbeat, then vaporized like mist; she sank against him, her lips parting at his command, her mouth an offering he claimed.

Alathea clung to her wits. She yielded all else without a fight, knowing any fight would be futile, but she held on to reason. About her, the world whirled; her senses rioted. He'd shocked her with his declaration, but she surprised herself even more.

She wanted him. Her hunger was too strong, too sharp in its raw newness, for her to ignore or mistake it. The arms locked about her were a welcome cage, the hard body pressed to hers the essence of dreamed delight. He plundered her mouth, ruthless, relentless, not gentle. She took him in, lured him further, to give and take and give again.

He took and exulted in the taking. She knew it. She sensed the surge of passion, his and hers, and reveled in her power. The heady wave grew into a vortex of heat, swirling about them, flames licking, touching, but not yet consuming. Then, to her surprise, the world steadied.

He lifted his head.

She felt him draw breath, his chest swelling against her breasts. It was an effort to lift her lids enough to see his face. Hard, each plane edged with desire, it gave her no clue to his direction. His eyes, glinting gold under lids as heavy as hers, were fixed on her hair.

His arms shifted. One hand splayed across her back, holding her against him. The other rose ...

To her hair.

"What ...?" She felt a brusque tug; satisfaction gleamed in his eyes. Glancing to the side, she saw her beaded cap in his hand. "Don't you *dare* throw that in the fire!"

His gaze returned to her face. "No?" Then he shrugged and tossed the cap to the floor. "As you will." His hand returned to her hair, rifling the soft mass, searching and plucking. Pins tinkled across the hearth.

"What are you doing?" She tried to wriggle, but he held her too securely. Then her hair fell free.

"You appear to have formed a grossly inaccurate opinion of what fascinates me. Arguing with you always was so much wasted breath, so I'll demonstrate instead."

"Demonstrate?"

"Hmm." He speared his free hand through her hair, spreading his fingers, combing through the long tresses, holding them out, watching them drift down as his fingers pulled free. "You never did understand why I hated your caps, did you?"

Mesmerized by the possessiveness investing his harsh features, Alathea didn't answer. He played with the silken mass, then he gathered half of it in his fist, tipping her head back.

"What else?" His gaze fastened on her eyes. "Ah, yes. Your eyes. Have you any idea what it's like to look into them? Not at them, but into. Whenever I do, I feel like I've fallen into some magical pool and lost myself. Certainly lost all sense." His gaze lowered. "And there's your lips." He took them in a swift, achingly incomplete kiss. "But we know why I like those." The arm about her eased, his hand drifted from her back. He still held her by her hair. "But I don't believe you have any idea about this."

Long fingers feathered her jaw, tracing from her chin to her ear. Then he cupped her face, holding her steady as he bent his head and followed the same line with his lips.

Alathea shivered.

"That's right. *Vulnerable.*" The word caressed her ear. "Not weak, but definitely vulnerable. Mine to seize."

Her lids fell as his lips brushed the sensitive skin beneath her ear, then slid lower, laying heat down the length of her throat. Her mind told her to correct him; she wasn't his.

Instead, when he fell to laving the tender spot at the base of her throat, she swayed into him. Her legs weakened. She clutched his lapels as her wits reeled.

He released her hair. His lips returned to hers and her hunger resurged. He matched it, fed it, incited her desire, then drank deeply, took, seized, claimed. Distracted, she had no inkling that his fingers had been busy until he closed his hands about hers and drew them down, then, breaking off their kiss, slipped her gown from her shoulders.

The ribbon straps of her chemise went, too. Her breasts, swollen and rosy-peaked, were in his hands before she lifted her lids, long before she drew in a breath.

He'd caressed her breasts before but only in the dark; she hadn't been able to see his hands cupping, caressing. She hadn't been able to see his face, to see desire engraved on his features, to see the fires of passion burning in his eyes.

His hands closed possessively.

"Beautiful," he murmured. "There is no other word. None to do you justice."

He bent his head; Alathea closed her eyes and struggled to hang on to her sanity as he feasted. With lips, tongue, and teeth, he worshipped, heaping pleasure upon pleasure until she gasped. The guttural sound he made rang with masculine satisfaction, then he returned to repeat the torture.

His touch was exquisite; helpless, she arched in his arms, offering, entreating, yet still aware of every nuance of every touch, of the meaning invested in each caress. Although the vortex of their passions whirled around them, they yet stood at the still eye of their storm.

Gabriel knew it. Never before had he attained such a high degree of arousal while still retaining such absolute control. Not with any other woman. The woman in his arms was special, but he'd known that all along. All his life, even though he hadn't understood.

Lifting his head, drawing his lips from the sweet mounds of her breasts, he steadied her. Sliding his hands to her back, he eased her gown and chemise further down. They gathered about her hips. Eyes wide, one hand on his shoulder for balance, she met his gaze, stunned understanding in her eyes.

His lips curved. He raised his hands to the backs of her shoulders, then skimmed them slowly down, tracing the long planes of her back, the supple muscles on either side of her spine. "I like the fact you're so tall. There's a lot of you, but you're so slender." He spread his hands, spanning the back of her rib cage. "I'm twice the size of you."

He closed his hands about her narrow waist. Possessive lust flared; he knew it glowed in his eyes. "Tall yet feminine. My ideal."

His gravelly tone shook her. She sucked in a shaky breath—

He kissed whatever she'd thought to say from her lips. Thoroughly. Then he pushed her gown and chemise over her hips. They swooshed down her legs to puddle on the floor.

"Gabri—"

He cut her off with another kiss. Luscious curves filled his hands; he was no longer interested in verbal communication. Deepening the kiss, he drew her hard against him, fingers flexing, kneading, learning anew. He knew the feel of her, the contrast of feminine firmness and softness, yet his senses seemed starved, urgently needy for more and yet more of her.

Fascination was too weak a word to encompass his obsession.

As for her legs ...

"Don't move." Closing his hands about her hips, he sank to his knees. He heard her indrawn breath and pressed a kiss to her waist, then trailed lower to lave her navel. Her hands had fallen to his shoulders, her fingers restless. As he evocatively probed the slight indentation, her fingers slid into his hair.

He paid homage to her legs, sliding his hands down, then up the long, graceful limbs. She quivered, muscles tensing. When he bent his head and nuzzled her taut belly, she gasped.

"Gabriel?"

The word was an aching whisper, laden with entreaty. Alathea could barely believe it came from her. Her body was hot, her skin flushed, her wits in disarray, yet she felt every touch, every caress keenly. Desire throbbed in the air, passion heated it; this time, there was no darkness to shroud her senses, no veil to obscure the reality.

She stood naked before him, held by the thought that her nakedness captivated him. His head against her stomach was a warm weight; the touch of his hands both soothed and excited. His hair, silky locks sliding over her flickering skin as he turned his head, felt so right.

His only response to her plea was a hot, wet, open-mouthed kiss pressed to her quivering belly just above the curls at its base. She shuddered, and clung to his skull. He shifted one hand to her bottom, shoring up her precarious balance while the fingers of his other hand trailed up and down the sensitive inner faces of her thighs.

He shifted fractionally lower.

She expected him to touch the soft flesh between her thighs. She waited, nerves tensing. Then he did, and she nearly died. The hot, wet sweep of his tongue, the subtle probing, nearly brought her to her knees. Her exclamation was incoherent.

"Shh." He caught her, steadied her. Grasping one of her knees, he lifted it over his shoulder. She had to shift her balance, curling that leg over his broad back, her fingers clenched on his skull. The position was more secure, but inevitably more intimate. Scalding hot, his tongue stroked her again. "I'm going to taste you."

Those mumbled words were all the warning she had before he did. Tasted, probed, stroked, lapped—whether she would have agreed to the intimacy was irrelevant. He simply took, and she gave.

Her nerves leaped, sensitized, excruciatingly aware; muscles tensed, clenched. Her wits reeled, yet some small part of her remained cogent, detached enough to catalogue his demonstration, sane enough to wonder if he had intended it that way.

Her very awareness was arousing; she could see and sense beyond the sensual plane. The air before her was cool, the fire behind her warm. And the man kneeling before her was the god of pure pleasure. He flayed her with it, lashed her with it, lavished it upon her until she sobbed, until her body became no more than a vessel of heated yearning.

She knew the instant his tongue and lips left her, felt the raw power as he surged to his feet. His hands closed hard about her thighs, and he lifted her.

Then he filled her.

The thick, solid length of him pressed in, breached the slight constriction, then slid up, in, thrust deep. With a gasp and a sob, she closed about him, sheathing him there, holding him there. His fingers flexed; she felt his chest strain. Locking her legs about his hips, winding her arms about his shoulders, she pressed herself to him, caught his head between her hands, and found his lips with hers.

The kiss was a true melding, drawn as much from her as from him; their bodies moved in similar harmony, in a slow, evocative rhythm as instinctive as their breathing. He lifted her; she slid sensuously down. She clung, then released; he withdrew, then returned.

It should, perhaps, have shamed her, this intimate yielding with her naked in his arms, her bare limbs wrapped around his fully clothed form. He'd only released his staff from the confines of his trousers. Every tiny movement rasped her sensitized skin with the fabric of his elegant evening clothes.

He'd planned it that way—at no stage did she entertain any other notion. He had said he would demonstrate his fascination; as he reveled in the slick heat of her body, drawing out every precious moment, holding the vortex at bay, she knew to her bones that he was playing no role.

She didn't need him to draw back from the kiss, chest laboring, eyes closed, concentration etched in every line of his face, to be convinced. Didn't need to feel her own body respond, undulating against him, upon him, to know she believed.

Didn't need him to lift his weighted lids, transfix her with a glittering glance, and say, "You think I know you, but I don't—I don't know the woman you've become. I don't know how it will feel to run my hands through your hair when it's warm from sleep, or what it will feel like to slide into you as you wake in the morning. I don't know how it will feel to fall asleep with you in my arms, to wake with your breath on my cheek. To have you naked in my arms in daylight, to hold you when you're big with my child. There are lots of things I don't know about you. I'll spend my life with you, and still not learn all I want to know. I don't care by what name you go—you're still the same woman. The woman who fascinates me."

She hushed him with her lips, but neither she nor he had the strength to prolong the kiss. They were clinging to sanity by their fingernails. She tucked her head down on his shoulder, nuzzled his neck, placed a breathless kiss on his heated skin.

His lips returned the pleasure, then he nipped lightly. "You like this, don't you?" His voice was broken, strained; he gave a hoarse laugh. "You're going to be the death of me in more ways than one."

She deliberately tightened about him, something she'd noticed gave him pleasure.

His head fell back and he groaned. Then he caught the trailing ends of her hair and tugged her head back so he could look into her eyes. "See? This is what you were made for—giving yourself to me."

She kept her lips shut. She was afraid he was right. With a flick of her head, she pulled her hair from his grasp. The sudden movement shifted her. She sank even deeper onto him, and reflexively tightened even more.

He sucked in a breath, then his lips were on hers, urgent and demanding. His control was gone. The vortex closed upon them; the flames roared.

Passion took them, lifted them high on a swell of pure need, then shattered them. Release was so profound, neither was aware that they sank to the floor. The only reality their senses permitted them was the knowledge they were together, and one.

"You called me Gabriel."

Slumped on his chest, still aglow in the aftermath, Alathea could barely think. "I've been calling you Gabriel in my mind for weeks."

"Good—that's who I am." Sprawled on his back on the sofa he'd carried her to, his hand lingered on her hair. "I'm not your childhood playmate. I'm your lover and I'll be your husband. I'm claiming the position." His hand closed on her nape, then gentled, stroked. "Just as my name doesn't really matter, what you call yourself changes nothing. You're the woman I want, and you want me. You're mine—you always were, and always will be."

The bone-deep assurance in his words struck Alathea to the heart; she stirred—

"No—lie still. You're not cold."

Her skin was still flushed. His body beneath her radiated heat. She wasn't cold—she was boneless, unable to summon the strength to reassert control and change direction. She was not even sure she wanted to.

They had, she recalled, once lain together on their backs looking up at the stars one summer night. They hadn't touched; instead, the tension between them had been so thick it had all but sparked. That tension had vanished completely. What surrounded them now was a well of peace, profound and enduring. Satiation deeper than she'd imagined could exist lapped them about; he seemed content to rest in its embrace, sharing the quiet.

She could hear his heart beating beneath her ear, slow and steady.

"Why are you here?"

He put the question evenly; mystified, she answered. "You brought me here."

"And you came. Now you're lying in my arms, totally naked—you took me willingly, willingly gave yourself to me, purely because I wanted you."

She felt far more at his mercy now than she had before. How could he know the confusion and uncertainty hovering in her mind? But it seemed he did.

"You're good at that—giving. And what you have to give, I want." His hand gently stroked her hair. "You're a sensual woman, a Thoroughbred in bed, and I certainly don't care how old you are. You haven't even been in training for long and you still make my head spin."

She shut her eyes. "Don't."

"Don't what? Speak the truth? Why, when we both know it?" His hand moved down, stroking her back, then he closed his arms about her. "You love to give, and the only man you'll ever give yourself to is me."

She didn't want to hear it because she couldn't deny it and it gave him far too much power over her. She struggled to sit up. "We have to go."

"Not yet." He held her easily and nuzzled her ear. Then his lips touched her skin, and lingered. "Just once more ..."

CHAPTER
Sixteen

The next morning, Alathea sat in the gazebo tucked to one side of the back garden and watched Gabriel cross the lawn toward her. Bright sunlight struck red and gold glints from his hair; she remembered the feel of it beneath her palms.

Eyes narrowed against the glare, she watched him exchange greetings with Mary and Alice, who were weeding the bed about the fountain. She had excused herself from gardening on the grounds of feeling under the weather. It was the truth; she'd barely slept a wink.

If she'd needed unequivocal proof that Gabriel had read her emotions accurately, the second half of their encounter in Lady Richmond's parlor had provided it. Even now, hours after the fact, just the thought of the suggestions he'd whispered in her ear, of what she'd willingly done and let him do to her, brought color surging to her cheeks. He'd wanted, and she had wanted to give. Last night, he'd introduced her to the ultimate in giving.

She wasn't hypocrite enough to pretend she hadn't enjoyed it, that the bliss she found in giving to him, whenever, however, brought the sweetest, deepest joy she'd ever known. In satisfying him, she found fulfillment. There was no other word, none that came close to describing the breadth and depth of what she felt. He'd labeled her a "giver;" she had to accept he was right. What she didn't—couldn't—accept was his extrapolation.

He was fascinated with her. That had been no act. He of all men would appreciate the irony that he should find her—a woman he'd known from the cradle—so physically enthralling. And despite what he'd said, her age did matter, but not in the way it would matter to the ton. Because she was older and where he was concerned more assured than any other lady he'd seduced, she was more challenging, more demanding of his talents. That, too, he would appreciate.

His fascination was real. Fascination did not, however, lead to marriage.

As he left the girls and, loose-limbed and confident, strode toward her, Alathea drew calm certainty about her. He was an exceptional practitioner of the sensual arts; he knew how to use his talents to pressure her, to cloud her reason. But she knew him too well—far too well—to swallow the tale that fascination was behind his determination to wed her. She thought too much of him—*cared* too much for him—to meekly fall in with his plans.

He reached the gazebo and trod up the steps. Ducking his head beneath the trailing jasmine that covered the small structure, he stepped into the cool shadows. Straightening, he met her gaze. Stillness gripped him. "What?"

Alathea waved him to the sofa beside her. She'd sent a note to Brook Street asking him to call. She waited while he sat; the wicker sofa was small—it left them shoulder to shoulder. He leaned back, stretching one arm along the sofa's back to ease the crowding. She drew breath and resolutely took the bit between her teeth. "There is absolutely no reason for us to wed. *No!*" She cut off his immediate retort. "Hear me out."

He'd tensed; his expression hardened but he held silent.

Alathea looked out over the lawn to where her stepsisters and stepbrothers chattered gaily. "Only you and I know about the countess. Only we know we've been intimate. I'm twenty-nine. As I keep trying to remind everyone, I've set aside all thoughts of marriage. I did so eleven years ago. I'm accepted as a spinster—your recent attentions notwithstanding, there's no expectation that I'll marry. Short of our liaison becoming common knowledge, which it won't for we're both too wise and too aware of what we owe our families and ourselves to bruit the fact abroad, then there's no need whatever for us to wed."

"Is that it?"

"No." She turned her head and met his gaze directly. "Regardless of what you decide is the right thing to do, I will not marry you. There's no reason for you to make such a sacrifice."

He studied her. "Why," he eventually asked, "do you think I want to marry you?"

Her lips twisted. She gestured to her stepsiblings, blissfully unaware of the clouds hovering on the family's horizon. "You want to marry me because of that same quality I counted on when, as the countess, I asked for your aid. I knew if I explained the danger to them, then you'd help. I've told you before—you're obsessively protective." He was her knight on a white charger; protectiveness was his strongest suit, and one of his most basic instincts.

He'd followed her gaze to the girls. "You think I want to marry you to protect you. Out of some notion of chivalry."

She'd tried to avoid that word; it sounded so melodramatic, even if it was the naked truth. Sighing, she faced him. "I wanted to trap you into *helping*—I never intended to trap you into marriage."

Gabriel searched her eyes, hazel pools of absolute sincerity. The vulnerability that had haunted him ever since he'd discovered the countess's identity evaporated.

She didn't know. She had no idea that he worshipped her, that his fascination was obsession, overwhelming and complete. He'd forgotten her naivete, that despite her age, despite knowing him all her life, in certain areas she was an innocent. She didn't know that she was so very different from all who had gone before.

He looked back at Mary and Alice while he mentally scrambled to reorient himself. "At the risk of shattering your illusions, that's not why I want to marry you."

"Why, then?"

He met her gaze. "You can hardly be unaware that I desire you physically."

Color touched her too-pale cheeks. She inclined her head. "Desire in our circles doesn't necessitate marriage."

She looked away, leaving him studying that all-too-revealing line of her jaw. Strength and vulnerability—she was a combination of both.

His reaction to the sight was immediate but no longer surprising—he now knew how primitive his feelings for her were. Last night, when she was fussing over her hair, trying to fashion it into some arrangement that would pass muster, he'd been visited by a violent urge to haul it all down again and march her through the house, past all Lady Richmond's guests, Chillingworth especially, so all would know that she was his.

His.

The powerful surge of possessiveness was achingly familiar. It was the same emotion she'd always evoked in him, the wellspring of that godforsaken tension that had gripped him whenever she was close. The emotion had clarified, crystallized. In unveiling the countess, other veils had been torn aside, too; he could now see his primitive impulse for what it truly was—the instinctive desire to seize his mate. *To Have and To Hold* was the Cynster family motto; hardly surprising he felt the impulse so keenly.

But how much was it safe to reveal to her? "How long have we known each other?"

"Forever—all our lives."

"Weeks ago, you told Chillingworth that our relationship had been decided for us. I agreed. Do you remember?"

"Yes."

"The earliest memory I have of you, you must have been all of two years old. I would have been three. From our cradles, our parents told us we were friends. I was twelve when treating you as a sister started becoming difficult. I never understood why—all I knew was that something was wrong. You knew it, too."

Her "yes" was a whisper; they were both looking back down the years.

"Remember that time we had to slip out of old Collinridge's barn by the back window and your habit got caught on a nail? Lucifer was already mounted, holding the horses—I had to catch your hips and hold you up so you could unhook the material."

He paused; a second later, she reactively shivered.

"Precisely. All that time, it was a peculiar blend of heaven and hell. I could never understand why I always gravitated to your side, always wanted to be near you, because whenever I was close, I felt ... violent. Crazed. As if I wanted to grab hold of you and shake you."

Her laugh was shaky. "I was never certain you wouldn't."

"I never dared. I was too afraid laying hands on you—touching you in any way—would drive me mad, that I would behave like some bedlamite. That one dance we shared was bad enough."

They both gazed blindly over the lawns, then he continued, "What I'm trying to point out is that I've felt … possessive of you for a very long time. I didn't know what the feeling was until after that night at the Burlington, but it isn't something that only recently evolved. It's been there, between us, growing stronger for over twenty years. If our parents hadn't set us up as brother and sister, that feeling would long since have resolved itself in marriage. As it is, your masquerade has opened our eyes and given us a chance to rescript our relationship into what it ought to be." He glanced at her; she was still stubbornly facing the lawn. "I'm more than sexually attracted to you—you're the woman I want as my wife."

She tilted her head. "How many women have you known?"

He frowned. "I don't know. I haven't counted."

She looked at him, one brow high, disbelief in her eyes.

He gritted his teeth. "All right. I did count at first, but I gave up long ago."

"What number did you reach before you stopped counting?"

"*That* is neither here nor there. What point are you trying to make?"

"Merely that you seem to like women but, until now, that liking hasn't prompted you to beat a path to the parson's door. Why now? Why me?"

He saw the trap but was ready to turn the questions to his advantage. "The now is simple—it's time." The fateful words, "*Your time will come,*" resonated in his mind. "I knew that at Demon's wedding. I just didn't know the who. You know how edgy Mama has been getting—much as it pains me to admit it, she's right. It *is* time for me to marry, to settle, to think of the next generation. As for the 'why you,' it isn't, as you seem determined to think, because you're a friend of the family and that because we've been intimate, I think I've ruined you and needs must make reparation."

His increasingly clipped tone had her glancing his way; he trapped her gaze. "What I'm saying is that you are the woman I want as my wife. Just that—I need no other reason." He paused, then continued, "You might have noticed I no longer suffer when I'm close to you. I can sit beside you, more or less at ease, no longer feeling caged to the point of madness, because I know I can take you in my arms and kiss you, that at some point in the not-overly-distant future, you'll lie beneath me again." He let his voice drop. "However, if you're witless enough to try to fight this—all that's between us—if you try to refuse me and smile instead at Chillingworth or any other man, then I can guarantee that what has been between us through the years will be as nothing to what will be."

She held his gaze steadily. "Is that a threat?"

"No. It's a promise."

She considered him, then opened her mouth—

He laid a finger across her lips. "I'm deeply attached to you, you know that. Now I'm no longer blinded and forbidden by preconception, I can admit it. I desire you sexually, but that's only the half of it. I want you because I can think of no other I would rather share my life with. We suit. We could be successful life-partners. We've never been friends, not really, but with the difficulty between us removed, that's another relationship within our reach."

Her eyes searched his—she was marshaling her arguments, still stubbornly resisting for all she was worth.

Releasing her lips, he traced her jaw, then let his hand fall to the sofa back. "Thea, no matter how you struggle to refute it, you know what's between us. It might have been cloaked and veiled for years, but now we've stripped away the disguise, you can see what it is as well as I." He held her gaze. "It's an ardent and undying passion, not just on my part but yours as well."

Alathea looked away. She didn't know what to do. It wasn't just her head that was spinning. His words had evoked so many emotions, so many long-buried needs and barely recognized dreams. But ... drawing herself up, she stated, "You're telling me your emotions are engaged."

"Yes."

"That what's between us demands marriage as its proper state—its necessary outcome."

"Yes."

When she stared into the distance and said nothing more, he prompted, "Well?"

"I'm not sure I believe you." Facing him, she hurried to explain, "*Not* about what's between us so much as why you believe we should marry." She searched his face, then, mentally girding her loins, she spoke bluntly. "We *do* know each other well—*very* well. You claim that the feelings that have always plagued us were due to frustrated desire, that what's between us is that— physical desire—and I accept that that's probably so. You've said that your emotions are engaged and I accept that, too. But what I don't know is: *Which* is the most prominent emotion?"

A scowl formed in his eyes. "Whichever emotion it is that prompts a man to marriage."

"*That's* what I'm afraid of. The emotion that's prompting, pressing, *spurring* you to marry me is the one dominant emotion you possess. You want to protect me. You've made up your mind that the right way forward is via the chapel and you're always successful once you fix your mind on a goal. Unfortunately, in this case, attaining your goal requires my cooperation, so I'm afraid your record of success is about to end."

"You think I made all that up."

"No—I think you were in the main sincere, but I don't believe your conclusions fit your facts. I think you're fudging. And if you want to know whether I think you would lie in pursuit of what you saw as a higher goal, then yes, I think you'd lie through your teeth." With her eyes, she challenged him to deny it.

Lips compressed, he held her gaze intimidatingly, but didn't.

She nodded. "Exactly. We know each other all too well. In creating the countess, I knew precisely what to say, how to pull the right strings to get you to do as I wished. I'm not so puffed up in my own conceit that I imagine you aren't clever enough to do precisely the same to me. You've decided we should marry, so you'll do whatever you need to to bring our marriage about."

He looked at her steadily. She'd expected an immediate reaction, possibly an aggressive one. His silent appraisal unnerved her. She could read nothing of his thoughts in his eyes.

Then he sat up. The arm along the back of the sofa slid about her; his other hand rose to frame her face. A split second and she was held, lightly, in his embrace.

"You're right."

She blinked. Was that a wry smile she saw in his eyes? "About what?"

His gaze lowered to her lips. "That I'll do whatever I must to bring our marriage about."

Alathea mentally cursed. She hadn't meant to phrase it as a challenge. "I—"

"Tell me," he murmured. "Do you accept that what's between us is an 'ardent and undying passion'?"

It was a struggle to draw breath. "Ardent, perhaps, but not undying. Given time, it will fade."

"You're wrong." He leaned closer and brushed her lips with his. The contact was too light to satisfy; all it did was make her hungry, too.

His breath was warm on her throbbing lips. "The ardency that flooded you last night when I filled you …" His lips touched hers again, another achingly incomplete kiss. "The passion that drove you to open yourself to me, to bestow whatever sensual gift I asked for. Do you think those will fade?"

Never. Alathea swayed. Her lids were so heavy, all she could see was his lips moving closer. Her hands, on his lapels, should have held him back; instead, her fingers curled, drawing him nearer. Her wits were drowning in a sea of sensual longing. In the instant before his lips completed her conquest, she managed to whisper, "Yes."

Lips touched, brushed, settled. An instant later, she surrendered on a sigh, giving him her mouth, thrilling to the slow, unhurried claiming. He touched every inch, then deliberately invoked the memory of their joining. Heady passion, ardent longing, had her firmly in their grip when he drew back and whispered against her lips, "Liar."

"Good morning."

Alathea looked up, and only just managed not to gape. "What are you doing here?"

Here was her office, her private, personal domain into which others ventured only by invitation. The room she had retreated to, ostensibly to tally the household accounts, in reality to search for some sure, safe, sensible path through her suddenly shifting world. Since their interlude in the gazebo, she was no longer sure what was real and what mere fanciful imaginings. As she watched Gabriel close the door, she resigned herself to making no progress on that front, not with him in the same small room.

"It occurred to me"—he scanned the room as he strolled toward her—"that with the Season at its zenith, we can expect Crowley to call in his promissory notes in about two weeks." Reaching the desk, he met her gaze. "It's time we started framing our petition to the bench."

"Only two weeks?"

"He won't wait until the very end. He's more likely to draw in his pigeons at the height of the whirl, when the ton provides maximum distraction. I suggest," he said, lowering his long limbs into the armchair facing the desk, "that you summon Wiggs. We'll need his input. I've brought Montague's figures."

Alathea considered him, entirely at his ease in her chair. He smiled at her winningly, his expression studiously mild. With awful calm, she rose and tugged the bell pull. When Crisp answered, she requested him to send for Wiggs. Crisp bowed and departed; she turned back to discover Gabriel eyeing the ledgers on her desk.

"What are you doing?"

"The household accounts."

"Ah." A smile flirted about his lips. "Don't let me disturb you."

Alathea vowed she wouldn't, something much easier said than done. Pen in hand, she forced herself to tally column after column. Despite her intentions, the figures showed a distressing tendency to fade before her eyes. At full stretch, her senses flickered. She bit her lip, clenched her fingers tighter on the pen, and frowned at her neat entries.

"Need any help?"

"No."

She completed three more columns, then carefully looked up. He was watching her, an expression in his eyes she couldn't place. "What?"

He held her gaze, then slowly lifted one brow.

She blushed. "*Go away!* Go and sit in the drawing room."

He grinned. "I'm comfortable here, and the scenery's to my liking."

Alathea glared at him.

The click of the latch had them both turning. Augusta's shining head appeared around the door. "Can I come in?"

Alathea beamed. "Indeed, poppet. But where's Miss Helm?"

"She's helping Mama with the placecards for the dinner." Shutting the door, Augusta came forward, studying Gabriel with the frank gaze of the young.

"You remember Mr. Cynster. His mama and papa live at Quiverstone Manor."

Gabriel lay there, a lazy lion relaxed in the chair, then he held out a hand. "That's a big doll."

Augusta considered, then turned Rose and held her out. "I bet you can't guess her name."

Gabriel took the doll; propping it on one knee, he studied it. "She used to be called Rose."

"She still is!" Augusta followed Rose, clambering onto Gabriel's lap.

As he settled her, he looked up—and met Alathea's astonished stare. He grinned and looked down at Augusta. "Did your sister ever tell you about the time Rose got stuck in that big apple tree at the end of your orchard?"

Alathea watched and listened, amazed that he still remembered all the details, and that Augusta, so often shy, had taken so readily to him. Then again, he did have three much younger sisters; he could probably write the definitive thesis on bewitching young girls.

Seizing opportunity, she quickly finished the accounts, then opened another ledger and settled to check through receipts. The activity used only a small part of her brain; the rest grappled with the problem of Gabriel, and what she could and should do about him. The sound of his deep voice, rumbling low as he charmed Augusta, was familiar and oddly comforting.

Two days had passed since they'd met in the gazebo, two days since she'd last been in his arms with his lips on hers. They'd met that evening at a ball; although he'd claimed two waltzes, he'd claimed nothing more. He'd appeared the next morning to stroll through the park by her side. She'd been ready to counter any possessive move he made, any maneuver to demonstrate his claim over her. He hadn't made one. Unfortunately, the understanding in his eyes warned her that he knew how she felt, how she would react; he was simply biding his time until the battlefield better suited his purpose.

Of that purpose there remained not a smidgen of doubt. Marriage. The notion—not of marriage but of marriage to him—deeply unnerved her. Just thinking of him now unnerved her in a way she'd never had to deal with before. Intimacy, and all the emotions wrapped up with it, had thoroughly disrupted her inner landscape. Yet if he'd allowed her to disappear as she'd planned, to fade out of his life, while she might regret the brevity of their association, she would, she felt sure, have remained inwardly steady.

Instead, she was whirling, her stomach often hollow, uncertainty and excitement an unsettling blend. What she felt for him now she couldn't put a name to—was afraid to put a name to, to even study it at all, not while she had to refuse him.

He'd decided to marry her because he desired her and because he wanted her as his wife. The reason behind that want he'd refused to clarify; she felt sure he was motivated by a compulsion to protect her.

The prospect of him marrying her with protection his true aim chilled her. He would be kind, considerate, generous—even a friend—but as time passed, he would cease to be hers alone. He would cease to be her lover. They would grow apart ...

With a little jerk, she returned to the present, to her office and the ledger open before her, to the rumble of Gabriel's voice and Augusta's piping prattle. Sucking in a breath, she held it, and tidied her pile of receipts.

She was *not* going to marry Gabriel—she couldn't let him sacrifice himself, or her. Turning him from his goal might not be easy, but marrying him would not be right, not for him or for her.

Marking off the last of the receipts, she opened a drawer and placed them in a box, then shut the drawer and shut her ledger. The slap of the pages brought Gabriel's and Augusta's heads up. Alathea smiled. "I have to talk business with Mr. Cynster now, poppet."

Sliding from Gabriel's lap, Augusta gifted her with a confident smile. "He said I could call him Gabriel. It's his name."

"Indeed." Rising and rounding the desk, Alathea hugged Augusta, then set her on her feet. "Off you go now—Miss Helm should be nearly finished."

Ducking around Alathea's skirts, Augusta waved to Gabriel and sang "Good-bye," then happily skipped to the door.

As it shut behind her, Alathea felt long fingers tangle with hers. She turned to discover Gabriel studying her hand, now entwined with his.

"What 'business' do you wish to discuss?" He looked up, invitation in his eyes.

One part of her mind urged her to whisk her hand from his, to whisk herself out of his orbit. The rest of her reveled in the warmth that flooded her as his fingers caressed her palm. Alathea studied the sleepy, languid beckoning in his eyes, and was deceived not at all. She looked at the wall clock. "Wiggs will be another twenty minutes, but we can make a start on a draft without him."

Looking back at Gabriel, she raised a brow and gently detached her hand. He grimaced but let her go. "All right. But you can write." He rose as she resumed her seat behind the desk. "We can start by noting the false claims we've identified."

Unsurprised to find herself his amanuensis, Alathea set a sheet of paper on the blotter. They listed Montague's calculations derived from the figures Crowley had provided Gerrard, comparing them with those Crowley had claimed. Gabriel stated and she transcribed, adding and correcting as they went. He paced back and forth behind her, between the desk and the window, stopping now and then to read over her shoulder. When they reached the end of Montague's findings, Gabriel halted beside her, scanning the list. His hand closed on her shoulder, close by her neck, on skin left bare by her summer morning gown.

His hand nestled there, strong fingers gentle on her skin.

"What next, do you think?"

Her composure shattered, unable to breathe, Alathea heard the mild words and realized with a hot rush horribly akin to mortification that he hadn't meant to discompose her. He'd simply touched her as a close personal friend might, without any sexual intention.

She was the one thinking of sexual intentions.

Before she could gather her wits, he tipped up her face. He studied it; she scrambled wildly to find some expression to mask the truth. Then his gaze turned intent, and she knew it was too late. The fingers at her throat moved again, this time deliberately.

Sensual awareness flared in her eyes. Gabriel saw it. His lips curved. "Perhaps"—he bent over her—"we should try this."

Her lips parted under his; her hand rose to cradle the back of his as he held her face steady. She gave her mouth freely as she always did; he took and drank and claimed. She was a delight in her sweet helplessness, her total inability to conceal her response, the womanly yearning that lay beneath the confidence of her years. Her tongue tangled with his; her fingers gripped his shoulder. Sliding his hand from her face, he lowered it to her breast, cupping the firm mound, then searching for its peak. Her hand followed his, cradling it still, feeling him knead and pleasure her. In one swift movement, he slipped his hand from under hers and reversed their positions, his hand covering and surrounding hers, pressing her palm to the heated flesh of her breast, guiding her fingers to her ruched nipple and squeezing them tight.

She gasped, swayed—

They both heard the creak of a board outside the door an instant before it opened.

Charlie looked in. "Hello!" He nodded to Gabriel, lounging against the window frame, then transferred his gaze to Alathea. "I'm going to Bond Street—Mama suggested I ask whether there's anything more we need for tomorrow night?"

Her pulse pounding, Alathea shook her head, fervently praying that, with her back to the window, Charlie couldn't see the flush heating her skin. "No. Nothing." Their ball would be held tomorrow night, formally introducing Mary and Alice to the ton. "All seems in hand."

"Good-oh! I'll be off then." With a wave, Charlie departed, shutting the door behind him.

Drawing in a much-needed breath, Alathea turned her head and met Gabriel's gaze. She frowned balefully. "*Stop* thinking about it!" Swinging back to the desk, she picked up her pen. "Aside from anything else, there's no lock on that door."

She heard his smothered laugh but refused to look his way. "I think," she said, stabbing the nib into the inkwell, "that next we should note all we've learned about Fangak, Lodwar, and wherever else it was."

He sighed dramatically. "Kingi."

Despite her hopes that all was in hand, the next morning saw a host of small commissions that simply *had* to be fulfilled. Leaving Serena in command, with Crisp and Figgs in their element, Alathea bundled Mary and Alice into the small carriage and escaped.

"It's a madhouse!" Face to the window, Alice peered back to where the red carpet was being shaken and swept. "If they put that out now, it'll be a mess by evening."

"Crisp will see to it." Alathea sank back against the squabs and closed her eyes. She'd been up since daybreak, and had already met with the caterers and the florist. All the major components for the evening were thankfully falling into place. Opening her eyes, she scanned the list she clutched in one hand. "Gloves first, stockings next, and then the ribbons."

*   *   *

The carriage bore them home an hour and a half later. Mary and Alice were bubbling with excitement; Alathea watched them with joy in her heart. No matter how tiring the day might be, tonight would be its own reward.

As they turned into Mount Street, she glanced out of the window—and saw Jeremy's head almost in line with hers. "What ...?"

Jerking forward, she stared, then leaned out of the window the better to view her youngest brother, laughing uproariously, arms flailing, seated atop a pedestrian curricle propelled full tilt down the pavement by Charlie and Gabriel.

She forebore to scream.

The carriage pulled up before their front steps. Mary and Alice tumbled out, paused but an instant to view Jeremy and company, then giggled and ran indoors.

Alathea descended from the carriage more slowly, then drew herself up and waited for the miscreants to arrive before her. They did so in an ungainly rush; for one instant she watched, horrified, expecting to see her worst nightmare unfold as, hauled to a halt, the unstable contraption slewed sideways, tipping Jeremy off the high seat—

Reaching forward, Gabriel caught him, swinging him clear, then setting him on his feet while Charlie neatly righted the curricle. Charlie and Gabriel grinned at her—Jeremy did his best to appear inconspicuous.

Alathea fixed her gaze on him. "I believe I had your promise on no account to ride this machine in town?"

Eyes downcast, Jeremy squirmed.

Gabriel heaved a sigh. "It was my fault."

Alathea looked at him. "Yours?"

"I arrived just as your footman was taking delivery and offered to show them how it was done."

"*You* rode it?"

The look he bent on her was dismissively superior. "Of course. It's easy. Would you like me to demonstrate?"

She nearly said yes. The notion of seeing him, hideously elegant as always, precariously perched on the awkward machine riding up and down the tonnish street was almost too good to pass up. But ... "No." She transferred her gaze to Jeremy. "That's not the point."

"Ah, but it is, because once I'd ridden to the corner, I simply put Jeremy on the seat and told him to hang on. It didn't occur to me that the machine had been bought for him but that he'd been forbidden to ride it."

Alathea caught the swift upward glance Jeremy shot her. She pressed her lips together, then explained, "The agreement I used to gain Serena's approval to buy the curricle was that Jeremy would only ride it on the lawns at the Park. He's prone to broken bones—to date, we've survived three broken arms and a broken leg. A collarbone in three pieces would never be welcome, but it would be even less welcome *today*."

Jeremy glanced up again; Alathea caught his eye. "You are extremely lucky that it was I who took Mary and Alice to the shops, and not your mama—she would have swooned had she seen your performance."

Jeremy shuffled his feet, but his eyes sparkled. A small smile played on his lips, just waiting to dawn. "But she didn't see it—you did. Wasn't it *grand*?" His smile broke free.

Alathea twisted her lips in an effort to hold back her own. "Potentially grand—you could do with a bit of practice, but don't you *dare* ride it here again."

"What about the back lawn?" Charlie asked. "That's thick—he wouldn't break anything if he fell on that."

"It's got a nice slope to it, too," Gabriel put in. "And I promise I won't let him career into the rhododendrons."

Faced with three male faces ranging in age from twelve to thirty but all with the same little-boy-pleading expression, Alathea threw up her hands. "Very well—I'll go and prepare Serena." She caught Gabriel's eye as she turned to the steps. "At least it'll keep you all out from under our feet."

His grin would have done his namesake proud.

Leaving them wheeling the curricle around to the back gate, Alathea crossed the threshold and entered a world of pandemonium. She first sought out Serena and reassured her of Jeremy's safety, embroidering on Gabriel's promise without a second thought as soon as she realized Serena was happy to place her trust in him.

For the next hour she was fully occupied dealing with queries from the caterers, the florist, and most importantly the draper. Her novel idea to decorate the huge ballroom with swaths of cerulean blue muslin, which could later be given as presents to the female servants here and at the Park, had been given form and style by the earnest young draper—the white-and-gilt ballroom looked like a vision of heaven.

"Perfect." With a brisk nod, she turned away from the sight. "Please send in your account promptly, Mr. Bobbins—we will only be in town for another few weeks."

Mr. Bobbins bowed low, incoherently assuring her that his account would be presented forthwith.

Alathea checked the supplies of salmon and shrimp with Figgs, then she and Crisp descended to the cellar. By the time they'd finished selecting the wines for the formal dinner preceding the ball, it was past noon. Retiring to her office, intending to do no more than catch her breath and check her lists for the next most pressing item, Alathea found herself drawn to the window.

On the lawn behind the house, Jeremy, Charlie and Gabriel were totally absorbed in the new toy. Gabriel had stripped off his coat; together with Charlie, he was coaching Jeremy in the difficult process of gaining his balance on the awkward machine. Alathea watched, quietly amazed at the patience Gabriel showed. None knew better than she that he was naturally impatient, yet in dealing with Jeremy he displayed both tact and steady encouragement, exactly what Jeremy needed. Under Gabriel's eye, he bloomed. Before she turned away, Alathea saw him free-wheel down the lawn, managing to steer the curricle away from the thick bushes.

As she left her office and plunged back into the melee, she reflected that, while he was not long on patience, Gabriel's second name could have been persistence, a fact she would do well to remember.

Half an hour later, he found her supervising the positioning of the trestles in the parlor they were converting into a supper room. Surveying the scene, he raised his brows. "How many cards did you send out?"

"Five hundred," Alathea absentmindedly replied. "God knows how we'll manage if they all arrive at once."

Gabriel studied her face, then calmly took her arm. Ignoring her resistance and her distracted scowl, he towed her to the side of the room. "Where's the petition."

"The petition?" She stared at him. "You can't mean to work on that *now*?"

"*I* can work on it. I can write, you know." Her frown suggested she wasn't convinced of it; he ignored that, too. "I'll take it home and continue framing our arguments." He glanced at the footmen and maids scurrying frantically about. "It's too noisy here."

She didn't look happy, but nodded. "It's in the top drawer of my desk."

"I'll take it." Gabriel started to leave, then halted. Ignoring the many about them, he caught her chin. "*Don't* run yourself ragged. I'll see you at dinner."

Before she could react, he ducked his head, kissed her quickly, and left. "Lady Alathea—is this where you wanted this table?"

"What? Oh ... yes, I suppose ..." Inwardly grinning, Gabriel headed downstairs.

CHAPTER
Seventeen

The formal dinner preceding a come-out ball was, in social terms, even more important than the ball itself. The earl, Serena, and Alathea had agreed that this dinner should be the most glittering affair regardless of cost, one by which the assembled leaders of the ton would remember the Morwellans. Alathea had personally overseen every detail, from the guest list Serena had organized and the stiff white stationery on which the invitations had been inscribed, to the gleaming crystal, the silver service, the Meissen dinner service, and the crisp white damask. The dishes in all twelve courses had been carefully chosen to complement one another in a parade of culinary delight. The wine was superb. Not one of the fifty guests seated about the long table would entertain the slightest suspicion of the economies normally practiced at Morwellan House.

From her seat midway down the table, Alathea watched the sixth course being laid out. All was proceeding smoothly, the babel prevailing on all sides—conversations, laughter, the constant clink of porcelain and silverware—a reassuring testament. Her father, presiding over the event from the table's head, looked magnificent; Serena, resplendent in navy silk at the other end, was his match. Opposite Alathea, spread between their guests, Mary and Alice conversed with simple charm. Charlie was seated farther along the table to her right. All three were dressed to perfection, each a paragon of tonnish expectations. In her amber silk gown, a beaded cap perched atop her coiffed hair, Alathea contributed her part to their sartorial facade.

Her heart lifted as she gazed about her. They'd done it—they'd come to London and, despite the difficulties, claimed their rightful place in society. As if to illustrate their success, Sally Jersey caught her eye and smiled and nodded. Seated further along, Princess Esterhazy had already regally signaled her approval. Only as she followed Sally Jersey's gaze to Serena did it occur to Alathea to wonder what it was both patronnesses were complimenting *her* upon. Their appreciation of the dinner and company they conveyed to Serena, of course. So what was it she'd done to attract their approbation?

She turned to Gabriel, seated on her left. She'd been so absorbed with the dinner itself she hadn't registered his appearing at her side to escort her into the dining room as anything odd. She'd grown accustomed to having him near, to resting her hand on his arm and letting him steer her through crowds. It wasn't until she'd caught Lucifer's questioning look halfway through the fourth course that she'd realized. One glance at Celia's face, at her intrigued expression, confirmed that their sudden penchant for each other's company had not escaped notice.

The suspicion that their ease in each other's company was not escaping *anyone's* notice suddenly assailed her. Before she had a chance to frame the question: "Did you plan this?" in any form likely to get an answer, Gabriel glanced at her and saw the frown in her eyes.

"Relax. Everything's going well." He indicated a dish of game. "This is excellent—what's in the sauce?"

Alathea looked at the dish. "Muscat grapes and pomegranate syrup." There was no point wrangling over how he'd come to be sitting beside her. He was there. She might as well take advantage. "How's the petition?"

He shrugged noncommittally. "We've made a good start."

"But not enough to be certain of a favorable judgment."

His lips twisted; he didn't answer.

Alathea forged on, her tone barely a whisper as she considered a dish before her. "Everything we have is open to argument—there's nothing cut and dried, no absolute and obvious falsehood. All our claims rely on the word of others, others we can't call on to verify the facts. Without a bona fide witness—without Captain Struthers—all Crowley need do is deny our claims. The burden of proof will rest on us." She helped herself to beans in white sauce and passed the dish along. "We have to find the captain, don't we?"

Gabriel glanced at her. "The case would be certain with him. Without him, it's going to be difficult."

"There must be something more we can do."

Again she felt his gaze on her face. "We'll find him." Beneath the table his hand closed about hers. His thumb stroked her palm. "But tonight, enjoy your success. Leave the captain and Crowley for tomorrow."

Unable to meet his eyes, she nodded and prayed her blush didn't show. His hand wrapped around hers had evoked a sensual memory of his body wrapped around hers, stroking hers ... When his hand slid away, she determinedly lifted her head and drew a steadying breath, looking along the table rather than at him.

"I take it Esher and Carstairs are both in earnest?"

Alathea refocused on Mary. Beside her, Lord Esher was quietly and persistently attentive, Mary sweetly appreciative. A similar scenario was playing out toward the other end of the table, where Mr. Carstairs sat beside Alice. "We believe so. Their parents were clearly pleased to be invited tonight." With a nod, Alathea indicated Lady Esher and Mrs. Carstairs; their husbands were farther down the table.

Gabriel followed her gaze, then transferred his attention to the dish she passed him. "Esher has a neat little property in Hampshire. He does well, and pays attention to his land. He's a likable chap with a sense of humor, but sensible and steady. From all I can gather, he's in a position to please himself—I doubt he'll cavil over Mary's lack of dowry."

"She does have a dowry."

"She does?" He hesitated, then asked, "How much?"

Alathea calmly told him.

"Just enough to ensure not even the most censorious raise a brow. You have covered all the cracks."

She inclined her head.

"Well, if Esher's unlikely to be concerned about money, Carstairs is even less likely to give it a second thought. While Esher's old money, well established, Carstairs is both old and new. They met at Eton and have been firm friends ever since, which should suit Mary and Alice admirably."

"They are very close."

"Carstairs's estate is just south of Bath—within easy visiting distance of Morwellan Park. His maternal grandfather had an interest in shipping, which Carstairs inherited. He's gaining a reputation as having a cautious interest in the right sort of ventures. He's ambitious in that area, and not about to become a silent partner."

The approval in his tone was clear; Alathea shot him a glance. "A useful contact for you, perhaps?"

Gabriel met her gaze. "Perhaps."

"How did you find out all this—about Carstairs and Esher?"

"I asked around. Quietly. I didn't think your father would have the right contacts to find out for you."

"He hasn't." Alathea hesitated, then inclined her head. "Thank you."

She looked away, along the table, ostensibly scanning the guests, in reality letting her gratitude flare, then fade. The reprobate beside her—he who knew her far too well—needed no encouragement. She tried not to dwell on how much easier her life was with him beside her, supplying the reassurances she needed but could not gain for herself. Having his shoulder to lean on was a far too seductive proposition.

Her wandering gaze reached Lucifer, sipping his wine, his gaze on her and Gabriel. His expression was quietly considering.

Smiling serenely, Alathea let her gaze wander on, only to encounter more considering glances. It took her a few minutes to realize why Gabriel and she were so persistently raising questions in so many minds. It was the way they conversed with each other. They were so attuned to each other's tone, to every nuance in the other's repertoire, that they rarely needed to look at each other to be sure of the other's meaning. They talked as two who knew each other well, as two who, in the ton's parlance, shared an understanding of long duration.

They talked like long-standing lovers.

The last course was being removed before she again turned to Gabriel. All the guests were repairing directly to the ballroom. He was already standing; he offered her his arm. She placed her hand on his sleeve and allowed him to raise her—as soon as she was on her feet, he grasped her hand, tucked it in his arm, his hand possessively over hers, and led her to join the queue exiting the dining room.

The message he was sending the interested observers all about them was crystal clear. Although he could be devilish enough when he wished, she was certain that, at present, he wasn't deliberately putting on a show. His behavior was simply an instinctive extension of how he now felt about her.

He caught her glancing at him and lifted a brow. "What?"

She looked into his hazel eyes, then, lips curving, shook her head and looked away. "Never mind."

There was no chance she could get him to change and, deep down, she knew she would miss their newfound closeness if he did.

The ballroom caused a sensation. Standing in the receiving line Alathea fielded numerous compliments on the unusual decor while helping Mary and Alice greet the more intimidating dowagers. Unfortunately, more than a few of the old battleships, when distracted from Mary and Alice, were only too ready to turn their cannons on her.

"Absolutely criminal," Lady Osbaldestone declared, scrutinizing her silk-clad figure through her lorgnette. "Waste, gel, *waste!*" One bony finger poked her in the ribs. "God knows *why* you've hidden yourself away, but it's past time some rake rattled your stays."

Others took a different tack.

"So, my dear, do you spend much time in charitable works?" Lady Harcourt, of similar age to Alathea, smiled insincerely. "It must be so nice to live a quiet life."

Alathea responded to all such queries with a serene smile and calm assurance. As soon as the incoming tide eased, Gabriel appeared and, with Serena's encouragement, drew her out of the line.

"But Mary and Alice—"

"Serena's with them. There's someone I want you to meet."

"Who?"

His Great-aunt Clara was a sweet old lady, although a trifle vague. She patted Alathea's hand. "Your sisters are lovely, dear, but we'll have to see you wed first."

"Precisely what I've been telling her," Gabriel put in.

Over Clara's head, Alathea narrowed her eyes at him.

"Indeed, yes," Clara said, and patted her hand again. "We'll have to find some nice gentleman for you—perhaps that nice Chillingworth boy."

The look on Gabriel's face was priceless; Alathea only just managed not to laugh. "I don't think so," she said, smiling at Clara.

"No? Well, then, let's see. Who else?"

Devil strolled up before Clara could consider other options. She released Alathea to clutch his sleeve. "Is Honoria here?"

Devil grinned. "She's on the other side of the room—I'll take you to her if you like."

"Oh, yes—so kind." Clutching her shawl with one hand and Devil with the other, Clara smiled in farewell and moved on.

"There are the Carmichaels." Gabriel directed Alathea's gaze to a couple whose country estate lay not far from Morwellan Park and the Manor. They headed toward them.

For the next twenty minutes, they moved through the ever-increasing crowd, stopping here then there to chat, always at Gabriel's direction. Only when she spied Lord Montgomery, then Lord Falworth through the sea of heads did Alathea realize what he was doing. With them constantly moving from one conversation to the next, her court was given no chance to gather about her.

Alathea swallowed her protest—she'd rather move through the crowd on Gabriel's arm than stand surrounded by her all-too-often vacuous court. Feigning ignorance of his high-handed manuverings was definitely the sensible course.

Then the musicians started up and the crowd magically parted, clearing a wide space. As both Mary and Alice had been given permission to indulge long since, the first dance was a waltz. Keen to see if her expectation that Esher would partner Mary and Carstairs would partner Alice would be fulfilled, Alathea eagerly accompanied Gabriel to the edge of the floor.

Sure enough, Mary and Esher took to the floor first, Mary blushing delightedly, her smile declaration enough, while Esher looked the picture of pride. Alathea smiled mistily as they waltzed past, then looked back up the room. Alice was already in Carstairs's encircling arms—both seemed lost in each other's eyes, oblivious to the crowd looking on.

Alathea sighed. With her sisters, her hand was played and she'd won—they would have the futures she'd wanted for them, and which they patently deserved. They'd be happy, and loved …

Alice and Carstairs waltzed past.

The next instant, Alathea, too, was on the floor, whirling in Gabriel's arms. Her eyes flew wide. There were as yet no other couples on the floor. "What?…"

Gabriel raised a brow. "My dance, I believe?"

She would have loved to tell him what she thought of his arrogance, but under the curious eyes of half the ton, all she could do was fix a smile on her lips and let him sweep her away. She did, however, glare at him.

He only smiled, gathering her closer as other couples took to the floor in their wake. He leaned closer as they went through the turn. "Don't tempt me."

The whispered words caressed her ear; Alathea shivered. "I should take umbrage."

"But you won't. You know I can't help myself."

She limited her response to a sniff; prolonging such a conversation would do nothing for her serenity. The nagging observation that she enjoyed waltzing with him, enjoyed the feel of his hand burning through the silk at her back, enjoyed the sense of being captive to his strength, whirled so effortlessly around the room, was more than distracting enough.

That her pleasure in life was increasingly dependent on him was a thought she wished she'd never had.

After the dance, they once more meandered through the crowd, chatting with acquaintances. They were leaving one group when Gerrard Debbington hailed Gabriel. Gabriel stopped; sidestepping this way, then that, Gerrard eventually reached them.

He smiled vaguely at Alathea.

She smiled brightly back, completely forgetting that she hadn't met him in the receiving line. "Hello."

Gabriel pinched her fingers and introduced them. Alathea continued to smile as if she commonly spoke to gentlemen she'd never met. Gerrard, thankfully, was too well brought up to comment.

He looked at Gabriel. "If I could have a word ... there's something you should know."

Gabriel gestured to Alathea. "Thea knows of my interests—she knows of Crowley. You can speak freely."

"Oh." Gerrard's smile hid his surprise. "In that case ... I was leaving Tattersalls yesterday when I literally bumped into Crowley. He was with a gentleman Vane said was Lord Douglas. Unfortunately, Vane and Patience were right behind me, and Patience spoke. From what she said, it was obvious she was my sister." He grimaced. "Only a sister would say something like that. As she was on Vane's arm, it wouldn't need any great intelligence to guess the connection. Vane said I should tell you and ask what you think."

"I think," Gabriel said, "that we should discuss the possibilities with Vane." He looked over the sea of heads. "Where is he?"

"Far left," Gerrard said, craning his head. "Close by the wall. Patience was with him."

Alathea spotted the purple plume Patience Cynster wore in her hair. "There—by the second mirror."

They headed that way but in tacking through the crowd, Gerrard forged ahead. Gabriel drew Alathea closer. "I need to talk to Vane about this— Gerrard could be in danger."

Alathea glanced at him, concern in her eyes. "From Crowley?"

"Yes. I need you to distract Patience while I talk to Vane."

"Why can't you talk about the matter in front of Patience? Gerrard is *her* brother, after all."

"That's why. And in case it's escaped your notice, Patience is increasing, so Vane will certainly not want her worrying over a threat to Gerrard that we're going to ensure never materializes."

"So you want me to distract her? To connive at keeping her in the dark over something she has a perfect right to know—" Alathea broke off, another idea overriding all thought of Patience's sisterly rights. "Tell me—if there was any threat to Charlie or Jeremy, would you tell me, or make sure I never heard of it?"

The way Gabriel's lips sealed into a thin line was answer enough. She narrowed her eyes at him. "Men! Why on earth you imagine—"

"Just tell me—who wants Crowley stopped?"

Alathea blinked. "I do."

"And who did you ask to stop him?"

"You."

"I vaguely recall stipulating that you had to obey my orders."

"Yes, but—"

"Thea, stop arguing. I need to talk to Vane and I don't want Patience unnecessarily upset."

Put like that ... "Oh, very well." She threw him a stern look. "But I don't approve."

They drew free of the crowd and advanced on Vane and Patience. With an assured smile, Alathea drew Patience aside; Gabriel hid a smile as he overheard her ask after Patience's condition. The perfect topic, the perfect excuse to exclude the menfolk from their councils.

The males in question quickly formed their own huddle.

"What do you think?" Vane asked.

"Altogether too dangerous. Crowley would have prised it out of Archie Douglas before they'd got to the first ring." Gabriel looked at Vane. "I take it Archie was sufficiently *compos mentis* to recognize you?"

"Definitely—he was remarkably sober, but then it was before noon."

Gabriel looked at Gerrard. "Nothing for it then—we've got to get you out of sight."

Gerrard shrugged. "I could go home to Derbyshire for a bit."

"No—too far. You have to be within reach of London and the courts. We'll need you as a witness to corroborate the details of the company's proposal to investors."

"How do you think Crowley will react?" Vane asked.

"I think," Gabriel replied, "that he'll pause and take stock. He's been in this game too long to act rashly. And he's very close to calling in his notes. I think he'll reason that Gerrard will have consulted me *after* the meeting—there's no reason he should suspect I knew anything about the meeting beforehand. Indeed, if Gerrard had mentioned one of Crowley's schemes to me *ahead* of any meeting, I would have advised against the meeting taking place. So he'll imagine I was consulted afterward, and that I've advised Gerrard against the investment. He hasn't heard from Gerrard again, and now he'll know why. He's so close to getting his hands on a small fortune, he'll be very hesitant over unnecessarily rocking his boat. I don't think he'll come searching for Gerrard yet, but I do think he will, and with a vengeance, the instant he hears there's a petition lodged against the company."

"How dangerous is he?"

Gabriel met Vane's gaze. "He'll kill without a qualm." Vane's brows rose. Gabriel continued, "The information I've received suggests he's plowed every last penny into this venture—if the company's notes fail, he'll be ruined. And he'll likely have some rather unsavory and irate creditors after him, too. Basically, I'd rate Crowley as more dangerous than a rabid rat cornered."

"Hmm." Vane's gaze shifted to his wife, chatting animatedly with Alathea three feet away. "I'm concerned about Patience. She seems rather pale, don't you think?"

Gabriel considered the bloom of health blushing Patience's fair cheeks. "Definitely peaked."

"A short sojourn in Kent would be just the thing to restore her. Fresh air, sunshine—"

"Scores of your workers in the fields surrounding the manor. Just what the doctor ordered." Gabriel swung to Gerrard, who had listened in silence. "Of course, as a dutiful brother, you'll accompany your sister into the country."

Gerrard grinned. "Whatever you say—I can sketch there as well as here."

Vane gestured to Patience and Alathea. "Shall we break the news?"

Ten minutes later, Gabriel and Alathea stepped once more into the crowd. Alathea smiled. "That was very thoughtful of Vane to be so concerned over Patience, even if there is no need. She's perfectly well."

"Yes, well, husbands have to do what husbands have to do, especially when they're Cynsters." Gabriel glanced at her. "Did you learn anything useful?"

"We were talking about pregnancy."

"I know."

Alathea took one more step, froze, then whirled on him. "What do you—? You don't—?"

He opened his eyes wide. "Don't what?" The musicians started up. Sliding one arm about her waist, he drew her to him, into his arms, onto the floor.

Staring straight over his shoulder, Alathea drew in a tight breath. Ignoring the color burning her cheeks, she categorically stated, "I am *not* pregnant."

His deep sigh feathered the curls about her ear. "Ah, well, one lives in hope."

His hand moved on her back in soothing little circles. Alathea bit her lip against a sudden compulsion to blurt out the truth—that she didn't know if she was or not. She was not, definitely not, going to talk about such things with him. Especially not with him.

"You will be pregnant with my child one day—you know that, don't you?"

She shut her eyes—tried to shut her ears to the words but they kept falling, straight into her mind, her heart, her empty, yearning soul.

"You love children—you want children of your own. I'll give you as many as you like."

They circled, neither paying any attention to the dance, moving to a tune heard on a different plane.

"You want to have my child—I want that, too. It'll happen one day, Thea— trust me, it will."

She shivered. To her immense relief he said nothing more but simply steered her around the floor. By the time the music ended and he released her, she'd regained her mental feet. She did not, however, meet his eyes; instead, she scanned the room. "I should check with Serena—"

"Everything's fine—she told me to keep you from worrying."

That had her searching his face. "She didn't."

"She did, and you know a gentleman should do everything in his power to satisfy his hostess."

Her pithy retort was cut off by the descent of Lord and Lady Collinridge, the neighbors who owned the old barn with the narrow back window. The Collinridges had known them both from childhood but hadn't met Gabriel for years; with a sweet smile, Alathea encouraged Lady Collinridge to twit her tormentor for all she was worth.

In the end, Gabriel invented a summons from his mother to escape, taking her with him.

"Jezebel," he whispered as they made their way through the crush, now as bad—as good—as any ball that Season. "You enjoyed that."

"You deserved that," Alathea retorted. A sudden press of bodies brought them to a temporary standstill, him behind her.

"Hmm—and what else do I deserve?"

Alathea swallowed a gasp as one large hand slid over her hip to perform a leisurely, all-too-knowing circuit of her silk-clad bottom.

Closing his hand, Gabriel lowered his head and whispered in her ear, "Perhaps you'd like to retreat to your office—I was, after all, ordered by your stepmother to do my very best to keep you amused."

Alathea couldn't resist the urge to tip her head back and meet his eyes. Under their heavy lids, they glowed with golden fire. There was absolutely no doubt of what he was thinking.

Her gaze dropped to his lips. Did temptation come any more potent than this?

The crush about them eased, and she managed to draw breath. "There's no lock on my office door, remember?"

She'd spoken before she'd thought—her cheeks flamed. The wicked chuckle he gave made her think of a buccaneer about to seize her, but his hand left her bottom—her fevered flesh—closing briefly, affectionately, on her hip before he released her. The flow of people resumed and they moved on.

Almost immediately they encountered Lady Albemarle, a distant Cynster connection, and stopped to chat. From her, they passed on to Lady Horatia Cynster.

"I have no idea," she responded to Gabriel's query, "if Demon and Felicity will return to town before the end of the Season. They're enjoying themselves hugely by all accounts. The last we heard, they were in Cheltenham."

They chatted easily for some minutes, then once again moved on. When the next lady with whom they paused to exchange greetings proved to be another Cynster connection, Alathea had to wonder. It was true there were a lot of Cynsters and many more family connections. Nevertheless ...

As they strolled on again, she caught Gabriel's eye. "You're not, by any chance, introducing me to your family?"

"Of course not—they already know you. And those who don't were introduced to you in the receiving line."

Alathea sighed exasperatedly. The look in his eyes, the set of his jaw, warned her any protest would be fruitless—his intention was fixed. The reins were presently in his hands and he was driving as hard as he could toward matrimony. She shook her head. "You're impossible!"

His lips quirked. "No. *You're* impossible. I'm merely immovable."

She tried to smother her giggle but failed.

"Lady Alathea!" Lord Falworth pushed through the crowd to bow before her. "Dear lady, I've been searching quite doggedly, I do assure you." He shot a censorious glance at Gabriel. "But now I've found you, I believe a cotillion is starting. If you would do me the honor?"

Alathea smiled. For all his foppish tendencies, Falworth was an amiable gentleman and an unexceptional partner. "Indeed, sir—it is I who would be honored." It was, perhaps, time she put some distance between herself and her self-styled keeper. "If you'll excuse me, Mr. Cynster?" With a nod for Gabriel, she placed her hand on Falworth's sleeve and let him lead her to where the sets were forming.

As soon as the dance started, her thoughts reverted to Gabriel, Falworth forgotten. No other gentleman could vie with her nemesis. There was—and very likely always had been—only one man for her, the man she'd been closest to all her life. And now he wanted to marry her. He cared for her, but not in a way she could accept as a safe basis for marriage. What she should do—how she could take charge of the situation and steer a safe course for them both—she had no idea. With every day that passed, the pressure to give in, to surrender and be his wife, grew.

Her one bulwark against that was simple but solid. Fear. An unconquerable, unquenchable fear of a pain so vast, so deep, she'd never be able to survive it. A pain she sensed rather than knew, one she could imagine but had never felt. The sort of pain that no sane person invited or permitted to threaten them.

That much she knew: She was too afraid to ever consent to their marriage if all he felt for her, bar transient desire, was mild affection and a duty of care.

As she circled and swayed through the figures of the cotillion, she considered that truth, and the fact that it meant she would never bear his child.

She would never, ever, have children of her own.

But that had been decided eleven years ago. Fate had yet to revoke her decree.

From the side of the dance floor, Gabriel watched as Alathea gracefully twirled. She was thinking of something, something other than the cotillion—there was a distance in her gaze, a closed calmness in her expression that meant she was mentally elsewhere. He was certain she was thinking about him. He wanted her to think of him, but … he had a strong suspicion that her thinking at present was not following the lines he wished. His instincts prodded him to press her, to seize her however he might. Some other emotion—a stronger emotion—warned him the decision was hers. And he knew just how easy she was to influence.

At present, his campaign was mired in circumstance and his quarry was proving elusive. Every time he thought he had her in his grasp, she drew away, hazel eyes wide, slightly puzzled, not convinced.

Nowhere near convinced enough to marry him.

That fact left him feeling caged and not the least bit civilized every time she moved away from his side. There was no convenient wall against which he could lean and guard her, so he prowled the edge of the cleared area, unwilling to be waylaid by any of the ladies intent on catching his eye.

He was successful in avoiding all the encroaching madams, but he couldn't avoid Chillingworth. The earl loomed directly in his path.

Their gazes clashed. By mutual accord, they swung so they stood shoulder to shoulder, gazing over the dance floor.

"I'm surprised," Chillingworth drawled, "that you haven't tired of this game."

"Which game is that?"

"The game of knight-protector, keeping the rest of us at bay." Chillingworth's gaze raked his face. "Being such a close friend of the family's, I can understand why you might feel compelled by the notion, but don't you think you're carrying the role a little far?"

"Now why, I wonder, should that so concern *you*?" Even as he asked the question, Gabriel felt an icy tingle at his nape.

"I would have thought that obvious, dear boy." Chillingworth gestured toward the dancers, careful not to indicate Alathea specifically. "She's an attractive proposition, particularly to one situated as I."

Every word deepened the chill now steadily coursing Gabriel's veins. The uninformed might imagine Chillingworth meant he was considering seducing Alathea because he was presently amorously free. Gabriel knew better. The earl was of their class, from the same social stratum as the Bar Cynster; he was their contemporary in every way. He abided by the same unwritten code Gabriel himself had honored all his adult life. Ladies of good family and good character were not fair game.

Alathea was unmistakeably both. Seducing her was not what Chillingworth had in mind.

His expression impassive, Gabriel looked over the dancers, his gaze fixing on Alathea's face. "She's not for you."

"Indeed?" Challenge rang in Chillingworth's tone. "I realize this may come as a surprise, especially to a Cynster, but the lady herself will ultimately be the judge of that."

"No." Gabriel uttered the word quietly, yet it held enough latent force to make Chillingworth tense. And wait.

Gabriel saw the danger clearly. Chillingworth was Devil's age but had yet to marry. He needed an heir, and for that he needed a wife. He could appreciate Chillingworth's taste in being attracted to Alathea; he was not, however, of a mind to approve.

Alathea loved him, but whether she knew that, or accepted it, he didn't know. She was headstrong and willful, used to charting her own course. She also had that streak of considered recklessness he'd always found alarming. He could never predict what it might lead her to do. She was finding coming to terms with the notion of marrying him difficult. If Chillingworth offered for her hand, might she accept to escape the impasse he'd created?

Despite loving him—or even because of it—might she think to set him free of the chivalric bonds she imagined compelled him by marrying Chillingworth instead?

Over the heads of the other dancers, Gabriel considered Alathea, and knew he couldn't risk it. She felt friendly toward Chillingworth. The earl could be charming when he wished and was, after all, a gentleman in the same mold as he. And Alathea was an earl's daughter. It would be a felicitous match all around.

Except for one thing.

Turning to Chillingworth, Gabriel met his gaze. "If you're imagining rectifying your lack of an heir through an alliance with the Morwellans, I suggest you think again."

Chillingworth stiffened; the look in his eyes suggested he could barely believe his ears. "And why is that?" he asked, his tone steely, his aggression poorly masked.

"Because," Gabriel said, "you would die before you laid so much as a finger on the lady in question, which might make getting your heir a trifle difficult."

Chillingworth stared at him, then looked away, resuming his previously noncombative stance. "I can't," he murmured, "quite believe you said that."

"I meant every word."

"I know." Chillingworth's lips quirked. "How enlightening."

"Just as long as you keep it in mind."

Chillingworth looked to where, the dance having ended, Alathea was strolling on Falworth's arm. Both he and Gabriel stepped out to intercept her. "I'll think about it," Chillingworth replied.

Alathea could not believe how easily Gabriel tracked her through the crowd; she and Lord Falworth had barely begun to stroll before he loomed from the throng. She was, consequently, especially delighted to see Chillingworth by his side.

"My lord." She gave Chillingworth her hand and smiled with real appreciation as he bowed. "I hope you note I took your comments to heart. I could do nothing about the number of guests, but there are many waltzes scheduled tonight."

Chillingworth sighed. "What manner of torture is that, my dear? I assume that, as usual, you have no waltzes free."

Alathea did not miss his sidelong glance at Gabriel. "Unfortunately not."

"However," Chillingworth continued, "unless my ears deceive me, that's a country dance starting up. Might I beg the pleasure of your company?"

Alathea smiled. "I would be delighted."

The dance was one that left them paired throughout. Chillingworth conversed easily on general topics. Alathea answered lightly, off the top of her head, her thoughts, as always, sliding back to Gabriel. She'd lost sight of him when the dance got under way; he was no longer where they'd left him. She wondered where he was, and what he was doing.

At the conclusion of the dance, she laid her hand on Chillingworth's sleeve. He led her from the floor, straight to Gabriel, who was waiting at the other end of the ballroom from where they'd parted.

Alathea resisted an urge to raise her eyes to the skies. Drawing her hand from Chillingworth's arm, she positioned herself between them, ready to jab an elbow into either of their ribs should they infringe her conversational standards.

Somewhat to her surprise, neither did. Chillingworth seemed careful, watchful. Gabriel was his usual arrogant self, the reality uncloaked given it was only Chillingworth, whom he patently regarded as an equal, with them. Then Amanda, escorted by Lord Rankin, joined them. A minute later, Amelia glided up on Lord Arkdale's arm.

"This is such a lovely ball, Lady Alathea." Amanda beamed her delight. "I'm enjoying myself hugely." The minx batted her long lashes at Rankin, who, all unknowingly, glowed.

"It's a crush—a positive crush," Amelia chimed in. "There are so many here." She smiled at Lord Arkdale. "Why, I've never had the chance to chat with Freddie here, before."

"I hope," Alathea cut in, preempting Gabriel, "that you're wise enough to take full advantage of the possibilities offered."

"Oh, indeed," Amanda assured her. "Our dance cards are full. We've danced every dance with a different gentleman."

"And spent every interval with still different gentlemen," Amelia added. Both girls softened the news of their deliberate inconstancy with a ravishing smile at their escorts. Neither gentleman was sure whether to preen or not.

"Incidentally, Gabriel, we haven't sighted Lucifer."

Amanda fixed her angelic blue eyes on her cousin's face.

"Is he here?"

"He was."

"He must have discovered something terribly interesting. Or someone," Amelia ingenuously announced.

"I saw Lady Scarsdale, and Mrs. Sweeney, too. She was wearing vermillion—a hideous shade. I don't think Lucifer would be with her, do you?"

"Perhaps he's with Lady Todd. I know she's here ..."

The twins continued artlessly speculating on Lucifer's current obsession. Their escorts were totally bemused. Gabriel was not, but neither was he willing to deflect their attention. Alathea bit her lip, and let the twins have their revenge.

Under cover of the girls' bright chatter, Chillingworth touched Alathea's arm. Turning, she encountered a slightly rueful expression in the earl's eyes.

"I fear I'm going to desert you, my dear, and leave you captive to this bevy of Cynsters."

Alathea smiled. "They are a riotous lot, but the twins, you see, are celebrating a family victory."

For an instant, Chillingworth's eyes held hers, then his gaze flicked to Gabriel, presently exchanging barbs with Amanda. Chillingworth looked questioningly at Alathea. "Cynster, too, I think?"

Alathea didn't know what to think—and even less what to reply.

Chillingworth relieved her of the problem by bowing. "Your servant, my dear. If you ever find yourself in need of help, know you have only to ask."

He then nodded elegantly and stepped away, disappearing into the crowd.

Puzzled, Alathea watched him go, then turned back to Gabriel and the twins.

The next dance was a waltz.

Without so much as a by-your-leave, Gabriel, his temper sorely tried by the twins, closed his hand about Alathea's and drew her onto the floor. His arm came around her, holding her close. Their gazes met.

She grinned, but said not a word. She relaxed, following his lead without conscious effort. Scanning the room as they twirled, she saw no indication of any problem; their ball was in full swing and all was well.

She was about to refocus on Gabriel's face when Lady Osbaldestone's flashed past. The gleeful expression in her ladyship's old eyes reminded Alathea of the approval of Lady Jersey, Princess Esterhazy, and the others. How many more had had their eyes opened tonight, their censorious minds alerted?

"This is dangerous—you and me." She looked at Gabriel. "We're going to end as a high treat for the scandalmongers."

"Nonsense. Who's been disapproving?"

No one. Alathea pressed her lips together. After a moment, she said, "I'm too old. The entire ton is expecting you to marry—they won't approve of your marrying me."

"Why not? It's not as if you're in your dotage, for heaven's sake."

"I'm twenty-nine."

"So? If that doesn't worry me, and you know damned well it doesn't, why should it concern anyone else?"

"Bachelors of thirty do not customarily marry spinsters of twenty-nine."

"Probably because most spinsters of twenty-nine are that for good reason." Gabriel caught her eye. "You're that for a completely different reason—a reason that is no longer valid. You've done what you needed to do—you've set your family back on their feet. You've held the fort until Charlie can take over, and trained him to do it." His voice lowered. "Now it's time to let go and live the life you should have lived. *With me.*"

Alathea remained silent, not sure she could trust her voice.

He continued, "I haven't detected the slightest hint of disapproval—quite the opposite. The senior hostesses all knew your mother—they're thrilled at the thought of you marrying at last. Along with the rest of the ton, they've never understood why you didn't marry. To them, the notion of your marrying me is highly romantic."

Alathea managed a sniff. After a minute, she risked a glance up.

Gabriel's gaze was gently ruthless. "They'll cheer the announcement, when you consent to let me make it. *They're* not standing in my way."

Only she was. Alathea looked away. There was, it seemed, to be no help from any quarter. She was swimming against a flood tide.

In the nearby card room, Devil Cynster, Duke of St. Ives, strolled up to the earl of Chillingworth, who was standing by a wall watching a hand of piquet.

"Amazing. I never thought to see you pull in your horns." Devil glanced pointedly toward the ballroom. "I find it difficult to believe there are *no* possibilities in there. If you don't look quick, you'll be cold tonight. I, at least, have a warm bed to hie home to."

Chillingworth looked amused. "And what makes you think I haven't? The only difference between you and me, dear boy, is that your bed will be the same tomorrow night, while mine has at least a chance of being different."

"On the other hand, there's something to be said for consistently high standards."

"At present, I'll settle for variety. That aside, to what do I owe this questionable pleasure?"

"Just checking on your current interest."

"To make certain we don't cross bows? Pull the other one."

Devil settled his shoulders against the wall. "Purely altruistic, on my part."

Chillingworth hid a smile. "Altruistic? Tell me, is it me you're interested in keeping whole, or another more nearly related?"

Devil studied the crowd in the ballroom through the arch directly before them. "Let's just say that I've no wish to see any misunderstanding cloud the otherwise congenial relationship between your family and mine."

Chillingworth said nothing for several minutes, also staring at the figures jostling in the ballroom. Then he shifted. "If I was to say that I have no intention of disrupting the harmony currently reigning between our houses, would you do me one favor?"

"What?"

"Don't tell Gabriel."

Devil turned his head. "Why?"

His lips quirking wryly, Chillingworth pushed away from the wall. "Because it's entertaining watching him rise to my bait, and," he murmured, just loud enough for Devil to hear as he moved away, "I consider that fitting consolation."

CHAPTER

Eighteen

Their ball had been held on Monday night. Alathea did not set eyes on Gabriel again until Wednesday. Ambling in the park behind his sisters and hers, closely escorted by Lord Esher and Mr. Carstairs, she was deep in disturbing thoughts of Crowley and the Central East Africa Gold Company when she heard her name called. Looking up, she saw the group ahead looking back at her. Heather Cynster pointed to the nearby carriageway—to where her brother held his team of restless bays, stamping impatiently. As she lengthened her stride, Alathea got the distinct impression that the horses were merely reflecting their master's state.

"Good morning." Tipping her head up, she looked into his face, some way above her, courtesy of his high perch phaeton. The carriage held the interest of the girls and their beaux, leaving her to deal with its driver.

He beckoned. "Come up. I'll take you for a tool around the avenue."

She smiled. "No, thank you."

He stared at her.

The others had heard.

"Go on, Allie! You'll enjoy it."

"We'll be safe enough."

"It'll just be for a few minutes."

"Carstairs and I will engage to watch over your charges in your stead, Lady Alathea."

Alathea kept her gaze steady on Gabriel's face. "When last did you drive a lady in the park?"

He studied her for an instant longer, then his lips thinned. "Hold 'em, Biggs." His groom leaped from the back and ran to the horses' heads. Gabriel tied off the reins and jumped down.

Without a word, he took her arm and waved the others on. Absorbed with their own concerns, the girls were happy to comply. By mutual accord, she and Gabriel waited until the group was far enough ahead so they could talk without being overheard, then set out in their wake.

"There's no reason you couldn't let me drive you about the park."

"I have no intention of letting you declare your hand in such a public fashion." She shot him a reproving glance. "I'm not going to be swayed by such manuevers."

"More fool you. How did you know, anyway?"

"Your mama is always full of your doings—yours, Lucifer's, and the rest of your cousins. The fact that none of you drive ladies in the park—ladies other than your wives—is well known to all, I gather."

Gabriel had been counting on it. "How does Gretna Green strike you? We could be there in two days."

"At present, I have matters to deal with here. As soon as those matters are settled, I intend retiring to the country once again."

"Don't wager your mother's pearls on it."

"Humph! Anyway, what have you learned? I take it you got my note last night?"

"Yes, but not until this morning. Last night I was busy trying to prise information from certain African dignitaries."

"What did they say?"

"Enough to unofficially confirm that at least four of Crowley's claims of governmental approvals and permissions are false. I'm working on turning unofficial into official, but no government bureacracy works quickly. We won't have any official support for our petition by the time we have to lodge it."

"And when's that?"

"I would advise against waiting longer than next Tuesday."

"That soon?"

"We can't risk Crowley calling in his notes, and I'd wager my bays he'll do it late next week." Gabriel glanced at Alathea, then continued, "The petition's all but ready. Wiggs's clerk should have finished it—as far as we've gone—by tomorrow. Wiggs will bring it to me. If we have no more to add, with your permission, I'll ask my solicitor to make an appointment for Tuesday morning with one of the judges of the Chancery Court to submit our case. We don't dare wait longer—fighting a rearguard action once the promissory note is executed and the call on funds made will leave us in a considerably worse position legally."

Alathea grimaced. "If that's how it must be ..."

"I'll alert Devil, and Vane, too. He'll bring Gerrard up to town when he's needed." His gaze on her face, her profile, Gabriel opened his mouth on the words: "Thea, it's a big risk," but left them unsaid. If he had considered all the dangers and alternatives, she would have, too. There was no danger to her—he would marry her in an instant, and rescue both her and her family from penury—she knew that without his stating it. But what of Morwellan Park, and the title, the long unbroken line of Morwellans stretching back through time? What of her family's pride? That was what she'd set out from the first to protect, and it wasn't something that could be rescued other than by risking all.

Her motives needed no explaining to a Cynster. All he could do was stand by her shoulder and do whatever he could to bring about her victory.

And, perhaps, provide a distraction. "Actually, the reason I came looking for you wasn't to tell you all that. I've tickets for Friday's performance of *The Barber of Seville*. I thought you and your family might like to attend."

Alathea stared at him. "Friday night's the last night—it's to be a gala performance."

"So I understand." The production had taken the ton by storm. The management had decreed the final performance would be a gala event, to thank both cast and patrons.

"But ... the gala was sold out within hours of the announcement last week. How on earth did you manage to get tickets for us all?"

"Never mind how I got the damned tickets! Will you come?"

"Speaking for myself, of course I'll come! As for the others, you can ask them yourself." Alathea waved ahead to where the group were gathered about the Morwellan barouche.

Gabriel was glad to see that his sisters had already said their good-byes and were heading for his mother's landau, drawn in to the verge a little way along. Celia saw him and waved but did not beckon him to attend her. Nor did she evince any surprise at seeing him again strolling with Alathea. Those facts declared that Celia, at least, understood his intention and approved; Gabriel knew he could rely on her for support should the need arise.

Joining the others before the Morwellan carriage, he smoothly issued his invitation, specifically including both Esher and Carstairs. Alathea looked at him curiously but said nothing. She didn't have to—everyone was eager to attend the gala performance of *The Barber of Seville*.

When she arrived with the others at the Opera House on Friday night, Alathea discovered Gabriel had not just secured tickets, but one of the two most sought-after private boxes overlooking the stage. He met them in the foyer, then with her on one arm and Serena on the other, led the way up the stairs and down the plushly carpeted first floor corridor to the gilded door giving onto the box overhanging the left of the stage.

Eyes swivelled as they took their seats, the tonnish occupants of the less-favored boxes craning to see who had commanded prime place on this, the most celebrated evening of the season. Whispers abounded as, head high, her expression serene, Alathea regally sat in one of the chairs at the front of the box. Serena sat beside her, turning to murmur her thanks to Gabriel as he settled in the chair behind and to the side of Alathea's.

Alathea would gladly have boxed his ears, but not in public. As it was, all she could do was smile and return the gracious nods of the ton's matrons. Mary and Alice, wide-eyed, took the other front-row seats beyond Serena. Esher and Carstairs sat behind them. His lordship leaned forward and engaged Serena in some discussion. Alathea turned to Gabriel, intending to inform him she would box his ears later, only to find him leaning closer, a frown in his eyes.

"My apologies. I didn't realize we'd attract *this* much attention."

Alathea grimaced, absolving him of intent. She refrained from acidly informing him that this was the degree of attention he, a Cynster, should expect in declaring his hand. "I take it," she whispered, glancing briefly at Serena to make sure she was occupied, "that you haven't heard anything of the captain."

"No." His gaze lifted to her forehead. The frown in his eyes intensified. "Stop worrying. One way or another, we'll see this through."

Willing away all external evidence of her state, Alathea sighed. "I've done all I can to be beforehand, just in case ..." She gestured helplessly. "I've paid all the accounts from the ball—the caterers, the milliners, the modistes—even the musicians. They all thought I'd run mad, demanding they submit their accounts immediately."

"I dare say. If you've paid them all outright, the Morwellans will be the only family in the ton to finish the Season with a clear slate."

"I thought it would be better—more ethical, in a way. I'd rather our honest creditors were paid before Crowley and his schemes lay claim to all we have."

Gabriel's fingers closed on her hand. She only just had time to brace herself against the sensation of his lips caressing the backs of her fingers.

"Relax. Forget the Central East Africa Gold Company. Forget Crowley, at least for tonight." With a nod, he indicated the stage; the curtain was rising to building applause. "I've brought you here tonight, and the only thanks I want is for you to enjoy yourself. So stop worrying, and do."

Turning her hand, he brushed her inner wrist with his lips, then released her. Alathea faced the stage as the house lamps were doused, and did as he asked.

It wasn't difficult—the production was a *tour de force*, the singers superb, the sets and orchestra unsurpassed. She had fallen in love with musical performances in those few short weeks when she'd first come to London. She'd felt starved ever since; the efforts of provincial theatres could not compare with the extravagantly superior London events.

Because of the additional scenes and special arias to be presented as part of the gala, there was to be only one interval, occurring after the second act. When the curtain swished down and the lamps flared to life, Alathea sighed contentedly and glanced back at Gabriel.

He raised a brow, then stirred his long frame. "Time to stretch our legs."

Alathea allowed him to draw her to her feet. She turned to Serena.

Her stepmother flicked open her fan and waved it before her face. "I'm going to rest here—you may all stroll the corridors, but do be back in good time for the next act." She smiled on them all, Esher with Mary on his arm and Carstairs beside Alice. Gabriel waved the others on ahead, then he and Alathea stepped from the box into a sea of parading humanity. There was nothing they could do but parade along with everyone else.

"Forget about watching the others," Gabriel advised. "But tell me, have they spoken yet?"

"*Both* have asked leave to call on Papa next Wednesday." Alathea smiled. "I understand they're very seriously preparing a joint presentation to win his consent. No one's had the heart to tell them there's no need. They're both dears, each in their own way."

"Just leave them to it. Marriage is, after all, a serious business, not something a gentleman should embark on without due consideration."

"Indeed? Then might I suggest—"

"No. You may not. Twenty-nine years of knowing you is consideration enough."

A footman in full Beefeater costume appeared before them, flourishing a tray of glasses; they each took one and sipped. Countess Lieven hailed them through the crush; by the time they gained her side and suffered through her observations, the bell summoning the audience back to their seats was pealing.

Ten minutes later, they regained their box and sank into their seats as the curtain rose. An expectant hush fell over the audience. Gabriel angled his chair so he could see Alathea's face, illuminated by the light from the stage. Then he settled to watch—not the performance but the expressions animating her features, the signs of joy, of sorrow, of delight evoked by the unfolding story. The performers held the ton in thrall, but for him there was only Alathea.

The second half of the program exceeded the expectations raised by the first; at the end the audience was on their feet, applauding wildly, flowers raining down as the soloists took their bows. Finally, it was over, and the curtain fell for the last time. Gabriel watched as Alathea heaved a deep sigh and turned to him, a smile in her eyes, her lips curved, all worries temporarily banished.

Reward enough.

The others were exclaiming, discussing various highlights. Tilting her head, Alathea studied him. Her smile deepened. "You needn't pretend you paid attention."

"One of the numerous benefits of knowing each other so well—there's no need to prevaricate."

She searched his face. "Why did you do this—go to all this trouble, indulge in what I'm sure will prove a shockingly hideous expense?"

He returned her gaze steadily. "You like music."

It was that simple—he let her read the truth in his eyes. Then she shivered. He reached for the shawl she'd left over her chair and held it up. She hesitated, then turned so he could drape it over her shoulders. Releasing the fine silk, he closed his hands about her shoulders; leaning closer, he murmured, "As with other pleasures, my reward is your delight."

The glance she threw him was arrested, her expression not one he could place. But he had no chance to probe in the short time it took to escort her down the private stairway to where their carriages waited.

As he handed her up to the same black carriage he'd handed the countess into weeks before, she squeezed his hand. Then she ducked and entered the carriage. He shut the door and stepped back as Folwell flicked the reins.

Alathea sank back in the carriage, frowning now the shadows gave her freedom to do so. Beside her, Alice chatted animatedly with Tony Carstairs, seated opposite. She left them to their dissection of the performance; there was another performance with which she was far more concerned.

A performance she was starting to think might not be an act at all.

If there was any possibility that that was so ...

It was time to face her fear and the emotion that gave it birth. Both were new to her. She'd pandered to the former, while pretending the latter didn't exist. She couldn't do so any longer.

She remained absorbed through the drive back to Mount Street, absentmindedly responding as, together with Serena and her stepsisters, she bade farewell to Esher and Carstairs in the front hall. She climbed the stairs, murmured her good nights, then surrendered to Nellie's ministrations, all the while analyzing each of their encounters, trying to see past his warrior's shield. Finally alone, she hitched a shawl over her nightgown and curled up on the padded seat before her window.

Morwellan House was over fifty years old, built on the foundations of a much older residence. Morwellans had owned the site for centuries. How much longer they would continue here was in the lap of the gods. Her own life, however, was in her hands. She stared at the old trees at the bottom of the back lawn, then heaved a deep sigh, crossed her arms on the stone window ledge, and settled her chin on her wrists.

When had she fallen in love with him? Had it been when she was eleven? Had he sensed it—was that what had first made him edgy when near her? Or had it been later? Had love bloomed unknown to her sometime in her teens? Or had a girlish fancy slowly developed into something more?

Unanswerable questions now. All she knew was that sometime, it had happened. It didn't, in truth, feel like something new so much as something newly discovered, a vulnerability she hadn't known she possessed until fate and circumstance had revealed it. That was bad enough, but there was more she'd yet to face. She loved him, but her love had not yet fully blossomed. It was still a bud, newly burgeoning after an extended winter; it had yet to open. She'd yet to experience the full expression of her love, the total spectrum of her need. But she could feel the force, the power swelling within the bud; if freed, it would sweep her will before it—it would become the dominant force in her life.

That fact only added to her fear.

The two threads of her worry—her family and her love—were headed for simultaneous resolution. Regardless of what transpired in the Chancery Court, he, she knew, would be there, ready to whisk her to safety be the outcome victory or defeat. If it be victory, he'd push for her surrender; if defeat, he'd wait for no permissions but simply claim her as his. From his point of view, all was straightforward; from hers, it was anything but.

Her fear she at least understood now that she'd acknowledged the strange notion of loving him. One benefit of being twenty-nine was that she knew herself well. Loving him as she knew she would if she allowed her love free rein would leave her wholly committed, totally enmeshed in their relationship. She wasn't capable of doing anything by halves—when she gave, she gave completely. If she gave her heart, it would be his, all his, forever. She hadn't done it yet, hadn't surrendered her love and her life into his keeping. If she agreed to be his wife, she would do precisely that.

But what would happen if he didn't love her?

The pain she feared flowed from that. She'd faced disappointment, misery and loneliness, the threat of servitude, of destitution, of seeing her loved ones in rags. She'd found strength when she'd needed it, yet she knew in her heart that the pain of his kindness would slay her.

For he would be kind, considerate, always gentle. Yet if he didn't love her in the same way she loved him, her love was of the sort that would destroy her from within. She couldn't contain it, simply hold it inside if there was no one to give it to, to lavish it upon. She'd waited too long for the bud to bloom—it would now bloom in glory, or wither and die. There was no other way. And if it died, so would she, in all ways that mattered.

Better the swelling bud froze again, and never bloomed.

She'd been certain he didn't love her. Not for a minute had she believed fate would be so amenable as to arrange for him to fall madly in love with her. Life had never been so kind. He cared for her, yes, just as he always had, in that guarded, rational way of his, where every emotion was nicely logical.

She was annoyed with him for that. How dare he be so logical when she felt so emotional? Yet that difference had seemed to confirm that love as she was coming to know it was not what he felt for her. He was presently in lust with her, he wanted to care for her, to protect her, to marry her, but he didn't love her. She'd held firm against his proposal, utterly certain she'd read him aright.

Until tonight.

It hadn't been the extravagance of the box, or even the fact that he didn't, as she well knew, appreciate music. The moment when her certainty had been rocked to its foundations was when he'd whispered, "As with other pleasures, my reward is your delight."

It was his tone that had struck her, so accustomed as she was to every nuance, every inflection he used. He'd uttered those words as if it was his soul speaking, not just his mind. The words had resonated within her, as if in that moment, heart spoke to heart.

Had she been wrong? Did he love her? *Could* he love her?

The question was: How to tell?

Raising her head, she looked up at the stars, at the moon slowly waning in the west. Asking outright was out of the question. If she wasn't prepared to confess her love for him out aloud, in words, then she could hardly expect him to do so. She felt far too vulnerable to make such a confession; she credited him with sensibility enough to feel much the same way. As for expecting him to go down on his knees and declare his heart ...

Lips curving, she uncurled her legs and rose. Sobering, she walked to her bed. She slipped between the sheets, no clever plan of how to prompt his confidence revolving in her head, yet on that she was determined. If there was any chance that fate had at last smiled and sent love to touch them both, she could not live without knowing.

The next morning dawned leaden, the skies gray, the light gray, all of a piece with her mood. Toying with her toast, conscious of the subdued nature of the conversations around the breakfast table, Alathea struggled to shrug off a deadening sense of aftermath. The triumph of their ball had been eclipsed by persistent worry over the looming prospect of their incomplete case failing to convince the Chancery Court to declare the Central East Africa Gold Company a fraud. The special magic of her night at the opera, with its seductive suggestion that perhaps, possibly, Gabriel, too, might be concealing the true nature of his feelings, had dispersed in the cold light of morning.

Despite numerous restless hours, she'd been unable to devise any plan guaranteed to make him lower his shield, the barrier with which, for as long as she'd known him, he'd protected his heart. She couldn't, despite their closeness, see into his soul.

She was no better—she'd always been careful to protect her innermost feelings. She wasn't about to drop her guard and let him see into her soul, either. Unfortunately, that seemed the one approach with any chance of success, but the risk ...

Inwardly heaving a sigh, she reached for the teapot. There *had* to be something she could do, some positive action she could take to slough off her dour mood, if not in unraveling the complexities of her nemesis-turned-lover-and-now-would-be-husband, then in pursuing their investigations.

There had to be something not yet done, somewhere not yet searched. Some stone as yet unturned ...

She looked at Charlie. "Have you and Jeremy visited the museum?"

"No." Charlie shrugged. "We did mean to while we were here, but ..."

Jeremy brightened. "Can we go today? The back lawn's too wet to run the curricle over it."

Alathea glanced at Mary and Alice. "Why don't we all go? We haven't gone out all together for weeks, and there's nothing else happening this morning."

A tug on her sleeve had Alathea turning. Augusta looked up at her, brown eyes wide. "Me, too?"

Alathea smiled; the grayness receded. "Indeed, poppet. You, too."

An hour later, Alathea stood in one of the cavernous halls of the museum, looking down at what purported to be a map of Central East Africa spread on a large table and protected by a glass case. Lodwar was marked, but neither Fangak nor Kingi, not even as Kafia Kingi, was shown. Worse, Lodwar appeared to be on the banks of a huge river—a river the explorer whose works she had studied had apparently missed seeing.

Alathea sighed.

She hadn't bothered with the museum before, reasoning that the clerk at the Royal Society would have mentioned any exhibits had there been any of use. In desperation, however, she'd been willing to draw a long bow. On inquiring of the custodian at the main door, and learning that the museum did indeed have an exhibit including a good map, her heart had leaped. Perhaps ...

She'd left the others wandering, Charlie and Jeremy among the military exhibits, Mary, Alice, and Augusta among the ancient pottery, and slipped into this hall—only to have her hopes dashed again. Other than the map, there was only a display of native artifacts, and a few watercolors of wildlife supposedly found in Central East Africa.

Her heart felt like lead. She'd lifted even this stone but, like all the rest, there was no help beneath it. With one last disgusted look at the unhelpful map, she stepped away—

She cannoned into a gentleman. "Oh!" Falling back, she clutched her slipping shawl.

"Beg pardon, m'dear." The gentleman bowed awkwardly. "I was so incensed by this trumpery stuff, I wasn't looking out as I should." His gesture took in the entire Central East African exhibit.

"On the contrary, it was I who didn't look." Alathea took in the man's shaggy brows overhanging features weatherbeaten to a walnut-brown. Grizzled whiskers framed them. His eyes were a washed-out blue, his old-style coat and corduroy knee breeches attire no longer common in town. The stance he adopted was unusual, too, his hands clasped behind his back, feet apart, legs braced.

Abruptly turning back to the exhibit, Alathea waved at the map. "Is this incorrect, then?"

His derisive reply came immediately. "Poppycock! All of it. It's nothing like that, upon my word."

"You've been there?"

"In between my sailings, when I have to wait months because of some flood or famine or skirmish between the tribes, an old prospector and I take to the hills. Why, we've crossed the whole continent a number of times." The sweep of his hand encompassed the area in which the interests of the Central East Africa Gold Company lay. "Not much improvement on the Great Desert, Central East Africa. Dusty wasteland, it is. This river shown here is nothing more than a trickle, and then only in the rainy season."

"You sail?" Alathea held her breath. "On a ship?"

"Aye." The man dragged his hat from under his arm and doffed it in a bow from a bygone age. "Captain Aloysius Struthers at your service, ma'am. Captain of the *Dunslaw,* sailing for Bentinck and Company."

Alathea exhaled, dragged in another breath and held out her hand. "Captain, you have no idea how glad I am to make your acquaintance."

Struthers looked taken aback, but instinctively grasped her hand. Alathea shamelessly held on to his. She cast a swift glance around. "If we retire to that bench, I'd like to explain. My interest is prompted by the Central East Africa Gold Company."

The change in Struthers's expression was instantaneous. "That blackguard, Crowley—" He broke off. "My apologies, ma'am, but when I think of the damage that jackal has done, it fair boils my blood."

"Indeed? Then you might be interested to learn that a friend and I have plans to bring his latest scheme to naught."

Slipping his hand from hers, Struthers offered his arm. "I'd be devilish interested in hearing from anyone ready to thrust a spoke in that brigand's wheel. But what's a lady like you doing mixed up with the likes of him?"

That took some time to explain. Alathea hesitated, but, in the end, revealed her identity. If she wanted Struthers's help, it was only fair to be frank. She outlined Crowley's scheme, then detailed all the false claims they'd uncovered. To her relief, Struthers grasped the situation quickly.

"Aye—that's his game, right enough. A bloodsucker, he is. He's swindled the colonists right and left all through that area. And what he's done with the local tribes ..." Struthers's expression hardened. "I won't sully your ears with the tales of his infamies, my lady, but if ever there was a blackguard overdue in hell, it's Ranald Crowley."

"Yes, well, I have to agree." Alathea thrust aside the idea of an opponent steeped in infamy. "Our problem, however, is that we have no absolute proof to disprove Crowley's claims. All our evidence is *surmised* from what we've learned from others. We desperately need someone who can appear before the judge and corroborate what we've learned—an eyewitness, as it were."

Struthers straightened. "Captain Aloysius Struthers is your man, my lady. And I'll do better than just give you my say-so. I know where I can get maps—signed maps, mark you. And if I ask around quiet-like, I'm sure I can get more on the holdings Crowley's claimed. They ring a bell, they definitely do. I'm not positive, but I think an old acquaintance holds the mining rights to those areas. I can ask, easily enough. You'll want as many nails in your hand as possible when the time comes to make sure Crowley's coffin's good and sealed."

Alathea didn't argue. The captain's reaction to Crowley, the grim look in his eyes every time he mentioned him, frightened her far more than her previous glimpse of the villain.

Struthers nodded decisively. "It'll be an honor to bring that blackguard down. Now." Briskly, he turned to Alathea. "How do I contact you when I've gathered my proofs?"

"The hearing will be on Tuesday morning ..." Alathea dug in her reticule and came up with a pencil. "In the judges' chambers at Chancery Court." The only paper she carried was the entry ticket to the museum; the back was blank.

She ripped it in half. "If you need to contact me before that, this is my direction." She wrote down her name and address. There was no point giving Gabriel's address; not only had the captain not met her knight, but her protector had a habit of galloping about town. At present, he was making a furious effort to prise some formal acknowledgment of the Central East Africa Gold Company's status from the African authorities' representatives in London. He didn't hold out much hope; neither did she. The captain was their best hope—their savior, indeed. If he needed to contact anyone, it had better be her; they couldn't afford to lose touch with him now. She handed him the scrap of paper. "Now, where are you situated?"

He gave her the address of a lodging house in Clerkenwell. "I find a different place every time I stay in London. I rarely stay long."

Alathea wrote down the address, then tucked the paper into her reticule. "You won't be sailing again before Tuesday, will you?"

"Unlikely," Struthers murmured, reading her address. Then he slipped the paper into his coat pocket. "Right, then. I'd better set to." They both rose. Struthers bowed to Alathea. "Never fear, my lady. Aloysius Struthers won't let you down."

With that, he clapped his hat on his head. With a grimly determined nod, he strode off.

Alathea watched him go. A rush of relief poured through her. Dizzy, she sank back onto the bench. Five minutes later, Mary, Alice, and Augusta found her sitting there, smiling.

"Yes," she replied in answer to their query. "We can, indeed, go home."

She sent a summons to Brook Street the instant they reached home; Gabriel arrived as they rose from the luncheon table. Barely giving him a chance to greet the rest of her family, Alathea dragged him out to the gazebo.

As if in tune with her mood, the clouds had rolled away. The others followed them into the sunshine, spreading out on the lawn to relax and play, but no one attempted to follow them into the shadowed privacy of the gazebo.

"I presume," Gabriel said, following her up the steps, "that you're about to reveal the nature of your 'fantastic discovery'?"

"Captain Aloysius Struthers!" Alathea whirled and sank onto the sofa. "I've found him."

"Where?"

"The museum." Gleefully, she recounted their meeting. "And he's not only agreed to testify as to the falsity of Crowley's claims, but he says he can lay hands on verified maps, and also on details of the relevant mining leases." She gestured expansively. "He'll be even more help than we hoped for." Gabriel frowned. Surprised, she asked, "What is it?"

He grimaced. "I'd be content with the captain simply turning up before the judge—with his testimony to anchor our case, we won't need anything more."

"It won't hurt to have a few more facts behind us."

"Hmm. Did Struthers tell you where he's staying?"

Alathea drew a folded sheet from her pocket. "I copied his address for you. Will you go and see him?"

Gabriel read the address; his expression turned grim. "Yes. If he'd been staying in Surrey, I wouldn't have bothered, but, as it is, I think a visit might be wise."

"Why?"

"To warn him. If he goes nosing about asking after maps and mining leases, he's liable to alert Crowley. We might be nearing the eleventh hour, but Ranald Crowley is not an opponent I'd ever turn my back on."

"Indeed not, but the captain seemed to know him well."

"Nevertheless, I'll speak to the captain. It won't hurt to underline the need for secrecy." Sliding the note into his pocket, Gabriel looked at Alathea, then turned and sat beside her. "Which brings me to another point."

Shuffling to make space for him, she looked at him questioningly.

"Don't go anywhere alone. Not until we have the decision handed down— no, not even then. Not until we know Crowley has left England."

"And I thought it was me who was melodramatic."

"I'm serious." Jaw setting, he took her hand. "Crowley is not some predictable English villain—he recognizes no law but that of the jungle. From the minute he learns of our plans until he returns to the jungle, or some other uncivilized place, you will not be safe." He trapped her gaze. "Promise me you won't go anywhere alone, and that, even in company, you'll restrict your outings to the purely social. No visits to the museum, or the Tower—no more searching at all. We have enough to defeat Crowley now. There's no reason whatever for you to place yourself in danger."

A gust of laughter had them both looking to where Charlie and Jeremy stood on the lawn, teasing Mary and Alice, seated on a rug.

"They're safe enough. While you remain within the ton, you'll all be safe— that's not an arena Crowley can move within without attracting immediate attention." Looking at Alathea, Gabriel squeezed her hand. "Promise me you'll take care."

Alathea looked into his eyes. She saw urgency and an unaccustomed softness in the hazel depths. "I'll be careful, but if—"

"No buts, no ifs." In a blink, all softness vanished from his face. Her knight-protector all but glared at her. "*Promise.*"

A demand, no plea. Alathea glared back. "I'll be careful. I won't do anything silly. With that, you'll have to be content. I've never been yours to rule."

His expression, the granite hardness in his gaze, gave credence to his low growl, "You're treading on thin ice."

Yes, but what was underneath? Desperate to know, once and for all, Alathea returned his gaze haughtily. "I am my own person—*not* yours."

Hazel eyes fell into hazel. A long moment passed, then he looked away. His expression hardened as he gazed at Jeremy and Alice, Augusta and Mary. "Let me tell you what's going to happen after we gain our judgment against the Central East Africa Gold Company.

"First, we're getting married. Not in any hole-and-corner fashion, but right here, in the heart of the ton. St. Georges Church one fine June morning. After that, we'll divide our lives between London and Somerset—the Season in London, and various trips as required for business, but we'll spend most of the year at Quiverstone Manor. Aside from anything else, from there you and I can keep an eye on Morwellan Park and lend a hand if Charlie needs it. And you'll be there to watch Jeremy and Augusta grow. We can sponsor Augusta for her come-out, and while in London you'll be able to catch up with Mary and Esher, and Alice and Carstairs.

"In between, you can learn about those of the Manor's tenants you don't already know, and help Mama with all the thousand and one things she does about the estate, so you'll be ready to step in when she eventually flags. And there are Heather, Eliza, and Angelica, who, as you well know, will be thrilled to call you sister. You could try teaching them not to giggle—God knows, Mama hasn't managed it yet.

"The east wing will have to be redecorated, too. I never did more than order the old furniture cleaned. I don't even know the state of half of it, although my bed there is sound enough."

Alathea swallowed the question, "Sound enough for what?" The answer was not long in coming.

"And if all that doesn't keep you sufficiently amused, I have a number of other distractions planned—at least three sons and any number of daughters." Turning his head, he met her gaze. "Yours and mine. Ours. Our future."

She held his gaze steadily, and prayed he couldn't see how much the thought tugged at her heart.

"Picture it—us sitting under the old oak on the south lawn, watching our children play. Hearing the shrill voices, the laughter, the cries. Picking them up to soothe them, to comfort them, or perhaps just to hold them." He searched her eyes, his own hard as agates. "You've always liked children, you always expected to have a tribe of your own. That was always your dream, your destiny. You gave it up for your family, but now fate's handing it back to you." His gaze raked her face, then, as if satisfied with what he saw, he sat back and looked across the lawn. "I know you too well to believe you'd turn your back on that dream a second time."

His confidence tweaked Alathea's temper, but she shrugged the temptation to ire aside. His words—his *pronouncement*—should have chilled her; there'd been no loverlike softness in his words. He'd been all warrior—logical, practical—her knight-protector carrying her off to a new beginning, for which she should be duly grateful and acquiesce to all his decrees.

It was enough to make her laugh, but she didn't. If he'd been charming, presenting his arguments with the light, airy touch of which she knew he was capable, her heart would have sunk without trace. That was how he behaved in matters that did not touch him deeply. Instead, he'd presented her with his warrior side, all impenetrable granite and impregnable shield. She had to wonder what he was shielding. Lifting her chin, she fixed her gaze on his profile. "And what about us? You and me. The two of us together. How do you see us?"

The question hit a nerve. His swift frown, an infinitesimal tensing of muscles otherwise under rigid control, told her so.

"I see us in bed," he growled, "and in a few other places, too. Do you want to know the details?"

"No. I'm quite imaginative enough to supply my own."

"Well, then." But his tone had softened, as if in thinking of her question, he'd seen more than he'd expected. "I imagine we'll ride like we used to, every day. You always liked riding—do you still ride a lot?"

After an instant's hesitation, she said, "I sold all the horses years ago."

He nodded. "So we'll ride every day. And, I just realized, you can help me with the estate accounts, which will leave more time for riding. And investing—studying the news, weeding out the rumors, checking with Montague and my other contacts. I manage all the Cynster funds. You've dabbled to good effect with the Morwellan treasury, such as it was, but I play a more aggressive hand."

"I'm not particularly good at aggression."

"You can take an interest in the defensive side, then—the bonds and capital." He gestured expansively. "That's how I see us."

Alathea waited a moment, then softly said, "You know perfectly well that's not what I meant. I wanted to know what you see *between* us."

His head whipped around and he scowled at her. "Thea—stop resisting. We'll be married soon. All I just said *is* going to happen—you know it is."

"I know nothing of the sort. Why do you imagine I'll agree to your dictates?"

He hesitated, his narrowed gaze locked with hers. Then he said, "You'll agree because you love me."

Alathea felt her lips part, felt her jaw drop. Horrified, she searched his eyes. The comprehension she saw horrified her even more. How *could* he know? She snapped her lips shut and fixed him with a militant glare. "*I'll* be the judge of whether I love you or not."

"Are you saying you don't?" His tone was a warning.

"I'm saying I haven't yet made up my mind."

With a disgusted snort, he looked away. "Pull the other one."

Although he'd muttered, Alathea heard him. "You *don't* know that I love you—you *can't* know!"

He looked her in the eye. "I do."

"*How?*"

After a moment, he looked away; this time, his gaze fastened on the jasmine, blooming in profusion over the gazebo, filling the arches, fragrant white blossoms nodding in the breeze. Catching a spray, he snapped it off. Looking down, he turned it in his hands, long fingers caressing the velvet-soft blooms. "How many men have you allowed to make love to you?"

Alathea stiffened. "You know perfectly well—"

"Precisely." He nodded, his gaze on the jasmine. "Only me. You don't know—"

Alathea waited; after a long moment, he drew breath and met her gaze. "I know you love me because of the way you give yourself to me. The way you are when you're in my arms."

"Well!" She fought down an urge to bluster. "As you're the only lover I've yet known—"

"Tell me,"—his steely words cut her off—"can you imagine being as you are with me, if it wasn't me with you but some other man?"

She stared at him. She couldn't begin to even form a mental picture; the idea was utterly foreign.

So foreign, she suddenly realized she'd lost sight of her agenda. "You're avoiding my point." It was a wrench to drag her mind from the avenues into which he'd lead it, to consider instead that if he knew she loved him, he'd be even more chivalrously inclined to wed her regardless of any other motive. The realization fueled a fresh rush of emotions, hope and frustration equally represented. Hope that the reason for his self-protective shield was a heart as vulnerable as hers; frustation over convincing him to lower his guard long enough for her to know.

She felt like clenching her fists, screwing her eyes shut, drumming her heels, and *demanding* he tell her the truth. Instead, she fixed her eyes on his and carefully enunciated, "I will not marry you until you tell me why you want to marry me, and place your hand on your heart and swear you've told me all—*every last one*—of your reasons."

Those who thought him the epitome of a civilized gentleman would never have recognized the harshly primitive warrior who now faced her. Luckily, she'd encountered him often enough not to quake.

"*Why?*"

The very air shivered beneath that one word, so invested with suppressed passions—anger, frustration, and barely leashed desire.

Alathea didn't blink. "Because I need to know."

He held her gaze for so long, she began to feel giddy, then he wrenched his gaze from hers and abruptly stood.

He looked out over the lawns, then glanced down at her. His expression was impassive. With a flick of his fingers, he tossed the sprig of jasmine into her lap.

"Don't you think we've wasted enough years?"

His gaze rose, touched hers, then he turned and strode down the steps.

Alathea sat in the gazebo mentally replaying their exchanges, wondering, if she had the chance, if she would say anything different, do anything different, or manage to achieve anything more.

At the end of an hour, she lifted the jasmine and inhaled the heady scent. She focused on the sprig, then, with a self-deprecating grimace, tucked it into her cleavage.

For luck.

She'd diced with fate for her sisters and won. She'd just played for her own future—had she told him she wasn't aggressive? She'd risked everything on a last throw.

She'd do it again in a blink.

With a sigh, she rose and headed for the house.

CHAPTER
Nineteen

Sunday evening. Gabriel let himself into his house with his latchkey. As he closed the door, Chance materialized from the back of the hall.

Gabriel handed him his hat and cane. "Is there brandy in the parlor?"

"Indeed, sir."

Gabriel waved a dismissal. "I won't need anything more tonight." He stopped with his hand on the parlor doorknob. "One thing—did Folwell bring his report?"

"Aye, sir—it's on the mantelshelf."

"Good." Entering the parlor, Gabriel shut the door and headed straight for the sideboard. He poured himself two fingers of brandy, then, glass in hand, lifted Folwell's missive from the mantelpiece and slumped into his favorite armchair. He took a long sip, his gaze on the folded sheet, then, setting both glass and note down on a side table, he pressed his hands to his eyes.

God, he was tired. Over the last week, aside from the time he'd spent with Alathea and a few restless hours' sleep, he'd devoted every waking minute to trying to shake formal statements—statements with legal weight—from a score of civil servants and foreign ambassadors' aides. To no avail. It wasn't that the gentlemen didn't want to be helpful; it was simply the way of governmental authority the world around. Everything had to be checked and triple-checked, and then authorized by someone else. Time, it seemed, was measured on a different scale in Whitehall and foreign parts both.

Sighing deeply, Gabriel stretched out his legs and leaned his head back, eyes closed. It wasn't his failure on the foreign front that was worrying him.

He'd called on Captain Aloysius Struthers that afternoon. Even from that short interview, it was clear that the captain was indeed the savior Alathea had thought him. His testimony, even in the absence of any further facts beyond those they'd already gleaned, would prompt the most reticent judge to a speedy and favorable decision. The problem was the captain had embarked on a crusade with all flags flying. He'd already contacted acquaintances in search of maps and mining leases.

Gabriel wasn't at all sure that was the way to sling a noose around Crowley's neck. Stealth might have been wiser.

He'd spent half an hour urging Struthers to caution, but the man hadn't wanted to listen. He was fixated on bringing Crowley down. In the end, Gabriel had accepted that and left, trying to ignore the presentiment of danger resonating, clarionlike, in his mind.

As long as Struthers appeared at Chancery Court on Tuesday morning, all would be well. Until then, however, the investigation and his nerves would teeter on a knife edge. One wrong move …

Opening his eyes, he straightened, reached for his glass, and grimly sipped. There was nothing more he could do tonight to bolster the Morwellan cause. It was, however, time and past that he attended to the other matter on his plate.

He was a coward.

A difficult fact for a Cynster to face, but face it he must. *She* had given him no choice.

He hadn't seen Alathea since their meeting in the gazebo the previous afternoon. Indeed, he didn't *want* to see her, not until he'd decided what to do, how to respond to her ultimatum. She made him feel so … *primitive*, so stripped of all his elegant attitudes, the patina of his social charm. With her, he felt like a caveman, one who had suddenly discovered heaven on earth was beyond the ability of his club to provide. He'd painted the details of their future life intending to lure her into admitting how desirable it would be, to show her how easily their lives would mesh. Instead, he'd opened his own eyes to how desperately *he* wanted all that he'd described.

He hadn't considered the details before—he'd known he wanted her as his wife and that had been enough. But now that he'd conjured up such visions in all their glory, they haunted him.

And pricked and prodded at his cowardice.

Was he going to risk that future—the glorious future that should be theirs—simply because he couldn't find the words to tell her what she wanted to know? Because the mere thought of what she truly meant to him closed his throat and rendered him incapable of speech?

But there *were* no words to encompass all she was to him, so how the devil *could* he tell her?

He swallowed a mouthful of brandy, and brooded on that fact. But he had to tell her, and soon. Patience had never been his strong suit—patience that entailed concommitant abstinence was utterly foreign to his nature. He'd endured more than a week without her; his stock of patience was stretched vanishingly thin. He certainly wasn't about to let the court case run its course and risk her slipping back to the country. If she did, he'd have to hie after her, and just think how revealing *that* would be to the now all-too-interested ton.

No—he had to speak before Tuesday morning. God knew how things would pan out after that, Struthers or no. And if, by some hellish twist of fate, things went awry and the decision went against them … if he waited until then to drum up his courage and speak, it might take forever to convince her he wasn't simply doing his all to whisk her into his protection. He'd probably go insane before he succeeded. Best to strike now, when their case looked strong, so she had less justification to attribute all his motive to his admittedly obsessive protective instinct. He wasn't sorry for that instinct—he wouldn't dream of apologizing for it—but he could see that in this case, it was going to get in his way.

So—how to tell her what she insisted on knowing before Tuesday morning?

He couldn't see himself doing the deed via a formal morning call, and trying to talk to her in the park would be insane. Reaching for Folwell's note, he scanned the list of Alathea's engagements. As he'd supposed, the next time he and she would unavoidably meet was at the Marlboroughs' ball tomorrow night.

They'd meet at Chancery Court the next morning.

Gabriel grimaced. How, between appearing in court and now, did fate expect him to declare his hand, let alone his heart?

"Send Nellie up to me, Crisp. I may as well get ready."

"Indeed, Lady Alathea. I believe Nellie's with Figgs. I'll inform her immediately." Crisp sailed on through the green baize door.

Alathea climbed the stairs, doggedly ignoring her constantly vacillating emotions. On the one hand, she felt almost hysterical with relief, buoyed to the point of frivolity over having the sword that had hung over the family's future for the past months all but effectively removed. The captain's testimony would carry the day against Ranald Crowley. There were moments when she had to concentrate to keep a silly grin from her face.

She had mentioned to her father and Serena that matters were looking up. A superstitious quirk had stopped her from assuring them that the family was finally safe. That she would do later in the week, the instant the judge handed down his decision.

But they were safe. She knew it in her heart.

Her heart, unfortunately, was otherwise engaged, not at all inclined to share in her imminent joy. On a matter that had, to her considerable surprise, come to mean more to her than even her family, her heart was troubled. Uneasy. Unfulfilled.

Reaching the top of the stairs, she released her skirts and sighed.

What was he up to?

She hadn't seen him, or heard from him since he'd left her in the gazebo, his harsh words "Don't you think we've wasted enough years?" ringing in her ears. So what now? Did he imagine she'd weaken and meekly acquiesce?

"Hah!" Lips compressing, she swept down the wing and flung open the door to her room. Nellie's footsteps came pattering after her.

"I want that ivory and gold gown—the one I was saving for a special occasion."

"Oooh!" Nellie darted to the wardrobe. "What's the occasion, then?"

Alathea sat before her dressing table; in the mirror, she considered the militant light in her eyes. "I haven't yet decided."

She wasn't going to do it—weaken and give in. She was going to be tenacious, stubborn—she was utterly determined. As far as she could see, *she* was the one who had taken all the risks thus far—in demanding his sworn motives, in being so naively transparent. It was time he did his part and told her the full truth.

A tap on the door heralded her bathwater. While Nellie oversaw the preparations, Alathea unpinned and brushed her hair, then wound it in a simple knot. Nellie came to fetch her usual bath salts; she mumbled through lips clamped about hairpins, "No—not those. The French sachets."

Nellie's brows rose, but she hurried to the drawer where the expensive birthday present from Serena was secreted. A moment later, a lush scent reminiscent of the countess's perfume wreathed through the room.

Nellie's face was gleefully alight; without further direction, she assembled all required to turn Alathea out at her finest—at her most seductive.

It was nearly an hour later before they were done. As she settled a gold cap on her hair, Alathea studied her reflection, trying to see herself through his eyes. Her hair shone, her eyes were wide and bright. Her complexion— something she rarely considered—was flawless. The years had erased all traces of youth from both face and figure, leaving both honed, refined. She touched her fingers lightly to her lips, then smiled. Swiftly, she scanned the expanse of her shoulders and breasts revealed by the exquisite gown, one Serena had forced on her earlier in the Season.

Sending heartfelt thanks winging her stepmother's way, Alathea stood. The gown rustled as the stiff silk fell straight, the gold embroidery at neckline and hem glittering. Stepping back, she turned, studying her outline, the way the gown caressed her hips. Determination glowed in her eyes.

As far as she was concerned the next move was Gabriel's, especially given he'd been so helpful as to make her declaration for her. Being naively transparent was bad enough—having one's transparency explained to one was infinitely worse.

She wasn't going to budge. He was going to have to convince her, utterly, completely, beyond a shadow—

"Here!" Nellie turned from the door to which a tap had summoned her. "Look what's come."

Alerted by the wonder in Nellie's voice, Alathea looked around.

Reverently holding a white-and-gilt box, Nellie gazed delightedly on what it contained. Then she beamed at Alathea. "It's for you—and there's a note!"

Alathea's heart leaped; her lungs seized. She sank back down on her dressing stool. As Nellie approached with the box, Alathea realized the reason for her awestruck expression. The box wasn't white—it was glass lined with white silk. It wasn't gilt, either—the decorations at corners, hinge and latch were all pure gold.

As Nellie gave it into her hands, Alathea could not imagine anything more exquisite. What on earth did it contain?

She didn't need to open it to find out. The lid was not lined. Through it, she saw a simple posy.

Simple, yes; in all other respects the posy was a match for the box. A group of five white flowers of a kind she'd never seen were secured with a ribbon of gold filigree. The posy nestled amid the white silk, all but hiding the note beneath. The petals of the flowers were lush, thick, velvety, the green of their stems a sharp contrast.

It was the most elaborate, expensive, extravagant come-out posy Alathea had ever seen.

Swivelling on the stool, she set the box on her dressing table and raised the lid. A drift of perfume reached her, sensual and heavy. Once inhaled, it didn't leave her. Carefully sliding her fingers beneath the flowers, she lifted the posy and set it aside. Then she drew out the note. Barely breathing, she opened it.

The message was simple—a single line in his bold, aggressive hand.

You have my heart—don't break it.

She read the words three times and still couldn't tear her eyes away. Then her vision misted; she blinked, swallowed. Her hand began to shake. Quickly folding the note, she laid it down.

And concentrated on dragging in her next breath.

"Oh, dear," she finally managed, and even that wavered. Blinking frantically, she stared at the posy. "Oh, *heavens*. What on earth am I to do?"

"Why you'll carry it, of course. Very nice, I must say."

"No, Nellie, you don't understand." Alathea put her hands to her cheeks. "Oh, how *like* him to make it complicated!"

"Him, who? Master Rupert?"

"Yes. Gabriel. He's called that now."

Nellie sniffed. "Well, I can't see why you can't carry his flowers, even if he is using some other name."

Alathea swallowed a hysterical laugh. "It's not his *name*, Nellie, it's *me*. I can't carry a girl's come-out posy."

He'd known, of course. She'd never had her come-out, never received a come-out posy, never had the opportunity to carry one.

"Damn the man!" She felt like weeping with happiness. "What am I to do?" She'd never felt so flustered in her life. She wanted to carry the flowers, to pick them up, rush out of the door like an eager young girl, and hurry to the ball just so she could show him—her lover—that she understood. But ... "The scandalmongers are watching us as it is." If she carried the posy, they'd be the *on-dit* of the night. Possibly the whole Season.

"Maybe I can wear them as a corsage?" She tried it, angling the flowers this way, then that, at her right, her left, in the center of her neckline.

"No." She sighed. "It won't do." One flower wasn't enough against the gold embroidery, but three, the number needed to balance the spray, was too much, too large. Far too visible. Aside from anything else, the spray would be in her constant vision—facing him over it, spending the evening with him by her side with his flowers so blatantly between them would be impossible. She'd never maintain her composure.

"I can't." Dismayed, she gazed at the beautiful blooms—at the favor her warrior had sent her as a token of his heart. She desperately wanted to carry them, but didn't dare. "Fetch a vase, Nellie."

With a disapproving humph, Nellie left.

Alathea cradled the posy in her hands, and let all that it meant wash through her. Then she heard Mary's and Alice's voices; blinking, sniffing, she gently laid the posy back in the box and set it to one side of the table. In a daze, she finished her toilette, clasping her mother's pearls about her throat, placing the matching drops in her ears, lavishly dabbing on the countess's perfume.

"Allie? Are you ready?"

"Yes. I'm coming!" Her wits whirling, she rose. Her gaze on the posy, cradled in its delicate box, she breathed in, exhaled, then picked up her reticule and turned.

"Hurry! The coach is here!"

"I'm coming." Reaching the threshold, Alathea lingered. Her hand on the door, she looked back at the delicate box he'd used to send her his heart.

Her gaze lifted to the mirror beyond, to her own reflection.

A moment later, she blinked. Leaving the door, she recrossed the room.

Halting before the dressing table, she picked up his note. She reread his message, then looked again at her reflection.

Her lips twisted, lifted. Tucking the note into her jewelry box, she raised her hands to her cap.

It took a moment to ease out the pins. Alathea ignored the chorus of calls wafting along the corridor. This time, her family could wait.

Laying aside the cap, she quickly unwound the posy. She wrapped the ribbon around the tight bun on the top of her head and tied it in a simple knot, the trailing ends interleaving with the surrounding curls. Fingers shaking, she separated three luscious blooms from the arrangement. By the time she'd threaded the stems into her thick hair and secured them with pins, she was smiling, her heart soaring, her face mirroring her joy.

Nellie rushed in, vase in hand, and abruptly halted. "Oh, my! Well, now! That's better!"

"Put the others in water. I have to rush." Whirling, Alathea squeezed Nellie's arm, then, breathless, ran to the door.

Brows high, Nellie watched her go, then, a broad smile wreathing her face, she bustled to the dressing table. She placed the two remaining blooms in the vase, then carefully carried it to the table beside the bed. Nellie wiped her hands and returned to the dressing table to tidy Alathea's combs and brush. She was about to turn away when the folded note poking out from Alathea's jewelry box caught her eye.

Nellie cast a glance at the door, then lifted the lid of the jewelry box and took out the note. She unfolded it, read it, then refolded it and replaced it. And chuckled delightedly. "You'll do, my lad. You'll do."

Gabriel saw his flowers in Alathea's hair the instant she appeared in the archway giving onto Lady Marlborough's ballroom. The sight transfixed him; joy, relief, and something far more primal locked his lungs. Pausing with her family at the top of the stairs, Alathea looked down, over the ballroom, but didn't immediately see him. His gaze didn't leave her as she slowly descended the broad sweep, one hand lightly skimming the balustrade as she searched the throng.

Then she saw him.

He drew breath and started toward her. His eyes didn't leave her face as he closed the distance between them; he had no recollection of those he passed as he cleaved through the crowd. He reached the newel post before her.

She descended the last steps, her gaze locked with his, pausing on the very last, higher than he, then she stepped down to the floor and angled her head so he could study the blooms.

"I couldn't carry them—you do understand?"

Triumph washed through him, a rolling wave that nearly brought him to his knees. "Your alternative is inspired." He took her hand; uncaring of any who might be watching, he carried it to his lips. His eyes held hers. "My lady."

Some magical force held them trapped, hazel drowning in hazel, so close they could sense each breath the other took, each beat of the other's heart. Neither could manage a smile.

"And about time, too, but *do* get a move on! There's a seat on a *chaise* over there I want to snare."

Alathea jumped and whirled. Gabriel looked up, into Lady Osbaldestone's black eyes. She grinned evilly and poked his arm. "Don't let me stop you in your rush into parson's mousetrap, but *do* get out of my way!"

They did; Lady Osbaldestone pushed past them and stumped into the throng. Gabriel turned as Alathea took his arm.

"We'd better do as she says."

Placing his hand over hers, he guided her into the already dense crowd.

"We were late," Alathea murmured. "Only by a few minutes, but it put us so far back in the queue of carriages ..."

"I was beginning to wonder if something had happened ..."

Something had. Alathea met his eyes; they were gently smiling, magnanimous in victory. She looked away. "You know, I would never have expected flowers from you."

She said nothing more; the muscles under her hand slowly tensed.

"There was a *note* with the flowers ..."

Alathea turned smiling eyes his way. "I know. I read it."

He drew her to a halt, his eyes searching hers. "Just as long as you *understood* it."

His tone held aggression, uncertainty, and a strong undercurrent of vulnerability. Alathea let her expression soften, let her guard down enough for him to see her heart in her eyes. "Of *course* I understood it."

He looked deep into her eyes, then he released the breath he'd held. "Just don't forget it. Even if you never hear or see the words again, they'll always be true. Don't forget."

"I won't. Not ever."

The noisy crowd around them had faded. For a moment, they remained in that world where only they existed, then Alathea smiled softly, squeezed his arm, and drew them both back to the present. She glanced about. "You could have chosen an evening more conducive to your declaration."

Gabriel sighed and they started to stroll. "Our whole courtship—no, our joint *lives* thus far have been dictated by circumstance. I'm looking forward to shaking free of the shackles and taking charge of our reins."

"Indeed?" Regally, Alathea exchanged nods with Lady Cowper. "Might I suggest that you resign yourself to sharing the reins?"

Gabriel shot her a glance; his brow quirked. "I'll think about it."

They strolled on through the crush, encountering no member of either of their families. "This is ridiculous," Alathea stated as the press of bodies forced them to a halt. "Thank heaven there's are only a few weeks to go."

"Speaking of time passing, has Struthers contacted you?" Surrendering to the inevitable, Gabriel drew her out of the parading crowd to a spot where they could stand and converse in reasonable comfort.

"No. Why? I thought you were going to see him."

"I did. I told him my address and to get in touch with me if he needed any help, but he hasn't."

"Well." Alathea shrugged and looked about. "Presumably that means all's well and we'll see him tomorrow in court." She smiled and held out her hand. "Good evening, Lord Falworth."

Falworth took her hand and bowed. Gabriel inwardly cursed. Within minutes, her entire court had gathered. They must have located her by tracking him, tall enough to be followed through the jostling throng. Lord Montgomery prosed on; Falworth and others attempted to capture the conversation and steer it in their own directions. A social smile on her lips, Alathea pretended to follow, nodding and murmuring at appropriate moments.

The first waltz and she would be his again. Unfortunately, Lady Marlborough was of an older generation; she'd scheduled a great many cotillions and even a quadrille amid a host of country dances. He'd be waiting a while for his waltz.

Meanwhile ...

"Dear Lady Alathea, I most earnestly implore your favor in this dance." Montgomery bowed low.

Mr. Simpkins regarded his lordship with unconcealed dislike. "Lady Alathea, you need only say the word. I would be honored to partner you." Simpkins's bow was abbreviated to the point of abruptness.

Alathea smiled serenely on them all, her gaze at the last touching Gabriel's.

"I fear, gentlemen," she said, turning back to her court, "that I will not be dancing, in general, this evening."

They all heard the qualification. They'd all seen that swift, shared glance. Now they all wondered. Furiously.

"Ahem." Lord Montgomery struggled not to glare at Gabriel. "Might one enquire …?"

Alathea waved at the crowd. "It's far too exhausting to even imagine fighting one's way to the dance floor." Again she favored them with a serene smile. "I prefer to enjoy your conversation and"—her gaze slid to Gabriel's face—"save my energies for the waltzes."

His expression inscrutable, he met her gaze, then arrogantly raised a brow. If her court had not yet got the message, the moment, heavy with blatant sensuality, should have opened their eyes. The warrior within him roared in triumph; he hesitated, then inclined his head and tore his gaze from hers. While his primitive self gloated at her gesture, it was doing nothing for his composure, further eroding the thin veneer that, where she was concerned, was all that hid his true feelings from the world.

Now she'd all but publicly declared that she was his, surely his possessiveness could relax, triumphant? Unfortunately, he felt anything but relaxed. Alathea reinstituted a conversation with Falworth, regally ignoring the not-quite-convinced looks on Montgomery's and Simpkins's faces. Gabriel tried to stand easily beside her and not think of what he'd rather be doing.

Both proved impossible. She'd been right. Marlborough House filled to the rafters was not a useful venue for what he would prefer to be doing with her, to her. Finding an empty parlor tonight would be impossible. Was there any other way they could steal an hour or so alone? With the conversations about them droning in his ears, he considered all the options, regretfully rejecting every one. He slanted her a glance. The instant she and her family were free of Crowley's threat, he would have to kidnap her, for a few hours at least. Long enough to soothe the beast within.

Thinking of how he would soothe his clamorous needs did nothing to ease them. Gritting his teeth, he wrenched his thoughts onto a different track. Struthers. He'd sent Chance to call on the old seadog at noon, offering his services in any helpful capacity. The captain had, not entirely unexpectedly, sent Chance off with a gruff but polite refusal. Chance had obeyed orders and kept watch on the run-down lodging house in the Clerkenwell Road. The captain had left late in the afternoon and headed for the City, then on toward the docks. Chance had faithfully tracked him, a talent learned in his previous existence, but the captain must have sensed he was being followed. He'd gone into a tavern and then disappeared. Chance had searched the three alleys the tavern gave access to, but hadn't been able to find the old man. Defeated, he'd returned to Brook Street to report.

If the captain was fly enough to lose Chance, then he could take care of himself. Presumably. The presentiment of danger that had struck Gabriel on first meeting the captain continued to nag at him.

Shifting, he glanced at Alathea. At least she was safe. From Crowley. She wasn't entirely safe—not in her terms—from him. They had nigh on a decade to make up for, and more than one event to celebrate. His gaze rose to her hair, to the gift he'd given her that had finally accomplished what he'd sought for so many years to achieve. He'd gotten rid of her damned caps. Never again would she wear one—he'd ensure she never even thought of it.

All of which added to his tension, to the impatience he could feel rising like a tide, a building pressure he could do nothing to release, not here, not now. He drew in an increasingly tight breath and refocused on her face, abruptly conscious that he was nearing the end of his severely strained tether. He glanced around at the gentlemen surrounding them; none posed as much of a threat to her as he.

Straightening, he shifted closer, all too aware of the countess's provocative perfume gently rising from her warm flesh. The thought of how much more strongly that scent would rise once her skin heated with passion had him clenching one fist.

Risking a scene at this point was senseless. He'd do better to take his clamoring instincts, possessive and otherwise, a short distance away.

A sudden gust of laughter from a nearby group had her court looking behind them. He seized the opportunity, touching the back of Alathea's arm, fingers light on the soft skin bare above her glove.

Vivid awareness streaked through him—and her. It was there in her wide eyes as she looked up. "What?"

The word was breathless; she was as giddy as he.

"I'd better circulate. I'll be back for the first waltz."

Her gaze dropped to his lips. They were so close, they could sense each other's breaths. She moistened her lips. "Perhaps," she whispered, "that might be … wise."

She lifted her gaze to his. Gabriel nodded.

He managed to turn away without touching his lips to hers.

Alathea watched him go, then, with an inward sigh, she returned her attention to her court as, the nearby ruckus abating, they turned back to her. She was relieved Gabriel had taken himself off; she'd sensed his suppressed tension. The fact that she now knew what caused it—what it truly was—did not make being its subject any less unsettling. Nevertheless, she would much rather have gotten rid of all her court, slipped away on his arm, and done all she could to ease him.

Keeping her social smile in place, she encouraged her court to entertain her. Her heart, however, wasn't in it. When a footman pushed through to her side, a folded note on a salver, that unruly organ leaped. Her first thought was that her warrior had found some bolt hole and was summoning her to his side.

The truth proved more disturbing.

Dear Lady Alathea,

I have secured all the information I sought and more. I have evidence enough to discredit Crowley's scheme but have been summoned back to my ship and must up anchor and depart on the morning tide. You must come at once—I must explain some of the details of the maps and documents in person, and it will be vital to your cause for me to make a signed deposition before witnesses, and leave the whole in your hands.

I implore you do not dally—I must weigh anchor the instant the tide turns. Take heart, dear lady—the end is nigh. All the necessary documents will shortly be in your hands and you will be able to send Crowley to the devil.

I have taken the liberty of sending a carriage and escort for you. You may trust the men implicitly—they know where to bring you. But you must come at once <u>or all may be lost!</u>

> *Your respectful servant,*
> *Aloysius Struthers, Captn.*

Alathea looked up. Her court were chatting among themselves, giving her a moment of privacy in which to read her note. She turned to the footman. "Is there a carriage waiting?"

"Aye, my lady. A carriage and a number of … men."

They'd probably be sailors. Alathea nodded. "Please tell the men I'll be with them directly."

The footman was too well-trained to show any reaction. He bowed and withdrew to do her bidding. Alathea touched Falworth's arm and smiled at Lord Montgomery, Lord Coleburn, and Mr. Simpkins. "I'm afraid, gentlemen, that I'll have to leave you. An urgent summons from a sick relative."

They murmured sympathetically; she doubted they believed her. Alathea inclined her head and left them. Stepping into the crowd, she lifted her head, scanning the throng. She couldn't see Gabriel.

"Damn!" Muttering under her breath, she started to quarter the room. He'd been tripping over her skirts for weeks. Now, when she needed him, he was nowhere to be found. The crowd was so dense, she couldn't be certain she wasn't crossing paths with him. She saw Celia, and Serena, and the twins, but their cousin was not to be found. Nor was Lucifer. Stepping onto the bottom of the ballroom stairs, Alathea cast an exasperated glance around, but could see no one—not even any of the other Cynsters—who might be of use.

"My lady?" The footman materialized at her elbow. "The men are very insistent that you leave right away."

"Yes, very well." With one last disgusted glance about the packed room, Alathea picked up her skirts, turned—and spied Chillingworth talking with a group of other guests in the lee of the stairs. "One moment."

She left the footman and plunged into the crowd. With a laugh and a bow, Chillingworth turned away from his friends as she pushed nearer. He saw her instantly.

He started to smile, then he took in her expression. He searched her eyes. "What's wrong?"

Alathea caught the hand he held out to her and pressed the note she held into it. "Please—see this gets to Gabriel. It's important. I have to leave."

"Where are you going?" Chillingworth closed his hand about both the note and her fingers. He glanced at the footman on the stairs as another liveried servant hurried down to whisper in the first's ear.

Alathea followed his gaze. "I have to go with someone—that's a message. Gabriel will understand." With a skill honed through years of wrestling with Cynsters, she twisted free of Chillingworth's grasp. "Just make sure he gets it as soon as possible."

The first footman had pushed through to her side. "My lady, the sailors are growing restive."

"*Sailors!*" Chillingworth grabbed for her arm.

Alathea eluded him. Pushing past the footman, she hurried to the stairs. "I haven't time to explain." She threw the words back at Chillingworth, following as fast as he could in her wake. "Just get that note to Gabriel."

Reaching the less-crowded stairs, she lifted her skirts and hurried up.

"Alathea! *Stop!*"

She didn't. She kept doggedly on to the top, then rushed through the archway and on out of the house.

Reaching the bottom of the stairs, Chillingworth stared after her. An influx of guests swept down, making it impossible for him to follow her. Other guests who'd heard him bellow cast him odd looks. His lips setting grimly, he ignored them. "Damn!" He looked at the note crumpled in his fist, then he turned and surveyed the throng. "Serve Cynster *bloody well* right."

He found Gabriel in the card room, shoulders propped against the wall, idly watching a game of whist.

"This"—Chillingworth thrust the note at him—"is for you."

"Oh?" Gabriel straightened. His tickle of presentiment changed to a full-blown punch. He took the note. "From whom?"

"I don't know. Alathea Morwellan charged me to see it to you, but I doubt it's from her. She's left the house."

Gabriel was busy scanning the note; reaching the end, he swore. He looked at Chillingworth. "She's gone?"

Chillingworth nodded. "And yes, I did try to stop her, but you haven't trained her very well. She doesn't respond to voice commands."

"She doesn't respond to *any* commands." Gabriel's attention was on the note. "Damn! This doesn't look good." His expression hardened. He hesitated, then handed the note to Chillingworth. "What's your reading of it?"

Chillingworth read the letter, then grimaced. "He's effectively told her to 'come immediately' three times. Not good."

"My feelings exactly." Retaking the note, Gabriel stuffed it into his pocket and pushed past Chillingworth. "Now all I have to do is figure out where the hell she's gone."

"Sailors." Chillingworth followed in Gabriel's wake. "The footman said the men waiting for her were sailors."

"The docks. Wonderful."

They were nearing the stairs when Chillingworth, still behind Gabriel, said, "I'll come with you—we can take my carriage."

Gabriel threw him a look over his shoulder. "I'm not going to feel *that* grateful, you know."

"My only interest in this," Chillingworth replied as they went quickly up the stairs, "is in getting the damned woman back so she can plague you for the rest of your life."

Reaching the top of the stairs, they made their way through the gallery, then descended the grand staircase and strode across the front foyer. They swept up to the main door, shoulder to shoulder—

Looking back over his shoulder, down the steps to the forecourt, Charlie Morwellan collided with them on the threshold. He fell back. "Sorry." He started to bow then recognized Gabriel. "I say—do you know where Alathea's gone?" He looked toward the road leading to the City. "I can't understand why she had to go with that rough lot—"

Gabriel grabbed him by the shoulders. "Where did they go? Did you get any idea?"

Charlie blinked at him. "Pool of London, Execution Dock, as a matter of fact."

Gabriel released him. "You're sure?"

Charlie nodded. "I was getting some air—terribly stuffy in there—and struck up a conversation with the sailor by the carriage." He was talking to two departing backs; Charlie started down the steps in their wake. "Here—where are you going?"

"After your sister," Gabriel ground out. He shot a glance at Chillingworth. "Which carriage?"

"The small one." Chillingworth was striding along, scanning the ranks of carriages drawn up along the road.

"I might have known," Gabriel muttered.

"Indeed you might," Chillingworth retorted. "*I*, at least, had plans for the night."

Gabriel had had plans, too, but—

"There it is!"

Together with a score of other coachmen, Chillingworth's coachman had left his master's unmarked carriage in the care of two of their number while the rest adjourned to a nearby tavern.

"I can run like the wind and 'ave your man here in a jiffy, guv'nor," one of the watchers offered.

"No—we haven't time. Tell Billings to make his own way home."

"Aye, sir."

The carriage was wedged between two others; it took the combined efforts of Gabriel, Charlie, and the two coachmen to clear the way sufficiently for Chillingworth to ease his carriage free. He waited only until Gabriel swung up to the box seat alongside him and Charlie leaped on the back before giving his blacks the office.

"Billings is going to have a heart attack." Chillingworth glanced at Gabriel. "But never mind that. What's going on?"

Gabriel told them, omitting only the extreme extent to which the Morwellans were at financial risk.

"So she thinks she's going to meet this captain?"

"Yes, but it's all too pat. Why tonight, the last night before the petition is lodged? I spoke with his shipping line only last Friday and they had no expectation of the captain sailing so soon. Struthers himself didn't expect to sail for weeks."

"This Crowley character. What's his caliber?"

"Dangerous, unprincipled—a gutter rat grown fat. One with no known scruples."

Chillingworth glanced at Gabriel, taking in the cast of his features, the granite-hard expression thrown into harsh relief by the street lamps. "I see." His own expression hardening, Chillingworth looked back at his horses.

"Alathea'll be all right," Charlie assured them. "No need to worry about her. She's more than a match for any rogue."

Unslayable confidence rang in his tone; Gabriel and Chillingworth exchanged a glance, but neither made any move to explain that Crowley was no mere rogue.

He was a villain.

"Pool of London," Chillingworth mused, reaching for his whip. "Vessels can leave directly from there."

With a flick of his wrist, he urged his horses on, clattering down along the Strand.

CHAPTER
Twenty

The coach carrying Alathea rocked and swayed as it rumbled along the dock. Clutching the window frame, she peered out on a world of dark shadows, of looming hulks rocking on the wash of the tide. Ropes creaked, timbers groaned. The soft slap of black water against the dock's pylons was as inexorable as a heartbeat.

Alathea's own heart was beating a touch faster, anticipation high but in this setting, tempered by caution and a primitive fear. She shrugged the latter off as the product of a too-vivid imagination. For centuries, convicted pirates had been hung off Execution Dock, but if ghosts walked, surely they wouldn't haunt a site so steeped in justice? Surely it was a good omen that it was to this place in all the dingy sprawl of the London docks that the captain had summoned her. She, too, sought justice.

The coach jerked to a halt. She looked out, but all she could see was the black denseness of a ship's side.

The carriage door was hauled open. A head swathed in a sailor's kerchief was outlined against the night. "If you'll be giving me your hand, ma'am, I'll be a-helping you up the gangplank."

While undeniably rough, the sailors had been as courteous as they knew how; Alathea surrendered her hand and allowed the sailor to help her from the carriage.

"Thank you." She straightened, feeling like a beacon in the dark of the night, her ivory silk gown shimmering in the moonlight. She hadn't worn cloak or shawl to the ball; the night in Mayfair had been balmy. Here, a faint breeze lifted off the water, brushing cool fingers across her bare shoulders. Ignoring the sudden chill, she accepted the sailor's proffered arm.

The dock beneath her feet was reassuringly solid, the wide planking strewn with ropes, pulleys, and crates. She was grateful for the sailor's brawny arm as she stepped over and around various obstacles. He led her to a gangway; she clutched the rope as they climbed, crossing the dark chasm above the choppy water between the dock and the hull.

She stepped onto the deck, grateful when it did not heave and tilt as much as she'd feared. The movement was so slight she could easily keep her balance. Reassured, she looked around. The sailor led the way to a hatch. As he bent to lift the cover, Alathea inwardly frowned. When the captain had said he plied cargo from Africa, she'd imagined a ship rather bigger. This vessel was larger than a yacht, yet ...

The thud of the hatch cover had her turning. The sailor gestured to the opening, lit by a lamp from somewhere below.

"If'n you'll just climb down the ladder, ma'am ..." He ducked his head apologetically.

Alathea smiled. "I'll manage." Gathering her skirts in one hand, she grasped the side of the hatch and felt for the top rung with her foot. Carefully placing her slippered feet, she stepped down the worn wooden rungs. A rope formed a handrail; once she'd gripped it, the rest was easy. As she descended, a corridor opened up before her. It ran the length of the vessel, with doors on both sides staggered along its length. The door at the very end was half open; lamplight shone from beyond.

As she stepped onto the lower deck and let her skirts fall, Alathea wondered why the captain had not come out to greet her.

The hatch clanged shut.

Alathea looked up. A thick iron bolt slid heavily across the hatch, locking it in place. She whirled, clutching the ladder's rope—

Her gaze locked on Crowley's face.

Through the open rungs of the ladder, he watched her, black, bottomless eyes searching her face, watching, waiting ...

Alathea's lungs seized. He was watching to see her fear. Waiting to gloat. Mentally scrambling, her wits all but falling over themselves in panic, she drew herself up, clasped her hands before her, and lifted her chin. "Who are you?"

She was pleased with her tone—regal, ready to turn contemptuous. Crowley didn't immediately react. A faint trace of surprise gleamed in his eyes; he hesitated, then deliberately stepped out from behind the ladder.

"Good evening, my lady."

Alathea was seized by an overwhelming urge to stuff him back behind the ladder. She was used to tall men, large men. Both Gabriel and Lucifer were as tall as Crowley, possibly even taller. But neither they nor any of the men she knew had Crowley's weight. His bulk. He was massive—a bull of a man—and none of it looked like fat. Hard and mean, his presence at close quarters threatened to smother her. It was an effort to bristle rather than flee. She raised one brow. "Are we acquainted?" Her tone made it clear there was no possibility of that.

To her increasing disquiet, Crowley's thick lips curved. "Let's not play games, my dear—at least, not *those* games."

"Games?" Alathea looked down her nose at him. "I have no idea what you mean."

He reached out, not quickly but without warning; there was nothing she could do—no space—to avoid the thick fingers that closed about her wrist. Her gaze locked on his, Alathea refused to let her rising panic show. Her chin set. "I have not the faintest idea of what you are talking about."

She tested his grip. It was unbreakable—and he wasn't even trying.

"I'm talking," he continued, ignoring her futile attempt to break free, "of the interest you've shown in the Central East Africa Gold Company." He brought his black gaze fully to bear on her eyes. "One of my enterprising schemes."

"I'm a lady of quality. I have absolutely no interest whatever in any 'enterprising schemes.' Least of all yours."

"So one would have thought," Crowley agreed equably. "It was quite a surprise to learn differently. Struthers, of course, tried to deny it, but ..." Locking his grip on Alathea's wrist, he drew her arm up, forcing her to face him.

"St-Struthers?" Alathea stared at him.

"Hmm." Crowley's gaze locked on her breasts. "The captain and I had a most satisfactory conversation." His gaze swept down, raking her insolently. "It was impossible for Struthers to explain why a paper bearing your name and direction in what was obviously a lady's hand was so carefully placed with his maps and the copies of those damned leases."

Returning his gaze to her face, Crowley smiled unpleasantly. "Swales remembered the name. After that, it wasn't hard to put two and two together. You Morwellans have decided to try to weasel out of honoring the promissory note your father signed." Crowley's gaze hardened. Fingers tightening on her wrist, he shook her. "Shame on you!"

Alathea's temper flared. "Shame on *us*? I hardly think the notion applies to chousing a cheat out of his ill-gotten gains."

"It does when I'm the cheat." Crowley's jaw set pugnaciously. "I know how to hold my own, and as far as I'm concerned, your father's wealth became *mine* the instant he signed that note."

He shook her again, just enough to let her feel his strength and how puny hers was pitted against it. "Family honor—*bah*! You can forget all concerns about that. You'll have more than enough to concern yourself with, with what I've got planned for you."

The pure malice in his snarl seized her; Alathea fought down her fear. Some fleeting flare must have shown in her eyes—his demeanor changed in an instant, the change itself so quick it was frightening. "Oh-ho! Like *that*, is it?" Eyes gleaming, he shoved her against the wall. "Well, then, let me tell you what I've planned."

He leaned closer; Alathea fought not to turn her head away, forced herself to meet his black gaze without a single flinch. He was breathing heavily, rather too fast even given his bulk. She had a nasty suspicion he was one of those men who found fear in others arousing.

"First," he said, enunciating each word, his eyes locked on hers, "I'm going to use you. Not once, but as many times as I wish, in whatever way I wish."

He looked down at her breasts, at the ivory mounds so enticingly displayed by her rich gown. Alathea felt her skin crawl.

"Oh, *yes*. I've always had a hunger to taste a real, bred-to-the-bone lady. An earl's eldest daughter will do nicely. Afterward, of course, even if you live, I'll have to strangle you."

You're mad. Alathea swallowed the words. His voice had deepened and slowed, slurring slightly. He continued to gaze at her breasts. She tried hard not to breathe deeply, but her pulse was racing, her mouth dry, her lungs laboring.

"Mind you"—his tone was that of one pondering aloud—"I suppose I could sell you to slavers if you survived. You'd fetch a good price along the Barbary Coast. They don't see many white bints as tall as you, but ..." He drew the word out, head tilting as he considered. "If I wanted to get a good price, I'd need to be careful not to mar the goods too obviously. That's hardly fun. And I would never be one hundred percent certain the threat was gone. No." Shaking his head, he raised his eyes to hers.

They were flat, bottomless, utterly without feeling. Alathea couldn't breathe.

His face a malignant mask, Crowley stepped back, hauling her away from the wall. "I'll get rid of you after I've had my fill. That way I won't need to exercise the least care in taking you." Abruptly changing directions, he thrust his face into hers. "A fitting punishment for your meddling."

With a leer and a laugh that echoed manically, he started along the corridor, dragging her behind him. "A fitting punishment, indeed. You can join your friend Struthers on the morning tide."

Alathea dug in her heels. "Struthers?" Throwing her weight against Crowley's pull, she managed to jerk him to a halt. "You killed Captain Struthers?"

Crowley scowled. "You think I'd let him go with all the information he had?" He snorted and pulled her on. "The captain has caught his last tide."

"He had information that threatened you, so you simply *killed* him?"

"He got in my way. People do disappear. Like him. Like *you*."

Alathea scratched at the hand locked about her wrist. "You're crazed! I can't just disappear. People will notice. Questions will be asked."

He threw back his head and laughed. The concentrated evil in the sound shook Alathea as nothing else had. The laugh ceased abruptly; Crowley's head snapped around. His black gaze pinned her. Unable to help herself, she shrank against the corridor wall.

"*Yes*." The word was vicious. Crowley rolled it on his tongue and smiled. "People will indeed notice. Questions will indeed be asked. But not, my beauty, the questions you think." He stepped closer, crowding her against the panelling, the gloating she'd noted before more pronounced. "I did a little checking of my own." His voice had lowered. Raising a hand, he went to caress her cheek. Alathea jerked her head away.

A second later, his hand closed like a vise about her jaw. Fingers biting cruelly, he forced her face to his. "Perhaps," he rasped, his gaze falling to her lips, "I'll keep you alive long enough to see it—what's going to happen to your precious family and who everyone will think is to blame."

He paused. His very nearness made Alathea feel faint. She tried not to breathe deeply, to smell his smell. The sheer bulk of him closed in on her. Her head started to spin.

His lips curved. "Your disappearance is going to coincide with the calling in of the promissory notes. I can guarantee your family is going to be beating off the bailiffs almost immediately. They'll be in turmoil. No one will know where you are, or what to make of your disappearance. All the precious ton will see is your family thrown out of their home in *rags* and you nowhere in sight." His gloating deepened. "I've heard there are offers in the wind for your sisters. Those offers will evaporate. Who knows?" He pressed closer, his gaze locking with hers; she felt the panelling hard against her spine. "If I enjoy breaking you, I might just send some 'gentlemen' I know to make an offer for your sisters. All *three* of them."

Alathea's temper erupted. "You *blackguard!*" With the full force of her arm, she slapped him.

Crowley swore and jerked back, hauling her arm up, pulling her off balance. Alathea screamed. He clapped a hand to her mouth and she kicked him.

That hurt her; the pain only infuriated her more and lent her strength. Swearing viciously, Crowley let go of her arm and caught her around the waist. She jabbed him in the ribs. He juggled her, then locked his beefy arms around her, trapping her with her back to his chest. Half lifting her, he bundled her down the corridor.

Toward the open door at the end.

Alathea wriggled and squirmed. No use. The man was as strong as an ox. She kicked back with her legs, but that was worse than useless. Dragging in a panicked breath, she thought back to her days of fighting with two young sprigs who had always been taller than she.

Gulping in another breath, she stretched and reached back. She grabbed Crowley's ears and tugged as hard as she could.

He howled and jerked his head back. Her nails scored his cheeks.

"*Bitch!*" His voice grated in her ear. "You'll pay for that. For every last scratch."

She could only be glad that, broad as he was, the corridor was too narrow for him to easily strike her. To do so, he'd have to risk letting her go.

Cursing freely, he half carried, half pushed her on before him. Alathea fought and twisted furiously, but did no more than slow him. His strength was overwhelming, suffocating; the notion of being trapped beneath him sent panic sheering through her.

Two yards from the open door, Crowley halted. Before she realized what he intended, he flung open another door concealed within the paneling and started to push her through.

Alathea saw the bed fixed against the wall.

She grabbed the door frame and redoubled her resistance, but inch by inch, Crowley forced her forward. Then he slammed his fist down on her fingers locked about the door frame.

With a yelp, she let go, and he thrust her across the threshold.

Footsteps pounded overhead. They froze, and looked up.

Alathea sucked in a breath and screamed for all she was worth.

Crowley swore. He shoved her into the room.

She tripped on her skirts and fell, but immediately scrambled up. *"Gabriel!"*

Crowley slammed the door in her face.

Flinging herself against the panel, Alathea heard a key scrape, heard the lock fall home. She crouched and put her eye to the keyhole.

And saw the paneling on the corridor's opposite wall. *"Thank God!"* Crowley had taken the key. She reached for a hairpin.

Outside the door, Crowley stared at the ladder. Footsteps moved over the deck above, checking one hatch after another.

"Gabriel?"

A smiling sneer curved his lips, then he laughed, turned, and strode for the open cabin.

Gabriel found the main hatch. He hauled on the heavy cross bolt and heard it grate. Swearing under his breath, he shot it fully back. Chillingworth appeared and helped him lift the hatch cover, easing it over. They looked down on a circle of lamplit corridor and the rungs of the ladder leading down. Looking at Chillingworth, Gabriel shook out his hands, then signaled that he was going down. His face felt expressionless. He had no difficulty acting nerveless. His blood was ice-cold, his veins chilled. He'd never known fear like this—a cold cramping fist closed about his heart. He'd known Alathea forever but he'd only just found her. He couldn't lose her now, not when he'd finally bitten the bullet and opened his heart—and she'd been poised to give him hers. No—he thrust the idea aside. It was unthinkable.

They were not going to lose each other.

He grasped the hatch's rim and swung himself into the hole. Locating the rungs, he quickly descended. He was so tall, he reached the floor before the corridor came fully into view. Stepping onto the lower deck, he looked straight along its emptiness—directly into the maw of the pistol Crowley had pointed at his heart.

Gabriel heard the trigger click. He dove for the floor.

The corridor wall exploded outward. A door swung across, blocking Crowley's shot. Alathea burst into the corridor. The door panel splintered beside her shoulder. She instinctively ducked.

The percussion of the shot boomed and echoed, the sound bouncing deafeningly around the corridor.

"Get down!" Gabriel roared.

Alathea looked at him, then at the door. They both heard Crowley curse, heard his pounding footsteps nearing. Alathea shrank back along the corridor wall.

Crowley slammed the door shut. He didn't look at Alathea but at Gabriel, coming to his feet, the promise of death in his eyes.

Crowley turned and raced back to the main cabin.

"Wait!"

Alathea heard Gabriel's bellow but she didn't even look back as she raced straight after Crowley. He would need to reload. Gabriel was unarmed. She could at least slow Crowley down.

She rushed into the cabin, expecting to see Crowley at the desk or bed, frantically reloading. Instead, she saw him fling the pistol across the room as he strode past the desk. Reaching the wall, he grasped the hilt of one of the twin sabers hanging in crossed scabbards between two portholes.

The saber left its sheath with a deadly hiss.

Alathea didn't pause—she flung herself at Crowley, trusting in her sex to keep her safe. It never occurred to her that Crowley might use the saber on her.

It did occur to Gabriel; he crossed the threshold just in time to see her grapple with Crowley, now brandishing a cavalry saber. One swing and he could cleave her in two—Gabriel died another death. He should have felt relieved when Crowley flung Alathea aside, much as an ox would swat a gnat. She fetched up hard against the wall, shocked, shaken, but essentially unharmed.

Gabriel saw it all in an instant—the instant before blind rage took possession of his senses. After that, all he saw was Crowley.

Crowley settled his weight evenly, taking a two-handed grip on the saber, his very stance declaring he'd never used one in battle.

Gabriel smiled a feral smile. Crowley shifted. Reaching out, Gabriel pushed a small table out of his way—it slammed against the wall. His eyes didn't leave Crowley's face. Slowly, he circled.

It was Crowley's move; he was the one armed. Despite his pugnacious expression, his overweening belligerence, uncertainty flickered in his eyes. Gabriel saw it. He feinted to his left. Crowley raised the saber and slashed—

Gabriel was nowhere near the space the saber whistled through. From Crowley's other side, he stepped inside his guard, left hand closing about Crowley's fists on the saber hilt, right fist slamming into the man's jaw. Crowley grunted. He tried to turn on Gabriel; Gabriel's hold on his fists prevented that, but Crowley's double-fisted grip also prevented Gabriel from gaining any hold on the hilt.

Crowley bunched his muscles to throw Gabriel off. Gabriel released him and spun away. Crowley slashed again and again, following Gabriel as he circled. Each slashing stroke threw Crowley off-balance. Gabriel feinted again; again Crowley fell for it. Gripping the saber hilt, Crowley's fists and all, Gabriel landed a swinging left on Crowley's jaw. Crowley roared and fought back. Wrenching the hilt free of Gabriel's restraining hand, he slashed and found his mark.

Ignoring the stinging bite of the sabre along his left arm, Gabriel flung himself at Crowley, locking both hands on the saber's pommel. Crowley was off-balance; Gabriel forced him back across the desk, pressing the saber closer and closer to his face.

Eyes locked on the blade inching nearer, Crowley gritted his teeth, gathered his strength, and shoved Gabriel and the blade to the side. Reading the move, Gabriel sprang back. The saber flew free, clattering on the floor.

Crowley reared upright—to be met by a solid punch to the gut. He bellowed and swung, starting after Gabriel, his clear intent to grapple with him.

Gabriel wasn't about to give Crowley the satisfaction of breaking his ribs. The man was a bruiser, the sort who'd learned his science in tavern brawls. Given his size and lack of agility, he relied on his brawn to win. In any wrestling match, Crowley would triumph easily. Fisticuffs, however, was another game entirely, one at which Gabriel excelled.

He landed blow after blow, focusing on Crowley's face and gut. Crowley laid not a finger on him. Crowley bellowed and raged, staggering into punch after punch. Gabriel concentrated on softening him up, on enraging him further. On finally beating him to the ground.

But the man's skull felt like rock; knocking him unconscious was not going to be accomplished by one lucky blow.

Backed against the wall, Alathea watched, her heart in her mouth, her breath suspended. Even to her untutored eyes, the fight was a battle between steely reflexes governing strength honed and refined, pitted against sheer brawn and a blind belief in the power of weight. Gabriel was clearly winning, even though he was now risking more to step closer, well within Crowley's reach, to where he could deliver his blows with more force. One of Crowley's swinging fists caught him as he retreated, snapping his head back. To her relief, Gabriel didn't seem to feel it, returning the blow with one that connected with a sickening crunch.

Crowley couldn't possibly last much longer.

Crowley must have come to the same conclusion. The vicious kick came out of nowhere. Gabriel saw it, but only had time to swivel. It caught him high behind his left thigh. Crowley clumsily pivoted. Gabriel lost his footing and fell.

Alathea smothered a scream.

Gabriel's head hit the desk's edge with a dull thud. He slumped to the floor and lay still.

Massive chest heaving, Crowley stood over him, fists clenched, blinking his piggy black eyes, both bruised and half-closed. Then his teeth flashed in a vicious smile. He looked around, then swooped on the saber, scooping it up, hefting the blade as he took up a stance beside Gabriel's twisted legs. Crowley shuffled his feet apart as he settled his hands about the saber's hilt.

Gabriel groaned. His eyes were closed, his shoulders flat to the floor, his spine twisted. He lifted his head slightly, struggling up onto his elbows, frowning, blinking dazedly, shaking his head as if to clear it.

Crowley's gloating expression filled his face. His eyes glittered. He smiled as he slowly raised the saber.

Alathea inched along the wall, unable to breathe, barely able to think through the flood of emotions swamping her. But fear and fury were the strongest; she knew what she had to do. Setting her teeth, she passed behind Crowley, creeping silently further along the wall.

Crowley stretched upward, raising the saber high above his head, tensing for the downward stroke—

Alathea leaped the last feet, grabbed the second saber, and yanked it from its sheath. The angry hiss filled the room.

Crowley's head snapped around. Teetering, he took an instant to regain his balance. He started to shift his bulk, to realign his saber, turning to swing at her—

The weight of the saber flying out of its sheath swung Alathea away from Crowley. With a gasp, she hauled on the heavy sword and sent it arcing back toward him—

Shoulders and torso still turning, Crowley raised his saber—

Gabriel finally refocused—what he saw stopped his heart. Hauling up his legs, he kicked at Crowley, catching him high on the thigh.

Crowley stumbled. His weight shifted. He staggered helplessly sideways toward Alathea, into the arc of her wildly swinging saber.

Powered by its own weight, the saber flashed in, burying itself in Crowley's side. Alathea gasped and released the hilt. The saber remained, its glistening tip barely disturbing the front of Crowley's coat, the hilt quivering behind his back.

Crowley's face leached of all color; shock overlaid all expression. He regained his balance, both feet settling square, the other saber held tight between his fists. Slowly, he looked down, then, equally slowly, turned his head and looked over his shoulder at the saber sticking out from his back. His expression said he didn't comprehend …

He shuffled his feet, turning to Alathea, still holding the other saber—

In a rush of footsteps, Chillingworth appeared in the doorway. He took one glance, raised his arm, and shot Crowley.

Eyes wide, Alathea made no sound as Crowley jerked. The ball had found its mark in the left of his huge chest. Slowly, he turned his head to stare uncomprehendingly at Chillingworth. Then his features blanked, his eyes closed, and he pitched forward.

Gabriel pulled his legs clear and struggled to sit up. Still dizzy, his head ringing, he leaned his shoulders against the side of the desk.

Chillingworth stepped into the room, frowning as he took in the saber sticking up from Crowley's back. "Oh. You'd already taken care of it." Then he looked at Gabriel, back at Crowley, then back to Gabriel, frowning even more. "How the devil did you manage that?"

Gabriel looked at Alathea's white face. "It was a joint effort."

Chillingworth followed his gaze to Alathea, still pressed back against the wall, her stunned gaze locked on Crowley's body.

Footsteps approached; Charlie looked in. "I heard a shot." Eyes growing round, he peered around Chillingworth. "I say—is he dead?"

Gabriel smothered a crazed laugh. "Very." His grim expression only tangentially due to the pain in his head, he studied Alathea, then softly asked, "Are you all right?"

She blinked, then she lifted her head and looked at him. "Of course I'm all right." Her gaze traveled over him. Wild concern flared in her eyes. Picking up her skirts, she leaped over Crowley's body. "*Good God*—the bastard cut you! Here—let me see."

Gabriel had forgotten about the cut on his arm. Now he looked and discovered his coat ruined, blood pouring afresh thanks to Alathea's probing. Crouched beside him, she was tweaking the slashed material, trying to see ...

"Can you stand?" She looked into his eyes, then grimaced. "No, of course, you can't. Here." She waved Chillingworth closer as she wriggled a shoulder under his. "Help me get him up."

Frowning, Chillingworth lent his aid.

"Just watch out for that damned dress." Hauled to his feet, Gabriel settled against the desk.

Alathea pressed close, pushing his hair out of his eyes to peer into them. "Are you all right?"

Exasperated, Gabriel opened his mouth to tersely inform her it would take rather more than a severe blow on the head and a shallow cut on his arm to incapacitate him. Then he caught a glimpse of the arrested expression on Charlie's face, and substituted, "Of course not." He gestured to the blood darkening his sleeve. "See if you can stop the bleeding. Just be sure you don't damage that gown."

The gown was a fantasy he had every intention of peeling from her, inch by sweet inch.

"Crowley must have some linen stored here somewhere." Alathea glanced at her brother. "Charlie—look around."

By the time Charlie returned, Alathea had eased Gabriel's coat off and laid bare the wound. It was a shallow but wide cut, lifting inches of skin but nowhere deep enough to be dangerous. It had, however, bled copiously and continued to do so.

"Here." Charlie handed Alathea a pile of clean shirts. He glanced at Crowley. "He won't need them anymore."

Alathea didn't spare a single glance for Crowley as she picked up a shirt and started ripping.

Straightening from examining the body, Chillingworth stepped around it. He glanced at Gabriel's wound, and stilled. Alathea bustled to the sideboard in search of water or wine. Chillingworth watched her go, then sent a disgusted glance at Gabriel.

Who met it with a bland if not challenging stare.

Chillingworth raised his eyes to the skies. Alathea returned, a bowl of water in her hands. Chillingworth surveyed the room. "While you're having your strength restored, perhaps Charlie and I should search."

"Good idea," Gabriel concurred.

"So what are we looking for?" Chillingworth rounded the desk.

"The promissory notes?' Alathea paused in her dabbing. "Would they be here?" She looked at Gabriel.

He nodded. "I think so. Presumably, the reason Crowley is here tonight and not in Egerton Gardens is because he got the wind up when he learned of our investigations." His expression grew grim and he glanced at Alathea. "I assume Struthers's activities kicked up too much dust. Did Crowley say?"

Alathea's eyes dimmed. "He killed the captain. He said so."

Chillingworth cast a dark glance at Crowley's body. "Obviously destined for Hades."

Gabriel caught Alathea's wrist. "Are you sure the captain's dead? Crowley didn't just say it to frighten you?"

Alathea shook her head sadly. "I think he's already thrown the body in the river."

Gabriel caressed her inner wrist, then released her.

Chillingworth grimaced. "Nothing we can do for the captain now. The villain's already savored his just deserts. The best way to avenge the captain's death is to make sure Crowley's scheme dies with him." He pulled out a desk drawer. "You sure these notes will be here?"

"I expect so." Gabriel looked around. "This is not a ship of any line—it's a privateer, and a small one at that, built for speed—for fleeing. My guess is that Crowley moved his operations here, ready to depart at an instant's notice. With Alathea and Struthers removed, he would plan on calling in the notes immediately, and leaving England as soon as he had his hands on the cash."

Alathea started to bind his arm. "Crowley did say he'd call the notes in immediately."

Chillingworth continued searching the desk. Charlie drifted off, saying he'd search the other rooms.

Just as Alathea was tying off her bandage, Charlie reappeared, dragging a small seaman's chest. He brandished a document. "I think this is what we're looking for."

It was—a thick stack of promissory notes filled the chest. Alathea held the one Charlie had brought in, and started to shake. Gabriel slid an arm around her waist, drawing her closer until she rested against him. "Take it home, show your father, then burn it."

Alathea glanced at him, then nodded. Folding the note, she handed it to Charlie with a strict injunction not to lose it.

Charlie shoved it in his pocket, then went back to reading the names on the handful of notes he'd extracted from the chest.

Chillingworth was doing the same. "He preyed on small fry, for the most part. From the addresses, some of these must be shopkeepers." He pointed to another pile he'd laid aside. "Those are the peers, but most are not the sort who usually invest in such schemes. And the amounts pledged! He'd have turned half of England insolvent."

Gabriel nodded. "Greedy and unscrupulous. That should be his epitath."

"So." Chillingworth restacked the notes. "What are we going to do? Burn these?"

"No." Alathea was frowning. "If we do that, then the people involved will never know they're free of the obligation. They might make decisions assuming they're in debt to Crowley, when that debt will never be realized."

"Are the addresses on all the notes?" Gabriel asked.

"Far as I can see," Charlie replied. Chillingworth nodded.

"Perhaps ..." Gabriel stared into the distance. "Find something to wrap them in. I'll take them to Montague. He'll know how best to return them to their owners, apparently properly and legally canceled."

"Our petition, if successful, will cancel the notes." Alathea looked at Gabriel.

He shook his head. "We won't be lodging it. We won't be doing anything to link ourselves with Crowley."

"No, indeed." Chillingworth glanced at the body on the floor. "So what should we do with him? Simply leave him here?"

"Why not? He's got enemies aplenty. He doubtless gave orders to his crew to stay away from the ship tonight."

"All except the guard," Charlie put in. "But he never even saw you."

Gabriel nodded. "Two of the sailors—the ones who delivered the note—will know Alathea was lured here, but no one will know anything more. No woman could have overpowered Crowley. When his men return to the ship, they'll find him here, alone and very dead. They'll assume Alathea left, and *then* someone killed Crowley."

"I sincerely doubt anyone will mourn him."

"Other than perhaps Archie Douglas, although even that's uncertain."

"Crowley probably had his hooks into him, too."

"Very likely." Gabriel considered, then continued, "It's my guess that without Crowley, and without those notes, the Central East Africa Gold Company will simply cease to exist. It has no capital, and Swales, from all I've been able to glean, is not the sort to drive this type of enterprise on his own."

Chillingworth considered, too, then nodded. "It'll do. We'll simply leave and take the notes, and get your Montague to return them to their owners."

They wrapped the notes securely in a blanket and Charlie carried them off the ship. Alathea helped Gabriel. Chillingworth was their lookout. When he joined the others in the shadows by his carriage, he nodded. "All clear."

Alathea sighed with relief. "Help me get Gabriel inside."

Chillingworth stared at her, then, hauling open the carriage door, cast a narrow-eyed look at Gabriel. "I assume," he asked in a sweetly innocent tone, "I should drive directly to his house?"

"Of course!" Alathea scrambled into the carriage, then turned and reached out to help Gabriel in. "I need to tend that cut properly as soon as possible."

Gabriel shot Chillingworth a wicked grin, then bent his head and stepped into the carriage. Chillingworth slammed the door shut. "Who knows," he said, loudly enough for Alathea to hear, "it might even need stitches."

With that, he climbed to the box seat, took up the reins Charlie was holding, and set his carriage rolling back to London.

CHAPTER
Twenty-one

Chillingworth let Gabriel and Alathea down in Brook Street.
"I'll go straight home," Alathea called to Charlie as she went up the
steps beside Gabriel, her grip on his arm firm and supporting. "I don't know
how long this might take. Tell your mama there's no need to wait up for me."

Gabriel grinned as he reached for his latchkey. He could just imagine
Chillingworth's face. Chillingworth had somewhat curtly offered to drive
Charlie back to Marlborough House. That probably entitled him to yet another
quota of Cynster gratitude. Given they could never be sure just how
incapacitated Crowley had been before Chillingworth shot him, tonight had
seen the earl's stocks rise high indeed.

Charlie called an acknowledgment. Chillingworth's horses stamped, then
the carriage rattled away. Sliding his key into the lock, Gabriel turned it.
Glancing at Alathea, he twisted the knob and opened the door.

This would, after all, shortly be her home. He was simply jumping the gun
a trifle. He wasn't, however, foolish enough to sweep her off her feet and carry
her over the threshold.

He let her shoo him in, instead, fussing like a mother hen.

Chance appeared at the end of the hall. He was in his shirtsleeves, clearly
taken aback to see his master returning so early. When he saw who his master
was with, he goggled, and started to silently back away ...

Alathea saw him and beckoned. "You're Chance, I take it?"

"Hmm." Chance ducked his head, warily edging closer. "That's me, mum."

Alathea shot him a sharp glance, then nodded. "Yes, well, your master has
been injured. I want a bowl of warm water—not too hot—brought up to his
room directly, with some clean cloths and bandages. And some salve, too—I
assume you have some?" All the while she'd been progressing down the hall,
towing Gabriel with her.

"Umm." Falling back before her advance, Chance looked helplessly at
Gabriel.

"This is Lady Alathea, Chance."

Chance bowed. "Pleased to make your acquaintance, mum."

"Indeed." Alathea waved him away. "I want those items, and I'll need your help upstairs momentarily." When Chance stared at her blankly, she leaned forward and looked him in the eye. "*Now*. Immediately. Sooner than soon."

Chance jumped back, all but tripping over his feet. "Oh! Right. Straight away, mum." He scurried through the baize door.

Alathea watched him go, then shook her head and tugged Gabriel on toward the stairs. "Your eccentricities never cease to amaze me." She proceeded to propel him up the stairs.

She couldn't have done it if he hadn't been willing—very willing—despite the fact that he hated being the object of any woman's fussing. Her fussing he was willing to endure given that she'd yet to make any formal statement—a clear and unequivocal acceptance of his heart.

He wanted to hear it, but she was perennially stubborn; encouraging her to let her feelings run riot, as they presently were, would make it all the harder for her to draw back, to balk at the final hurdle. So he meekly climbed the stairs, biding his time, letting her imagine he was weak. He did feel a little lightheaded, relieved that it was over, that Crowley was dead, never to darken their horizon again, and eager, buoyed with anticipation like some callow youth at the realization that she was his.

All he needed now was to hear her admit it.

"Here." He stopped by his door and leaned against the door frame, letting her turn the knob and set the door wide. Without the slightest hesitation, she urged him inside, steering him to the wide bed.

She pushed him to sit on its side. Her fingers going to the improvised bandage, she glanced frowningly at the door. "Where is that man?"

"He'll be here in a moment." Gabriel stood to ease out of his coat. She stripped it from him and promptly pushed him back down again, then busily set about unlacing his cuffs.

Gabriel twisted his lips to hide a grin. How far would she go if he let her?

"Are you in pain?"

Hurriedly straightening his lips, he shook his head. "No." He searched her face, drowned in her eyes, in the concern that filled them, the love that gave it birth. "No." He reached out and closed one hand over hers. "Thea, I'm all right."

Frowning, she shook off his hand and slapped a palm to his forehead. "I hope you don't develop a fever."

Gabriel dragged in a breath. "Thea—"

Chance rushed in, balancing a bowl of water on his wrists, a towel over one arm, cloths balanced upon it, with a pot of salve clutched in his other hand. "Is this all you wanted, mum?"

"Indeed." Alathea nodded approvingly. "Just bring that table nearer. And the lamp, too."

"Oooh! Lot of blood there." Chance moved the table closer. He glanced at Alathea. "Perhaps you'll want some brandy, mum? To clean the wound?"

"An excellent idea!" She lifted her head. "Is there any here?" Her glance fell on the decanter on the dresser.

Gabriel stiffened. "No! That's—"

"Perfect!" Alathea enthused. "Bring it here."

"Thea ..." Horrified, Gabriel watched Chance dart to the dresser and bring back the decanter filled with superbly aged French brandy. "I really don't need—"

"*Do* be quiet." Alathea stared into his eyes, peering into one, then the other. "I keep worrying you'll start raving any minute. Please—just let Chance and me fix this. Then you can rest. All right?"

He looked into her eyes—she was perfectly serious. Gabriel bit his tongue, glanced at Chance, then nodded.

For the next fifteen minutes, he suffered their combined ministrations. He'd forgotten that Chance had reason to want to repay him with kindness. Sitting silent on his bed, he was smothered by kindness, by concern, by love. It was pleasant, even if he felt a fraud.

With Chance's help, Alathea stripped off his shirt, then gently tended his wound, apparently unaffected by the sight of his bare chest. Gabriel itched to change that, but ... Chance was still in the room. Alathea lovingly cleansed the long cut, then bathed it.

He kept his gaze glued to her hair. Despite all she'd gone through, the three blooms were still firmly in place, his declaration acknowledged. He wasn't about to remove them, not intentionally. Not until he'd had their promise converted into words. Multiple times. While she fussed over his arm, he fell to rehearsing all that was to come, and how best to wring from her the words he wanted to hear without disturbing those blooms.

Leaving his arm to dry, she straightened and stepped closer, the warmth of her breasts bare inches from his face. He tried not to breathe while she investigated the bump on his head.

"It's the size of a duck egg," she pronounced, suitably horrified.

Gabriel shut his eyes as she probed, and tried not to groan. The cool cloth she laid upon the bump helped, easing the dull ache in his head. There was only one remedy for the ache in his groin. When she finally turned her attention to binding up his arm, Gabriel caught Chance's eye. It took a moment for Chance to understand his message. When he did, he looked shocked, but when Gabriel scowled, he hurriedly collected the cloths, towels, and bowl and eased himself out of the door.

The click of the latch coincided with Alathea's benedictory pat to the knot she'd tied in the bandage around his arm. "There." She lifted her gaze to his face. "Now you can rest."

"Not yet." Gabriel clamped his hands about her waist and took her with him as he fell back on the bed. Her surprised yelp was smothered as he rolled, shifting them further onto the cushioned expanse, simultaneously trapping her beneath him.

"Be careful of your arm!"

"My arm is perfectly fine."

She stilled beneath him. "What do you mean, it's 'fine'?"

"Just that. I did try to tell you. It's only a surface cut—I'm not likely to die from it."

She scowled at him. "I thought it was serious."

"I know." Bending his head, he nibbled at her lips. "That did become apparent."

He surged over her; the sensation of her long, supple form tensing beneath him sent a wave of primitive possessiveness through him. A possessiveness colored by desire, by need, and by another emotion almost too vital to contain.

Still frowning, she braced her hands against his bare chest. "It must hurt. Your head *must* be throbbing."

"It aches, but it's not my skull that's throbbing." He shifted suggestively, thrusting his hips to hers.

Her eyes widened slightly as she shifted beneath him to cradle his erection at the apex of her thighs. Confirming his state. The look she sent him was the epitome of feminine—wifely—resignation. *"Men!"* With renewed vigor, she pushed him back and struggled to sit up. "Are you all the same?"

"All Cynsters, certainly." Gabriel rolled to the side, watching bemusedly as she reached for her laces. She was doing it again—taking a tack he hadn't foreseen. It took him a moment to fathom the why and wherefore, then he decided to follow her lead. He reached for her laces. "Here, let me."

He'd fantasized about peeling the white-and-gilt gown from her; in it, he could easily see her as some priestess, some pagan female designed to be worshipped. As he eased the gown from her shoulders, he worshipped, his lips anointing each silken inch of skin revealed. She shivered. Surging up beside her, he filled one hand with her breast, the soft flesh firming at his touch, heating as he kneaded. His other hand rose to cradle her head, long fingers searching for the pins that anchored the tight knot of her hair, careful not to dislodge the three white flowers adorning her crown—the evidence of his adoration. Her hair fell loose; his fingers tightened about her nipple. On a moan, she let her head fall back, offering her lips. He took them, took her mouth greedily, hungrily, aware there was no longer any need to hold back. She was with him. The same need drove them both, a fervent desire to hold, to possess, to reassure their souls they had survived the threat whole, still hale. To take a first tantalizing taste of the future, of the freedom to love that they'd won.

His plans degenerated into a sweet, reckless flurry of searching hands, of incoherent, breathless moans, of sweet caresses and heated kisses, of urgent fingers and quivering flesh. They stripped each other of every last stitch, content only when they lay skin to skin, long limbs entwined, cocooned within the chaos of his covers. He gathered her to him, moving over her, surrounding her. With one stroke, he sheathed himself in her heat.

She gasped and welcomed him in, her body arching, tensing, easing, then melting about him. Her surrender was implicit. Gabriel held tight to their reins. Tonight, he wanted explicit. So he rode her slowly, joining with her in long, slow, rolling thrusts, melding their bodies as they would meld their lives—deeply, completely. When he would have risen over her, she clung to him, holding him to her. He acquiesced and stayed, their bodies in contact from chest to knees. She undulated beneath him, all shifting silk and velvet lushness, a glory of womanly need.

He filled her again and again, until she gasped and clung.

He stilled, savoring her glorious climax, luxuriating in her satiated sigh. He waited until she'd softened fully beneath him. Then he moved again.

Still slow, still unhurried. He had all night and knew it. Not even this—the glory of her giving—was going to distract him tonight.

It was a minute or two before she stirred, before her body instinctively searched for, then found his steady rhythm. Her lids lifted, just enough for her to stare at him. Her tongue touched her lips; he delved deeper and she arched.

A glint of surprise glowed in her eyes.

An instant later, he felt her hands trailing, gently questing down the planes of his flexing back, down to caress his pulsing flanks.

She caught his gaze. "What?"

His grin was partly grimace, over gritted teeth. She was warm and soft and so inviting beneath him. "I want to hear you say it."

The words were low, gravelly, but sufficiently distinct. She didn't ask what it was he wanted to hear.

Beneath him, beneath the steady, relentless onslaught, she stirred. "I have to go home."

He shook his head. "Not until you say the words. I'm going to keep you here, naked and hot and needy, until you admit you love me."

"Needy? It's not me—"

He cut the words off with his lips. When he'd wiped them from her tongue and her brain, he drew back, rising up on his braced arms to drive deeper into her slick heat.

She gasped, panted, bit back a moan. Writhed just a little. "You ... you know I do."

"Yes. I know. Even if I hadn't known before, I'd certainly know now, after your performance tonight. Now even Charlie and Chillingworth know."

Her state made her slow to respond. She stared at him, blinked, then weakly asked, "*What?* Why should they think ...?"

He couldn't grin, although he wanted to. It was hard enough to find the strength to answer. "You half killed a man to save me tonight, and for the last two hours, you've been fretting and fuming over what anyone could see was little more than a scratch. You nearly made poor Chillingworth bilious."

Alathea wished she could summon a glare, but her body was prey to the sweetest heat, her senses far too interested in the glory building between them. Her mind was clinging to sanity by a thread. "I didn't know it was just a scratch. I was being led by the nose—"

"You were being led by love." He lowered his head and found her lips in a kiss laden with sensual promise. "Why don't you just admit it?"

Because she'd only tonight come to a full understanding of what this joint love of theirs entailed. The shared joy countered by the fear of loss—the sudden desperation when he, her life, had nearly been slain before her. There was a lot more to loving than she'd imagined. Loving this deeply was a frightening thing.

Lifting her head, she brushed her lips along his jaw. "If it's so obvious ..."

He lifted his head out of her reach. "Obvious it might be. I still want to hear you say it."

He was filling her with long, slow, languid thrusts, enough to keep her fully aroused but not enough to satisfy. Her temper, unfortunately, was thoroughly subsumed by desire. "Why?" She arched, desperate to lure him deeper yet.

"Because until you do, I can't be sure you know it."

She opened her eyes fully and looked into his. Beneath his heavy lids, she could detect not the slightest glimmer of humor. He was serious. Despite all, despite the way her heart ached simply when she looked at him. "*Of course* I love you."

The set of his face—features etched with passion but with his expression somehow driven—didn't change. "Good. So you'll marry me."

There was no question in the words. Alathea sighed, struggling not to smile. He wouldn't appreciate it. The reins were in his hands and he was driving hell for leather for the church.

He didn't even appreciate her sigh. He stilled within her, looking down at her almost grimly. "You're not leaving this room until you agree. I don't care if I have to keep you here for weeks."

Despite her best efforts, her smile dawned, even though she knew the threat was not an empty one. He would do it if she pushed him.

He was a Cynster in love.

Letting her smile deepen, she reached up and brushed aside the lock of hair hanging over his forehead. "All right. I love you, and I'll marry you. There—is there anything more I need say to get you to go faster?"

She only just glimpsed his victorious smile as he bent to kiss her, but see it she did. She made him pay for his smugness by demanding more and even more of his expertise.

She nearly drove them both insane with wanting.

But it was worth it.

Later, when they lay wrapped in his sheets, not asleep but too deeply sated to move, Alathea lay with her head on his shoulder and hazily considered a lifetime filled with such peace.

For it was peace that filled her, an unutterable sense of having found her true home, her true place—her true love. That his love surrounded her, and hers him, she had not the smallest doubt. Only that, a deeply shared love, could fill her heart to this extent, so that she could not imagine any joy more fulfilling than lying naked in his naked arms, his breath a soft huff in her ear, his arm heavy about her waist, his hand splayed possessively over her bottom.

They were so alike. They would need to go slowly into their future, eyes open, careful not to step on each other's toes. There would be adjustments to be made by both of them—that was implicit in their natures. Yet while that future beckoned, rising like a new sun on their horizon, she was too comfortable, too sensually sated, to attend to it just yet.

She was comfortable, yes, and that was a discovery. That even now, fully aware of the latent strength in the body beneath hers, in the muscled arms that yet held her so gently, in the steel-sinewed limbs that pressed all along her length, even now, she was soothed, relaxed. Aware of the crisp hair beneath her cheek, exquisitely aware of his hair-dusted limbs tangled with hers. Aware to her soul of the warmth within her, of the firm member angled against her thigh. The entire reality left her deeply content.

Profoundly happy.

In bliss.

She closed her eyes and indulged.

He eventually stirred, his arms tightening about her, tension returning to his limbs. He held her close, then pressed his lips to her temple. "I'm never going to let you forget what you said."

Alathea smiled. Was she surprised?

"So." He shook her fractionally. "When are we getting married?"

They had, apparently, arrived at the church.

Opening her eyes, she dutifully turned her mind to weddings. "Well, there's Mary and Esher, and Alice and Carstairs, too. A joint wedding might be best."

His snort said no. "They may be your stepsisters, but they're sweet, innocent, and full to bursting with the usual romantic notions. They'll take months to decide on the details. I have absolutely no intention of waiting on their decisions. You and I are getting married first." He tightened his grip on her. "As soon as possible."

Alathea grinned. "Yes, my lord."

Her teasing tone earned her a finger in her ribs. She gasped and squirmed; he sucked in a breath. He settled her again, his touch converted to caress, idly fanning her hip.

"I've already spoken to your father."

Alathea blinked. "You have? When?"

"Yesterday. I saw him at White's. I'd already arranged to send you the flowers."

His hand continued its slow stroking, soothing, subtly calming.

Alathea looked into the future, the future he was so swiftly carrying her into. "They'll miss me. Not just the family but the household—Crisp, Figgs and the rest."

The slow stroking continued. "We'll be close—only a few miles away. You'll be able to watch over them until Charlie takes a bride."

"I suppose …" After a moment, she added, "Nellie will come with me, of course, and Folwell. And Figgs is your housekeeper's sister, after all."

"Tweety's sister?"

"Hmm. So I'll certainly hear of any problems."

"*We'll* hear of any problems. I'll want to know, too."

She lifted her head to look into his face. "Will you?"

He trapped her gaze. "*Anything* that happens in your life from now on, *I* want to share."

She studied his eyes, read his feelings on the years gone by, on the question that would always be with him—could he have saved them those eleven years if he'd known, if he'd opened his eyes and truly looked at her?

She lifted her hand to his cheek. "I don't think anything serious will happen, not with both of us watching."

Stretching up, wantonly undulating in his embrace, she pressed her lips to his. He lifted her and settled her, stomach to ridged abdomen, then filled her mouth with caresses that stirred her to her toes.

She was simmering when he drew back. Brushing his lips across her forehead, he murmured, "I fantasized for weeks about having the countess reveal herself to me." His palms skimmed down her naked back to cup her bottom, making it abundantly clear just how forthcoming he'd wanted the countess to be. "Are you disappointed?"

His hands closed possessively. He shifted her, then rocked his hips, his erection parting her curls, impressing her belly. Alathea caught her breath.

He chuckled. "The revelations I've suffered were better by far than any fantasy." She looked up; he trapped her gaze. "I love you." The words were simple and clear. He searched her eyes, then his lips relaxed. "And you love me. As revelations go, those are hard to beat."

Alathea tucked her head into the hollow of his shoulder so he couldn't see her eyes as the words slid through her, into her heart. After a moment, she sighed. "I still can't quite believe that our troubles are all over, that Crowley is dead. We don't need to worry about him anymore—I don't have to worry about the family's finances any more."

Abruptly, she stiffened and went to sit up; Gabriel restrained her. She lifted her head. "The notes! Charlie has ours, but all the rest ... we left them in Chillingworth's carriage."

Gabriel started to stroke her again. "He'll send them around. Don't worry. Stop worrying. You've been worrying for the past eleven years. You don't need to worry about *anything* anymore."

Alathea subsided back into his arms. "That's not going to come easily, you know."

"I'm sure I can find any number of engrossing subjects with which to distract you."

"But you manage your own estate—there won't really be anything for me to do estate office-wise."

"You can help. We'll be partners."

"Partners?" The idea was strange enough to have her lifting her head to look into his face.

He continued to stroke her bare back. "Hmm."

She frowned. "I suppose ..." Turning over, she settled comfortably, wrapping her arms over the hand he splayed over her waist. "I'll do the household accounts, of course. Or does your mother do those?"

"No—by all means, you can do them."

"And if you like, I can do the estate tallies. Or does your father do those?"

"Papa handed over the Manor estate to me two years ago. Neither he nor Mama is any longer involved."

"Oh." Alathea wriggled. "So it's just the two of us, then?"

"Mmm. We can divide the duties any way we like."

She drew in a breath. Held it. "I'd like to continue actively managing my own investments. As I did with my family's funds."

Gabriel shrugged. "I can't see why not."

"You can't?" She tried to look up at him but he held her fast. "I thought you'd disapprove?"

"Why? From all I saw, you're good at it. I'd disapprove if you weren't. But if we're going to be partners generally, there's no reason we can't be real partners in that sphere, too."

Alathea relaxed. After a moment, she murmured, "Who knows? We might even be friends."

Gabriel closed his arms about her. "Who knows? Even that." It was a peculiarly attractive thought. "I'd enjoy that, I think."

Another moment passed, then she murmured, "So would I."

Lips curving, Gabriel tightened one arm about her, splaying his other hand over the smooth curve of her belly. "Given our present circumstances, I suggest we concentrate on the most pertinent—the most immediate—aspect of our partnership."

She sucked in a breath as he slid his fingers further, twining through the springy curls to reach the softness they shielded. With one broad finger, he stroked. She shuddered.

"I really think you need to pay more attention to this." With a grin, he rolled and lifted to come over her. She reached for him and found him. It was his turn to groan.

"Convince me."

The words were a challenge—precisely the sort she knew his Cynster soul delighted in. He threw himself into meeting it, heart and soul.

When she was writhing beneath him, hot and ready and yearning, he filled her with one long thrust. Braced above her, he watched her face as, eyes closed, head thrown back, she arched and took him in. His flowers still glowed against the rich brown of her hair. He withdrew and thrust slowly again, just to watch her accept him, to see the flowers quiver, then he settled to a steady, easy rhythm, rocking her relentlessly, taking the longest route he knew to heaven.

She gasped, clung, but there was a subtle smile flirting about her lips. He bent his head and laved one furled nipple, then nipped it. "By the time Jeremy and Augusta have grown, I can guarantee that if you pay attention to this aspect of our partnership, you'll have a tribe of your own to watch over in their stead."

Her lids lifted fractionally; she seemed to be weighing his words. "A tribe?"

She sounded intrigued.

"Our own tribe," he gasped as she tightened about him.

Alathea grinned. Reaching up, she curved her hand about his neck and lifted her lips to his. "Just as long as that's an iron-clad guarantee."

The laughter started in his chest, erupted in his throat, then spilled over to her. They shook and clung, giddy as children. Then abruptly the laughter was gone; something much stronger swirled wildly about them, through them, then closed upon them and lifted them from the world.

Finally they settled to sleep, the city silent about them, the future settled, their hearts at peace.

Alathea slid into Gabriel's waiting arms and felt them close about her. Whatever the future, they'd create it together, manage it together, *live* it together. That was so much more future than she'd ever thought she'd have.

She slid her arms about him, hugged him once, then relaxed, content in his embrace.

The next morning, Lucifer stood on the front steps of the Brook Street house and watched the departure of the lady who, somewhat to her surprise, had spent the night warming his bed. And him. Raising a hand in salute as her carriage rumbled off, he turned inside, letting his victorious smile show. She'd proved a challenge but he'd persevered and, as usual, triumphed.

Success had proved very sweet.

Replaying honeyed memories, he headed for the dining room. Breakfast was just what he needed.

Courtesy of Chance, the door was ajar. Lucifer pushed it wide; it swung open noiselessly.

On a scene guaranteed to freeze the blood in his veins.

Gabriel sat at his usual place at the head of the table, sipping coffee. On his right sat Alathea Morwellan, dreamily staring straight ahead, a tea cup in one hand, a piece of nibbled toast growing cold in the other.

She looked radiant. And a trifle flushed. As if ...

Stunned, Lucifer looked again at Gabriel. His brother appeared a great deal too well fed for someone just about to tuck in.

The dread conclusion hovering in his mind grew weightier, steadily taking on substance.

Gabriel sensed the draft from the door and looked up. He met Lucifer's astonished gaze with one of transparent unconcern, raising a querying brow as he gestured to Alathea. "Come welcome your sister-in-law-to-be."

Lucifer plastered a smile on his face and stepped across the threshold. "Congratulations." Alathea, he noted, still looked a trifle lightheaded, but then, he knew his brother. "Welcome to the family." Leaning down, he gave her a brotherly buss. He couldn't help muttering as he straightened, "Are you sure you haven't both run mad?"

It was Alathea who frowned him down. "*We* were never the ones to run mad, as I recall."

Lucifer abandoned that tack, along with any hope of ever understanding. He made all the right noises, said all the right words, while he floundered to make sense of any of it. Alathea and Gabriel? He knew he wasn't the only one who had never thought it. Which just went to show.

"The wedding," Gabriel informed him, "will be as soon as we can arrange it, certainly before we or the Morwellans, or indeed, the rest of the ton, desert the capital."

"Hmm," Lucifer returned.

"You will be there, won't you?"

At Alathea's pointed look, Lucifer summoned a smile. "Of course."

He'd be there to see his brother, the last of his confreres still free, take up the shackles of matrimony. After that, he'd leave.

He was going to disappear.

London—indeed, the ton in its broadest sense—was far too dangerous for the last unmarried member of the Bar Cynster.

The Season ended as it always did, with a rash of tonnish weddings, but this year, amid the many, one stood out, very definitely "the wedding of the Season." The tale of how Lady Alathea Morwellan had turned her back on her own prospects to help her family in the country, only to return eleven years later to tame the most distantly aloof member of the Bar Cynster, fired the romantic imagination of the ton.

St. Georges Church off Hanover Square was filled to bursting on the day Lady Alathea took her vows. The crowd outside the church was just as dense, those not invited to the festivities finding reason to be passing at the time. Everyone craned to catch a glimpse of the bride, regally radiant in ivory and gold, three unusual flowers anchoring her long veil. As she appeared at the top of the church steps on the arm of her proud husband, flanked by a troop of imposing Cynster males and a bevy of beautiful Cynster wives, the crowd let out a communal sigh.

It was just the sort of fairytale romance the ton and all of London delighted in.

At three o'clock, long after the crowds had retreated to savor all they'd seen, to recount the details and embellish their memories, Gabriel was still giving thanks that they'd managed to fight clear of the crowd of well-wishers before the church and repair to Mount Street for the wedding breakfast.

Standing by a window in the drawing room of Morwellan House, he peered through the fine curtains, reconnoitering the street. There was a small crowd waiting to watch them leave, but it was manageable.

"Almost free?"

Gabriel turned as Demon strolled up. His cousin looked disgustingly pleased with himself; Gabriel reasoned that Demon was yet too newly wed for his expression to ease into the deeply content expressions Devil and Vane now habitually wore. Richard was harder to read, but the glow in his eyes when they rested on Catriona was equally revealing. Gabriel knew a vain hope that *he* would not be quite so easy to read. "Almost." He turned back to the window. "Add the guests inside and it'll still be a goodly crowd, but hopefully we'll make it away in reasonable time."

"Where are you headed? Or is it a secret?"

"Only from Alathea." Briefly, Gabriel outlined his plans to whisk Alathea off on a quick tour of the shires, visiting cities like Liverpool and Sheffield that she'd never visited before but that featured prominently in his business dealings.

"We'll end by going directly to Somersham for this summer celebration our mamas have planned."

"Miss that at the risk of your life—or worse."

Gabriel grinned. "Richard's obviously taking no chances." He nodded to where his cousin's black head was bent over his wife's fiery locks.

"Not on any count," Demon agreed. "He says they'll be on the road north the day after the celebrations. He's not at all sanguine about having Catriona traveling in the condition she'll be in then."

"I'm sure Catriona will have everything precisely planned. Even if she hasn't, she'll just pass a decree and matters will fall out as she wishes—comes of being Lady of the Vale."

"Hmm. Still, I can understand Richard's feelings."

Gabriel glanced at Demon, wondering if that meant …

Before he could form a suitable question, Alathea appeared.

She swept into the room, and his heart stopped. She'd changed into a traveling gown of watered mulberry silk, the high upstanding collar a frame for her hair, rich and lustrous in the afternoon light. Her mother's pearls were coiled about her throat, the matching drops in her ears. She wore no other decoration, acquiescing to his anathema toward anything covering the glory of her hair. No other decoration except for the three white blooms fixed in a spray trailing over one breast, a filigree gold ribbon looped between.

They were the flowers from her veil, the flowers he'd sent her that morning, with another note even simpler than his last.

I love you.

That was all he'd wanted to say, but he knew as only a Cynster could that he'd be looking for ways to tell her that for the rest of his life.

She scanned the room, saw him, and immediately smiled. Her fine eyes bright, she glided to his side.

Gabriel raised a brow as she slid her hand onto his arm. "Ready?"

She wrinkled her nose at him. "We have to give Augusta and Jeremy a few more minutes."

Not even that news could dim his anticipation; he knew his wife well enough to know the younger Morwellans would not have stepped over the line. All he wanted to do was to leave, and have her to himself again.

Flick, Demon's young wife, joined them in a froth of blue skirts, face animated, her eyes lit with an inner glow—an inner glow, Gabriel suddenly realized, now he'd grown accustomed to the sight in Alathea's eyes, that all the Cynster brides shared.

Interesting.

"Come on!" Flick claimed Demon's arm. "It's almost time for them to leave."

"Why are you so afire?" Demon asked. "It's not as if you need to catch any bouquets."

"I want to see who *does*." Flick tugged. "The steps are filling up."

Demon gave a little ground, looking back at Gabriel. "Where's Lucifer?" His demonic grin surfaced. "Thought I'd give him a little advice."

Gabriel scanned the crowd, then lifted a brow at Demon. "I suspect he's already fled."

Demon snorted. "Fool!" He cocked a brow at Gabriel. "Care to wager it'll do him no good?"

Gabriel shook his head. "Some things are meant to be."

Demon acknowledged the comment with a swift smile and a nod, then surrendered to Flick's impatience.

Gabriel turned his gaze on Alathea, and simply smiled. After a moment, she looked up at him. "Ready?" he asked.

She held his gaze. "Yes."

"At last." He covered her hand where it lay on his sleeve.

They walked out of the room, out of the house, and set out on a journey to last the rest of their lives.

All About Love

The Bar Cynster Family Tree

(at the beginning of this story)

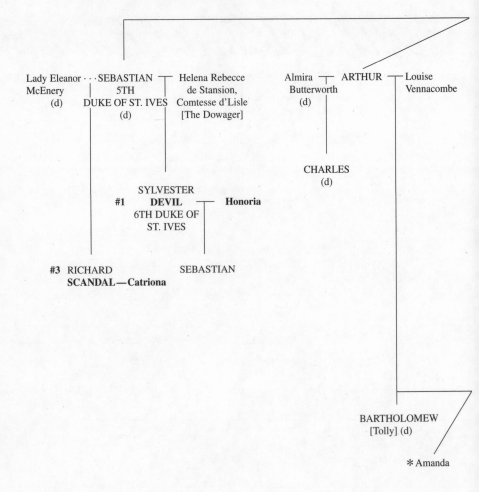

Lady Eleanor · · · SEBASTIAN ─┬─ Helena Rebecce
McEnery | 5TH   de Stansion,
  (d)   DUKE OF ST. IVES   Comtesse d'Lisle
             (d)   [The Dowager]

Almira ─┬─ ARTHUR ─┬─ Louise
Butterworth   Vennacombe
(d)

CHARLES
(d)

SYLVESTER
    #1   **DEVIL** ─┬─ **Honoria**
6TH DUKE OF
ST. IVES

#3   RICHARD   SEBASTIAN
SCANDAL—Catriona

BARTHOLOMEW
[Tolly] (d)

＊Amanda

THE BAR CYNSTER SERIES

#1 *Devil's Bride*	#4 *A Rogue's Proposal*
#2 *A Rake's Vow*	#5 *A Secret Love*
#3 *Scandal's Bride*	#6 *All About Love*

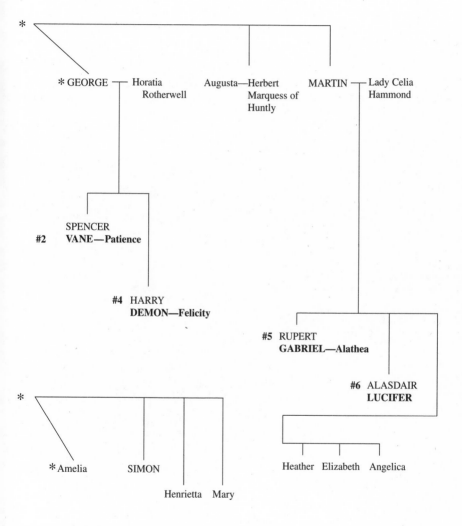

* GEORGE —— Horatia   Augusta—Herbert   MARTIN —— Lady Celia
              Rotherwell   Marquess of   Hammond
                              Huntly

SPENCER
#2   VANE—Patience

#4 HARRY
    DEMON—Felicity

#5 RUPERT
    GABRIEL—Alathea

#6 ALASDAIR
    LUCIFER

* Amelia   SIMON   Heather Elizabeth Angelica

              Henrietta Mary

MALE CYNSTERS named in capitals   * denotes twins

CHAPTER
One

June 1820
Devon

A bstinence.

It didn't even *sound* comfortable.

Alasdair Reginald Cynster, widely known, with good reason, as Lucifer, pushed the word from his mind with a disgusted snort and concentrated on turning his pair of highbred blacks down a narrow lane. The lane led south, toward the coast; Colyton, his destination, lay along it.

Around him, early summer clasped the countryside in a benevolent embrace. Breezes rippled the corn; swallows rode the currents high above, black darts against the blue sky. Thick hedges bordered the lane; from the box seat of his curricle, Lucifer could only just see over them. Not that there was anything to see in this quiet rural backwater.

That left him with his thoughts. Holding the blacks to a slow but steady pace along the winding lane, he considered the unwelcome proposition of having to survive without the type of feminine company to which he was accustomed. It wasn't a pleasant prospect, but he'd rather suffer that torture than risk succumbing to the Cynster curse.

It wasn't a curse to be trifled with—it had already claimed five of his nearest male relatives, all the other members of the notorious group that had, for so many years, lorded it over the ton. The Bar Cynster had cut swaths through the ranks of London's ladies, leaving them languishing, exhausted in their wake. They'd been daring, devilish, invincible—until, one by one, the curse had caught them. Now he was the last one free—unshackled, unwed, and unrepentant. He had nothing against marriage per se, but the unfortunate fact—the crux of the curse—was that Cynsters did not simply marry. They married ladies they loved.

The very concept made him shudder. Its implied vulnerability was something he would never willingly accept.

Yesterday, his brother, Gabriel, had done just that.

And that was one of the two principal reasons he was here, going to ground in deepest Devon.

He and Gabriel had been close all their lives; only eleven months separated them. Other than Gabriel, the one person he knew better than anyone in the world was their childhood playmate Alathea Morwellan. Now Alathea Cynster. Gabriel had married her yesterday, and in so doing had opened Lucifer's eyes to how potent the curse was, how irresistible it could be. Love had bloomed in the most unlikely ground. The curse had struck boldly, ruthlessly, powerfully, and had conquered against all odds.

He sincerely wished Gabriel and Alathea joy, but he had no intention of following their lead.

Not now. Very possibly not ever.

What need had he of marriage? What would he gain that he didn't already have? Women—ladies—were all very well; he enjoyed dallying with them, enjoyed the subtleties of conquering the more resistant, encouraging them into his bed. He enjoyed teaching them all he knew of shared pleasure. That, however, was the extent of his interest. He was involved in other spheres, and he liked his freedom, liked being answerable to no one. He preferred his life as it was and had no wish to change it.

He was determined to avoid the curse—he could manage very well without love.

So he'd slipped away from Gabriel and Alathea's wedding breakfast and left London. With Gabriel married, he'd succeeded to the title of principal matrimonial target for the ladies of the ton; consequently, he'd dismissed all invitations to the summer's country house parties. He'd driven to Quiverstone Manor, his parents' estate in Somerset. Leaving his groom, Dodswell, a local, there to visit with his sister, he'd left Quiverstone early this morning and headed south through the countryside.

On his left, three cottages came into view, huddled around a junction with an even narrower lane that ambled down beside a ridge. Slowing, he passed the cottages and rounded the ridge—the village of Colyton opened out before him. Reining in, he looked about.

And inwardly grimaced. He'd been right. From the looks of Colyton, his chances of finding any local lady with whom to dally—a married one who met his exacting standards and with whom he could ease the persistent itch all Cynsters were prey to—were nil.

Abstinence it would be.

The village, neat and tidy in the bright sunshine, looked like an artist's vision of the rustic ideal, steeped in peace and harmony. Ahead to the right, the common sloped upward; a church stood on the crest, a solid Norman structure flanked by a well-tended graveyard. Beyond the graveyard, another lane ran down, presumably joining the main lane farther on. The main lane itself curved to the left, bordered by a line of cottages facing the common; the sign of an inn jutted over the lane just before it swung out of sight. Nearer to hand was a duck pond on the common; the blacks stamped and shook their heads at the quacking.

Quieting them, Lucifer looked to the left, to the first house of the village standing back in its gardens. A name was carved on the portico. He squinted. *Colyton Manor*. His destination.

The Manor was a handsome house of pale sandstone, two stories and attics in the Georgian style with rows of long pedimented windows flanking the portico and front door. The house faced the lane, set back behind a waist-high stone wall and a large garden filled with flowering plants and roses. A circular fountain stood at the garden's center, interrupting the path joining the front door and a gate to the lane. Beyond the garden, a stand of trees screened the Manor from the village beyond.

A gravel drive skirted the nearer side of the house, eventually leading to a stable set back against more trees. The drive was separated from a shrubbery by an expanse of lawn punctuated here and there by ancient shade trees. Somewhat overgrown, the shrubbery extended almost to where the curricle stood; a glimpse of water beyond suggested an ornamental lake.

Colyton Manor looked what it was, a prosperous gentleman's residence. It was the home of Horatio Welham—the reason Lucifer had chosen Colyton as his temporary bolt hole.

Horatio's letter had reached him three days ago. An old friend and his mentor in all matters pertaining to collecting, Horatio had invited him to visit at Colyton at his earliest convenience. With the grande dames turning their sights on him, convenient had been immediately—he'd grasped the excuse to disappear from the social whirl.

At one time he had haunted Horatio's house in the Lake District, but although he and Horatio had remained as close as ever, over the three years since Horatio had moved to Devon, they'd met only at collectors' gatherings around the country and in London; this was his first visit to Colyton.

The blacks shook their heads; their harness clinked. Straightening, gathering the reins, Lucifer was conscious of a welling impatience—to see Horatio again, to clasp his hand, to spend time in his erudite company. Coloring that anticipation was Horatio's reason for asking him to visit—a request for his opinion on an item that, in Horatio's words, might tempt even him to extend his collection beyond his preferred categories of silver and jewelry. He'd spent the drive from Somerset speculating on what the item was, but had reached no conclusion.

He'd learn soon enough. Clicking the reins, he set the blacks in motion. Turning smartly in between the tall gateposts, he drew the curricle up by the side of the house with the usual crunching and stamping of hooves.

No one came running.

He listened—and heard nothing but the sounds of birds and insects.

Then he remembered it was Sunday; Horatio and all his household would be at church. Glancing up the common, he verified that the church door stood ajar. He looked at the Manor's front door—it, too, stood partially open. Someone, it appeared, was home.

Tying off the reins, he jumped down and strode along the gravel path to the portico. Ablaze with summer blooms, the garden caught and held his gaze.

The sight teased some long-buried memory. Pausing before the portico, he struggled to pin it down.

This was Martha's garden.

Martha was Horatio's late wife; she'd been the anchor around which the Lake District household had revolved. Martha had loved gardening, striving through all weathers to create glorious displays—just like this. Lucifer studied the plantings. The layout was similar to the garden in the Lake District. But Martha had been dead for three years.

Outside of his mother and aunts, Lucifer had felt closer to Martha than any other older woman—she'd occupied a special place in his life. He'd often listened to her lectures, whereas to his mother he'd been deaf. Martha had not been related—it had always been easier to hear the truth from her lips. It was Martha's death that had lessened his enthusiasm for visiting Horatio at home. Too many memories; too acute a sense of shared loss.

Seeing Martha's garden here felt odd, like a hand on his sleeve when there was no one there. He frowned—he could almost hear Martha whispering in her soft, gentle voice.

Abruptly turning, he entered the portico. The front door was half open; he pushed it wide. The hall was empty.

"Hello! Is anyone about?"

No response. All he could hear was the summer buzz outside. He stepped over the threshold and paused. The house was cool, quiet, still … waiting. Frowning more definitely, he strode forward, bootheels clacking on black-and-white tiles. He headed for the first door on the right. It stood open, pushed wide.

He smelled blood before he reached the door. After Waterloo, it was one scent he'd never mistake. The hairs at his nape lifted; he slowed.

At his back, the sun glowed bright and warm—the cold quiet of the house intensified. It drew him on.

He halted in the doorway, his gaze drawn down to the body sprawled a few feet inside the room.

His skin turned cold. After an instant's hiatus, he forced his gaze to travel the old, lined face, the straggly white hair covered by a tasseled cap. In a long white nightshirt with a knitted shawl wound around heavy shoulders, twisted onto his back with one arm outflung, bare feet poking out toward the door, the dead man looked as if he might be asleep, here in his drawing room surrounded by his antique tomes.

But he wasn't asleep—he hadn't even collapsed. Blood still seeped from a small cut on his left side, directly beneath his heart.

Lucifer dragged in a breath. "*Horatio!*"

On his knees, he searched for a pulse at wrist and throat, and found none. Hand on Horatio's chest, he felt a lingering warmth; slight color still graced the old man's cheeks. Mind reeling, Lucifer sat back on his heels.

Horatio had been murdered—minutes ago.

He felt numb, detached; some part of his brain continued cataloguing facts, like the experienced cavalry officer he'd once been.

The single killing stroke had been an upward thrust into the heart—like a bayonet wound. Not much blood, just a little ... oddly little. Frowning, he checked. There was more blood beneath the body. Horatio had been turned onto his back later—originally he'd fallen facedown. Catching a glimpse of gilt under the shawl, Lucifer searched with fingers that shook—and drew out a long, thin letter knife.

His fingers curled around the ornate hilt. He scanned the immediate area but could see no sign of any struggle. The rug wasn't rumpled; the table between the body and the rug appeared correctly aligned in its normal place.

The numbness was wearing off. Emotions welled; Lucifer's senses flickered, then flared to life.

He was cursing beneath his breath; he felt like he'd been kicked in the gut. After the serenity outside, finding Horatio like this seemed obscene—a nightmare he knew there'd be no waking from. Deadening loss engulfed him; his earlier anticipation lay like bitter ashes on his tongue. Pressing his lips tight, he drew in a deep breath—

He wasn't alone.

In the instant he sensed it, he heard a sound. Then came a clunk and a scuffle behind him.

He sprang to his feet, gripping the letter knife—

A heavy weight crashed down on his skull.

It hurt like hell.

He lay slumped on the floor. He must have gone down like a sack of bricks, but he couldn't remember the impact. He had no idea whether he'd lost consciousness and only just regained it, or whether he'd only just reached the floor. Exerting every last ounce of his will, he cracked open his lids. Horatio's face swam into—and out of—focus. Closing his eyes, he bit back a groan. With luck, the murderer would think he was insensate. He almost was. The black tide of unconsciousness surged and dragged, trying to suck him under. Grimly, he resisted its pull.

The letter knife was still in his fist, but his right arm was trapped beneath his body. He couldn't move. His body felt like a lead weight he was trapped within; he couldn't defend himself. He should have checked the room first, but the sight of Horatio, lying there still bleeding ... *damn*!

He waited, oddly detached, wondering if the murderer would stop to finish him off or just flee. He hadn't heard anyone leave, but he wasn't sure he could hear at all.

How long had he been lying there?

From behind the door, Phyllida Tallent stared wide-eyed at the gentleman now stretched lifeless beside Horatio Welham's body. A squeak of dismay escaped her—the ridiculous sound prodded her into action. Dragging in a breath, she stepped forward, bent, and wrapped both hands around the pole of the halberd now lying across the fallen man.

Bracing, she counted to three, then hauled. The heavy head of the halberd rose. She staggered, boots shuffling as she fought to swing the unwieldy weapon aside.

She hadn't meant it to fall.

Having only just walked in and discovered Horatio's body, she hadn't been thinking at all clearly when the stranger's footsteps had sounded on the gravel outside. She'd panicked, thinking him the murderer returning to remove the body. With all the village in church, she couldn't imagine who else it could have been.

He'd called a "Hello," but so might a murderer checking to see if anyone else had come upon the scene. She'd frantically searched for a hiding place, but the long drawing room was lined with bookcases—the only gap that would have hidden her from the door had been too far away for her to reach in time. Desperate, she'd secreted herself in the only available spot—in the shadows behind the open door, between the frame and the last bookshelf, squeezing in alongside the halberd.

The hiding place had served, but once she'd realized from his actions and his muttered expletives that this man was no murderer, and after she'd debated the wisdom of showing herself—the daughter of the local magistrate and quite old enough to know better than to slip into other peoples' houses dressed in breeches to search for still other peoples' misplaced personal belongings— once she'd got past all that and realized that this was murder and she'd gone to step forward to make herself known, her shoulder had nudged the halberd.

Its descent had been inexorable.

She'd grabbed it and fought vainly to halt it or deflect it; in the end, all she'd been able to do was twist it enough so that the heavy blade had not struck the man's head. If it had, he'd have died. As it was, the hemisphere at the side of the iron axe-head had connected with a sickening thud.

With the halberd finally angled to the side, she lowered it to the floor. Only then did she realize she'd been repeating a breathless litany: *Oh, God! Oh, God! Oh, God!*

Wiping her palms on her breeches, sick to her stomach, she looked at her innocent victim. The sound of the halberd connecting with his skull echoed in her ears. It hadn't helped that he'd chosen that precise moment to leap to his feet. He'd come up propelled like a spring, only to meet the halberd going down.

He'd hit the floor with a sickening thud, too. He hadn't moved since.

Steeling herself, she stepped over the pole. "Oh, God—*please* don't let me have killed him!" Horatio had been murdererd, and now she'd murdered a stranger. What was her world coming to?

Panic gnawing at her nerves, she sank to her knees; the gentleman lay slumped forward, facing Horatio ....

Lucifer sensed a presence approaching. He couldn't hear, he couldn't see, but he knew when they knelt at his back. The murderer. He had to assume that. If only he could gather enough strength, even to lift his lids. He tried, but nothing happened. Unconsciousness welled, lapping about him—he refused to let go and sink under. There was a roaring in his head. Even through it he knew when the murderer reached out. The roaring in his head escalated—

Fingers—*small* fingers—touched his cheek gently, hesitantly.

The touch blazed across his brain.

Not the murderer. Relief swept through him, and relentlessly carried him into the black.

Phyllida traced the fallen man's cheek, mesmerized by the stark beauty of his face. He looked like a fallen angel—such classically pure lines could not possibly be found on mortal men. His brow was wide, his nose patrician, his thick hair very dark, sable black. His eyes were large under arched black brows. His lids didn't flicker; her stomach clenched tight. Then she saw his lips, lean and mobile, ease, softening as if he'd exhaled.

"Please, please, don't die!"

Frantically, she searched for a pulse at his throat, ruining his cravat in the process. She nearly fainted with relief when she found the throbbing beat, steady and strong. *"Thank God!"* She sagged. Without thinking, she carefully rearranged his cravat, smoothing the folds—he was so beautiful and she hadn't killed him.

Wheels crunched heavily on the gravel drive.

Phyllida jerked upright. Her eyes flew wide. The murderer?

Her panicky wits calmed enough for her to distinguish voices as the conveyance rolled on around the house. Not the murderer—the Manor staff. She looked at the unconscious stranger.

For the first time in her life, she found it difficult to think. Her heart was still racing; she felt lightheaded. Dragging in a breath, she fought to concentrate. Horatio was dead; she couldn't change that. Indeed, she knew nothing of any relevance. His friend was unconscious and would remain so for some time—she should make sure he was well tended. That was the least she should do.

But here she was in Horatio's drawing room, in breeches, instead of being laid down on her bed at the Grange with a sick headache. And she couldn't explain why, not without revealing her reason for being here—those misplaced personal belongings. Worse, they weren't hers. She didn't actually know why they were so important, why their revelation was to be avoided at all costs, which made it all the more incumbent on her not to reveal their existence. Aside from anything else, she'd been sworn to secrecy.

Damn! She was going to be discovered any minute. Mrs. Hemmings, the Manor housekeeper, would even now be entering the kitchen.

Think!

What if, instead of waiting here and landing herself in a morass of impossible explanations, she left, cut home through the wood, changed, and returned? She could easily think of an errand. She could be back in ten minutes. Then she could make sure Horatio's body had been discovered, and oversee the tending of the stranger.

That was a sensible plan.

Phyllida clambered to her feet. Her legs wobbled; she still felt woozy. She was about to turn away when the hat on the table beyond Horatio's body caught her eye.

Had the stranger carried a hat when he'd entered? She hadn't noticed it, but he was so large, he could have reached forward and put it on the table without her seeing.

Gentlemen's hats often had their owners' names embroidered on the inside band. Stepping around Horatio's body, Phyllida reached for the brown hat—

"I'll just go up and check on the master. Keep an eye on that pot, will you?"

Phyllida forgot about the hat. She shot through the hall, out of the front door, then raced across the side lawn and dove into the shrubbery.

"Juggs, open this door."

The words, uttered in a tone Lucifer usually associated with his mother, jerked him back to consciousness.

"Nah—can't do that," a heavy male voice answered. "Mightn't be wise."

"Wise?" The woman's tone had risen. After a pause, during which Lucifer could almost hear her rein in her temper, she asked, "Has he regained consciousness at all since you picked him up from the Manor?"

So he was no longer at the Manor. Where the hell was he?

"Nah! Out like a light, he is."

He wasn't, but he might as well have been. Beyond hearing, his senses weren't functioning well—he couldn't feel much beyond the massive ache in his head. He was lying on his side on some very hard surface. The air was cool and held a hint of musty dust. He couldn't lift his lids—even that much movement was still beyond him.

He was helpless.

"How do you know he's still alive?" The woman's imperious tone left little doubt she was a lady.

"Alive? 'Course he's alive—why wouldn't he be? Just swooned, that's all."

"*Swooned*? Juggs, you're an innkeeper. For how long do swooned men stay swooned, especially if they're jolted about in a cart in the fresh air?"

Juggs snorted. "He's a swell—who knows how long they stay swooned for? Right liverish lot, they are."

"They found him slumped by Mr. Welham's body. What if he hasn't swooned but sustained some injury?"

"How could he have sus—got any injury?"

"Maybe he fought with the murderer, trying to save Mr. Welham."

"Nah! That way, we'd have his nibs here and someone else the murderer—that'd make two people coming in separate from outside in one day with no one seeing either of 'em, and that just plain doesn't happen."

The lady lost all patience. "Juggs—*open this door*! What if the gentleman dies, all because you decided he'd swooned when that wasn't so at all? We have to check."

"He's *swooned*, I tell you—not a mark on him that Thompson or I could see."

Lucifer gathered every last shred of his strength. If he wanted help, he was going to have to assist the lady; he didn't want her going away defeated, leaving him with the uncaring innkeeper. He lifted one hand—his arm shook ... he forced the hand to his head. He heard a groan, then realized it was his.

"There! *See?*" The lady sounded triumphant. "It's his head that hurts—the *back* of his head. Why, if he'd simply swooned? Quickly, Juggs—open the door! There's something very wrong here."

Lucifer let his hand fall. If he could have, he would have roared at Juggs to open the damned door. Of course there was something wrong—the murderer had coshed him. What on earth did they think had happened?

"Maybe he hit his head when he fell," Juggs grumbled.

Why the hell did they imagine he'd fallen? But the jingle of keys pushed the thought from Lucifer's mind. The lady had won; she was coming to his aid. A lock clanked, then a heavy door scraped. Quick footsteps briskly crossed stone, heading his way.

A small hand touched his shoulder. A warm, feminine-soft presence leaned near.

"Everything will be all right in a moment." Her tone was low and soothing. "Just let me check your head."

She was hovering over him; his senses had returned enough to tell him she wasn't as old as he'd thought. The realization gave him the strength to lift his lids, albeit only a fraction.

She saw and smiled encouragingly, brushing back the lock of hair that had fallen across his brow.

The pain in his head evaporated. Opening his eyes further, Lucifer drank in the details of her face. She was not a girl, but she would still qualify as a young lady. Somewhere in her early twenties, yet her face held more character, more strength and blatant determination than was common for her years. He noted it, but it was not that that held him, that captured his awareness to the exclusion of the debilitating pain in his head.

Her brown eyes were large, wide, and filled with concern—with an open empathy that reached past his cynical shields and touched him. Those lovely eyes were framed by a wide forehead and delicately arched brows, by dark hair, almost as dark as his, cut short to curve about her head like a sleek helmet. Her nose was straight, her chin tapered, her lips ...

The sudden surge of sensual thoughts and impulses for once didn't sit well: Horatio was dead. He let his lids fall.

"You'll feel much better directly," she promised, "once we move you to a more comfortable bed."

Behind her, Juggs snorted. "Aye—he's that sort of gentleman, I'd wager. A murderer and the other, too."

Lucifer ignored Juggs. The lady knew he was no murderer, and she now had the upper hand. Her fingers slid through his hair, carefully feeling around his wound. He tensed, then bit back a groan when she gingerly probed. ·

"See?" She pressed aside his hair so the air touched his wound. "He's been hit on the back of the head with something—some weapon."

Juggs harrumphed. "P'rhaps he hit his head on that table in the Manor drawing room when he swooned."

"Juggs! You know as well as I do this wound is too severe for that."

Eyes closed, Lucifer breathed shallowly. Pain was rolling over him in sickening waves. In desperation, he conjured the image of the lady's face, struggled to concentrate on that and hold the pain at bay. Her throat had been slender, graceful. That augered well for the rest of her. She'd mentioned a bed—He broke off that train of thought, once again disconcerted by its direction.

" 'Ere, let me see," Juggs grudgingly said.

A heavy hand touched Lucifer's skull—his head exploded with pain.

"Papa, this man is seriously injured."

His guardian angel's voice drew Lucifer back to the living. He had no idea how much time had elapsed since last he'd been with them.

"He's been hit very violently on the back of the head. Juggs has seen the wound, too."

"Hmm." Heavier footsteps approached. "That right, Juggs?"

A new voice, deep, cultured, but tinged with the local county accent—Lucifer wondered just who "Papa" was.

"Aye. Looks like he's been coshed good and proper." Juggs—the clod—was still with them.

"The wound's on the back of his skull, you say?"

"Yes—here." Lucifer felt the lady's fingers part his hair. "But don't touch."

"Papa" thankfully didn't. "It seems very sensitive—he regained consciousness for a moment, but fainted when Juggs touched his head."

"Hardly surprising. That's quite a blow he's taken. Administered with that old halberd of Horatio's by the look of it. Hemmings said he found it beside this gentleman. Given the thing's weight, it's a wonder he isn't dead."

Letting his hair fall, the lady stated, "So it's obvious he's not the murderer."

"Not with that wound and the halberd lying beside him. Looks like the murderer hid behind the door and coshed him when he discovered the body. Mrs. Hemmings swears the thing couldn't have fallen on its own. Seems clear enough. So we'll just have to wait and see what this gentleman can tell us once he regains his senses."

Precious little, Lucifer mentally answered.

"Well, he's not going to get better lying in this cell." The lady's voice had developed a decisive note.

"Indeed not. Can't understand what Bristleford was about, thinking this fellow was the murderer who'd swooned at the sight of blood."

Swooned at the sight of blood? If he'd been able, Lucifer would have snorted derisively, but he still couldn't speak or move. The pain in his head was just waiting for a chance to bludgeon him into unconsciousness. The most he could do was lie still and listen, and learn all he could. While the lady held sway, he was safe—she seemed to have taken his best interests to heart.

"I thought Bristleford said he had the knife in 'is fist."

That came from Juggs, of course.

"Papa" snorted. "Self-defense. Had a moment's warning the murderer was behind him and grabbed the only weapon to hand. Not much use against a halberd, unfortunately. No—it was obvious someone had found the body and turned it over. Can't see the murderer bothering—it wasn't as if Horatio would have been carrying any valuables in his nightshirt."

"So this man is innocent," the lady reiterated. "We really should move him to the Grange."

"I'll ride back and send the carriage," "Papa" replied.

"I'll wait here. Tell Gladys to pile as many cushions and pillows as she can into the carriage, and ..."

The lady's words faded as she moved away; Lucifer stopped trying to listen. She'd said she'd stay by him. It sounded like the Grange was "Papa's" residence, so presumably she lived there, too. He hoped she did. He wanted to see more of her once the pain had gone. The pain in his head, and the pain around his heart.

Horatio had been a very dear friend—how dear he hadn't realized until now, now that he was gone. He touched on his grief, but was too weak to deal with it. Shifting his mind away, he tried to find some way past the pain, but it seemed to feed on the effort.

So he simply lay there and waited.

He heard the lady return; others were with her. What followed wasn't pleasant. Luckily, he wasn't far removed from unconsciousness; he was only dimly aware of being lifted. He expected to feel the jolting of a carriage; if he did, the sensation didn't make it past the pain.

Then he was on a bed, being undressed. His senses flickered weakly, registering that there were two women present; from their hands and voices, they were both older than his guardian angel. He would have helped them if he could, but even that was beyond him. They fussed and insisted on pulling a nightshirt over his head, being inordinately careful of his injured skull.

They made him comfortable in soft pillows and sweet-smelling sheets, then they left him in blessed peace.

Phyllida looked in on her patient as soon as Gladys, their housekeeper, reported that he was settled.

Miss Sweet, her old governess, sat tatting in a chair by the window. "He's resting quietly," Sweetie mouthed.

Phyllida nodded and went to the bed. They'd left him sprawled on his stomach to spare his sore head. He was much larger than she'd realized—the broad expanse of his shoulders and chest, the long lines of his back, the even longer length of his legs—his body dominated the bed. He wasn't, perhaps, the largest man she'd seen, but she suspected he should have been the most vital. Instead, a sullen heaviness invested his limbs, a weighted tension quite unlike relaxation. She peered at his face; the section she could see was pale, still starkly handsome but stony, lacking all sense of life. The lips that should have held the hint of a wicked smile were compressed to a thin line.

Sweetie was wrong—he was unconscious, not truly resting at all.

Phyllida straightened. Guilt swept her. It had been her fault he'd been hit. She glided back to Sweetie. "I'm going to the Manor—I'll be back in an hour."

Sweetie smiled and nodded. With one last glance at the bed, Phyllida left the room.

"I really couldn't say, sir."

Phyllida entered the Manor's front hall to find Bristleford, Horatio's butler, being interrogated by Mr. Lucius Appleby directly before the closed drawing room door. They both turned. Appleby bowed. "Miss Tallent."

Phyllida returned his nod. "Good afternoon, sir." Many local ladies considered Appleby's fair good looks attractive, but she found him too cold for her taste.

"Sir Cedric asked me to inquire as to the details of Mr. Welham's death," Appleby explained, clearly conscious of the need to excuse his intrusion. He was secretary to Sir Cedric Fortemain, a local landowner; no one would be surprised at Sir Cedric's interest. "Bristleford was just telling me that Sir Jasper has declared himself satisfied that the gentleman discovered by the body is not the murderer."

"That's correct. The murderer is as yet unknown." Unwilling to encourage further discussion, Phyllida turned to Bristleford. "I've asked John Ostler to tend the gentleman's horses." His *magnificent* horses—even to her untutored eye, the pair were expensive beauties. Her twin brother, Jonas, would be over to see them just as soon as he learned of their existence. "We'll put them in the stables here—the stables at the Grange are full now my aunt Huddlesford and my cousins have arrived."

They'd arrived that afternoon, just as she'd been rushing off to rescue the unknown gentleman; because of her useless cousins, she'd been too late to save him from Juggs's clutches.

Bristleford frowned. "If you think that's best ..."

"I do. It seems obvious the gentleman was coming here to visit—presumably he was a friend of Mr. Welham's."

"I don't know, miss. The Hemmingses and I haven't been with the master long enough to know all his friends."

"Quite. No doubt Covey will know." Covey was Horatio's valet and had been with him for many years. "I take it he's not back yet?"

"No, miss. He'll be devastated."

Phyllida nodded. "I just looked in to pick up the gentleman's hat."

"Hat?" Bristleford stared. "There was no hat, miss."

Phyllida blinked. "Are you sure?"

"Nothing in the drawing room or out here." Bristleford looked around. "Perhaps in his carriage?"

Phyllida fabricated a smile. "No, no—I just assumed he must have had a hat. No cane, either?"

Bristleford shook his head.

"Well, then, I'll be off." With a nod for Appleby, who returned it politely, Phyllida walked out of the house.

She paused beneath the portico, looking out over Horatio's gorgeous garden. A chill washed down her spine.

There had been a hat—a brown one. If it didn't belong to the gentleman and hadn't been there when the Hemmingses and Bristleford discovered the body …

The chill intensified. Lifting her head, Phyllida glanced about, then walked quickly to the gate and hurried home.

The pain in his head grew worse.

Lucifer tossed and turned, struggling to escape the needles driving into his brain. Hands tried to restrain him; gentle voices tried to soothe him. He realized they wanted him to lie still—he tried, but the pain wouldn't let him.

Then his guardian angel returned. He heard her voice at the edge of his awareness; for her, he found strength and lay still. She bathed his face, neck, and the backs of his shoulders with lavender water, then placed cool cloths over his wound. The pain ebbed, and he sighed.

She left, and he grew restless again. But before the pain could peak, she returned and changed the cloths, then sat beside the bed, one cool hand on the back of his wrist.

He relaxed. Eventually, he slept.

When he awoke, she was gone.

It was dark; the house was quiet, slumbering. Lucifer lifted his head—the pain stopped him. Gritting his teeth, he shifted onto his side; raising his head just a fraction, he looked around. An older woman in a mobcap sat slumped in an armchair by the window. Focusing his hearing, he could detect gentle snores.

The fact that he could reassured him. Setting his temple back down on the pillow, he took stock. While still painful when he moved, his head was otherwise much better. He could think without agony. He stretched, flexing his limbs, careful not to shift his head. Relaxing again, he did the same with his senses; all seemed in working order. He might not yet be hale, but he was whole.

That established, he reconnoitered his surroundings. Bit by bit, the immediate past cleared and his memories fell into coherent order. He was in a chamber comfortably furnished in a manner befitting a gentleman's residence. Recollecting that "Papa" had been called upon to pass judgment over his involvement in Horatio's death, "Papa" might well be the local magistrate. If so, he'd made contact with the one gentleman above all others he needed to know. As soon as he was well enough to lift his head, he intended finding Horatio's killer.

His thoughts paused ... he pushed them in a different direction. His guardian angel wasn't here—doubtless she was asleep in her bed ...

Not that direction.

Inwardly, he sighed. Then, closing his eyes, sinking into the bed, he opened his mind and let his grief take him.

Let sorrow for the good times he would not now share with Horatio rise and spill over—let grief for the passing of one who had, in one way, been a kind of father, well and pour through him. No more the joy of shared discoveries, the eager quest for information, the shared hunt to pin down some elusive provenance.

The memories lived, but Horatio was gone. A formative chapter in his life had ended. It was difficult to accept that he'd reached the last page and now had to close the book.

Grief ebbed and left him empty. He'd seen death too many times for the shock to hold him for long. He came from a warrior caste; unjust death was the trigger for one of his most primal responses. Revenge—not for personal satisfaction, but in the name of justice.

Horatio's death would not go unavenged.

He lay in the soft sheets while grief transmuted to anger, eventually coalescing into icy resolution. His emotions hardened, he mentally returned to the scene, replaying every step, every recollection, until he came to the touch ...

Fingers that small belonged to a child or a woman. Given the fascination behind the touch—one he recognized instinctively—he would wager his entire collection that a woman had been there. A woman who was not the murderer. Horatio might have been old, but he hadn't been so infirm that a woman could have stabbed him so neatly. Few women would have the strength, or the knowledge.

So—Horatio had been murdered. Then *he* had entered and the murderer had coshed him with the halberd. Then the woman had entered and found him.

No—that couldn't be right. Horatio's body had been turned onto its back *before* he'd arrived; he agreed with "Papa"—it hadn't been the murderer who'd done that. The woman must have, then she'd hidden when he appeared.

She must have seen the murderer strike him, then leave. Why hadn't she raised the alarm? Some man called Hemmings had done that.

Something more than the obvious was afoot. He revisited the facts, but couldn't shake that conclusion.

A board in the hallway creaked. Lucifer listened. A minute later, the door to his room opened.

He remained relaxed on his side, lids lowered so he appeared asleep, but he could see through his lashes. He heard a soft click as the door shut, then footsteps padded across the floorboards; a pool of candlelight approached.

His guardian angel came into view. She was in her nightgown.

She halted six feet away, studying his face. One hand held the candlestick; the other rested between her breasts, anchoring her shawl. It was the first time he'd seen all of her; he didn't try to stop himself looking, noting, assessing. Her face was as he recalled, wide eyes, tapered chin, and sleek dark hair giving an impression of intelligence and feminine resolve. She was of average height, slender but not thin. Her breasts were full and high, nipples just discernible beneath the shawl's fringe. He couldn't judge her waist under the nightgown, but her hips were neatly rounded, her thighs sleek.

Her feet were bare. His gaze locked on them, tantalizingly revealed, then concealed beneath her nightgown. Small, naked, intensely feminine feet. Slowly, he dragged his gaze back up to her face.

While he'd studied her, she'd been studying him. Her dark eyes roamed his face, taking in, it seemed, every line. Then she turned away.

Lucifer bit back an urge to call to her. He wanted to thank her—she'd been a madonna of kindness and caring—but if he made a sound, he'd scare her out of her wits. He watched her stop by the sleeping woman; setting her candlestick down, she lifted a blanket, shook it out, then tucked it around the other woman. As she turned away, candle once more in hand, the soft light lit her smile.

She started for the door, but, as if she'd heard his silent plea, she halted before she passed the bed. She looked his way, then, hesitantly, drew nearer. And nearer.

Holding the candle aside so his face was screened by her body, she rested against the bed a foot away and studied his face anew. He fought to keep his lids steady; he could only just see her face. Her eyes were fathomless, her expression unreadable.

Then she released her grip on her shawl. Slowly, she reached out. With her fingertips she lightly traced his cheek.

Lucifer felt like he'd been branded—and he recognized the brand. He surged up on one elbow, seizing her wrist, transfixing her with a glare.

She gasped; the sound echoed through the room. The candlelight wavered wildly, then steadied. Eyes dilated, she stared at him.

He tightened his grip and held her gaze. *"It was you."*

CHAPTER
Two

Phyllida stared into eyes so vibrant a dark blue they were nearly black. She'd seen them earlier, but they'd been hazed with pain, unfocused; they'd been startling enough then. Now, focused mercilessly on hers, clear and brilliant as a dark sapphire, they stole her breath away.

She felt like she'd been the one hit by the halberd.

"You were there." His gaze held her trapped. "*You* were the first to reach me after the murderer hit me. You touched my face, just as you did then."

She kept her expression blank. Thoughts popped up, then sank, flotsam thrown up by her whirling mind. His fingers clamping about her wrist had shocked her; they'd locked before she could react. She twisted her arm, trying to ease from his hold; he tightened his grip enough for her to sense his strength and the futility of struggling.

She felt lightheaded. She'd forgotten to breathe.

Dragging her gaze from his, she did. Staring at his lips, she wondered what to say. How could he know just from a touch? He had to be guessing.

Draped in shadow, his face was even more compelling than she recalled. The impact of him—his conscious physical presence—was potent; he appeared altogether more dangerous, and he'd appeared dangerous enough before. He was decently covered in one of her father's nightshirts, but the collar was open, exposing a V of chest—dark hair curled invitingly in the gap.

The realization that she was standing by a gentleman's bed staring at his chest, in the small hours, in her nightgown, slammed into her. Heat prickled across her skin. Gladys was near, but …

She glanced across the room. As if sensing her hope that Gladys wouldn't wake and hear him, he eased onto his back, pulling her across him.

Phyllida bit back another gasp. "Be careful of your head," she hissed.

His eyes gleamed. "I'll be careful."

His voice was deep; it almost purred. He kept extending his arm, the one shackling her wrist. She had to lean across him, balancing the candlestick in her other hand. Inexorably, he drew her on.

She swallowed as her breasts neared his chest. Heart thudding, she scrambled onto the bed.

He smiled in triumph. "Now you can tell me what you were doing so secretively in Horatio's drawing room."

The command was blatant. Phyllida lifted her chin. At twenty-four, she wasn't about to be bullied. "I don't know what you mean." She tried to slide her wrist free, to no avail. Kneeling beside him on the bed, one hand locked in his, the candlestick in the other, was not a position of strength. She felt like a supplicant.

His expression hardened. "You were there. Tell me why."

She looked down her nose at him. "I fear you're still delirious."

"I wasn't delirious before."

"You kept talking about the devil. Then, when we assured you you wouldn't die, you asked for the archangel."

His lips thinned. "My brother's known as Gabriel, and my eldest cousin is Devil."

She stared at him. Devil. Gabriel. What was *his* name? "Oh. Well, this idea you have is nonsense. I know nothing about Horatio's murder."

She met his gaze on the last, and fell into the blue. It was the most peculiar sensation; the nerves under her skin, all over her, tingled. Warmth spread through her. The sense of being held captive grew. The odd notion that her nightgown was transparent she dismissed as ridiculous.

"You weren't in Horatio's drawing room when I was lying on the floor?"

The words were soft, subtly challenging; an undercurrent of danger rippled beneath. Held trapped by his gaze, by his hold on her wrist, Phyllida pressed her lips tight and shook her head. She couldn't tell him—not yet. Not until she'd spoken with Mary Anne and been released from her oath.

"So these fingers"—deftly, he altered his grip so his fingers wrapped around hers—"weren't the ones that touched my cheek as I lay beside Horatio?"

He raised her hand, then looked at it; she looked, too. Long, tanned fingers surrounded hers. His hand swallowed hers in a warm clasp. That clasp firmed; slowly, he lifted her fingers to his face. "Like this." He touched her fingertips to his cheek, then drew her hand down.

His stubble had grown, prickling against the pads of her fingers; the sensation only emphasized the fact that the sculpted lines were not rock but living flesh. Fascinated anew, Phyllida watched her fingers trace, drifting down, following her gaze to the tempting line of his lips ... then she realized he'd slackened his grasp. Her fingers were tracing on their own.

She snatched her hand away, but he was quicker. His fingers shackled her wrist again.

"You were there." His tone was grimly determined; conviction resonated through it.

Phyllida looked into his deep blue eyes; every instinct she possessed urged her to flee. She tugged. "Let me go."

One black brow rose. He considered—heart thumping, she wondered what alternatives he was weighing. Then his lips eased; the intensity of his gaze didn't. "Very well—for now."

She tried to draw her hand free but he didn't release it. Instead, he raised her fingers—this time, to his lips. His gaze remained locked on her face; she prayed her reaction—panic melded with insidious excitement—didn't show.

His lips brushed her knuckles—she lost her breath. His lips were cool yet her skin burned where they'd touched. Eyes wide, she felt her senses sway. Before she could drag in a steadying breath, he turned her hand and pressed a burning kiss into her palm.

She snatched her hand back—he let her go, but reluctantly. Backing off the bed, she stood; her gown fell to decently cover her legs. From not breathing at all, she was now breathing too rapidly.

Satisfaction gleamed in his eyes.

Lifting her head, she gathered her shawl, hesitated, then haughtily nodded. "I'll check on you later in the morning."

She turned to the door. A wave of peculiar heat washed over her. Without risking a backward glance, she escaped.

Lucifer watched the door close. He'd let her go. That hadn't been what he'd wanted to do. But there was no need to rush, and matters might have rushed rather more than was wise if he'd kept her kneeling on his bed.

He inhaled deeply and could smell her still, sweet feminine flesh warm from her bed. Her nightgown had been totally opaque, but the material had lovingly outlined every curve it touched. Once she'd released the ends of her shawl, his distraction had been complete.

If the older woman hadn't been in the room ...

A minute passed; then he shook aside his thoughts. Tactically, it hadn't been wise to so blatantly display his intent. Luckily, his guardian angel seemed committed to taking care of him, despite the threat she now clearly perceived.

Her last words had been more declaration than statement, uttered as much for her benefit as for his. If she'd found him struck down in Horatio's drawing room but had been forced, for whatever reason, to leave him there, her stance was understandable. She felt guilty. No matter how difficult he proved, she would try to do the right thing.

In that respect, he already felt certain of her—she was a woman who would strive to do what she deemed right.

He stretched, easing muscles that had tensed; then he shifted onto his side, the better to spare his head. It still ached, but, true to form, while she'd been in the room, he hadn't been aware of it.

All he'd been aware of was her.

Even before she'd touched his face.

But the knowledge that it was she who had knelt beside him in Horatio's drawing room and traced his cheek with that hesitant, wondering touch had powerfully focused the attraction he'd been doing his best to decently ignore.

The revelation meant he no longer needed to feign indifference; his attraction, her fascination, and her consequent skittishness were going to prove exceedingly helpful.

She knew something—he'd read that much in her wide dark eyes. They were easy to read; her face was not. Her expression had remained open but uninformative, her emotions screened. Even when he'd kissed her hand, only her eyes had flared. She seemed contained; judging by all he'd seen, she was used to being in control, in command.

Whatever the case, she wasn't about to disappear; he'd have time to pursue his questions, and her. None knew better than he how to persuade women to do what he wanted, to give him what he wanted—that was, after all, his specialty. And after he'd learned what she knew of Horatio's murder ...

He drifted into sleep and dreamed.

At eleven o'clock the next morning, Phyllida marched into the bedchamber at the end of the west wing. She held the door wide so Sweetie, followed by Gladys carrying a laden tray, could enter.

"Good morning." She addressed the room in general, as if the large body lying in the bed hadn't immediately captured her entire attention.

As per her instructions, Sweetie had fluttered down to find her the instant their patient awoke. Phyllida knew he was awake—she could feel that midnight-blue gaze on her face, and on the rest of her, now unexceptionably garbed in a morning gown of sprigged muslin. It was infinitely easier to assert control while properly dressed.

"Good morning. Ladies." The deep, reverberating words were accompanied by a graceful nod. Phyllida resisted the urge to frown. That direct "Good morning" had been for her; the "Ladies" and the nod had been for the others.

Wrapping her habitual calm, collected demeanor about her, she followed Gladys to the bed, ignoring the heat still lingering in the center of her palm. Just as she was going to ignore him. She was determined not to succumb to the foolish fascination that had overcome her last night.

"We've brought you some broth, which is just what you need to set you up again." She let her glance slide over him, a confident smile on her lips; she made sure not to meet his eyes.

"Indeed?"

Sweetie and Gladys preened; a swift glance showed he was smiling at them. "Indeed," she averred, with rather more steel. "How is your head?"

"Considerably improved." He glanced at her. "Thanks to you."

"Indeed, yes!" Sweetie twittered. "So very right of dear Phyllida to insist you be brought here. Why, you were quite out of your senses, dear."

"So I understand. I do hope that, in my delirium, I said nothing to distress you."

"Of course not, dear—do set your mind at ease on that score. Gladys here and I have *brothers*, so you may be sure you surprised us not at all. Now, let me help you ..."

He struggled to sit up; Sweetie grasped his arm and tugged. Phyllida plumped his pillows, careful not to touch his shoulders. Once he was settled, Gladys deposited the tray on his knees.

"Thank you."

The smile that went with that left both Gladys and Sweetie happily dazed; Phyllida mentally frowned. The man was past dangerous. His next words confirmed it.

"This is excellent broth. Did you make it?"

Gladys confessed; pink with pleasure, she excused herself to return to her duties, pausing at the last to assure him that, should he require anything further, he only had to ask.

Phyllida inwardly sniffed. She stepped back from the bed, biding her time, letting him eat. He did so smoothly, steadily—she could detect not the smallest tremor in his hands. Strong, long-fingered, inherently graceful, they plied the spoon and broke the bread.

"Good heavens!" Sweetie fluttered. "We forgot the butter. I'll fetch some right away." She rushed out the door.

Phyllida found herself staring at the closing door before she had time to protest. Being alone with a gentleman in his bedchamber was unquestionably improper. Still, what harm could befall her? He was more or less tied to the bed. And she was quite capable of keeping him in his place, disturbing blue gaze or no. There wasn't a man in the district she couldn't manage, and despite his elegant facade, he was just a man. Folding her arms, she faced the bed. "I daresay you have a number of questions—"

"Oh, I do."

She inclined her head, avoiding his eyes. "I'll attempt to answer them while you eat. You need to build your strength." He nodded in acquiescence; she continued. "You are presently at the Grange, my father's house. It lies south of the village. You were found at the Manor, which as you probably recall lies on the village's north boundary."

"That much I remember."

"My father is Sir Jasper Tallent—"

"Is he the local magistrate?"

She frowned. "Yes."

"Has he any idea who killed Horatio?"

Phyllida pressed her lips together, then relented. "No."

"Do you?"

She'd looked at him before she'd thought; his gaze locked with hers. Phyllida looked into eyes diabolically blue, took in the hard lines of his face, the unwavering determination, the hard mask that concealed his intention not at all. "No."

He held her gaze for a moment longer, then inclined his head. "Perhaps not."

She almost sighed with relief.

He looked down at his soup. "You do, however, know something."

His conviction rang absolute. Phyllida nearly threw her hands in the air—there was clearly no point in arguing. She gripped her elbows and looked past the bed at the window. After a moment, she said, "I daresay you're ravenous, but at this stage, you would be unwise to bite off more than you can chew. Your constitution may be excellent, but the blow you suffered was severe—you'll need time to recover full use of your faculties."

From the corner of her eye she saw his lips twitch, felt his gaze drift assessingly over her. She mentally replayed her words and felt pleased with them. A subtle warning and a clear statement she would not bow to *force majeure*. With most men, just the question of what she really meant would be enough to keep them puzzled and no more threat to her.

"My faculties," he murmured, "are returning in leaps and bounds."

Suggestive and openly threatening, the shocking warmth in his voice slid over her skin, a wanton, explicit caress.

Without thought, she sucked in a breath and whirled to face him, as if he were a predator. She was suddenly sure he was. "You'll need to be careful."

She kept her expression blank, her tone direct.

He opened his eyes wide; innocence wasn't what she saw in them. "Shouldn't you check my wound?"

"Your wound needs nothing more than time to heal." No power on earth would get her closer to the bed—closer to him. Phyllida frowned, and held tight to her role. *She* was in charge, not he. "Papa would like you to join us for afternoon tea, if you're able."

His smile made her nerves tingle. "I'm able."

"Good." She turned to the door. "I'll have your bags brought up—as a precaution, we left them downstairs."

"Precaution?"

"Why, yes." Reaching the door, she looked back. "We kept your clothes from you in case you turned difficult over remaining abed."

His lips curved; his eyes glinted. The combination looked positively wicked. "Lying abed is one of my favorite pastimes. However, if I'd wanted to get up, the mere absence of clothes wouldn't have deterred me." His gaze slid over her; his voice deepened. "Not in the least."

Gripping the doorknob, Phyllida met his gaze blankly and prayed she wasn't blushing. "I'll let Papa know you'll be joining us later. Your name?"

His untrustworthy smile deepened. "Lucifer."

Phyllida stared at him; even with the width of the room separating them, all her instincts were screaming, warning her not to call his bluff. Any of his bluffs.

Some part of her knew he wasn't the sort who bluffed.

It went seriously against her grain to let him trifle with her and escape retribution, but arguing would simply be playing into his hands. She forced herself to incline her head and evenly state, "Sweetie—Miss Sweet—will return shortly. She'll take away your tray."

On that note, she opened the door; with a regal nod, she left.

*   *   *

Later, after he'd bathed and dressed, Lucifer sat on the window seat in his bedchamber and looked north, over a dense wood. Through the shifting canopies he could occasionally glimpse the gray slate roof of the Manor.

Gaze fixed, he thought of Horatio, and of Martha, and of what he should do next, how best to move forward. Horatio's death was an accepted fact in his mind, but the tale had only just begun.

It was quiet beyond the open window. The snoozy quality of a summer's afternoon blanketed the village, yet somewhere in that peace a murderer waited, and watched and worried. Horatio's death had not been neat. Not only had he, Lucifer, stumbled on the scene far too soon, but so, too, had Phyllida Tallent.

Lucifer pondered that last, and all that it might mean.

A knock interrupted his reverie. He faced the door, keen to see if intuition proved correct. "Come in."

Phyllida entered; he smiled in private triumph. Retreating earlier and leaving the field to him must have been difficult; despite her wariness, he'd predicted she wouldn't stay away. She glanced around the room, then discovered him. She hesitated, then, leaving the door wide, crossed toward him. Frowning, she studied his face, his eyes. He let her draw near before smoothly rising—no sudden movements.

Her lovely eyes widened. She immediately halted. "Ah ..." From four feet away, she stared up at him, her expression a telltale blank. Her gaze drifted, passing over him, then she wrenched it back to his face. And caught him returning the favor. Her eyes snapped even as her expression smoothed to impassivity. "Are you sure you've recovered enough to join us downstairs?"

He continued to smile, relishing her resistance. "I'm quite recovered enough to brave a drawing room." The frown in her eyes deepened; he added, "My head only aches—it no longer throbs."

"Well ..." She searched his eyes once more. "I'm afraid my aunt and cousins have arrived for the summer, and, of course, they're agog to meet you. You must promise you won't overtax yourself."

Fussing was not something he readily endured, yet the idea that she'd elected herself his keeper, and was determined to do her duty despite the urgings of her common sense to keep a safer distance between them, was oddly satisfying. Oddly endearing. He smiled charmingly, too wise to smirk. "If I weaken and need support, you'll be the first to know."

She glared, but the concern in her dark eyes was very real. As was her suspicion.

"Very well." She lifted her head. "And now, if you please, your real name?"

Lucifer looked down at her; he made no attempt to disguise the tenor of his smile. "I told you. Lucifer."

She met his gaze directly. "No one is called Lucifer."

"I am." He stepped forward; she backed.

"That's ludicrous. That cannot be your real name."

He continued his advance; she continued to fall back.

"It's the name I'm known by. There are many who would tell you it suits me." He held her gaze and continued his prowling stroll. "If you ask anyone in the ton for Lucifer, they'll instantly send you to me."

Her eyes had grown wider—their expression informed him she'd never encountered a man such as he. She was both fascinated and defensive—and, he suspected, disapproving. Desire flared; he tamped it down, kept that truth from his eyes. That he delighted in transforming disapproving ladies into wanton houris was a truth she didn't need to know.

He took the last step that backed her over the room's threshold. Glancing about, she discovered herself in the corridor. She stiffened; the look she threw him as she stepped aside was distinctly irate. And not a little surprised. He hid a grin. It seemed likely that no one had ever managed her as he just had. He'd herded her out of the room—no hands, no voice—simply him. And there was hay yet to be made on this fine summer's day.

Closing the door, he looked down at her. "You shouldn't be alone with me. Especially not in a bedroom."

She held his gaze; he struggled to keep his eyes on hers rather than focus on her swelling breasts, rising as she drew in a long, rigidly controlled breath. Lips compressed, she held it in, along with her temper.

Not at all innocently, he raised a brow at her.

Her eyes spat sparks. So fleeting was the sight, he could almost think he'd imagined it; his body's reaction confirmed he hadn't. In the next instant, her eyes once more dark pools of calm composure, her expression, as it so often was, deceptively serene, she inclined her head and turned down the corridor.

"Thank you for the warning." Her words drifted back to him. "You may tell Papa your name directly. If you'll follow me?" Head high, she moved toward the stairs.

Lucifer watched her hips sway, unconsciously seductive, the delectable hemispheres of her derriere and the graceful lines of her legs occasionally outlined by her gown. Lips lifting, he stepped out in her wake, very ready to oblige.

The room she led him to gave onto the back lawn and onto the terrace along the side of the house. The long windows were open, letting the balmy breeze bring the summer day inside. A family group was gathered about the tea trolley, stationed in front of a *chaise*. A middle-aged lady with a hard expression wielded the teapot; beside her, a dandy, her son by his features, lounged petulantly. On her other side, a younger gentleman slouched— another son, this one sulky. No wonder the lady looked so worn down.

Two other gentlemen stood beside the *chaise*. The younger, an insouciant male version of Phyllida, grinned engagingly. The older man, large and dressed in country tweeds, studied Lucifer from under shaggy brows.

Preceding Lucifer into the room, Phyllida waved to this gentleman. "Papa?"

Lucifer joined her as she halted before her father. She slanted him a glance. "Allow me to present …"

He smiled, then turned to her father and held out his hand. "Alasdair Cynster, sir. But most call me Lucifer."

"Lucifer, heh?" Sir Jasper shook hands without any evidence of disquiet. "What names you youngsters do take. Now! How're you feeling?"

"Much better, thanks to your daughter's care."

Sir Jasper smiled on Phyllida, who had turned to the tea trolley. "Aye, well, that was a nasty blow, no doubt of that. Now let me make you known to m'sister-in-law; then we'll take our tea and you can tell me all you know about this distressing business."

His sister-in-law, Lady Huddlesford, summoned a smile and held out her hand. "I'm delighted to meet you, Mr. Cynster."

Lucifer politely shook hands. Sir Jasper gestured to the dandy. "M'nephew, Percy Tallent."

Percy, it transpired, was her ladyship's son by her first marriage to Sir Jasper's late brother. One minute of affected conversation and Lucifer had Percy pegged—he was on a repairing lease. Nothing else could account for his presence in rural Devon. His sullen half brother, Frederick Huddlesford, openly stared at Lucifer's well-cut coat, hard pressed, it seemed, to marshal the words for even a simple greeting.

With a nod, Lucifer turned to the young man so like Phyllida, who promptly grinned and stuck out his hand. "Jonas. Phyllida's little brother."

Clasping the proffered hand, Lucifer smiled and raised his brows. Loose-limbed, with the same careless grace that characterized his sister, Jonas stood a good six inches taller than she. Lucifer glanced at her as she straightened from the tea trolley. For all his transparent, good-natured insousiance, Jonas didn't appear younger than she.

Phyllida caught his glance; her chin rose. "We're twins, but I'm the elder."

"Ah. I see. Always the leader."

Her brows rose haughtily. Jonas chuckled.

So did Sir Jasper. "Quite, quite. Phyllida keeps us all in line—don't know what we'd do without her. Now"—he waved to a grouping of chairs at the end of the room—"let's move down there and you can tell me what you can about this terrible business."

As he turned, Lucifer felt Phyllida's gaze on his face.

"Indeed, Papa. I do think Mr. Cynster should sit down. I'll bring you your cups."

Sir Jasper nodded. Lucifer followed him down the room. They settled in wing chairs angled to each other, a small table between. The length of the room assured them of privacy; the others watched them go, their curiosity palpable, then reluctantly returned to their own company.

As he gingerly rested his head back on the chair's cushion, Lucifer considered Sir Jasper. His host was a type he knew well. Men like him were the backbone of county England. Bluffly good-natured, genial if unimaginative, they were, nevertheless, no one's fools. They could be counted on to hold the line, to do whatever needed to be done to keep their community stable, yet they had no taste for power; it was appreciation of their comfort plus trenchant common sense that drove them.

Lucifer glanced at Phyllida, busy at the tea trolley. Like father, like daughter? He suspected so, at least in part.

"So"—Sir Jasper stretched out his legs—"are you familiar with Devon?"

Lucifer went to shake his head, but stopped. "No. My family home lies north of here, to the east of the Quantocks."

"Somerset, heh? So you're a west countryman?"

"At heart, but I've lived in London for the last decade."

Phyllida arrived with cups on saucers; she handed one to each of them, then whisked back up the room. Sir Jasper sipped; Lucifer did, too, conscious of reawakening hunger. An instant later, Phyllida reappeared with a cake plate piled high. She offered it around, then subsided onto a love seat beside her father's chair, and patently settled to listen.

Lucifer glanced at Sir Jasper. His host was aware of his daughter's presence, and clearly saw nothing odd in her being privy to his investigations. His flippant remark about her being a born leader was not, it seemed, far from the mark.

Hands folded in her lap, she sat quiet and contained. Lucifer studied her as he consumed a piece of cake. She wouldn't see twenty again, but how much older was she? Her cool composure he suspected was misleading. Jonas's age was easier to estimate; his body was still all long bones and spare frame. He was in his early-to-mid twenties, at least four years younger than Lucifer's twenty-nine.

Which made Phyllida the same.

And a puzzle. There was no ring on her finger, nor had there ever been one. He'd noted that last night; even in extremis, his rakish instincts hadn't failed him. She was twenty-three, twenty-four, and still unwed. Definitely a puzzle.

She was aware of his scrutiny, but not a smidgen of that awareness showed. The urge to shake her—to see her lose that cool control—flared. Lucifer looked down, set aside his cake plate, and picked up his cup.

Sir Jasper did the same. "Now, to business. Let's start with your arrival. What brought you to the Manor yesterday morning?"

"I received a letter from Horatio Welham." Lucifer settled his head back on the cushion. "It was delivered in London on Thursday. Horatio invited me to visit the Manor at my earliest convenience."

"So you were previously acquainted with Welham?"

"I've known Horatio for over nine years. I first met him when I was twenty, while staying with friends in the Lake District. Horatio introduced me to serious collecting. He was my mentor in that field and became a close, very trusted friend. Over the years, I frequently visited Horatio and his wife, Martha, at their house by Lake Windemere."

"Lake District, was it? Always wondered where Horatio hailed from. He never said and one didn't like to pry."

Lucifer hesitated, then said, "Horatio was deeply attached to Martha. When she died three years ago, he couldn't face living alone in the house they'd shared for so long. He sold up and moved south. Devon appealed because of the milder climate—he used to say he chose to move here because of his old bones and because he liked this village. He said it was small and comfortable." *With no managing local mesdames.* Lucifer glanced at Phyllida—how had Horatio viewed her?

Her eyes had grown dark. "No wonder he never spoke of his past. He must have been deeply in love with his Martha."

Lucifer inclined his head, then looked at Sir Jasper.

"Would any of Welham's servants know you?"

"I don't know who he kept on. Is Covey still with him?"

"Yes, indeed."

"Then he knows me, certainly." Lucifer frowned. "If Covey's here, why did the servants suspect me of killing Horatio? Covey knows how long I've known Horatio and the nature of our relationship."

"Covey wasn't here," Phyllida said. "He visits an old aunt in Musbury, a village nearby, every Sunday. By the time he returned, you were here at the Grange."

"Covey would be very cut up by Horatio's death."

Phyllida nodded.

Sir Jasper sighed. "No getting any sense out of him yesterday—I did try. Daresay he's still feeling it today."

"Covey was devoted to Horatio over all the years I knew them."

Sir Jasper threw Lucifer a shrewd glance. "Quite—no reason to suppose Covey knows anything about his master's death." He sat back. "Now, let's see. This is your first visit to Colyton?"

"Yes. Until now, matters never fell out suitably for a visit. Horatio and I discussed it, but …We met at least every three months, sometimes more frequently, in London and at collectors' gatherings around the country."

"So you're a collector, too?"

"I specialize in silver and jewelry. Horatio, on the other hand, was an acknowledged expert on antique books and a highly regarded authority in a number of other areas, too. He was an inspired teacher. It was an honor to have learned from him."

"Were there others who learned from him?"

"A few, but none who remained so closely in touch. The others took up collecting in Horatio's own spheres, and so became competitors of sorts."

"Could one of them have killed him?"

Lucifer shook his head. "I can't imagine it."

"Other collectors? Jealous ones, perhaps?"

Lucifer waved a negative. "Collectors might metaphorically kill for certain items, but few actually do. For most collectors, half the joy is displaying your acquisitions to other collectors. Horatio was highly respected and well liked among the fraternity; his collections were well known. Any item of his unexpectedly surfacing in someone else's collection would draw immediate attention. As a motive for murder, a known collector wanting to gain a particular piece is unlikely. We can, however, check for missing items, although it will take time. Horatio kept meticulous records."

Sir Jasper was frowning. "We knew Welham was a collector and dealer, but I, for one, had no notion he was so highly regarded." He glanced at Phyllida.

She shook her head. "We all knew he had visitors from outside—beyond the local area—but no one here knows much about antiques. We had no idea Horatio held such a prominent place in that sphere."

"I think," Lucifer said, "that that was part of the attraction of Colyton. Horatio liked being 'one of the locals.' "

Sir Jasper nodded. "Now you mention it, he became 'one of us' very quickly. Hard to believe it's only been three years. He bought the Manor and rebuilt and refurbished it. He put in that garden—his pride, it was. Used to potter in it for hours—his success turned some of the local ladies green. He always did all he could—went to church every Sunday, helped out in many ways." Sir Jasper paused, then quietly concluded, "He'll be missed."

They sat silently for a moment, then Lucifer asked, "If he always went to church, why was he at home yesterday? I hadn't sent word I was coming."

"He was ill," Phyllida said. "A bad cold. He insisted the others go as usual, and that Covey was not to disappoint his aunt. Mrs. Hemmings said she left him reading upstairs."

"So"—Sir Jasper shifted in his chair—"let's recount what happened as we know it. You arrived on a social visit—"

"That's not quite true—or not all of the truth. I left Horatio's letter in Somerset, so you'll have to bear with my paraphrasing, but he specifically asked me to visit because he wanted my opinion on some item he'd discovered. He was obviously excited by it—the impression I received was that it was a wholly unexpected find. The inference was that he personally felt sure the item was authentic, but wanted a second opinion."

"Any idea what this item was?"

"No. The only thing I can be sure of is that it wasn't silver or jewelry."

"But those are your specialties."

"Yes, but Horatio wrote that if the item was authentic, it might even tempt me to expand my collection beyond silver and jewelry."

"So it was a desirable piece?"

"My interpretation was that it was desirable and valuable. The fact that Horatio asked me to appraise something not in my area of expertise, when he could easily have invited the opinion of any of the established collectors of whatever type of collectible it is, suggests that the item was one of those finds that no sane collector tells anyone he has until he's established ownership and perhaps arranged greater security. Horatio might have been old, but he was still very sharp."

"But he told you—why not others?"

Lucifer met Phyllida's dark gaze. "Because for various reasons, among them our long friendship, Horatio knew he'd be safe telling me. Indeed, I might be the only one he mentioned the item to at all."

"Would Covey know of it?"

"Unless his duties have changed, I doubt it. Covey helped Horatio with arrangements and correspondence but was never involved with the actual dealing or assessing."

Sir Jasper mulled over their words. "So you came here to meet with Horatio and view this new item of his." He looked at Lucifer, who nodded. "You drove into the village ...?"

Lucifer leaned back, his gaze fixed above Phyllida's head. "I passed no one on the road, nor did I see anyone about. I turned into the drive ..." Simply and succinctly, he described his movements. "And then someone hit me over the head and I collapsed beside Horatio."

"You were hit with an old halberd," Sir Jasper said. "Nasty weapon—you're lucky not to have died."

Lucifer lowered his gaze to Phyllida's calm face. "Indeed."

"This letter knife Horatio was stabbed with—do you recall it?"

"It was his—Louis Quinze—he'd had it for years."

"Hmm—so that's not this special item." Sir Jasper kept his gaze on his boots. "So as things stand, you have no idea who might have killed Welham?"

Phyllida stared into deep blue eyes and prayed her welling panic didn't show. It hadn't occurred to her, not until he started recounting his movements, that, in truth, Lucifer held her in the palm of his hand. If he told her father that someone had been there after the murderer had struck, and that he was convinced—no, he *knew*—that that person was she ...

Her father would instantly know she'd lied—not by act but by omission. He'd realize her uncharacteristic surrender to a headache last Sunday morning had been a ruse, that it would be easy for her to cut through the wood and reach the Manor without being seen. That she'd known no one else should have been in the house.

What he wouldn't understand was why—why she'd done it and then so deceitfully kept silent. And that was the one thing she couldn't tell him, couldn't yet explain—not until she was released from her oath.

The dark blue gaze never wavered. "No."

She breathed shallowly and waited, knowing he knew, knowing he was debating whether or not to expose her. To her father, one of the few people whose good opinion mattered to her.

Time slowed. As if from a distance, she heard her father ask the fateful question, the one she'd realized he would eventually ask. "And there's nothing else bearing on this matter you can tell me?"

Lucifer's eyes held hers steadily. Giddiness threatened.

It suddenly occurred to her to consider the next step: What if he didn't tell?

"No."

She blinked.

He held her gaze for an instant longer, then glanced at her father. "I have no notion who killed Horatio, but, with your permission, I intend to find out."

"Indeed, indeed." Her father nodded. "Commendable goal." He looked up, and frowned.

"Good gracious, Jasper!" Lady Huddlesford swept forward. "You've been interrogating Mr. Cynster for quite long enough. His poor head must be aching."

Lucifer rose, as did Sir Jasper.

"Nonsense, Margaret, we have to sort this matter out."

"Indeed! I haven't been so shocked in years. The very thought of a London cutthroat slipping into the village and stabbing Mr. Welham is more than enough to overset me."

"There's no reason to think it was someone from London."

Lady Huddlesford stared at her brother-in-law. "Really, Jasper! This is such a sleepy little place—everyone knows everyone. Of *course* it must be someone from outside."

Phyllida sensed her father's resistance. He doggedly held to the logical approach, which meant that at any second he was going to turn to her and ask if she knew of anyone local with a reason to wish Horatio dead.

She didn't, but her answer might come close to being a lie. An outright lie. She avoided prevarication on principle, except in pursuit of the greater good. As her gaze touched Mr. Cynster—Lucifer—she acidly wished she'd made no exception. Just look where it had landed her.

First swamped by guilt. Now chin-deep in his debt.

Percy sauntered up to them. Phyllida glanced his way, then let her gaze drift to Lucifer. Percy was unwise to stand beside him; the comparison left Percy looking like a pasty-faced, effeminate weakling. Percy was pasty-faced, but otherwise presentable—it was the competition that served him so ill.

Her aunt continued to proclaim the impossibility of the murderer being local. Phyllida grasped the moment when she paused for breath. "I must call on Mrs. Hemmings, Papa, to make sure she has all she needs for the wake. I also need to stop at the church and speak with Mr. Filing."

Her nemesis spoke. "Perhaps I could accompany you, Miss Tallent?"

"Ah …" Transfixed by blue eyes that warned her there was no alternative to his company, Phyllida bit back a refusal, couched as a polite reminder about his head.

His lips curved; his gaze remained steady. "I know I promised not to overtax myself, but as I'll be in your company, there's surely no risk."

He'd kept her secret; now she had to pay the price. She inclined her head. "If you wish. A walk in the fresh air might ease your head."

"An excellent notion." As Lucifer straightened from bowing to her aunt, her father caught his eye. "Give you a chance to get the lay of the land, heh?"

"Indeed." The reprobate turned to her, a definite glint in his eyes. He smiled and gestured elegantly. "Lead on, my dear Miss Tallent."

CHAPTER

Three

She took him to the Manor by way of the lane through the village; it was too dangerous to walk through the woods with a predator, especially one in whose power she now was. Her father, of course, had no idea—he was impressed with the fiend, she could tell.

As she walked through the sunshine with him prowling beside her, she grudgingly admitted that if he hadn't been such a threat to her, she might have been impressed, too. He felt just as he ought to about Horatio. But being managed was a novel experience for her, one she didn't like. However, he hadn't done the unforgivable and given her the ultimate ultimatum—that either she tell him the whole truth, or he would tell her father she'd been in Horatio's drawing room. She was therefore willing to humor him.

She glanced at him. His dark hair shone mahogany brown in the sun. "You forgot your hat."

"I rarely wear one."

So much for that. She walked on. The village proper lay just ahead.

Lucifer looked at her; her bonnet shielded her face from his view. "I think"—he waited until she glanced up at him—"that, given we've formed an alliance of sorts, you'd better tell me what happened after I was discovered."

She studied his eyes, then faced forward. "You were discovered by Hemmings, Horatio's gardener. Mrs. Hemmings, the housekeeper, went upstairs, imagining Horatio to be there. Hemmings went into the drawing room to lay the fire. He raised the alarm and Bristleford, Horatio's butler, sent for Juggs and Thompson."

"To take me, as the murderer, into custody?"

Her bonnet bobbed. "Bristleford was overset—he thought you were the murderer. There's a cell beneath the inn where prisoners are held awaiting transportation to the assizes. Thompson's the blacksmith—they used his dray to shift you."

"And where were you?"

She glanced swiftly at him, then away. A full minute passed before she said, "I was laid upon my bed with a sick headache—that was why I hadn't gone to church."

When she said no more, he prompted her. "You appeared in the cell insisting I wasn't the murderer."

"I didn't know whether you remembered."

"I remember. How did you come to be there?"

"I often borrowed books of poetry from Horatio. I recovered from my headache and thought I'd fetch a new volume. But just as I reached our front door, Aunt Huddlesford's carriage drew up. I'd forgotten she was arriving that morning, but all the arrangements were already in place—or so I thought."

The irritation in that last reached Lucifer clearly. "But ...?"

"Percy and Frederick—I wasn't expecting them. They don't usually favor us with their gracious presence."

"I'd wager Percy's on a repairing lease."

"Very likely, but their arrival meant that I had to wait until our staff returned from church to give orders for extra rooms, and entertain them and Aunt Huddlesford until Papa and Jonas appeared."

"And when that happened?"

"I left as soon as I could, but when I reached the Manor, you'd already been taken away."

"Is this the inn?" Lucifer stopped; Phyllida did, too. The building beside them was a half-timbered structure, worn and a little shabby but still serviceable.

"Yes—the Red Bells."

"And Juggs is the innkeeper."

She started walking again. "He gets paid for holding prisoners, so you shouldn't judge him too harshly."

He swallowed his response to that. "What happened next?"

"I made sure they'd sent for Papa, then I came to the Bells." She glanced at his face. "How much do you remember?"

"Not all of it, but enough. You stayed until your father arrived, and then he rode home and was to send the carriage. The next thing I remember clearly was ..."—he studied her eyes while he replayed his memories—"waking up in the witching hour."

"Yes, well, that's really all there was to it." Looking ahead, she paced on. "You were restless, but your skull was intact—it was all just the pain."

Lucifer glanced at her. Why hadn't she taken the opportunity to tell him of her vigil by his bed? He'd put her in a position of being grateful to him; why hadn't she evened the score?

They strolled past a succession of neat cottages and on around the curving lane. The Manor came into sight.

"Very well," he said. "I now know your story. I also know that you were in Horatio's drawing room before I entered, and that you were there after I was hit."

"You know nothing of the sort."

He looked smugly superior—she was watching from the corner of her eye.

"You can't possibly tell it was me from a mere touch." The glance she flung at him was both irate and uncertain.

"I can. I did. I know it was you."

"You can't be sure."

"Hmm ... perhaps not. Why not touch me again, just to see if I'm certain?"

She stopped and faced him, latent sparks in her eyes—

"Hoi! Miss Phyllida!"

They swung around. A heavy man in a leather apron and vest was lumbering down the common toward them.

"The blacksmith?"

"Yes—Thompson."

Thompson approached. His gaze on Lucifer, he nodded respectfully. "Sir." He nodded at Phyllida, then looked back at Lucifer. "I just wanted to apologize, like, for any bruises you mighta taken when we dumped you in my dray. 'Course, we thought you was the murderer and you weren't easy to lift, but I wouldn't want no hard feelings."

Lucifer smiled. "None taken. I don't bruise easily."

"Well." Thompson blew out a relieved breath and grinned back. "That's all right, then. Not but what it was no fit welcome to the village, 'specially not with a bash on the head an' all."

Phyllida inwardly squirmed. She glanced up the lane toward the Manor.

"Has Sir Jasper got any clues as to this murderer, then, sir?"

Her "No" clashed with Lucifer's "None"—Phyllida nearly outwardly squirmed when she realized the question had not been addressed to her.

With a subtly amused glance, Lucifer added, "Sir Jasper's investigations are proceeding."

"Aye, well ..."

Phyllida waited while Thompson pointed out the forge on the far side of the common and assured Lucifer that he could count on him for any assistance, either in laying the murderer by the heels or with his horses.

With a final nod, Thompson took himself off back over the common.

She stepped out again; Lucifer prowled by her side, his stride an exercise in effortless grace. He murmured, "It seems a peaceful little place."

"Usually." She glanced up and found him scanning the common and the church on the crest.

They avoided the duck pond and its vocal inhabitants and reached the Manor's gate. She opened it and stepped through; Lucifer had to duck the trailing fingers of wisteria hanging from the framing arch. She led the way around the small fountain. Gaining the porch, she realized he'd fallen behind. Looking back, she saw him studying a bed of burgeoning peonies. His gaze moved on to a bed of roses and lavender; then he glanced up, saw her waiting, and lengthened his stride.

He joined her on the porch, but glanced back at the garden.

"What is it?"

He looked at her, his expression closed, his eyes screened. "Who did the garden?"

"Papa told you—Horatio. Well"—she glanced at the beds—"Hemmings helped, of course, but Horatio's was always the guiding hand." She studied his face. "Why?"

He looked at the garden. "When they lived in the Lake District, Martha did the garden—it was hers, totally. I would have sworn Horatio wouldn't have known a hollyhock from a nettle."

Phyllida considered the garden with new eyes. "All the time he was here he was most particular about the garden."

After a moment, Lucifer turned; she noted his closed face. Swinging around, she led the way inside.

The house was silent; they walked quietly forward, halting level with the open drawing room door. Horatio's coffin rested on the table just beyond the spot where they—yes, *they*—had found his body. For a moment, they both simply looked, then Phyllida led the way in.

A yard from the coffin, she stopped. It suddenly required effort to breathe. Long fingers touched hers; instinctively, she clung. His hand closed about hers, warm and alive. He stepped forward to stand beside her. She felt his gaze on her face. Without looking at him, she nodded. Side by side, they stepped to the polished wooden box.

For long moments, they stood gazing down. Phyllida drew comfort from the peaceful expression that had settled on Horatio's face. It had been there when she'd found him, as if his departure from this world, although violent and unexpected, had been a release. Perhaps there truly was a Heaven.

She'd liked him, approved of him, and was sad that he was gone. She could say good-bye and let him go, but the manner of his going was not something she could let be. He'd been murdered in the village she'd virtually managed for twelve years; that she'd been the one to find him, already gone and beyond her help, had only increased her outrage.

It was as if something she'd worked for all her life—the peace and serenity of Colyton—had been violated, tainted.

The memory returned to her, crystal-clear, that moment when she'd found Horatio dead. She felt again her shock, the chill touch of fear, the paralyzing fright when she'd realized she'd heard no one leaving ...

Lifting her head, she stared down the room. She'd only just remembered.

She'd come to the drawing room from the back of the hall; before that, she'd been in the kitchen. Even from there, if anyone had left the house, she would have heard them cross the hall or cross the gravel. No one had. She'd idled in the hall, then decided on searching the drawing room.

How long had all that taken? How long had Horatio been dead before she'd found him?

What if the murderer hadn't left but had still been in the drawing room when she'd entered?

She focused on the gap between two bookcases, almost at the end of the room. It was the only hiding place the murderer could have used.

He *must* have been there. That was the only explanation for the disappearing hat. There was certain to have been a gap between her exit and Hemmings deciding to lay the fire. Mrs. Hemmings would have been upstairs. A small window of opportunity, but the murderer had grasped it, and his hat, and disappeared without a trace.

Phyllida drew in a breath; the warmth of Lucifer's hand clasped around hers anchored her, steadied her. She looked down at Horatio's lined face and made a vow—a binding, resolute vow—that she would find whoever had hidden between the bookcases and watched her discover Horatio's body.

This was one murderer who would not escape.

Even as she made her silent declaration, she was aware another, very similar one was being made not a foot away. Lucifer's words to her father had rung with determination; she needed no convincing that he would regard his vow as seriously as she regarded hers.

They could work together—together they might succeed. Alone, even with her father's support, bringing a murderer to justice might well be more than she could accomplish. Despite his dubious talents, she was certain the reprobate beside her could achieve anything he set his mind to. So ...

She slanted a glance at him. She needed to tell him all that had happened, even to admitting that it was she who had hit him over the head. Confessing to that wouldn't be comfortable, but he needed to know.

He especially needed to know about the hat.

Which meant she had to speak with Mary Anne straightaway.

She took in Lucifer's bleak expression, the planes of his face harsh without any lurking laughter to soften them. His large eyes were hooded. He'd been much closer to Horatio than she had.

Sliding her fingers from his, she retreated and left him with his grief.

Lucifer heard her go. Part of his mind tracked her movements; part of him relaxed when she turned deeper into the house. He remembered she'd mentioned speaking with the housekeeper. Reassured, he returned his attention to Horatio.

Their last farewell—there wouldn't be another. He let the memories spill through his mind, like water running through his fingers. Their shared interests, their successes, their mutual appreciation, the long afternoons spent on the terrace overlooking Lake Windemere. All good times—there'd been none bad.

At the last, he drew in a deep breath, then laid a hand atop Horatio's, clasped on his chest. "Go twit Martha on her pansies. As for revenge, leave that to me."

Vengeance might be the Lord's, but sometimes He needed help.

As he turned away, his gaze fell on the bookshelves lining the walls. Idly, he strolled along them, tracing the spines of volumes here and there, remembered friends. Toward the end of the room, he noticed three volumes jutting out from their shelf. He slid them back in, aligning them. He looked back along the tome-lined wall. How appropriate for Horatio to spend his final hours here, surrounded by his dearest possessions.

He was standing before the long windows, looking out on the garden that so puzzled him, when a discreet cough sounded in the doorway. He turned; a thin, spare man, hunched into his coat, was staring at the coffin. Lucifer left the window. "Covey. Pray accept my condolences. I know how attached you were to Horatio—and he to you."

Covey blinked watery blue eyes. "Thank you, sir. Miss Tallent told me you were here. I regret that it's such a dreadful occasion that sees you with us ... again."

"A dreadful business, indeed. Do you have any idea ...?"

"None at all. I had no inkling, no reason to suppose ..." He gestured helplessly at the coffin.

"Don't blame yourself, Covey—you couldn't have known."

"If I had, it wouldn't have happened."

"Of course not." Lucifer interposed himself between Covey and the coffin. "Horatio wrote to me about some item he'd discovered that he wanted my opinion on. Do you know what it was?"

Covey shook his head. "I knew he'd found something special. You know how he'd get—his eyes all lighting up like a child's? That's how he was for the past week. I hadn't seen him so excited for years."

"He didn't mention anything at all about it?"

"No, but he never did, not with his special finds. Not until he was ready to tell all; then he'd lay all the proofs out on his desk and explain it all to me." A wistful smile touched Covey's lips. "He'd take great delight in that, even though he knew I understood not one word in three."

Lucifer gripped Covey's shoulder. "You were a good friend to him, Covey." He hesitated, then added, "I'm sure Horatio will have made provision for you in his will, but whatever happens, we'll sort something out. Horatio would have wished it."

Covey inclined his head. "Thank you, sir. I appreciate the reassurance."

"One thing. Have any of the other dealers stopped by recently? Jamieson? Dallwell?"

"No, sir. Mr. Jamieson stopped by some months ago, but we've seen no one recently. The master hasn't—hadn't—been so active in dealing since we'd moved south."

Lucifer hesitated. "I imagine I'll be staying at the Grange for the next few days."

"Indeed, sir." Covey bowed. "If you'll excuse me, I'll return to my tidying."

Lucifer nodded in dismissal, wondering who Horatio's heirs would be. He made a mental note to have a word with them regarding Covey's long service and devotion. Returning to the window, he considered Covey's description of Horatio's recent excitement.

If he could understand why Horatio had been killed, he would know who had killed him. The "why" was the key. It seemed possible, even likely, that the "why" was the mysterious item Horatio had discovered; his violent death had followed so soon after the discovery. If the mysterious item was the key, then the murderer might have come from beyond the local area, as Lady Huddlesford insisted was the case. Luckily, they were deep in the country—"outsiders" were noticed. He was sure he'd been noticed, perhaps not in Colyton, but certainly along the way.

Turning, he scanned the room. Horatio might have concealed his latest find in plain sight, amid the treasure trove of his collection.

When Phyllida returned to the drawing room, she found her nemesis examining the halberd responsible for the dent in his skull. He looked at her. "Was it always kept here—behind the door?"

"I understand so."

He studied her, then looked at the axe-head. Raising the halberd, he let it fall to his other hand, watching how the weighted head swung. "I would have thought, if it had fallen or been wielded with intent ..."

Then the axe should have cleaved his skull in two. Phyllida didn't want to think about it. "This part here"—she pointed to the rounded side—"was apparently what connected with your head."

"Indeed?" He hefted the weapon fully upright, then looked at her. "How did it fall?"

She met his eyes directly—and said nothing.

He held her gaze, and let the tension stretch.

And stretch ...

She lifted her chin. "I have to go to the church to sort out the flowers for the funeral, and then I must speak with the curate. You can stay here, if you like."

Lucifer replaced the halberd. "I'll come with you."

He'd said his last good-bye to Horatio.

Contained and uncommunicative, she led the way through the garden. As they rounded the fountain, he paused. "The flowers for the church—use some of these peonies. They were Martha's favorites."

She stopped and glanced back at him, then at the flowers. Then she nodded and continued on.

They crossed the lane and started up the common. The expanse of green was kept clipped by the sheep allowed to graze over it; it rose in a gradual slope from the lane to the crest on which the church stood.

Lucifer matched his long strides to Phyllida's and breathed deeply. The air was fresh, sun-warmed; the scents and sounds of a June afternoon ebbed and flowed around them. The ache in his head was subsiding, and the best distraction Colyton had to offer was walking beside him.

He was intrigued, and couldn't entirely understand why. Indeed, he wasn't sure he approved. His preference, until now, had been for ladies of more bountiful charms, yet Phyllida Tallent's slender grace acted powerfully on his ever-ready male senses. Being so easily aroused by a gently reared, intelligent, and stubborn virgin, one who was making no effort to attract him at all, had to be fate's idea of a joke. Perhaps being hit on the head had affected him more than he'd realized.

Whatever the cause, walking beside and a little behind her left him all too aware whenever the frolicking breeze plastered her gown to her legs and bottom, or when it flicked at the hem of her skirt, exposing slim ankles. Her svelte figure contained a suppressed energy one part of him—the wild, untamed pirate part of him—instantly recognized; he longed to wind it tight, then release it before plunging into its core.

Climbing the hill was easing his head at the expense of intensifying the ache in his loins. An ache destined to remain unrelieved. Drawing a bracing breath, he looked ahead, and deliberately shifted his thoughts.

She preceded him into the church and went straight to the altar. Picking up a vase, she headed through an open door into a small side chamber.

He lounged against a pew. The small church was well endowed with carvings and stained glass. The oriel window above the entrance was particularly pleasing. It was fitting that Horatio's funeral would be held here; Horatio would have appreciated the church's beauties.

A beauty of a different sort swept back in and effortlessly recaptured his attention.

Phyllida jumped when large hands covered hers as she wrestled with the urn on the font.

"Let me."

She did. The reverberations of his voice played up and down her spine and left her nerves jangling. Wordlessly, she led the way through the vestry and out through the open back door. She indicated the pile of dead flowers. "Just toss them there."

He did. She retrieved the urn from his hands; without being asked, he wielded the pump handle so she could rinse it. With a nod of thanks, she swept back into the vestry; swiping up a cloth, she vigorously buffed the urn.

He halted in the doorway, almost blocking out the light; propping one shoulder against the frame, he watched her.

The vestry suddenly seemed very small. Awareness prickled over her skin.

"The funeral will be tomorrow, late morning. I'll send flowers over first thing—in this weather, they wilt so quickly." She was babbling. She'd never babbled in her life. "Especially if they're not picked before the sun strikes them."

"Does that mean you'll be flitting among the flowers at dawn?"

She wanted to look at him but didn't. "Of course not. Our gardener knows just how I like them picked."

"Ah. No need, then, to get up too early."

It was his tone, the deep resonance in his voice, that gave his words their full meaning. For an instant, she froze, her hands on the urn, then she sucked in a breath, grasped the urn, set it on the shelf, and swung to face him. Her expression, she was sure, remained calmly superior, unruffled, and serene. No one in the village ever saw beyond that, which made protecting herself and managing them very easy.

His gaze, however, settled on her eyes. He saw further, deeper—she wasn't at all comfortable with what he might see. "I need to speak with Mr. Filing, the curate. Given your injury, you should rest for a few minutes. I suggest you sit in a pew in the cool of the church. I'll collect you when I've finished with Mr. Filing."

He continued to study her face, her eyes. After an unnerving moment, he glanced back outside, over his left shoulder. "Is that the curate's house?"

"Yes. That's the Rectory."

He straightened away from the doorframe; the movement did nothing to reduce the sense of entrapment she felt. "I'll come with you."

Phyllida drew in a breath, and held it. With anyone else she would have argued, but there was an undercurrent in his voice that warned her she had no chance of swaying him. Not without a fight—and fighting with him was too dangerous. "As you wish."

He moved back and she stepped past him, into the sunshine. She led the way down the winding path to the Rectory, snug in a hollow just below the crest. Shutting the vestry door, he followed on her heels.

His intention was impossible to mistake. He knew she was hiding something; he was going to cling to her side—unnerve her as much as he could—until she told him what it was. Or until he uncovered her secrets for himself.

The latter, Phyllida decided, was not a fate to tempt. How soon could she see Mary Anne?

Lucifer followed her to the Rectory, too conscious of the lithe grace of her stride, the unfettered freedom with which she moved. To senses steeped in consideration of the feminine, she registered as something beyond the norm. Infinitely more desirable, and infinitely more elusive.

Why, he wondered, did she not wish him to be a party to her meeting with the curate?

That gentleman had seen them coming; he stood waiting for them at his front door. Fair, pale, and slightly built, his clothes fastidiously neat, Filing had the appearance of a gentleman aesthete. He greeted Phyllida with a smile, one that held the warmth of long-standing friendship.

"Good morning, Mr. Filing. Allow me to present Mr. Cynster, an old friend of Horatio's."

"Indeed?" Filing offered his hand; Lucifer shook it. "Such a sad occurrence. It must have been a shock to discover Horatio slain."

Lucifer inclined his head.

"As you'll have heard, the funeral's tomorrow morning. Perhaps, as an old friend, you'd like to give the eulogy?"

Lucifer considered, then shook his head. "With this knock on the head, I'm not sure I'll be up to it, and frankly, I think Horatio would consider his connection with the people here of more importance to him over these last years than his professional associations."

And he suspected he'd be of more use to Horatio by studying those attending the funeral.

"I see, I see." Filing nodded. "Well, then, if there's no objection, I'll give the eulogy myself. Horatio and I often shared a glass of port of an evening. He had a wonderful collection of ecclesiastical texts and kindly gave me free rein to browse through them. He was truly a gentleman and a scholar—that will be the theme of my eulogy."

"Very apt." Lucifer turned his gaze on Phyllida, and waited; Filing did the same.

Her expression calm, her eyes watchful, she glanced at him. "There are a number of organizational matters I must discuss with Mr. Filing."

Lucifer nodded, as if giving her permission to speak. Shifting back, he let his gaze roam the common, down to the cottages lining the lane.

"Our discussion will take a few minutes. Perhaps you should rest on that bench over there."

The bench was halfway down the slope overlooking the duck pond, well out of hearing range. He frowned and glanced at her. "It might be wiser if we descend together. Just in case I'm overcome with giddiness."

Her annoyance reached him in a wash of heat; anger glowed momentarily in her eyes. But she inclined her head, her expression cool, unconcerned—a perfect social mask. Filing glanced back and forth; he sensed something, but couldn't define it. Couldn't see past her facade.

Lucifer wondered why *he* could—and why he wanted to see so much further, to know so much more.

She turned to Filing. "About the flowers for tomorrow ..."

Fixing his gaze down the common, Lucifer let their discussion flow past him. There seemed a great deal to be said about the flowers. Then, with not the slightest shift in her tone to mark the shift in her subject, she continued. "Which brings us to our other business."

Lucifer suppressed a cynical smile. She was good. Unfortunately for her, he was better.

"You have the collection complete, I believe?"

From the corner of his eye Lucifer saw Filing nod—and shoot a glance at him.

"I assume you foresee no difficulties in the distribution to those deserving?"

"No," Filing murmured. "All seems ... straightforward."

"Good. Our next outing will be as scheduled. I've had a letter confirming there's been no change to the plans. If you could pass the word on to those interested?"

"Of course."

"And do remind them that we'll need the group assembled in good time— we can't wait for stragglers. If they're not there from the very first, then we really cannot include them in the group, so they'll miss out on the benefits of the excursion."

Filing nodded. "If any want to argue that point, I'll suggest they speak with Thompson."

Phyllida shot him a glance. "Do." She straightened. "Until tomorrow, then."

Lucifer returned his attention to her, then nodded a farewell to Filing.

Phyllida gestured down the common. "We should get back—you really should rest your head."

He fell into step beside her; they descended the slope at an easy pace.

What in all Hades was the woman up to?

He assumed he was supposed to imagine that they'd been discussing some excursion for Filing's parishioners. He might have believed it but for her dogged attempts to keep the knowledge from him. While the correct interpretation presently eluded him, he couldn't believe it was anything heinous or illegal. She was the magistrate's daughter, devoted to good works, and Filing was patently honest and upright. So why didn't she want *him* to know what she was about?

If she'd been younger, he would have suspected some lark. Not only was she too old for that, but her behavior tended to the mature, the managing; she was no irresponsible hoyden.

The mystery about her had just deepened; the urge to take her somewhere private, back her against a wall, and keep her there until she told him all he wished to know, grew with every step.

He glanced at her and was rewarded with a full view of her face as she lifted it to the breeze, shaking back her tangling bonnet ribbons. He drank in her features, the resolution in her face, the challenge implicit in the defiant tilt of her chin. Facing forward again, he reminded himself that she was a gently reared virgin—no fit prey for him. She was not a woman with whom he could dally.

He would learn her secrets, then he'd have to let her go.

They stepped into the lane. A carriage was drawn up just ahead, the occupants—a large gentleman and an older lady—patently waiting to speak with them.

"Sir Cedric Fortemain and his mother, Lady Fortemain," Phyllida supplied sotto voce.

"And they are?"

"Cedric owns Ballyclose Manor—it lies over the hill past the forge."

They neared the carriage. Sir Cedric, in his late thirties and already tending portly with a florid face and thinning hair, rose and bowed to Phyllida, then leaned over the side to shake her hand.

Phyllida performed the introductions. Lucifer bowed to her ladyship and shook hands with Cedric.

"I hear you were the first to discover the body, Mr. Cynster," Lady Fortemain said.

"Shocking business!" Cedric declared.

They chatted inconsequentially about London and the weather; Lucifer noted Cedric's gaze rarely left Phyllida. His comments were a touch too patronizing, a touch too particular. When, contained and unresponsive, she stepped back, preparing to leave, Cedric caught her eye.

"I'm pleased to see, m'dear, that you're not rambling about the village on your own. There's no telling but that Welham's murderer is still about."

"Indeed!" Lady Fortemain smiled at Lucifer. "So comforting to see you're keeping an eye on dear Phyllida. We'd be devastated were anything to happen to our village treasure."

That was accompanied by a beam of sincere approbation, which brought a frown to the village treasure's eyes. "We must be getting on."

Lucifer bowed to Lady Fortemain, exchanged nods with Cedric, then strolled beside Phyllida as she crossed the lane to walk along the cottages' front fences. "Why," he murmured, "does Lady Fortemain think you a treasure?"

"Because she wants me to marry Cedric. And because I helped her to find a ring she misplaced at the Hunt Ball one year. And once I guessed where Pommeroy was hiding one of the times he ran away, but that was years ago."

"Who's Pommeroy?"

"Cedric's younger brother." After a moment, she added, "He's much worse than Cedric."

The rattle of carriage wheels came from behind them; they both slowed, stepping further to the side of the lane. The carriage swept past; a hatchet-faced, stony-eyed lady gazed haughtily down on them.

Lucifer raised his brows as the carriage rattled on. "Who was that harbinger of sunshine and delight?"

He looked across in time to see Phyllida's lips twitch. "Jocasta Smollet."

"Who is?"

"Sir Basil Smollet's sister."

"And Sir Basil is?"

"The gentleman approaching us. He owns Highgate, up the lane past the Rectory."

Lucifer studied the gentleman in question; he was neatly, even severely dressed, and of an age similar to Cedric. But where Cedric's expression had been choleric yet open, Basil's was guarded, as if he had a lot on his mind, but was above explaining himself to anyone.

He tipped his hat in greeting. Introduced, he shook hands with Lucifer.

"Dreadful business, this. Sets the whole village on its ears. No rest for any of us until the villain's caught. Pray accept my condolences on the death of your friend."

Lucifer thanked him. With polite nods to them both, Basil continued on his way.

"Punctilious," Lucifer murmured.

"Indeed." Phyllida stepped out again, looked ahead, and slowed. "Oh. Dear."

The words were uttered through her teeth; she might as well have cursed. Lucifer considered the cause of her consternation. Red-haired, in his late twenties, the gentleman strode toward them with a purposeful air. Only just taller than Phyllida, he was plainly dressed in corduroy breeches and riding boots, topped by a loose, flapping coat.

Phyllida's chin rose; she moved forward decisively. "Good day, Mr. Grisby." She inclined her head, her intention plainly to continue on her way.

Grisby planted himself directly in front of her. Phyllida halted and smoothly turned to Lucifer. "Mr. Cynster, allow me to present Mr. Grisby."

Lucifer nodded coolly. Grisby hesitated, then curtly responded. He returned his gaze to Phyllida. "Miss Tallent, please allow me to escort you home." The glance he shot Lucifer brimmed with poorly concealed dislike. "I'm surprised Sir Jasper hasn't forbidden you to roam, what with this knife-wielding murderer on the loose."

"My father—"

"One never knows," Grisby sententiously continued, "from what direction danger may come." Pugnaciously, he reached for her arm.

Phyllida reached for Lucifer's.

Bending his arm, covering her hand with his, Lucifer drew her closer. He caught Grisby's gaze, all humor flown. "I assure you, Grisby, that Miss Tallent is in no danger from knife-wielding felons, or any others, while in my care." He'd only been waiting for some sign from Phyllida before stepping in; if he hadn't been feeling his way, Grisby would already be flailing in the duck pond. "We're on our way back to the Grange. You may rest assured I will see Miss Tallent safe into Sir Jasper's keeping."

Grisby flushed.

Lucifer inclined his head. "If you'll excuse us?"

He gave Grisby no choice, solicitously steering Phyllida, censoriously haughty, down the lane. He kept her close, her skirts brushing his boots. Under his hand, her fingers fluttered. They strolled on; eventually her fingers relaxed under his.

"Thank you."

"It was entirely my pleasure. Aside from being an insensitive clod, who, exactly, is Grisby?"

"He owns Dottswood Farm. It's up past the Rectory, beyond Highgate."

"So he's a prosperous gentleman farmer?"

"Among other things."

Her disgusted tone gave him his clue. "Am I to understand Mr. Grisby is another aspirant to your fair hand?"

"They all are—Cedric, Basil, and Grisby."

Her tone wasn't improving; Lucifer raised his brows. "You have cut a swath through the local ranks."

She cast him a repressive glance, one his aunt, the Dowager Duchess of St. Ives, could not have bettered, then, head high, looked forward.

The common ended just ahead where the lane leading to the graveyard and the forge joined the village lane. Along the lesser lane lay a row of small houses, bigger than the cottages but not as large as the Manor or the Grange. Each house had its own garden with a fence and a gate.

A gentleman stepped through the nearest gate; in breeches, stockings, and high-heeled shoes, he minced down the lane toward them. In a bottle-green coat with a bright yellow-and-black kerchief tied in a floppy bow and sporting a periwig, the gentleman was unquestionably the most colorful figure Lucifer had seen for many a long year.

He glanced at Phyllida; she was deep in thought, her gaze fixed ahead; she'd yet to see the gentleman.

"I hesitate to ask, but is the gentleman to our right another of your suitors?"

She looked. "No, thank God. Unfortunately, that's the best I can say for him. His name is Silas Coombe."

"Does he always dress like that?"

"I've heard that in earlier years, he dressed as a macaroni. These days, he contents himself with adopting all the extremes of fashion and wearing them all at once."

"A gentleman of independent means?"

"He lives off inherited investments. His main interest in life is posturing. That, and reading. Until Horatio arrived, Silas had the most extensive library in the area."

"So he and Horatio were friends?"

"No. Quite the opposite." She paused as the gentleman neared; he crossed the corner of the common, sparing them not one glance. They continued to stroll; as they left the village behind, Phyllida mused, "In fact, Silas is possibly the only one in the locality who sincerely hated Horatio."

"*Hated* Horatio?" Lucifer shot her a glance. "Horatio wasn't an easy person to hate."

"Nevertheless. You see, for years, Silas had touted himself as a renowned antiquarian bibliophile. I think it was his ambition, and here in the country there was no one to challenge his claim. Not that it meant anything to anyone else, but it meant a lot to Silas. Then Horatio arrived and exploded his myth. Horatio's library eclipsed Silas's completely and Silas did not know books as Horatio did. Even to us, untutored though we are, the difference was obvious. Horatio was genuine; Silas, a poor imitation."

The Grange drive appeared before them; as they turned through the gateposts, Phyllida drew her hand from his sleeve and turned to face him. "You don't think ...?"

He met her gaze. "I don't know what to think. At the moment, I'm merely gathering information."

"Silas is effeminate. I wouldn't think him very strong."

"Weaklings can kill quite effectively—rage can lend strength to the most ineffectual."

"I suppose ..." She frowned. "But I still can't see Silas stabbing anyone."

He was silent for a moment, then asked, "So who do you think killed Horatio?"

The question hung between them; she lifted her head and looked him in the eye. "I don't know who killed Horatio."

She enunciated each word clearly. Their gazes held; it was she who turned away. Head high, she continued down the drive. After a moment, he fell in beside her, his stride longer and slower than hers. "Tell me, how many more are there in the locality—people like the Fortemains who would have known Horatio socially?"

"Not that many. You've met about half." They continued strolling down the winding drive, hemmed in by trees on all sides. Phyllida drew in a breath. "Do you seriously think someone from the village killed Horatio?"

She glanced up; Lucifer caught her eye. "Horatio was killed by someone he knew well—someone he let get close to him, well within arm's reach." When she frowned, he added, "There was no sign of any struggle."

Her frown cleared as she remembered; refocusing, she saw the intensity in his gaze and looked away. "Perhaps it was someone he knew from outside— another collector."

"If so, we'll find out. I'll be making inquiries in all the surrounding towns."

They walked on in silence. She felt his gaze on her face. They'd gone another fifty yards before he asked, "Indelicate question though it is, why, with so many suitors, aren't you married?"

She glanced up but could see nothing in his eyes beyond simple interest. The question was indeed impertinent, yet she felt no compunction in answering; she knew the answer so well. "Because every man who has ever asked for my hand has wanted to marry me to suit his own ends—because having me as his wife would improve his lot. For Cedric and Basil, marrying me would be sensible—I'm suitable, I know the locals, and I could manage their households with my eyes shut. For Grisby, I can add that marrying me would be a step upward socially—he's ambitious in that sphere."

She looked up and discovered Lucifer studying her. After a moment, he asked, "Don't you have any wishes, any requirements of marriage—anything they might provide you?"

She shook her head. "All they can offer is a household and a position—I already have both. Why marry and take a husband when I'd gain nothing I desire in the process?"

His lips twitched, then curved into a smile. "How very clearheaded of you."

The dangerous purr had returned to his voice; there was a look in his eyes she didn't understand. Facing forward, she kept strolling.

The house lay just ahead, screened by the last bend, when he stopped her with a hand on her arm. She faced him, her question in her eyes. He looked down at her, his gaze disturbingly direct. "What actually happened?"

Phyllida held his gaze and thought about telling him. But it was a case of all or nothing—she'd seen enough of him to know she would have to tell him all once she admitted that she was there. He wouldn't let her keep anything back. And for once in her life, she doubted her ability to stand against a man.

This man was something else—some different species she hadn't before encountered. She was old enough, wise enough, to recognize the difference and acknowledge in her mind that she'd be unwise to challenge him.

Of course, not telling him was a blatant challenge, but that simply had to be. She would not break her word. She might prevaricate for a good cause, but her oath was absolute, and a vow given to a friend was sacred.

"I can't tell you. Not yet." She turned away. He stopped her, long fingers closing around her elbow. Her temper flared; she looked up at him. "I've kept my part of the bargain."

He blinked. "What bargain?"

"You didn't tell Papa you believed that I was there, in Horatio's drawing room, and so I took you around the village, introduced you to Horatio's acquaintances, and answered your questions about them."

He frowned, the gesture more evident in his eyes than on his face. His hold on her arm anchored her before him; she didn't bother trying to wriggle free. He studied her eyes and she let him; emotionally, she had nothing to hide.

"Is that why you thought I invited myself along?"

"That, and so you could try to trip me up. Why else?"

He released her, but his gaze held hers. "Couldn't I have wanted to spend time in your company?"

She stared at him. The suggestion was so unexpected, she couldn't at first imagine it. Then she did, and the truth washed over her—she would have liked it if he had. If he'd simply wanted to spend a summer afternoon strolling with her around the village, idly commenting, relaxed in her company. Her chest tightened; haughtily, she turned away. "You didn't. That wasn't why you came walking with me today."

Lucifer heard the calm statement but left it unchallenged. He watched her walk away, and let the impulse to correct her fade. She was such a contrary female—handling her was difficult, not to say dangerous; she was so different from the women he knew. God knew, he'd never before been so attracted to a virgin.

A stubborn, willful, innocent, headstrong, intelligent, far-too-untouched-for-her-own-good virgin.

It made everything so much more complicated.

CHAPTER
Four

H e caught Phyllida up as she negotiated the last bend in the drive. The side lawn of the Grange opened before them; a knot of people were gathered around tables and chairs, enjoying the late afternoon. They both halted, but they'd been seen; Lady Huddlesford beckoned imperiously.

"Who are they?"

"Some of the half you've yet to meet." Phyllida searched the group; then she saw Mary Anne and felt giddy with relief. "Come. I'll introduce you."

They crossed the lawn. Lady Huddlesford, presiding over the gathering from a chair at a wrought-iron table, beamed delightedly. "Mr. Cynster! Excellent! I was just telling Mrs. Farthingale ..."

Phyllida left Lucifer to fend for himself, something he was patently well able to do; he smiled, effortlessly charming, and the ladies all preened. Directing a general smile on those present, she strolled to Mary Anne's side.

Mary Anne stared at Lucifer. "He's ..." She gestured.

"From London." Phyllida slipped her arm through Mary Anne's. "We need to talk."

Mary Anne turned huge blue eyes her way. "Did you find them?" she whispered as they turned from the group.

Mary Anne's fingers clamped like talons around her wrist; something close to panic filled her eyes. Phyllida inwardly frowned and drew her on. "The rose garden's more private. Pretend we're simply strolling."

Luckily, the entire gathering—Mary Anne's mother, Mrs. Farthingale, Lady Fortemain, Mrs. Weatherspoon, and a gaggle of other ladies, with Percy and Frederick for leavening—was hanging on Lucifer's every word. Phyllida glanced back as she and Mary Anne entered the yew walk that led to the rose garden. Lucifer's attention appeared fully engaged.

Surrounded by thick stone walls, the rose garden was a secluded paradise of lush growth, vibrant splashes of color, and rich, exotic scents. The instant they entered its privacy, Mary Anne's public demeanor crumbled. She swung to face Phyllida, gripping her hands tightly. "Say you found them! *Please* say you did!"

"I looked, but ..." Phyllida frowned. "Come—let's sit down. We need to discuss this."

"There's nothing to *discuss!*" Mary Anne wailed. "If I don't get those letters back, my life will be *ruined!*"

Phyllida towed her to a seat set against the wall. "I didn't say we won't get them back—I promised we would. But there's been a complication."

"Complication?"

"A large one." Over six feet tall and difficult to manage. Phyllida sat on the seat and pulled Mary Anne down beside her. "Now, first, are you absolutely sure Horatio was the one your father sold the writing desk to?"

"Yes. I saw Horatio take it away last Monday."

"And you definitely, positively, hid your letters in the secret drawer in the desk? You haven't by accident left them somewhere else?"

"They were too *dangerous* to leave anywhere else!"

"And it is your grandmother's traveling writing desk that we're talking about, with the rose leather on the top?"

Mary Anne nodded. "You know it."

"Just checking." Phyllida considered Mary Anne, considered how much to tell her. "I went to Horatio's on Sunday morning to search for the desk."

"And?" Mary Anne waited; then understanding dawned. Horror replaced her panic. Her mouth opened, then closed, then she squeaked, "You witnessed the murder?"

"No, not exactly."

"Not exactly? What does that mean? You saw something?"

Phyllida grimaced. "Let me tell it from the beginning." She related how she'd invented a sick headache, then dressed in boots and breeches—Jonas's castoffs that she often wore when engaged in nonpublic activities that might necessitate running. "Sunday morning was the perfect time because there shouldn't have been anyone at home."

"But Horatio was sick."

"Yes, but I didn't know that. I slipped through the wood and searched that outbuilding he used as his warehouse, then I went in through the kitchen and searched the storerooms. They were filled with furniture as well. I didn't see your grandmother's desk anywhere, so I assumed it was somewhere in the main rooms. I went back through the kitchen, into the hall—"

"And you saw the murderer."

"No. I found Horatio just after he'd been killed."

"After the murderer had hit Mr. Cynster and left him for dead."

Phyllida gritted her teeth. "No. I got there before Mr. Cynster."

"You saw the murderer hit Mr. Cynster?"

"No!" She glared at Mary Anne. "Just listen."

In the baldest terms, she recounted what had happened. By the time she finished, Mary Anne had traveled from horror-struck to aghast. "*You* hit Mr. Cynster?"

"I didn't mean to! The halberd tipped and fell—I stopped it from killing him."

Mary Anne's face cleared. "Well, he's obviously recovered. He must have a thick skull."

"Perhaps. But that's not the complication." Phyllida caught Mary Anne's eye. "He knows I was there."

"I thought he was knocked unconscious."

"Not entirely—not at first."

"He saw you?"

Phyllida described what had happened.

Mary Anne bent a look of utter disbelief upon her. "He couldn't possibly tell from a touch. He's bamming you."

"That's what I thought at first. But he *knows*, Mary Anne—he knows and he wants to know what happened."

"Well, why not just tell him that yes, you were there, and tell him what happened and that you had to leave?"

Phyllida fixed her with a direct look. "I haven't admitted that I was there, because as soon as I do he's going to want to know *why*."

Mary Anne blanched. "You can't tell him that!"

"He's determined to find out what happened—he's investigating Horatio's murder. From his point of view, he needs to know everything that happened that morning."

"But he doesn't—he doesn't need to know about my letters." Mary Anne's lower lip protruded. "And he can't make you tell him."

"He can."

"Nonsense." Mary Ann tossed her head. "You're always the one in charge—you're Sir Jasper's daughter. You can just look at him haughtily and refuse to say anything. How can he force you to tell?"

"I can't explain it, but he will." She couldn't describe the sensation of being mentally stalked, trapped, and held, the pressure of knowing he was waiting, watching ... patient now, but how long would that last? On top of that, she felt she *should* tell him, that he deserved to know. "He hasn't yet threatened to tell Papa that he knows I was there, but he could—he knows he could. It's like Damocles' sword hanging over my head."

"That's just melodramatic. He's pressuring you. He doesn't have any evidence you were there—why would Sir Jasper believe him?"

"How often do I succumb to sick headaches?"

Mary Anne pouted; her expression turned obstinate. "You can't tell him about my letters—you *swore* you'd tell no one."

"But this is *murder*. Horatio was killed. Mr. Cynster needs to know what happened and what I saw." She hadn't mentioned the brown hat; that would only distract Mary Anne, who was distracted enough as it was. "He needs to know about your letters so he can be sure they aren't anything to do with why Horatio was killed."

Mary Anne stared at her. "*No!* If you tell him about the letters, he'll think Robert killed Horatio."

"Don't be silly. Robert wasn't anywhere near ..." Phyllida stared at Mary Anne. "Don't tell me Robert was here on Sunday morning."

"I walked home after church—it was a lovely sunny day." Mary Anne slid her eyes from Phyllida's. "We met in the Ballyclose wood."

"It's impossible that Robert killed Horatio and then made it there to meet you, so he can't be the murderer."

"But we can't tell anyone we met in the wood!"

Phyllida swallowed a groan. She wasn't getting anywhere; she tried another tack. "What is *in* these letters?" She hadn't asked before—before, it had only mattered that Mary Anne was hysterical and getting the letters back—an easy enough task, it had seemed—would calm her down. She'd given her oath not to reveal the existence of the letters to anyone without a second thought. But now Horatio's murder had turned her simple plan to retrieve Mary Anne's letters into a nightmare—and she was still bound by that oath.

Mary Anne picked at her skirt. "I told you—they're letters I sent Robert that he gave back, and some he sent to me."

Robert Collins was Mary Anne's intended, not her betrothed. Her parents had stood firm against the match since Mary Anne and Robert first met at the Exeter Assembly when Mary Anne was seventeen. Robert was an articled clerk in a solicitor's office in Exeter. His fortune was nonexistent, but once he took his final exams next year, he would be able to practice and thus support a wife. Through the years, Mary Anne's devotion to Robert and his to her had never wavered. Her parents had hoped the attachment would wane. However, they'd known better than to feed their daughter's stubbornness; assuming that with Robert in Exeter, physical meetings would be rare, they'd allowed the usual exchange of correspondence.

The existence of the letters would therefore surprise no one; it was the content that constituted the threat. Phyllida wasn't, however, convinced that the threat was all that serious—not compared with murder. "I can't see why telling Mr. Cynster that your letters were the reason I was in Horatio's house, searching for them because they'd been accidentally put in the writing desk and then forgotten, is going to cause a scandal."

"Because if you tell him that, he'll want to know why you—or, more to the point, I—didn't simply call and ask Horatio for them."

Phyllida grimaced. She'd asked precisely that question when Mary Anne, distraught and barely coherent, had come to her for help. The answer had been that Horatio might look at the letters before he handed them over—and then he might hand them to Mary Anne's parents instead.

"And," Mary Anne continued, her tone increasingly obstinate, "if Mr. Cynster is half as clever as you think him, he'll guess why I want them back so desperately. He's investigating—if he finds them, he'll read them."

"Even if he does, he wouldn't hand them to your parents." Phyllida glimpsed a way out. "Wait—what if I make him *promise* that if I tell him all and he finds the letters, he'll hand them to me without reading them?"

Mary Anne frowned. "Do you trust him?"

Phyllida returned her gaze steadily. She trusted Lucifer to find Horatio's killer if that were humanly possible. She would trust him with any number of things. But could she trust him with Mary Anne's secret? She still didn't know what was in those damned letters. "These letters—in them you described what happened at your meetings? How you felt—that sort of thing?"

Tight-lipped, Mary Anne nodded; she was clearly not going to say more.

A few kisses, a cuddle or two—how scandalous could that be? "I'm certain that even if Mr. Cynster read the letters, they wouldn't shock him. And he's a stranger. He'll leave after Horatio's murderer's found and we'll never see him again. There's no reason he'll feel any great need to hand even the most scandalous letters to your parents."

Mary Anne pondered. "If you tell him about the letters, you wouldn't tell him they were scandalous?"

"Of course not! I'll tell him they're private letters you don't want anyone else reading." Phyllida waited, then said, "So—can I tell him?"

Mary Anne shifted. "I ... I want to talk to Robert." She lifted eyes clouded with worry to Phyllida's face. "I haven't told him the letters are missing. I want to know what he thinks."

Oh, how she wished she could infuse a little of her own steel into Mary Anne's backbone. But Mary Anne was, beneath her social veneer, nearly frantic with worry. Phyllida sighed. "All right. Talk to Robert. But *please* talk to him soon." She swallowed the words *I don't know how long I can hold Mr. Cynster at bay.*

She looked up—and discovered the wolf a lot closer than she'd thought; her heart leaped to her throat, then somersaulted back into place.

He stood fifteen feet away, framed by the arch leading into the garden. White roses nodded above his dark head, the delicate blooms emphasizing his strength and the latent power in his stance. Hands in his trouser pockets, his gaze was fixed on them. Phyllida was relieved to see the tails of his coat settle—he'd only just arrived.

Summoning a serene smile, she rose and strolled toward him. "We've been catching up. Have they let you escape?"

His dark blue eyes watched her approach. He waited until she halted before him to say, "I escaped a while ago to check on my horses."

His gaze went beyond her; Phyllida turned as Mary Anne nervously joined them. "Allow me to present my close friend, Miss Farthingale."

He bowed gracefully.

Mary Anne bobbed a curtsy. "I should return to my mother—she'll be wanting to leave."

He stepped aside and Mary Anne slipped past him. She glanced at Phyllida. "I'll let you know as soon as I can."

With that, she hurried away. Phyllida suppressed a grimace. From under her lashes she glanced at her nemesis. Drawing his gaze from Mary Anne, he fixed it on her. He studied her face; she kept her expression calm and collected. Lifting her lids, she gave him back stare for stare.

After an instant of hesitation; he raised one dark brow. "My horses? No one here seems to know where they are."

"They're in the Manor's stables. There wasn't enough space here, while the stables there were empty. I asked John Ostler from the Red Bells to look after them. He's very good with horses."

He considered her, then nodded. "Thank you for arranging it. Now"—he looked toward the lawn—"I'd better head back to the Manor."

There was a slight frown in his eyes; Phyllida didn't think it was due to worry about his horses. He took a step—she put a hand on his arm. He glanced at her, brows rising. She searched his eyes. "Are you in pain?"

After a moment, he inclined his head. "A little."

"I don't suppose you'd consider waiting until tomorrow to see your horses?"

"No." His lips curved just a little at the ends. "You know how gentlemen are about their horses."

She pressed her lips tight and considered. "There's a shortcut through the wood. It's much faster than going via the village."

His interest was immediate; his speculation that that was the route she'd used to go from the Grange to the Manor on Sunday morning gleamed in his eyes. "Where does this shortcut start?"

Phyllida hesitated, but only for a moment. If his head was aching, she couldn't let him walk through the wood alone. She turned away from the lawn. "I'll show you."

He followed her through the wood, claiming her hand often, helping her over roots and up and down rocky dips. The path was clear, but not designed for strolling; long before the Manor's roof came into sight, Phyllida was wishing she was in her boots and breeches. Then she wouldn't have needed to let him take her hand—wouldn't have been so conscious of his strength prowling at her heels, all but surrounding her every time he steadied her.

She wouldn't have been so conscious that he could physically manage her without any difficulty at all.

Despite the fact she was neither tall nor large, she'd never felt at a physical disadvantage with any other man.

As they reached the trees bordering the back of the Manor and stepped into the mild sunshine, she reminded herself that this man was different—he was like no other she had met before, altogether a very different proposition.

She'd do well to remember that.

"Your horses will be in there." She indicated the stone stables that stood to one side. "I'll let the Hemmingses and Bristleford know you're here." Evening was approaching. "John will probably look in shortly."

She headed on through the kitchen garden, aware that Lucifer's dark gaze lingered on her before he turned to the stables.

The Hemmingses were in the kitchen, Mrs. Hemmings cooking, Hemmings by the fire. Hemmings immediately went out to the stables. Phyllida discussed the preparations for Horatio's wake, then excused herself and went into the house, ostensibly to take a last look at Horatio.

She did. Then she looked around the drawing room and Horatio's library across the hall. Mary Anne's grandmother's traveling writing desk had to be somewhere. It was small enough and ornate enough to be placed on a side table as an ornament, especially in a house full of antiques. Phyllida searched, but didn't find it. Going back down the hall, she checked in the dining room, then in the back parlor and its adjoining garden room. In vain.

Returning to the hall, she halted at the foot of the stairs and looked up. The thud of a drawer being shut reached her ears. Covey, most likely, tidying his late master's effects. Phyllida grimaced. The desk had to be upstairs. There were bedrooms on the first level with attics above. Covey and the Hemmingses had rooms in the attics, but that would account for only part of the space. She would have to find time, and some excuse, to search upstairs.

Retreating through the kitchen, she bade Mrs. Hemmings an absentminded farewell and strolled out into the kitchen garden, pondering the how and when. No answers leaped to mind.

Standing before the stables, Lucifer watched her amble along the path. He'd glimpsed her in one of the back rooms. What had she been doing there? Yet another question to which she'd be giving him an answer. Soon.

His blacks were eating their heads off; John Ostler had just left. Hemmings nodded and headed back to the house. Phyllida looked up as Hemmings passed her, smiled a vague greeting, then saw Lucifer waiting. She moved forward more purposefully and joined him. "Ready?"

He fell into step beside her. "You were right—John Ostler knows his horses."

She smiled; her gaze lingered on his eyes, then slid over his face. "How's your head?"

"Better."

She looked ahead. "The fresh air should help."

They walked into the wood and cool silence enveloped them. The westering sun threw slanting beams through the trees, golden shafts to light their way. The bustle of day faded as evening approached; birds settled on boughs, into nests; soft cooing filled the air.

Nearing the Grange, they reached a spot where the path dipped sharply. Phyllida halted, assessing it. Lucifer stepped past and over the gap; turning, he held out a hand. She took it and leaped—her narrow skirt restricted her stride; her sole slipped in the leaf mold lining the dip's edge.

He caught her around the waist and swung her clear. She landed against his chest.

The unexpected contact shocked them both. He heard her indrawn breath, felt the tensing of her spine. Felt his own inevitable reaction. She looked up, lustrous brown eyes wide ... the procession of emotions through their depths held him spellbound.

Wonder—fleeting, innocent thoughts of what it might be like ...

Her fingers, spread across his upper chest, fluttered, then stilled.

Her gaze dropped to his lips; his dropped to hers.

Her lips parted, just a little.

He bent his head and covered them.

They were petal-soft, and sweet—a delicate, fresh sweetness that hinted, not of innocence, but of innocent pleasures.

He hadn't intended this. He knew he should stop, draw back, let her escape even if she didn't know enough to run. He didn't. Couldn't. Couldn't bear to release her without tasting her, without giving his clamoring senses at least that much reward.

No easy task, to take that much in a first kiss without frightening her. The implicit challenge tantalized.

He kept the caress gentle, undemanding, waiting with the patience of one who knew for her curiosity to overcome her scruples. It didn't take long—she was inherently confident, with little reason to doubt her ability to cope, even if, in this arena, she was out of her league. Just how out of her league was not a point she appreciated. Not yet.

When her lips firmed, tentatively molding, gently returning his kiss, the pirate within him gloated. He swooped, but was careful to disguise his attack. Skillfully fanning her interest, teasing, tantalizing, he set himself to captivate with simple kisses laced with potent temptation.

The promise of something new, illicit, sensual—a taste she'd not tried before.

She sank into his arms. He closed them around her, aware to his bones of her warmth, of the enticement of her soft flesh. He breathed deep and her scent wreathed through him—his arms locked. He shackled the sudden urge to seize. Instead, he traced her lower lip with his tongue, and waited.

She hesitated for a heartbeat, then parted her lips. He traced their contours, encouraging her further, until, almost giddy with need, with triumph, he could enter and taste her as he wished.

One taste was what he'd promised himself; he savored the moment, then, reining in his rakish impulses, drew back.

Their lips parted, by half an inch. Their breaths mingled; she didn't draw back. Her hands were fisted on his lapels. Her lids were heavy, veiling her eyes. As he watched, they lifted and she met his gaze.

Her eyes were darkened, sultry, yet filled with innocent surprise, and with a womanly wondering ...

He kissed her again, not, this time, for his pleasure but for hers. To show her just a little more of what could be, a little more of the wonder.

Phyllida tightened her hold on his lapels and gave herself up to the kiss, to the slow surge of his tongue, the intimate caressing and exploring. Warmth seeped through her; a sharp lick of sensation whipped to her toes and slowly curled them.

His head angled over hers and she clung; he deepened the kiss and she willingly followed. For years, she'd dreamed of being kissed like this, kissed as a woman, a woman desired. It was frightening and enticing. She couldn't breathe, she couldn't think. She certainly wasn't in control. Instead of scaring her, that thrilled her. Foolish, certainly, yet she felt no fear. Only a wanton eagerness.

Lips and mouths melded; tongues tangled, sliding, caressing ... for one magical instant, the world fell away.

He tasted of heat and wildness, of something primeval, something barely tamed. Male—hard where she was soft, beast to her beauty. She sensed the leashed power simmering beneath his lips, held back behind his experienced facade.

Then he started to draw back, to retreat and end the kiss.

It was a surprise to realize she'd stretched up on her toes, that she'd pressed herself against him. Her knees had weakened, her skin felt too hot, her wits were whirling. His chest was a solid wall supporting her; she spread her fingers and pressed, enthralled by the resilient hardness beneath the crisp layers. His arms had locked, iron bands caging her; she didn't care.

She wanted to hold him, to prolong the precious moment—she knew she couldn't. She didn't know how.

On the instant their lips would have parted, he paused. Then he returned, surging deep, a swift, hard invasion that mentally rocked her—the hidden power she'd sensed was no lie.

Then he lifted his head and straightened, and she was standing on her feet, his hands rising to close about hers, clenched again on his lapels. She blinked and released her grip, then drew her hands from under his.

Dazed, she met his eyes, and wasn't at all certain what she saw. Something dark and dangerous prowled behind the blue. "Why did you kiss me?"

That was suddenly very important to know.

He didn't smile, didn't try to turn the awkward question aside with some glib and charming quip. His eyes held hers; they'd widened slightly at her question—she could almost believe he was as dazed as she.

"Because I wanted to." His voice was gravelly; he blinked, drew breath, and added, "And to thank you for your help—yesterday and today." He met her gaze. "Regardless of all else, I sincerely appreciate all that you've done."

Lucifer tried to find a charming smile and couldn't, so he clung to impassivity and gestured, urging her ahead of him along the path.

With one last, wondering glance, she acquiesced. He followed, breathing deeply, thanking his stars that she'd accepted his answer. Walking before him, she couldn't see the effort it took for him to reshackle his demons. He hoped she never guessed how close she'd come to meeting them.

At least he'd answered her truthfully. About that first kiss. There was no need for her to know his reasons behind the second, and even less his reasons for the third. He couldn't remember the last time he'd warned a woman away, but for her own safety, she should keep her distance.

Frowning, he strolled at her heels, through the gathering gloom. He'd taken what he'd wanted, that one simple taste, but what had it cost him?

He wasn't sure he wanted to know.

They'd reached the Grange lawns when he closed his fingers around her elbow and drew her to a halt. She faced him, brows rising, her expression all but blank. The shadows were too dense for him to read her eyes. "I kissed you because I didn't want you seeing me as some ogre, bent on browbeating the truth out of you." Releasing her, he held her gaze. "I'm not the enemy."

She studied his face, then her lips lifted as she turned away. She stepped out, heading for the house. Her cool words drifted back to him. "I didn't think you were."

CHAPTER

Five

Phyllida knew why he'd kissed her. He wasn't an ogre, he wasn't her enemy, but he was a masterful seducer. She was a novice in that sphere, yet she realized he'd kissed her to rattle her, to weaken her resolve so she'd tell him all she knew. She'd asked him why, but she'd known the answer the instant she'd voiced the question.

Seated in the second pew, she glanced across the aisle of the church to where Lucifer sat. His expression was impassive as he listened to Cedric read the lesson. Covey hunched beside him; farther along, Mrs. Hemmings wept into her handkerchief. Hemmings patted her arm awkwardly. White-faced, Bristleford stared straight ahead. While the rest of those present might have lost a friend and a neighbor, Covey, the Hemmingses, and Bristleford had lost a beloved master and their livelihoods had been rendered uncertain.

Phyllida returned her gaze to Lucifer's face—it wasn't expressive, yet she encountered no difficulty in following his thoughts. They were presently centered on the coffin resting before the altar, jeweled by shafts of light playing through the stained-glass windows. His thoughts, however, were not on Horatio but on who had put him in the box.

She faced forward once more. Cedric continued to drone. She let her mind slide back to its most urgent consideration—how to deal with Lucifer.

That name was the one that sprang to mind; it suited him so well. She'd known what type of man he was the instant she'd set eyes on him, although she hadn't fully appreciated the whole until she'd encountered him fully dressed and fully conscious. Then, what he was had been obvious.

The reason matrons preened and women lost their wits when he smiled was blatantly apparent—he didn't hide his light under any bushel. Even more to the point, his powerful aura of masculine energy, raw edges smoothed by graceful elegance, hadn't come about by accident—it was even more than cultivated—it was part of a practiced art.

An art he intended practicing on her.

Luckily, she knew it. She was confident and in control of her world, bar him. And his kisses hadn't rattled her in the least. She hadn't expected them, but, on consideration, she hadn't been surprised. He'd thought about kissing her when he'd held her trapped on his bed the night before. The woods had simply been a more amenable venue.

Would he kiss her again? The question hovered in her brain. She'd enjoyed the experience; she hadn't felt the least bit threatened, or coerced, or even in danger. But wishing for more might be tempting fate.

Besides ... She glanced sideways to where a small man in severe black sat, pinched features blank. Mr. Crabbs was Horatio's solicitor, come from Exeter to read the will. And in Mr. Crabbs's train had come his clerk, Robert Collins.

With luck, this evening, after speaking with Robert, Mary Anne would release her from her oath. Then she could explain to Lucifer what had happened in Horatio's drawing room and they could join forces to track down Horatio's murderer.

That was her aim and she wasn't about to be deterred, even if succeeding meant dealing with the devil. He was definitely the most fascinating devil she'd ever met, and deep down, she was convinced he'd never hurt her.

Impatient, she waited for Cedric to have done.

When the service was over, Lucifer stepped forward with Cedric, Sir Jasper, Thompson, Basil Smollet, and Mr. Farthingale; they hefted the coffin and slowly carried it out to the graveyard. During the short burial ceremony, Lucifer noted the faces of the men he'd not yet met as they stood about the graveside. Was the murderer present? The ladies did not join them, but gathered in a dark group just beyond the side porch of the church.

When earth rained down on the coffin, Lucifer joined Sir Jasper and Mr. Farthingale. As they walked back to the church, he learned enough to place Mr. Farthingale as a minor Sir Jasper—backbone of the county, absorbed with his land and family, unlikely to have any connection with Horatio's murder.

Together with the rest of the men, they joined the waiting ladies; family groups formed and started down the common. Sir Jasper led the way, Jonas beside him. Phyllida followed; Lucifer fell in beside her. She slanted him a glance; her eyes held no hint of censure or trepidation. If anything, they held a question: What next?

"If you'd be so kind as to introduce me to those I don't know ...?"

She inclined her head regally. "Of course."

She acted as if he'd never kissed her. Lucifer hid a frown.

Followed by, as far as he could tell, the entire congregation, they went through the Manor gate, crossed Horatio's garden, and filed into the house.

The wake was the perfect opportunity, not just to meet the locals, but to have them explain their relationship to Horatio. Most discussed their last meetings with him without prompting, and aired their views on his murder.

Phyllida hovered near, graciously steering people his way, in each case providing him with the right information to place the person in the context of village life and establish his or her connection with Horatio. If he'd thought she'd played any role in Horatio's murder, he'd have been suspicious. Instead, he stood by the side of the room and appreciated her social skills.

"Mr. Cynster, allow me to present Miss Hellebore. She lives in the cottage immediately next door."

Lucifer bowed over Miss Hellebore's hand. Old with a sweet, lined face, she stood no higher than his shoulder.

She clutched his hand. "I was in church when it happened—*so* unfortunate. I might have heard something otherwise. They'd just dropped me off before they found you—what a to-do *that* was! But I'm so glad, dear, that you were not the one." She smiled vaguely, her eyes dimming. "Horatio was a dear soul. Such a worry, this happening."

Her voice faded; Phyllida took her other hand and patted it reassuringly. "You needn't worry, Harriet. Mr. Cynster and Papa will find out who did it, and then all will be peaceful here again."

"I do hope so, dear."

"There's some asparagus on the table—would you like some?"

"Oh, yes. Which table?"

With a glance that said she'd be back, Phyllida steered the old lady away.

Lucifer watched them go. Despite the fact that Phyllida was unmarried and neither the oldest nor the most established lady in the room, it was to her the locals unhesitatingly turned—for reassurance, for order. Her character, her personality, cast her in the role—that calm, collected air of being perennially in control.

The desire to see her in an uncontrolled frenzy surfaced—again. He swiftly doused it and looked away.

"Mr. Cynster." Jocasta Smollet, as haughty as when she'd passed them in the lane the previous evening, approached on the arm of Sir Basil. She extended her hand.

Basil performed the introductions.

"I do hope," Jocasta said, "that you'll be remaining in Colyton for a few days yet. We'd be pleased to entertain you at Highgate—I'm sure there's little else hereabouts to interest a gentleman such as yourself."

If Jocasta's nose rose any higher, she'd tip backward.

"I'm unsure how long I'll be staying." Lucifer watched Phyllida returning through the crowd. She didn't see Jocasta until she was almost upon them. Her smile faded; she changed tack so she could slide past them.

Calmly, he reached out, caught her hand, and drew her to his side. Setting her hand on his sleeve, he looked at Jocasta. "Despite the unfortunate circumstances, I've enjoyed meeting those round about. People have been very welcoming." He glanced at Phyllida. "Miss Tallent has been particularly helpful."

"Indeed?" There was a wealth of meaning in the word. Jocasta drew herself up and stiffly inclined her head. "Dear Phyllida is so good to everyone. If you'll excuse us, I really must speak with Mrs. Farthingale."

She glided away. Basil, embarrassed, didn't follow. He chatted inconsequentially; Lucifer determined that he'd been in church when Horatio had been murdered.

When Basil moved on, Lucifer looked down at Phyllida. "Why does Miss Smollet so dislike you?"

She shook her head. "I really don't know."

Lucifer glanced across the room. "There are three gentlemen I've yet to meet."

The first proved to be Lucius Appleby. Phyllida introduced them, then left to chat with Lady Fortemain. Lucifer made no effort to disguise his purpose. Appleby answered directly, but was hardly forthcoming.

Collecting Phyllida, Lucifer guided her down the room. "Is Appleby always so reserved? So self-effacing?"

"Yes, but he's Cedric's secretary, after all."

His eye on their next target, Lucifer murmured, "What was Appleby before he became Cedric's secretary? Has he ever mentioned?"

"No. I assumed he always was a clerk or something similar. Why?"

"I'm sure he's been in the army. He's the right age—I just wondered. Now, who's this?"

A moment later, Phyllida said, "Allow me to present Pommeroy Fortemain, Sir Cedric's brother."

Lucifer held out his hand.

Pommeroy's eyes bulged; he edged back. "Ah ..." Wide-eyed, he looked at Phyllida. "I mean ... well ..."

Phyllida sighed exasperatedly. "Mr. Cynster did not murder Horatio, Pommeroy."

"He didn't?" Pommeroy glanced from one to the other.

"No! This is Horatio's wake, for heaven's sake! We wouldn't knowingly have invited the murderer."

"B-but ... he had the knife."

"Pommeroy"—Phyllida spoke very distinctly—"no one knows who the murderer is, but the one thing we *do* know is that it could *not* be Mr. Cynster."

"Oh."

After that, Pommeroy behaved reasonably, answering Lucifer's questions with, if anything, an overeagerness to please. He'd accompanied his mother to church on Sunday and, he assured them, knew nothing about anything.

"That last is unfortunately true." Obedient to the touch on her arm, Phyllida moved to the side of the room.

"So I'd gathered." Lucifer was looking ahead. "Our last potential suspect is scanning the bookshelves."

She'd guessed who it was before they stepped around the Farthingales and came face-to-face with Silas Coombe, fingering a gold-plated spine. He snatched his hand back as if the book had bitten him and stared at them, blank-faced.

"Good day. Mr. Coombe, is it not?" Lucifer smiled. "Miss Tallent mentioned you know something of books. Horatio's amassed quite a collection, don't you think?"

His glance along the shelves clearly invited Silas's opinion. It was a masterly stroke. Phyllida practiced self-effacement while Silas waxed lyrical, putty in the hands of a gentleman he didn't even realize was his interrogator.

"Well, I don't normally confess this, but you're a gentleman who knows a bit about life." Silas lowered his voice.

"Not much of a churchgoer, you understand. Got out of the habit in my youth—can't see the point in rubbing shoulders with all the starched-up matrons, not at my age. I've better things to do with my time."

Silas's gaze ranged the nearby shelves. "I don't suppose you have any idea who will inherit these, do you?"

Lucifer shook his head. "No doubt we'll learn soon enough."

"Ah, yes—the solicitor fellow's here, isn't he?" Silas scanned the room, then frowned. "He's staring at you."

Lucifer looked; Phyllida did, too. It was instantly apparent that Mr. Crabbs was hovering, hoping for a word.

"If you'll excuse us," Lucifer murmured, "I'll see what he wants."

The instant they stepped away, Crabbs headed toward them. Lucifer stopped by the bookshelves and waited. Crabbs smiled perfunctorily as he joined them.

"Mr. Cynster, I just wanted to be sure that it would be convenient to read the will immediately the guests leave."

"Convenient?" Lucifer frowned. "For whom?"

"Why, for *you*." Mr Crabbs searched Lucifer's face. "Well, dear me—I assumed you knew."

"Knew what?"

"That, barring some minor bequests, you are the sole principal beneficiary of Mr. Welham's will."

Crabbs's statement had been uttered within the hearing of Lady Huddlesford, Percy Tallent, and Sir Cedric and Lady Fortemain. Within seconds, all of Colyton had heard the news. The wake terminated as if a gong had sounded. People quickly took their leave, their alacrity plainly due to a wish to have the unexpected details of the will disclosed as soon as possible.

Despite the fact that the reading had been attended by very few, for the last hour the attention of Colyton had been focused on Horatio's library.

Pushing back from the desk, Lucifer laid the will down.

He'd just finished going through it a second time with Crabbs, making sure he understood the details. For someone familiar with the complex assignment of a ducal purse, Horatio's stipulations were straightforward. Leaning back in the leather chair, Lucifer scanned the room.

At one corner of the desk, Crabbs sat checking documents. At the sideboard, his assistant, Robert Collins, was carefully packing a satchel. The Hemmingses', Covey, and Bristleford had slipped out after the reading, all intensely relieved, all clearly pleased with the outcome.

For himself, Lucifer was … faintly stunned.

"Ah-hem."

He looked at Crabbs, then raised a brow.

"I was wondering if you planned to sell the Manor. I could get matters started if you wish."

Lucifer stared at Crabbs without seeing him. Then he shook his head. "I don't intend to sell."

The statement surprised him more than Crabbs, but when impulse struck this strongly, it rarely served to fight it. "Tell me." He refocused on Crabbs. "Were there any others who might have expected to inherit?"

Crabbs shook his head. "There was no family—not even any legal connections. The estate was Mr. Welham's outright, his to leave as he pleased."

"Do you know who Horatio's heir was, who was in line for the estate, before this present will was drawn up?"

"As far as I'm aware, there was no previous will. I drew this one up three years ago, when Mr. Welham came into these parts and engaged me to act for him. He gave me to understand he had not made a will before."

Later, with the shadows lengthening, Lucifer strode back to the Grange through the wood. Hands in his pockets, gaze fixed on the ground, he stepped over roots and ditches blindly, his mind engrossed with other things.

Crabbs had taken his leave, retreating to the Red Bells. Given he was not presently residing under the Manor's roof, Lucifer had not invited him to stay there. He hadn't wanted to impose the duty of entertaining the solicitor on Bristleford, the Hemmingses and Covey, not tonight.

He'd instructed Crabbs to contact Heathcote Montague, man of business to the Cynsters. With Montague involved, the formal transfer of the estate would be accomplished quickly and efficiently. Lucifer made a mental note to write to Montague.

And Gabriel. And Devil. And his parents.

Lucifer sighed. The first tugs of the reins of responsibility. He'd avoided them most of his life. He couldn't avoid them now. Horatio had bequeathed them to him—the responsibility for his collection, the responsibility for the Manor, for Covey, Bristleford, and the Hemmingses. Together with the responsibility for his garden.

That last worried him more than the others combined.

Horatio had trained him in how to oversee a collection; his family had prepared him to manage an estate and servants. No one had ever taught him about a garden, much less the sort of garden Horatio had created.

He had a very odd feeling about the garden.

The path joined the Grange shrubbery, leading into a maze of interconnecting walks. Lucifer checked he was taking the right one, then paced on, deep in thought.

Until a fury in patterned cambric came storming through a gap in the hedge and walked into him.

Phyllida lost all her breath in the collision. Even before she'd glanced up, her senses had recognized whose arms had locked around her. If she'd been the type of female who gave way to every impulse, she'd have shrieked and leaped away. Instead, she fixed him with a glittering glance and stepped back.

His arms fell from her. The reprobate had the gall to raise one arrogant black brow.

"My apologies." Calmly correct, she whirled around and headed for the house.

He fell in beside her as she walked, with ladylike gentility, along the path. His gaze lingered on her face; she refused to look at him—refused to see if his lips were straight and what type of amusement lurked in his blue eyes. The fiend had just made her life immeasurably more difficult.

His, too, did he but know it.

"You do that very well."

The murmured words were deliberately provocative.

"What?"

"Hide your temper. What was it that set you off?"

"An acquaintance who's being particularly trying. Actually, it's three acquaintances." Him, Mary Anne, and Robert. He'd inherited the Manor, Mary Anne had been thrown into a tizzy on the grounds that he might decide to stay, and Robert had unhelpfully confirmed that as fact.

She'd hoped the funeral would convince Mary Anne that her letters were a minor matter compared to murder. Instead, thanks to Mary Anne's sensitivities, she was now further away from being able to tell Lucifer why she'd been in Horatio's drawing room than she had been that morning. Fuming, she'd left Mary Anne and Robert by the fountain and stalked off. Only to run into Lucifer.

A sudden flush ran down her body at the memory of the impact. Under his elegant clothes he was all hard muscle; despite the fact she'd been going at full tilt, he hadn't even staggered. She glanced at him. "I take it you have, indeed, inherited the Manor?"

"Yes. There are apparently no relatives, so ..."

They stepped onto the lawn. Phyllida fixed her gaze on the house. "If I might make so bold, what are your plans? Will you sell, or live here?"

She felt his gaze on her face but didn't turn to meet it.

"You may be as bold as you like, but ..."

His tone had her glancing quickly his way.

He smiled. "I was on my way to discuss matters with your father. Perhaps you could take me to him?"

Sir Jasper was in his library. Lucifer was unsurprised when, after showing him in and then disappearing, Phyllida returned with a tray bearing glasses and a decanter.

"Well, so you're now a landowner in Devon, heh?"

"Shortly to be so, it seems." Lucifer accepted the glass of brandy Phyllida brought him. She handed a similar glass to her father, then retired to the sofa facing the chairs he and Sir Jasper occupied.

"Any thoughts on what you'll do with the property?" Sir Jasper regarded him from under shaggy brows. "You mentioned your family's estate is in Somerset ..."

"I have an older brother—the family estate will go to him. In recent years, I've lived primarily in London, sharing my brother's house."

"So you have no other establishment demanding your attention?"

"No." That was something Horatio had known. His gaze on the brandy swirling in his glass, Lucifer added, "There's nothing to stop me from settling in Colyton."

"And will you?"

He looked up, into Phyllida's eyes. It was she who had, with her habitual directness, asked the simple question.

"Yes." Raising his glass, he sipped, his gaze never leaving her. "I've decided Colyton suits me."

"Excellent!" Sir Jasper beamed. "Could do with a little new blood around here." He went on at some length, extolling the benefits of the area; Lucifer let him ramble while he tried to understand the irritation in Phyllida's brown eyes. Her expression calm, she sat watching her father, but her eyes ... and a downward quirk at one corner of her lovely lips ...

Sir Jasper wound to a halt; Lucifer stirred and faced him. "One point I wanted to mention. I consider Horatio's bequest a gift, one I couldn't comfortably accept if I hadn't done everything I could to bring his murderer to justice."

Sir Jasper nodded. "Your feelings do you credit."

"Perhaps, but I'd never feel at ease in Horatio's house, owning his collection, unless I'd turned every stone."

Sir Jasper eyed him shrewdly. "Do I take it that's a warning you intend turning every stone?"

Lucifer held his gaze. "Every rock. Every last pebble."

Sir Jasper considered, then nodded. "I'll do whatever I can, but as you doubtless appreciate, it won't be easy to lay this murderer by the heels. The bare fact of the matter is no one saw him."

"There may be other proofs." Lucifer drained his glass.

Sir Jasper did the same. "We can hope so." As Phyllida collected the empty glasses, he added, "You may investigate as you wish, of course. If you need any formal support, I'll do all I can." He stood. "Horatio was one of us. I suspect you'll find you'll have any number of people willing to help you find his murderer."

"Indeed." Lucifer rose, his gaze resting on Phyllida. "I'm hoping that will be the case."

He wanted her help in catching Horatio's murderer. He'd all but asked for it.

She wanted to help him. Even if he hadn't asked, he would have received her assistance.

Unfortunately, the promise of the morning, when she'd hoped to be able to tell him all soon, had given way to the frustration of the afternoon, which was now to be crowned by the disaster of the evening. For some ungodly reason, and she used the term advisedly, her aunt had decided to host an informal dinner for a select few who had attended the funeral. A funeral dinner. Phyllida wasn't impressed.

She'd had a good mind to wear black, but compromised with her lavender silk. It was one of her most flattering gowns and she felt in need of the support.

She was the last to enter the drawing room. Lucifer was there, startlingly handsome in a midnight-blue coat the exact same shade as his eyes. His hair appeared black in the candlelight; his ivory cravat was an exercise in elegance. He stood with her father and Mr. Farthingale before the hearth; from the instant she'd stepped over the threshold, his gaze had remained fixed on her.

Regally inclining her head, she went to join the Misses Longdon, two spinsters of indeterminate age who shared a house along the lane to the forge.

They were sixteen at table. After checking with Gladys, Phyllida took her seat. Lucifer was at the table's other end, at her aunt's right and flanked by Regina Longdon. Regina Longdon was all but deaf, which left Lady Huddlesford with little competition. Mary Anne and Robert were both too far away to engage in conversation. Or persuasion. With nothing else to do, Phyllida applied herself to overseeing the meal.

Her father never dallied long over the port; he led the gentlemen back into the drawing room a bare fifteen minutes after the ladies had settled themselves. Those fifteen minutes had been spent listening to Mary Anne play the pianoforte. As soon as the gentlemen appeared, Mary Anne closed the instrument and came forward to join the conversing groups. Phyllida closed in on her.

Mary Anne saw her coming; agitation instantly filled her blue eyes. *"No!"* she hissed, before Phyllida could say a word. "You must see it's impossible. You have to find the letters—you *promised!"*

"I would have thought that by now you'd see—"

"It's *you* who don't see! Once you find the letters and give them back to me, *then* you can tell him, if you're so sure you must." Mary Anne literally wrung her hands, then her gaze flicked past Phyllida. "Oh, heavens! There's Robert—I must rescue him before Papa corners him."

With that, she all but fled across the room.

Phyllida watched her go, not entirely able to hide her frown. She'd never seen Mary Anne so overset. "What on earth is in those letters?"

Swinging to face the room, she scanned the guests to see if any needed her hostessly attention, only to discover Lucifer crossing the room toward her, the look in his eye signaling that he required precisely that. She waited; he halted beside her, and joined her in considering the room.

"Your bosom-bow, Miss Farthingale—what's the situation between her and Collins?"

"Situation?"

He glanced at her. "Farthingale looked ready to have an apoplectic fit when Collins arrived with Crabbs. Mrs. Farthingale looked thoroughly taken aback, and then grimly, tight-lippedly, resigned. I've been following your father's lead in stepping in with distractions all evening—it would be helpful to know what game we're all playing."

Phyllida met his eyes. "Star-crossed lovers, but we're hoping this version will end without tragedy." She looked across the room to where Robert Collins was speaking with Henrietta Longdon, who happened to be sitting beside Mary Anne on the *chaise*. "Mary Anne and Robert have been sweethearts since they first met. That was six years ago. They'd be perfect for each other but for one thing."

"Collins has no fortune."

"Precisely. Mr. Farthingale forbade the connection, but despite Robert living in Exeter, meetings always seem to occur, and Mary Anne has remained absolutely adamant."

"For six years? Most parents would have yielded by now."

"Mr. Farthingale is *very* stubborn. So is Mary Anne."

"So who'll win?"

"Mary Anne. Luckily, quite soon. Robert will shortly complete the requirements for registration. Crabbs has already offered him a place. Once Robert is practicing, he'll be able to support a wife, and then Mr. Farthingale will capitulate because he won't have any choice."

"So Farthingale's apoplexy is all for show?"

"In a way. It's expected, but it's not as if Robert isn't presentable." He might be too meek, too conservative, too nonassertive, but his birth was acceptable. "That said, the Farthingales wouldn't have expected Robert to be here this evening. Everyone hereabouts knows the situation; we all avoid doing anything to exacerbate it."

"What happened tonight?"

Phyllida looked at Lady Huddlesford, holding court by the hearth. "I'm not sure. It's possible my aunt, who spends two or three months here every year, forgot and innocently invited Robert along with Crabbs."

"But ...?"

Phyllida's lips twitched. "Under that careworn exterior, she's rather a romantic. I suspect she imagines she's easing the star-crossed lovers' path."

"Ah."

The syllable was heavy with worldly cynicism. Phyllida glanced up—and saw Percy bearing down on them.

He nodded to Lucifer, his gaze fixed on her. "I wonder, cuz, whether I could have a private word with you?"

About what? Phyllida swallowed the ungracious reply. "Of course."

Percy smiled at Lucifer. "Family business, don't y'know."

Lucifer bowed.

Inclining her head in reply, Phyllida put her hand on Percy's sleeve and let him escort her through the open French doors and onto the terrace. Withdrawing her hand from his arm, she walked to the balustrade.

"Not there." Percy gestured along the terrace. "They can see."

Phyllida heaved a mental sigh and obliged, hoping Percy would cut line, tell her what he wanted, and let her return to the drawing room. If she got Robert alone, she might be able to salvage something from today. Robert might be meek, but he was also stultifyingly conservative, and as an almost solicitor, he should be law-abiding. Perhaps she could convince him—

"The thing is …" Percy halted outside the darkened library windows. Tugging down his waistcoat, he faced her.

"I've been watching you and thinking. You're what? Twenty-four?"

Leaning back against the balustrade, she stared at him. "Yes," she admitted. "Twenty-four. What of it?"

"What of it? Why, you should be married, of course! Ask m'mother—she'll tell you. You're all but on the shelf at twenty-four."

"Indeed?" Phyllida considered explaining that she was quite happy on her shelf. "Why should that concern you?"

"Of course it concerns me! I'm the head of the family—well, once your father shuffles off, I will be."

"I have a brother, remember?"

"Jonas." With a wave, Percy dismissed Jonas. "Thing is, you're here, unmarried, and there's no sense to it, not when there's an alternative."

Phyllida debated. Humoring Percy was probably the fastest way to bring this scene to an end. Folding her arms, she settled against the balustrade. "What alternative?"

Percy drew himself up and puffed out his chest. "You can marry me."

Shock held her speechless.

"I know it's a surprise—hadn't thought of it myself until I came down here and saw how it was. But now I can see it's the perfect solution." Percy started to pace. "Family duty and all that—offering for you is what I should do."

Phyllida straightened. "Percy, I'm perfectly comfortable here—"

"Precisely. That's the beauty of it. We can be married and you can stay down here in the country—daresay your father would prefer it. He wouldn't want to have to run the Grange without you. On the other hand, *I* don't need a hostess. I've never had one." He nodded. "I'll be perfectly happy rattling 'round London on my own."

"I can quite see that. Let's see if I fully understand your proposal." Her terse accents had Percy tensing. "Are you, by any chance, currently at *point-non-plus*?"

Stony-faced, Percy glared at her.

Phyllida waited.

"I might, at present, have outrun the constable a trifle, but it's merely a temporary setback. Nothing serious."

"Nevertheless. Now, let's see … you came into your inheritance from your father some years ago and you have no further expectation from our side of the family."

"Not with Grandmother making you her beneficiary and Aunt Esmeralda leaving her blunt to you and Jonas."

"Quite. And, of course, when Huddlesford dies, his estate will pass to Frederick." Phyllida fixed her gaze on Percy's now petulant face. "Which means that beyond any inheritance from your mother, who everyone knows enjoys the best of health, there's no pot of gold waiting just over your horizon." She paused. "Am I right?"

"You know you're right, damn you."

"And am I also right in thinking that the cent-per-cents will no longer advance you funds—not unless you can show them some evidence of further expectations—like a wife with various inheritances attached?"

Percy glowered. "That's all very well, but you're straying from the point."

"Oh, no! The point is you've run aground, and you're looking to me to tug you out of the mire."

"And so you *should*!" Face mottled, fists clenched, Percy stepped close. "If I'm prepared to marry you out of family duty, you should be pleased to marry me and resurrect my fortunes."

Phyllida shut her lips on an unladylike utterance. She gave Percy back stare for glare. "I will *not* marry you—there's absolutely no reason that I should."

"Reason?" Percy's features contorted. "*Reason*? I'll give you reason."

He grabbed her, clearly intending to kiss her. Phyllida jerked back and wrestled half out of his hold. She'd never been afraid of Percy; he was three years older, but she'd run rings around him from her earliest years—she'd grown accustomed to treating him with contempt.

To her shock, he was much stronger than she'd realized. She struggled, but couldn't break his hold. With a growl, he hauled her back into his arms, cruelly pressing her back into the balustrade, trying to force her face to his—

Suddenly he was gone, literally plucked off her.

Phyllida collapsed against the balustrade, dragging in air, one hand at her heaving breast. She stared at Percy, dangling, choking, at the end of one long, blue-suited arm.

"Is there a pond or lake closer than the duck pond? I believe your cousin needs to cool off."

Tracking along his arm, Phyllida located Lucifer's face in the dimness. Then she looked back at Percy, feet still swinging helplessly four inches clear of the flagstones. His face was turning purple. "Umm—no."

Lucifer's lip curled. He shook Percy, then flung him away—he landed with an "Ooof!" and a clatter of limbs. He lay wheezing on the flags, shaking his head weakly, not daring to look up.

Reluctantly accepting that that was the worst he could do, Lucifer slammed a door on the chaos of emotions whirling inside him and looked at Phyllida. She was still breathing rapidly, but her color, as far as he could judge in the poor light, was acceptable. Her gown and hair were still neat—he'd been in time to spare her that much of the ordeal. He resettled his coat and cuffs, then offered her his arm. "I suggest we return before anyone else misses you."

Looking up at him, she swallowed, then nodded. "Thank you." Placing her hand on his arm, she straightened, stiffening her spine and lifting her head.

Her mask of calm composure slid into place, hiding her shock—the sudden comprehension of her physical vulnerability—that had, until that moment, sat naked on her face.

It was not a look he had ever liked seeing on any woman's face. He would have given a great deal to have saved her from the realization entirely. She shouldn't need to know that men could physically harm her. Her physical safety, here in her home, in and around the village, was something she'd taken for granted all her life. Percy had violated the "comfort" she had alluded to—the sense of security she enjoyed in this place.

As for Percy's so elegant proposal, just the thought of it made Lucifer see red. Grimly clinging to his own mask of calm indifference, he steered Phyllida along the terrace. They reached the French doors and she stepped into the light. He let his gaze slide over her, from her pale, hauntingly lovely face, over the slender frame and feminine curves concealed beneath lavender silk, down to the tips of her satin slippers. Other than her breathing, still too shallow, there was no overt evidence of any distress.

Chest tightening, he looked into her eyes. They were shuttered, all emotions locked away.

As he handed her over the threshold, then followed, Lucifer wondered if it was too late to slip out again and thrash Percy to within an inch of his life.

CHAPTER

Six

The emotions stirred by the incident on the terrace did not rapidly subside. Later that night, with the moon riding the sky, Lucifer paced before his bedchamber window.

Tomorrow, he'd remove to the Manor. Tomorrow, he'd start investigating Horatio's murder with a great deal more intensity than he'd yet employed. Horatio had been killed on Sunday morning. Tomorrow would be Wednesday. The first rush of shock and speculation would have died; people would have had time to think and, he hoped, remember.

Pausing before the window, he glanced out. The moon broke free of the wispy clouds and shone down; the night was a cauldron of shifting shadows stirred by the pale light.

A figure left the house, striding purposefully across the back lawn. Lucifer stared. A low cap hid the man's head—or was it a youth? The stride was swinging, graceful, and easy, long legs encased in breeches and boots. A hacking jacket hung to hip length. Jonas?

The figure neared the entrance to the shrubbery; the graceful stride faltered, slowed.

That instant of hesitation ripped the veils from Lucifer's eyes. "What the devil …?"

He didn't wait for an answer. His quarry was into the wood before he had drawn close enough to be sure of not losing her. He trailed her; he wanted to see where she was going.

And then he would want to know why.

He would have wagered a great deal that her goal would be the Manor—she knew he would be taking up residence there tomorrow. Instead, she turned left off the main path onto a narrower one heading into the village.

He followed, closing the gap so he could keep her in sight; the path twisted through the trees—it would be easy to lose her. Head down, she tramped along, apparently absorbed in her thoughts.

The path became an alley running between two cottages to join the lane. Without pause, Phyllida crossed the lane and continued up the common.

Lucifer hung back in the alley, letting the distance between them increase. The common was open ground, and there was little doubt now of her destination. She was making for the church.

Her peculiar conversation with the curate replayed in his mind. What in all Hades was going on?

On reaching the graveyard, he saw faint light spilling from the church's side door. Using gravestones for cover, he crept closer, exercising greater caution than before.

Phyllida was no longer alone.

A tall gravestone stood by the path leading from the side door; concealed in its shadow, Lucifer watched Phyllida standing beside Filing in the narrow porch before the open door. Both had ledgers in their hands; heads down, they were making notes, occasionally comparing entries.

Lucifer looked down the path to the lane bordering the graveyard. The lych-gate was shrouded in gloom; eyes straining, he could make out shapes and movement in the lane beyond. Then figures separated from the shadows and came up the path—men toting small barrels, boxes, packages. They passed his hiding place. Swiveling, Lucifer watched as Phyllida checked each box and barrel, speaking in low tones to the men and to Filing.

Then the men carried their loads into the church.

Lucifer slumped back, his shoulders against the gravestone. *Smuggling?*

The daughter of the local magistrate running a smuggling gang, aided and abetted by the local curate?

It was too hard to swallow, especially given what he knew of the daughter of the local magistrate.

Phyllida checked each item brought to the church door against the bill of lading. Beside her, Mr. Filing created a separate list, noting which men were assisting tonight and who brought what up to the crypt.

One of the men, Hugey, held a package up for her perusal. "This be almost it."

Phyllida nodded. "Good. That can go down now."

Hugey bobbed his head and trudged past them. She heard his boots clatter on the stairs down to the crypt.

"This be the last for tonight." Oscar, another heavy, hulking man, sat a barrel on the step.

Oscar was the leader of the band and a solid supporter of their enterprise. Smiling, Phyllida bent to check the barrel's markings. "A quiet and uneventful night?"

"Aye—just how I likes it." Oscar grinned back. At Phyllida's nod, he hefted the barrel to his shoulder. "I'll stow this, then we'll be away."

Phyllida closed her ledger and turned to Mr. Filing.

He smiled. "It's all running so smoothly."

"Thank heaven." Phyllida headed for the crypt stairs. "I want to get these figures into the accounts." She and Filing stood back as Oscar and Hugey came back up the stone steps. With nods and good-byes, the men trudged down the path to join the others. They would quietly disperse, returning the ponies to their respective stables, then go home to their cottages and their beds.

It would be an hour or so before she could do the same. Phyllida led the way down into the crypt. "I expect to be busy over the next few days, so I'll bring all the accounts up to date and work out the payments in advance. That way, once you've collected the money, you can disburse the men's share without having to find me first."

"A very good notion." Filing looked around as they reached the crypt floor. "I'll just make sure everything's where it ought to be."

Phyllida crossed to the sarcophagus she used as a desk. It was built flush to the wall, with various niches carved above it, presumably for offerings. The niches presently contained a set of ledgers, assorted writing implements, and the other paraphernalia she required to keep the accounts. There was a wooden stool beside the sarcophagus; she drew it out and sat, winding her boots around the stool's legs. Moving the lamp that had been left on the sarcophagus to a higher perch on a stack of boxes nearby, she checked that the light thrown on her ledger was even, then settled to her task.

Behind her, Filing moved between the rows of goods which largely filled the crypt. Phyllida transcribed numbers, then worked through the calculations. The sound of something sliding on stone reached her. She glanced back at the stairs. No one came down. Then Filing stepped out from one row, concentrating as he counted boxes. He rounded the next row; Phyllida turned back to her columns.

Fifteen minutes later, the intensity of light increased. Phyllida looked up. Filing stood beside her.

"Everything's as it should be. Thompson and I should encounter no problem sorting the next delivery."

"Good." Phyllida looked at the ledger before her. "I'll be a little while yet, so I'll wish you a good night."

She glanced up. Filing frowned.

"I don't like to leave you here at this hour, alone ..."

"Nonsense!" Phyllida made the disclaimer with a confident smile, although, for the first time in her life, she wasn't sure she wanted to be alone, away from her home at this hour. She wasn't, however, about to display her fear—doubtless an irrational one—to Mr. Filing.

"I'll be perfectly all right and, truth to tell, I work faster in complete silence. If you shut the church door, no one's likely to come in. I'll be quite safe." She returned her attention to the ledger. "I'll probably only be another fifteen minutes."

Mr. Filing hesitated, but she'd spoken realistically. Why would anyone climb to the church so late at night?

"Very well—if you're sure ...?"

"I'm sure."

"Then ... good night."

"Good night." Phyllida nodded without looking up; as she corrected a figure, the light from Mr. Filing's lamp receded. A moment later, she heard him on the stairs, then heard the scrape of the church door closing.

She was alone.

In silence, her concentration absolute, she finished adding the figures in five minutes, then calculated and recorded the payments due to the men in another five. Pleased, she sat back, surveying her handiwork.

A shadow loomed on the page.

With a gasp, she swung around—

Lucifer stood beside the lamp, arms crossed, dark blue eyes narrowed. Her heart thudding in her throat, she stared at him.

"Would you care to tell me what this is all about?"

She drew breath into her lungs—and narrowed her eyes back. "No. And might I suggest that, given you intend to reside in this village, you'd do well not to prowl around at night scaring the occupants out of their wits!" She'd started her tirade evenly; the last word was shrill. Swinging back to stare at her ledger, she concentrated on breathing. Grabbing a piece of blotting paper, she blotted her figures.

After a moment, he replied, "You might have momentarily been frightened, but you haven't lost your wits. And you may as well tell me what's going on, because you know I won't leave you be until I know."

She did know that; he wasn't easily deflected. And there really was no reason he couldn't know the truth, especially as he was remaining in Colyton. Shutting the ledger, she returned it to its niche. "I'm running an import business."

He hesitated, then asked, "Is that the new name for smuggling?"

"It's all perfectly legal." Rummaging in a niche, she drew out a sheet of printed paper and handed it to him.

He took it and read, "The Colyton Import Company." He looked up. "A legal importing company that operates in the dead of night?"

His incredulity was transparent; nose in the air, she slid from the stool. "There's no law against it."

She reached past him for the lamp—he anticipated her and lifted it. Laying the paper on the sarcophagus, he waved her to the stairs. Head high, she led the way; as she climbed she became increasingly conscious of the side-to-side sway of her hips. She scampered up the last stairs, but with one step he was beside her, looking beyond her to the church door. Phyllida shut the small door to the crypt; he extinguished the lamp, set it aside, and pulled open the church door. Together, they went out into the night.

He tugged the door shut. She felt his gaze on her face.

"Explain."

Phyllida headed for the common. He fell in beside her, his dark presence more comforting than unnerving. He had the sense not to repeat his command; if he had, she might not have obliged. "This is a smuggling coast. There's always been smugglers here, running goods either heavily taxed or, in more recent times, prohibited because of the war with France. The end of the war led to trade resuming, so the goods previously prohibited could once again be openly imported."

Leaving the graveyard, she continued down the common. "Virtually overnight, smuggling was no longer, or only marginally, profitable. Selling smuggled goods became difficult because merchants could buy the same goods legally at a reasonable price—there was no longer any incentive to take risks. Most of the smugglers are farm laborers—they turn to the night trade to supplement their incomes and support their families. Suddenly, that extra income was no longer there, and the whole"—she gestured—"*balance* of things hereabouts was in jeopardy."

They crossed the lane and headed down the alley; she waited until they were in the wood before continuing. "The only way I could see to help was to set up the Colyton Import Company. Papa knows all about it—it's entirely legitimate. We pay our excise duties to the Revenue Office in Exeter. Mr. Filing is an accredited collector."

He was following close at her shoulder, head bent as he listened. She glanced his way and saw him shake his head.

"Legitimized smuggling." Through the gloom, he caught her eye. "You arranged it all?"

She shrugged. "Who else?"

A fair answer, Lucifer supposed, but it led to the next question. "What do you get out of it?" An impertinent question, but he wanted to know.

"Get out of it?" The concept puzzled her; she halted and looked at him, then moved on again. "I suppose peace of mind."

Not what he'd expected. Excitement, the thrill of being in charge, something along those lines, but …"Peace of mind?"

"Just consider the alternative to smuggling in these parts." Her voice hardened. "We're two miles from a coast riddled and raked with reefs and sandbars."

"Wrecking?" His blood ran cold.

"That's what happened before. I wasn't having it happening again—not with Colyton men." Even through the dark, she exuded determination. Now he understood. Peace of mind.

"So instead, you organized this entirely legitimate enterprise." Not a question but a statement, one tinged with surprise and more definitely with approval.

She inclined her head.

They walked on in silence as he digested it all. "But why work at night?"

The sound she made, half snort, half sigh, was distinctly patronizing. "So it *looks* like the men are still smuggling, of course."

"Why is that important?"

"It isn't, not to anyone but them." Resigned frustration colored her tone. "Other than myself, only Papa, Mr. Filing, Thompson, and the men involved—and now you—know that the business is legal. In the company's name, I organize the rendezvous with the ships—most French captains are happy to unload without having to lay into an English port. The gang keeps the rendezvous and brings the goods up to the church—"

"And you store them in the crypt."

She nodded.

"What happens then?"

"Mr. Filing takes the signed bills of lading to the Revenue Office and pays the duties owed, then brings back the stamped clearances. Thompson isn't involved with the incoming goods, but his brother, Oscar, is the gang's leader. Once Mr. Filing has the clearances, the gang comes back one night and loads the goods onto Thompson's dray. The next day, Thompson drives the goods into Chard, where the Company has an arrangement with one of the major merchants. He sells the goods on commission and the funds come back to Mr. Filing, who pays the men their share." She gestured. "That's it."

"But why do the men pretend they're still smuggling?"

"They pretend they're still members of the brotherhood essentially to save face. They've got used to a regular income and a comfortable existence free of any threat from the Revenue, but the mystique of smuggling runs deep in these parts—they don't want it known they're no longer involved, no longer taking risks. There are other smuggling gangs still operating in the district. The gang that operates to the west of Beer is all but legendary."

Eyes on the ground, she strode on. "When I suggested the Company, the men were adamant that they'd only be part of it if the legality of the operation was kept secret. I had to agree to them continuing to operate like smugglers."

She shot him a glance; he sensed her contemptuous air. "Male egos are nonsensical things."

Lucifer grinned. The woman came out night after night to spare those selfsame male egos. He looked ahead. The Grange shrubbery was just discernible through the gloom.

Crack!

He reacted instantly, grabbing Phyllida, hurling them both forward.

A long groan and the sounds of roots and earth tearing followed them down; the next instant, with a massive *crash!* a dead tree thumped down across the path where a few seconds before they had stood. One skeletal branch trapped Lucifer's boots. Turning, glancing back at the tree, he kicked and the brittle twigs snapped.

He'd flung them against the rising bank that bordered the path at that point, Phyllida first, his body protectively over hers. They'd landed roughly horizontal, stretched full length on a narrow shelf in the bank. Lucifer slowly turned over, assessing their state. He slipped and slid down, ending on the path, flat on his back.

Phyllida, who'd been trying to push herself away from the bank, lost his support behind and beneath her. With a muffled shriek, she followed him down. She landed on top of him, her shoulder digging into his chest.

He winced. Gasping, she wriggled around; they ended literally nose to nose, lips and eyes mere inches apart.

They both froze, stilled ... waiting ... thinking ...

He started to raise his arms to close them about her, then stopped. Percy had grabbed her only hours before and tried to force his attentions on her. He wanted to seize, to hold, to capture, but the last thing he wanted was to remind her of Percy.

His night vision was good. Her face was a pale oval, her expression not her usual serene mask but carefully blank. Eyes wide, she was staring at his face. Considering ... wondering ...

He knew what he'd like her to consider—what he wanted her to wonder. "I believe"—his voice had deepened—"that I deserve a reward for that."

Phyllida stared at him and tried to marshal her wayward wits. His hands were at her waist, but not gripping. She lay fully upon him; he lay passive beneath her. She knew that he was infinitely more dangerous than Percy. Why, then, did she feel so much safer, all but in his arms, lying atop him, entirely alone in the dark wood late at night?

It was a conundrum, one she felt she should solve. But she couldn't, not now, not with his dark gaze on her eyes, with the hard warmth of him beneath her, threatening, in the most tempting way, to surround her.

He did deserve a reward. If she'd been alone, she would have stopped and looked around, and probably have ended being hurt. Even killed. He deserved a reward, and she didn't even have to think to know what it was he would like.

His wish was the glint in his eyes, the tension in the hard body beneath her—an almost discernible hum of desire. Of its own volition, her tongue came out; she licked her lips, leaving them slightly parted.

His gaze lowered; her lips throbbed. She waited ...

His gaze rose to her eyes. He held her gaze, then slowly raised one brow.

You may be as bold as you like ...

His earlier words returned to her; their true meaning—the meaning his deep, purring, seductive voice had invested them with—rang crystal-clear. She hesitated no longer. Framing his face with her hands, she set her lips to his.

They felt as they had before, alive, firm, tempting; they made her lips tingle. She kissed him and he kissed her back, pressure for pressure but no more. She kissed him again and the same thing happened—she was in control. Some part of her mind tried frantically to remind her just how dangerous he was; the rest gloried in the unexpected possibilities. There were so many things she'd always wanted to know, sensations she'd wanted to experience.

She traced his lower lip with her tongue and he obediently parted his lips. She ventured in and was immediately lost in a carnival of delicious delights, slipping from one to the next and back again. Whatever she asked, he gave; wherever she ventured, he followed. The texture of his tongue against hers, the heated wetness of the kiss, were all still new to her. She reveled in each novel delight, then, confident and secure, explored further.

Lucifer lay there and let her have her way with him. He had to concentrate to maintain his passive state, given she was a mature twenty-four and every development in their kiss apparently necessitated a wriggle or a squirm.

Luckily, she provided a distraction, too—her naivete coupled with her blatant curiosity left him wondering what the local gentlemen had been doing for the past six years. Asking for her help, apparently—certainly not kissing her. Especially not kissing her as she deserved to be kissed.

She was twenty-four—the warm swells that tantalizingly brushed his upper chest, the warm weight of her hips pressed to his waist, the long sweeps of her thighs riding down, over his hips—He abruptly cut off that train of thought and focused again on her hungry lips, on satisfying her and satisfying himself.

He felt they'd succeeded very nicely when she finally raised her head.

Phyllida looked down at him, and felt her heart thud. Her skin, all her nerves, had come alive; she was intensely aware of his body, and hers, of the masculine power he exuded yet controlled so effortlessly. It surrounded her, yet she didn't feel trapped, didn't feel like pulling away. She felt like plunging deeper in.

Temptation might well be his middle name.

She frowned, then struggled, just a little. "Let me up."

His lips curved. "I'm not holding you."

She stared at him; heat rose in her cheeks. His hands on either side of her waist might be burning her—they weren't gripping her. She tried to push away, to roll off him. His fingers gripped lightly and he lifted her from him.

Scrambling upright, she brushed herself down, tugged her cap firmly on her head, then, with barely a glance to confirm he was on his feet, she strode on toward the house.

Lucifer followed, careful, even in the darkness, not to grin too triumphantly. Close behind her as they navigated the shrubbery, he felt more than victorious. He felt honored, curiously so, as if she'd bestowed something on him that was worth more than words could define. In one way, she had— she'd gifted him with a degree of trust she'd never given to any other man.

He'd invited it, true, but it wasn't something he could have forced from her. Inordinately pleased with himself, and her, he stepped onto the back lawn.

She'd trusted him in one way—that augered well for his plan, a plan that was simplicity incarnate. She knew something about Horatio's murder and she was a sensible, intelligent female; the only reason she hadn't told him all was because she didn't yet trust him that far. Once she'd learned more of him and convinced herself that he was an honorable man, then she would tell him her secret. Simple.

Grinning, he walked on by her side.

His next thought came out of nowhere, unheralded—unwanted. It destroyed his triumph, leaving a bitter taste on his tongue. Was he any better than the others who courted her, not out of real desire, but out of a desire for something she could give them?

The question clanged in his brain. The sensual memory of her body lying flush atop his washed over him.

Jaw setting, he willed both memory and question away.

The house rose before them, silent and still. Without words, they made their way inside, and parted for what was left of the night.

CHAPTER
Seven

L ate the next morning, Lucifer walked into the front corner bedchamber at the Manor and looked around. His brushes were on the dresser. If he opened the wardrobe, he would, he was sure, find his coats neatly hanging. Covey had been busy.

He'd breakfasted at the Grange with Sir Jasper and Jonas; Phyllida, he assumed, had still been abed. Or perhaps, after last night, she'd decided to avoid meeting him quite so soon. If so, he was grateful. Taking leave of his host, he'd walked through the woods to the Manor to take up the reins Horatio had willed him.

After speaking with Covey, Bristleford, and the Hemmingses, assuring them that he would, indeed, be residing permanently at the Manor and that he was happy to have them continue in their present positions, he'd allowed himself to be shown around the house and had chosen this room as his.

Leaving Mrs. Hemmings and Covey to organize and fuss—which had reassured them as no words could—he'd settled in the library to write letters. One to his parents, one to Devil, one to Montague, and a summons to Dodswell to join him here. He didn't know where Gabriel and Alathea were, so he couldn't write to them. Had it really been only four *days* since their wedding? It felt like weeks.

Leaving the letters for Covey to take to the Red Bells for collection, he'd wandered up here.

He'd chosen this room because of the windows, the light. The room Horatio had occupied, similarly large but at the back, was shady and quiet.

Here, the front windows looked over the flower garden, the drive, and the gates to the lane, while the side windows gave views of the shrubbery, the lawns, and the lake. Between the side windows sat a large four-poster bed invitingly arrayed with plump pillows and a rich red-and-gold tapestry bedspread. Curtains of the same fabric were gathered at the four corners and tied back with tasseled gold cords.

All the furniture gleamed; the faint scent of lemon polish hung in the air.

Walking to the window facing the common, Lucifer gazed out, mentally assembling a plan, one that didn't involve pressuring Phyllida Tallent into telling him all she knew. She could come to trust him of her own accord; he refused to seduce her into it.

Shaking aside all memories of last night, including the hours during which he'd been unable to sleep, he focused on the lane. He recalled driving into the village, halting, and looking around … he'd seen no horse or carriage, no one on foot ….How had the murderer left the scene?

"If by horse …" Crossing to the side window, he studied the shrubbery.

Two minutes later, he was striding across the side lawn. The shrubbery entrance was wide but shaggy; inside, the hedges were overgrown. Making a mental note to speak to Hemmings about hiring more help for the grounds, Lucifer pressed on along a path leading, he hoped, to the lane.

He discovered an archway in the hedge running parallel to the lane. Pushing through, he found himself on a narrow path winding between the shrubbery hedge and the hedge bordering the lane. Topping him by more than a foot, both hedges were so poorly tended that arching new growth met and tangled overhead. Even though the path was wide enough to walk freely, when he'd stopped in his curricle only yards farther along the lane, he hadn't had any inkling this path was here—it had appeared that the shrubbery hedge and the lane hedge were one and the same.

Presumably the path started by the Manor's drive. Turning, Lucifer paced in the other direction.

He found what he'd suspected he might just beyond the shrubbery. The side and back shrubbery hedges met in a corner; a grassy area wide enough to accommodate a horse lay between the back of the shrubbery and a briar-filled ditch marking the edge of a paddock. Hard by the lane, the ditch closed over and the path led on, hugging the lane hedge to swing out of sight around a bend.

Turning his attention to the grassy area, he looked, then squatted and parted the grass to study the impressions in the earth beneath.

A horse had stood there, not long ago. He didn't think it had rained since Sunday. As the grass sprang back, he saw that some tufts had been chomped. So—a horse had stood there recently, for at least a little while. Why?

There seemed only one likely answer.

Lucifer rose and continued along the path. He was out of sight of the shrubbery when he came upon a place where the lane hedge had partly died. There was a gap, wide enough for a horse to push through.

Twigs were snapped on both sides of the gap. He twisted one free and studied it. It had broken, not this morning, not even yesterday, but not long ago.

From the other side of the hedge came a rustle of skirts, a quick, light step. Lucifer looked up. His senses prickled.

The steps halted. A small hand appeared, fingers extended to touch a broken twig.

The owner of the hand stepped into the gap.

She gasped and nearly stepped back when she saw him.

Lucifer stared at her.

Phyllida stared back.

For one wild moment, her consciousness of their kiss in the night flared in her eyes; he felt the same awareness tug, hot and strong, in his gut. Then she blinked and looked down—at the twig he still held in his fingers. Her gaze swung up to his face. "What have you found?"

Sharing would make her trust him sooner. He glanced back down the path. "I think a horse was ridden through here and left waiting at the back of the shrubbery."

She pressed into the gap, craning to see; the curve of the lane prevented that. "The back of the shrubbery?"

"There's a clearing there."

"Show me." She began to push through the hedge. Branches grabbed at soft curves protected only by her delicate blue gown.

"No!" He waved her back. "Use your parasol as a shield."

She looked at him inquiringly. He showed her how; holding the open parasol before her, she maneuvered through the hedge without sustaining any serious damage. Shaking out her skirts, she raised the parasol again. "Thank you."

He said nothing but waved her down the path; it wasn't his pleasure—he wasn't at all sure he wanted her this close, alone and private again. He had to keep reminding his rakish senses that she was more innocent than her behavior painted her. Not an easy task when he could all too clearly remember the sensations of her lips on his, her tongue … He shook his head. "The clearing's beyond those briars."

She stopped at the spot. He hunkered down and showed her what he'd found, the clear impressions made by front hooves neatly shod.

"Can you tell anything from the hoofprints?"

He shook his head and stood. "The back hooves were on harder soil, and the horse was here long enough to shift about a good deal. There's no imprint with any distinctive mark." He frowned, still looking down. "But the shoes are good quality—clean, good lines."

"So it's unlikely to be a workhorse, a plow horse …"

"No, but any decent mount would fit the bill." He moved back, onto the path. Phyllida joined him. Without further words, they strolled toward the Manor.

Temptation whispered; Lucifer ignored it. He glanced at her; there was no evidence of awareness in her face—but then, there rarely was. Her face was a mask; only her eyes would tell him what she was feeling, and she was being careful not to meet his gaze. Being very careful not to touch him as they strolled.

He looked forward and drew in a breath. "Let's hypothesize that on Sunday morning, the murderer rode here, pushed through the hedge, and left his horse waiting at the back of the shrubbery while he went on to the Manor. Where could he have ridden from?"

"You mean from which towns?"

He nodded.

"Lyme Regis is close, about six miles, but the route is by the coast, so if they'd come from there, they would have ridden through the village." She glanced at him. "Old Mrs. Ottery lives in the cottage by the Bells. She's chair-bound and spends her Sunday mornings looking out over the common. She swears no one rode through the village."

Lucifer eyed her calm profile. "If not Lyme Regis, where else?"

"Axminster is the closest town, but it's not very large."

"I passed through it on my way here. Chard is further, but might be worth considering. I saw a few stables there."

"Chard is the most likely place where someone from outside would hire a horse to ride here. The mail coaches to Exeter stop there."

"Very well. Let's consider nearer at hand. Who rides in from this end of the village?"

She glanced at him; a frown filled her eyes. "The households of Dottswood and Highgate—their lane joins the main lane back by the first cottages."

Lucifer remembered the lane beside the ridge. "Who else commonly rides into the village?"

She hesitated. They'd passed the archway into the shrubbery; the end of the path lay just ahead. "Most of the men living outside the immediate village ride in. Papa and Jonas rarely ride in the village. Silas Coombe and Mr. Filing I've never known to ride at all. All the rest, even Cedric, would normally ride in."

Stepping through the ragged entrance to the path, she halted on the lawn. He followed, glancing around. They were some yards from the main gates, the hedge bordering the lane still to their immediate right. The gravel path leading to the front door started twenty paces away.

He returned his gaze to Phyllida. "Could a man from any of the other estates—not Dottswood or Highgate—easily circle the village and reach the lane at that spot?"

"Yes. Bridle paths link all the lanes, although you'd have to be a local to know them."

No one wanted to think the murderer was a local, yet ... "Ignoring that gap in the hedge, could the horse have been ridden to that clearing from the other direction?"

"By coming up the field?" When he nodded, she shook her head. "That field—in fact, all your fields—runs down to the river. The Axe. It's not far and it's too deep to ride across without getting thoroughly wet. To come along this side of the river, they'd have to cross the Grange fields first—a lot of fields, most bordered with briar ditches."

Lucifer looked across the drive to the colorful blooms nodding in Horatio's garden. "So we're looking for some outsider who hired a horse, most likely in Chard, and rode in, then out, or it could have been any of the local gentlemen."

"Bar Papa, Jonas, Mr. Filing, and Silas Coombe. And the other gentlemen who were at church, of course."

He'd forgotten. "Basil and Pommeroy. I haven't checked the others, but that should narrow the list."

Phyllida threw him a glance. "Don't count on it."

Lucifer grinned. He was about to twit her on the comment when the rumbling of a carriage reached them.

They glanced toward the lane, then looked at each other. Their gazes met, held …

Without a word, they stepped into the drive—into the open. Where anyone could see them and no one could suggest they'd been "private."

They were standing in the middle of the drive, facing the gate, when the carriage slowed and halted.

Lady Fortemain leaned over the side and beamed. "Mr. Cynster. *Just* who I was looking for!"

Lucifer quashed an urge to flee. With an easy smile, collecting Phyllida with a glance, he strolled to the barouche.

"I've just heard the *wonderful* news!" Lady Fortemain's eyes gleamed. "Now you've decided to remain among us and fill the void left by dear Horatio's passing, you must—positively you *must*—allow me to host an impromptu dinner to introduce you to your neighbors."

He'd been born in the country and lived among the ton; there was no need to ask how Lady Fortemain had heard.

She leaned forward, including Phyllida in her bright gaze. "Our summer ball is just over a week away—I'll send you a card, of course. But I thought, seeing as we're so very quiet hereabouts, that there would be no harm in holding a small dinner tonight."

"Tonight?"

"At seven—Ballyclose Manor. You can't miss it—just take the lane past the forge."

Lucifer hesitated for only an instant; such a gathering would provide excellent opportunities to further investigate his neighbors' activities last Sunday morning. He bowed to Lady Fortemain. "I'd be honored."

Delighted, her ladyship turned to Phyllida. "I'm just going to Dottswood and Highgate, dear, and then I'll be calling at the Grange. I'm expecting everyone to attend—your papa and brother, as well as dear Lady Huddlesford and her sons. And, of course, you, my dear Phyllida."

Phyllida smiled. To Lucifer, the gesture was superficial—mild, distant, it said nothing of her thoughts.

Her ladyship saw it otherwise; she beamed warmly at Phyllida. "Perhaps you'd like to accompany me to Dottswood and Highgate, and thence to the Grange?"

Phyllida's smile didn't waver as she shook her head. "Thank you, but I must call on Mrs. Cobb."

Lady Fortemain sighed fondly. "Always so busy, dear. Well, I must leave you and spread the word." She tapped her coachman; she waved as the carriage jerked forward. "Until seven, Mr. Cynster!"

Lucifer raised his hand in salute; smiling, he watched the carriage rumble away. Then he turned to Phyllida, unsurprised to find that her smile had faded, leaving a frown investing her dark eyes.

"So why aren't you delighted?" He gestured to the flower garden; brows rising haughtily, she strolled beside him onto a secondary path that wound its way through burgeoning beds to the central fountain.

He waited—he had no intention of withdrawing the question. He wanted to know the answer.

After a moment, she pulled a face. He inwardly blinked—she rarely displayed her feelings so blatantly.

"Would *you* be delighted to know you were destined to spend the entire evening listening to a pompous windbag?"

"Which windbag is that?"

"Cedric, of course." They strolled on, she admiring the blooms, he, more covertly, admiring her. Her consciousness of their interlude the previous night was still there, but had faded, receded, as they'd talked. Stopping to examine a rose, she went on. "I told you Cedric wants to marry me—Lady Fortemain is determined that I should marry him. That alone would render this impromptu dinner less than appealing, but, of course, Pommeroy will be there, too, doing his best to be off-putting."

"Why off-putting?"

"Because he *doesn't* want Cedric to marry me."

"Pommeroy wants to marry you, too?"

She smiled. "No—it's simpler. Pommeroy doesn't want Cedric to marry at all. There's fifteen years between them—Pommeroy therefore has expectations that Cedric's long bachelorhood have fueled."

"Ah."

They wandered on through the garden; Lucifer said nothing more. Her tone whenever they touched on the subject of marriage grated, although why he, of all men, should feel compelled to defend the institution was difficult to comprehend. Or, more to the point, he didn't want to comprehend the reasons behind the impulse, to study his motives too closely. Yet the fact remained.

Courtesy of her self-centered suitors, she'd developed a cynical, not to say negative, view of marriage that seemed considerably more cynical and deeply entrenched than his own. He, at least, knew all marriages were not like those offered her. Did she? "When did your mother die?"

Halting by the fountain, she blinked at him. "When I was twelve. Why?"

He shrugged. "I just wondered."

She bent to sniff a burst of lavender spikes. Leaning one shoulder against the fountain's rim, he watched her.

After a moment, he said, "This garden ..."

She glanced up at him, her face shaded by her parasol, her expression serene yet interested, eyes dark, unknown and unknowing ...

That dark gaze caught him. She was aware of him, yet so ... innocent of all else. All that she had a right to know, to experience—all she deserved to enjoy.

"I haven't any idea how to ... manage it." He heard his words as if from a distance.

She smiled and straightened. He pushed away from the fountain.

Turning toward the gate, she gestured to the glorious displays on all sides. "It isn't that hard." Pausing beneath a delicate arch covered with rioting white roses, she looked back at him. Her smile curved her lips, still warmed her eyes. "Horatio learned how—I'm sure you could, too. If you truly wished to."

Lucifer halted beside her; for a long moment, he looked into her eyes. Her dark gaze was direct, open, honest—assured and confident and also so aware. A bare inch of air was all that separated his body from hers, nevertheless, she stood, a serene goddess as yet untouched, certain, not of his control, but hers. "If I were to ask, would you help me?"

His voice had deepened, his tone almost rough. Tilting her head, she studied his eyes. Her answer, when it came, was considered. "Yes. Of course." Smoothly, she turned away. "You have only to ask."

Lucifer stood beneath the arch watching her hips sway as she headed for the gate. Then he stirred and followed.

Lady Fortemain's dinner proved more interesting than Phyllida had expected, even if, for the most part, she was relegated to the status of mere observer. From the side of the Ballyclose drawing room to which she'd retreated to escape Cedric's patronizing possessiveness, she watched Lucifer move gracefully through the gathering.

At dinner, she'd been seated at Cedric's right at one end of the long table; Lucifer had been guest of honor at the other end, beside their hostess. He'd returned to the drawing room with the rest of the gentlemen a good half hour ago. Since then, he'd been on the prowl, indefatigably hunting, yet no one seemed defensive in the least.

He would pause beside a group of gentlemen and, with some question or comment, neatly cut his quarry from the pack. A few questions, a smile, perhaps a joke and a laugh; having got what he wanted, he'd let them return to the group and he'd move on, an easy smile, his elegantly charming air, masking his intent. Why they couldn't sense it, she did not know; even from across the room, his concentration reached her.

Then again, she knew what it felt like to be stalked by him, to be the focus of that intensely blue gaze. She hadn't expected to meet him that morning; throughout the interlude, she'd waited for him to pounce, to once again ask what she knew of the murder. She'd hoped he wouldn't, that he wouldn't mar the moment—the odd sense of ease, of shared purpose, that seemed to be growing between them. To her considerable surprise, he'd walked her to the garden gate, held it open, and let her escape with nothing more than a simple good-bye.

Perhaps he, too, hadn't wanted to disturb the closeness that had enveloped them in Horatio's garden. His garden now.

She watched him weave through the other guests. That sense of closeness puzzled and intrigued her. Lifting her head, she considered the other gentlemen—all her prospective suitors and the others from the village—all men she'd known most of her life; the exercise only emphasized the oddity. She'd known Lucifer for a handful of days, yet she felt more comfortable with him, less inhibited, infinitely freer to be herself. With him she could be open, could speak her mind without any mask, any concession to society. That he saw through her mask had certainly contributed to that, but it wasn't the whole explanation.

Jonas was the only other person she felt that comfortable with, yet not by the wildest stretch of her imagination could she equate the way she reacted to Lucifer with her all but nonreaction to her twin. Jonas was simply there, like some male version of herself. She never wasted a moment wondering what Jonas was thinking—she simply knew.

She also never worried about Jonas—he could take care of himself. Lucifer was similarly capable. The same could not be said of anyone else in the room. Perhaps it was that—that she considered Lucifer an equal—that made her feel so at ease with him?

Inwardly shaking her head, she watched him prowl the room. Sometimes she could tell what he was thinking; at other times—like in the garden this morning—the workings of his mind became a mystery, one she itched to solve. Regardless of the danger she knew that might entail.

Putting out a hand, Mrs. Farthingale stopped him. He paused, smiling easily, exchanged some glib quip that had her laughing, then smoothly moved on. As far as Phyllida could tell, his sights were set on Pommeroy.

She left him to it, turning to greet Basil as he strolled to her side.

"Well." Taking a position beside her, Basil scanned the room. "There are some who are now wishing they'd been more regular in their devotions."

"Oh?"

"I overheard Cedric speaking with Mr. Cynster—they were discussing estate management and Cedric mentioned he'd started using Sunday mornings to tackle his accounts."

"Cedric wasn't at church last Sunday?"

Basil shook his head. His gaze shifted to Lucifer. "I have to say, I'm quite impressed with Cynster. I suspect he's gathering information as to who might have killed Horatio. Thankless task, of course, but his devotion does him credit. Most would accept the inheritance and let be. Nothing to do with him, after all."

Phyllida viewed Lucifer with increasing appreciation. It had never occurred to her that he wouldn't pursue the murderer, yet Basil was right. Most men would have shrugged and let be. Indeed, she suspected Basil would have shrugged and let be, and Basil was the most morally upright of her suitors.

At no time had she doubted Lucifer's resolve. He'd called Horatio friend and she'd known without question that he valued friendship highly. He was that sort of man—an honorable man.

Inwardly, she grimaced. She wasn't, to her mind, acting honorably at present—she was caught on the prongs of an honor-induced dilemma, damned if she did and damned if she didn't.

"Is Lady Huddlesford planning a long stay?"

Phyllida replied; conversing with Basil was always stultifying, given there was no chance of any challenging surprise. Mundane topics were Basil's specialty, but at least he was innocuous.

That changed when Cedric came charging up, much in the manner of a lowering bull. His short neck contributed to the unflattering image.

"I say, come and talk to Mama." Cedric grasped her elbow. "She's on the *chaise*."

Phyllida stood her ground despite his tug. "Did Lady Fortemain ask to speak with me?"

Cedric's face darkened. "No, but she's always pleased to speak with you."

"I daresay." Basil's expression turned as haughty as his sister's. "Miss Tallent, however, might prefer to converse with someone who actually wishes to converse with her."

Miss Tallent would prefer an empty room. Phyllida swallowed the words. "Cedric, what were you doing last Sunday morning?"

Cedric blinked at her. "Sunday? While Horatio was being murdered?"

"Yes." Phyllida waited. Cedric responded well to directness. Subtlety was entirely beyond him.

He glanced at Basil, then back at her. "I was doing the accounts." He paused, then added, "In the library."

"So you were in the library at Ballyclose all morning?"

He nodded, his gaze straying to Basil. "From before Mama left until after she got home."

Phyllida artfully sighed. "So you couldn't have seen anything."

"Seen what?"

"Why, whatever there was to be seen. The murderer must have slipped away somehow." She glanced at Basil. "You were in church." She looked from one to the other. "Of course, you do both hire laborers who might have been out and about—or their children. Papa would be very grateful for any information."

"I hadn't considered that." Basil drew himself up. "I'll ask around tomorrow."

"So will I," Cedric growled.

"If you'll excuse me, I must have a word with Mary Anne." Phyllida left Basil and Cedric scowling at each other. If any of their farm workers had seen anything useful, she could be assured they would learn of it and come to lay the information at her feet.

She'd glimpsed Mary Anne and definitely wanted to speak to her, but Mary Anne didn't want to be spoken to. Short of chasing her around the room, there was nothing Phyllida could do. Robert had returned to Exeter. Halting, she considered the crowd, wondering who else she might conscript. Would anything be gained by enlisting the ladies of the village?

"Miss Tallent. I've been waiting for an opportunity to speak with you."

Whirling, Phyllida came face-to-face with Henry Grisby. "Good evening, Mr. Grisby." She inwardly sighed; she'd managed to avoid him thus far.

Henry bowed. "My mother sends her greetings. She heard about the recipe for gooseberry tart that you gave the Misses Longdon. Mama wondered if you'd be so kind as to share the recipe with her."

"Of course." Phyllida added it to her mental list. Recipe for cough syrup for Mrs. Farthingale; speak to Betsy Miller, one of Cedric's tenants who Lady Fortemain believed was having difficulties; recipe for Mrs. Grisby; letters for Mary Anne; one murderer for Lucifer.

Henry tried to catch her eye. "My mother would be deeply honored if you would call at Dottswood."

Phyllida looked at him. Henry's eyes met hers, then slid away. "I don't think that would be appropriate, Henry." *He* would be deeply honored; Mrs. Grisby would not.

He regarded her challengingly. "You call at Ballyclose and Highgate."

"To visit with Lady Fortemain and old Mrs. Smollet, both of whom have known me from the cradle."

"My mother's lived here all your life, too."

"Yes, but ..." Phyllida searched for a polite way to point out that Mrs. Grisby, at present, was not pleased with her. Mrs. Grisby, who rarely ventured beyond Dottswood Farm and therefore relied on Henry for her view of village life, was intractably opposed to Phyllida marrying Henry. Being Henry's mother, it had not occurred to her that Phyllida was of a similar mind. In the end, Phyllida simply looked Henry in the eye and said, "You know perfectly well your mother would not be pleased if I called."

"She would be pleased if you accepted my proposal."

Another lie. "Henry—"

"No—listen. You're twenty-four. It's a good age for a woman to marry—"

"My cousin informed me just yesterday that at twenty-four, I was firmly on the shelf." Percy might as well be useful for something.

Henry scowled. "He's got rocks in his head."

"The pertinent point you fail to grasp, Henry—you and Cedric and Basil, too—is that I intend to cling to my shelf for all I am worth. I like it there. I am not going to marry you or Cedric or Basil. If you could all regard me as an old maid, it would simplify matters considerably."

"That's nonsense."

Phyllida sighed. "Never mind. I'm prepared to wait you out."

"Ah, Mr. Grisby."

Phyllida turned to find Lucifer almost upon them. His dark blue eyes met hers; a rush of prickling warmth washed over her skin. Halting beside her, he looked at Grisby and smiled—like a leopard eyeing his next meal. "I understand," he purred, "that you've been agisting on some of the Manor's fields."

It was clear Henry would have preferred to scowl; instead, he nodded stiffly. "I keep part of my herd on some of the higher fields."

"The fields overlooking the river meadows? I see. Tell me, how often do you shift the herd?"

Despite Henry's resistance, Lucifer extracted the information that Henry's herds had been rotated last on Saturday; on Sunday, both Henry and his herdsman had worked in his barns. The questions were sufficiently oblique that Henry didn't recognize their intent.

He still glowered; he had not expressed any great joy at the news that Lucifer was to join their small community.

Henry's visual daggers bounced harmlessly off Lucifer's charm. He glanced at her. "I wonder, Miss Tallent, if I might avail myself of your understanding of the village. A small matter of traditions." He looked at Henry. "I'm sure Mr. Grisby will excuse us."

Left with no choice, Henry gave an exceedingly stiff bow and pressed her fingers too fervently. Phyllida tugged her hand free and placed it on Lucifer's sleeve. He led her away, strolling easily. She glanced up at him. "On what subject did you wish to ask my advice?"

He smiled down at her. "That was a ruse to whisk you away from Grisby."

Phyllida wondered if she should frown. "Why?"

He stopped before the French doors that opened to the terrace. "I thought you might be in need of some fresh air."

He was right; the night air outside was wonderfully balmy, warm against her skin. The terraces at Ballyclose were handsome and wide; they ran around three sides of the house. Lucifer and Phyllida strolled through the twilight.

"Are there many who were not at church last Sunday?" she asked.

"More than I'd expected. Coombe, Cedric, Appleby, Farthingale, and Grisby, and they're just the ones here tonight. If I included those not of the gentry, the list would be longer, but I'm concentrating on Horatio's peers."

"Because whoever it was struck from so close to him?"

"Precisely. More likely someone he regarded at least as an acquaintance."

"Why were you after Pommeroy? I thought he accompanied Lady Fortemain to church."

"He did. I wanted to ask if he'd spoken to Cedric or Appleby when he returned. It seems they were both out."

"Out?" Phyllida slowed. She looked at Lucifer.

He raised a brow. "What?"

Phyllida halted. "I suggested Cedric and Basil ask their farm workers if they'd seen anyone—meaning the murderer—about on Sunday morning."

"An excellent notion."

"Yes, but while discussing last Sunday, Cedric stated quite definitely that he'd been in the library all morning and was there when his mother returned."

Lucifer looked into her eyes, then shrugged. "Both Cedric and Pommeroy could be telling the truth. Cedric could have left after he heard his mother return, but before Pommeroy went looking for him."

Relieved, Phyllida nodded. "Yes, of course."

They started strolling again, then Lucifer asked, "What's the name of the head groom here?"

A knot of suspicion pulled tight in Phyllida's chest. But he was right—they had to be sure it wasn't Cedric. "Todd. He'd know if Cedric had taken a horse out."

"I'll speak to him—perhaps tomorrow."

Phyllida said nothing. The seriousness of the murder seemed to be growing. How terrible for the village if the murderer was one of them.

How horrible if that suspicion firmed, but they never learned who.

"You're very determined to find Horatio's murderer."

"Yes."

One word, no embellishments. It didn't need any. "Why?" She didn't look at him, but continued to stroll.

"You heard me explain it to your father."

"I know what you told Papa." She walked a few more paces before she said, "I don't think that's all your reason."

His gaze slid over her face, sharp, not amused. "You're an exceedingly persistent female."

"If your middle name is Temptation, then mine is Persistence."

He laughed; the sound tugged at something inside her.

"All right." He halted and looked down at her. She raised a brow at him, then turned to pace back toward the drawing room. He fell in beside her. "I'm not sure I can explain it simply. Not in a way that'll sound rational to you. But it's as if Horatio was mine—part of me—certainly under my protection, even if that wasn't actually so. His murder is as if someone has taken something from me by force." He paused, then went on. "My ancestors conquered this country—perhaps it's some primitive streak that hasn't fully died. But if anyone dared take one of theirs, vengeance, justice, would have been guaranteed."

After a moment, he glanced at her. "Does that make any sense?"

Phyllida arched a brow. "It makes perfect sense." His ancestors might have conquered the land, but hers had civilized it. Horatio's murder violated her code in precisely the same way it offended his. She understood his feelings perfectly—indeed, she shared them.

She halted. For a moment, she stared straight ahead, then she drew in a deep breath. "There's something I must tell you." She turned to him—

"*There* you are, Mr. Cynster!"

Jocasta Smollet swept up to them, flashing stiff silks and feathers. "We were all wondering where you'd disappeared to. So naughty of Phyllida to monopolize your time."

That last was said with open spite. Phyllida silently sighed. "We were about to return inside—"

"No, no! So much more pleasant out here, don't you agree, Miss Longdon?" Jocasta turned to the French doors as the Longdon sisters stepped through, followed by Mrs. Farthingale and Pommeroy. Others joined them, milling about, exclaiming at the pleasantness of the evening.

Phyllida shot a glance at Lucifer; he caught it. *Later?* was what his look said.

Almost imperceptibly, she nodded; it didn't really matter if she told him tonight or tomorrow.

She was threading through the guests, wondering where her father was, when someone grabbed her sleeve and unceremoniously tugged.

"Please, Phyllida, *please*! Say you've found them."

Phyllida turned, and watched Mary Anne's face crumble.

"You haven't, have you?"

Taking Mary Anne's arm, Phyllida drew her into the shadows by the house. "Why *are* you in such a panic? They're just *letters*. I know you've worked yourself into a pelter over them, but truly, nothing terrible will come of it even if someone else discovers them before I do."

Mary Anne swallowed. "You only say that because you don't know what's in them."

Phyllida opened her eyes wide and waited. She couldn't be sure, but she thought Mary Anne blushed.

"I ... I can't tell you. I really truly can't. But"—she was suddenly talking so fast she tripped over her words—"I've had the most *horrendous* thought." She grabbed Phyllida's hands. "If Mr. Cynster finds them, he'll give them to Mr. Crabbs!"

"Why would he do that?"

"Mr. Crabbs is his solicitor—he knows him!"

"Yes, but—"

"And even if he only gives them to Papa, now Papa will show them to Mr. Crabbs—they met at the Grange last evening. You *know* Papa would do *anything* to stop Robert from marrying me!"

Phyllida couldn't argue with that, but ..."I still don't see why—"

"If Mr. Crabbs reads the letters, he'll expel Robert from the firm! If Robert doesn't complete his registration, we'll *never* be able to get married!"

Phyllida started to get an inkling of what might be in the letters. She wished she could reassure Mary Anne that it really wasn't that serious—not compared to murder. Unfortunately, she wasn't sure herself just how damning the revelations might be—not to Mr. Crabbs.

Mary Anne tried to shake her. "You have to get the letters back!"

Phyllida focused on her face, on the huge eyes overflowing with so much panic it was evident even in the gloom. "All right. I will. But I haven't even seen the desk yet. It's not downstairs anywhere, so I'll have to wait for a time when the upper floors are clear."

Mary Anne drew back, making a heroic effort to reassemble her previous, subdued expression. "You won't tell anyone, will you? I don't think I could *bear* it if I couldn't marry Robert."

Phyllida hesitated; Mary Anne's eyes widened. Phyllida sighed. "I won't tell."

Mary Anne's lips lifted in a pathetically weak smile. "Thank you." She hugged Phyllida. "You're such a good friend."

CHAPTER
Eight

"What was it you wanted to tell me?" Lucifer glanced at Phyllida, perched beside him on his curricle's box seat. "When we were talking on the terrace last night."

They were on the road to Chard, his blacks pacing eagerly, a picnic hamper in the boot. He'd called at the Grange midmorning and without much difficulty prevailed upon Phyllida to join him on his investigative excursion.

He'd given her a few miles to broach the subject, but she hadn't.

The breeze flicked her bonnet ribbons as she glanced his way, giving him the barest glimpse of her face. "The terrace?"

Her tone suggested she couldn't recall the moment. "You *said* there was something I should know."

His tone stated he wouldn't forget.

After a moment of tense silence, she lifted her chin. "I have it now. I wanted to tell you that I feel just as strongly over unmasking Horatio's murderer as you do, and that you may count on me for whatever aid I can give."

He narrowed his gaze on the sliver of pale cheek that was all he could see beneath her bonnet rim. Eventually she glanced up, avoiding his gaze. There was nothing to be read in her calm expression. Bowling along with the blacks in an exuberant mood and his hands consequently full, his chances of forcing her to meet his eyes were slight.

He eyed her bonnet with increasing distaste. "I already knew you want to catch Horatio's murderer, and I fully intend to call on you for assistance. I'm doing precisely that at this moment."

He got another fleeting glance. "By taking me along so I can help question the stable masters?"

"And anyone else you can think of."

"Hmm." She sounded mollified, although he couldn't think why.

Who had invented poke bonnets? Any reasonably tall gentleman had the devil of a time seeing a lady's face when she was sitting or standing next to him wearing one.

He glanced at her again. She was surveying the fields and hedgerows, transparently enjoying the outing. He doubted Cedric or Basil, much less Grisby, had thought to squire her about, to woo her. More fool they.

His thoughts returned to the previous evening. Damn Jocasta Smollet. She'd interrupted at precisely the wrong moment. Jocasta clearly harbored some deep antipathy toward Phyllida, although no one, not even Basil, seemed to know why. But Jocasta had achieved what she'd wanted. She'd clung to his side for the rest of the evening; he'd lost sight of Phyllida when the crowd had invaded the terrace.

He'd seen her briefly in the hall as they'd all prepared to depart; she'd given no indication of having any burning information to convey to him.

He hadn't imagined that moment on the terrace. She'd been about to entrust him with the truth. Something had happened to change her mind, yet she hadn't retreated from trusting him. He tried to imagine what could hold enough power to prevent a woman like her from doing something he was increasingly sure she felt she should. She wanted to tell him, but …What was it that had stopped her?

The question went round and round in his mind but found no ready answer.

Chard appeared before them. They'd driven straight through Axminster and made for the larger town.

Phyllida straightened as they passed the first houses. "There's three stables here. Perhaps we should start at the one furthest north?"

They did. No gentleman had hired a horse on the Saturday or Sunday in question. No unknown gentleman had stayed at the inn. They drove back into the town. The other two stables were off the main street. After receiving negative answers at the Blue Dragon, they left the curricle there, the blacks resting, and strolled to the Black Swan.

"Nah!" The innkeeper shook his head. "We got two nags, but there's rarely much call for 'em. Later in summer, p'r'aps, but right now we haven't hired a horse to any gen'leman for months."

In answer to their second question, he opened his eyes wide. "Ain't *seen* any gen'leman—nought but the locals—not for weeks."

As they stepped outside, Phyllida murmured, "We don't get many visitors down here."

"Which means any visitor would have been noted." Taking her arm, Lucifer turned her toward the Dragon. "I think we can conclude no visitor used Chard as a base."

They strolled along; Phyllida halted when they reached the Dragon. "This hasn't taken us long. If we drive back and check at Axminster, and then drive down to Axmouth and check there, then if no one's seen any unknown gentleman about … well, it really leaves few options."

"Honiton, perhaps."

"Perhaps. But why would anyone come from that direction?"

"I understand the tendency to imagine any nefarious wrongdoers essay forth from London. That isn't, however, necessarily true."

"Is it likely the person who killed Horatio came from Honiton or Exeter—from somewhere to the west?"

Lucifer fell silent. Phyllida watched him. "Well?"

He refocused. "I was trying to recall if any collectors, or anyone connected with collecting, lived out that way."

"And?"

"I'd have to agree that if the murderer rode in from beyond the village last Sunday, then they probably came from the east. Nevertheless, we'll need to check Honiton, but we can do that some other day." Looking up, he saw a dapper little man hurrying across the street, flourishing a piece of paper to attract their attention. "Who's this?"

Phyllida turned. "Mr. Curtiss—he's the merchant the Colyton Import Company deals with."

Mr. Curtiss reached them; he nodded politely to Lucifer, then beamed at Phyllida. "Miss Tallent—well met! I wanted to send this"—he held out a letter—"to Mr. Filing. My customers have been very pleased with the quality of goods Mr. Filing's company provides. So rare to find quality one can rely on. I've decided to increase our order. With word getting around, I'm sure I can sell more. If I could presume—I know you assist Mr. Filing—could you see this missive reaches him?"

Smiling serenely, Phyllida took the letter. "Of course, Mr. Filing will be thrilled." She tucked the letter into her reticule.

Mr. Curtiss bowed. "A pleasure, my dear. Do convey my best wishes to Sir Jasper."

"I will, indeed."

With a nod to Lucifer, Mr. Curtiss, still beaming, withdrew.

"Mr. Filing's company?" Lucifer asked as they entered the Dragon's courtyard and headed for the curricle.

Phyllida unfurled her parasol. "Of course. No mere female could operate an import company."

Lucifer smiled. "Naturally not."

He handed her into the curricle. Minutes later, they were bowling back toward Axminster. "Tell me—just so I don't inadvertently cause a problem. Am I right in assuming no one other than those involved knows of your involvement in the Company?"

"Of course not. There's no reason for others to know. In fact, not all of the men know—most think Filing runs it and I'm just his amanuensis. I'm not *sure* how much Papa understands …"

He could imagine. She was the linchpin, the person around whom all else revolved, yet she preferred anonymity. Her tone, subtly amused, said as much.

Her role, however, extended much further than the company. He'd been in Colyton only a few days, yet he'd lost count of the times he'd seen someone—man, woman, even child—approach Phyllida with some request.

He'd never seen her turn anyone down.

The impulse to watch over people, to be actively involved, doing, helping, was one he understood. In his case, it derived from *noblesse oblige*—part learned, part inherited, part instinctive. Phyllida's impulse was, he suspected, wholly instinctive. Wholly giving. He was, however, getting the distinct impression that the village took her—and her help—for granted. "How long have you been ruling the roost at the Grange?"

The glance she slanted him was sharp. "Since my mother died."

Twelve years? No wonder her influence was so pervasive. She waited, but he said nothing more, content to drive through the sunshine with her beside him. And to consider …

Her impulse to help him would lead her to tell him whatever she knew soon enough. She was too intelligent to hold back information that would allow a killer to run loose; he accepted that she did not know the murderer's identity. She had a clue, nothing more; the best way forward was to continue his inquiries and keep her closely involved. Ironically, the less he learned, the more she'd feel compelled to resolve whatever matter was preventing her from being open with him, and to tell him all she knew.

That was how to proceed on that front. For the rest, now that he'd committed to residing in Colyton …

He had a house—one too large for just him. It was a family house—a family was what it needed. That was what Horatio would have envisioned. *He* certainly hadn't envisioned a family, not before he'd come to Colyton. But now he was here, and Horatio was gone, but the Manor still stood along with its garden.

The outlying houses of Axminster appeared—a welcome distraction. They were thorough in their inquiries, but, as they'd assumed, no gentleman visitor had ridden through or driven through Axminster on Sunday morning.

" 'Cept for you." The grizzled veteran slouching outside the small inn eyed him suspiciously.

Lucifer grinned. "Quite. I drove through that morning. But you're sure no one else was before me?"

A quick shake of the head. "Don't get that many carriages or horsemen going south of a Sunday. I'da noticed. And I was here from first light."

Lucifer nodded and tossed him a coin. The man caught it deftly and bowed to them both.

Phyllida led the way back to the curricle. "Where now?" he asked as he lifted her up.

"South. To the coast."

She directed him down a road; a mile or so south, a river came into view, winding along to their right.

"Is that the Axe?" When she nodded, he asked, "Are those my fields on the other side?"

"Not yet, but a little further and they will be."

They rattled through the early afternoon, the lush green of the river valley about them. The sun was screened by light clouds; it was warm but not hot.

The first intimation that the coast was near was a cool breeze. They rounded a curve—at a crossroads before them stood an old inn.

Phyllida pointed to the left. "That's the road to Lyme Regis. If anyone came past from Lyme on Sunday morning, the children would have noticed."

"Children?"

A tribe ranging in age from about twelve to two, mostly girls. He left the questioning to Phyllida, content to lean against a stone wall and watch.

The innkeeper's wife had looked out at the sound of their wheels on the cobbles. She recognized Phyllida and came forward, beaming, wiping her hands on her apron. Without waiting for assistance, Phyllida jumped down. In seconds, she and the woman were discussing what sounded like the recipe for some poultice.

The innkeeper stuck his head out; Lucifer waved him away, tied the blacks to the rail, then settled to observe.

Laughing, Phyllida gestured to an opening in the worn stone wall. The woman nodded and smiled; together, she and Phyllida strolled through. Lucifer trailed after them. Stopping in the gap, he leaned against the wall.

Beyond lay the remnants of a garden, stunted by the sea breeze whipping across the open fields. A vociferous crowd gathered around Phyllida, greeting her shrilly; she laughed, patted heads, tweaked braids. Then she sat on a stone bench in the sun and the children pressed around her.

He couldn't hear what she asked, how they answered. He didn't bother trying to hear. Instead, he drank in the sight of Phyllida with the children like fairies surrounding their queen, all eager for her blessing.

She gave it unstintingly with smiles, laughter, and an effortless understanding. With sincere interest and a deep caring. It glowed—in her eyes, like an aura all about her. The children, the woman, basked and drew it in; Phyllida simply gave.

He was sure she didn't realize—she certainly didn't realize how much he could see.

Finally, after much teasing, she stood and the children, made to mind by their mother, let her go. She strolled toward him, still smiling softly, her gaze on the path. As she neared, she looked up. He kept his expression impassive. "Did they see anyone?"

She shook her head. Looking back, she waved, then, side by side, they headed for the curricle.

"They were out on Sunday morning. It was glorious weather, if you recall. They play out there most of the time. The chances of anyone slipping by and being missed by all those sharp eyes ..."

He handed her up to the seat. "So we've accomplished what we set out to do—we've confirmed no visitor, no one from outside, rode into Colyton on Sunday, at least not from the east."

Phyllida was silent as he set the blacks in motion and turned them out onto the road. "Now where? I'm ravenous. We need a place to do justice to Mrs. Hemmings's picnic."

She pointed south. "Down to the coast. It's wonderful on the cliffs."

The road took them down through the village of Axmouth, then wound up onto the cliffs. She directed him along a rutted track that led to a stand of scrubby trees. "We can leave the horses here. It's not much further."

Carrying the basket, he followed her onto the windswept cliff. The view was magnificent. He stopped to drink in the majestic sweep of the cliffs westward. The Axe spilled into the sea virtually at their feet, distance miniaturizing the houses of Axmouth. The estuary itself was peaceful, but beyond the breakers the Channel swell ruled, surging powerfully.

The gray-green sea stretched to the horizon; the cliffs dominated on either side. Phyllida stood watching a little way ahead; when his gaze reached her, she smiled and beckoned with her head. She led the way around a hillock; a patch of grass lay protected by the hillock, large boulders, and trees. It was a pretty spot, partly sheltered yet still open, still blessed with panoramic views.

"Jonas and I found this place when we were children." Phyllida drew the rug from the basket, then spread it on the grass. As she straightened, Lucifer's hand appeared before her. She hesitated, then put her fingers in his and let him hand her down to the rug. He placed the basket beside her. She busied herself unpacking and arranging their feast.

He lounged on the other side of the basket and reached for the bottle wrapped in a white napkin. Sliding it free, he rummaged for the glasses. When she finished laying out their repast, he had a glass ready to hand to her.

"To summer."

She smiled and clinked glasses, then sipped. The wine slid down her throat, cold and refreshing; a tingle slithered down her spine. A whisper of anticipation echoed in her mind while a pleasurable warmth spread through her.

They ate. He seemed to know her needs before she did, offering her rolls, the chicken, pastries. At first, she felt unnerved; then she hid a self-deprecatory smile. He wasn't deliberately trying to rattle her—he wasn't even aware he was. Such attentions were simply second nature to him.

Not so to her. No other man treated her like that—ready with a steadying hand, a protective shoulder, not out of any intent to impress her but simply because she was she.

It was unnerving, and rather nice.

"Does the Colyton Import Company bring its goods ashore near here?"

She waved to the west. "There's a path to the beach a little way along. It's easy to find; there's a knoll beside it. If we need to light a beacon, we put it up there."

"How dangerous is it along this stretch?"

"Not too bad if you know it. But there are reefs close."

"So the Colyton men go out and bring the goods in?"

"They've been sailing these waters since they could stand. There's very little risk for them."

She repacked the basket. The wind was freshening, tugging at napkins, but it was still pleasant beneath the screened sun. She'd left her parasol in the curricle and was glad she had. She couldn't have used it in this wind.

With everything returned to the basket, she stood. The wind frolicked about her face, flirting with her hair, teasing the ribbons of her bonnet. Lifting her face, she drew in a deep breath, then wrapped her arms about her. She'd worn a lilac cambric carriage dress, normally perfectly adequate in this weather, but here the wind rushed at her, sliding chill fingers through the fabric and along her body.

Beside her, Lucifer uncoiled his long length and stood.

She shivered.

An instant later, warmth fell around her; his coat settled over her shoulders. "Oh—" She half turned. He'd sidestepped the basket and now stood just behind her. She met his gaze briefly and prayed her reaction didn't show. She managed a small smile. "Thank you."

His body heat was trapped in the fabric; it slid like a warm hand down her spine. She turned further toward him. "I'm really not that cold. You'll freeze without your coat."

Before she could slide out of it, he caught the lapels and drew the coat more firmly around her. "I'm not cold."

Taking a firm hold of her wits, she looked up, into his eyes. "Are you sure?"

Even as the words left her lips, she sensed the answer. She couldn't have missed it—his hard body was near enough to feel his heat, the all-too-tempting warmth. The wind pushed her, urging her into it. Into his arms.

His eyes, intensely blue, searched hers; his lips kicked up at the ends. "Why," he murmured, his hands sliding from between them, his head bending nearer, "do you think they call me Lucifer?"

If she'd been wise, she'd have stepped smartly back and told him she had no idea. Instead, she stood still, face tilted up, and let his lips settle on hers.

The kiss was pure heat—a source of wonderful warmth. It spread through her; she could almost believe she was thawing—nerves stretching, unfurling, luxuriating. The kiss teased, tantalized. She moved closer, drawn to him, needing to feel his chest solid against her breasts. They tingled, then ached, yet it wasn't with pain. His shirt was under her hands; she spread her fingers, feeling the fine fabric shift like a veil over hard muscle, over the roughness of hair; the flat disk of his nipple burned under her palm.

She felt that tempting power surge through him. She parted her lips and opened her mouth to him, and shuddered when he entered. So hot. She drank it in; she wanted more. She pressed her palms to his chest, pushed them up to his shoulders. Everywhere she touched was like a furnace, the steady pulsing heat of hot coals.

Her breasts were pressed to that heat; his hands had slipped beneath his coat and fastened about her waist. He held her tight against him, his thighs like granite columns on either side of hers. He was hard, ridged, rampant against her belly.

A wanton urge to shift her hips and caress that rampant hardness gripped her; in something near panic, she tamped it down, like putting out a fire. The flaring urge died; she sighed into his mouth and sank a little more against him.

He shifted, one hand rising to her throat. She felt a tug—he was pulling at her bonnet ribbons. She drew back from the kiss—the bow under her chin unraveled—

"Oh!" She grabbed at her hat as the wind whipped it from her head. She whirled and caught it.

Her feet twisted in the rug; she tipped backward, stumbled, and crashed into Lucifer. He caught her, tried to steady her, took a step back—

They tumbled over the picnic basket, large and solid in the middle of the rug. Lucifer ended sitting behind it with her in his lap. Shaking with laughter. Swinging his legs free of the basket, he lifted her—and turned her and sat her back in his lap.

He grinned at her. "We seem to be making a habit of landing on the ground with you on top of me."

She blushed. She should definitely have made every effort to struggle free, to escape from his arms and stand up. Safe. Instead, she sat there, warm to the core, her gaze fastened on his lips, a mere inch in front of her nose.

"Here—let me have that." He tugged her bonnet from her nerveless fingers; bemused, she watched as, reaching around her, he tied the ribbons around the basket's handle. "Now you won't worry about losing it."

He was a man who definitely understood women.

He straightened, his gaze fastening on her lips. He bent his head, fingertips sliding across the sensitive skin beneath her chin. She swallowed. "I'm not sure this is a good idea."

"Why not?" His lips brushed hers lightly—too lightly to satisfy the hunger welling inside her.

"I don't know." She couldn't drag her gaze from his lips.

They murmured, "Do you trust me?"

Her heart was pounding in her ears. Her lungs were so tight she couldn't breathe. She couldn't think, but she knew the answer. "Yes."

His lips lifted. "Then relax." They closed the distance and brushed hers; his voice was a whisper in her mind. "And let me show you what you want to know."

It was easy, so easy to do just that, to give him her mouth, to let herself flow, boneless in his arms. They held her, but not tightly. She felt cradled, protected, cared for.

Worshipped.

The thought floated through her mind as his fingers gently trailed her cheek. The touch was as wondering as hers had ever been; she suddenly understood how he had known it had been she who had touched him in Horatio's drawing room. She'd never forget his touch, either—it was such a revealing, oddly innocent, gesture.

His fingers drifted lower and he framed her jaw, his tongue surging boldly. Not innocent at all. She met him, knowing now what he wanted, what he liked. A dangerous knowing—so tempting to use it, to learn a little more. Her hands lay passive against his chest—she pushed them up, over his shoulders, fingers spreading over the powerful muscles, then sliding further to tangle in his hair.

It was soft, silky, black as a night sky. She sank her fingers into the thick locks, holding tight as he slowly, unhurriedly, plundered her mouth, taking, certainly, but giving more.

Addictive. Another word that drifted through her mind. It had to be that— the sweetest craving—that held her to the kiss even when he released her jaw.

Forbidden—he was surely that. She shouldn't be kissing him at all, yet the idea of stopping seemed totally foolish, something she never was. His fingers trailed, just the tips tracing tantalizingly down her throat, tightening nerves she hadn't known she possessed. His fingers trailed on, lower; flames followed, heat spread.

Her breast was swollen long before he touched it; once he had, she didn't want him to stop. His touch was light, excruciatingly insubstantial—she wanted more, much more.

Experienced—thank heavens he was that. His hand settled, hard palm cupping the weight of her breast. Delight was all she felt as his fingers firmed, then eased. His hand shifted, caressed. She sighed into their kiss and sensed his satisfaction, felt the hand at her back firm.

The kiss grew more demanding, a fire that needed tending. She gave it her full attention, only dimly aware when the warmth of his hand about her breast slid away.

Need was growing within her, but for what she didn't know. The compulsion was not one she recognized. Then she felt the top button of her bodice give, and knew. A thrill of pure excitement raced through her. That was what she needed—a scandalous need, assuredly, yet ... her breasts were swollen, aching with the heat of their kiss. Her wits were awash on the swelling tide that lapped about them. A languorous thing, it whispered promises of things she'd never known, of pleasure beyond imagining.

The touch of cool air on her breasts, the light tracing of his fingers as he brushed her bodice wide, drew her from the mesmerizing warmth of their kiss. She should stop him, she knew it, yet ... she couldn't recall why. There was no threat, no danger—he'd told her to trust him and she did. If she wanted this to end, wanted to bring the simple pleasure to a halt, she only had to say.

She didn't say—she had no reason to. She wanted to know, to feel, to be touched and savored. Just once to be a woman desired.

He gave her what she wanted, that and much more.

She hadn't known that his lips would feel like that, there. That the hot wetness of his mouth could scald her so and rip her wits away. Hadn't known that her body could grow so hot and heavy, so wanton with desire.

It was desire that thrummed through her, that pounded in her blood, that rose to every touch, every tantalizing caress. His lightest touch was sharp delight; more explicit caresses left her senses reeling. Heated pleasure was what he conjured; purposely, he wrapped her in it, pressed it upon her, and let it sink into her.

Until she was filled with it, until her mind rode on the warm waves and her body was melting.

His lips returned to hers, and she welcomed him back. His hand closed possessively about her naked breast and her body sang.

He drew back from the kiss, just enough to look down at her. He studied his hand, firm and still about her breast; her flesh filled and heated even more. His gaze lifted to rove her face, her eyes. He glanced past her.

His gaze steadied, fixed beyond her. Then he blinked; she saw his eyes widen and alter focus, saw his features harden. She felt the changing tension in his body.

Lucifer looked back at her—and tried to think. Tried to breathe past the tightness in his chest. She lay relaxed in his arms, her nipple furled between his fingers, her skin hot silk against his palm. He felt dazed. Rational thought had left him long ago; desire rode him—potent temptation flicked a whip.

He knew what he wanted, the need sharp as spurs, as clamorous as any demon.

A tempest was bearing down on them, racing over the sea, piling thunderheads before it, yet looking into her eyes, drowning dark beneath heavy lids, with her body supple and heated in his arms, he wasn't sure in which direction danger lay.

It had been a long, long time since he'd surrendered so completely that he'd lost all sense of self-protection.

Stifling a curse, he bent his head and kissed her, passion-deep, fire-hot. He closed his hand over her breast, fingers kneading, tightening … then easing. He drew back—from the kiss, from the caress, his fingers reluctantly leaving her. He brushed a last kiss to her lips as he drew her bodice closed.

Her eyes blinked wide, revealing surprise … disappointment.

Features setting grimly, he nodded out to sea. "There's a storm blowing in—we have to go back."

CHAPTER

Nine

L ate the next morning, Lucifer tramped through the wood behind the Manor and tried not to think about the previous day. He'd told Phyllida the truth; they'd had to go back, to retreat. He'd gone charging into unchartered terrain, far too fast for her, and much too fast for him.

Thank God for storms.

He'd started today with breakfast at a table too empty for his liking. He'd never lived alone; the solitary life did not suit him. He'd repaired to the library and started sorting through Horatio's desk. He'd spent two hours reading accumulated correspondence.

After that, he'd had to get out. Walking through the wood to explore the lay of his land all the way down to the Axe seemed a sensible, and sufficiently physical, exercise.

He felt like the energy of last night's storm was bottled up inside him.

The storm had brought rain; they'd gained Colyton in the teeth of a downpour. Although the sun was now out, the wood remained damp; the tang of rain-washed greenery rode the light breeze. He'd headed east from the rear of the stable block, leaving the lake on his left. The trees ahead thinned; he'd trudged for less than half a mile. Fifty paces more and he stood on the edge of a wide field, gently sloping down; beyond lay a lush meadow. Beyond that lay the Axe, a gray-blue ribbon glimmering in the sunshine.

He ambled down the sloping field. A flash of movement to his left caught his eye. He looked, then halted.

Phyllida was marching—no, *storming*—through his field. Her skirts frothed about her, whipped by the violence of her stride. Her gaze was fixed in front of her. Her dark hair gleamed. She held her poke bonnet in both hands.

She was mangling the bonnet, twisting it, hands clenched on the brim.

He stepped out to intercept her.

She didn't see him until he was almost upon her. She recoiled, eyes flaring, one hand rising to her breast. A squeak escaped her; it would have been a scream if she hadn't recognized him and smothered it. Gulping in a breath, she stared up at him through huge dark eyes.

"What's wrong?" He smothered an urge of his own—to haul her into his arms. "What happened?"

She dragged in another breath and looked at her bonnet. She was shaking. "Look!" She thrust her finger through a hole in the crown. "The ball just missed my *head*!"

Her tone made it clear she wasn't shaking with fear. She was shaking with fury. She whirled and looked back the way she'd come. "How *dare* they!" If both hands hadn't been clenched on the bonnet, she would probably have shaken her fist. "Stupid hunters!"

The words trembled; she bit them off and hiccuped.

Lucifer reached out and wrapped his hand around one of hers, tugging until she released the bonnet. He enveloped her small hand in his and drew her to face him.

Her expression was blank, not calm and serene but blank, as if she couldn't maintain her usual mask but was fighting not to let her feelings show. Her eyes, wide and dark, were turbulent, awash with emotions. Fear was there, very real; she was using her fury to counter it.

He drew her nearer still, until she stood close enough to feel his heat and the shield of his physical presence. She was wound tight, her control so brittlely fragile he didn't want to risk even putting an arm around her; she wouldn't thank him if she broke. "Where did it happen?"

She dropped her gaze to his chest, drew a tight breath, then gestured with her bonnet. "Back there. Two fields back." After a moment, she added, "I was returning from visiting old Mrs. Dewbridge—I go there every Friday."

A chill touched his spine. "*Every* Friday morning?"

She nodded.

His grip on her hand tightened; he forced himself to relax it. He looped her arm through his. "I want you to show me where."

He turned her back along the track, an old right-of-way. She resisted. "It's no use—they won't still be there."

"I know." He kept his tone calm, even; that wasn't how he felt, but it was what she needed. "I just want you to show me where you were. We won't go any further."

She hesitated, then nodded. "All right."

He guided her along and helped her over the stile. A sliver of blue fabric was caught in the crossbar where she'd ripped her gown in her haste.

Despite her fury, she'd been very frightened.

She still was.

They reached the boundary of the next field and she stopped. "I was there." She waved with her ruined bonnet. "Right in the middle of the field."

Lucifer held her hand and looked, gauging distances. "Can I have your bonnet?"

She handed it to him; he took it and raised it—there were *two* holes punched through the crown. Without a word, he handed it back. His face felt like stone. She'd glanced down at the critical moment; the ball had entered through the back of the bonnet just below the crown seam, then exited through the bonnet's top, on the other side of the seam. "Let me check your head."

"I didn't get hit," she grumbled, but she let him look.

Her hair lay like mahogany silk, sleek and undisturbed—no wound. He imagined the way her bonnet would sit, then touched his fingers to her hair. Grit, very fine, came away on the pads of his fingers. He sniffed them. Powder—the bullet had come that close.

He looked back at the field. The path didn't run directly across but angled away toward the river. "Did you hear anything? Glimpse anyone?"

"No, but ..." She lifted her head. "I ran. Silly, I know, but I just did."

Running might have saved her life. He said nothing, just drew a breath and held it until his violent reaction faded. She'd been walking this way; the only possible place of concealment was a copse on the far side of the field.

"I'll walk with you to the Grange."

The glance she shot him said she felt she should protest. Instead, after a moment's hesitation, she inclined her head and acquiesced.

Sir Jasper was out when they reached the Grange. Lucifer delivered Phyllida into Gladys's hands, making sure, despite Phyllida's dismissive remarks, that Gladys understood that her mistress had had a severe shock.

He left with Phyllida glaring at him; he didn't care. She was safe.

He strode back to the Manor via the wood, and was pleased to find Dodswell had arrived with the rest of his horses. Dodswell had paced the string well; they had enough in reserve to go for a quick gallop.

Taking Dodswell with him, he rode back to the copse. Dismounting at the edge of the field, they tethered their mounts while he told Dodswell what they were looking for.

They found it close by one side of the copse, the side screened from the walking track.

"Just the one horse." Dodswell examined the hoofprints in the rain-softened earth. "Nice, clean front shoes."

Lucifer stared at the ground farther back. "I can't find any impressions of the back hooves."

"Nah. That turf there's too thick, more's the pity."

Grimly, Lucifer nodded at the hoofprints they had found. "What do you make of them?"

"Decently looked-after horse, fresh shoes, no nicks or cracks, well-filed hooves."

"A gentleman's horse."

"A horse from a gentleman's stable, anyway." Dodswell studied Lucifer's face. "Why are we interested?"

Briefly, Lucifer told him of the horse that had stood at the back of the Manor's shrubbery. Told him who had a hole in her bonnet. He didn't tell him why.

"Wasn't no hunter. What would they be shooting at? No quail or skeet yet, and they'd be too far from the wood for pigeons. Rabbits won't be out at present." Grimfaced, Dodswell scanned the area. "Nothing here to shoot at."

Only one female given to solitary walks and addicted to doing good deeds by a regular schedule. Lucifer looked at the hoofprints and tried to ease the tension in his shoulders. "Let's get back. We've learned all we can here."

Bristleford was waiting when he walked into the front hall.

"Mr. Coombe has called, sir. I put him in the library."

"Thank you, Bristleford." Lucifer walked straight to the library door and opened it. Silas Coombe jumped back from one of the bookshelves, his hand raised. Lucifer would have wagered Horatio's entire collection that Coombe had been fingering the gold-encrusted spines. Face impassive, he nodded, shut the door, and stalked to the desk. "Gold leaf doesn't wear all that well—but then, you'd know that, wouldn't you."

He arched a brow at Coombe, who drew himself up and tugged at his waistcoat; its black-and-white horizontal stripes made him appear more rotund than he was.

"Oh, quite. Quite! I was just admiring the tooling." He approached the desk.

Waving him to a chair, Lucifer sank into the one behind the desk. "Now— to what do I owe this pleasure?"

Coombe sat, making a great show of settling his coattails. Then he looked at Lucifer. "Naturally, I feel Horatio's loss keenly. I daresay I'm one of the few hereabouts who truly appreciated his greatness."

A wave indicated the room about them; Lucifer was left in no doubt that in Coombe's eyes, Horatio's greatness had resided in his possessions. Coombe's gaze drifted along the shelves. "It must be quite puzzling to you that someone would spend his life gathering all these musty tomes. Such a fantastic number of them."

Lucifer kept his expression impassive. He'd told only Sir Jasper and Phyllida of his interest in collecting; clearly, neither had talked.

"Now, it may seem odd to you, but I've an interest in books myself, as you might have heard around the village. I'm viewed as quite the eccentric because of it, y'know."

"Indeed?"

"Yes, oh, yes. Now, to come to my point, I realize you'll want to be rid of these—doubtless you'll start clearing them soon. They take up such a great space. All through the ground floor and even, I daresay, abovestairs?"

Lucifer pretended not to hear the question.

"Yes, well." Coombe shifted, tugging at his coat. "That's where I believe I could help you."

He sat back and said nothing more. Lucifer was forced to ask, "How?"

Coombe leaned forward like a well-rehearsed puppet. "Oh, I couldn't take them all, of course! Dear me, no! But I would like to add just a few of

Horatio's books to my collection." He brightened. "In memorium, you might say. I'm sure Horatio would have wanted it that way."

Smiling, Coombe sat back again. "I'll just come and take a look at the books as you're packing them—I wouldn't want to inconvenience you."

"You won't." Lucifer tried to imagine Coombe with a knife in his hand. The picture wasn't convincing. If there was any man in the village liable to swoon at the sight of blood, he would have bet it was Coombe. Still, he hadn't been in church last Sunday. "I haven't thought about selling the books, but if I do, I'll probably call in an agent from London."

A frown creased Coombe's brow. "I hope that you'll agree, when the time comes, to grant me first refusal?"

Lucifer shrugged. "I'll have to see how things fall out. Some agents may not take the commission if they believe the juiciest plums have already been picked."

"Well, my word!" Coombe puffed like an agitated hen. "I must say, I think Horatio would have wanted me to have some of his gems."

"Is that so?" His dry tone had Coombe deflating. He held the man's gaze. "Unfortunately for you, Horatio is no longer here. I am." He rose and tugged the bellpull, then looked at Coombe. "If there's nothing else, I've a considerable amount of business awaiting my attention."

The door opened; Lucifer glanced up. "Ah, Bristleford—Mr. Coombe is leaving."

Coombe got to his feet, face mottling. But he drew himself up and bowed from the waist. "Good day, sir."

Lucifer inclined his head.

As Coombe neared the door, Lucifer signaled to Bristleford; Bristleford almost imperceptibly nodded, then ushered Coombe out and shut the door.

Lucifer was sorting correspondence when Bristleford returned.

"You wanted something, sir?"

"Send Covey to me."

"At once, sir."

Covey slipped into the room some minutes later. Lucifer sat back. "I've a job for you, Covey."

"Yes, sir?" Covey stopped before the desk, hands clasped before him.

Lucifer glanced at the bookshelves. "I want you to take a complete inventory of all Horatio's books."

"All of them?" Covey looked at the long, high bookshelves.

"Start in the drawing room, then in here, then in the other rooms. For every book I want the title, publisher, and date of publication, and I want you to check for inscriptions or page notes. If you find any notations, set those books aside and show them to me at the end of each day."

Covey squared his shoulders. "Indeed, sir." He was transparently pleased to be following orders again. "Shall I use a ledger for the list?"

Lucifer nodded. Collecting a fresh ledger and a pencil from a chest, Covey headed for the drawing room. Lucifer watched the door close; he sat back—leather squeaked.

The books he'd found misaligned in the drawing room—now he thought of it, they'd been tight in the shelf. They couldn't have accidentally slid forward.

Now Silas Coombe was requesting first dibs on Horatio's books. Could Coombe be the murderer?

Lucifer looked down at the pile of correspondence he'd stacked on the blotter. He had other questions, too, at present equally unanswerable.

What was it Horatio had wanted him to appraise?

And where on earth was it?

Late that evening, he stood looking out from his bedchamber window, watching the moonlight play over the common. He'd spent half the afternoon searching the house in the hope that something, some piece, would strike him as unfamiliar and unique enough to have been Horatio's mystery item. He'd learned the extent of his inheritance, but was no nearer to solving the mystery.

The house was a treasure trove, understated in its magnificence. Every piece had a history, had a value greater than its functional worth. Yet, as was common with many great collectors, Horatio's best items were used as they'd been designed to be used, not hidden away. So where was his mystery item? In full view? Or hidden away in some other item designed to provide a hiding place?

That was a possibility. Lucifer made a mental note to check.

Identifying the mystery item—possibly the reason Horatio had been killed—was only one of his problems. The most pressing, the most critical, was learning why some man, riding a horse that might well have been the same horse that had waited in the shrubbery while Horatio was killed, had attempted to kill Phyllida.

Lucifer rotated his shoulders, trying to ease the knots that had been there since late afternoon, when he'd gone back to the Grange to speak with Sir Jasper.

And Phyllida, of course, but she hadn't been there.

Not in the library, not in the drawing room, not lying on her bed prostrate with shock. The damned woman had ordered out the carriage and gone to visit some other deserving soul. At least she hadn't walked.

Of course, she'd been the first to Sir Jasper with the story—her version had stressed that it had been some misguided hunter; she had clearly downplayed her fright.

He'd tried to correct those impressions, but had been severely handicapped by two things. First, as Sir Jasper did not know of Phyllida's presence in Horatio's drawing room, he therefore had no reason to suppose Horatio's killer would have any interest in her. Without telling Sir Jasper all, without exposing Phyllida, there was no point making the connection between the horses, and without that, his ability to invest the situation with suitable gravity was severely compromised.

The second obstacle was the fact that Sir Jasper had been well trained to accept everything his daughter told him, at least about herself. With all that against him, shaking Sir Jasper out of his complacency and into a sufficiently protective frame of mind had been beyond him. All he'd managed was to convey his own deep unease over the shooting, and over Phyllida's safety in general.

Sir Jasper had smiled too knowingly and assured him that Phyllida could take care of herself.

Not against a murderer. He'd held the words back, but only just.

He'd stridden back through the wood in something perilously close to a temper; the emotion had converted to a nagging disquiet by the time he'd reached the Manor.

Gazing out at the moonlit common, he felt decidedly grim. Tomorrow, he'd find her—

A figure crossed the lane and started up the common.

Lucifer stared. He knew what he was seeing, but his brain refused to take it in. *"Damnation!* What in *Hades* does she think she's *doing?"*

Swinging on his heel, he went to get an answer.

She was standing on the side porch, ledger in hand, when he reached the church.

Phyllida saw him emerge from the shadows, large, dark, and menacing, like a god not at all pleased with a disciple. She lifted her chin and fixed him with a warning glance; Mr. Filing stood beside her.

"Mr. Cynster!" Filing shut his ledger.

"It's all right," she reassured him. "Mr. Cynster knows all about the Company and how we operate."

"Oh, well, then." Reopening his ledger, Filing smiled at Lucifer. "It's quite a little enterprise."

"So I understand." Lucifer didn't return the curate's smile. He stalked past Filing, circled her, and halted on her other side, hands on his hips, doing an excellent imitation of a disapproving deity. "What are you doing?"

He'd bent his head so his words fell by her ear in an angry rumble. She didn't look up. "I'm checking the goods against the bill of lading—see?" She demonstrated as Hugey lumbered up with a box. "Put that to the left of the Mellows' sarcophagus."

Hugey nodded circumspectly to the looming menace beside her and headed into the church.

Oscar took his place, eyeing Lucifer more directly. She felt forced to introduce them. Oscar bobbed his head, his arms locked around a small tun.

Lucifer nodded. "You're Thompson's brother, I hear."

"Aye, that be right." Oscar grinned, pleased to have been known. "Hear tell you've decided to make Colyton your home."

"Yes. I don't plan to leave."

Bent over her ledger, Phyllida pretended not to hear. Oscar shuffled on to be replaced by Marsh. He coughed and she had to introduce him, too. Before the night's cargo was stored, all the men had been introduced to Lucifer; he'd been accepted by them all far too easily for her liking.

She glanced at him as she headed for the crypt—and had to grudgingly admit that he was a commanding figure, especially in the shadowy night. Like his namesake, dark and forbidding, he followed her down the stone stairs.

Nose elevated to a telling angle, she pointedly settled to her accounts. He hovered for a moment, then made his way to where Mr. Filing was shifting boxes. She heard him offer to help, heard Filing's ready acceptance. Boxes scraped on stone; she concentrated on her figures.

Finally shutting the ledger, she stretched her back; only then did she realize Lucifer and Filing had finished moving boxes long before. Turning, she saw them leaning against a monument, talking earnestly. Filing was facing away from her; Lucifer's voice was too low for her to hear.

Quickly clearing her "desk," she went to join them.

Lucifer watched her approach. "So, other than Sir Jasper and Jonas, Basil Smollet and Pommeroy Fortemain, the bulk of the males were not at church."

Filing nodded. "Sir Cedric is an irregular attendee, as is Henry Grisby. The ladies I can count on"—he smiled at Phyllida—"but I'm afraid the males of the parish are rather more recalcitrant."

"Inconvenient, in this case."

Phyllida looked at Filing. "Indeed. I've entered everything. All is in order, so I'll bid you a good night."

"And a good night to you, my dear."

Filing bowed. Phyllida smiled and turned away.

Lucifer straightened. "I'll walk you to the Grange."

She wasn't the least bit surprised to hear that. She inclined her head and started up the stairs. "If you wish."

She led the way out of the church and onto the common. He lengthened his stride until he was pacing beside her, almost shoulder to shoulder. Her skin prickled; awareness rushed over her and left all her nerves standing on end.

Their mad dash from the cliffs to Colyton—a careening drive—had left no time, let alone breath, for embarrassment or consciousness, but once she'd regained her bedchamber, consciousness had swamped her. She'd been sure she could not possibly meet his eyes again—look at his lips again—not without blushing so fierily everyone would guess why. She'd almost made up her mind to avoid him—certainly to avoid his arms.

Then someone had shot at her and he'd arrived—and she'd wanted nothing more than to fling herself into his arms and feel safe. The urge had been so strong she'd quivered with it; only by a supreme effort had she quelled it.

It was utter nonsense to feel so—to feel that the only place she would truly feel safe was in his arms. Dangerous, too, when she knew his interest in her was transient. Once she told him what she knew, he would have no reason to seduce her.

She'd spent the afternoon lecturing herself, pointing out that she'd survived perfectly well until now, that she would still be safe in the village. All she needed to do was exercise a little extra caution and all would be well. She'd find Mary Anne's letters, tell Lucifer everything, then they'd unmask the murderer and life could go on as it had before.

Except that Lucifer would be living in the village. He wasn't going to leave. She wouldn't be able to avoid him.

There was only one solution—to behave with her usual confidence and pretend nothing out of the ordinary had happened on the cliff. Pretend he didn't affect her at all.

Not too easy when he was glowering at her.

"You can't possibly be so witless as to believe that it was some benighted huntsman who shot at you."

"You can't argue that it's not a possibility."

"It became much less of a possibility when we found hoofprints, just like those behind the Manor's shrubbery, beside the copse in that field."

Her stride faltered; she slowed. "Someone rode there ... it could still have been a huntsman."

"There was nothing to hunt in the field."

Except her. A cold hand gripped her nape; icy fingers trailed her spine. Phyllida suppressed a shiver. She continued walking. Her mind darted, sifting, rearranging the known facts in light of that new one.

She'd almost convinced herself it *had* been a careless hunter—despite her instinctive fear, there'd been no logical reason to think otherwise. Now ... could the murderer be trying to kill her?

Why? She'd seen the hat, true, but it was just a brown hat—she'd know it again if she saw it, but she couldn't recall seeing it before. She'd kept her eyes peeled, but she hadn't sighted it again. In fact, until they'd confirmed otherwise, she'd assumed some outsider must have ridden in and stabbed Horatio. That no longer seemed likely. If Lucifer was correct and the same horse that had been tethered by the shrubbery on Sunday had been by the copse this morning, then she could only agree with him.

The murderer was a local and had tried to kill her.

He must think she could identify him, but surely not because of the hat? He'd have burned it by now, and as she hadn't said anything, it must be obvious she hadn't recognized it. Was there something else she'd seen?

Frowning, she walked on.

A disgusted sound came from beside her. She felt Lucifer's gaze on her face and swiftly banished her frown.

"I should tell your father of your connection with the murder."

She rounded on him. "You haven't?"

He scowled at her. "No—but I should. I *will*, if that's the only way to ensure you remain safe."

She breathed easily again. "I'll take care."

"Take *care?* Just look at you! Traipsing about in the dead of night—alone!"

"But no one knows I'm out here."

"Except all those involved."

She snorted softly. "None of them is the murderer and you know it."

A charged silence ensued.

"Are you going to tell me that no one ever notices the light shining from the church every few nights?"

"Of course they notice—they think it's smugglers."

"So everyone knows you're there."

"No! No one even *imagines* I'm there—I'm a *woman*, remember?"

That shut him up. Only for a moment. "Believe me, that's one thing I'm highly unlikely to forget."

She tripped. He caught her arm, hauling her up, swinging her to him. She steadied, facing diagonally down the common. "Good Lord!" She stared. "A light just winked in your drawing room."

They both froze, staring down at the Manor. All was dark, then a pinprick of light flashed again. Before they could blink, a faint glow suffused the windows of the drawing room. A lamp had been lit and turned low.

Phyllida sucked in a breath. "It must be the murderer!"

"Stay here!"

Releasing her, Lucifer plunged down the slope.

"Hah!" Phyllida headed after him, in his wake, trusting that if there was a place to stumble, he'd find it first.

They skirted the duck pond, then picked their way across the lane, careful to avoid loose stones. Gaining the cottages' front fences, they hugged the shadows, ducking low as they rushed along the Manor's garden wall. Lucifer reached the gate before her; he stood and swung it open—

It creaked.

The sound seemed loud enough to wake the dead.

Lucifer flung himself up the path, gravel crunching under his feet. Phyllida followed at his heels.

The light in the drawing room abruptly died.

They skidded up against the front door, Lucifer juggling a set of unfamiliar keys. From within came the sound of footsteps fleeing across the tiles. Lucifer stopped, lifted his head, listened …

He swore and shoved the keys back in his pocket. He focused on her. "Dammit! Stay here!" He turned and charged along the front of the house.

Phyllida followed.

Lucifer rounded the corner and stopped; Phyllida cannoned into him. Steadying herself against his back, hands clutching his coat, she peered around his shoulder—

And caught a glimpse of a fleeing figure at the edge of her vision. "There!" She pointed.

The moon sailed free as the man fled across a stretch of open lawn. He was heading for the shrubbery.

"Stay here!" Lucifer took off after him.

Phyllida hesitated. There were only two other exits from the shrubbery—one to the lake, one … She looked at the entrance to the narrow path beside the lane. Dragging in a quick breath, she raced for it.

It was the fact that she wasn't following him that made Lucifer glance back. At first, he couldn't see her—then he did; she was a shadow streaking across the stretch of lawn by the main gates. His heart stopped.

"No!" he roared. "Come back!"

She dove into the dark entrance of the path.

Swearing violently, he swerved and headed after her.

He plunged along the path. It twisted and turned, a tunnel whose walls were impenetrable black, whose ceiling was the night sky obscured by dark branches. He could barely see the ground beneath his pounding feet. Branches grabbed at his coat; he pressed on at full tilt.

Phyllida was fast—faster than he'd expected—unencumbered as she was by skirts. She was still ahead of him, but he thought he could hear her footfalls over his own and the pounding in his ears.

The pertinent question was not how fast she was, but how fast the murderer was. And whether he was armed or not.

Would they reach the end of the shrubbery in time?

Would he catch Phyllida before she ran headlong into the murderer's arms?

Then he rounded a bend and saw her; exerting every last ounce of strength, he forged ahead. He caught up with her where the shrubbery hedges ended; shoulder to shoulder, they burst into the clearing beyond.

The mocking thud of retreating hooves greeted them.

They halted, sagged. Chest heaving, hands on his hips, Lucifer looked at Phyllida. Half bent over, hands on her knees, she puffed and puffed.

He waited, then asked, "Did you recognize him?"

She shook her head, then straightened. "I barely glimpsed him at all."

They'd been too late to even catch a glimpse of the horse. Beneath his breath, Lucifer swore. He scowled at Phyllida, then brusquely gestured back up the path. He'd give her his opinion of her behavior later—after he'd caught his breath.

They retraced their steps. At the end of the path, they emerged onto the lawn. Phyllida looked ahead, sucked in a breath, and stepped back.

Lucifer halted. Dodswell and Hemmings were prowling the lawn. Inwardly sighing, he murmured, "Stay here." He began to walk forward, then paused and added, "You don't want to know what I'll do if you are not in that precise spot when I get back."

He thought he heard a haughty sniff, but he didn't look back. Pushing into a lope, he crossed the lawn, waving when Dodswell saw him.

"An intruder—I gave chase but lost him." He waited until Hemmings came up, then said, "I'm going to prowl around a bit more. You can check through the house, see how he got in and out, then lock up. I've got my keys—we can compare notes in the morning."

Both Hemmings and Dodswell were in their nightshirts; they nodded and started toward the house.

Lucifer waited until they'd gone indoors, then turned and headed back to the path.

CHAPTER

Ten

Phyllida was waiting where he'd left her, just inside the entrance to the path. Arms folded, she might have been scowling at him; he couldn't be sure in the dark.

He halted beside her, looming over her, deliberately intimidating. She gave not an inch.

"Do you always have such difficulty following orders?"

"There are very few people who give orders to me."

They stood, gazes locked, then he stepped back and gestured to the lawn. "I'll walk you through the wood."

She glanced at the house. "It might be better to go through the shrubbery and out by the lake path."

He waved her on, and followed.

Phyllida retraced their steps, then turned into the shrubbery, all too conscious of the poorly suppressed male energy prowling at her back. She tried to tell herself he was doing it only to intimidate, to pressure her into revealing all and following his orders henceforth, but she knew it wasn't that. If he'd wanted to intimidate her, he would have been more forthright.

Not that the sense of something dangerous, something violent and not fully under control, stalking on her heels, wasn't intimidating enough.

They skirted the lake and traversed the wood in silence. She paused when they reached the Grange's shrubbery, but he frowned and waved her on.

The back lawn lay just ahead when he caught her arm and drew her to the side, onto one of the connecting paths. He released her; she faced him, her back against the hedge, luckily one of a small-leaved conifer. Neatly trimmed, it formed a cushion at her back. He leaned one shoulder into the hedge, just beside hers, and looked down at her. "When are you going to tell me what it is you know?"

She wished she could read his eyes, but they were lost in shadow. He stood there, so close, yet there was no sense now of intimidation. Invitation was what reached her. No pretense, no guile, simple dealing, him and her. To her, that was so much more appealing. She blew out a soft breath. "Soon."

"How soon?"

"I can't say, but not long. A few days, perhaps."

"Is there anything I can do to shorten the time?"

"If I could tell you …" She paused. "But I can't. I gave my word."

"Is this knowledge of yours the reason the murderer now has you in his sights?"

"I don't think so. I can't see how it could be any threat to him."

He considered, then nodded. "I'll make a bargain with you." He straightened, and suddenly the sense of physical menace was back; a leashed predator stood before her.

"I'm not aware of any need to make any bargains."

"Believe me, there's a need."

The growl in his voice warned her against challenging the statement. "What, then?"

"I want a promise from you that until we've laid this murderer by the heels, you will not roam about alone, either by day or by night."

She lifted her chin. "And in return?"

"In return, I won't tell your father that you were there, and know something to the point."

She relaxed. "You won't tell Papa anyway."

He frowned; his eyes narrowed. "Are you so sure you're prepared to risk it?"

She was, but this didn't seem a wise time to admit it. "I'll be careful." She would have moved on again, but he was in the way.

" 'Careful.' " His features hardened. "Someone tries to kill you and you talk of being *careful*? I should tell your father and have him lock you in your room."

"Nonsense! We can't be absolutely certain it was the murderer who shot at me."

"Who else? And don't say it was a hunter."

"There's no *reason* for the murderer to kill me!"

"He must think there is." He searched her face. "This thing you know must identify him."

"Well, it doesn't." She didn't try to hide her chagrin. "I thought at first it might, but I can't see how it can, not now."

"It doesn't matter whether it identifies him or not, only that he believes it might. That's enough to put you in danger." As he said the words, Lucifer felt their weight—for the first time fully realized their truth. She was in danger. Real, acute danger. She could be killed by the same killer who'd taken Horatio from him.

He drew a tight breath. "You have a choice. Either you can promise me you won't set foot outside the Grange except on urgent matters, and then only with a male escort, or we can go inside right now and speak with your father and lay all the pertinent details before him."

For once, she allowed her irritation to show. "This is ridiculous. *You* are not my keeper."

He stared down at her, and let that point lie.

"I'm going inside."

He didn't move.

She glared, then darted out—

He wrapped an arm around her waist, swung her back to the hedge, then trapped her against it. He looked into her smoldering eyes. "You are not safe." He'd meant from the murderer, but it suddenly occurred to him that he was speaking literally. He lowered his head. "You're a woman—the murderer's a man." He breathed the words along her cheek, his lips tracing down to her jaw. Her scent rose, wreathed his senses—and ensnared him.

Muscles bunched, locked. The temptation to taste her rose within him, more compelling than ever before. On the hedge beside her shoulder, his fist clenched as he fought the urge—and won.

He was a man, too. In the heat of the moment, he'd overlooked that fact. Steeling himself, tightening his reins, he tensed to draw back.

"Kiss me."

The words were a whisper in the dark, a soft plea so unexpected he felt stunned. Raising his head, he looked at her face, unsure he'd heard aright.

His jacket had been open; her hands had come to rest on his shirt-clad chest. Now they slid to his sides, gripping, urging him nearer.

"Kiss me again." He saw her lips move as she stretched up; they touched his jaw. "Kiss me like before … just once more …"

She didn't have to ask a fourth time, but it wouldn't be just one kiss. Bending his head, capturing her lips, he assumed she knew that, that her last words were simply part of her entreaty. He wanted to kiss her a million times, over and over again. He'd never get tired of her taste, of the sweet, innocent, trusting way she yielded her lips, her mouth.

She did it again and captured his senses. He fell into the kiss, into her.

He was ravenous.

The springy hedge was soft enough to press her into. He did; the feel of her supple body taut against his inflamed his need. Her hands slid further, searching, then spreading over his back. She clung and he kissed her more deeply. His hunger exploded. She arched against him, instinctively offering, and then she kissed him back.

She was still new to the game, enough so to distract him. He took the time to coax, to tease, to tutor, until, lips melded, tongues tangling, they were satisfied with the depth of the shared intimacy.

It wasn't enough—not for him.

It wasn't enough for Phyllida, either. When he ventured nothing more but simply remained, a hot, vibrant, intensely exciting male all but wrapped around her in the dark, she presumed it was her turn to take the lead. Sliding her hands around from his back, savoring the hard muscles, the tension she felt invest them as she stroked, she searched and found the buttons of his shirt. Quickly, she worked her way up, sliding the small buttons from their moorings, all the while kissing him, taking him in, then returning his hot caresses with heated caresses of her own.

The give-and-take—the reciprocity of it all—was something she hadn't foreseen. It intrigued her and spurred her on. He'd seen her breasts, stroked them, played with her nipples; it had all been gloriously pleasurable. Now was her chance to return the gift.

The last button gave; she slipped her hands inside the soft fabric. Splaying her fingers, she pressed her palms to the broad muscle that was the equivalent of her breasts.

He reacted as she had; a sharp tensing all but instantly converting to heat, to a curious thrumming resonance of the flesh. Pleased, she caressed, shifting her hands, fingers flexing, digging in, releasing; she wondered if that thrumming resonance was desire—his desire.

Hair rasped against her palms. She found the flat disks of his nipples, so unlike hers yet they still budded as hers did. She played, intrigued by the discovery, by the welling reaction she sensed in him. Their lips remained fused, her mouth trapped beneath his. She sensed his control, his holding back. Boldly, she caressed him with hands and tongue and tempted him more.

The dam broke; heat washed through her in a burning tide.

She'd been right—it was desire; she knew it in her bones. It filled her, warmed her. She basked in its heat and bravely drank it in, as much as he would give her.

She wanted this—desperately wanted to know about all the things she'd feared she never would. She wanted to feel, wanted to know what mutual desire was like, how it felt to burn with that flame.

Tonight might be her last chance to find out—once she told him her secret, he would no longer be interested in her, not like this. He would have no cause to compel her, no reason to seduce her. Once she found the letters, she would have to tell him all; the instant she did, this brief moment—her opportunity to be the object of a man's desire—would be over.

She didn't want it to pass. The realization shook her; she pushed it aside, too confusing to deal with now. Now when she had so many new sensations, not just physical but ethereal, to deal with. To experience, to understand—it was like plunging into a new world with new wonders, new customs. There was so much she had to learn.

He pressed her back into the hedge; his hands tugged at her shirt. It didn't button down the front. She sank back, easing her hold on him. He yanked the shirt from her breeches and then his hands were underneath it.

They encountered the bands wound tight over her breasts; his hands froze. She thought she heard him groan. Then his hands slid around, locking over her back, and he hauled her against him. That she understood. She pulled her hands free, wound them around his neck, and pressed herself to him, giving him back kiss for wild kiss, caress for heated caress.

She wasn't sure her feet were touching the ground. She didn't care. All she wanted was to get closer, to combine her heat with his.

His hands slid lower, over her hips, until they cupped her bottom. He lifted her against him, into him. His desire was very evident. She let her body press like a hand to him, as if with her soft stomach she could caress him there.

Something changed. Not in a flash, but in a steady rush of power. Something new rose between them, something so vital, so intense, she ached to hold it, to know it. She tightened her arms about his neck and kissed him more deeply, sharing the driving need. He kissed her back. The power swelled and spread through them until she was glowing with it, aching with it, and he was the same.

Their lips parted. They both needed to breathe. A curious hiatus held them; she glanced at his face. His eyes were shut; his breathing was as ragged as hers. What next? She had no idea. She was quite sure he did.

She brushed her lips against his. "Teach me."

His harsh laugh was mostly groan. "Dammit—I'm trying to *spare* you!"

"Don't." She would have frowned, but his eyes were closed. Was he being chivalrous? Or pigheadedly protective? Was there any difference? And did she care? "Stop making my decisions for me."

"You don't even know—"

"Stop arguing and *show* me." She kissed him—hard, forcefully. He reacted instantly and kissed her back fiercely. Her head spun. She didn't draw back, she refused to retreat—she kept kissing him, sinking against him, using her body against him. She sensed the moment when she won, when desire triumphed over whatever misguided male notions he'd held.

A shudder went through him, then heat and glory welled between them again, even more powerful than before.

The tenor of their kiss changed—the giving and taking shifted to some deeper level of intimacy. She gave readily, took gladly, and refused to back away.

A deep sigh coursed through him and his hands firmed about her bottom. His fingers flexed, then kneaded; heat spread in a prickly wave over her skin.

He backed her further into the hedge. One hand cradling her bottom, he held her there, pinned by his weight, while, with fingers quick and sure, he undid the buttons closing her breeches.

She should have been shocked, but she wasn't—she wanted to know. Now. Tonight. Here. With him.

Long fingers splayed over her stomach; they gently pressed and she lost her breath. His lips firmed and she took her breath from him, and rode the spiraling sensation of his touch, of his exploration.

He didn't hurry. He took the time to savor, to learn. Nerves tightening to excruciating sensitivity, she followed his every move.

Followed his fingers through the springy thicket of her tangling curls, felt the long slide of his fingers between her thighs. Sensed the heat, the curious dampness he encountered, thrilled to the flash of pure sensation that speared her when he caressed, then fondled.

His knowing fingers touched her, parted her, explored her—waves of pleasure rose and swamped her. They pushed her on. On toward something; the urge to reach it grew, swelled, until a near-mindless want consumed her.

She didn't know what she wanted; she was sure he did. Holding tight to him, to their anchoring kiss, she tilted her hips, opening herself to his hand, begging ... she knew not for what.

He cupped her, fingers sliding slick in a soothing caress; then, very slowly, he entered her.

So slowly she felt the intrusion keenly—no force, no pressure, just the yielding of her body to his penetration. He reached deep, then stroked.

The heat within her tightened, coalesced, then contracted even more. He stroked again, finger within her, thumb upon her—she would have gasped, cried out, but he drank the sound. And stroked again.

Her heat fractured, imploded, then erupted. Hot glory and pleasure spilled down every vein. Fierce delight, tangible in its sharpness, ran across her skin, through her body, scattered her wits and left her senses sighing.

Clinging tightly, she gave herself up—to him, to the splendor of desire.

Lucifer watched her face as the pleasure rolled through her, his awareness centered within her, savoring the rippling caresses as she eased. Every demon he possessed was slavering, expecting its customary reward; he didn't know how he was going to hold them back, only that he would.

Somewhere, a line had been crossed, some Rubicon beyond which there was no turning back. He didn't know where or when, but there was no longer any point pretending he hadn't, at least partly deliberately, taken the fatal step. Whether it had been fifteen minutes ago, when the realization that he'd already nearly lost her had hit, whether Horatio's garden was to blame, or the inheritance as a whole—or if he'd decided in that instant when first he'd laid eyes on her face—didn't matter. She was his. So the only matter he had to concentrate on right now was not giving in to his demons.

Not easing her breeches farther down, lifting her, and taking her here, now, against the hedge.

Studying her face, eyes closed, her expression beatifically serene, helped— so did easing his fingers from her, gently drawing them from between her thighs.

Her musky scent rose, teasing, taunting his demons. He slammed a mental door on them, shut his ears to the howls.

He'd have her—he'd decided that days ago, even if he hadn't let himself think of it—but not here, not tonight. For all that she'd insisted, she deserved better than a shrubbery hedge. And he seriously doubted, when the time came, that once would be enough—not now. He'd known from the first that abstinence was not a good idea.

A whole night. If he exercised appropriate caution and skill ...

Leaning into the hedge beside her shoulder, he was still watching her, her breeches done up, his hand resting on her hip on top of her loose shirt, when she drew in a deeper breath and opened her eyes.

She blinked. Her gaze flew to his face.

Even in the dimness, he saw awareness bloom; through his hand on her hip he felt tension reinvest her spine. She stared into his eyes, then swiftly scanned his face before once more meeting his gaze.

His lips curved, not so much a smile as a gesture of intent. He leaned into her. "That was just the appetizer."

He brushed a kiss across her swollen lips, then captured her wide-eyed gaze. "Next time, I'll have you naked, on a bed, and I won't let you go until I've had you. Multiple times."

At eleven the next morning, Phyllida closed the side door of the church and started down the path. The vases were done for the services tomorrow—one item she could cross off her list.

Jem, the Grange's youngest groom, was lounging in the lych-gate; he straightened as she neared. She'd requested his presence on her errand to protect her from the murderer or to protect her from Lucifer—she wasn't sure which. If the latter, then she'd failed. A pair of blacks pranced before the lych-gate; she had not the slightest doubt who would be holding their reins.

Jem opened the gate and she stepped into the lane. Lucifer was listening to Thompson, standing beside the curricle, but his blue gaze was all for her.

Thompson saw her and broke off to nod.

Lucifer seized the opportunity. "Good morning, Miss Tallent. Would you prefer to drive back to the Grange?"

No one would believe her if she said she wouldn't; in truth, she was perfectly amenable to meeting him again. In public. "Thank you." She sent Jem home, then strolled to the curricle's side. Although still engaged with Thompson, Lucifer held out a hand as she neared. She considered it, then calmly put her hand in it and allowed him to help her up. In public, she'd be safe.

Settling beside him, she shamelessly eavesdropped.

"So you want new locks on all the doors and windows, the kind that can't easily be slipped."

Lucifer nodded. "I haven't any idea how many will be needed, but I want every window secured."

"Aye, well—no point otherwise." Thompson straightened. "I'll be along this afternoon to count up. I knows just the sort you want, but it'll take a week or more to get 'em in. Come from Bristol, they do."

Lucifer nodded. "Get the job done as fast as you can."

"I'll do that." With respectful nods to them both, Thompson stepped back.

Lucifer clicked the reins and the blacks stepped out. He glanced at her, but had to look back to his horses. They passed Jem, swinging down the lane. "You have no idea," Lucifer said, "how pleasantly surprised I am to see you with Jem in your train."

"Why? I didn't say I wouldn't."

"You didn't say you would, either, and you are the most contrary female I've ever met."

She couldn't decide whether to be pleased or insulted. "Why are you ordering locks? Because of last night?"

His gaze touched her face. "Because of the intruder."

A *frisson* of awareness raced through her; she carefully kept it from her face. She wasn't going to let what had happened last night inhibit her from continuing with their joint investigations. She had a shrewd notion he'd be quite happy to see her retreat from the field, a victim of consciousness. But last night had come about by her insistence; just because he'd given her precisely what she'd wanted—even though, as he'd observed, she hadn't known for what she was asking—she wasn't about to convert into some mindless ninny.

She wasn't about to let his warning about the next time worry her, either. It would be up to her if ever there was a next time, and she hadn't yet made up her mind.

Shocking, of course, but there it was. She should be swooning, not sitting beside him, calmly if warily. She might not have appreciated last night's possibilities, not until she'd been in the middle of them, but she was twenty-four. She knew what he'd meant by his final words.

They'd been uttered like an oath. One that had carried a great deal of conviction. After a tense moment, face hard, all angular planes, he'd stepped back and let her slip past him, out onto the lawn. She'd looked back just once and seen him standing, a dark, forbidding shadow at the entrance to the shrubbery. Lucifer, indeed. All hot desire.

Temptation *was* his middle name.

And she'd felt safe, utterly and completely safe—safe not just physically, but at some much deeper level—while in his arms.

Why that should be so was a mystery, but it was pointless to cavil. Just how far that sense of safety might tempt her she didn't know, but in all her twenty-four years, he was the first to make her feel that being a woman desiring and desired was an experience available to her.

Deep in her mind lay a very strong feeling that just as he was the first, he might also be the last.

"The intruder"—she grabbed the curricle's rail as he took the corner into the main lane—"how did he get in?"

"There was a window with a loose latch—the one in the dining room facing the side lawn."

"So that's how he got out so fast." After a moment, she asked, "Do you think he'll return?"

"Not immediately, but sometime. Whatever he was after, he hasn't found it. If it was enough to commit murder for, then he'll be back."

"Are you sure the intruder is the murderer?"

He grimaced. "No. But unless there were *four* people visiting Horatio on Sunday morning—the murderer, you, me, *and* the intruder—and we've found absolutely no trace of the murderer, then the intruder is the murderer."

The gates of the Manor appeared around the bend; he didn't slow. "Bear with me." He flicked her a glance. "Bar your father and brother, you're the only sane and definitely innocent person I can talk to about this, and for obvious reasons, I can't yet talk to your father or brother."

She regarded him calmly.

He had to look to his horses. "I believe Horatio was killed because of some book. Everyone knew that on Sunday morning, the Manor should have been deserted. The downstairs doors were never locked. The murderer—a local who was not at church—left his horse behind the shrubbery and went to the drawing room. He started examining books, pulling them from the shelves— then Horatio disturbed him. On Monday afternoon, I noticed three books not properly pushed in."

"Where?"

"Bottom of the last bookshelf against the inner wall."

Near the gap where she'd surmised the murderer must have hidden. "So— the murderer is after a book."

"Or something in a book."

"Could the book be the item Horatio wanted you to appraise?"

"No. Horatio wouldn't have asked me to appraise a book. *He* was the foremost authority in the field. If he'd found something spectacular, and all the signs suggest he had, he wouldn't have needed my opinion to be sure."

They'd reached the road to Axmouth; he slowed and turned the curricle. When they were rolling back to Colyton, Phyllida asked, "Why did you say something *in* a book?"

"Many books are valuable, not because of the book itself, but because of what's subsequently been written in them. Sometimes it's the notational information that adds the value, but most often it's the identity of the writer."

"You mean inscriptions—that sort of thing?"

"Inscriptions, instructions, messages—even wills. You'd be amazed at what you come across."

"So at present it appears that the motive for the murder is some information noted in a book?"

"That's my best guess." The Grange gates loomed; deftly, he turned through them.

"What about the item Horatio wanted you to look at?"

"That remains a mystery. The fact that Horatio was killed just after he'd discovered it is looking more and more like coincidence. No one beyond myself and Covey knew he'd found anything. Covey knows no more than I."

"We'll have to search all the books."

"I have Covey doing that. He's used to handling old and valuable tomes— he'll be careful yet thorough."

He drew up before the Grange steps; the blacks pranced. Phyllida climbed down without assistance. On the steps, she turned and met his blue gaze. "Thank you." She didn't add anything more.

One black brow arched; he searched her face, consideration in his eyes.

She smiled, inclined her head, and turned toward the door. "Until next time."

She didn't look back to see how he reacted, but his wheels didn't start turning until she'd stepped over the threshold and Mortimer was closing the door behind her. Still smiling, she headed for her room. Why she was teasing him, she didn't know. She knew it wasn't safe.

She didn't know if she was teasing, either.

By the time she reached her room, her smile had converted to a frown. Lucifer was focusing on Horatio's books, which meant he'd be unlikely to go inspecting a writing desk. But he'd ordered new locks and he'd order them used, at least until the murderer was caught.

So she had a week's grace—the time it would take for the locks to arrive. She would have to search the Manor's upstairs rooms one night soon. Mrs. Hemmings had told her Lucifer had taken the room at the front right corner, leaving Horatio's room as it was.

Phyllida grimaced. "All I can do is pray that damned writing desk is not in the front corner bedroom."

CHAPTER
Eleven

Not to be outdone by the Fortemains, the Smollets had arranged to host a dance that evening. It was a large affair with guests driving in from miles around. Many Lucifer hadn't met; he spent half the evening being introduced and exclaimed over—he was the main attraction, after all.

While doing the pretty, he kept an eye on Phyllida. She'd arrived in good time with her father, brother, and Miss Sweet. Lady Huddlesford had swept in later, Frederick at her heels. Percy Tallent had not appeared.

In her gown of bronze silk, a simple gold chain around her throat and gold drops in her ears, Phyllida was the least fussily dressed woman in the room, and easily the most stunning. She drew many men's eyes, yet few, Lucifer realized, properly appreciated the sight. Cedric, Basil, and Grisby—those he paid most attention to—clearly viewed Phyllida as a desirable chattel, one that, if possessed, would add to their consequence. None of them seemed to see *her* at all. Fools, the lot of them.

Her expression serene, she did her best to ignore them, chatting instead with the many others present—doubtless dispensing aid and succor in various forms. Yet she could not entirely avoid her would-be suitors.

She danced the first dance with Basil, their host. By dint of superior strategy, Lucifer avoided the reciprocal fate; Jocasta Smollet danced the measure with Sir Jasper. Phyllida then danced a cotillion with Cedric; later, he saw her going down a country dance with Henry Grisby.

Her attitude at the conclusion of the dance—that of relief that her duty had now been done—failed to puncture Grisby's self-absorption. Less than impressed, Phyllida retreated to speak with the Misses Longdon.

From the side of the room, Lucifer watched her, and considered his best avenue of approach.

"There you are!"

He turned as Sir Jasper joined him.

"Wanted to ask—have you uncovered anything about this blackguard who stabbed Horatio?"

"Nothing positive. There's no evidence anyone rode in from beyond the village, at least not from the east. I've yet to check in Honiton, but at present, all signs point to the killer residing locally."

"Hmm. This intruder you surprised last night ...?"

"May well be the murderer."

Sir Jasper let out a long sigh. He looked away, over the room. "I'd hoped, y'know, that it wouldn't be someone from round about. But if they're still searching ..."

"Precisely. It can't be anyone from far afield. They'd be noticed."

"By the same token, given the way we all go about down here, riding day in, day out, it'll be hard to pin anyone down."

Lucifer inclined his head in agreement.

Sir Jasper remained beside him, a frown gathering on his face. Eventually, he drew breath and faced Lucifer. "This business of that hunter shooting at Phyllida ..."

"Exactly what I want to know, too."

Sir Jasper and Lucifer glanced around as Jonas ambled up. Hands in his pockets, he met Lucifer's gaze. As usual, he appeared relaxed, ready for any lark. It occurred to Lucifer that, as Phyllida's calm serenity was often a mask, so, too, Jonas's insouciant good humor concealed something more. There was certainly nothing insouciant in his hazel eyes.

"I know Phyl *said* it was a hunter, but I can't see it myself. Ridiculous time and place to go shooting. And whyever did she burn that bonnet?"

"She burned her bonnet?" Sir Jasper gazed across the room at his daughter.

"So Sweetie said." Jonas studied Phyllida, too.

"Why on earth would she do that?"

Because she'd been frightened and destroying the bonnet had been her way of putting the incident from her. Lucifer could understand that. For all her intransigence, Phyllida was too intelligent not to be afraid.

"What I want to know is: Is she in any danger?"

It was Jonas who voiced the question. To Lucifer's relief, it wasn't directed specifically at him; he couldn't answer truthfully. He shifted; it went against his grain to keep Sir Jasper and Jonas in the dark. To his mind, they had a right to know—had a right to protect daughter, sister.

Lips shut tight against any unwary word, he canvassed his options, but there wasn't any way to warn them that it looked like the murderer was indeed after Phyllida—they'd immediately ask why. "I saw her out walking, coming back from the church. I noticed she had a groom with her."

"Did she? Now that's a first." Jonas glanced at him. "I wonder why."

"Perhaps the shock of being shot at." Lucifer kept his tone light. "Who knows what goes on in the minds of women?"

Sir Jasper snorted. Jonas grinned.

After a moment, Sir Jasper said, "I don't like this business of a murderer running loose among us. No telling where it might end. I might just have a word with the male staff—no need to let Phyllida know."

"A general increase in watchfulness wouldn't hurt."

"She'll hear of it," Jonas said. "You know she will. Then she'll just reorganize things her way."

"Humph!" Sir Jasper's frowning gaze remained on his daughter. "I'll do it anyway. With luck, by the time she learns of it, we'll have this miscreant by the heels."

Lucifer hoped so. Leaving Sir Jasper and Jonas, he strolled down the room to negotiate with the musicians laboring in a corner. After that, he headed toward the *chaise* Phyllida was sharing with the Misses Longdon.

He bowed to all three ladies. They had barely exchanged five words before the opening bars of a waltz filled the room. The Misses Longdon tittered; neither danced, but they eagerly scanned the room to see who of their neighbors would partner whom.

Lucifer caught Phyllida's eye and bowed again. "If you would do me the honor, Miss Tallent?"

She inclined her head and gave him her hand. He raised her and drew her into the dance, into his arms. The Misses Longdon twittered furiously.

Phyllida danced well and was thankful for it—at least she didn't need to mind her steps. One less problem on her plate. The most pressing, literally, had her trapped in his arms and was whirling her effortlessly around the floor. For some silly reason, her wits and her senses seemed intent on following her feet into some realm of giddy delight, and that was far too dangerous.

There was an aggravated frown in Lucifer's eyes, a tightness about his lips, a tension in his body as it tantalizingly brushed hers—unquestionably all danger signs. She kept her expression mild, her gaze on his face.

"I've just had a most *uncomfortable* conversation with your father and brother."

She felt her eyes go round, her jaw drop. "How on earth did Papa, let alone Jonas, learn of last night?"

Lucifer stared at her, then his lips thinned. "We weren't discussing our interlude in the shrubbery. They don't know about that."

Phyllida sagged with relief. "Thank heavens!"

Lucifer all but shook her as they went around the turn.

"We were discussing whether you are in danger. Which you are."

"You didn't tell them?" She searched his eyes.

They glittered back at her. "No, I didn't. But I should."

"There's no reason for them to be worried—"

"They have a right to know."

She narrowed her eyes at him. "I don't want them to know. It's pointless. As you saw, I'm perfectly capable of taking appropriate steps, and with luck I'll be able to tell you all soon, and then, one way or another, we'll catch the murderer and all will be well."

He studied her face, her eyes. "It would be better if you told me what it was you saw in Horatio's drawing room."

She considered it.

I saw a brown hat.

A brown hat?

Just a brown hat. I didn't recognize it and no one's worn it since.

Then it can't be that that the murderer's worried about. What else happened? What were you doing? Why were you there?

"I can't tell you. Not yet."

His gaze remained steady, vibrant dark blue, focused on her eyes. "I think you can."

His voice was soft, low; it sent shivers down her spine. Her impulse was to lift her chin and step back from his arms; before she could, he drew her nearer.

Near enough so the silk over her breasts brushed his coat with every breath; close enough so that his hard thighs brushed hers at every turn.

She was suddenly very conscious of just how physically powerful he was—although he never hid it, he hadn't before projected it, not like this. Some part of her mind was pointing frantically, urging her to understand how threatening he could be, and give in. Instead, she simply frowned at him. "Not yet. I'll tell you as soon as I can."

Her tone was calm and even. An expression of surprise—as if he couldn't quite believe his ears—passed swiftly through his eyes. Then the blue hardened. Slowly, arrogantly, he lifted one black brow.

She knew that look—could interpret it with ease. "Nothing you can do will change my mind."

The music stopped; they swirled to a halt by the side of the floor, but he didn't let her go. His hand at her waist burned through the silk, threatening to bring her hard against him. He lowered their linked hands, lacing his fingers through hers, and looked into her eyes. "Nothing?"

Just that one, soft word.

Phyllida suddenly felt faint. Her knees felt weak. If she didn't say something soon, he was going to kiss her—right here in the Smollets' ballroom in front of half the county. He would do it, and delight in the doing. Her heart was thudding; her eyes were trapped in midnight blue. She couldn't think—not well enough to concoct any evasive plan. And she couldn't break away.

His gaze grew more intent; his lips lifted a little at the corners. The hand at her back tensed—

"Ah, Phyllida, my dear."

It was Basil. He walked toward them, not looking at them but surveying his guests. Lucifer was forced to release her. Phyllida edged back.

Reaching them, Basil glanced at them and smiled perfunctorily. "I wonder, my dear, if I could prevail on you to give your opinion of the punch. I'm just not sure ..."

"Of course!" Seizing Basil's arm, Phyllida turned him. "Where's the punch bowl?"

She steered Basil down the room, away from Lucifer, and didn't once look back.

Despite that, she knew he watched her—kept watching her, waiting for another chance at her. No matter where in the room she went, she felt his gaze on her. Consequently, she was forced to conscript some gentleman—one of her village suitors or one of the others from farther afield who would gladly pay court to her if she gave the slightest sign—as bodyguard. They, unfortunately, didn't know they were guarding her.

One, a Mr. Firman from Musbury, insisted on fetching her a glass of punch; he left her by a window. Phyllida scanned the crowd; she couldn't see Lucifer. But the sense of being in danger grew … retreating to the withdrawing room seemed a good idea. She turned toward the door—

And walked into a familiar chest.

She all but leaped back. She glared at him. "Stop it!"

He raised his brows, all innocence. "Stop what?"

"This! You know you can't"—she gestured with both hands—"*seduce* me in a ballroom."

"Who wrote that rule?" He studied her eyes, then added, "I'll admit it's a greater challenge, but …"

His voice had deepened to a suggestive purr. Phyllida flashed him a repressive look and turned to scan those nearby, hoping to see Mr. Firman or some other useful soul …. Robert Collins was standing quietly by the wall.

Lucifer had followed her gaze. "I thought the hostesses hereabouts didn't encourage Mr. Collins."

"They don't and Jocasta's no different, she's just more cruel. She knows inviting Robert will irritate Mr. Farthingale, reinforcing his opposition, which quite ruins Mary Anne's delight in having Robert here. Robert, of course, is helpless to decline the invitation—he gets so few opportunities to see Mary Anne in such surrounds."

Phyllida was conscious that, just for a moment, Lucifer's attention drifted from her. She glanced at him; he was studying the guests.

"Miss Smollet," he murmured, "seems to have a rather peculiar notion of what constitutes entertainment."

Phyllida quietly humphed. She was saved from having to find some other distraction by Mr. Firman's return. He handed her her glass; to gain a moment, she introduced him to Lucifer, only to discover that Mr. Firman had been waiting to talk to Mr. Cynster all evening.

Mr. Firman, it transpired, was the owner of a cattle stud.

Phyllida learned that that was a subject on which Lucifer wished to extend his knowledge. Not only did Mr. Firman talk, but Lucifer listened and asked questions.

The opportunity was too good to pass up. Phyllida edged away; Lucifer shot her a glance but was trapped in the ongoing discussion. Mr. Firman was not someone he wanted to offend.

Phyllida gave her glass to a footman, then joined Robert Collins by the wall.

He glanced at her—there was a painful intensity in his eyes that Phyllida didn't like to see. He pressed her hand. "Mary Anne told me about the letters."

He looked across the room to where Mary Anne stood chatting with two young ladies. "How I *wish* I'd never urged her to write to me."

The bitterness in his words had Phyllida frowning. "It's the letters I wanted to speak to you about."

Robert's head whipped around, hope naked in his face. "You've found them?"

"No. I'm sorry ..."

Robert sighed. "No—*I'm* sorry. I know you will and I'm grateful for your help. I've no right to press you." After a moment, he asked, "What did you want to know?"

Phyllida took a deep breath. "I have to ask you this because it's important, and whenever I try to talk to Mary Anne on the subject, she becomes quite hysterical. But I need to know this, Robert—and if I don't get a sensible answer, I don't know that I can keep searching for those letters in secret. So tell me—what is it about them that makes them so dangerous to you and Mary Anne?"

Robert stared at her, the image of a rabbit cornered. Then he swallowed and looked away. "I can't tell you—not in so many words."

"Generalizations will do—I'll extrapolate."

He fell silent; eventually he said, "Mary Anne and I have been meeting secretly for nearly a year. You know how long we've waited and ..." He dragged in a breath. "Anyway, Mary Anne used to fill in the time between my visits by writing to me about our last meeting—about what we'd done and what we might do the next time—well, she wrote in a very *detailed* way." He cast Phyllida an anguished glance.

She met it, blank-faced. After a moment, she said, her tone flat, "I think I understand, Robert."

Thanks to Lucifer, she now had some inkling of what could transpire between a lady and a gentleman where desire was involved. And she had no doubt Mary Anne desired Robert—she always had. Phyllida cleared her throat.

"I used to bring the letters with me to our next meeting and we'd try to ... well ..." Robert hauled in another breath and rushed on. "So you see, if Mr. Farthingale got hold of the letters, it would be very ... bad. But if he showed them to Mr. Crabbs—if *anyone* showed them to Mr. Crabbs ..."

"Hmm." A vision of the starchily conservative, stern-faced solicitor flashed into Phyllida's mind.

"I wouldn't get my registration, and then we'd never be able to marry." Robert looked at her, his plea in his eyes.

She forced a reassuring smile. "We'll find them."

Robert squeezed her hand. "I can't thank you enough—you're such a good friend."

Phyllida took back her hand, and wished she could be a bad friend. But she couldn't. On top of that, she'd given her word. She turned from Robert—and found Lucifer almost upon her.

She met his eyes. "No!"

A violin sang—they both glanced toward the musicians. Then Phyllida looked back. She considered Lucifer, then stepped closer and flicked a hand against his chest. "Waltz with me."

He looked at her, arrested. "Why?"

"Because you might as well be useful and I don't want to waltz with anyone else."

His arm closed around her and he steered her into the whirl. His eyes searched hers. "You're trying to distract me."

"Perhaps." She was also trying to distract herself, and he was simply perfect for the task.

How *could* Mary Anne have been so idiotic as to write such things down? Love-induced stupidity—that was the only reason Phyllida could imagine.

The sun shone brightly, the air was fresh and clean as she strolled briskly down the common. Behind her, the Sunday-morning congregation was streaming home. Ten paces to her rear, Jem strode, her concession to male notions of feminine vulnerability. Her aunt and the rest of the females of the Grange were rolling home in the carriage, but she had elected to stroll back via the wood.

And the Manor.

All the Manor's household bar Lucifer had been in church, even the newcomer, his groom. Bristleford had informed her that Mr. Cynster had elected to watch over the house in light of the recent intrusion.

Phyllida wondered if that was the real reason or whether, given his name, he would prove any less irregular than the other gentlemen of the parish when it came to Sunday services.

Her parasol protecting her from the sun, she crossed the lane and turned toward the Manor. Nearing the front gate, she slowed, considering what excuse to give for calling.

From the shadows beyond the open front door, Lucifer watched her hesitating by the gate. He'd been deep in Horatio's ledgers when some force had metaphorically jogged his elbow, breaking his concentration. He'd glanced up, then stood and strolled to the library window. His gaze had been drawn to the figure heading purposefully down the common, neatly encased in Sunday ivory, her parasol shading her face, Phyllida's destination wasn't hard to guess.

He'd waited in the hall—he didn't want to seem too eager to see her. That wouldn't help his cause. His gaze lingered on her figure, on the sweet curves of breast and shoulder, on the dark hair that framed her face. With the glory of Horatio's garden between them, he studied her, then stepped forward.

She saw him and straightened; her grip on her parasol tightened. Not fear but alertness—a keen anticipation he could feel. He crossed the garden but stopped short of the gate, halting beneath the rose-covered archway. There was a convenient spot where his shoulder could prop; availing himself of it, he crossed his arms and looked at her.

She studied him, trying to gauge his mood. He gave her no assistance.

She tilted her head, her eyes on his. "Good morning. Bristleford said you'd stayed to watch the house. I take it the intruder didn't reappear?"

"No. All was quiet."

She waited, then said, "I was wondering if Covey had discovered anything—any wildly precious volume or one containing a reason for murder."

How much to tell her? "Have you ever heard any rumors concerning Lady Fortemain?"

Her eyes widened to dark saucers. "Lady Fortemain? Good heavens, no!"

"In that case, possibly."

Phyllida waited. When he continued to simply stand there, his gaze steady, his face uninformative, she prompted, "Well? What was it?"

A moment passed before he answered, "An inscription in a book."

So she had imagined. "What did it say?"

"What did you see in Horatio's drawing room last Sunday?"

Phyllida stiffened. The undercurrents in the present scene were suddenly clear. "You know I can't tell you—not yet."

His eyes were very dark; they remained fixed on her face. "Because it concerns someone else?"

She pressed her lips together, then nodded. "Yes."

They stared at each other across the gate to Horatio's garden. He stood relaxed but still, dark, dangerous, and devilishly handsome, framed by white roses. The sun beat down on them; the breeze wrapped them in its warmth.

Then he stirred, straightened. His eyes hadn't left hers. "Someday I hope you'll trust me."

He hesitated, then inclined his head, turned, and walked back toward the front door.

Three paces and he stopped. He spoke without turning. "Walk back through the village. Until the murderer's caught, the woods and the shrubberies are no place for you."

He waited for a heartbeat, then continued on.

Phyllida watched until he'd disappeared into the house. Then she turned. Her mask firmly in place, she beckoned to Jem, who had hung back on the common, and set off—through the village.

Of course she trusted him—he *knew* she did! Phyllida slapped the brass vase she'd just emptied down on the vestry table, then swept back into the nave. She headed for the font.

The flowers she'd arranged on Saturday had only just lasted through Sunday. Wrapping both arms around the heavy urn, she hefted it. Balancing the weight carefully, she slowly edged toward the vestry and the open door beyond; the last thing she needed was dirty water streaks down the front of her muslin gown.

That would be the last straw.

How could he not know that she trusted him? He did know—he *must*, after their little interlude in the shrubbery. He knew, but he was using the question of trust—her trust in him—as a lever to pressure her.

He wasn't really talking about trust at all—he was talking about dominance. About the fact that she hadn't weakened and told him what he wanted to know. If he wanted to discuss trust, what about him trusting *her*? She'd told him she couldn't tell him, but that she would as soon as she could, and that what she knew was of no consequence anyway!

And just what had he meant by his parting comment about shrubberies not being safe for her?

"I'll go into the shrubbery any time I like."

The words, uttered through clenched teeth, echoed in the empty vestry. Feeling ahead with one foot, she located the threshold, then stepped out into the grassy area at the back of the church.

The sky was overcast, at one with her mood. Peering around the urn, she turned toward the pile of discarded flowers—

Black cloth fell over her head.

The weight of a rope fell against her collarbone.

The next instant, it jerked tight.

And tightened.

She flung the heavy urn aside—it clanged against a headstone. Lashing back with her elbows, she connected, and heard a satisfying "Ouff!"

It was a man, and he was bigger, heavier, and stronger than she was. She didn't stop to think; years of wrestling with Jonas flared in her mind. She scrabbled at the rope with both hands, bending forward from the waist, hauling on the rope, forcing the man to reach over her, forcing him off-balance. Before he could pull back on the rope, she straightened. The back of her head hit his jaw. More important, the rope eased enough for her to hook her hands inside it.

He brutally yanked it back again, but she pulled with all her strength, dragged in a breath, and screamed.

The scream bounced off the church walls; it echoed from the stones all around them.

A door crashed; footsteps pounded, heading their way.

A rough curse fell on her ears. Her attacker flung her aside.

Phyllida fell over a grave. Rough stone grazed her calf, then she toppled, catching her upper arm on another sharp stone edge before tumbling blindly back. She landed across a marble slab, still shrouded in the heavy black cloth, the rope still hanging around her shoulders.

"Here! You! *Stop!*"

Jem's yells broke through Phyllida's stunned daze. She heard him run past and on down the path. Struggling to rise, she batted at the black fabric hanging heavily all about her. Panic clawed at her throat. She couldn't break free.

Then she heard another curse, more forceful, more virulent. Heavy footsteps strode quickly toward her.

Before she could gather her wits, she was swept up like a child in a pair of strong arms, then he sat, and she was deposited in his lap.

"Stop struggling—you're only tangling it. Hold still."

Her panic left her in a rush. She started to shiver. The rope was unwound from her shoulders. The next instant, the black shroud was lifted away.

She stared into Lucifer's face, blue eyes dark with concern.

"Are you all right?"

She drank in the sight of his face for one more moment, then slid her arms around him, ducked her head to his chest, and clung. His arms closed comfortingly about her. He rested his cheek on her hair and rocked her.

"It's all right. He's gone." He held her tight, safe. A minute passed, then he asked, "Now tell me, are you hurt?"

Without lifting her head, she shook it. She gulped in air and struggled to find her voice. "Just my throat." Her voice was hoarse from the scream and from the rope. She put a hand to her neck and felt roughened skin and the puffiness of swelling.

"Nothing else?"

"Just a graze on my leg and a bruise on my arm." She didn't think she'd hit her head on the slab, but her leg was stinging. Lifting her face, fists clenched in his coat, she peeked at her legs—her skirts were rucked up to her knees.

She blushed and tried frantically to flick them down.

Lucifer caught her hand, returned it to his chest, then reached out and straightened the flowing muslin for her. He noticed the graze and paused. "It's just a scratch—no blood." He arranged her skirts so they covered her calves.

Then he looked up, his gaze fixing on the path leading down to the lych-gate. "Here they come."

He looked down at her, then his arms tightened and he rose to his feet. Settling her in his arms, he set out, negotiating the narrow path between the graves to the grassy area by the vestry door. He stopped and waited. Mr. Filing and Jem joined them.

Thompson was with them, a heavy hammer in one hand. "What's to do?"

"Someone attacked Miss Tallent." Lucifer glanced back at the slab where he'd left the black cloth and rope. "Filing—if you would?"

Frowning, clearly upset, Mr. Filing was already on his way. He returned a moment later, distress very evident on his face. "This is my robe." He held up the black shroud, shaking it so it fell into a more recognizable shape. "And this"—he held up the rope; it was gold, about half an inch thick—"is the cord from one of the censers!"

Outrage rang in his tone.

"Where were they kept?" Lucifer asked.

"In the vestry." Filing looked at the open back door. "Good God—did the blackguard attack you in the church?"

Phyllida shook her head. Trying to hold it steady and not rest it on Lucifer's chest was an effort. "I was clearing the vases. I walked out ..." She gestured to the area beyond the open door. She swallowed, and it hurt.

Lucifer was frowning at her. "Filing, I think we should take Miss Tallent back to the Rectory so she can rest. We can discuss the matter more fully there." He glanced at Jem and Thompson. "I take it he got away?"

Jem nodded. "I barely got a glimpse of him. He was already through the lych-gate when I got here."

"Where were you?"

Phyllida waved. "I told Jem he could sit out at the front of the church and watch the ducks. I never imagined ..."

"Indeed." Lucifer tightened his hold on her, tipping her slightly so it seemed natural to lean into his chest.

"I heard the scream and grabbed my hammer and came running," Thompson said, "but by the time I got to the lane, he was in the wood."

"I followed into the wood a ways," Jem said, "but then I couldn't tell which way he'd gone."

Lucifer nodded. "You did well. If he's following his usual pattern, he would have had a horse waiting. No sense running on."

Jem ducked his head, clearly relieved.

Filing had taken the robe and cord back into the vestry; now he fetched the urn, emptied it, and returned that, too, to the church. Phyllida watched as he shut the vestry door; the curate's face was pale and set.

Lucifer turned and headed toward the Rectory. Filing caught him up and fell in just behind; Jem and Thompson brought up the rear.

As they started down the sloping path, Phyllida leaned closer and whispered, "I'm sure I can walk. You don't need to carry me."

Lucifer's eyes met hers; the look in them suggested she'd missed the point entirely. "I do need to carry you." His jaw tightened; he looked ahead. "Believe me, I do."

They trooped into the Rectory; Lucifer made for the *chaise* in the parlor. He lowered Phyllida, laying her along it so she could lie back. The loss of his heat, his muscled strength protectively around her, made her tense. She fought the urge to cling. She'd never clung to any man in her life.

But sudden panic rose as he drew his arms from her and straightened. Fright flowed like a chill through her and she shook. She knew he was frowning down at her, but she didn't meet his eyes.

Mr. Filing appeared with a glass of water. Gratefully, she took it and sipped.

Lucifer stepped back, then prowled around the *chaise*. Without looking, she knew he came to stand just behind her, a protective presence hovering over her.

Mr. Filing paced back and forth before the hearth. "This is shocking—most shocking. That anyone would *dare*—!" Words failed him; pressing his hands together in silent prayer, he stood for a moment, then turned to Phyllida. "Perhaps, my dear, you could tell us what happened."

Phyllida took another sip of water. "I was emptying the vases—"

"Do you always do that on Monday mornings?"

She glanced up and back at Lucifer. "In this weather, yes. Mrs. Hemmings brings flowers up on Tuesday, and then I change the vases again on Saturday. That's what we usually do—last week was different because of Horatio's funeral."

Lucifer looked down into her wide eyes, still dark, still huge, still frightened. "So it was common knowledge that you'd be at the church, most likely alone, with the vestry door open this morning?"

Phyllida hesitated, then nodded. She looked at Filing.

"If we could start at the beginning," Filing suggested. "You reached the church ...?"

Phyllida sipped, then lifted her head. "I reached the church and as usual entered through the main door from the common. I left Jem outside, sitting on the steps."

"There was no one inside?" Filing asked.

Phyllida shook her head. "I picked up the vase from the altar and carried it through to the vestry. I opened the vestry door, propped it open, and took the vase out to empty it. Then I took it back inside."

"You didn't see or hear anyone about?" Lucifer asked.

"No. But ..." Phyllida glanced up at him. "I was ... absorbed. Someone might have been near, but I wasn't paying attention."

The fleeting awareness in her eyes told him what she'd been absorbed with—she'd been annoyed at him, which was exactly what he'd intended. He'd wanted to irk her, to prod the temper he'd sensed and occasionally glimpsed behind her calm facade; wanted to bring it to life and use it to get her to tell him the truth. Instead, he'd distracted her and made her an even easier target for the murderer.

No more games. Jaw setting, he looked at Filing as Phyllida did the same.

"And then ...?" the curate prompted.

Phyllida drew in a deeper breath. "I fetched the urn. It's heavy and cumbersome—I have to wrap both arms about it. I reached the door and stepped out ..." She paused, then went on. "That's when the cloth fell over my head. Then the rope—" She broke off and took another sip of water.

"Quite, quite," Mr. Filing soothed.

After a moment, she added, "He was behind me. I struggled, then I screamed—I heard a door crash."

"That was here." Filing glanced at Lucifer. "Mr. Cynster and I were considering the list of men who did not come to church last Sunday when we heard your scream."

"What happened next?" Lucifer asked.

"He flung me aside and ran off." Phyllida glanced back at Lucifer. "I never saw him."

He looked down at her. "Think back. He was standing behind you—how tall was he?"

She considered. "He was taller than me, but not as tall as you." She glanced across the room. "About Thompson's height."

"Did you get any sense of build?"

"Not as heavy as Thompson"—her gaze swung to Filing—"but not as slim as Mr. Filing."

Lucifer turned to Jem, standing by the door. "Does that sound right for the glimpse you caught, Jem? A man about Thompson's height but of average weight?"

Jem nodded. "Aye. And he had brown hair—leastways, not dark like yours."

"Good. What about clothes? Any idea?"

Jem scrunched up his face. "Neat. Couldn't rightly say gentl'man or not, but neat. Not a smock or anything shabby."

Lucifer glanced down at Phyllida. She'd gone quiet, withdrawn. She was not moving, barely breathing. "Phyllida?"

She raised her face; her eyes were drowning dark pools filled with revisited fear. "A coat," she said, then shivered and looked away. "When I was struggling … I think he was wearing a proper coat."

Lucifer left Phyllida with Filing and strode back to the Manor to fetch his curricle. Returning to the Rectory, he carried Phyllida out to the carriage, ignoring her hissed protests, and set her gently on the seat.

When he flung a rug over her knees, she stared at him. "It's summer," she said as they rattled down the Rectory drive.

"You're in shock," he replied, and said nothing more.

Silence was definitely wise; God alone knew what might tumble out if he let the chaos of emotions inside him free.

He concentrated on driving as quickly as he dared; he wanted her safe indoors again as soon as possible. They reached the Grange gates in a few minutes; a minute later, he pulled up before the steps.

Phyllida flicked back the rug and clambered out before he could tie off the reins. Jem, who had hustled back earlier, came running; Lucifer threw him the reins and followed Phyllida. He caught up with her on the porch.

She stopped him with a look. "I am not going to faint."

This was her home; she should be safe here. "All right." His tone was grudging, precisely how he felt. He looked up as Mortimer opened the door. "Miss Tallent has been attacked—she'll need Gladys and Miss Sweet. If Sir Jasper's at home, I'd like to speak with him immediately."

An hour later, Lucifer stood before the window in Sir Jasper's study and stared out over the Grange lawns. Behind him, seated in the big chair behind his desk, Sir Jasper raised a glass and sipped, then sighed heavily.

Summoned by a horrified Mortimer, Miss Sweet and Gladys had descended on Phyllida and borne her off upstairs. Lady Huddlesford had swept majestically after them, declaring her intent to see that her niece did not play fast and loose with her nerves. Whose nerves, Lucifer wasn't quite sure.

Miss Sweet had popped her head into the study half an hour ago. She'd informed them that Phyllida was resting quietly on her bed and had agreed to the wisdom of remaining there for the rest of the afternoon.

That much he'd accomplished. She was fussed over and safe, at least for the time being.

Lucifer turned. Sir Jasper had aged years in the past hour. The lines in his face had deepened; fretful worry had taken up residence in his eyes.

"What's this place coming to, that's what I'd like to know." Sir Jasper set his glass down with a snap. "Dreadful business when a lady can't go to fix the church flowers without being attacked, what?"

Lucifer opened his mouth, then shut it. Again he felt compelled to bite his tongue. Telling Sir Jasper that the attack was not general but quite specific might dampen his concerns as local magistrate, but would only escalate his fatherly fears.

Sir Jasper fixed him with a frowning glance. "From what you said, it seems unlikely this was some itinerant laborer passing through. Not a gypsy or a tinker."

"No. Phyllida's impression that the culprit wore a coat tallies with Jem's description of him being neatly dressed. In Jem's words, 'not a smock or anything shabby.' "

"Hmm." After a long moment of staring into space, Sir Jasper looked at him. "Any chance this attack is connected to Horatio's murder?"

Lucifer looked down into eyes that were very like Phyllida's but had seen a great deal more. "I can't say."

That was the literal truth.

He turned back to the window. He felt even grimmer than his grim expression showed. "With your permission, I'd like to talk to Phyllida tomorrow morning." He glanced at Sir Jasper, meeting his gaze. "There are a number of matters I'd like to discuss with her, and if I could speak with her privately, I think there are various points we might clarify."

Sir Jasper held his gaze, then turned back to his desk. "Privately, heh? Well, you might be right—not easy to get her to open her budget." He paused, then asked, "Should I mention you'll be dropping by to speak with her?"

Lucifer looked out of the window. "It might be better if my visit came as a surprise."

CHAPTER
Twelve

Midnight. Phyllida lay in her bed and listened to the clocks throughout the Grange chime. The last echoes died and left her in silvered darkness.

She'd slept through half the afternoon, then, after dinner, she'd been harried and hounded until, simply to gain some peace, she'd retired early to her room and her bed. She'd slept. Now she was wide awake.

Nothing hurt. The scrape on her calf and the bruise on her arm were distant irritations.

Her thoughts were more tortured.

Being shot at across a field was something she'd been able to push aside—despite the evidence of the horse Lucifer had uncovered, it *could* still have been a hunter. Being shot at was distant; she hadn't seen her attacker.

At the church, she hadn't seen him, but she'd felt him.

Felt his strength, and known the threat was real.

Fear. She could still taste it at the back of her tongue. She'd never known real fear before—not here in her peaceful, maybe not quite happy but content, existence.

That existence was under threat; she felt it like cold iron at her back. Her life was not something she'd thought of before—she'd taken it for granted. Just like all those around her. How ironic.

She didn't want to die. Especially for no reason. Especially at the hands of some cowardly murderer. Lucifer had been right. The murderer obviously thought she knew more than she did. He was after her in earnest.

Dragging in a breath, she held it, forced the chill from her skin, waited until the shivery tremors had died. She couldn't go on like this—she hated the sense of not being in control, of not being safe. She hated the taste of fear.

So—what to do?

It should have been an easy question; thanks to her promise about Mary Anne's letters, it was anything but. Phyllida lay on her back and stared up at the shadows dancing on her ceiling.

She would bet her best bonnet Lucifer would be back tomorrow morning; this time, he wouldn't let be. He'd insist she tell him all, and if she refused, he would speak to her father. She felt confident in predicting how he would react, certainly in those circumstances where honor and duty ruled. He might be many things, a reprobate, a rake, an elegant charmer of questionable constancy, but at his core he was a gentleman, one of the highest caliber.

It would not be in his lexicon to allow her to endanger herself—that was how he would see it. That, for him, would be the crux of the matter, regardless of how she felt.

After nearly being strangled, she could hardly argue. She would have to tell him all tomorrow. She would tell him about the hat—and then she would have to tell him about the rest, too.

But what of her promise to Mary Anne, her sworn oath that she'd say nothing to anyone about the letters?

What price an oath to a friend?

She'd never imagined facing such a decision. Finding the letters should have been so easy. Even now, if only she could search upstairs at the Manor. She'd been thinking of going one night, when the servants were abed. She knew which room to avoid, but the other rooms ...Mary Anne's grand-mother's traveling writing desk had to be in one of them. She doubted it had been put in the attic. No—it would be sitting on some chest somewhere, looking dainty and delicate, just waiting for her to retrieve the letters ....

Lifting her head, she looked across her room. The moonlight was bright; she could see her dresser clearly, even make out the scrollwork around her mirror's rim.

She pushed up onto her elbows.

Before tomorrow morning dawned and brought Lucifer with it, she had at least four hours of deep night. Time enough to search the first floor rooms at the Manor, find the letters, and return home. And the window in the Manor's dining room still had a loose latch.

She flung aside the covers. If she didn't find the desk tonight, then tomorrow she'd tell Lucifer all and ask for his aid in finding the letters. Despite Mary Anne's and Robert's paranoia, she felt confident that if he bothered to read them at all, the contents of the letters would gain no more than a raised eyebrow from Lucifer; she couldn't imagine him giving the letters to Mr. Crabbs.

But for Mary Anne, and to honor her promise, she'd make one last attempt to find the letters.

Struggling into her clothes, she glanced out at the shifting shadows of the wood. She'd be safe. No one, not even the murderer, would imagine she'd be out tonight.

She was still repeating that thought when she reached the edge of the wood and looked across at the Manor. She'd worked her way farther around the house; across the lawns stood the dining room. To reach the corner window, she'd have to pick her way across the gravel drive.

Steeling herself, she started across, carefully placing each foot before transferring her weight to it. Luckily, her enforced sleep and the brisk walk through the wood had left her physically alert. She reached the beds before the dining room with barely a crunch.

The latch was certainly loose; just a jiggle and the window swung wide. She hauled herself up onto the wide sill, then sat and swung her legs in.

Easing down to the floor, she closed the window, then listened. The house was asleep—she could feel the silence like a heavy cloak hanging undisturbed all around her. Shadows draped the furniture, rendered deeper by the moonlight slanting through the uncurtained windows. Like all the ground-floor rooms, this room was lined with bookcases. Once her eyes had adjusted enough to pick out the books, she moved silently around the large table.

The door to the front hall stood wide; beyond was a sea of shadows. She paused before the doorway, gathering her courage.

Movement. Just by the foot of the stairs. She froze.

A foot above the floor, a disembodied plume came swaying through the shadows, then the cat lifted its head; its eyes gleamed.

She sagged with relief. The cat considered her, then, unperturbed, paced down the hall, tail raised, still swaying.

Phyllida dragged in a calming breath. It had to be a good sign—a cat would sense any evil intruder. Presumably she was the only intruder tonight. She hadn't expected the murderer to be here, yet ...

Putting the nagging worry aside, she crossed the hall, treading lightly, then started up the stairs. She trod close to the banister to minimize the chance of any telltale creak. Reaching the landing, she paused and looked up.

The gallery above was dense with shadow. She took a moment to reorient herself. The last time she'd been upstairs at the Manor was before Horatio had bought it. She knew he'd remodeled and refurbished extensively, but the basic layout of the rooms remained unchanged.

On the way through the wood, she'd distracted herself by planning her search. Horatio had been ill for a week before his death. He'd written to Lucifer in that time, and he'd always had a deal of correspondence. He might have been using the desk himself.

The idea had given her heart. There was no point looking anywhere else before she searched Horatio's room, so she would search it first, even though it was separated from the room Lucifer occupied only by a narrow dressing room.

Reaching the head of the stairs, she stepped into the corridor. Hugging the wall, she slid along, tensing with each footstep, praying for no creaks. The door to the front corner room loomed out of the darkness; it was shut.

She halted, sparing a moment to take it in and breathe a little easier. The image of her nemesis sprawled on his stomach in the big bed at the Grange flashed into her mind. She'd survived the sight once. Even more to the point, tonight she wasn't going to open his door.

She swiveled her gaze to the opposite door, the one to Horatio's room. It stood open—another piece of luck. Mrs. Hemmings had told her that, other than tidying, they'd left the room as it was. Confidence welling, Phyllida resisted the urge to hurry; keeping to her careful glide, she covered the last yards to the door and moved inside.

Halting, she listened, senses straining for any sound, any hint she'd alerted anyone to her presence. Around her, the huge house remained silent, inanimate yet with a presence of its own. Nowhere in that presence could she sense any threat.

Drawing in a steadying breath, she looked around. The room was large, the curtains drawn. She could see enough to avoid the furniture, but not enough to be certain what it was. Grasping the doorknob, lifting to minimize any scrape, she eased the door into its frame. She didn't push it fully closed, didn't want to risk the sound of the bolt falling home. But it was shut enough for her purpose, wedged tight enough that it couldn't swing open.

She still needed to move quietly, but she no longer needed to skulk. Surveying the room, she blew out a breath. Searching thoroughly was going to take more than a few minutes.

The huge bed stood foursquare between twin windows overlooking the lake. A large blanket chest stood at its foot; another heavy chest stood back against one wall. There were two large tallboys, both with deep lower drawers, and three huge armoires. The traveling writing desk could be in any one of them.

An escritoire filled one corner; a comfortable armchair sat before the hearth. The long bay window overlooking the kitchen garden was fitted with a window seat.

Moving past the bed, Phyllida parted the curtains at one side window. The moon was high; silver light streamed in. She looked up—the curtains hung from large wooden rings; both rings and rod were polished from frequent use.

Holding her breath, she drew the curtains evenly back. The rings didn't rattle. Exhaling, she circled the bed and did the same with the other side window, then, for good measure, with the bay window as well.

The result was good—not daylight, but sufficient to search without worrying that she would knock something she hadn't seen to the floor. Fate was on her side tonight. Confidence brimming, she knuckled down to her task.

The desk was nowhere in open sight, but both Mrs. Hemmings and Covey had tidied—they might have tidied it away. Phyllida started with an armoire. The deep shelf at the top looked promising; she fetched the chair from the escritoire and checked, but the shelf held only boxes. The chest by the wall held only clothes. She spent minutes wrestling out the bottom drawers of the tallboys, all without making a sound; they were filled with books. The other two armoires were similarly disappointing. By the time she reached the blanket chest, her spirits were sinking. The chest was filled with blankets and linen.

Closing the chest, she sank down on it. The confidence that had fired her thus far—the conviction that tonight she had to find the letters and would—had faded. Yet as she glanced around the room, she couldn't quite believe that the desk wasn't here. She'd felt so sure it would be.

Her scan of the room had her swiveling around; she ended staring at the bed. She rose and looked under it.

Nothing. Heaving a dejected sigh, she clambered to her feet. One boot toe scraped on the polished boards; the sound wasn't loud, but she warned herself to be careful. She still had to search the rest of the rooms on this floor.

She headed for the door, then halted. What about the curtains—would anyone notice if she didn't close them? She frowned at the wide bay window and decided those curtains, at least, she would have to close.

Only fear of detection kept her from trudging dejectedly across the floor. Rounding the window seat, she reached up to the curtains bunched at that end. Her gaze fell on the window seat. Her hand froze on the curtain.

The window seat was a chest in disguise. The padded, chintz-covered top was hinged. Hope flared anew. Phyllida left the curtains wide and moved to the center of the window seat. Sliding her fingers under its edge, she gripped, then lifted. The long seat lifted up.

It was a weight, but she eased it over—at the very last, her fingers slipped and she lost her grip. The padded edge hit the windowsill with a muted thud. Muted enough to ignore. Phyllida looked down at the length of dark chest and prayed: *Please, let it be here.*

The interior of the chest was deeply shadowed. The lid shaded it and the side windows were too far away to throw much light inside. She would have to search by feel.

She started at one end. The chest was divided into three compartments. Finishing one, she stood and massaged her back, taking a few steps before bending to the compartment at the other end. That, too, proved disappointing.

Standing before the middle section—the last place in this room left to search—she stared into the shadowed chest. Then she sighed, bent, and reached into it.

Her fingers touched polished wood. Her heart leaped. Instantly, she quelled it, reminding herself of the need for care. If she shifted wooden objects around, there'd be bumps and knocks—just the sort of sounds to wake people she didn't want to wake. Like one blind, she felt with her hands, fingers outlining the shapes for her mind.

Walking sticks. A shooting stick. Wooden boxes—could this be it? No— too small. She reached further, easing her fingers between the boxes, trying to ascertain if there was a bigger boxlike object underneath.

Her fingers touched the planks at the bottom of the chest.

At the same instant, a light breeze wafted past her cheek, stirring her hair. Phyllida froze.

No window was open. The only door was the one to the corridor—the one she'd wedged shut.

That door, behind her, was now open.

Slowly, she straightened. Her wildly flickering senses screamed the information that there was someone in the doorway, blocking it. The murderer?

She felt him step forward and whirled—

"Well, well. Why am I not surprised?"

Her breath came out in a rush. Her mind all but wilted with relief. *Thank God, thank God*—the refrain filled her head, then abruptly died.

Her eyes flared wide, then wider; her wits tripped over themselves, then seized. Her lungs already had; they squeezed tight. She stood and simply stared.

Lucifer was standing just inside the room. His broad shoulders did indeed block the doorway. The moonlight washed over him, lovingly illuminating every muscle, every angle, every plane.

He was naked.

One part of her mind wanted to ask where his nightshirt was; the rest considered the point irrelevant. Wherever it was, it wasn't on him, and that was all that mattered.

Her gaze slid helplessly over him, from his face, limned in silver, over his shoulders, his chest. The muscles of chest and forearms were shaded by dark hair, while those of shoulders and upper arms formed smooth, sculpted curves. She could imagine their heat beneath her palms. The band of hair across his chest coalesced to a dark line that trailed down, over his ridged abdomen. His waist was narrow, as were his hips. She couldn't stop herself; she didn't even try. Her gaze lowered. Her mouth dried.

She felt her lips part, her jaw drop; she couldn't summon a single coherent thought. By the time her gaze reached his bare feet, her face was aflame.

In his right hand he was carrying a naked sword, its edge winking silver in the moonlight. He held it in a relaxed grip, as if he were used to wielding it. It was presently pointing at the floor.

Not so that other part of him, equally naked, equally unsheathed. That was pointing—

She wrenched her gaze upward and fixed it on his face. Even then, she couldn't breathe. She could feel his gaze like a living thing, a warm weight on her skin. He was watching her, considering her, his eyes heavylidded.

Then he smiled, a flash of white in his dark face. It wasn't a comforting smile. With the sword in his hand, he looked like a pirate. A naked pirate. Fully aroused. With wicked thoughts filling his mind.

He stepped forward; she stepped back—the backs of her booted calves struck the chest.

Without taking his eyes from her, he reached behind him and closed the door. The click of the latch sounded loud in the suddenly warm dark.

"I suppose," he murmured, his voice deep, his tone languidly conversational, "that you're going to be stubborn and refuse to tell me what you came here looking for."

What she came here looking for. The letters? An alternative truth rose in her mind; she quickly buried it.

He stalked slowly toward her; she struggled to keep her gaze on the naked blade—the one the moonlight was glinting on. She'd seen Jonas in various stages of undress, but nothing had prepared her for this.

The letters. She'd intended telling him about them in the morning. Why not now? She looked into his face. He was close enough now that she could see his eyes glinting, could appreciate the subtle changes—changes she'd seen before.

Desire—he desired her with an almost brutal intensity. A thrill slithered down her spine. What was he planning—what would he do to her if she refused to tell?

"I …" Her voice wavered; abruptly, she lifted her chin and looked him in the eye. "I don't want to tell you yet."

He halted in front of her, a yard away. He held her gaze, then his lips curved. His expression held no disappointment, only a keen anticipation.

"I'll just have to torture it out of you, then."

The intent was there, ringing in his voice, yet the promise was not one of pain but of pleasure—pleasure too tempting to resist, too powerful to withstand. The threat filled her mind with images of warm flesh, hard muscle, silk sheets, and burning touches.

She licked her lips. "Torture?"

His eyes had never left hers. They searched briefly, then he nodded. "Hands up."

The sword flashed upward between them. Phyllida jumped.

"Up." He gestured with the sword.

Frowning inwardly, she raised her hands, palms facing him, up to shoulder level.

"Higher."

The sword flashed again; she frowned openly, but raised her hands to head height.

The sword tip hovered level with her nose, then slowly lowered … she followed it with her eyes. It stopped, resting on the top button of her shirt, just above her breasts.

She looked up—the sword flashed. Openmouthed, she watched as the button rolled over the floor and under the bed. "*What* …?" The word came out as a strangled squeak.

She looked back at his face.

He grinned. "I've always wanted to do this."

The sword flashed again—once, twice—*pong, ping*. Her shirt gaped fully open. Instinctively, she reached to pull it closed.

"Oh, no." The sword flickered warningly before her, quicksilver in the moonlight. "Keep your hands up." He paused, studying her face. "You're not ready to confess yet, are you?"

She looked into his eyes, glinting beneath heavy lids, pure temptation in the night. If she told him all, he'd stop. If she told him, he wouldn't have any reason for continuing … and then she'd never know. "No."

His head tilted, just a little; his gaze grew more intent. He hesitated, then asked, "Are you sure?"

The words were quiet, direct; she understood what he was asking. The night shimmered around them, filled with desire so potent she could taste it. It didn't all come from him. They stood three feet apart, bathed in moonlight, he completely naked, she in breeches with her shirt gaping. And both of them were thinking of taking that next step—of closing the distance between them, of feeling skin against naked skin.

Her fingers itched, her palms burned, her skin heated.

"I'm sure." She heard the words, felt them fall from her lips, sensed them deep inside her. She was sure—she wanted to know and with him she could learn and still feel safe. If the murderer had been a better shot, or if she hadn't fought so hard this morning, she might have died not knowing; that seemed a fate too sad, too pathetic, to contemplate. Lifting her chin, she fixed him with a direct and, she hoped, challenging look. In for a penny, in for a pound. "What next?"

Humor lit his face, then was gone. "If you're not going to confess, then you'll have to do exactly what I say." The "exactly" was invested with particular emphasis. "To begin with, you have to stand ... absolutely ... still."

His gaze dropped as he said it. The sword flashed again—a quick zigzag. The two buttons closing her breeches flew off into the night.

The breeches gaped. Phyllida sucked in a breath and fought the urge to lower her hands.

"Keep them up," he murmured as if reading her thoughts. "Now ... what have we here?"

His deep purr made her toes curl. His gaze remained fixed below her waist.

The sword rose, its tip lifting one side of her jacket. His gaze rose with it to lock with hers. "Slip it off. One arm at a time. Keep the other hand up."

She kept her expression bland; her nerves were skittering. Her stomach was one tight knot. His face right now branded him all pirate—all male predator—but it was desire that burned in his eyes. She did as he said, sliding the jacket off—it hit the window seat behind her. The instant it did, he was busy with the sword again, tangling it in one side of her loose shirt. He lifted, and drew the shirt—slowly—from her breeches, then slid the fabric over her shoulder, tugging it sideways until the seam lay over her upper arm, trapping her arm by her side. He repeated the exercise, trapping her other arm in the same way.

That accomplished, his gaze did not return to her face but fastened on her breasts, firmly bound in linen bands.

Phyllida swallowed.

"You were brave coming here tonight." Eyes narrowing, he brought the sword tip in to rest at the top of the band between her breasts. "Brave—and reckless."

He lifted his gaze to hers fleetingly, then drew the sword down and away. She glanced down. He'd sliced cleanly through just one layer.

"Take a deep breath—now!"

His voice rang with such command that she'd obeyed before she'd thought. The bands slipped, slid, then unraveled in a rush. They clung for an instant, then gave up their hold, collapsing around her waist.

Leaving her breasts naked, exposed to his gaze. She quaked; she couldn't bring herself to look into his face.

But she knew he was looking—she could feel the warmth of his gaze. A slow flush suffused her. Her nipples crinkled, then puckered tight.

He moved then, transferring the sword to his left hand. He stepped closer—his lower body came into view and she quickly raised her gaze. To his chest, to the fascinating pattern of silver-etched muscle and shadow. He bent his head; his lips traced lightly along her temple. He shifted closer, so that all along one side she could feel his heat.

She was breathing quickly, as if she'd run a race.

His right hand rose; he trailed the backs of his fingers along her collarbone, then reversed his hand. It lowered; she watched him cup her breast, then slowly close his fingers about it. His voice was a dark whisper, his lips close to her ear. "Now let's see how much of my torture you can take, before you beg for mercy."

His fingers tightened; she looked up on a gasp. His lips closed over hers.

Lucifer took her lips, took her mouth. He deliberately let passion flare, let the smoldering embers catch fire, then drew back.

He was operating on instinct, primal instinct—a primitive blend of wants, needs, and desires. He wanted her—wanted to possess her, to brand her unequivocally his. After the shock of the morning, and the consequent realization that he'd come within minutes of losing her—of never having her at all—he needed to make her his.

But he also needed her with him, needed her to share the moment fully, needed her to want him as much as he wanted her. To desire him as deeply as he desired her. He desired her as he had no other—wanted her and needed her in myriad ways, some entirely new to him. That emotion he'd hoped never to feel had sunk its claws deep, so deep he didn't even want to shake free.

He was a willing captive—he wanted her to be one, too.

So he drew back from the kiss until their lips parted, not even by an inch but enough to breathe. Enough for her to be fully aware, to feel, to know. To watch from beneath heavy lids.

His hand at the back of her waist still held the sword; the hilt was pressed to her back. Releasing her breast, he slipped his fingers into the folds of her bands; slowly, he drew the linen strip free, then let it fall to the floor. He splayed his hand across her naked midriff, then, lightly caressing her breast on the way, trailed his fingers to her shoulder. He traced the bare roundness; her skin shimmered pale in the moonlight. Instinct prodded; he bent his head. With his lips, he followed the line his fingers had laid over her shoulder, then continued lower, fingers artfully stroking, lips following, until he cupped her breast and lifted the tight peak to his mouth.

Her gasp shivered through the room. Her knees weakened; he tightened his arm about her, bringing her hip against his thigh. He'd warned her he would torture her and he did—rasping her sensitive flesh with his tongue, then suckling hard enough to make her cry out.

The evocative sound ripped through him and set his instincts racing. He shifted across her, trapping her thighs between his, and turned his attention to her other breast, repeating the torment until her hands, trapped low by her shirt, reached for him. Her fingers gripped, then sank into his flanks.

He raised his head and kissed her, took all she offered, all she gave; the flames of desire licked hotly, hungrily. Lifting the sword, he stood it in the open chest behind her. Then he spread his hand across the back of her hips and drew her fully against him.

She murmured, not in protest but in discovery. He held her close, letting her feel the flagrant promise of his body, the heady certainty of pleasure to come.

Her clothes chafed. He lifted his head, then lifted both hands to her shoulders, caressing briefly before sliding his hands down her arms, taking the shirt to her wrists. Her eyes were open but screened beneath lids sensuously heavy; her breathing was rapid, shallow. He paused, hands light on hers. She drew in a deeper breath, held it, and drew her hands from his, tugging them from the sleeves.

He held the shirt until she was free, then dropped it in the chest behind her. Closing his arms around her, he slid his palms along her back, urging her to him, glorying in the exquisite sensation of her silken skin, already heated, brushing, then settling, then sinking against his chest.

She looked up at him briefly; her gaze came to rest on his lips. Her hands rested lightly on his arms; she pushed up, fingers tracing, flexing, over the muscles, then up and over his shoulders. Stretching on her toes, she lifted her lips and touched them to his.

He waited; their breaths mingled. Then she angled her head and kissed him. He opened his mouth and welcomed her in, teasing and tempting her. He held tight to their reins and let her play, let her explore, let her learn.

When she was totally enthralled, he closed both hands about her waist, then slid them lower, easing her breeches down. They didn't fall from her—she was too curvaceous for that—but they now gaped front and back. Their kiss had become a heated melding; he caressed her boldly, then slid both hands deep beneath her breeches and closed them about the firm hemispheres of her bottom. Her skin was flushed; he kneaded, deliberately possessive. Her hands clenched on his nape, then speared into his hair and fisted.

She moved against him, her body lifting, caressing—a siren's song as old as time. He understood; gliding one hand from her bottom, over the curve of her hip, he splayed his fingers over her stomach, pressing until she moaned and repeated her instinctive demand. Then he gave her what she wanted.

He'd caressed the soft flesh between her thighs before; Phyllida wanted to feel the magic again. He traced and played, then entered her, one finger sliding deep and stroking, but it wasn't enough—not nearly enough.

She wanted more, much more—she knew exactly what she wanted.

Drawing back from the kiss, she lifted her weighted lids and looked down. Then she reached down, and closed her fingers gently about him. He tensed; the fingers caressing her slowed. Fascination washed over her.

So hard, so male, yet so delicate. Her fingers brushed, reached, traced, lingered on the softest skin she'd ever touched, then she closed her hand again.

A groan reached her. She glanced at his face just as he raised his head. The moonlight highlighted features set, hard-edged, etched with desire. She tightened her grip and watched his face grow taut, felt his body react.

It was too tempting not to experiment. To see just how much tenser she could make him, how much pleasure she could lavish on him with just that simple touch. Rigid became more rigid; his whole body hardened against her.

He drew in a huge breath, looked down at her, then his head swooped and he took her lips, her mouth, in a kiss that poured fire down her veins. His hand left her; his fingers locked around her wrist and he drew her hand from him. He bent, wrapped both arms around her hips, and lifted her against him.

She didn't want to end that kiss; she framed his face with her hands and, now above him, kissed him hungrily as he walked to the bed. He stopped by its side; he juggled her—she felt him blindly groping, then he flung the covers back. His arms locked her to him. Holding her tight, he kissed her back—a heated duel ensued—it quickly spun out of control. Desire raged through them in a hot tide.

He pulled back with a gasp. He stared up at her face, his breathing ragged, his eyes black pools. They searched her face, her eyes. She looked steadily back at him, her pulse racing, her breathing fragmented.

He reached up again as if to kiss her, but held off with less than an inch between their lips.

"Tell me you want this as much as I do."

A command and a plea—she heard both, felt both.

She slid her hands into his hair. "I want it more." She kissed him ravenously, letting all she felt flow freely, letting the wild desire, the wanton rush of feeling, the excitement, the sensual joy, the anticipation, pour from her to him.

He drank it in, then broke from the kiss and tossed her across the bed. His brief laugh was harsh. "That's impossible."

She didn't argue, but he was wrong. He'd done this before; he knew what was to come, but she'd never experienced it. And she wanted to—with him, tonight.

It felt right, so very right.

He reached for her boots; she let him slide them off. He reached for her breeches and she lifted her hips. He pulled the breeches from her, then let them fall, his gaze locked on her.

She lay naked—as naked as he—and let him look.

He couldn't seem to look away. He knelt on the bed, first one knee, then the other. A ripple of excitement shivered down her spine as he crawled on all fours to come over her. Then, slowly, he lowered himself to her.

It was a shock—a sensual shock—feeling his hard weight settle upon her, sensing his strength, the reined power in his body, feeling the rasp of crisp hair against her sensitive skin. He caught her hands and moved them to his shoulders. He looked into her eyes, then dipped his head.

"We're going to take this slowly. Very, very slowly."

Was he murmuring to her, or repeating an injunction to himself? His lips brushed hers, then slid along her jaw until he nuzzled her throat. His hands pressed down into the mattress, easing beneath her. They traced down her back, caressing as they went. They stopped at her hips, closing possessively.

"This is going to hurt. You know that, don't you?"

She lay beneath him, feeling his heat surround her, feeling her own heat rise in response. His hips lay across her thighs, his erection hot and heavy between them. She closed her eyes and whispered, "Yes."

He said nothing more, asked nothing more. His hands slid lower, tracing the backs of her thighs, then gripping and parting them. He settled between, reached between.

He caressed her, over and over until she thought she'd scream. Her body arched beneath his and still he stroked, probed. She was slick and wet, all but melting when he withdrew his hand; gripping her hips, he eased into her.

It did hurt, but from the first touch of that incredibly soft skin at the entrance to her body, where she so longed to feel him, she knew she couldn't live without having him inside her. The conviction was so strong that despite the discomfort, she tilted her hips to urge him in.

He stilled, fingers clamping hard about her hips, anchoring her. "No—just lie still." The words were strained, uttered against her throat. He waited until she eased back before pressing inward once more.

Slowly, steadily, he filled her. She felt her body stretching and marveled. Then he stopped. He lifted his head, found her lips, and kissed her deeply. She responded eagerly, breathless and yearning—quite for what, she wasn't sure.

She had only an instant's warning—the sudden coiling tension that gripped him. He drew back and thrust into her.

Her scream spilled into their mouths; she arched beneath him, but almost immediately the sharp pain receded. She eased back, into the bed, tensed muscles gradually releasing. He lay still, upon her, within her, and kissed her. She kissed him back, letting him catch her up in the caress, willingly following his lead.

His experienced lead; she realized that when he finally lifted his head. Her body felt invaded, he lay heavy within her, but the pain was gone. He looked down at her, dark eyes glinting. His expression was one she'd never seen before, set and locked, passion-driven. He searched her face—she had no idea what he saw, but it seemed to reassure him. Bending his head, he set his lips to hers. Her hands resting lightly on his shoulders, she gave herself up to the kiss, up to him. Then he moved.

Until he did, the sensation of being so stretched, so filled, hadn't fully registered. As he withdrew, then returned, riding her slowly, the sensual realization impinged again and again.

Her body stirred beneath him. She found his rhythm and matched him, rising to meet him. The effortless joining, the repetitive glide of his body into hers, became her reality. His body shifted against hers, crisp hair rasping her sensitized skin. She slowly heated as if he were fanning a furnace deep within her. Her senses swirled, whirled; the surge of his tongue into her mouth mirrored his possession of her body.

She was his—her fingers tightened, sinking into the muscles of his upper arms. She held tight as the world fell away and only they remained, skin to heated skin. Desire lapped, a warm sea washing over them, through them.

He said it would be slow—she'd felt no sense of urgency, not at first. But something—some compulsion, some blinding physical need—was steadily swelling inside her. Something hot, tight, coiling inside her—with every thrust he touched it, stoked it, fanned the flames higher.

She drew back from the kiss with a gasp; pressing her head back, into the bed, she arched and struggled to breathe, struggled to urge him nearer. Deeper. She needed him there, deep and hard—suddenly, she was sure of it.

He raised up, arms bracing, lifting his chest from hers; his next thrust rocked her.

She gasped again; her fingers trailed, nails sharp, down his chest. The crisp hair that brushed her palms focused her mind on the feel of crisp hair rasping between her widespread thighs. Spreading her hands, she ran them over his ribs, then around—the heat inside her coiled tighter, almost painfully tight … she rose, hands sliding to his back, then clinging tight as she lifted her lips to his.

He took them in a kiss that was almost savage—his weight shifted. He leaned on one arm, his other hand curving over her bottom, tucking her hard against him, holding her there as he thrust deeply—again, again.

The heat inside her exploded; her lower body clenched. A silvery sensation, brittlely intense, speared through her, then the spasm dissolved in a burst of glory. A river of feeling welled and washed through her, soothing away her compulsive heat, leaving a different warmth in its place.

She clung to him and rode the warm tide.

He laid her down, then followed, but he rolled onto his side, then onto his back, taking her with him. She ended sprawled atop him with him still hard within her. She'd melted—she couldn't move. Resting her head on his chest, she lay and luxuriated in heavenly delight.

How much time passed before her wits reengaged and she realized she still lay naked atop him, with his hand lazily, yet somehow intently, stroking her naked bottom, she didn't know. The realization was suddenly there, along with another—he was still hard within her, filling her. His body was still strung tight with that tension she now recognized. He hadn't …

She lifted her head and looked into his face. He studied her eyes, then raised a brow. She blushed, grateful he couldn't see it in the moonlight. "What now?" Presumably there was a next step.

His lips curved, his eyes glinted. "I did say we'd take it slowly."

Her skin was still heated, dewed where he caressed; in contrast, the air felt cool. She had felt relaxed to her toes, but tension was returning along with her wits. She licked her lips. "What does that mean?"

His wicked smile flashed. "It's easier to demonstrate."

He reached down and curled his hands around her thighs. He tugged, and she let him bend her knees up, shift her and mold her—she ended sitting astride him, knees bent, calves tucked to his flanks, hands on his chest, looking down at him. His face held more pain than smile as he lifted her hips slightly, then let her sink down again.

"Oo-oooh." Exhaling slowly, she closed her eyes and let her head fall back.

"Does that hurt?"

"Hurt?" Opening her eyes, she looked down at him. She couldn't find words to describe how it felt. "It doesn't hurt."

"Good." He lay back, sinking deeper into the bed beneath her. "So do it again."

She did, lifting up without his help, although his hands still rode her hips, guiding her. He would let her rise only so far before he stopped her. She sank down and watched his lids fall, watched desire deepen the lines in his face. A new eagerness gripped her—she rode him slowly, concentrating on the feel of him pressing into her softness, concentrated on caressing him like that.

The tension investing his body increased; she felt it through her hands, through her thighs—saw it in his face. She was heating, too. His hands left her hips to close over her breasts; his fingers played—her urgency grew.

Then he rose beneath her and brought his mouth to her breasts. Sharp sensation speared her; she nearly died. Nearly saw rapture again. She clung desperately to her wits as he laved, sucked, teased. The wet spots felt cool against her burning skin.

One hand returned to her hip—he gripped and slowed her. Slowed her until she was nearly frantic, mindless with the need to take him deeper, harder, faster. She spread her thighs and pressed down on him. She rose again—he halted her and pressed her down. And took one turgid nipple into the hot wetness of his mouth and suckled.

She cried out and plunged down, pressing him high inside her. Her world came apart, fragmenting into glimmering shards of rapturous wonder. They penetrated her skin, spread, and melted, until she was a mass of glowing heat with him hard and vibrant at her core.

With a sob, she put her arms around his shoulders, held his head to her breast, curled herself around him, and clung tight.

Gradually, he moved back, drawing her down with him. His breathing was harsh in her ear. Every muscle in his body was locked tight.

"Why?" She whispered the word against his skin.

Lucifer lay beneath her and couldn't think enough to form a coherent thought. "I wanted you more than once, but ..." He lost the thread. She was hot and so tight around him. He brushed a kiss to her temple. "In a moment." His voice was a gravelly rumble, almost hoarse with need.

He'd wanted her more than once, but she'd been untried, untutored. If he'd had his wicked way with her, he'd have had her three times, and she'd have cursed him in the morning. Instead, once inside her, he'd stayed deep, moderating the length and thus the force of his thrusts to minimize the abrasion and pressure to her delicate flesh. So he'd been able to enjoy having her come apart in his arms with him sunk inside her twice … thus far.

Lifting her, he withdrew from her, sliding from beneath her. She murmured, tried to clutch and hold him. He soothed her with a kiss along her back. "You have to do all I say, remember?"

She slumped onto her stomach. "So what should I do?"

He reached for a pillow. "Absolutely nothing. It's my turn now."

She lay boneless and let him lift her hips and stuff the pillow beneath them. He knelt between her legs and bent one slender limb, nudging it to the side, knee almost level with her waist. Then he touched her, leaned over her, and slid home.

Her breath fell from her in a gasping moan.

"Did that hurt?"

She shook her dark head and pressed back against him. He took what she offered, sinking deeper into her body. Arms braced, he lowered his head and dropped a kiss on her shoulder.

"Just lie still and let me love you."

She did—he would have thanked her if he'd been able to form the words. Instead, he thanked her with his body. She lay hot, naked, and completely open before him; he filled her, his hips pressed to her firm derriere, the smooth hemispheres glowing palely in the moonlight. The curves caressed him, her body welcomed him, enclosing him in slick, sweet heat. The musky scent of her rose and wreathed through him; he drew it deep, and felt the beast within him slip its leash.

Beneath him, he felt her stir. She didn't move, but her body tightened about him. He reacted instinctively, pressing his hips to her bottom, thrusting deep, rotating just enough to lift her hips in a roll.

She caught her breath and pushed back, then eased down again. He gritted his teeth, withdrew further, held back, then filled her slowly. He sank home, rolled, withdrew—she moaned.

Filled with feminine entreaty more primitive than words, the sound shredded his much-tried control. He rode her hard, plunging even deeper; she met him, urging him on. He'd meant to be gentle, but she was wild and wanton—he responded in the same way.

She shattered beneath him in a climax so intense he felt it in his bones. She spasmed so hot and tight about him, he thought he'd lose his mind. And then he did. Lost all touch with reality as he lost himself in her. Lost his soul to her heat, lost his heart to her.

CHAPTER

Thirteen

Phyllida woke. She lifted her lids; through the nearby window she could see the sky. A gray light washed over the darkness, presaging dawn, but dawn was not yet here.

Her lids fell; she snuggled deeper into the warm cocoon of the covers. Every muscle in her body felt stretched, released. The heavy arm across her waist was comforting.

She half sat up with a jerk—or would have, but that hairy arm tensed and held her down.

Lying on her side, she sent her senses searching. Lucifer lay sprawled on his stomach alongside her, one arm flung over her. And he was awake. And naked. And so was she. Escaping this while maintaining her composure was not going to be a simple matter.

Unfortunately, rack her brains though she did, she could recall no teachings on the etiquette of leaving a gentleman's bed. If he'd been asleep, she'd have slipped away—and worried about meeting him face-to-face later. Fully clothed, she'd have managed with tolerable calm.

But naked? With him naked beside her?

If she lay there thinking about it anymore, she'd end in a witless panic. She turned; his arm slid over her waist. On her back, she glanced sideways at his face, half buried in the pillow. "I have to go."

Only one of his eyes was visible; it opened and regarded her—far too intently for her liking.

"You haven't yet told me what you were looking for, which is presumably why the murderer is after you."

"It's not, but it's nearly dawn. I have to get through the wood and into the Grange. If you call later this morning, I promise I'll tell you everything."

He didn't lift his head—he just shook it. He looked stunningly handsome with his black hair rumpled; had she done that? Her fingers itched.

"I was going to come and interrogate you this morning, but the present situation has a great deal to recommend it in terms of extracting information."

She frowned. "What do you mean?"

"I mean that you won't be leaving this bed until you've told me all."

"Don't be silly—I have to leave before your household gets up. You won't want your servants to know I'm here."

Lucifer shrugged. "If you don't mind, why should I?" He was going to marry her; in the circumstances, everyone would turn a blind eye.

She stared at him, blank-faced, then her eyes flashed. "Well, I *do* mind!"

She tried to push his arm from her. He sighed and turned—and drew her into his arms. She quieted. He rolled her until she lay on her side, all but nose to nose with him, his arms locked around her, her legs tangled with his, his erection pressed to her soft belly. He looked into her eyes. "In that case, you'd better start talking."

Her expression was impossible to read; only her dark eyes, still wide, still lustrous with lingering satiation, showed her awareness of his state. Of his unstated threat. Her lips firmed, obstinate to the end.

He held her gaze and waited, while the sun rose.

Phyllida capitulated. "I've been searching for a packet of letters. Not mine—someone else's."

"Mary Anne's."

The leap of logic was hardly great. "Yes. She hid the letters in her grandmother's writing desk, and then her father sold the desk to Horatio and it was delivered here before Mary Anne realized."

"What's so threatening about these letters?"

"I don't know. All I know is that Mary Anne and Robert are desperate to get them back without anyone knowing anything about them, much less reading them."

He searched her eyes. "You promised not to tell anyone?"

"I swore I wouldn't reveal the existence of the letters to anyone at all."

After a moment, he nodded. "All right. So you were looking for the letters …" His gaze sharpened. "That's why you were in Horatio's drawing room on Sunday last."

Phyllida sighed. "Yes." It felt good to be able to tell him. And he'd understood about her promise; she'd thought he would. "I was searching for the writing desk and walked into the drawing room—and saw Horatio lying there, dead."

"Where was I?"

"You hadn't arrived yet. I'd just turned Horatio over and realized he really was dead when I heard you striding up the path."

"And?"

"I thought you might be the murderer coming back for the body. I hid."

A frown formed in his eyes. "Where?"

She kept her eyes glued to his. "Behind the door."

His eyes hardened; so did the planes of his face. The arms about her tightened. She'd imagined telling him that she'd been the one who had hit him with the halberd a hundred times, but she'd never imagined doing it while naked in his arms.

"*You* hit me?"

"I didn't mean to! I realized you weren't the murderer and stepped forward to speak to you, and the halberd overbalanced."

He stared into her eyes for a long, long minute; then the muscles in his arms relaxed. "You tried to stop it. That's why it didn't kill me."

She let out the breath she'd been holding. "I tried, but I *couldn't*. I only managed to turn it a bit." The remembered panic washed through her; it must have shown in her eyes.

He bent his head and touched his lips to hers. "It's all right." His hands smoothed over her back. "A bit was enough."

The comfort in his tone, in his touch, wiped away all resistance. She relaxed in his arms. Her gaze dropped to his lips. "Well, now you know."

His lips quirked. "I now know a great deal that I didn't go to bed knowing, but ..."

She blushed and looked back at his eyes—away from those devilish lips. "I don't know why the murderer is after you."

"I think it's because of the hat." She told him, describing it briefly. "But I don't know whose it was, and I haven't seen it since."

A board creaked directly above them. They both looked up. Phyllida paled. "Oh, Lord!"

Lucifer pulled her to him and kissed her soundly, long and deep, his hands playing over her back, her bottom. Then he released her. "Go."

Dazed and blinking though she was, she didn't wait to be told twice. She scrambled from the bed. Her breeches were at her feet; she swiped them up and sat to struggle into them. Crossing his arms behind his head, he lay back and watched her.

She stuffed her feet into her boots, then raced across the room and grabbed her shirt. Neither shirt nor breeches had buttons anymore. Horrified, she turned to him, arms wide, demonstrating. He raised a brow.

She glared, picked up her jacket, and shrugged into it. She stooped to pick up her bands, stuffed them in a pocket, then made for the door, one hand clutching the jacket closed, the other beneath it, holding up her breeches.

"I'll call on you later in the morning. Don't go *anywhere* before then."

His tone gave her pause; from the door, she looked back, then nodded, hauled it open, and fled.

Lucifer listened, but she was quiet as a mouse. None of his household were yet up—he always heard them going down the stairs. She'd be safe getting out of the Manor and safe enough through the wood; no one could know she'd spent the night in his bed. Both attacks on her had been planned; their murderer was not the sort to hang around on the off chance where someone might see him and grow suspicious. She'd be safe getting home; he trusted her to reach her room undetected, not that it was of any truly great moment, but she would worry if she were seen.

The thought gave him pause. He lifted the sheet and looked down. Blood spotted both sheets.

He lowered them, then looked across the room to his exceedingly sharp cavalry saber, standing propped in the chest. Obviously, he'd been unable to sleep, thought he'd heard a noise, and gone to investigate, carrying the saber. He'd nicked his leg, but hadn't noticed in the dark. Then he'd decided to try out Horatio's bed, to see if sleep came easier there. It had. Simple enough.

Leaning back, he closed his eyes and let his mind revisit the night. His lips curved in a wicked smile.

"I want to ask for your daughter's hand in marriage."

The words were amazingly easy to say. Lucifer turned from the window overlooking the Grange lawns and faced Sir Jasper.

Seated behind his desk, Sir Jasper beamed. "Excellent!" Then his smile faded. He cleared his throat. "Of course, Phyllida herself will have the final say. Headstrong female. Runs her own life, y'know."

"Indeed." Lucifer claimed a chair facing his father-in-law to-be. "Apropos of that, it appears her suitors to date have left her with a distinctly jaundiced view of marriage."

"Indeed, indeed—she's been adamant she'll have none of it." Sir Jasper eyed Lucifer consideringly. "Not sure if it's some odd kick in her gallop or not having a mother for so long, or what, but there it is—she declares she has no interest in marrying."

"With due respect, she's been given little incentive to be interested. Everyone expects her to marry, assumes she will, and her suitors have sought to turn that to their own advantage." Lucifer paused, then added, "Few women appreciate being taken for granted."

Especially not intelligent ladies of managing disposition. "Because of that," he continued, "while I wished to make my intentions known to you, I have not yet spoken to Phyllida. We first met only nine days ago, and although I'm sure of my own mind on the matter, I'm equally sure that the way to gain Phyllida's agreement to the match lies in giving her time to convince herself of its rightness."

"So you propose waiting before putting the question to her, heh?"

"I propose wooing her before, metaphorically, going down on bended knee. A few weeks—I'm in no urgent hurry." An all-too-physical memory of Phyllida beneath him seared across his brain; he blocked it off, ignored his reaction, and continued. "I believe the most inimical step I could take at present would be to press my suit."

If he did, she'd immediately want to know why—why he wanted to marry her. He'd be forced to trot out all the conventional reasons, which would paint him in precisely the same unappealing colors as all her other suitors. The reasons were sound, but he knew they were not what she would want to hear. She would not be swayed by them.

He did have one obvious reason no other had ever had—he'd bedded her and therefore should, by all honorable tenets, make all right by marrying her. Although in some respects—the ones pertaining to honor—that struck a chord with him, it wasn't, to his mind, a wise or valid reason to advance in support of his cause.

No woman wanted to hear that she was being married because of honor's dictates. To let Phyllida believe that—to even suggest it—would be both cruel and cowardly. It was nowhere near the truth. He'd bedded her *because* he intended to marry her, not the other way around.

"I believe," he said, "that a course of gentle persuasion is in order."

Sir Jasper nodded. "You may be right. Can't hurt to try that tack." He looked at Lucifer; his expression hardened. "I won't hide it from you—right now I'd appreciate all the help I can get with Phyllida. This business of her being attacked—very possibly twice—has me more than worried. Can't see rhyme or reason to it myself."

"I think we must assume that the attacker is Horatio's murderer. There's no reason to believe Colyton is harboring two men with malicious intent. But the reason he attacked Phyllida is certainly a mystery."

"She says she has no idea why he wants to kill her."

"Hmm. I will, of course, be continuing my investigations into Horatio's murder. With your permission, I'll extend that to include the attacks on Phyllida. It must be the same man."

"Hard to get one's mind around any of it, but yes, I agree. It's most worrying."

Lucifer rose. "Again with your permission, I'll keep an eye on Phyllida. I'll be better placed than others to do so."

Sir Jasper rose, too, shrewd consideration in his eyes. He regarded Lucifer, then nodded and held out his hand. "Whatever permission you need, consider it given. No one I'd rather welcome as a son."

Lucifer grasped Sir Jasper's hand.

"Well, then," Sir Jasper said. "Now you can get to it with a clear conscience, what?"

Suppressing a smile, Lucifer inclined his head. "Indeed."

He left Sir Jasper's study, fully intending to get to the matter forthwith. His conscience, however, wasn't entirely clear. He was concealing his real reason for marrying Phyllida; he intended to do so indefinitely. He knew what it was, yet he could barely let the concept take shape in his brain—stating it out aloud, to her or even to himself, would remain, he was convinced, forever beyond him.

It was simply too much to ask. Not now. Not ever.

He found the object of his thoughts—the object of his lust, his desire, and a great deal more—in the rose garden. She was lopping blooms and laying them in a basket. He stood under the arched entrance and watched her. Watched the sunlight play on her dark hair, striking red lights in the silky strands. Watched the pale gold gown she wore swing and sway around the slender body that had writhed beneath him last night.

Pushing away from the archway, he stepped down to the flagged path.

Phyllida rounded a bush and saw him. She waited, watching him approach with the graceful strength of some large hunting cat. As always, he was the picture of male elegance, this time in a dark coat over pale breeches that molded to his thighs before reaching into polished Hessians. Her heart thudded as he neared; she seized the moment to calm it and strengthen her hold on her emotions. She knew exactly where she stood, where he stood; she would not allow herself to imagine anything more. She inclined her head. "Good morning."

He halted a foot away and studied her eyes. "Good morning."

There was a light in his eyes, a sliding purr in his voice that warmed her more than the sun. She looked at the bush and concentrated on snipping a nicely opened rose. "Have you found the letters by any chance?"

"I looked, but I couldn't find any writing desk, not on the first floor and not in the attics, either. Are you sure it's not downstairs?"

She frowned. "I don't think I missed it."

"Perhaps you should visit the Manor this afternoon and check the downstairs rooms."

She glanced up, then nodded. "It would be a relief to solve at least one mystery."

"As for the question of who murdered Horatio—tell me what happened from the time you walked into the front hall to the time you left the Manor."

"I already told you."

"Humor me. There could be something, some little thing, that you'll remember this time."

Laying the clippers in the basket, she turned. She recounted her movements as they strolled to the arbor at the end of the garden.

"So reaching for the hat was the very last thing you did?" He handed her to the stone seat in the arbor.

"Yes. I thought it was yours."

"Mine?" He sat beside her. "My coats are either black or dark blue. What would I be doing with a brown hat?"

"I didn't know your sartorial preferences at the time." She paused, holding tight to her calm, looking at the roses nodding in the heat rather than at him. "Anyway, I went back in the afternoon to arrange about your horses. I thought I would fetch the hat for you. I asked Bristleford. He was certain there'd been no hat in the drawing room when they found Horatio's body."

"And mine."

She inclined her head. "And yours."

She waited for him to say something about how he'd come to be a "body." Instead, he sat silently for some minutes, then said, "It has to be the hat. The murderer must be convinced you'll recognize it."

"But I haven't. That ought to be obvious by now."

"True, so he must think you *will* recognize it—that you'll suddenly remember. Which means—" He stopped.

She looked at him. "Means what?"

He met her gaze. "That it's someone you've seen often, in that hat."

"So"—she drew a tight breath—"definitely no stranger."

"It's someone you know."

The words hung in the air between them, chill despite the heat. Phyllida held herself rigidly upright and fought the sudden urge to take refuge in his arms. The seat was short; he'd stretched one arm along its back, behind her shoulders. His chest was temptingly near. The impulse to lean into him, to press her shoulder to his chest, to feel his arms close about her, waxed strong.

She knew what it felt like to be held in his arms. It felt safe. But ... she wasn't the clingy sort.

She was about to look away, to switch her gaze to the safe subject of the garden, when he shifted. His arm left the seat back and curled about her shoulders; his other hand tipped up her face. His lips were on hers before she knew it, and then she was kissing him back.

When he raised his head, she frowned at him. "What was that for?" She wriggled upright.

Lucifer released her. He searched for a light answer; only the truth filled his mind. "Reassurance. You looked frightened."

She gazed into his eyes, then lightly shivered and looked away. "I am frightened—a little."

"A little frightened is wise, but the murderer is not going to have you, too."

She slanted him a glance. "You sound very sure."

"I am."

"Why?"

"Because I won't allow it."

Before she could utter the "Why?" he could see in her dark eyes, he drew her to him and kissed her again. After an instant's hesitation, she relaxed and let herself flow into the kiss. The rose garden was private; too tempting. Her bodice was open, his fingers fondling one breast when she pulled back on a gasp and looked down.

"What are you doing?"

He circled her nipple with one fingertip. "I'm sure you can guess."

The gaze she lifted to his face was shocked. "But ... I've told you all I know."

She drew back; he let his hand fall. Puzzled, he tried to see her eyes as she fussed, rebuttoning her gown. Her expression was still calm, if just a little determined. Determined about what, he couldn't guess. "What—?"

"There's nothing I've left out." Gown neat again, she picked up the basket and stood. "You know it all."

Rising, too, Lucifer was certain that last wasn't true. An unwelcome suspicion formed in his brain.

Lifting her head, she stepped out. "I assure you there's nothing more to be gained from continuing to seduce me."

She'd taken only two paces when his fingers locked around her elbow and he swung her back.

"What did you say?" Eyes narrowed, he looked down at her.

She returned his gaze; irritation swam in her eyes. "You heard perfectly well." She twisted her arm; he let her go.

"Why do you think I seduced you?"

She drew herself up—suddenly, he could no longer read her eyes. "You seduced me in order to learn what you wanted to know. Now I've told you all, there's no need ..." She gestured and swung away.

"That isn't why I seduced you."

His tone stopped her. She took a deep breath, then turned to face him.

"Why, then?"

Her challenge rang clearly. Yet she'd asked the very question he didn't want to face, the one he couldn't bring himself to answer truthfully. He looked into her dark eyes, and he didn't want to lie.

A gong bonged, the sound carried on the breeze from the house. They both looked, then Phyllida turned. "That's the gong for lunch." After an instant's hesitation, she walked on.

A moment later, he caught up and fell in beside her.

She didn't speak again until they were climbing the steps from the sunken garden. "If you meant what you said about allowing me to search the Manor, I'll come by this afternoon."

"I meant what I said, but we can walk back together." Lucifer halted on the top step. "Your aunt invited me to lunch."

Phyllida turned toward the house. "How convenient."

His hand on her arm halted her. She glanced back.

He held out a small pouch. "Before we go in, you'd better take these."

Puzzled, she took the pouch. And felt the buttons inside. Heat rose to her cheeks. "Thank you." Without meeting his eyes, she tucked the pouch under the roses in her basket, then continued along the walk.

Three hours later, Phyllida sat in a chair before the desk in the Manor's library, carefully scanning entries in the ledger open on her lap. Seated in the chair behind the desk, Lucifer watched her from beneath his lashes.

They'd left the Grange after lunch and walked to the Manor through the wood. All the way, Phyllida had maintained her usual calm composure, answering when spoken to but otherwise treating him—reacting to him—as if he were any other reasonably intelligent gentleman. She hadn't, admittedly, attempted to treat him with the dismissive air she employed with her other suitors, but by the same token, she definitely wasn't treating him like the man she'd shared a bed with last night.

He'd spent enough nights with more than enough women to know how they should greet him the next day.

Not Phyllida.

Irritation simmered, fed by frustration. He'd turned away from seducing her into telling him all, yet because of her rash actions, and his reactions, he now appeared to have done just that. If truth were told, *she* had seduced *him* into seducing her. It hadn't been his doing that she'd turned up at the Manor in breeches after midnight, searching Horatio's room. Once he'd found her—well, what was he supposed to have done? Bowed and shown her the door?

Suppressing a snort, he tried to focus on the ledger before him. The undeniable fact that he'd used his wish to learn her secret as camouflage, a superficial, flippant covering for the deeper, darker truth, continued to niggle and irk. The situation and Phyllida had conspired to trip him up; the reality of his need, the driving urge to make her his, had completed his downfall.

Why had he seduced her? Because he'd wanted to—*needed* to. If he told her that, she'd sniff and look away, and continue believing the worst.

His gaze flicked to her; he was careful not to stare too intently.

At least she was here, safe and, for the moment, occupied. She'd gone around the downstairs rooms, but the writing desk had not materialized; she'd returned dejected, making sounds about going back to the Grange. He'd suggested she look through Horatio's ledgers to see if he'd sold the desk.

He was also going through the ledgers, searching for any entry that might qualify as Horatio's mystery item. He hadn't found anything yet.

His gaze fastened once more on Phyllida's calm face. He definitely did not like being classed with her other suitors, those who wanted her for material or social reasons, reasons that had little to do with her fair self. They were the ones who had made her lose faith in marriage. The fact that she believed he was like them irked—indeed, irked worse because, from her point of view, he'd been exploiting her, the woman—her emotions, her femaleness—all those qualities the others failed to even see.

Even if she hadn't accused him of that, he didn't like the idea that, in her mind, she might.

How to correct her misconception? There really was only one answer. Having successfully seduced her once, he was going to have to do it again. And the bar on the jump had just been raised. Indeed, now he thought of it, she'd just become an even greater challenge.

The thought made him feel immeasurably better. He thrived on challenges.

Focusing on the page before him, he realized it was the one he'd been on when Phyllida had walked into the room. Stifling a sigh, he fixed his gaze on it, and scanned.

Minutes later, the latch clicked; Bristleford walked in. "Mr. Coombe wishes to speak with you, sir. Shall I inform him you are engaged?"

"Coombe?" Lucifer glanced at Phyllida. "Show him in, Bristleford."

Bristleford withdrew, closing the door. In reponse to Phyllida's pointed look, Lucifer murmured, "Coombe called a few days ago wanting first refusal on Horatio's books."

"You're going to sell them?" She looked shocked.

Frowning fleetingly, Lucifer shook his head; his gaze swung to the door as it opened. Silas Coombe minced in; Bristleford shut the door.

"Coombe. You know Miss Tallent, of course." Rising, Lucifer held out his hand.

Silas bowed extravagantly to Phyllida, who nodded. Then he grasped Lucifer's hand.

"What can I do for you?" Lucifer waved Silas to a chair.

"I won't keep you long." Silas glanced at Phyllida as he sat, then faced Lucifer. "As I mentioned, I'm interested in acquiring selected works from Horatio's collection. As you're a busy man and will doubtless have many other calls upon your time, I wondered if I might propose an accommodation that would suit us both."

"What accommodation?"

"I would be prepared to act as your agent in selling the collection." Silas rushed on. "It will be a very large job, of course, quite a commitment in time, but in the circumstances, I feel the arrangement will serve us both."

For a long moment, Lucifer said nothing; then he asked, "Let me see if I understand your proposal correctly. You're suggesting I should consign Horatio's entire collection to you, and you would arrange the sales for a commission. Is that right?"

"Precisely." Coombe beamed. "It'll make life much easier for you, especially with settling in—new county, new house." His gaze drifted to Phyllida, then he looked back at Lucifer. "Why, I'll even arrange to have the books removed to my house in the interim."

"Thank you, but no." Lucifer stood. "Contrary to your expectations, I have no plans to dispose of any part of Horatio's collection. Indeed, if anything, I shall be adding to it. Now, if there's nothing else?"

Forced to rise, Coombe stared at him. "You don't mean to sell?"

"No." Lucifer rounded the desk. "Now, if you'll excuse us, Miss Tallent and I have various accounts to check." He steered Coombe to the door.

"Well! I mean—well, fancy that! It never occurred … I do hope I haven't given the wrong impression …"

Coombe's protestations died away. Lucifer handed him to Bristleford, waiting in the hall, then shut the library door. He strolled back to the desk. Phyllida was sunk in thought. "What?" he asked.

She glanced up, then waved at the door. "I was just thinking. I don't think Silas has ever worn brown."

Lucifer resumed his seat behind the desk.

Phyllida continued to frown. "What was he after the first time he called?"

"A book—at least one. Other than that, he was exceedingly careful to give no indication."

"Hmm."

Lucifer waited, but she said nothing more. After another minute of puzzled frowning, she returned to the ledger in her lap.

An hour later, Phyllida snapped the last of the recent ledgers closed. "Horatio did not sell that writing desk."

Lucifer looked up. "In that case, it must still be here somewhere."

"Humph!" Placing the ledger on the desk, she glanced at the window. "I'll search upstairs tomorrow, but I should return home now."

Lucifer rose as she did. "I'll walk back with you."

She looked at him. "I'm perfectly capable of walking through the wood on my own."

His jaw set. "I daresay." Rounding the desk, he waved her to the door. "Nevertheless, I'll accompany you."

She held her ground and held his gaze.

He stood there, rocklike, and looked calmly back.

When it became clear he was prepared to stand there all night, she lifted her chin, turned, and swept to the door.

She left the house with him prowling at her heels.

Lucifer didn't let her get out of arm's reach. If anything happened to her ...

It was just as well she couldn't see his face. If he looked half as grim as he felt, she'd probably stop and demand to know his problem. Not something he could easily explain without telling her she was his. She hadn't realized it yet, but she would. By the time he finished seducing her again, she would be perfectly ready to marry him without any further explanations.

He certainly didn't need any further discussion, not with himself or with her. His role felt just right—it fitted him like a glove. Protecting women had always been his role. Even those he tempted to his bed—there was more than one form of protection. But this, following on a woman's heels ready to screen her from any danger—this was him. The essential him. A part of him that needed—demanded—almost constant exercise. He'd never gone for long without a woman to protect.

The twins, his fair and beauteous cousins, had most recently been his release, but they'd turned into harpies and insisted he leave them to their own devices. Under considerable duress and the none-too-subtle threat behind the smothering attention of society's mesdames, he'd retreated to Colyton—only to discover here the perfect answer to his need.

What, after all, was he supposed to do with his life if not to have a wife—and a family, too—to protect? What else was he, under the elegant glamour, if not a knight-protector? Until the twins had refused him and his cousins' marriages had left him too exposed to brave the ton, he hadn't fully appreciated his own nature.

To Have and to Hold, the Cynster family motto—he understood it now, appreciated all that it meant.

For him, it meant Phyllida.

He followed her through the shadows of the wood, and considered how best to break the news to her.

Phyllida plunged a gladiolus spike into the heart of the vase and stepped back. She eyed the arrangement through narrowed eyes, studiously avoiding the lounging presence darkening the vestry door. Collecting a handful of cornflowers, she started setting them in the vase.

She'd arrived at the Manor midmorning and searched the first-floor rooms, all except Horatio's and Lucifer's. Horatio's she'd already searched; Lucifer's … she didn't need to check there. While not large, the traveling writing desk wasn't so small it was difficult to see.

"How thorough was your search of the attics?"

He seemed to be following her train of thought. "Very thorough. So now you've looked, and I've looked—the desk isn't there."

She didn't look at him—she'd sworn she'd give him no encouragement. If he insisted on clinging to her skirts against her clearly expressed, not to say forcefully stated, wishes, she wasn't going to put herself out to entertain him.

Descending from the attics, disappointed yet again, she'd run into Mrs. Hemmings in the front hall. The housekeeper had been flustered. She had a pot of jam at the crucial stage and didn't dare leave it, but she hadn't yet done the church flowers. Hemmings had picked the best blooms that morning; they were in a pail in the laundry.

She'd gladly agreed to do the vases. The notion that the murderer might be haunting the church she'd dismissed as irrational; a brisk walk up the common followed by the soothing ambience of the church had sounded just perfect. Unfortunately, the door to the library had been open. Lucifer had materialized in the doorway—he'd insisted on coming, too.

A short argument had ensued. Once again, she'd lost. It was becoming a habit—one she indulged in with no one else. Losing arguments was not her forte.

By not one word would she encourage him further.

Sticking a finger in the vase, she checked the water. "Too low." Grasping a jar, she walked to the door, looked out, then stepped into the sunshine. She crossed the few feet to the pump—and listened to hear if he followed. No sound—he must still be brooding darkly in the doorway.

Indeed, he seemed to find her as irritating—that was not the right word, but it was something very similar—as she found him. Irritating, puzzling, unaccountable. Utterly impossible to comprehend.

She filled the jar, then lowered the pump handle. As she turned away, her gaze swept the graveyard—a vase on a grave had blown over. She tsked and went over to the grave. Righting the vase, she filled it from her jar and resettled it against the gravestone. Straightening, she approved of the alignment, then turned to retrace her steps.

In the lane beyond the lych-gate, Silas Coombe clicked sedately along in his high-heeled shoes.

Phyllida hesitated, then waved. He didn't see; she put the jar down on a nearby slab and waved both arms.

Silas noticed—Phyllida beckoned.

She thought furiously while he made his way under the lych-gate and up the path. Halting before her, he bowed extravagantly, flourishing a silk handkerchief.

When he straightened, she was smiling. "Mr. Coombe." She curtsied—Silas liked the formalities. "I was wondering … I couldn't help but overhear your conversation with Mr. Cynster last afternoon." She summoned her most sympathetic expression. "He seems quite set on not selling any of Horatio's treasures."

"Indeed." Silas frowned. "A great pity."

"I hadn't realized you were interested in Horatio's volumes." Sinking onto the marble slab, she gestured, inviting Silas to join her. "I had thought your own collection was quite extensive in its own right."

"Oh, it is—indeed, it is!" Silas flicked his coattails and sat beside her. "Just because I wish to purchase one or two of Horatio's more interesting tomes is not to say my own collection needs them for validity."

"I had wondered …"

"No, no! I do assure you. My collection is quite worthy as it stands!"

"So what is it that attracts you to buying certain of Horatio's books?"

"Well—" Silas blinked. "I …" He focused on her face, then leaned closer, raising a finger to tap the side of his nose. "There's more reason for buying a book than just to read it, m'dear."

"Oh?"

"Can't say more." Silas sat back, clearly pleased with Phyllida's intrigued expression. "But I'm not one to be interested for no reason, m'dear."

"A mystery," Phyllida murmured. "I do so love secrets. Surely you could tell me—I would tell no one else."

Striving to appear foolishly fascinated, she leaned closer, then wished she hadn't. Silas blinked; the look in his eyes changed. His gaze lowered to her lips, then drifted lower still.

Phyllida fought a blush—fought the urge to jerk upright. Leaning forward as she was, the scooped neckline of her gown was revealing more to Silas than she'd intended. But … Silas knew something. "Isn't there anything you'd like to tell me, Silas?"

She uttered the question gently, encouragingly. Silas wrenched his gaze up to her face. Then he grabbed her.

Phyllida gasped and tried to straighten, but Silas had his arms around her.

"My dear, if I'd known you preferred more elegant men—more sophisticated gentlemen—I'd have gone down on my knees years ago."

"Mr. Coombe!" Crushed against his chest, Phyllida dragged in a breath. His cologne nearly suffocated her.

"My dear, I've waited and watched—you'll need to forgive the strength of my passions. I know you're unversed in the art of—"

"*Silas*! Let me go!"

"Coombe."

The single word fell like the sound of doom. A vengeful, threatening doom.

Silas started. He uttered a sound like a shriek, released her, and leaped to his feet—almost landing against Lucifer. Silas whirled, clutching his chest, ruining his floppy bow. "Oh, my! My word. You—you startled me."

Lucifer said nothing at all.

Silas looked into his face and started to back down the path. "Just having a friendly word with Miss Tallent. No harm in it—none at all ... you'll have to excuse me." With that, he whirled around and clattered down the path as fast as his high heels would allow.

Still seated on the slab, Phyllida watched him go. "Good Lord."

She knew when Lucifer's gaze left Silas's retreating figure and fixed on her. "Are you all right?"

The words sounded like they'd been said through clenched teeth. She regarded him calmly and stood. "Of course I'm all right."

"I assume the impression Coombe was laboring under was mistaken?"

She shot him a frosty look, straightened her skirts, lifted her head, pointedly stepped past him, and headed up the path. "Silas knows something—something about one of Horatio's books."

He fell in beside her, a large, hard, darkly masculine presence pacing by her shoulder. "Perhaps I should pay him a visit. I'm sure I could persuade him to reveal his precious secret."

There was a wealth of menace in his tone; Phyllida was grateful Silas wasn't there to hear it—he'd have fainted on the spot. "Whatever it is may have nothing to do with Horatio's murder. We know Silas is unlikely to be the murderer, and he certainly isn't the man who attacked me—he's too short." She paused before the vestry door and glanced at Lucifer. "You can't go around intimidating everyone into doing as you wish."

His midnight-blue eyes met hers. The message in them was simple: *You think not?*

Raising her chin, she stepped into the vestry—and stopped dead. He walked into her—she would have fallen but for the arm that wrapped around her, effortlessly lifted her, then put her down two feet farther into the room.

She caught her breath and swung around. "I left the water jar outside."

He raised one hand—it held the water jar.

"Thank you." She took it—her fingers brushed his. She blocked the sensation, wiped her reaction from her mind. Turning to the vase, she filled it.

The sense of menace behind her didn't abate.

"Don't do that again."

"Don't do what?"

"Slip away where I can't see you."

Amazed, she turned. "*Where you can't* ... Who appointed you my keeper?"

His face hardened. "Your father and I—"

"*You discussed this with Papa?*"

"Of course. He's worried. I'm worried. You can no longer"—he gestured sweepingly—"waltz around the village as if you don't have someone trying to kill you."

"You have absolutely no right to—to *dictate* to me!" She whirled, snatched up the vase, and headed into the nave. "I'm my own person and have been for years. I'm *astonished* Papa—" She broke off; she couldn't think of words to express the jumble of her feelings. Not precisely betrayal, but certainly a sense of having been handed over …

She plonked the vase down on the shelf beside the pulpit, breathed in, then rearranged the disturbed blooms.

She didn't need to think to know where Lucifer was—she could feel him right behind her. After a moment, he stepped around to her side. She felt his gaze on her face, sensed him trying to glimpse her eyes. She refused to look at him.

Finishing the flowers, she brushed her hands, then tensed to step away—

Hard fingers slid beneath her chin; he turned her face to his.

He held her gaze, studied her eyes. "Your father is seriously worried about you. So am I. He cares for you …" He paused, then his face hardened. "And just so you can get your astonishment over all at once, your father has agreed to let me watch over you. In his words: 'Whatever permission you need, consider it given.'"

She stared at him—into that harsh face, all hard angles and planes, into his eyes, filled with ruthless candor. A weight—some power—amorphous but unrelenting, invincible, inescapable, settled around her and held her. She didn't need to wonder if he was telling the truth—his eyes told her he was.

"And what of *my* permission?" Her voice was calm, steady—much more so than she felt. Her heart was thudding in her ears, in her throat.

His gaze held hers, then it lowered. To her lips.

"As far as I'm concerned, I have your permission already."

The words were dark and low. The weight around her closed in.

Phyllida stiffened. Lifting her chin from his fingers, she looked him in the eye. "In that, you're quite definitely mistaken."

She stepped past him, out of the circle of that dark embrace, and walked—calmly—out of the church.

CHAPTER
Fourteen

A fter lunching alone, Lucifer strode into the wood and headed for the Grange. Phyllida had insisted on returning home immediately after leaving the church. He'd insisted on accompanying her. He'd seen her onto the Grange's front porch, then returned to the Manor via the wood. Now he was retracing his steps—because he couldn't bear the thought of her being simultaneously in danger and out of his sight.

Ten days since they'd first met, and look what he'd been reduced to.

He'd already visited Silas Coombe. Although almost incoherent, Silas had said enough to convince him he knew nothing about any specific volume in Horatio's collection; he'd simply hoped to lay his hands on some treasures at bargain prices. Silas was not the murderer.

Lucifer swung along the leaf-strewn path; he moved quietly, an innate hunter. There was a point where the path curved sharply, thick bushes limiting the view ahead. He rounded it—and stopped, just in time to avoid mowing Phyllida down.

She ran into him instead.

He caught her, steadied her—he had to fight not to close his arms around her. Her breasts pressed to his chest were a remembered delight; lust, desire, and that simple need she and only she evoked poured through him.

She must have felt his instant reaction. Her breath caught in her throat, then she stiffened, dragged in a breath, and stepped back.

"My apologies." She sounded breathless; she didn't meet his eyes as she flicked her skirts straight. Lifting her head, she looked past him. "I was on my way to your house."

He felt her gaze touch his face; his own gaze was fixed on the empty path behind her. She hadn't brought any escort. His temper rose; hot words burned his tongue—an elemental need to lash her with them gripped him.

He swallowed the words, resisted the urge; the effort left him feeling like a beast caged. At least she'd been coming to see him. After this morning, he should probably be grateful.

Stepping aside, he gestured her on. He fell in behind her, on her heels, and waited to hear why she wanted to see him. To say she understood? To admit that she was wrong to wander about alone and that she appreciated his watchful care?

They reached the edge of the trees and she walked into the sunshine. "I came to ask," she said, "if you would mind if I look through the outbuilding and storerooms." She surveyed the former across the kitchen garden. "They're stuffed with furniture—it's possible I missed the writing desk when I searched that Sunday."

Lucifer looked at her face, but she didn't—wouldn't—look at him. After a moment, he drew breath. "If that's what you wish, then by all means ..." With a bow that was cuttingly polite, he waved her on. "You will, however, have to excuse me—there are other matters requiring my attention."

She inclined her head haughtily and headed for the outbuilding. He watched until she entered it, then turned to the house. He marched through the kitchen, curtly dispatched Dodswell to keep watch on the outbuilding, then retired to the library, leaving strict instructions he was not to be disturbed.

Phyllida stepped into the outbuilding and finally managed to draw a full breath. Her nerves were still twitching; she stood in the silence and willed them to settle.

What was going on? In the space of a few days, her life had changed from humdrum to unpredictable, from mundane to exciting, from sleepy to intense. And it had very little to do with Horatio's murder. That might be part of the drama about her, but it was not the source of the whirlwind of change.

A hot wind named Lucifer.

Luckily, he'd left her alone. If he'd stayed, she—or he—would not have been able to resist reopening their unfinished discussion. The result would not have been a happy one. She was still smarting from learning that he'd discussed her safety with her father rather than with her. No one—not Cedric, not even Basil—had simply and so arrogantly *assumed* control of her.

The thought made her so angry, she thrust it aside, bundled the whole question of Lucifer away. She looked around. The long building was filled with boxes and furniture stacked along the walls and also down the center, leaving a path circling the room.

She'd searched here first on that fateful Sunday. She'd thought she'd been efficient, yet, as she studied the jumble, hope flickered to life. The traveling writing desk wasn't big—about twelve inches wide, twelve deep, maybe nine inches tall at the back. The sloping lid had leather the color of rose lavender set into it. A handsome piece, she could recall seeing it on Mary Anne's grandmother's knees innumerable times.

She could have missed it. Determination renewed, she started checking each stacked piece, each box, moving counterclockwise around the room. Her eyes searched; her hands touched, reached, poked.

Her mind wandered.

She should never have allowed him to seduce her, of course, but even now she didn't—couldn't—regret that night.

She had wanted the experience, had yearned for the knowledge. Thanks to him, she'd got her heart's desire. That, however, should have been the end of it—a bargain of sorts, an exchange completed. One night filled with passion for the answers he'd wanted. The exchange had been made, yet something lingered.

Something else. And she wasn't even sure it had been born of that night. His possessiveness was a tangible thing—she had to wonder, given his recent behavior, if it had been there before and their night of passion had been driven both by his wish for answers and by his wish to ...

Lips thinning, she shook her head. If he'd thought that would help his cause, he would need to think again. She wasn't a possession—not his, not any man's, not even her father's. She was herself—her own woman—and she would remain so, come what may.

As long as she stayed out of his arms so she wasn't visited by that all-but-overwhelming compulsion to spread her hands over his chest, she'd be safe. Safe from him. As for the murderer, they'd have to work together to ensure he was caught. On that they did not differ. Regardless of what lay between them, finding the murderer remained a shared goal.

That thought was comforting—she didn't want to ponder why. Shifting her mind back to the task at hand, she continued steadily searching.

She was almost at the far end of the building when Lucifer paused in the doorway. He saw her and stopped, hesitated.

He wished he knew what he was doing—what he was going to do. He was operating totally on instinct, an instinct that told him she didn't understand. She thought he'd seduced her for information. Regardless of the truth of that, did she seriously imagine that after that night he'd simply shrug and walk away? That he'd stop wanting her?

While he did not wish to examine, much less explain, his deeper motives, he was more than willing to correct that particular misconception.

Stepping over the threshold, he closed the door. Light slanted through narrow windows set high in the walls; Phyllida did not notice the dimming of the light behind her. He strolled toward her, watching her shift a box and peer under a table. She bent over; lilac muslin pulled tight over her hips. He considered the sight as he neared.

She straightened; he heard her sigh. Then she replaced the box and stepped back. Into him.

She tripped backward over his boots. His arm about her, his hand splayed across her midriff, he steadied her against him. She caught her breath; dark hair sliding like silk over his shoulder, she looked up, into his face.

Their eyes met, held for an instant, then her gaze lowered to his lips. His gaze slid to hers, then to the expanse of ivory breasts revealed by her neckline. The sweet mounds rose and fell. He bent his head, turning her to him.

She stopped him, her fingers light on his cheek.

He held her in one arm, her breasts against his chest, her thighs between his. Her lips were parted, her eyes wide; her gaze was fixed, not on his eyes, but on his lips.

"Why?" The whispered question overflowed with genuine puzzlement. She lifted her eyes to his.

He looked into them and searched for a true answer. "Desire." He lowered his head. "Hasn't anyone told you of that?"

He kissed her; she kissed him back, not hungrily so much as wonderingly. Her lips were soft and full, warm, tempting. They parted tentatively—a hesitant invitation; when he immediately accepted, she softened in his arms, surrendering her mouth, inviting further conquest.

Conquest of whom, by whom, was moot; he pushed the question aside and sank into her, into the delight of her, letting the feel of her awaken him fully, letting his desire for her unfurl. It was a deliciously wicked moment, and even more delicious in its promise. He closed his arms about her, bringing her fully against him. The kiss deepened; their senses swirled, whirled, waltzed.

When they came up for air, she didn't pull away. Her dark eyes searched his face, then settled once more on his lips. "Is this desire?"

"Yes." He brushed her lips with his. "But there's more. You've heard the music, but that's just the introduction. There's more steps, many more movements to the dance."

She hesitated; desire shimmered about them, a silvery anticipation hovering, waiting ... She drew a short breath. "Show me."

He drew her closer; she let him. Let him hold her hard against him so her breasts caressed his chest and her thighs met his. His hands firmed about her waist; hers slid up to his shoulders. Their gazes were locked on each other's face; slowly, he bent and covered her lips with his.

Phyllida gave her mouth, her body, readily, too intrigued, too enthralled to draw away. Walk away. Did he truly desire her? No one else ever had. Was it possible? Was it desire that lingered after their night of passion?

Those weren't questions she could leave unanswered, yet it wasn't them alone that drove her. Drove her to spread her hands and flex her fingers, sinking them into the broad muscles of his shoulders as she stretched upward against him. Their kiss deepened, heated, and she wanted to get closer, to feel his desire as more than heat—as flesh and blood, muscle and skin, hunger and yearning.

Desire flowered between them, not just his, but hers, too—a new, very delicate bud. He skillfully coaxed it and she knew he did, knew he was waiting for it to bloom. When it did, in a rush of warmth and longing that flowed over her skin, he drew back from the kiss, lips sliding to trace her jaw, then her throat, as if he could taste it.

Their breaths mingled, warm, rushed, eager yet controlled. His lips touched hers again. "Open your bodice for me."

A warm shiver skittered over her skin. She glanced down; three buttons fastened the front of her gown. His arms eased. Her pulse sounded heavy in her ears as she lowered her hands and set her fingers to the buttons.

She knew what she was doing; she knew why she was doing it. There was something here, between them, that explained all—excused all. Something that prompted her to feed his desire, and hers.

The third button slipped free and the gown gaped, revealing her chemise, fastened with a row of tiny buttons. She unfastened them, too. After an instant's hesitation, she drew the layers aside; she could feel his gaze on her breasts as she bared them. A heated touch, it swept them and they swelled.

She would have looked up, but he bent his head, his temple against hers as his hand rose to caress her. The arm about her tightened, holding her hips against him; his fingers touched, traced, then fondled.

He'd touched her breasts before, but only in the night when shadows had shrouded them, hiding so much from her view. His face, close by hers, showed his leashed desire in the hard angles and planes, in the dark glow of his eyes beneath their heavy lids, in the sensual line of his lips.

He touched her gently, the pads of his fingers warm and vital, circling her aureoles, teasing her nipples into bud with just a brush. He watched as her skin heated, then glowed, brought to life by his ministrations; she watched, too, watched the reverence with which he invested each caress, not seizing but worshipping—a different face of desire.

She lifted one hand to his cheek, then turned his face so she could see his eyes. They burned darkly, turbulent yet banked. Controlled. He turned his head and pressed a kiss to her palm. She stretched up and kissed him, soft, deep, as temptingly as she could, then she drew back, leaned back, pressing her breast into his hand.

She didn't need to spell out her invitation; his head bent and his lips fastened on her heated flesh, hot, wet, burning. He kissed, licked, and she shuddered, fingers tangling in his hair. She closed her eyes, waiting … she tensed, nerves jumping when he rasped one nipple with his tongue. Then he took her into his mouth and her body melted, then tightened as he suckled, only to ease again.

The level of heat between them rose steadily; desire thrummed. She felt it in her fingertips, felt it spread under her skin.

He raised his head and drew her close, his breathing as unsteady as hers. He breathed deeply, chest expanding, coat rasping against her naked breasts. Lips close by her ear, he murmured, "Do you want more?"

"Yes." The word left her lips as she lowered her hands. She plucked the sapphire pin from his cravat, anchored it in his lapel, then tugged at the folds around his throat. At the edge of her vision, she saw his lips curve. Cravat loose, she started on his shirt buttons and flicked him a glance. "What?"

The curve deepened into a wicked smile. "Not quite what I had in mind, but … do carry on."

She did, tugging his shirt loose and baring his chest. She stared. Moonlight had not done him justice—not at all. There was a warm tone to his skin that made her palms ache; she set them to the heavy muscle band across his chest and pressed, stroked outward. He closed his eyes. She stroked down, fascinated by the contours, the ridges, by the contrast of smooth skin roughened by crisp hair. He was heavy yet lean, sleek but solid. So very real.

She skimmed her hands back up to the flat disks of his nipples; greatly daring, she pressed closer, nearer, bringing her breasts, bare and sensitive, against his lower chest. Her skin tingled; her breasts ached. Easing them against him, she circled his nipples with her thumbs.

His hands clenched at her waist; he bent his head. His lips traced a line from her temple to her ear. He gave a short laugh—a little harsh, a little shaky. "My turn."

He drew her closer, his hands sliding down her back. At the backs of her thighs, he stroked her skirts upward, not lifting them but frothing them until they spilled and fell over his hands—leaving his hands beneath her skirts, riding over bare skin.

She caught her breath—he stroked—heat washed over her in a prickling wave. Her senses focused on the areas he touched; she leaned her head against his chest, slid her arms around him, and let her senses follow his lead.

He cupped her bottom, fingers tracing, learning, then caressing until she shuddered and clung. Head bowed against his chest, she put out her tongue and licked—and felt him tense. She turned her head and found a nipple, and licked again. His hands clenched, then eased, then kneaded provocatively.

He bent his head and breathed against her cheek, "More?"

She nodded, eyes shut as she savored the feel of him wrapped all around her—savored the building urge to have him closer still. "I want you inside me." The words left her lips before she'd thought; she might have blushed, but she was already so warm she couldn't tell. But she didn't take the words back; she couldn't lie. Not about this. "Is all this desire?"

"Yes." After a moment, he added, "This, and what's to come."

He looked up, then under her dress, his hands rose to fasten about her hips. He backed her, steering her a few steps past a rolltop desk to where a high sofa table stood by the aisle; the table touched the back of her waist.

"I take it that's not the desk in question."

Fingers on the buttons closing his buckskin breeches, she barely glanced at it. "No." She looked back at his waist. "Wrong sort of desk."

He looked down; his fingers tightened on her hips. "No—not yet."

"Yes. Now."

He didn't argue—he moved his hands. One to her bottom, splaying, then pressing and lifting to tilt her hips. His other hand slid down her stomach until his fingers tangled in her curls, then he touched her.

Sensation speared her. She slumped, her head against his chest. "No." But her protest lacked strength. Another argument she'd lost. She licked her lips, her senses already following the drift of his wicked fingers. "If you ... I won't be able to think, later."

"You will." He pressed a kiss to her temple. "I promise." His fingers stroked. "This time, you'll know it all." Gently, he probed the soft flesh between her thighs, then bent his head and nudged hers; his lips found hers in a languid, open-mouthed kiss that was hot enough to scald. "Open for me."

The whispered words sighed through her. She moved her feet, then, as she felt him reach between her thighs, she curled one ankle around his booted calf; that gave her better balance.

"Yes." The encouragement came with another kiss. She ran her hands, trapped between them, up over his chest, his shoulders, and clasped them at his nape. Her breasts tingled, abraded by his hair-roughened chest; exquisitely sensitive, they felt hot and tight. The kiss ended and he laid his cheek against hers; she glimpsed his face, eyes closed, expression blank.

She rested her head on his chest and gave herself up—to him, to the thrills of sensation his fingers pressed on her, to the desire that beat about them, strong and growing stronger.

He held it back—held her anchored, safe from being taken and consumed too soon. She wanted to know, to learn, to experience desire in its full glory, so he reined himself in, and reined her in, too, so she could feel and know all that was, and anticipate all that would be.

He'd touched her before as he was touching her now, yet only now did she fully realize, fully feel, the true intimacy. The slickness of her flesh, its swollen state, the growing sense of aching emptiness—these had happened before, yet only now did she appreciate them.

"Desire," she breathed; it wasn't a question.

She lifted her head and looked into his face. She stretched up and kissed him. Brief, hungry. Their lips parted. She leaned her forehead against his jaw, and he slid one finger slowly into her.

She closed her eyes and felt her body tighten, clasping him within her. Her eyes opened and she relaxed, then he stroked. His lips brushed her temple. "You do that when I enter you."

He continued to stroke slowly, then withdrew and explored, only to return to slide within her again. Whether he was learning her or teaching her, she wasn't sure, but she felt every touch, every circling glide.

Heat fell from them in waves; desire rode the tide. She could feel it all around them, a welling sea rising to swamp them. It beat in her blood and his, in an increasingly compulsive tattoo.

It was she who lifted her head and breathed, "Now."

From beneath heavy lids, he looked at her face, then met her eyes. His were so drowning a dark blue they seemed black. His fingers didn't cease their slow, repetitive motion. "Can you think enough?"

For a moment, she was lost, then she remembered. She drew in a short, tight breath and nodded. Tracing one hand slowly down his chest, she felt at his waist, then slipped the buttons free.

Hot, iron-hard, he filled her hand. She closed her fingers slowly, then slid them down, then up, marveling anew at the contrast of velvety softness encasing rigid strength. She ran her finger around, then over, the broad head.

His breath shivered by her ear. Fingers closing, she looked up; eyes shut, his expression was tight, fraught.

"Does that hurt?"

"No."

Smiling, she looked down and closed her hand again.

He bore with her torture for only a minute more.

"Enough." His hands left her, then gripped her hips. He lifted her and balanced her on the edge of the sofa table.

She grabbed his shoulders; she wasn't far enough back to sit securely. Wild panic gripped her—exhilaration and anticipation raced through her. But she didn't want to lose her wits—not yet. There was more she'd yet to see, more she'd yet to appreciate. She wanted it all—every moment. She sucked in a breath. "How?"

Her question snapped his attention back to her face; he met her gaze—in his eyes she saw the fight he waged to releash his need, to bring it back under control. He paused, then drew in a long breath and nodded. "Wait."

Fingers sinking into his shoulders, she did.

He lifted her skirts and chemise, pushing them back, catching them under her so they pulled tight across her hips and stomach. She looked down and blushed; the dark locks below her stomach curled wildly, a soft nest between her bare thighs. Her stockings were gartered just above her knees; hands closing on the bare skin above her garters, he eased her thighs wide and stepped between. He'd loosened his breeches, releasing himself fully.

She ran her hand down, fingers trailing the length of his chest, then down still farther, until she coiled her fingers around his length. He caught her wrist and moved her hand away. He grasped her hips, drew her right to the table's edge, then held her there.

He stepped closer and she caught her breath.

"Watch."

She did.

Lucifer watched her, watched the total absorption in her face as he pressed against her soft flesh. He found her entrance, and let her feel the pressure build before, with a gentle nudge, he slipped inside. Only a fraction. Just enough for her to catch her breath, then shudder and tense. He waited, expecting her to relax again. Then he realized.

"It won't hurt—not this time. Not ever again." He whispered the words against her hair and willed her to believe them. His control was exceptional, but so was she—exceptionally hot, exceptionally wet, exceptionally trying. "When you relax, I'll slide into you—you already know I'll fit."

She let out a shuddering breath. "Yes."

He felt her body ease, little by little, around him. At last she was open and accepting. Slowly, very slowly, he pressed into her.

Head bowed, she watched him enter her, ultimately sliding home. She shivered. He pressed deep, then settled her. Then he withdrew. Because she was watching, he withdrew all the way, then reentered her and slowly sank home. She watched him penetrate her twice more before, with a shuddering gasp, she broke.

He was waiting when she clutched his shoulders and lifted her head blindly. He caught her, caught her lips in a searing kiss, and let their reins loose. She came to him like a wanton, eager, abandoned. She pressed herself to him, bare breasts hot against his chest, nipples tight, taunting as she shifted with each thrust.

"Put your legs about my hips."

She did; wrapping her arms about his shoulders, she lifted herself against him. He spread his hands beneath her bottom and held her as he thrust deep, then withdrew, only to return harder, deeper. She clung to him; he filled her mouth, filled her body, bathed in her wet heat.

That heat was exquisite, burning bright, hot enough to cinder their senses. He shattered deep within her, drowning in her glory. An instant later, she followed, shuddering in his arms.

He held her close; she curled around him, resting her head on his shoulder. Their hearts thundered; his chest swelled as he dragged in a breath. He eased her down, resting the backs of his hands on the tabletop, then placed a soft kiss in her hair.

For long moments, they remained still in the silence, locked in the comfort of that intimate embrace.

Phyllida couldn't believe the depth of the pleasure that washed through her. She was floating on a sea of golden joy, anchored, held safe in his arms. Throughout the entire interlude, that was how it had been—desire, intimacy, pleasure, and joy, all safe in his arms.

They still surrounded her. Beneath her cheek, she could hear his heart beating strongly, gradually slowing as they returned to earth. Her only wish was that, rather than here, still clothed, they were naked in his bedroom. Then there would be no reason to pull away—to disturb the moment. She could lie in his arms forever, bask in his heat forever. Play desire with him forever.

Only it hadn't, really, been play. The desire that had held them, driven them, and, at the last, consumed them—that desire had been very real. Hers and his—theirs.

She lay in his arms, and wondered just what lesson he'd really meant her to learn.

"Where are you leading me?" The most pertinent question.

"You know where."

In her heart, she did. She had known, but not believed. Now she had to. "Where?"

Better he say it, so she couldn't pretend otherwise.

"I would never have made love to you if I didn't intend to marry you."

He hadn't wanted to tell her—she could imagine why. "I haven't agreed."

He let the silence stretch, then he pressed a kiss to her hair. "I know—but you will."

CHAPTER
Fifteen

"You said Covey had uncovered something about Lady Fortemain. I forgot to ask—what was it?"

Seated at his desk, a stack of books before him, Lucifer glanced across the Manor library to where Phyllida sat on a straight-backed chair facing one of the bookcases. She was working along one shelf, checking each book for notations, then entering the book's details in a ledger. Covey was working likewise around the drawing room. Lucifer had started on the shelves behind the desk.

"It was an inscription in a book. 'To my dear Letitia, with fond memories of our recent time together, etc. Humphrey.' I understand Lady Fortemain's husband was Bentley. It appears Horatio bought some volumes from the Ballyclose library and that book was among them."

Phyllida looked at him. "Well, it's hardly a sensation to find such an inscription. I daresay it dates back to before Lady Fortemain married."

"The book was published after Cedric was born."

"Oh."

"Indeed. However, we haven't stumbled on any other such protestations of affection for her ladyship, so I'm not setting much stock in that at present."

Phyllida swung back to the bookshelf. After a moment, she shrugged and continued her cataloguing. Lucifer returned to his.

His campaign to win her, to woo her into marrying him, was progressing in a slow if not steady manner. He hadn't intended to state his decision to marry her so soon, but their interlude in the outbuilding had made it imperative she know—so she couldn't imagine he'd had any other motive in seducing her. Again. He was well aware that repeating the exercise had been easy only because she desired him with an uncomplicated directness that, at least while in his arms, she made no effort to deny.

He'd worried that after they'd left the warm stillness of the outbuilding, she'd grow skittish and even more difficult. Instead, she'd unsettled him with her continuing calm, as if she were coolly considering him and the question he hadn't yet asked. He wouldn't ask—not until he was sure of her answer; that was the strategic course. As long as she hadn't refused him, he could continue to press his suit, albeit carefully.

He wasn't fool enough to take gaining her agreement for granted; she had an entrenched belief that marriage was not for her. Her cool appraisal suggested he'd made her revisit that belief, but she hadn't yet changed her mind.

He needed to tread warily. Seducing a lady into matrimony was not a game he'd played before; he wasn't sure of the rules. But he'd never yet failed in a seduction—he wasn't going to start with Phyllida Tallent. How to seduce a lady of managing disposition? Thanks to her previous suitors, she had no appreciation of her womanly charms, much less their effect on him; the notion that her sweet self held the power to sway him was bound to be attractive. He'd need to make an effort to be more manageable than he was, but if that was her price, he'd pay it. He'd unblinker her vision, show her what might be, then leave her to convince herself how desirable that was.

Desire, in all its forms, was on his side. He only had to touch her to feel it flare—sometimes he only had to meet her dark eyes to be conscious of their mutual need. He could afford to give her time to decide that, despite her qualms, marrying him was an excellent idea.

For the past two days—yesterday and today—he'd pursued the strategy of propinquity, the notion that being constantly with him would help quell whatever qualms she possessed. On both mornings, he'd called at the Grange after breakfast; yesterday, after finishing her search of the outbuilding and storerooms, she'd joined him here. They'd spent the hours since making inroads into Horatio's book collection. Unexpectedly, they'd stumbled on a shared interest, stopping every now and then to exclaim over some plate in an old tome, to share some discovery. Her excitement yesterday over the illuminations in a prayer book had had him smiling—he'd caught a glimpse of his own youthful enthusiasm in her face. Thus must Horatio have seen him. They'd parted that evening when he'd walked her home before dinner, closer, more relaxed, the understanding between them broadening, deepening.

Propinquity was definitely working. It hadn't escaped him that, just now, she'd felt sufficiently comfortable to not bother looking at him when asking her question. A sign of growing ease. Little by little, even if she didn't know it, she was leaning his way.

They broke for lunch, a cold collation Mrs. Hemmings had laid out in the dining room. Afterward, returning to the library, they found Covey stacking books on the desk.

"I've finished one wall in the drawing room. These are the books with notes written in them—I forgot to give them to you the last couple of days."

"That's all right, Covey. We'll go through them now—it'll give us a break from the shelves." Lucifer lifted a brow at Phyllida.

She nodded and headed for the desk. They settled in, he behind the desk, she in a comfortable chair before it, and knuckled down to decipher the often illegible notations.

"Hmm." Phyllida sat up and scanned the desk, picked up a scrap of paper, placed it as a bookmark in the book on her lap, then set the book on the floor by her chair.

She glanced up; Lucifer looked his question.

"A recipe for plum sauce—I must take a copy."

Lucifer smiled. They returned to the books. Companionable silence wrapped around them. The clock on the mantelpiece ticked on.

Then Phyllida sat up. Lucifer glanced at her; she was frowning. "What?"

"This has another inscription to Letitia from Humphrey. 'To my dearest heart, my love, my life.' It's dated February 1781."

After a moment, Lucifer asked, "How old is Cedric?"

Phyllida looked at him. "In his late thirties."

Lucifer raised his brows and held out a hand for the book; when Phyllida gave it to him, he set it aside. "One to think about later."

Five minutes later, Phyllida humphed. "This is another one 'to my dearest Letty.' The wording is quite ... warm. It's signed 'Pinky.' "

"Date?"

"1783."

Lucifer added that book to the "later" pile.

Fifteen minutes later, the pile had grown by three more volumes. Handing over the last, a book of poetry sent to dearest Letty from a gentleman who'd signed himself "Your fated lover," also with a date of 1781, Phyllida viewed the pile with consternation. "This is really rather worrying."

Lucifer eyed the stack of books with notations they'd yet to check. "From what we have already, it would appear Cedric, certainly, has cause to be concerned over what might be found in Horatio's collection."

Phyllida stared at him. "You mean that Cedric might not be Sir Bentley Fortemain's legitimate son?"

Lucifer nodded. "If that could be proved, and if Sir Bentley's will is the usual simple affair, then Pommeroy could claim that Sir Bentley's estate should be his."

"Pommeroy is not fond of Cedric."

"So I gathered. That gives Cedric a definite motive to clandestinely remove books from Horatio's collection."

Silence fell. Phyllida stared at Lucifer; he looked steadily at her. "I can't believe Cedric's a murderer."

"What does a murderer look like?"

"Even worse, Cedric wears brown. Most of the time. I know he wears brown hats."

"Think back—have you ever seen him wearing the hat you saw in Horatio's drawing room?"

Phyllida considered, then shook her head. "I can't recall seeing him in that particular hat."

"Are you sure you'd remember it?"

"The hat? Yes, definitely. I looked directly at it. I nearly picked it up. If I saw it again, I'd know it."

Lucifer sat back. "If Cedric's our murderer, he won't still have the hat."

"No. He'll have got rid of it. Cedric may bluster, but he's not stupid." Phyllida frowned. "Did you ask Todd who rode out from Ballyclose that Sunday morning?"

"Dodswell asked. Unfortunately, Todd not only went to church, but then visited his brother-in-law's farm. He has no idea who rode that morning." Lucifer considered. "Could Cedric have been the intruder we chased?"

Phyllida grimaced. "Cedric used to be more athletic. If pushed, he could probably run as fast as the intruder."

"So Cedric's a possibility."

Phyllida fell silent; after a moment, Lucifer prompted, "Penny for your thoughts."

She glanced at him, then looked away. "Cedric wants—wanted—to marry me. If he's the murderer, then ..."

Lucifer glanced at the clock, then stood and rounded the desk. "Come on." He held out his hand.

Phyllida looked up, her fingers slipping into his even without the answer to the question in her eyes.

Lucifer looked down at her. "You've forgotten the summer ball at Ballyclose Manor tonight."

"Good heavens!" Phyllida glanced at the window. "I *had* forgotten." She looked at Lucifer. "Perhaps ...?"

He met her gaze. "We'll need to go carefully, but we can certainly test Cedric's interest in Horatio's books, and all they may contain."

Five hours later, stylishly gowned in pale blue silk, Phyllida stood by the side of the Ballyclose ballroom and watched the only one of her suitors who had succeeded in getting her to consider marrying him. He was standing across the room, charming the Misses Longdon; clinging to the shadows thrown by a large palm, she considered his tall frame, considered the dark locks rakishly framing his brow, the elegant black coat and trousers set off by his ivory cravat and an ivory silk waistcoat. Along with most of the women in the room, she savored the aura of strength and masculine confidence he so effortlessly exuded.

She'd hoped distance would help her gain perspective. With an inward sniff at her own susceptibilities, she forced her gaze from him and scanned the room. She'd sent Basil to fetch her a glass of orgeat; she hoped he would find some distraction along the way.

She needed time to think. Spending day after day by Lucifer's side was undeniably pleasant, but it made thinking sensibly about him difficult. And she definitely needed to think—about him, about marrying him. About what she wanted, about if she would.

His statement that he would never have seduced her if he hadn't intended to marry her had opened her eyes, not to his motives but to hers. *She* would never have *allowed* him to seduce her if she hadn't already loved him, even if she didn't understand what love was.

She'd always found the subject of love—love between a man and a woman—confusing.

Her mother had not lived long enough for her to form any useful view of her parents' marriage. The only other married couple she knew well were the Farthingales, and their relationship was based on mutual acceptance, not on any stronger emotion. Lady Fortemain's apparent excursions outside matrimony only muddied the waters further—she had always viewed her ladyship as the epitome of a gentlewoman.

No one had explained love to her. As for her reaction to Lucifer, she'd been suffering from self-assured blindness, convinced such an emotional development—the sort that looked set to bind Mary Anne and Robert for the rest of their lives—could never happen to her.

Out of the blue, it had. Lucifer had arrived and affected her life like an earthquake—everything had changed and was still changing. The new landscape hadn't yet taken final shape. She hadn't yet allowed it to do so.

Desire might have temporarily fogged her brain—it still did with just a touch, just one look from those midnight-blue eyes—but she was still her own woman, still in charge of her life. Letting the matter slide as she had with her other suitors was not an option with Lucifer. She couldn't ignore him; he'd created and occupied a place in her world that none of the others had. He was her lover.

He was, however, a great deal more.

A ruthless pirate at heart, a protective tyrant—all that she could easily see. She'd also experienced his gentleness, his tenderness. In teaching her of his desire and hers, he had, time and again, put her needs ahead of his wants. She might have been innocent, naive, a virgin, but she'd overheard enough over the years to know not all men were so considerate. With him, it had gone far beyond consideration—he had cared.

The emotion, the impulse, was so much a part of her, she'd recognized it instantly with no possibility of error. He cared for her. That truly unnerved her—everyone else expected her to be the one who cared.

She had wondered whether he'd seduced her intending to use the fact to pressure her into marriage, yet he hadn't done so. She was under no illusion that he expected to win her, to ultimately gain her agreement to their wedding, but she'd read his character accurately—he'd play fair. He was so much stronger than she, yet in his arms she never felt threatened. In his arms she felt safe—safe from everything, even him. So it was still her life, her choice, although he would do all he could to influence it.

It was still possible to say no, to turn her back and retreat to safer ground, but she was no longer the woman she'd been when he'd arrived, and so much of what he was offering was tempting. But there was one major hurdle to accepting that new future: How would their marriage work? If like the Farthingales' or Lady Fortemain's, then her answer would be no. He'd asked her what she wanted of marriage. She'd always known what she didn't.

She couldn't make up her mind, not without the answer to that major question. Could it work? Could she retain her sense of self while being the object of his overpowering protectiveness and the associated, highly possessive ramifications? Could she accept being cared for, rather than being the active carer? Could she adjust? Could he? If both of them were willing ... that raised the question of how willing he was.

When he'd asked what she wanted of marriage, she hadn't had a clue. Now she did. She wanted to share. She wanted to work together, live together, love together—to make a difference together—to share his life and have him share hers. That was a prize worth the risk of binding herself to a protective tyrant.

If she told him what she wanted, would he give it? Would he let her take the driving seat sometimes? Was he truly capable of sharing the reins?

Smiling, she turned to greet Basil, all her questions still weaving through her mind.

Basil had brought her orgeat; she rewarded him with the next dance. Lucifer had strolled up the instant she'd stepped into the ballroom; they'd agreed to let the ball get under way before sounding Cedric out. So they were both dancing, chatting, and waiting for the time to pounce.

Lucifer watched Phyllida curtsy and link hands with Basil, then was forced to pay attention to his own partner, a Miss Moffat. Lady Fortemain had been exceedingly busy on his behalf—she'd invited every unmarried young lady for miles around. He was sorely tempted to tell her she didn't need to bother. He knew who his wife would be.

The word used to make him shudder; it no longer did. He was beyond fighting this fate—it was too desirable to reject. But he knew his social role and he played it well, charming the ladies, conversing with the gentlemen, acting as the perfect guest. Around him, the large crowd swayed and dipped. Lady Fortemain had pulled out all the stops; the occasion exuded a festive air. Her neighbors had joined in enthusiastically; the faces about him glowed.

The Grange household was well represented. Sir Jasper stood chatting with Mr. Farthingale and Mr. Filing. Mrs. Farthingale and Lady Huddlesford were similarly occupied. Jonas, Percy, and Frederick were engaged on the dance floor. Percy had condescended to attend. Frederick was making an effort to be pleasant. Jonas, on the other hand, had an easy smile on his face—only his eyes flicking every now and then to Phyllida gave him away.

Lucifer twirled Miss Moffat; he could dance a cotillion without thought. Like Jonas's, his thoughts were on Phyllida and the man who had her in his sights. He had spoken to Jonas. If, for some reason, he wasn't watching Phyllida, then Jonas would be. No matter her intentions, no matter her fear, she too often forgot the danger. The village was her home; she'd been safe here for all her twenty-four years. It was hard to change a lifetime's habit. So he or Jonas would keep watch over her until the danger was past.

This was the second cotillion, the fourth dance; as he changed sides in the set, Lucifer scanned the crowd.

Cedric was standing in a patriarchal pose, watching his guests with an approving eye. Lady Fortemain was the center of a knot of voluble ladies. Pommeroy was dancing despite the exigencies of his ridiculously high cravat. Lucius Appleby was lending his assistance entertaining the guests and doing a much better job than Pommeroy.

The local ladies considered Appleby an enigma; Lucifer read the signs with ease. Appleby ranked as handsome; despite his reserve and an attitude that suggested he had no interest in stepping over anyone's line, his success with the ladies was assured. A Miss Claypoole was dancing with him, eyes and lips smiling. Appleby deflected her interest with a confidence that had Lucifer wondering.

With a flourish, the cotillion ended; Lucifer bowed and excused himself from Miss Moffat's side.

He headed for Phyllida's. She welcomed him with a smile that warmed him and a look so eager he pressed her fingers warningly. He exchanged nods with Basil.

"How opportune, Mr. Cynster. I was about to mention that I understand Phyllida's been forced to spend the past two days at the Manor for safety's sake. That must be both boring for Phyllida and a distraction for you, what with all you have to do to settle Horatio's estate." With a patronizing air that stated louder than words that he believed every word he said, Basil smiled at Phyllida. "I'll send the carriage around tomorrow morning, my dear. Mama would be delighted to have you spend the day."

Lucifer glanced at Phyllida's face, calm as always, and resisted the urge to applaud. She returned Basil's smile. "Thank you, Basil, that's a kind thought. But I have other plans for tomorrow."

"Indeed?" Basil clearly considered asking what; instead, he said, "Then perhaps—"

"The day after tomorrow is Sunday, so that's out of the question. After that … well, the endeavors with which I'm assisting Mr. Cynster have yet to be completed, so I'll still be helping him at the Manor."

Her tone as she uttered that last sentence was enough to give even Basil pause. After a moment, he bowed. "My apologies, my dear, if I did not properly understand—"

There was no apology in his tone, only irritation and faint rebuke; Phyllida stopped him with a raised hand. "There's a great deal you fail to properly understand, Basil, usually because you don't wish to understand it."

A violin hummed, then screeched. Phyllida turned to Lucifer. "I believe that's our waltz commencing."

Lucifer bowed and took her hand. He nodded to Basil. "You'll excuse us, Smollet."

No question, of course; Basil bowed stiffly. With a bob, Phyllida turned on Lucifer's arm and let him lead her to the floor. She went into his arms, following his lead without thought; after a moment, she felt his hand stroke her back.

"Relax."

She threw him a glance—one she knew he would interpret correctly. "Where he ever got the idea that he *owned* me, that he could simply appropriate me and dictate my life, I have no notion."

Lucifer said nothing. He drew her closer, just enough so their bodies brushed lightly as they whirled. She softened, relaxing into his embrace.

"Not all men are like that, surely?" She glanced around them. "Well, of course they're not, but just look at Basil, and Cedric, and Henry Grisby. No woman of sense would marry such a man." After a moment, she added, "Perhaps it's something in the water hereabouts."

Lucifer held her protectively tighter as they went through the turn, then he murmured, "Appleby. How long's he been with Cedric?"

"Appleby?" Phyllida scanned the dancers. "He's been here ... well, it seems a long time, but he only joined the household last February. Why?"

"I wondered before if he'd been in the military—I think he must have been. He seems popular with the ladies."

"He is. They approve of his style and his person, and his behavior is such as must please."

"You don't sound particularly taken."

"I've never seen the attraction, I must confess."

Lucifer was glad to hear it; her tone left no doubt she found the other ladies' interest puzzling. Her comments on Basil were less reassuring.

"I think," she said, "that it's time to speak to Cedric."

Lucifer glanced at their host, now listening to Lady Huddlesford. "At the end of this dance. Follow my lead."

"What tack do you intend to take? You can hardly walk up and ask if he was aware he might be illegitimate."

"I thought I'd ask if he was interested in acquiring any of Horatio's tomes." Lucifer looked to where Silas Coombe, resplendent in a green silk coat and a canary-yellow waistcoat, stood conversing. "How likely is Coombe to have mentioned to anyone that I don't intend to break up Horatio's collection?"

"Silas is an inveterate gabblemonger."

"In that case, I'll have to watch my phrasing."

The music ended. Lucifer released Phyllida, raised her from her curtsy, then tucked her hand in his arm and strolled toward Cedric. He was with Lady Huddlesford. Everyone exchanged bows; then her ladyship, overwhelming in bronze bombazine, regally glided away.

Cedric smiled at Phyllida, then looked at Lucifer. "Well, sir, I hope our simple country gathering measures up in some small way against what you're accustomed to."

"It's been a thoroughly felicitous evening," Lucifer returned. "Your mother is to be congratulated, as I've already told her."

"Indeed, indeed. Mama delights in these sorts of affairs. She used to be a feature in the capital before the pater's health forced them to retire here. You may be sure she's pleased to have reason to entertain in such style again."

"If that's so, then I'm pleased to have been of service." Lucifer considered the bluff geniality that colored Cedric's expression. Was it a facade, or his true nature? "I don't know if you've heard, but I've decided to keep Horatio's library essentially intact."

"Ah, yes! I did hear Silas bemoaning that fact. He seemed to think some of Horatio's collection would be better housed with his own."

"Unfortunately for Coombe, my mind is made up, in the general sense. However, in checking Horatio's records, I noticed he'd acquired some volumes from your library."

Cedric was nodding. "Before his death, the pater—greatly taken with Horatio, he was—went through the library and sold quite a few tomes to him."

"Indeed. As your father is now dead, and as I'll be preserving the collection more as a memorial to Horatio than from any real interest of my own, I wondered if you wished to repurchase any of those books. At the same price Horatio paid your father, of course."

Cedric pulled a face. "Not much of a book man myself. I always thought it wise of the pater to get rid of a few of the books. There's a blessed lot left if you're interested."

Lucifer smiled easily. "It's not my field."

"Ah, well, worth a try." Cedric turned to Phyllida. "Now, my dear, we've been neglecting you shamefully. I hear you've been spending your days at the Manor."

Cedric glanced at Lucifer; Phyllida stiffened. If he intimated she just sat there, twiddling her thumbs …

Cedric looked back at her. "Daresay there's all manner of things you've been helping Cynster with, heh?"

Her stiffness easing, Phyllida inclined her head. "Indeed." She glanced at Lucifer. "All manner of things."

Lucifer's dark eyes smiled at her, then his gaze went past her and he bowed. "Miss Smollet."

Phyllida turned as Jocasta joined them. Jocasta exchanged greetings with Cedric, then glanced at her. Phyllida inclined her head.

Jocasta mirrored the movement, then, smiling a touch brittlely, fixed her gaze on Lucifer. "I understand, Mr. Cynster, that you're considering life as a farmer. Basil tells me you're talking of setting up a stud."

"It's one of the possibilities I'm investigating. The fields and meadows of the Manor are currently underused."

"True, very true." Cedric frowned. "Tend to forget how much land there is, back of those woods of yours."

Lucifer regarded him. "Have you been that way recently?"

Cedric shook his head. "Can't recall being down that side of the valley for over a year. Not hunting country."

"Cedric hunts with the local pack," Jocasta said. "Will you be joining them, Mr. Cynster?"

Lucifer smiled. "I only ride hounds to ride, rather than to hunt."

Phyllida swallowed the observation that, for him, a fox was the wrong sort of prey. She stood and pretended to listen while inwardly she plotted. Eventually, Lucifer excused them; they left Jocasta with Cedric. Her hand on Lucifer's sleeve, she strolled with him through the milling crowd.

"Was it my imagination, or was Cedric less … fixated on you than when last we met?"

Phyllida blinked. "Now you mention it, yes. In fact, he seemed rather relaxed. He didn't seem perturbed that I've been helping you at the Manor."

"You know him better than I, but I would almost say he was *relieved* you were spending so much time at the Manor."

Phyllida looked forward. Lucifer was right. And how did she feel about that? "If he's relieved, then I'm relieved." She glanced at Lucifer. "I've known Cedric all my life. I've always considered him a friend; I never wanted him as a suitor."

Lucifer held her gaze, read her eyes. "And you don't think he's a murderer, either."

"No." She sighed. "It's so horrible, knowing how you feel about people but logically knowing it's possible."

"I detected not the slightest degree of consciousness over the books, or about my fields beyond the wood."

"No, that was simply Cedric. What you see is what there is."

"Speaking of facades"—Lucifer steered her toward the side of the room—"Jocasta Smollet was making an effort to be conciliating. I can't help suspecting she's the victim of some sad story." She struck him as a woman who'd missed her chance at happiness, yet still searched for it every day. "Perhaps that's the reason for her normally acid tongue."

Gaining the side of the room, Phyllida faced him. "Having usually been a target for her acid tongue, but then, almost everyone in the village is, you know, I hadn't really thought of it, but she does seem sad. I've never seen her smile or laugh, not happily, not for years."

"You don't know her story?"

"No. And that's really rather odd, because if I don't know, then it must be a secret, and in a village this size … that's amazing."

For a moment, they both pondered, then Phyllida shook aside her thoughts and looked into Lucifer's face. "I think we should search Cedric's room for the hat."

Lucifer's blue gaze fixed on her eyes. "Why? I thought we'd agreed he'd passed our tests."

Phyllida grimaced. "I *like* Cedric. I don't want him to be the murderer. Or my attacker. But you know as well as I do that beneath Cedric's genial *bonhomie* is an intelligent man, and the threat implied by those inscriptions is a real motive for him. It would destroy his life." She gestured about them. "It would destroy all this. And this simple country life is important to Cedric."

She studied Lucifer's face, then narrowed her eyes. "And despite what you just said, you haven't crossed him off the top of our list of suspects."

Lucifer's lips thinned. "No, but—"

"We owe it to ourselves, the village, and Cedric to turn every possible stone to determine whether he's the murderer or not."

"Searching his room for the hat." Lucifer fixed her with a gaze too patronizing for her liking. "As you yourself pointed out—"

"I know he *should* have got rid of it, but what if he hasn't? This isn't London—decent hats aren't easy to come by. He might have laid it aside, intending to get rid of it, but I've made no mention of the hat—even of being there that Sunday. He might reason nothing will ever come of it. Who knows—he might even have forgotten about the hat. It might be something quite different that he thought I saw."

She turned toward the ballroom door. "If you wish to remain here, *I* will go and search Cedric's room."

She took one step. Long fingers curled about her elbow and stopped her in her tracks.

"Not. Alone." The two words rumbled just above her ear; they carried a weighted warning she could not have described in words, but her senses translated effortlessly. She waited, her gaze fixed on the door.

A sigh brushed her ear. "Where is Cedric's room? Do you know?"

"Upstairs to the right—the last door along the corridor."

"Very well." He drew her to face him. "In a moment, we'll part. I'll head for the refreshment table. You stroll a little—not enough to get caught—then go out as if heading for the withdrawing room. I'll be watching. I'll give you enough time to reach Cedric's room, then I'll follow."

Phyllida looked at him. "You've done this before."

He simply smiled, then he bowed and they parted.

Phyllida followed his instructions to the letter—not something that came naturally, but she could see no good reason to do otherwise. He'd agreed to search Cedric's room—that was what mattered. And not only in terms of their investigation. It meant he could be reasoned with, which, did he but know it, was a definite point in his favor.

Henry Grisby tried to solicit her for the next dance; she politely declined and headed for the withdrawing room. No one was about to see her glide up the stairs. Once in the gallery, she turned right. She reached Cedric's room; her hand was on the knob when she heard a distant footfall. Glancing back, she saw Lucifer step up from the stairs.

He saw her; she waved, then opened the door and walked in. Less than a minute later, he joined her, easing the door closed behind him. Phyllida watched him straighten, watched him prowl toward her, his gaze scanning the room; it came to rest on her.

Moonlight slanted through the uncurtained windows and lit his face. She suddenly recalled how he had looked three nights before, when he had crossed such a room toward her. The same heavy-lidded eyes, the same sensual lips. His gaze dropped to her lips; she could swear he was having the same sensual, wicked thoughts.

Her breath caught in her throat.

He stopped before her, less than a foot away. His heat reached her; his gaze rose to her eyes. He studied them. His hand rose; one thumb brushed her lips and she shivered.

His lips curved, just a little—not taunting, but self-deprecatory. "Hats," he murmured. "Where would Cedric store his hats?"

Phyllida blinked. Weakly, she waved to a small door. "In his dressing room. There's a hat shelf."

Lucifer looked at the small door, half ajar, then back at her, one brow rising.

"This was Sir Bentley's room—he was ill for years. I often visited."

Phyllida bustled to the door, ignoring the tempting warmth that had slid under her skin. She tried to ignore the presence following at her heels, but that was beyond her.

Lucifer stepped into the dressing room—long and narrow, it ran the length of the main bedroom. A hat shelf was fixed along the wall facing him at head height. It was packed with hats.

"This *isn't* London." He glanced at Phyllida. "Cedric owns more hats than any gentleman of fashion I know."

"All the more reason to check—it looks like he's never thrown one away in his life."

That was true. Phyllida couldn't reach the hats. He stood there, her assistant, and handed them to her, one by one. She took each specimen in both hands, studied it, held it at arm's length, then shook her head and handed it back. In the moonlight streaming through the high single window, all the hats appeared the same color—brown.

Slowly, they progressed the length of the shelf. With a sigh, she handed the last hat back and shook her head. He was reaching up to the shelf, setting it back, when a faint sound—not a click, not a tap—reached his ears. He froze.

Phyllida froze, too, head tilted. Then she looked at him. He held a finger to his lips, then turned.

The bedroom had two doors—the one they'd entered by, near to the wall of the dressing room, and another, leading to the adjoining room, presumably a sitting room. They would have heard someone coming along the corridor. Had someone just entered from the sitting room?

Cedric? But would a host leave a country ball?

If he was a murderer, he might.

Lucifer drew in a breath and stepped into the bedroom.

A rush of air, a faint whistle, warned him—he ducked back—a heavy rod cracked across his left shoulder.

The impact drove him to his knees; he caught himself, bracing with his right arm on the doorframe, and saw a man's figure, shrouded in shadows, whip around the door into the corridor. The sound of fleeing footsteps thudding on the corridor runner reached them.

"Good Lord! He's getting away!" Trapped behind him, Phyllida lifted her skirts and leaped over him.

He caught her in mid-leap and hauled her back. "*No!*"

She fell on him. "But—" She wriggled furiously, silk skirts a-froth in his lap. "I might catch him!"

"Or he might catch *you!*" He tightened his arm around her and she quieted. "Oh."

"Oh, indeed." Teeth gritted, he shifted her so her hip wasn't grinding into him, then tried to ease his shoulder.

She turned to him. "He was waiting."

"With this." Lucifer reached out and pulled a cane toward them, then lifted it so they both could see. The top of the cane was a lion's head, brass and very heavy.

"It usually sits in the corner by the door." Phyllida looked at the corridor door, and tried not to think about what might have happened if Lucifer's reflexes hadn't been so honed. If he hadn't ducked and the cane had connected with his skull, he might have died, or at least lost consciousness. Leaving her facing the murderer.

She turned to Lucifer and saw the same realization in his gaze. "We have to get back to the ballroom."

CHAPTER
Sixteen

"Jonas, I wonder if we might have a word." Phyllida by his side, Lucifer smiled at the two young ladies with whom Jonas had been conversing.

The young ladies giggled; they bobbed curtsies, then bustled away, casting coy glances over their shoulders.

Jonas met Lucifer's eyes. "Any trouble?"

"As a matter of fact, yes." Lucifer smiled as if they were bandying observations.

Jonas looked at Phyllida. "I thought Phyl was with you."

"I was," Phyllida put in. "But that's not the trouble."

Jonas raised a brow. Phyllida looked away and decided to leave the explanations to Lucifer.

"Did you notice any of the gentlemen slipping away about fifteen minutes ago?"

Jonas raised both brows. "Cedric left, then Basil left. Filing had left before that. And Grisby, too. There had to be others missing as well, because there was a dance and there weren't many couples on the floor and not many men standing out. Lady Fortemain was beating the bushes."

"Has Cedric returned?"

"He came back a few minutes ago—Basil returned a bare minute before that. They both looked a trifle choleric. I haven't seen any others slipping back, but I wasn't watching." Jonas looked at them. "What happened?"

Briefly, Lucifer told him. Phyllida scanned the room, trying to determine which gentlemen were present. The crowd was still considerable. "Do you think," she said, when Lucifer fell silent, "that we might engineer a trap?"

They both looked at her, identical expressions of male incomprehension on their faces, as if she'd spoken in an alien tongue.

"What sort of trap?" Lucifer eventually asked.

"I didn't get a glance at the murderer this time and you only got the barest glimpse. He must know that—there's no reason for him to flee. Assuming he's still present, perhaps we can encourage him to show himself again."

Lucifer stared at her. "With you as bait?"

"If you both keep watch, then there's no reason I should be in any danger."

"If we're both watching—if either of us is anywhere near—he won't make a move. We've known from the first he's not stupid."

"You don't need to hover so obviously. There's more dances to come. Everyone will expect us to separate."

Lucifer quelled his rising panic and studied Phyllida's calm face. What she was suggesting was ... reasonable. He couldn't give way to his instinctive urge to plant his foot solidly and say no. He didn't dare. "*If* you promise to remain in the ballroom—"

"I fully intend to remain in sight." She tilted her chin challengingly; her dark eyes flashed a warning. "I'm perfectly capable of playing my part. All you need do is watch from a distance. Now, I'll take myself off."

She drew her hand from his sleeve—he had to fight the urge to grab it back. With a gracious nod and a smile, she turned and strolled into the crowd.

Lucifer watched her go. Under his breath, he swore.

Jonas humphed. "I wish you'd said no."

He hadn't had a choice. Not if he wanted her to marry him.

"I'll go watch from the other side of the room." Jonas ambled off.

Phyllida danced and chatted, and danced some more. She circulated through the room at her brightest, her most charming. She spoke again to Cedric, Basil, and Grisby. She pretended to a faulty memory and conversed with Silas as if their meeting in the graveyard had never been.

All for nought. No gentleman approached her with any, even slightly nefarious, proposition.

At one point, Lucifer stopped by her side. "Enough. I don't like this. He'll be feeling under pressure. He might be at his most dangerous."

"He's more likely to be off-balance and at his most vulnerable." She strolled on, not waiting to hear his opinion of her logic.

Fifteen minutes later, Lucifer joined the circle about Phyllida; with practiced ease, he excised her from it. Her hand on his sleeve, he ambled down the room. "I think we should call it a night." He had had enough. He could feel the tension locked between his shoulder blades; his left shoulder was aching as well. "If he hasn't approached you by now, there's no reason to think he will."

She stopped and swung to face him. Her expression was calm and serene; her eyes glinted dangerously. "You know perfectly well that, other than finding that hat, we have no evidence to identify our man. There's not much we can do other than tempt him to try again. Here, where I'm surrounded by friends, is the safest place to do it. You're here; Jonas is here. This is too good an opportunity to pass up."

She held his gaze steadily; Lucifer swallowed a low growl. He was feeling increasingly caged. "This is *not* a good idea."

Her chin rose; her eyes flashed. "This is *my* idea and it's a perfectly sensible one."

With that, she swanned off.

Lucifer gritted his teeth and let her. It was that or risk showing her how mildly possessive her other suitors truly were. Compared with a Cynster, they did not rate. Fate had to be laughing hysterically.

Jaw clenched, he strolled to a wall and propped his uninjured shoulder against it. He watched her dance another country dance, then she chatted with a group of ladies. After that, she drifted. Then he saw her hesitate, looking down the room. He followed her gaze—he couldn't see whom she was staring at.

Then she stepped out; from her stride, she'd either seen something or had an idea. He wasn't enamored of her ideas. Chest tightening, he started after her.

He lost her in the crowd. Panic sank its claws deeper. He stopped and looked over the heads—he saw Jonas. Jonas shook his head. He'd lost her, too. Lucifer cursed, turned, and glimpsed her. At the other end of the ballroom, she stepped onto the terrace beside Lucius Appleby.

Appleby? Lucifer didn't stop to consider her reasoning. He doubted Appleby had invited Phyllida outside. If he had, she wouldn't have gone. No, she'd inveigled him out, God only knew why. But outside with only one gentleman was impossibly dangerous. Who knew who might be concealed by the night?

The distance to the nearest French door seemed a mile—a mile of obstacles, all smiling and nodding and wanting to chat. He reached it—it was locked. He had to plunge down the side of the room to the doors through which Phyllida and Appleby had disappeared, all without raising a dust.

He gained the terrace; Jonas, who'd been even farther down the room, was following. He glanced around and caught the smallest, most fleeting glimpse of blue skirt disappearing around the far end of the terrace. He strode after her, making no attempt to mute his footsteps. Rounding the corner, he discovered Phyllida a few yards away, leaning back against the balustrade, talking with Appleby, who was standing before her.

Behind the balustrade was a thicket of bushes, just the right sort to conceal a man with a knife.

Lucifer reached out, locked a hand around Phyllida's wrist, and yanked her to him, away from the bushes. He ignored her shocked expression and turned to Appleby. "Do excuse us, Appleby. Miss Tallent is just leaving."

Appleby returned his look blank-faced, the epitome of a well-trained employee. With the barest nod, Lucifer turned, let Phyllida get a good glimpse of his face, then stalked back around the corner of the terrace, dragging her with him.

"What are you doing!" she hissed. She twisted her wrist; he tightened his grip and strode on.

"I'm saving you from yourself! What the devil did you think you were doing, going off outside like that?" He pulled her close, moderating his stride so his body shielded her as much as was possible. "It's black night out there!" He waved at the lawns rolling away from the terrace. "He could take a shot at you without risk of being seen."

She glanced at the lawns. "I hadn't thought of that."

He ground his teeth. "Well, *I did*. That's why I made you promise not to go out of the ballroom."

"I didn't promise." Her nose rose. "I said I'd remain in sight. I thought you were watching."

Her tone, hinting at sudden vulnerability, made him bite his tongue. "I *was* watching. So was Jonas. But we both lost you for a moment, and then you were stepping outside. We nearly lost you altogether."

The thought made his blood run cold. It made his voice deeper, darker, a great deal more menacing. "I repeat, what the *devil* did you think you were doing?"

He stopped; she stopped, too, and faced him, head up, gaze direct. Her tapered chin was set. "I admit I forgot about the dark, but my reasons were perfectly sensible. I couldn't think where else to take Appleby."

"So this *was* your idea?"

"Of course! Appleby is the one person most likely to know which men had slipped out and returned. He's Cedric's right hand—he helps with all the arrangements and acts as Cedric's second. If Cedric left the room, then Appleby would have been alerted and watching the other guests in case someone needed anything."

"So," Lucifer grudgingly extrapolated, "Appleby's unlikely to be the murderer. He would have been on duty, as it were—"

"Precisely! So I was in no danger from him. Appleby doesn't like me any more than I like him, so I wasn't risking receiving any unwelcome advances. And you did say he'd been in the military, so he was probably the safest person, aside from you, to be with on the terrace."

Lucifer bit back the information that she wouldn't have been safe with him—still wasn't safe with him. He gestured brusquely toward the ballroom. "Let's get inside."

With a distinctly irate sniff, Phyllida turned. He wrapped the wrist he still held about one arm and stalked beside her. Jonas had stuck his head out, seen them, and gone in again. As they neared the open door, Lucifer asked, "Well? Did Appleby know anything to the point?"

Phyllida stepped over the threshold, nose in the air. "No."

"I wondered if you'd care to accompany me on a drive to Exeter."

Phyllida jerked her head up, only just managing to smother her gasp. Lucifer stood not two feet away. How had he got so close?

He raised one dark brow; reaching out, he took the flower basket from her nerveless fingers. She forced her gaze to a rosebush; cupping one bloom, she snipped it. As she laid it in the basket, she said, "If you can wait until I put these in water, then yes. A drive would be pleasant, and there are a few people I should see in Exeter."

Lucifer inclined his head. "For the pleasure of your company, I'll wait."

Twenty minutes later, he handed her into his curricle, then stepped up to the box seat, sat, picked up the reins, and gave his blacks the office. As he tooled the carriage down the drive, he knew relief.

Phyllida sat beside him, self-contained, a touch aloof—but she was there. After his performance last night, he hadn't been at all sure of his reception; he'd been prepared to kidnap her if she hadn't come of her own accord. But she had, thank heaven. She'd even come without a bonnet.

The blacks swept out of the Grange drive; he glanced at her—she had deployed a parasol to shade her fair skin from the summer sun, but he could see her face. He scanned her features, noted the line of her lips, the set of her chin, then gave his attention to his horses.

After last night, he would have to watch his every step.

They rattled on through the countryside in silence, a silence that became progressively more companionable as the miles fell beneath the blacks' hooves. The sunshine seemed to wilt her starchiness; when they reached Honiton, she spontaneously pointed out the sights.

He'd taken the more northerly route so they could check at the inns in Honiton, just in case a gentleman had hired a horse on the Sunday Horatio had been killed. Phyllida directed him to the appropriate establishments, then left him to make the inquiries. As they'd expected, there was no news to be had. Leaving Honiton, they bowled along the highway to Exeter.

The road was in good condition and the blacks were fresh. They leaned into the traces and the curricle flew. The wind of their passing whipped at Phyllida's hair. The speed was exhilarating, the warmth of the sun relaxing— she couldn't help but lift her face to the breeze and smile.

"Why are we going to Exeter?"

She waited, eyes half shut, lips curved; she felt Lucifer's gaze roam her face, then he answered. "I need to call on Crabbs and, for completeness' sake, we should check the stables. Then I thought we could have lunch by the river before heading back along the coast road."

Phyllida nodded. "That sounds pleasant."

"You mentioned there were some people you wished to see?"

"I'd like to call at the Customs House, a courtesy to preserve contact with Lieutenant Niles. And while you're consulting with Mr. Crabbs, I'll have a word with Robert." She glanced at Lucifer, but he merely nodded.

"If you like, we can go to the Customs House first."

She shook her head. "The livery stables first, then Mr. Crabbs, then the Customs House, then lunch at the Mermaid." She slanted Lucifer another glance—this time he caught it. She searched his eyes, then smiled and looked ahead. "Jonas tells me they have the best ale in Exeter. We can leave directly from there along the coast road."

Lucifer grinned. "Agreed." He slowed the blacks as the first houses appeared. "Now, my dear, which way?"

Phyllida directed him with an airy enthusiasm which warmed him as much as the sun. They called at the livery stables and received the same answer—no gentleman had hired a horse that Sunday. Continuing on to Mr. Crabbs, Lucifer went with that venerable gentleman into the solicitor's private sanctum, leaving Phyllida to dally in the outer office, where Robert Collins worked at his desk. Fifteen minutes later, Lucifer emerged to find Phyllida smiling serenely and Robert looking less tense than before.

Exchanging bows with Crabbs, who punctiliously took his leave of Phyllida, they strolled out to the pavement, where an urchin held the blacks. Lucifer tossed the boy a coin, then handed Phyllida up. "What did you say to Robert? Does he know I know about the letters?"

"Not precisely." Phyllida gathered her skirts so he could sit beside her. "I told him you were letting me search for the writing desk. He's been terribly worried over the whole business."

"So I noticed." Lucifer wondered about the letters, but let the matter slide. "Where's the Customs House?"

It stood on the quay, a few minutes down a sloping cobbled road from the High Street. Lucifer eased the blacks down the steep slope. The quay lined the River Exe; boats were tied to it, bobbing on the tide. Lucifer drew up before the handsome, two-storied brick building Phyllida pointed out. A cabin boy was slouching nearby. His eyes lit at the sight of the blacks; Lucifer waved him over.

There was an inn farther along the quay, tucked into the hill behind it. The sign of a mermaid swung outside. Lucifer instructed the boy to walk the horses to the inn and hand them to the ostler.

"This won't take long," Phyllida said as he helped her down to the cobbles.

She led the way into the building and walked directly to the counter along one wall. "I'd like to speak with Lieutenant Niles, please. If you would tell him Miss Tallent is here?"

The man behind the counter eyed her as she stripped off her gloves. "The Lieutenant's busy. He only handles business matters here."

Phyllida lifted her head and fixed the man with a direct glance. "This is business."

Strolling up in her wake, Lucifer came to stand directly behind her. He looked at the clerk.

The clerk met his eyes, then swallowed and glanced at Phyllida. "I'll tell him. Miss Tallent, you said?"

"Indeed." Phyllida waited until the clerk had disappeared through a door before looking over her shoulder at Lucifer. "What did you do to him?"

Lucifer opened his eyes wide. "Nothing." He smiled. "Just me being me."

Phyllida searched his face, then humphed. She turned back to the counter as the door beside it opened. A gentleman in the uniform of the Revenue Service came striding out, smiling, his hands outstretched.

"Miss Tallent." He grasped her hand, then looked past her to Lucifer.

"Good morning, Lieutenant Niles." Phyllida gestured at Lucifer. "Allow me to present Mr. Cynster. He's come to live in Colyton."

"Oh?" All innocent inquiry, Niles shook Lucifer's hand.

"Does that mean you'll be taking an interest in the Colyton Import Company?"

"A benign interest," Lucifer returned. "Purely in an advisory capacity."

He knew when Phyllida let out the breath she'd held. Niles turned back to her and she reclaimed his attention. "I just wanted to check the overall totals with you, and whether we need to change any of our payments."

"Indeed, indeed." Niles waved them to the door. "If you'll just come this way?"

He bowed them into his office, then he and Phyllida settled to a brisk discussion of the various goods the Company had brought in and expected to bring in in the near future, and the levels of the duties payable on the differing cargoes. Lucifer sat back and listened, intrigued by how, once she'd been given the opportunity—given the right to lead—Phyllida managed the interview, and Niles, so well. She was a businesswoman to her toes.

He was inwardly smiling by the time she'd finished with the Lieutenant. Tucking a list of the latest tariffs into her reticule, she stood, turned, and caught his eye. She waited until they'd taken their leave of Niles and were out on the quay before asking, "Now, what so amuses you in that?"

"Nothing at all. I'm appreciative, not amused. It just occurred to me that, in the same way I could be of assistance to you with the Company, you, too, could to great effect assist me with my business." Taking her arm, he turned her toward the Mermaid.

"Business?" She looked up at him. "What sort of business do you engage in?"

It took all of lunchtime and more to tell her. By the time he'd finished and they were in the curricle heading east along the road that would eventually take them home along the coast, she was intrigued.

"I had no idea. I thought you were a London swell—that all you ever did was waltz around ballrooms and charm ladies."

"I do that, too, but one has to have something to do to while away the days."

"Humph." She shot him a measuring glance. "So this interest of yours in a cattle stud is quite genuine?"

"Given I've now got the land, it seems a pity not to use it, and establishing a stud seems the farming equivalent of being a collector."

"I hadn't thought of it in quite those terms, but I suppose that's true." Phyllida looked ahead.

Then she gripped his arm. "Stop!"

Drawing on the reins, Lucifer looked at her. "What?"

She'd swiveled around on the seat, staring back along the road. Reins tight, Lucifer shifted and also looked back. A tinker was ambling along, heading into Exeter.

"The hat!" Phyllida swung to face him, eyes wide. "That tinker's got *the hat!*"

He turned the horses and set them trotting back along the road. "Quiet," he warned Phyllida as they drew level with the tinker. She stared hard at the man—at his hat—but didn't argue. Lucifer drove a hundred yards farther on, then turned the curricle again. He drove back, almost to where the tinker slogged along, then drew rein.

"Good day."

The tinker stopped and touched the brim of the hat—the hat that even the most cursory glance declared was not his.

"Good day to you, sir. Ma'am."

"That hat," Phyllida said. "Have you had it long?"

A wary look passed through the tinker's eyes. "I found it, fair and square. I didn't steal it."

"I didn't think you had." Phyllida smiled reassuringly. "We were just wondering where you found it."

"Along the coast a ways."

"How far back? Before Sidmouth?"

"Aye—it was a ways before. I'd left Axmouth and decided to go inland a bit. There's a sleepy little village there, name of Colyton."

"We know it," Lucifer said.

"I sharpen knives." The tinker gestured to the packs on his back. "After I finished in the village, I headed on, west, then northwest—there's a path leads on to Honiton, which was my next port o'call. I found the hat along the way, a bit out of Colyton."

Phyllida nodded. "You must have gone up the lane, past the church and the forge—up the hill—"

"Aye, that's right."

"And then there's a bit of a dip, a shallow valley, you eventually get to the next ridge—stop me when I get to where you found the hat—and then there's tall gateposts, and then the lane narrows, and winds down and around toward the sea—"

"That's it! That's where I found it. It was rolling along at the bottom of the hedge just short of where that seaward leg ends. I picked it up, dusted it off— wasn't no name in it. I looked around, but there was no house or hut for miles. Then I walked but a few yards on and the lane turned into a path and swung northwest for Honiton."

The tinker beamed at Phyllida; she beamed back.

"Here." Lucifer held out two guineas. "One for the hat, one for your help. You'll be able to buy yourself a good cap, find a comfortable room, and have a good dinner and a few drinks on us."

The tinker's eyes, fixed on the largesse, gleamed. "My lucky day—the day I found that hat." He handed it to Phyllida.

Lucifer handed over the coins. "And which day was that—the day you found the hat?"

The tinker screwed up his face. "I left Axmouth on a Monday, and spent a day between there and in and about Colyton. I slept in the lych-gate and set out for Honiton early the next morn—that was when I found the hat."

"So you found it on Tuesday?"

"Aye, but not this Tuesday. 'Twould have been the one before that—I was nearly a week in Honiton, and then I went down to Sidmouth."

"Tuesday before last." Lucifer nodded. "Our thanks."

The tinker looked down at the coins in his hand. "I'm thinking 'twas my pleasure entirely."

They left him bemused by his good fortune; Lucifer set the blacks pacing smartly, then glanced at Phyllida.

She was holding the hat in her lap, staring down at it. "No wonder we couldn't find it—never saw it. He must have got rid of it straightaway."

Her tone was distant. Lucifer frowned. "Those tall gateposts you mentioned—that's the entrance to Ballyclose Manor, I take it."

Phyllida nodded.

"So what is at the end of the seaward leg of the lane?"

She exhaled. "It's a rear entrance to Ballyclose. It's not even a gate, just a gap in the hedge, but it's been there forever. Everyone who rides at Ballyclose uses it to come and go unless they're riding directly into the village."

"So if someone was out riding from Ballyclose and didn't want to return by riding through the village, they'd use that entrance?"

"Yes."

The tone of the word had Lucifer glancing at Phyllida again. "What are you thinking?" He couldn't tell from her face.

She drew in a breath. "It must be Cedric after all."

He looked to his horses. "There are other possibilities."

"Such as?"

"That it's not Cedric's hat, for a start."

Phyllida held the hat up, turning it around. "Just because I can't recall seeing him wearing it doesn't mean it isn't his. You saw how many hats he has. I didn't recognize half of them."

"Equally, just because he has a hat fetish doesn't mean that one's his." Lucifer looked at the hat again. "I really don't think it is."

"If I can't be sure, I can't see how you can be."

Lucifer swallowed his explanation of why he didn't think the hat was Cedric's—he was, after all, only guessing. After a moment, he said, "Very well, consider this. The murderer, not Cedric, knows that the books in Horatio's library leave Cedric with a real motive for killing Horatio, which, I admit, is more than we've been able to uncover for anyone else. The murderer, however, has another motive—one we have no idea of. Needing to get rid of the hat, he plants it at a place where enough people come past, so that, at some time, it'll be discovered and all will point to Cedric, not him."

Phyllida stared at him. "That's tortuous reasoning. Do you really think anyone actually thinks like that?"

Lucifer shot her a glance. "Our murderer has eluded us multiple times—he's ruthless, clever, and without compunction. He probably has the sort of mind that works like that all the time."

"Hmm." Phyllida looked down at the hat. "Or he could simply be Cedric."

Lucifer let out a long sigh. "I have serious difficulty casting Cedric in the role. Not because I don't think he could do it, but because I don't think he *would*."

"I can't imagine him as a murderer, either, but ..." Phyllida looked up; her gaze fixed forward. "I think we should go directly to Ballyclose."

"Why?"

"Because of this." She brandished the hat. "I cannot bear to go on thinking Cedric might be the murderer, and just not knowing. I want to find out—with this—now."

"What on earth do you plan to do? Barge in and ask him if the hat's his?"

Phyllida lifted her chin. "Precisely."

"Phyllida—"

Lucifer argued, reasonably, then not so reasonably; Phyllida held firm. She wanted the matter settled, one way or another, today. In the end, Lucifer looked at the hat in her lap, then, lips compressed, shook his head and faced forward.

"Very well," he growled after a tense minute had crawled by. "We'll go to Ballyclose, and *you* can do the talking."

Nose in the air, Phyllida inclined her head, accepting his terms.

They rolled onto the gravel circle before Ballyclose's front steps half an hour later. A groom came running; Lucifer handed over the reins. He handed Phyllida down; she preceded him up the steps.

The butler smiled and bowed them in. He showed them into the drawing room, then went to confer with his master. He returned a moment later. "Sir Cedric's in the library, if you would care to join him there, miss. Sir."

Lucifer gave Phyllida his hand; she rose from the chair she'd only just sunk into. Carrying the hat before her, she led the way to the library. The butler held the door wide; Phyllida swept through. Cedric was seated behind his desk; he smiled and rose. Phyllida swept straight to the desk and plunked the hat down in the middle of Cedric's blotter.

Cedric stared at it.

Standing poker-straight before the desk, Phyllida almost glared at him. "Is this hat yours, Cedric?"

Startled, Cedric blinked at her. "No."

"How can you be sure?"

Cedric glanced at Lucifer, who had halted behind Phyllida, then, warily, looked at her again. Moving slowly, he reached for the hat, lifted it, and placed it on his head.

It was Phyllida's turn to stare. "Oh."

The hat sat on Cedric's head, propped high, well above his ears. It was patently too small for him.

All the steel went out of Phyllida; groping for a nearby armchair, she sank into it. Then she covered her eyes with her hands. "Thank God!"

Lucifer closed a hand on her shoulder briefly, then held out his hand to Cedric. "There is a sane explanation."

"Glad to hear it." Cedric shook hands, then removed the hat and studied it. "Not but what this does look familiar."

Phyllida removed her hands from her face. "Do you know whose it is?"

Cedric grimaced. "Can't place it this minute, but it'll come back to me. I usually notice hats."

Lucifer flicked Phyllida a glance; she met it, but only briefly.

She looked at Cedric. "It's very important that we find out whose hat that is, Cedric."

He looked at her, then at Lucifer. "Why?"

They told him.

"The inscriptions," Lucifer said, having tactfully explained their existence, "did give you an apparent motive for wanting to remove books from Horatio's library and, potentially, to do away with Horatio."

Cedric blinked. "Because they might call my paternity into question?"

Phyllida nodded. "And therefore, Pommeroy could claim Sir Bentley's estate."

Cedric regarded her for a moment, then coughed and glanced down the room. He lowered his voice. "Actually, that wouldn't work. Papa worded his will specifically, naming me his principal heir. And as for Pommeroy, while there might be a question over my paternity, there's absolutely none about his. He's not Papa's son."

"He's not?" Phyllida looked horrified.

Cedric shook his head. "Not common knowledge, of course. Mama wouldn't like that."

"Indeed not." Phyllida blinked, then dazedly shook her head.

"So, you see, laboring under that misapprehension as we were ..." Lucifer continued their explanation, omitting nothing. The ridiculous sight of the hat perched on Cedric's head had effectively removed him from their list of suspects. Cedric took the information that he'd topped the list for some time relatively well. When, cheeks rosy, Phyllida apologized, he waved it aside.

"You had to suspect everyone who wasn't at church that Sunday. As it is, I can't account for my time—"

"Perhaps you can't, but I can."

Both Lucifer and Phyllida turned. Jocasta Smollet rose from a wing chair facing the windows some way down the room. She'd been sitting, hidden from sight when they'd entered.

Cedric got to his feet. "Jocasta—"

Jocasta smiled at him—it was the most natural expression Lucifer had yet seen on her face. "Don't fret, Cedric, but I'm not going to stand by and see your reputation sullied even by suspicion purely on account of my brother's pride. If we're truly to break free of it, then we may as well start as we mean to go on."

Coming to stand beside Cedric, Jocasta looked at Phyllida, and at Lucifer, who had also risen. "Cedric," she said, "was with me that Sunday—the Sunday morning when Horatio was killed."

The announcement was so unexpected, Phyllida simply stared. Cedric harrumphed, then pulled up a chair for Jocasta. "Here—sit down."

She did; Cedric and Lucifer resumed their seats.

Jocasta folded her hands in her lap and regarded Lucifer and Phyllida calmly. "Cedric wished to speak with me about our future—Sunday morning, when both Mama and Basil were in church, was the only time that was possible. He rode up shortly after the carriage left for church. The stable lad who took his horse would remember. We met privately, but our housekeeper, Mrs. Swithins, was in the next room and the door was ajar. She can confirm that Cedric was with me for more than an hour. He left just before the carriage returned from church."

"My dear, if we're going to tell them that much, then we should tell them the rest." Cedric turned to Lucifer and Phyllida. "Jocasta and I were close— oh, for many years. But when I asked for her hand eight years ago, Basil would have none of it. He and I have our differences." Looking down, Cedric shrugged. "Basil wouldn't hear of us marrying, and, well, I dug in my heels and words were exchanged. And then Mama heard of it and she wasn't in favor, either, and things fell into a heap. Jocasta and I stopped seeing each other—we've avoided each other for years. But then Mama started insisting that I marry"—he glanced at Phyllida—"specifically, that I marry *you*, my dear. Yet the more time I spent with you, the more I thought of Jocasta. I realized she was the only woman I wanted for my wife." He looked at Jocasta, then held out a hand; she took it and smiled.

Face alight, Jocasta said, "Cedric tried to talk to Basil last night, but he's still very set against the marriage." She glanced at Cedric and squeezed his hand. "But we've decided not to waste any more years. Regardless of what Basil and Mama may say—"

"Or my mama, either," Cedric put in.

Jocasta inclined her head. "Regardless, we've decided to marry."

Phyllida found she was smiling. She rose; Jocasta rose, too. Phyllida embraced the older woman, touching cheeks. "I'm so pleased for you."

Jocasta's smile was a little crooked, but she met Phyllida's eyes. "Thank you. I know I haven't been the kindest of souls over the years, but I hope you understand."

"Of course." Beaming, Phyllida turned to hug Cedric. "I wish you both joy."

"Very kind of you, m'dear." Cedric patted her shoulder. "Well"—he blew out a breath—"at least you'll know why, if Mama comes screaming to cry on your shoulder."

Phyllida grinned.

Lucifer shook hands with Cedric and Jocasta, wishing them both well; then he and Phyllida took their leave.

"Well!" Phyllida said as he tooled the carriage down the drive. "Jocasta and Cedric! Whoever would have thought it."

Lucifer kept his mouth shut.

An instant later, Phyllida sighed. "Basil is going to have an apoplectic fit." She smiled and leaned back, the murderer's brown hat, temporarily forgotten, in her lap.

CHAPTER
Seventeen

The next day was Sunday. Lucifer strode briskly up the common. An onshore breeze flirted with fleecy clouds in the pale blue sky. The last stragglers were making their way into the church; Lucifer joined them, sliding into a pew at the rear.

Scanning the congregation, he searched for Phyllida. He'd driven her home the previous afternoon; they hadn't discussed their next meeting. Leaving Dodswell watching the Manor, he'd come to ask her to spend the day with him, looking at books, reading inscriptions, strolling the lawns ... whatever she wished to do.

He located Sir Jasper. Lady Huddlesford and Frederick sat beside him. Miss Sweet was there, too. He couldn't see Phyllida. Or Jonas.

The organ swelled; the congregation rose as Mr. Filing and the small band of choristers paraded in. Lucifer hesitated, then left his seat; he made his way as unobtrusively as he could down the aisle to Sir Jasper's side.

Sir Jasper smiled.

"Phyllida?" Lucifer mouthed.

Sir Jasper leaned close and whispered, "Headache. She's resting at home."

Headache. Lucifer drew breath, then nodded and retreated. At the rear of the church, he hovered by the last pew, then turned and quit the church.

Face setting, he strode back down the common even faster than he'd gone up. There was nothing—nothing—to suggest that Phyllida didn't have a headache. Women did get headaches; they also used the term to excuse other, less mentionable ailments. When he reached the Grange and discovered Phyllida laid down upon her bed, he'd be able to accept her indisposition as truth and the nagging worry rising like a tide in his mind would subside.

Until then, with a killer on the loose, focused on her, his imagination was primed and ready to bolt. Reaching the lane, he broke into a lope.

From the church, it was faster to reach the Grange via the lane. Within minutes, he was turning through the gateposts. Gaining the front porch, he rang the bell, then opened the door and walked in. "Phyllida?"

A door opened; Jonas emerged from the library. He stared at Lucifer, consternation showing through his usual benign mask. "She's not with you?"

Lucifer opened his mouth; Jonas stopped him with an upraised hand. "I walked Phyllida to the Manor via the wood. I just got back. She said you don't normally go to church and that you'd be there."

Lucifer grimaced. "Normally, but today I walked up to the church to meet her."

Jonas grinned. Lucifer turned back to the door. "I left Dodswell at the Manor, so there's no harm done." In the doorway, he paused and looked back. "Did she give any particular reason for wanting to see me?"

Still grinning, Jonas shook his head. "Nothing she wanted to share with me. But she was carrying that brown hat, and her reticule, too, and a parasol. I assumed she wanted you to take her somewhere."

"Hmm. No doubt I'll learn where soon enough." With a nod, Lucifer stepped back through the door and closed it behind him.

Take her somewhere. As he strode around the Grange and into the wood, he tried to imagine where Phyllida had in mind. He'd assumed they were at a temporary standstill with their investigations, that they'd need to consider the question of where next. Presumably Phyllida had already done so and had come up with an answer.

He knew where he would like to take her, but that didn't require either parasol or reticule. She didn't normally carry either when visiting the Manor.

He lengthened his stride. A few paces later, he started to jog. The path through the wood was too uneven to risk a flat-out run. The tide of impending panic hadn't receded in the least—it was welling even higher.

He did run through the kitchen garden, slowing only once inside the house. Dodswell met him in the front hall.

One look at his face, and the tide rushed in.

"Thank Gawd." Dodswell held out a note. "Miss Phyllida was here looking for you."

"I've been looking for *her*." Lucifer unfolded the note. Another note contained within it fell into his hands. Phyllida had written:

L—our tweeny brought this up just before I was to leave for church—she said she answered a tap on the back door and found it on the step. As you will see from the note, it appears we might at last have found Horatio's murderer, or at least someone who knows to whom the brown hat belongs. Molly is Lady Fortemain's seamstress. I intended asking you to accompany me to the rendezvous, however, that was not to be, and Jonas had already left before I realized you weren't here, and I didn't wish to take Dodswell and leave the Manor unguarded. If I haven't returned by the time you come back from church, perhaps you can meet me there, or on the way back. P.

A postscript containing a set of directions followed. Lucifer turned his attention to the other note, the one Phyllida had received. "Miss Tallent" was inscribed on the front in an obviously feminine hand. He opened the note. It read:

Dear Miss Tallent,
As you know, I work at Ballyclose, and I heard as how you was asking after who owned a certain brown hat. I know of a gentleman who has lost a brown hat, but I am not sure as it would be right to say who he is, not unless I am sure it is his hat.
I dont want it known, not by anyone, especially not this gentleman, that I am talking to you. I dont get much time away, but I can slip away from the house on Sunday while they are all off at church. If you want me to look at the hat you have and see if it is the one I am thinking of, then if you meet me at the old Drayton cottage during Sunday service, I will try to help you.

Yrs respectfully, Molly

The note looked genuine. The words were carefully inked; it was easy to imagine a seamstress laboring over its composition.

Lucifer waited for his panic to recede. It didn't. Some primitive part of him was on full alert, prodding like some diabolical demon with a fiery prong for him to move—fast. His body was tensed, tight with the need to fly into action.

He swore and juggled the notes.

Was it intuition that urged that she wasn't safe, that she was, in fact, walking into danger? Or was it instinct, elemental, primal, that insisted she was not truly safe except when in his care?

Or was it simply panic, the black fear that, at any time she was out of his sight, she might be taken from him?

He thrust the questions aside and tried to make sense of Phyllida's directions. The old Drayton cottage stood some way north of the fields bordering the lane to Dottswood and Highgate. He'd heard it described as abandoned. While his logical mind reiterated that all would be well, that the murderer could not know that Phyllida was out walking alone that way, even his logical mind had to admit the Drayton cottage sounded an odd rendezvous for some woman walking from Ballyclose to suggest.

Who knew what went on in the minds of women?

His own words uttered earlier in relation to Phyllida. He thrust the notes into his pocket. "I'll follow Miss Tallent."

Dodswell nodded. "Aye. I'll wait here and keep an eye out."

The way was clear to the point where the narrow ridge lane met the village lane. Thereafter, Lucifer checked Phyllida's instructions frequently as he strode along walking paths, over fields, across stiles, past copses. The sun rode the sky and beat down on his shoulders. It would have been a pleasant walk if he hadn't been so tense, if he hadn't been striding so fast.

Rounding a copse, he paused to consult Phyllida's note. The breeze shifted—he smelled smoke.

Head up, he sniffed—and caught the scent again. He glanced at the note, then stuffed it into his pocket and started to run.

He had one more field to cross; the abandoned cottage supposedly lay in a clearing beyond. He broke through the hedge and ran full tilt through the knee-high crops. Trees screened what lay ahead, but the smoke was more definite on the breeze. He vaulted the gate and plunged into the trees. A greedy crackling reached his ears.

Bursting from the trees, he saw the cottage standing on a low crest above him, already well alight. The front door stood open; as he raced up the flags of an old garden path, he registered the fact that the door was propped open. Windows were open, too.

The roof was old thatch, brittle and dry; flames were already thrusting through it. The open windows and door fed the inferno.

Smoke billowed out at him as if trying to drive him from the door. He coughed, turned away, dragged in a breath, then dove in.

His eyes watered; even ignoring that, he could barely see. Smoke curled and eddied, a tangible shroud growing thicker by the minute. He felt walls to his right and left. A corridor. Head down, hand outstretched, his handkerchief held to his nose and mouth, he felt along it.

Wood—a doorframe. He went to turn into the room. His feet struck something; he lurched and fell to his knees.

Flames raced across the room's ceiling with a whooshing roar. They licked over the top of the doorframe, voraciously reaching for the sustaining air outside.

On his hands and knees, Lucifer coughed. He'd lost his handkerchief; he could barely breathe. His lungs already felt raw.

What had he tumbled over? He reached out blindly; he could have wept with relief when his hands closed over a leg—a female leg. Phyllida—or the seamstress? He reached further, going quicker and quicker, tracing the body, until he got to her head. Her hair.

Phyllida. The feel of the silken fall under his palm was a remembered delight. The shape of her skull cradled in his hand was imprinted on his brain.

Phyllida.

The relief was so great, for an instant he stopped, head down, and struggled to take it in. She lay facedown, still breathing, but barely.

He could barely breathe himself; he couldn't concentrate, could hardly think.

A long, groaning creak sounded overhead; a sharp crack like a pistol shot echoed. Another gout of whooshing flames seared the air above them, eating it up. The heat intensified, beating down on them, scorching, shriveling.

He could no longer expand his chest. Taking shallow little breaths, he staggered to his feet, not straightening. Bending over Phyllida, he grasped her waist, then struggled and shrugged and wrestled her over his shoulder.

A shower of cinders rained down as he turned to where he knew the door was. He staggered two steps and fetched up against the doorframe. Phyllida hung down behind him, her head bumping on his lower back. He kept his hold on her legs and shuffled into the corridor. Step by shuffling step, he headed for the front door. No point looking up—the ceiling glowed red behind the blanket of smoke that lay thick and heavy all about them.

He bounced off the corridor wall, then half tripped and fell. He put a hand out—and grasped the edge of the front door. His head was swimming. For an instant, he remained, dazed, sick, reeling. Above, something popped, then snapped. Burning wood rained down. A piece struck his hand; more bits hit Phyllida's skirts. He gasped, but caught no air, then frantically brushed the burning fragments from Phyllida. Her skirt was scorched, but hadn't caught alight.

A draft of cool air wafted to him. The flames above and behind them roared.

Lucifer dragged the taste of survival deep, held it in, and struggled to his feet.

He stumbled across the threshold and got three steps along the path before he collapsed again. They were out of the worst, but not free. They were still too close.

Coughing, almost retching, he looked back, blinking his stinging eyes. The front doorway was haloed in flame, bright and hungry. The open windows were belching smoke; behind their sills, flames danced.

If Molly the seamstress was in there, he could do nothing to save her.

He looked down at Phyllida. She'd slipped from his shoulder when he'd fallen and now lay unconsious beside him. He hauled in a breath and felt it score its way into his lungs. Gasping, he rose—to his knees. He couldn't manage his feet.

Head whirling, he wrapped an arm around Phyllida and locked her to his side, dragging her with him as he crawled off the path, onto the lawn, taking the most direct route away from the house. He reached a point where the lawn sloped down toward the trees. He lay down, pulled Phyllida's unconscious form to him, cradling her face into his chest, protecting her head and shoulders with his arms—then he rolled.

Their momentum carried them most of the way down; they fetched up on a shallow shelf of mossy grass, well away from the burning cottage.

Lucifer lifted his head and looked back at the cottage. Flames shot through every window, greedily licking up the outside walls. It was the ultimate death trap.

Phyllida lay unconscious, barely breathing beside him. Still alive.

He exhaled, closed his eyes, and flopped back on the grass.

The wind shifted, carrying the taint of smoke as far as the common. A fire in the country at this time of year triggered an immediate response. Men came running with pitchforks, sacks—anything they could lay their hands on.

The Thompson brothers were the first to come thundering up. Others arrived on foot, still others on horses, some saddled, some not. Grooms, stable lads, footmen, and their employers all turned out. Lucifer glimpsed Basil stalking the scene, shouting orders. Coat off, Cedric wielded a pitchfork, breaking up thatch as it fell away, dispersing it so those with sacks could beat the flames to death.

Focused on the cottage, no one saw them. Lucifer lay still, head pounding, too weak to move, and listened to the almost indiscernible huff of Phyllida's breathing. The sound held him to consciousness, to some degree of lucidity.

Then the flames started to falter, running out of fuel. The cottage had burned more or less to the ground. Thompson retreated into the garden to catch his breath, and saw them.

He let out a surprised "Oy!" and came lumbering down the slope.

Others turned, saw, and followed. Lucifer braced. He waved Thompson to him; with the big man's help, he managed to sit. The backs of his hands were scorched, as were the pads of his fingers. His hair had largely escaped, but his coat was ruined, shoulders and back pocked with burns and scorch marks. A crowd gathered about them—Oscar, Filing, Cedric, Basil, Henry Grisby, and more. Every face was shocked, deeply and utterly shocked. Clearing his throat, Lucifer managed to say, "I found her unconscious in the cottage. It was already well alight."

Filing pushed through and went to his knee beside Phyllida. She lay on her stomach, her face to the side. Gripping gently, Filing raised her shoulder just enough to confirm she still lived, still breathed. He eased her back to the cushioning moss. "We'll have to get you both out of here—Phyllida needs to be back at the Grange."

Lucifer closed his eyes. The world was still swaying. "Sir Jasper?"

"The Grange household left the church before the alarm was raised."

Lucifer wasn't sure if that was good or not. Sir Jasper would have been shaken, but he could still have counted on the older man to take charge. He himself was not up to it at present.

Basil hunkered down beside Phyllida. He stretched out a hand and lifted a fallen lock of her hair back from her face. His face was set, blank with shock. Phyllida's hair was scorched here and there; her blue gown had fared worse, even worse than Lucifer's coat. Thankfully, she'd worn a cambric walking dress, not one of her thin muslin gowns. With luck, she would escape any major burns. Basil's hand shook as he drew it back; he had paled.

So, too, had the others. Henry Grisby caught his breath and volunteered, "Dottswood's closest. I've a farm cart I can bring up the old lane. It'll still be a way away, but ..." His voice trailed away.

Filing nodded. "Yes, Henry. That's the best suggestion. Go, now."

Henry nodded. He drew back, his gaze on Phyllida. Then he turned and started climbing the slope, slowly, then more quickly. At the top, he broke into a run.

"Terrible, terrible." As shaken as the rest, Cedric straightened; the effort he made to regain his composure was visible. He looked at Lucifer. "Was it about that hat?"

Lucifer looked at him, then glanced at the smoldering cottage. "I believe she had the hat with her."

Phyllida regained consciousness on the journey back to the Grange. The gentle rocking of the cart, the freshening breeze, tugged her back to reality. She opened her eyes and was immediately beset by a paroxysm of coughing.

A large hand closed over hers.

"It's all right. You're safe."

She looked up; through stinging tears, she saw the face that, in the moment she'd thought would be her last, had been the only face in her mind. Her last instant of lucidity had been filled with regret—regret for what they wouldn't have a chance to share. Closing her eyes, she let her head slump and gave silent thanks. Fate had been kind—they still had their chance.

Sliding her fingers in his, she clung. "Who saved me?" His coat was burned, an unsalvageable wreck.

"Hush—don't talk."

She heard a rustle on the cart's seat; then Henry Grisby's voice reached her. "Lucifer saved you—thank God."

His tone was fervent. Lucifer had, it seemed, been elevated from demon to god, at least in Henry's eyes.

Not only in Henry's eyes. Phyllida squeezed Lucifer's fingers, inexpressibly relieved to feel them firm and strong around hers.

The hours that followed were a confusion of sounds perceived through a haze—her lungs felt tight, dizziness threatened, she couldn't stand or speak, she could barely move, not even her head. Her eyes burned, but at least she could see—at least she was still alive.

Every time her mind touched on that, she wept—tears of joy, of relief, of emotion too overwhelming to contain.

Her father was shocked, shaken. She tried to reassure him but had no idea if what she said was even coherent. Jonas carried her upstairs, but it was Lucifer who lingered, leaning over her bed, stroking her hair back from her face. Behind him, Sweetie, Gladys, and her aunt rushed and fussed and spoke in whispers. Lucifer leaned close, his face soot-streaked, his expression softer than she'd ever known it.

He touched his lips to hers. "Rest. I'll be here when you wake. Then we'll talk."

Her lids drifted closed of their own accord. She thought she nodded.

Evening shadows were playing across her room when she awoke. For long minutes, she simply lay there, thrilled by the fact of being alive.

With the help of Sweetie and her aunt, she'd stripped off her ruined clothes, then bathed. She'd had Sweetie snip the scorched locks from her hair. Gladys had produced a salve. After annointing every minor burn and scorched spot, she'd donned a fine cotton robe and lain down on her bed.

They'd left her and she'd slept. It had been like falling into a deep well, black, soundless, undisturbed.

She felt a great deal better. Gingerly, she eased up to sit, then, encouraged, swung her legs over the side of the bed. Holding onto the bed, she stood. Her limbs seemed in working order. A twinge here and there, the scorches and bruises, too, but nothing incapacitating.

A cough caught her; rasping pain gripped her lungs. She clung to the bed, struggling to master her breathing. Her throat felt scorched; it hurt to breathe other than shallowly. If she drew a deeper breath, coughing threatened.

Once the paroxysm faded, she straightened and walked, carefully, to the bellpull.

Her little maid, Becky, came up. Twenty minutes later, Phyllida felt human again—resurrected. In a gown of soft lavender trimmed with a flounce and a narrow band of darker ribbon, with a gauzy scarf around her throat and perfume dabbed liberally, hair neat and sleek once more, she felt ready to face what lay beyond her door.

The maid opened it for her. Before she could cross the threshold, Lucifer was there.

He frowned. "You should have rung. I would have—" He stopped, then grimaced. "Got Jonas to carry you down."

Phyllida smiled; with her heart and soul in her eyes, she smiled into his. Then she let her gaze roam, drinking in the fact that he, too, had rested and recovered. He was wearing a coat of that particular shade of dark blue that best set off his eyes and made his hair appear blacker than jet. The sight erased a lingering worry in her heart; only with its easing did she realize it had been there.

"You shouldn't be walking."

His voice was rough and raspy. She studied his hard face, then calmly said, "Why not? You are."

He scowled, trying to read her eyes. "I wasn't knocked unconscious."

She raised her brows. "Was I?"

"Yes."

"Well, I'm conscious now. If you'll just give me your arm, I'm sure we'll manage."

He did. He hovered solicitously down the stairs and all the way to the library, but, as she'd predicted, they managed perfectly well.

Pausing before the library door, she let her gaze linger on his face. Raising a finger, she traced his cheek, as she first had two weeks ago. "When we work together we're invincible."

She'd intended the comment to refer to their descent; hearing it, she realized it applied to much more.

She lifted her eyes and he met them, his blue gaze steady. He trapped her hand, pressed a kiss to her palm. "So it would appear."

He held her gaze for a moment longer, then reached past her and opened the library door.

Her father rose as they entered. So, too, did Cedric. Jonas was standing by the long windows.

"My dear!" Sir Jasper came forward, hands outstretched, concern very evident in his face.

Phyllida put her hands in his. "Papa." She returned his kiss. "I'm feeling much better, and I really should tell you what happened." Her voice was as raspy as Lucifer's.

"Humph!" Sir Jasper looked at her, shaggy brows drawn down. "You're quite sure you're up to it?"

"Quite sure." Retaking Lucifer's arm, she allowed him to steer her to the *chaise*. She nodded to Cedric.

Handing her to the *chaise*, Lucifer murmured, "I thought Cedric should be here—there are points he might be able to help us with."

Phyllida nodded and settled back. Before she could blink, Lucifer lifted her ankles and swung her feet up. Previously, she'd have glared and swung them back down. Now she just wriggled into a more comfortable position.

"Well, then." Clearing his throat, her father sat in a nearby chair. "If you're determined to explain it tonight, we'd better start, heh?"

"Perhaps"—Lucifer took the chair beside the *chaise*—"to save Phyllida's throat, I could fill in the background, then she need only describe the events only she knows."

Sir Jasper turned his gaze expectantly to Lucifer. Cedric, in another armchair, did the same. Jonas held to his position by the windows, his attention fixed on Lucifer.

Lucifer settled back. "To begin, there are some elements in our investigations which concern others not implicated in Horatio's murder or the subsequent attacks on Phyllida, but to whom we, Phyllida and I, owe a certain measure of confidentiality." He looked at Sir Jasper. "If you will accept some of our discoveries without detailed explanations of how we made them, then we can preserve those confidentialities without prejudicing our account."

Every inch the magistrate, Sir Jasper nodded. "Sometimes that's the way of things. If mentioning unnecessary details will trouble someone who has done no wrong, then there's no need for me to know."

Lucifer nodded. "On that basis, then. Phyllida saw a hat at the murder scene soon after the murder, but later that hat disappeared. Bristleford and the Hemmingses never saw it. It was not Horatio's. When the attacks on Phyllida became obvious and concerted, she concluded that the hat would identify the murderer—or so the murderer believes. There's nothing else Phyllida knows that could explain the murderer's interest in her."

"Did Phyllida recognize the hat?" Sir Jasper asked.

Lucifer shook his head. "She has no idea whose hat it is, but even though she has obviously not remembered—given she's raised no hue and cry—as evidenced by his continued attacks on her, the murderer's convinced she will, at some point, recall, and she's therefore a continuing threat to him."

"How did the murderer know Phyl had seen the hat?"

The question came from Jonas; Lucifer turned to look at him. "We don't know. We can only assume that, from hiding, he saw her take note of it."

Turning back to Sir Jasper and Cedric, Lucifer continued. "Phyllida kept her eyes open for the hat—a brown one. Simultaneously, I was pursuing the idea that something in Horatio's library was behind his death. For instance, some information hidden in a book that the murderer wished to hide. We found such information. Unexpectedly, we also found the brown hat.

"Both the information and the brown hat led us to Cedric, but when we confronted him with both, it was quickly proved that he wasn't the murderer. The hat didn't fit, and the information wasn't as vital as it had seemed. Cedric also has a solid alibi for the time when Horatio was killed. We established all that yesterday, by which time it was evening.

"This morning, before church, Phyllida received this note." Lucifer drew the note from his pocket and handed it to Sir Jasper. Sir Jasper read it, then, his expression hardening, passed it to Cedric.

Sir Jasper looked at Phyllida. "So you didn't have a headache?"

Phyllida colored and shook her head. "Molly asked for no one to know. I got Jonas to take me to the Manor, intending to show only Lucifer and have him escort me to the cottage."

"But I wasn't there—I'd gone to look for Phyllida."

"I assumed," Phyllida said, "that the note was genuine, so when Lucifer wasn't at the Manor, I went on to the cottage alone, reasoning that I'd be safe, as the murderer could not know I was out, walking that way."

Cedric handed the note back to Sir Jasper. "Whoever wrote it, it wasn't Molly. She's in Truro visiting her family, and, on top of that, the girl doesn't read or write much above a few words. Mama's forever lamenting that she has to make the lists of stuffs to buy herself."

"So," Lucifer continued, "someone wrote the note making sure it looked innocuous, unthreatening, but also believable. Phyllida knew Molly; we'd found the hat near the back of Ballyclose Manor. No one saw who left the note here—Jonas checked with the staff indoors and out."

Sir Jasper humphed. "Whoever he is, he's clever and very careful not to be seen."

"Which suggests," Jonas put in, "that if he was seen, most people would know who he was."

Lucifer nodded. "My thoughts exactly. It's someone widely known in the village. That's inescapable."

"So what happened next?" Sir Jasper addressed the question to Phyllida. All eyes swung to her.

She drew in a breath, careful not to make it too deep. "I reached the cottage. The front door was open as if someone was waiting inside. I went in, calling for Molly, but there was no reply. I went into the parlor and stopped just inside the door. There was no one about ..."

Phyllida had to stop to take another breath, to break the hold of the paralyzing fear, to remind herself she'd survived. Lucifer rose and came around the *chaise* to perch on the back. He reached down and took her hand, his fingers curling over hers. She glanced up—his expression was closed, but she drew strength from his touch.

She looked at her father. "I was about to turn back to the door. A black cloth dropped over my head. Hands closed around my throat and squeezed—I struggled, but it was no good. He held on, but the cloth was too thick—he couldn't strangle me through it."

Lucifer glanced down. There were bruises about her throat, just blossoming, largely hidden by the scarf she'd wound around her neck.

"He ... I think he lost his temper. He swore and muttered about me leading a charmed life, but his voice was so ... so *fraught*, through the material I couldn't recognize it."

"But it was the same man who attacked you before?" Sir Jasper asked.

She nodded. "The same man who attacked me in the graveyard." She hesitated, then went on. "He still held me, but he took away one hand. I heard a scrape ... I jerked back." She looked up at Lucifer. "I think he hit me with something."

With one finger, Lucifer touched the bump behind her ear. He'd discovered it while in the farm cart. "Here." An inch farther forward—where the murderer had been aiming—and he'd have killed her. As it was, the blow had been glancing.

Eyes too wide, Phyllida looked into his face. "I don't remember anything more. Not until I woke up in the cart."

Lucifer would have liked to smile, just a little, to reassure her. He couldn't. "You were unconscious. He assumed that you'd die in the fire."

"I nearly did."

Lucifer tightened his hold on her hand. He looked at Sir Jasper. "I was following Phyllida to the cottage—I smelled the smoke." He briefly described how he'd found her. "And then, thankfully, the others arrived."

Head bowed to his steepled fingers, Sir Jasper pondered, then he regarded Phyllida and Lucifer. "The brown hat?"

Phyllida glanced at Lucifer. "I dropped it in the cottage."

Lucifer shook his head. "I didn't see it. The smoke was so thick I only found Phyllida by touch. I think we can assume the brown hat is now cinders."

Sir Jasper addressed Phyllida. "Any sense in making a list of all the local men who wear brown hats?"

"I already did that. Even with the hat in my hand, I couldn't remember it on any of them."

Sir Jasper grimaced. "In that case, I don't think there's any point raising a hue and cry for a man who wears a brown hat. That would cover half the county. Even *I* wear brown hats."

"I agree." Lucifer glanced at Phyllida, then at Sir Jasper. "Much as I hate to say it, we're no nearer to identifying the murderer than we were when Horatio died. We had the brown hat—I was going to suggest that we take it around the village. While Phyllida couldn't place it, others might. Cedric even thought it was familiar. But the murderer acted. Whoever he is, he's clever and able to act decisively under pressure. If we'd started showing the hat around, he might well have been unmasked. Instead, he struck boldly and removed the hat, and nearly removed Phyllida, too. He's ruthless and very dangerous. And we have no clue who he is."

"Only," Jonas said, "that he probably still believes that, at some point, Phyl will remember who owned the hat."

Phyllida sighed. "The truth is, I never will. As far as I know, the first time I saw that hat was on Horatio's drawing room table after he'd been killed."

That conclusion did not make anyone feel more comfortable. Lucifer eventually put their helplessness into words. "All we can do is pray that the murderer realizes that Phyllida is no threat to him."

CHAPTER
Eighteen

Cedric excused himself and returned to Ballyclose. At Sir Jasper's urging, Lucifer stayed to dine at the Grange.

The meal was a family affair. All present were subdued, reflecting on Phyllida's near escape. Even Lady Huddlesford spoke rarely, and then in a quiet tone quite different from her usual imperiousness. The only moment of interest arose when Percy declared he'd decided to leave the next day for "the congenial company of some friends in Yorkshire." The announcement was met with blank silence, then everyone returned to his meal.

When the ladies retreated to the drawing room and the port was set upon the table, Percy excused himself and retired to pack.

Frederick moved to a chair next to Jonas. "I say, terrible business. Is there anything I can do?"

The question—surely the first intimation that Frederick thought of anything beyond himself—arrested the three other men. Then Sir Jasper harrumphed, but kindly. "Nothing I can think of, m'boy. Nothing to be done—nothing we can do at present."

Lucifer wasn't so sure. His gaze on Jonas, he spoke to Sir Jasper. "I wonder, sir, if I might have a private word."

Jonas rose. "Come on, Frederick. Let's go pot some balls."

Frederick murmured his farewells and followed Jonas out of the room.

His face tight with worry, Sir Jasper turned to Lucifer. "Thought of something, have you?"

"In a way, yes. Lady Huddlesford mentioned earlier that you were expecting guests tomorrow."

Sir Jasper looked blank, then consternation filled his face. "Damn! Forgot. My sister, Eliza, her husband, and their brood arrive tomorrow. They come for a few weeks every summer." He looked at Lucifer. "Six children."

"Although I'm sure she'll declare otherwise, I doubt Phyllida is up to coping with such an invasion at present."

"Indeed, not—the four girls are a handful. Drive us insane. They tend to cling to Phyllida."

"Not this time."

"No. You're right. Although how to keep them from bothering her ..." Sir Jasper shook his head. "I won't hide it from you, m'boy—I'm deuced worried about Phyllida."

"As am I. Which is why I'd like to suggest that Phyllida stay as a guest at the Manor for as long as this murderer is on the loose, for as long as we have reason to think her in danger. I realize the suggestion is somewhat unusual, but I've already made plain my intentions toward her and they haven't changed. For her part, Phyllida is aware of them."

"She hasn't refused?"

"No, but she has yet to agree." Lucifer sat back. "However, in this, I'm thinking primarily of her safety. After the incident of our nighttime intruder, I ordered locks for all the doors and windows at the Manor. They've arrived— Thompson started installing them yesterday. He's completing the task as we speak. Once that's done, the Manor will be thoroughly secure. The Grange is not." He shrugged. "Most country houses aren't."

"True. So little need, generally speaking."

"Exactly, but this isn't a usual case. There's also the fact that my staff have no other guest to deal with, so they'll be on hand to ensure Phyllida is cared for and protected at all times. Of course, I would imagine Miss Sweet would accompany Phyllida; thus, the proprieties will be observed."

Sir Jasper humphed. "Very neat. For myself, given the seriousness of the situation, I'm grateful for the suggestion and to hell with the proprieties. But the ladies set such store by 'em, best to do what we can to preserve them."

"My thoughts exactly."

Sir Jasper looked at Lucifer, then nodded. "As I said before, whatever permission you need, consider it given." He paused, then asked, "Do you think she'll agree?"

Lucifer's expression remained impassive. "You may leave that to me."

"Where are you taking me?" Phyllida looked up, into Lucifer's face, and waited for an answer. With her cradled in his arms, he was striding through the shrubbery. They'd set out for a moonlit stroll around the back lawn, but then he'd scooped her up into his arms and turned between the hedges.

Her throat was still sore; despite having slept for half the day, she was tiring. She'd only just remembered to give orders for rooms for her aunt and family to be prepared for their arrival tomorrow. While she'd been talking to Gladys, Lucifer had chatted to Sweetie, then strolled up and inveigled her into believing that a turn about the gardens in the cool of the night would help her still difficult breathing.

An image of Sweetie's face as, parting from Lucifer, she'd turned to go upstairs suddenly glowed in Phyllida's mind. She tightened her arms about Lucifer's neck. The end of the shrubbery was approaching. "Stop."

He didn't. He kept straight on through the gap in the hedges and onto the path through the wood.

Phyllida inwardly sighed. She relaxed her arms. "You're taking me to the Manor. Why?"

For a moment, he didn't say anything; then he stopped in a spot where the moonlight beamed down. He could see her face bathed in silver; she could barely see his as he looked down at her.

"You're going to let me take care of you."

She wasn't sure there was a question involved. She tried to think what her answer should be. She was the one who cared for everyone else—she couldn't remember the last time someone had set themselves to care for her.

He shifted her weight in his arms, gathering her closer, tightening his hold—not enough to make her feel trapped, just enough to make her feel totally secure. Totally safe.

"You have to let me protect you."

Those words were softer, more like a plea.

She tried to read his eyes, but couldn't. There was, however, no one more capable of protecting her than he.

And she knew she needed protection.

She'd wondered how she was going to fall asleep, tired though she was. The fear and panic that had swamped her in the cottage hovered, a shadow at the edge of her mind. She would sleep much better knowing he was near.

Besides, if she wanted a marriage of sharing, of give and take, then perhaps this was one of those times she should give ... and take. "Very well." An instant later, she added, "If you wish to."

His soft snort suggested, strongly, that her qualification was absurd. He started forward again.

"Sweetie's packing your things. She'll stay, too, so there'll be no scandal. She'll drive around in the carriage. We'll be safe through the wood—no one could know we'd be out here."

Phyllida considered that. "Our man—the murderer—has been like that, hasn't he? All his attacks have been carefully planned. Even that time at Ballyclose, it was almost as if he'd been watching. It was all too neat."

Lucifer nodded. "He knew we were looking for brown hats and that Cedric had a shelfful, and that you'd know Cedric wore brown hats. Everyone knew we'd both be at Ballyclose that night."

"That suggests the murderer knows the Ballyclose household well. He knew where Cedric kept his hats."

"True, but you mentioned that Sir Bentley was ill for some time. I take it he held court in his bedroom and that many of the local gentry attended."

Phyllida grimaced. "Yes, but the murderer also knew of Molly. He knew she existed and that I knew her, too."

Lucifer frowned. "You're right."

Some minutes later, he stepped out from the trees. Ahead, the Manor stood pale and solid, a modern castle. Welcoming lights shone from the kitchen; one hung over the back door, which swung open as they neared. Mrs. Hemmings looked out and beamed.

"Welcome, Miss Phyllida, and right glad we be to see you safe and sound." She stood back and let Lucifer past, then followed hard on his heels. "Now, you just let the master carry you on up to the old master's bedroom—it's the biggest and I've done my best to make it seem homey. The bed's nice and big. All you need do is lie back and let us all take care of you."

The eager anticipation in Mrs. Hemmings's voice was impossible to mistake. As Lucifer started up the stairs, Phyllida looked into his impassive countenance—and wondered just what she'd agreed to.

Three hours later, Phyllida lay in the big bed in Horatio's old room—the bed that, unbeknownst to Mrs. Hemmings, she'd occupied once before—and listened to the deep bongs of the longcase clock on the landing send waves through the silence of the house.

Twelve resonating bongs, then silence returned, deeper, thicker than it had been before. Beyond the Manor, the village and its surrounding houses lay sleeping. Somewhere lay a murderer, asleep—or awake?

Wriggling onto her side, she closed her eyes and waited for sleep to reclaim her. Instead, black filled her mind—the black of the shroud—she could feel his hands on her throat!

Her eyes flew open. She was breathing too fast, too shallowly. Her skin felt cold; all warmth had drained away.

She shivered and drew in a breath, then exhaled and threw back the covers.

She moved quietly but not silently along the corridor, eyes open to their widest extent, ready to speak—or squeak—if necessary. She remembered the sword Lucifer had carried the last time they'd met in the dark. She didn't know how good his night vision was.

His door stood open. She halted in the doorway; she hadn't been in this room before. All the curtains were open letting starlight stream in; the moon had waned. Shadows lay thick, but she could make out the chests that stood between the windows, with what she assumed were items from Horatio's collection arrayed on their tops. Tallboys and armoires lined the other walls. A long wall mirror hung opposite the bed—a huge four-poster with curtains cinched by tasseled cords at each post.

The rich covers were half turned down; white sheets and pillows filled the bed above. In their midst, Lucifer lay sprawled on his stomach, much as he'd been that first night at the Grange. The only difference was, this time he was wearing no nightshirt. Full knowledge of what wouldn't be covered blossomed in her mind. She hesitated, uncertain what to do next, but she had no intention of retreating.

She'd made up her mind, although she wasn't sure when. Perhaps when she'd woken in the cart and found him beside her, her savior, her protector who had faced death for her and rescued her from its vicious teeth. Perhaps later in the wood when she'd heard his plea, heard his heart speak without any social glamor to shield it. Or maybe it had been when she'd realized that it was the facet of his care she found most difficult to accept—his possessive protectiveness—that had given her a second chance at life and love. Whenever it had been, her decision was made.

Her time alone—managing alone, being alone, sleeping alone—had come to an end. She was here to let him know.

Whether he'd been asleep or not, she had no idea, but he slowly rose on one elbow and studied her.

"What is it?"

His voice was even, a little hoarse, but whether from the smoke or something else, she couldn't tell.

Barefoot, she padded over the threshold, then paused, turned back, and shut the door. Clutching her robe around her, she walked—heart in her mouth—to the side of the bed. She stopped a foot from it. The bed was a mass of shadows; she couldn't see his face.

She licked her dry lips, then drew breath and lifted her chin. "I want to sleep with you." She meant more than just sleep, but surely he'd understand.

For one instant, he just stared at her, then his smile flashed. "Good." He lifted the covers beside him. "I want you to sleep with me, too."

A sigh of relief escaped her, chased by a shivery, anticipatory tingle. She shrugged the robe off her shoulders. It fell to puddle at her feet.

Noting his suddenly arrested state—the locking of muscles throughout his large body at the sight of her naked limbs—she shyly slid into his bed.

He let go of the sheets. And reached for her.

"You've just made my favorite dream come true."

She reached for him and drew him to her. "Do you think you can return the favor?"

He looked into her face. "I'll do my very best." He lowered his head. "You can count on it."

That first kiss sealed that promise; she felt it in her bones. Warmth unfurled between them, driving out her chill. She sank into it, offering her mouth and more. Although he claimed her lips, tangled her tongue, mesmerized her wits with slow, tantalizing surges, with one hand framing her face, the other trapped next to her shoulder, he remained beside her, his body a hot line alongside hers, but not touching.

She wanted to touch, to feel, to explore. She wanted to give herself to him and take all he would give in return. There was something very liberating in the thought, a free exchange that, ultimately, would balance, with body, mind, heart, and soul all freely offered on the scales. She turned and pressed, stretched upward against him, matching her body to his.

He gave a wicked chuckle, one not entirely steady. Closing his arms around her, he shifted onto his back, urging her across him. She followed his lead, quite content to sprawl atop him. Much easier to explore from there.

She took his urging as invitation. Wriggling until she straddled his hips, knees bent, calves gripping lightly along his flanks, she braced her arms, palms flat on his chest, and lifted up—so she could survey her prize.

His chest had always fascinated her—the sharp contrasts of smooth, lightly tanned skin and crisp black hair, the palpable weight of muscle and the heavier, harder curves of bone. Fingers splayed, she pressed, glorying in the resilience of muscle, the solid resistance of bone. Then she softened her touch and went searching, caressing lightly, then lovingly, across the broad muscles, down over his ribs, across the ridges of his abdomen. Only her position stopped her from reaching further, but she had all night.

"None of your chest was burned." Her sighing comment reeked with satisfaction.

"No real burns. Just the backs of my hands got scorched."

She examined his hands as he held them up. "Do they hurt?"

He skimmed his palms down her back. "Not enough to stop me from touching you."

She responded to the long, artful caress with a low, murmurous moan.

Of their own volition, her hands stroked upward again to cover his flat nipples. She let her fingers tease and draw, then circle, roll—until his nipples were as tight as hers.

That seemed fair. She smiled and leaned forward, remembering what else he liked to do to her. And how much she liked his doing it. Presumably the same actions worked in reverse. The way he stiffened even before her tongue touched convinced her that was true. She licked, laved, then nipped lightly. That last made him jerk. His hands gripped her hips, fingers sinking in, but he made no effort to stop her.

So she played, fingers firm on one bud while she tortured the other with lips, tongue, and teeth. Then she switched hand and head, trailing wet, openmouthed kisses across his chest on the way. She settled to her task and thought she heard a low moan. He was burning up beneath her, his skin fire-hot everywhere she touched.

A wicked thought occurred. She pressed her body lower, so that her breasts caressed his lower chest and the backs of her thighs moved against his hips, the hot, wet, aching flesh at the juncture of her thighs a bare inch above his flat stomach. Just out of reach of the ultimate prize.

Then she moved. Sliding her body from side to side, she caressed him.

He sucked in a breath; his body tensed beneath her. She sensed his struggle to lie still. His fingers flexed on her hips, tightening before he forced them to relax ... she felt their touch drift upward, over her shoulders. She suckled one nipple lightly, then tightly. He arched beneath her. His fingers tangled in her hair, clutched—then he drew her away, turning her face to his.

He swooped—his lips closed on hers in a searing kiss so full of heated passion it stole her breath. The kiss went on and on. He started to turn, to roll her beneath him. She pulled away, hand on his shoulder pressing him back. She shook her head, then found her voice, a little hoarse, like his. "Not yet."

He was tempted to disobey—the tension in his body told her that—but after a fraught moment, he eased back to the bed. His eyes, dark in the night, watched her; his gaze held a heat all its own. His chest rose and fell beneath her hands. "All right. For now."

She smiled and made the gesture beatific, then ducked her head to lick first one aching nipple, then the other. Then she shuffled her legs, her hips, farther down his body, lifting slightly to accommodate the hard shaft of rampant flesh that thrust upward so aggressively from its thicket of black hair, then lowering again so she caressed it, too, sliding the slick, swollen flesh between her thighs down from its broad head all along its ridged length.

A heartfelt groan was her reward; his body bowed, head and shoulders pressing back in reaction. "Dammit! You're an innocent—I know you are."

"Hmm." Innocent she might be, but she had a few ideas.

She put them into action. Her body and mouth moving on him, over him, slowly and in concert, seemed almost more than he could stand. His fingers gripped her shoulders, then tightened about her head—even then, he remembered and avoided the bump on one side. She'd started the evening with a mild but persistent headache. It had disappeared the instant their naked bodies had touched.

She wasn't about to let a few bruises stop her learning all she wanted to know. Only her breathing was still a restriction, and even that was easier now. Shallow little breaths. A little panting. All that she could manage.

Her hands continued their exploration; her mouth followed them down his body. She shifted lower, lower, until her swollen breasts brushed his rock-hard thighs.

The sheet was pushed behind her, leaving him fully exposed so she could worship by starlight. Resting her cheek on his hip, she traced, circled, then closed her hand around him. She'd done that before—it wasn't that which made him so tense. It was the anticipation that where her fingers went, her lips, her mouth, would follow. Lips curving, she let her fingers play.

Lucifer lay back and tried to think of England. The only part he could remember was a certain bed in Devon. His fingers sifted through Phyllida's hair, sliding through the sable silk, tracing her skull—tightening when he couldn't help himself. Her touch wasn't so much artful as wondering, naive, enthusiastically natural. His body reacted, helplessly in thrall.

She was a warm, supple, rounded weight lying across his thighs. Her head lay heavy to one side of his groin, her hand cupping, her fingers gliding over her current obsession. He felt possessed, as if in permitting it—letting her have her way—he'd somehow surrendered to her.

He had. He just hadn't told her so in words. Only groans.

Then she shifted and he felt her breath on him, an insubstantial warmth brushing him to even more painful erection. She was going to kill him, not with need, but through the violent clash of powerful emotions—the gut-wrenching desire to have her take him in her mouth, the fear she wouldn't, the suspicion she had no idea she could, and the nearly overwhelming, protective urge that insisted that she shouldn't. It was enough to drive a man insane.

Then she raised her head, not moving closer but over. Her fingers traced his throbbing head again, fascination very clear in her touch. Then she bent her head.

Every muscle in his body locked tight at the first touch of her lips; she trailed openmouthed kisses around, then down, then licked, gently, then more firmly, as if she liked his taste. Then her tongue went questing and he thought he might die. His chest hurt—he dragged in a quick breath—

Without warning she took him into her mouth, closed that hot, wet sweetness around him, taking just a little, then, deliberately, more. For a definable instant, he lost touch with the world and floated in a sensual heaven. He felt her tongue curl, around, then about. He slumped back, easing muscles he hadn't known he'd tensed. He was breathing raggedly and they'd only just begun. He knew that for a fact; it made him feel light-headed. His hands sifted through her hair, caressing, tensing responsively as she tightened, sucked, kissed, then went back for more.

He was clinging to sanity by his fingernails, guiding her, just a little—it was too much, too precious, to break the moment, but ... she was wearing him down.

Tightening his stomach, he half sat and reached down and around to grasp her hips. "Enough." He barely recognized his voice, so rough, so low. She looked up, releasing him; the loss of her wet heat was almost painful. She slid her palms to his chest, bracing to push him back down. He gathered her in his arms, lifted her to his chest, then rolled and trapped her beneath him.

One hand on his shoulder, she met his gaze. Her eyes were dark pools, wide and lustrous. That was all he could see in the starlight. But he could sense something else in that dark gaze, a weight of instinctive feminine knowledge, of innate womanly need.

"I haven't finished yet," she murmured, and the sound was close to a purr. Her gaze lowered to his lips as she spoke. She licked hers.

The knowledge that she was responding instinctively didn't help at all. "No," he agreed, "but it's my turn now."

He bent his head and took her lips, and she surrendered her mouth readily. Sliding her arms around his neck, she leaned back against the bank of pillows. Her body softened under his.

His turn. His turn to worship, to visit pleasure on her heated flesh. To lave and lick and suckle until she gasped and arched beneath him. When her breasts were swollen and aching, he moved lower, anointing the skin over her ribs, past her waist to her navel, then lower still, over the flickering tautness of her stomach to the thatch of dark curls at its base.

Her fingers sank into his shoulders at the first delicate probing of his tongue. Hands trailing down from her hips to grip her buttocks, he kneaded, then slid his palms even lower, over the backs of her thighs. Grasping gently, he urged them wider. She hesitated, then, with a gasp close to a sob, she parted them. Gripping her hips again, he bent his head. He licked, and her fingers clenched in his hair.

She was a delight—wanton in her passion, open and eager in her desire to be his. All his. He claimed every last slick inch, tasted every soft fold. Her essence swirled through his senses and sank deep.

He wound her tight, then tighter, calling on experience to further her horizons, ruthlessly sending her spinning, then reeling her back the instant before she went over the edge.

Some primal need drove him. She'd come to him, offered him all she was, knowing what his demands would be—not just of the flesh but of the soul. Her own actions made it clear she wanted to plunge headfirst into their new life; that was so much like her, so much a reflection of the directness he prized in her, that he was more than willing to teach her how to fly and extend himself to be her safety net, at least in this arena.

For the rest—the emotional adjustments, the more subtle changes—whether he would teach her or she him was moot. Perhaps they'd learn together. But for tonight, she'd chosen to open her arms to passion. His, and hers.

He stoked both and let her feel the power rise, the insatiable hunger, the greedy need, the hot urgency that poured like molten gold down their veins.

And then he joined with her. Bracing his arms, he held himself above her and filled her with long, steady strokes. Eyes closed, he concentrated on the rhythm, concentrated on the hot embrace of her body, on their pulsing, driving need. He felt her hands, fingers extended, trail down his chest. Cracking open his lids, he looked down. Eyes shut, head thrown back, pressed into the pillows, she was lost in their union. Caught in the sensual waves that rolled through him, through her, she surrendered and rode the tide. Every thrust lifted her, rocked her breasts, her hips, shifted her head against the pillows. Her dark hair rasped softly, silk against linen, again and again.

Her breath came in little pants. She lifted her hips and met him, took him in, accepted him deep, then let him ease back so he could love her again.

They were drowning in each other, drowning in a sea of desire so intense it was close to rapture. Then that, too, swirled into the mix, into their bodies, into their blood. And took them.

He felt her shatter beneath him, felt her hands clutch, her body cling. Then she eased, her heated softness rippling about him in the ultimate caress. Head back, eyes shut, he clung to the moment; then his own release swept through him. He shuddered and filled her, then slowly collapsed, turning, taking her with him, holding her close, wrapping her limbs about him.

He would never let her go.

On the cusp of oblivion, Phyllida felt him within her, hot and liquid at her core. With her hands, her arms, her body, she held him tight. If she was his, then he was hers. And he'd definitely lived up to her dreams.

She woke to find herself high in the bed. His head against her breast, his arms wrapped around her waist, he was a warm, solid mass of muscle trapping her mostly beneath him.

She was curiously comfortable and not in the least sleepy—presumably the afternoon's rest had been enough. She felt relaxed. No specter of death could possibly haunt her, not in his bed. Raising one hand, she lifted a dark lock from his forehead, smoothing it back amid the rest.

He stirred, tensed for an instant, then, eyes still closed, hugged her and placed a deliberate kiss on the nipple all but against his lips. "Very nice."

Phyllida laughed. He sounded like a very large human cat, purring with masculine satisfaction. Shifting, he freed a hand from beneath her, then settled back, head cradled on one breast, his hand on the other. He touched her gently, soothingly—not so much with desirous intent as for sensual comfort. She had no difficulty making the distinction.

Content, she lay back, luxuriating in the warm caresses, in the golden glow of the moment that still held them. Fingers stroking his hair, she set her mind free—free to feel, to think. To wonder. "I think I love you." It had to be that, this golden feeling.

The lazy drift of his fingers ceased. "Why aren't you sure?"

She answered truthfully. "I don't know what love is." Lifting her head, she peered at his face. "Do you?"

He met her gaze, eyes dark, mysterious. Then he looked at his fingers, lying on her breast, and started to gently stroke once more.

She smiled and leaned back on the pillows, her gaze lost in the shadows of the canopy above. She didn't press for an answer. If she didn't know, why would he?

Then again ... "Do you love me?" She didn't look down but she felt him look up.

After a moment, he said, "Can't you tell?"

"No."

She waited. He shifted, lifting his head, moving back just a little. She felt his gaze on her face; it lingered for some time, then swept down, over her breasts, over her waist, over her hips, down her long legs. It returned, but stopped at the top of her thighs. The hand at her breast firmed. His touch changed.

"I'll have to demonstrate, then."

"Demonstrate?"

"Hmm. Cynsters are better with actions than words."

He proved it. The night became a heated odyssey through realms of passion, desire, sensation, anticipation, hunger, and need. He drew from them both and created the landscape, then guided her through it, ever onward to peaks gilded with ecstasy.

Each touch became invested with more than just feeling, each joining with more than the physical fact. Sensations battered at them, emotions drove them, onward, upward, to impossible bliss.

At the last, she shattered and drank it in, and felt it sink into her bones. A heartbeat later, he joined her. They clung, and the wave washed over them, through them, then the tension slowly drained. Her lips curved. She leaned her forehead to his. He traced her face, then touched his lips to hers in a chaste, final kiss.

Their pact was sealed.

Giddy with release, relaxed beyond this world, they slumped together, drew the sheets up, and slept in each other's arms.

* * *

At ten the next morning, Lucifer left the Manor and set off for the old Drayton cottage. The night had given him more than he'd thought he'd ever have, but it had also left him with much to think about. Possessing for such as he always entailed a certain responsibility—the obligation to take due care. How much did he care for Phyllida? There wasn't a word to encompass the reality.

He strode out, drawing the morning air deep, letting it clear his mind. He'd been up since dawn when he'd lifted Phyllida, still asleep, from the cocoon of his bed and carried her to her own. She'd clutched at him as he'd placed her between the cold sheets. He'd stayed with her, sharing his warmth, until the first sound of his awakening household had sent him back to his bed.

His extremely rumpled, storm-tossed bed. God only knew what Mrs. Hemmings would make of it, but he was quite sure she wouldn't imagine the truth. Or, at least, nothing like the whole truth. That was hard enough for even him to believe.

Underneath her serenely decorous facade, Miss Phyllida Tallent was a wanton in disguise. He now knew that for a fact, and very comforting it was. He'd strolled into her room after breakfast, having been informed by Sweetie that her erstwhile charge had agreed to rest quietly for the morning but was suitably attired to permit of a visit. So he'd visited and with just one look, one wicked, suggestive grin, had sent a wave of heat rising to her cheeks.

She'd glared, then had to hide it as Sweetie bustled in. He'd stayed long enough to assure himself that Phyllida was indeed well; with carefully worded replies, she'd given him to understand that she was suffering more from sexually induced lethargy than from fire-induced trauma.

He'd been careful not to smile too triumphantly, or to show his relief. He'd explained where he was headed and why, then left her sewing on the buttons he'd sliced off the week before.

Striding along the tracks, he followed the acrid smell of burned thatch. The day was cool, so peaceful, when yesterday had held so much panic.

And resulted in so much being resolved.

In actions, at least—intentions declared but not stated. He understood what Phyllida had meant to tell him—at least, he thought he did. What he was far less sure about was why she'd made her decision.

Who knew what went on in the minds of women?

After all these years, he really ought to have a clue.

She'd asked whether he knew what love was. He knew what he felt for her—the compelling need to know she was well, safe, and happy, the joy he felt when she laughed, when she smiled. He knew how his gut knotted when she was in danger and how his nerves flickered when she was away from his side. He knew the pride that warmed him as he watched her going about her daily round, so competent, so caring, so giving in that managing yet selfless way that was so uniquely hers. Knew, too, the overwhelming impulse to cosset her, to protect her emotionally and physically, to care for her. To meet her every need, to give her all she could ever desire.

So, yes, he knew about love. He loved her and always would. She loved him, too, but didn't know it—couldn't see it—even though she wanted to see, to know.

Could he teach her what love was?

He could hear fate cackling in the wings, but he shut his ears and set his jaw. If that was what Phyllida wanted, someone to show her, to point out the truth in such a way that she could see it, too, then ...if he wanted their marriage to be what it could be, it behooved him to do it.

Decision made—simple, easy. She wasn't the only one who could act decisively.

He emerged from the last copse and looked up; the blackened ruin of the cottage stood on the crest, still smoking, charred timbers listing crazily against the summer sky. He heard a grunt and saw Thompson grappling with a crowbar at one side of the shell. An instant later, Oscar joined him.

Lucifer strolled up the path and around to where they worked on the one wall still standing. They both stopped and nodded, leaning on their tools.

"Miss Phyllida?" Oscar asked.

"She's well. Still resting, but I doubt there'll be any lingering effects."

"Best not be," Thompson growled. "But we've got to find this maniac. Doesn't look like he's about to stop."

"I came up to take a look around." Lucifer looked at the half-collapsed wall. "Do you need a hand?"

"Nah." Thompson turned back to the wall. "We'll have this down soon enough. If we left it standing, sure as the sky is blue, some of the tykes would come up to play, and then we'd have an accident."

He leaned on his crowbar and a burned log split.

Lucifer stepped back. "I'll leave you to it." He glanced around, then walked down the overgrown track toward Dottswood, the way most of the locals had come running yesterday. A little way down, he stopped and turned; eyes narrowed, he surveyed the cottage. If he'd been the murderer ...

Two minutes later, he started back up the slope, then cut around, away from the front of the cottage, circling through the overgrown trees and shrubs at its rear.

He found what he'd been certain he would—and just a little more—in a small clearing tucked away behind a stand of rhododendrons run wild. He stared, then hunkered down and looked more closely, hardly daring to believe their luck. Then he stood and went to fetch Thompson.

Thompson came; Oscar followed. The three of them stood behind the rhododendrons and stared down at the clear impression of a horse's hooves—all four of them.

"Ordinary-sized beast, but well set up." Thompson knelt to inspect the indentations. He traced one with a broad fingertip. "Better yet—it's my own work, that is."

"You're sure?"

"I'm sure." With a grunt, Thompson got to his feet. "I'm the only one hereabouts who uses those particular nails. See the odd-shaped heads?"

Both Lucifer and Oscar looked, and nodded.

"And that left back shoe?" Lucifer asked.

"Gets better'n better, it does. I haven't seen this horse recently, but I'm going to soon, and then we'll have our man." Thompson nodded at the left back hoofprint. "That shoe's going to come off any day."

Lucifer had to wait until later that evening when Sweetie retired and he and Phyllida were finally alone in the library before he could tell her the news.

"Don't mention it to anyone," he warned. "Thompson has customers from beyond Lyme Regis, so it's not possible to search for the horse. We have to wait for the shoe to fall and the animal to be brought in. Only you, me, Thompson, and Oscar know of it—we've agreed to say nothing, so there's no possibility the murderer will realize and take the horse somewhere else."

Phyllida sat in the armchair by the desk, her face, for once, awash with emotions. "Soon, Thompson said?"

"It depends on how often the horse is ridden. If it's ridden every day, Thompson says in less than a week. Ridden less, and it'll be longer, but he doesn't expect that shoe to stay on much above a fortnight."

She considered, then asked, "And it's been the same horse every time?"

"I believe so." Lucifer frowned. "Just to be sure, I'll send Dodswell to look at the latest prints. The others would all have washed away by now."

"I really don't believe we have more than one phantom horseman in the village," Phyllida returned. "He always hides his horse, too, doesn't he?"

"He makes sure it isn't somewhere where a chance passerby would see it. That suggests the horse, too, would identify him, which makes our prospects of catching him at last look good." Lucifer met Phyllida's gaze. "It's ironic. He tried to kill you and succeeded in destroying the one piece of hard evidence we had. But in doing so, he's given us another piece of even better evidence. We might never have traced the hat. It's unlikely we won't trace the horse."

Phyllida blinked. "I didn't think of that."

Lucifer rose and circled the desk. "I think we need to think of that." Halting before Phyllida, he hunkered down so his face was level with hers. "This murderer, whoever he is, has shown himself capable of the most ruthless acts. Murdering Horatio. Trying to kill you." Reaching out, he smoothed her hair, then cupped her face lightly. "We can't take any chances for the next few weeks."

Phyllida looked into his eyes, then smiled. She leaned forward and touched her lips to his. "You're right."

Lucifer blinked. His hand remained about her face, stopping her from retreating. He held her gaze. "I'm not letting you out of my sight."

Phyllida's smile softened. "Is that a promise?"

Lucifer studied her eyes, then drew her nearer. "A sworn oath."

Five minutes later, distinctly breathless, she drew back, tried to frown at him, and lifted the book that had fallen, forgotten, in her lap. "We haven't finished these yet." She held the book like a shield between them.

Lucifer glanced at the pile of tomes with inscriptions that Covey had left stacked between the desk and the chair.

"We might have nearly identified Horatio's murderer, but we've yet to find any explanation for why he's so interested in Horatio's books." Phyllida picked up the top volume and slapped it against Lucifer's chest.

He grimaced and took it. "As you say." He rose.

Phyllida looked up at him. "Have you any idea what that item was that Horatio wanted you to look at?"

Lucifer shook his head. "That, too, remains a mystery. It's possible we'll never know what it was Horatio had found."

"Don't give up hope." Phyllida handed him two more books. "Not when there's so many places still left to search for clues."

Smiling, Lucifer returned to the desk. "Speaking of searching, you still haven't discovered that writing desk and the oh-so-important letters."

"I know." Smiling, Phyllida shook her head. "When Mary Anne visited this afternoon, she never mentioned the letters, even when Mrs. Farthingale left us alone. All she could talk about was the fire, and me staying here with you."

"Perspective," Lucifer said, sitting down and opening a book. "It comes to us all."

Phyllida humphed, then settled to deciphering notations.

An hour later, they called a halt. The house was already secured for the night; Dodswell had stuck his head into the library and reported that fact. All they had to do was to turn out the lamps, collect their candles from the table in the hall, and climb the stairs.

They turned along the corridor. All about them was quiet and still. Sweetie had the other back corner room at the end of the other corridor. When they reached the point where they would part, each to their separate rooms, Phyllida halted. She glanced at Lucifer. "You're the experienced one. Your room or mine?"

Lucifer looked into her dark eyes, lit by the candle flame. It was on the tip of his tongue to inform her that in this particular arena, the one they were playing in, he was no more experienced than she.

Except, perhaps, that wasn't quite true.

He was a Cynster. He had generations of love matches behind him. These days, love matches abounded all around him. It was something in the blood, something not even he could resist. He'd grown up knowing of no other sort of marriage. It was the only sort that would do for him.

He bent his head and kissed her lightly. "Are you sure?" He breathed the question over her lips, then eased back.

Her hand had fisted on his lapel; she held him near, her eyes locked on his. Then her gaze dropped to his lips. Hers, he noted, curved gently. "Yes," she whispered. "I'm sure."

"Your room, then, for now. We'll have the rest of our lives to enjoy mine."

CHAPTER

Nineteen

Early the next morning, Lucifer stood at his bedchamber windows and looked out over Horatio's garden. The sight soothed him, helped clear his mind and focus his thinking.

He couldn't ask Phyllida to marry him—not yet. Not while the murderer was still loose, with her very much in his sights. The man had to be growing desperate; that gave him an overwhelmingly powerful reason for wanting Phyllida completely within his protective care. If he asked her to marry him now ... no. He wasn't going to risk it. He would not give her even the flimsiest reason to imagine his proposal had any motive bar one.

She wanted to learn about love—so be it. He would make sure she saw it clearly, uncamouflaged, undisguised. Make sure she learned enough so she would recognize it instantly, so that no possibility of confusion would exist when he finally asked her to be his.

He took a determined breath, then exhaled. His gaze was drawn to the jeweled tapestry below, bedewed and glittering with the first touch of the morning sun. A self-conscious smile tugged at his lips. Turning, he grabbed his coat, shrugged into it, and headed downstairs.

When Phyllida joined him at the breakfast table half an hour later, a spray of summer blooms lay beside her plate. She blinked at them; hesitantly, with one fingertip, she touched the velvet petal of a perfect white rose. Then she glanced up at him as, having held her chair for her, he moved back to his. "I didn't know you'd been out."

"Only for those. Only for you." He sat. "Through one impulsive act, I've shattered my suave London persona. I filched the shears from the garden room. When I came back in, the Hemmingses were turning the place upside down looking for them. I'd forgotten today is the day Mrs. Hemmings does the church flowers."

Phyllida raised the fragrant blooms to her face to hide her smile. As well as the white rose, there was rose lavender and honeysuckle, all set off with violets. "Thank you," she murmured. "I appreciate the sacrifice."

He reached for the coffeepot. "Strange to tell, it didn't hurt at all."

That made her giggle. Laying aside the spray, making a mental note to set it in a vase by her bed—the bed they presently shared—she helped herself to toast. "What now? We can't simply sit on our hands for the next two weeks and hope everything comes right in the end."

Lucifer hesitated, then said, "I sent a letter off yesterday while you were busy with the Farthingales. The contents aren't important so much as any results it might bring."

"Results?"

"I wrote to my cousin Devil. He'll be at Somersham at present—that's in Cambridgeshire. I gave him a brief outline of what's happened here, and the names of the gentlemen we've not yet eliminated."

"What do you expect him—Devil—to do?"

"Ask questions. Or have other people ask them. That's something Devil does well. He'll be discreet, but if there's any useful information lying about the capital, you can rest assured Devil and his troops will find it."

"His troops?"

"Whoever he calls on."

Head tilted, Phyllida regarded him. "What aren't you telling me?"

Lucifer grinned. "Devil is the Duke of St. Ives. If he wants something, he'll get it."

"Ah." Phyllida nodded. "I take it he's a despot. Is he a close relation?"

"First cousin."

Her face blanked. "You're first cousin to a *duke*?"

Thankful that Sweetie was twittering about outside, helping the Hemmingses, Lucifer nodded. "Don't let it bother you."

It was obvious it did. "If you're a near relative of a duke—"

"Near but a long way from the title, so I can marry as I choose." Brows rising, he added, "Not that any of us ever do anything else."

Frowning, Phyllida studied him. "You're serious."

"There's no reason to hold my birth against me."

She glared, but let the point slide. "So you've asked your cousin for help—"

"And I think, now matters have reached this pass, that it's time to inform Horatio's peers of his murder and appeal for their help."

"Other collectors like Horatio?"

Lucifer nodded. "I know most of them. Covey will have the addresses. I'll write and ask if they can shed any light on what might be in Horatio's collection that could have led to his murder, and also if they know of any special item he might have recently discovered."

"Would you like me to help?"

"If you would, we'd get the letters out faster. There must be someone who knows something to the point."

Phyllida looked at him, so large and darkly handsome he dominated the room. "I should help Mrs. Hemmings with the church vases—I didn't clear them yesterday."

"Mrs. Hemmings can take Sweetie—they'll be delighted to relieve you of the burden." Lucifer returned her gaze steadily; he reached out and closed his hand over hers. "I don't want to keep you locked inside like some maiden in a tower, but until we have this man in keeping, you should not go out on your usual errands. No church flowers, no Colyton Import Company. No visiting Mrs. Dewbridge or any of your other old ducks. No excursion that anyone could predict or anticipate."

She stared at him. "What does that leave?"

Later that afternoon, she found herself on the box seat of his curricle with the blacks trotting smartly along the lane. Despite her position, she was surrounded by male—Jonas to one side, Lucifer on the other, and as Jonas was handling the ribbons, Lucifer had stretched one arm behind her along the seat. There was absolutely no doubt she was safe from the murderer. As she watched Jonas work to keep the blacks in line, she wasn't so certain she was safe from her twin landing them all in a ditch.

Lucifer seemed much more sanguine, issuing instructions and explanations in a relaxed tone. Phyllida watched and listened. When they reached the end of the lane and Lucifer took back the reins and wheeled his pair, she held out her gloved hand commandingly. "My turn."

They both looked at her. Their jaws set.

She ignored that and all other evidence of masculine disapproval, along with all their arguments. She drove the curricle back into Colyton and felt a great deal better for the outing.

The days that followed settled into a rhythm—an uneasy one. After penning missives to all Horatio's known associates, they refocused their attention on the large number of books not yet inspected.

"It's amazing how long it takes to do just one shelf."

"Indeed," Lucifer returned without looking up. "I don't want to know how many shelves there are."

The activity ate the hours; visits from others punctuated the sessions and, in some measure, relieved the tedium. Her father stopped in, bright and surprisingly sprightly—all for show, she could tell. Worry and deep concern lurked in his eyes, permanent residents; she wished she could send them away. All she could do was smile and squeeze his hand, and let him know she was happy. That, at least, seemed to honestly cheer him.

Jonas was frequently on hand, but she didn't count him a visitor. He was like a shadow, simply there; she didn't need to entertain or even consider him. Others, however, proved much more distracting.

Her aunt Eliza called with her brood, a noisy invasion. She was guiltily grateful when Lucifer, abetted by her aunt Huddlesford, shooed the children across the lane to the duck pond. Eliza remained to squeeze her hand, comment on Lucifer's handsomeness, and set her mind at rest; they were remaining at the Grange for only eight days.

Lady Fortemain was an early caller. While shocked by the attempt on

Phyllida's life, she clearly believed fate had made some monumental mistake in having Lucifer, rather than Cedric, save her. Beyond that, however, she was cloyingly solicitous, insisting she would send a footman with some of Ballyclose's damson jam.

Cedric and Jocasta, Phyllida had expected; their newfound happiness radiated from them and made her smile. They were concerned, but not smotheringly so—their visit was a definite success.

Not so Basil's. He called when Lucifer had, at her insistence, gone to have a word with Thompson. Basil's concern for her health was clearly genuine, but he found her presence under Lucifer's roof difficult to comprehend. Luckily, Lucifer returned before she lost her temper; he clarified matters—Basil departed with no false illusions.

They were just the first. Mr. Filing visited regularly, as did the Farthingales. Henry Grisby called twice, bringing daisies; he spoke reasonably and made no unwelcome protestations. Phyllida thought better of him than she previously had. Wednesday brought a deluge—all the older ladies and women Phyllida visited came to call, to hear how she was faring, to press their advice and cast measuring glances at Lucifer. All brought gifts, little tokens of affection—a crocheted pot warmer, a sprig of broom tied with ribbon, a pot of salve for her scorched skin. When old Mrs. Grisby herself stumped up the front path, Phyllida felt overwhelmed.

The ladies fussed and fretted and clearly enjoyed it immensely; she could not find it in her to push them away. When they finally left, all pressing her hands and beaming their approval, she slumped back in an armchair and looked at Lucifer. "What on earth has got into them?"

He smiled and sat on the chair's arm. "You have."

"Me? Nonsense! *I'm* the one who takes care of *them,* not the other way about."

Lucifer put an arm around her and hugged, then dropped a kiss on her hair. "True, but unless I miss my guess, this is the first time in recent memory that you've needed to be taken care of. They're seizing the opportunity to let you know how much they—to borrow Lady Fortemain's phrase—treasure you. They want to pay you back."

Phyllida humphed. Beneath his arm, she wriggled. "It was uncomfortable, being the object of their ... care."

Lucifer's arm tightened, then eased. "For some, it is difficult—sometimes very difficult—to let someone take care of them. Yet sometimes that's precisely what the other person needs most. Caring for them means letting them care for you."

Phyllida turned her head and looked up at him. His dark blue eyes met hers without guile. Then his lips curved, not teasing but inviting her to laugh with him—the joke, after all, was on them.

There was a bustle in the hall, Mrs. Hemmings coming to clear the tea tray. Lucifer lifted one hand, tapped a finger to the tip of her nose, then rose and left her.

* * *

Day followed day. Despite the activities that filled their time, there was an inescapable sense of waiting for something to happen—for that horseshoe to fall. It was as if they were living through some hiatus, the dead calm before a storm. As the week lengthened, the tension grew.

On Friday, a packet arrived with "St. Ives" boldly scrawled across one corner. Seated at his desk behind a stack of tomes, Lucifer broke the seal. Phyllida watched as he spread out the sheets, many more than one.

He read the first, started on the second, then stopped. Refolding the second and subsequent sheets, he slipped them into his pocket, leaving the first sheet on the blotter. "It's a progress report from Devil. He's got Montague following up the names I sent." Lucifer glanced at Phyllida. "Montague's the family's man of business. He's exceedingly thorough. If there's anything to be learned in the City, he'll find it."

Lucifer looked back at the note. "At first sounding, however, the names rang no bells. Devil has recruited one of my other cousins—Harry, better known as Demon. He was kicking his heels down in Kent with his older brother, so Devil sent him word and Demon's now in London, haunting the taverns off Whitehall, looking up all our ex-guardsmen friends."

"Why the Guards?" Phyllida asked.

"Not the Guards. He wasn't a guardsman."

"Who? Appleby?"

"He's one of the men we have to check on."

"But—"

"But you decided he wasn't the murderer because he should have been in the ballroom doing his duty in Cedric's place while we were dodging the murderer upstairs?"

Phyllida grimaced. "I suppose you're going to say that's an assumption, and as we don't *know* he was in the ballroom, then he might have been the villain?"

"There's also the fact that the note from Molly looked as if a female had written it. That it was supposed to be labored over helped, but not many men would have thought of it."

"But someone who spent his life writing and reading letters might have thought of it."

"Precisely."

"Why were you so sure Appleby was in the army?"

"It's his stance, the stiffness in his shoulders, the way he bows. It's something learned, and the place you learn it is on the drill field. I'd wager he was in the infantry."

"So, again: Why the Guards?"

"Ex-Guards. Plenty of those about who served with us at Waterloo. They're now secretaries and aides-de-camp to the generals and commanders. They're the ones with access to the records. Demon will find out which regiment Appleby served with, and who his immediate superior was, and have a chat with the man. If he says Appleby's straight as an arrow, we'll have at least learned that much."

Phyllida studied Lucifer's face. "You think it's him."

Lucifer grimaced. "I think the murderer has shown an odd combination of planning carefully, acting ruthlessly, but being so cautious, his caution has interfered with his success. When things go wrong, he doesn't lose his nerve. He acts, but he misses opportunities and doesn't quite succeed in his purpose."

He swiveled to face her. "That's a good description of the characteristics of a regimented foot soldier, one who's reasonably clever. They always have a plan; they don't like operating extemporaneously. They're cautious. And although they don't lose their nerve when things go wrong, their responses aren't always the most likely to succeed—because they haven't had time to plan."

"You sound like you know a lot about soldiering."

"I *saw* a lot of soldiering—a lot of infantry fighting—at Waterloo."

She remembered the saber. "You were in the cavalry."

He nodded. "We played by different rules—following plans was never our forte. Making it up as we went was much more our style."

"Why couldn't it be Basil? He's cautious."

"He was in church when Horatio was murdered, but I'm not taking any chances and assuming it's Appleby." Lucifer caught Phyllida's gaze. "With luck, we'll have proof of who it is soon enough."

By Sunday night, she felt wound tight—waiting for that proof to arrive. Lucifer understood. In that peaceful hour after the sun had set but darkness had yet to descend, he drew her outside to stroll in the scented sweetness of Horatio's garden.

Her hand in his, she walked beside him down the gravel paths. Apart from the main ones from the gate and the side of the house to the front door, there were many others winding through the carefully tended beds.

"He might be out there." Phyllida looked at the shadows deepening beyond the trees.

"He isn't. We don't make a habit of walking in the garden of an evening."

"We don't make a habit of anything anymore—" Phyllida caught herself and amended, "Not outside."

Lucifer laughed; the sound was like a warm hand sliding comfortingly down her back, an invitation to relax. Phyllida breathed deeply—the scent of night stock wreathed around them. "He hasn't gone away."

"No."

They knew that because, just that morning, Dodswell had reported that someone had tried to force the dining room window, the one that used to have a faulty latch. They'd all gone to look, even Sweetie. There'd been scrapes on the window frame and gouges in the earth where the man's heels had dug in, but no clear footprints.

Phyllida exhaled, long and slow. "It's been a week."

"Only a week—Thompson said it might take two." Lucifer drew her closer and turned down another path. "Did you read Honoria's missive?"

The rest of the packet that had come from the duke had proved to be a long letter from the duchess to her. Lucifer had remembered to give it to her after they'd discovered the attempted break-in. Given what Honoria had written, she had to wonder if he would otherwise have "remembered" it at all.

It had certainly distracted her. Honoria had opened by saying that she realized she might be a trifle precipitate in welcoming her to the family, but if they were so unwise as to live their lives according to their menfolk's whims ... from there, the letter had got only more interesting. Phyllida smiled. "You have a fascinating family."

"A big one, certainly, especially if you add all the connections."

"You mentioned a brother—Gabriel."

"He's a year older than me." Lucifer glanced at her as they strolled. "He got married a few weeks ago—the day before I arrived here."

"The day before?"

"Hmm. Gabriel and Alathea—we used to be a threesome when we were young. When they married and left London, I felt like they'd gone off on some adventure and left me behind. Instead, here I am, with you, neck-deep in adventure." He glanced at her again. "Heart-deep in something more."

She wasn't yet ready to inquire into that last statement. "Do you have other brothers and sisters?"

"Three sisters—they're half my age. Heather, Eliza, and Angelica. Gabriel is harboring fond hopes that Alathea will succeed in teaching them not to giggle."

Phyllida smiled. "They'll grow out of it."

"Hmm—that's not something we like to envisage. We don't, as a rule, deal well with our sisters growing up."

Alerted by his tone, she studied his face. "Now who are you thinking of?"

He looked at her, then grimaced. "Two of our cousins—the twins. Due to a sad accident some years ago, they haven't any older brother to watch over them, so we all do. Did."

"We?"

He slanted her a glance. "Didn't Honoria mention the Bar Cynster?"

Phyllida smiled and looked ahead. "She did, as a matter of fact. Very interesting, I found it."

Lucifer snorted. "Don't read too much into it—those days are gone."

"Really?"

"Yes—really!" He frowned. "Though I'm not at all happy about the twins."

"According to Honoria, the twins are quite capable of managing their own lives, and if you mention interfering, I'm to remind you of that fact."

"With all due respect, Honoria is a duchess, and Devil's her duke. She's never set foot in the ton without him metaphorically if not physically at her elbow. Not quite the same as swanning through the ballrooms totally unprotected."

"I'm to tell you your cousins are sensible young ladies and they'll manage perfectly well."

"I know—but I don't have to like it."

His disgusted tone very nearly had her laughing. She glanced at him. "What are you going to be like with your own daughters?"

"I shudder to think." He looked at her. "Of course, I'll need to beget them first."

He drew her nearer, one arm sliding around her waist, then his hand spread, warm and alive, over her hip, urging her back against him. The gravel path ended in an arbor framed by a bed of rioting peonies. They halted. Holding her before him, he bent his head; his lips touched, tracing lightly, laying a line of heat from temple to ear, then down the curve of her throat to where her pulse beat hotly.

"How many children would you like?" Her whisper was a little shaky.

"A dozen would be nice." He murmured the words against her throat, then turned her and brushed her lips. "But at least one boy and one girl, I think."

Phyllida settled in his arms and lightly kissed him back. "At least."

He stood with his arms loosely about her, their bodies just touching. There was honeysuckle close; the perfume drifted over them, subtly tempting. The same scent wreathed their bed. His palms moved, just a little, on her back. He looked into her face. "Have I told you the story about this garden?"

Night was falling, slowly closing about them, gently creeping over the land.

"Story?" Enough light remained for them to see each other's face, and the expression in each other's eyes.

"When I first came here, the garden caught me." He looked around. "Even before I'd gone into the house, I stopped and stared. Then I realized it was Martha's garden."

"Martha—Horatio's wife?"

"Yes. This is a copy of the garden she designed and grew beside their house overlooking Lake Windemere."

"Horatio re-created it here?"

"Yes, and that truly puzzled me. That first day, before I went inside, I felt as if Martha was trying to tell me something. Later, I thought it must have been some presentiment that Horatio was dead. Later yet, I realized it wasn't that at all."

Lucifer returned his gaze to Phyllida's face. "It was Martha who always created things—as women do. She created the atmosphere that filled their house, created the garden that surrounded it. Horatio knew nothing about gardening—I can still see them walking arm in arm down the paths with Martha showing him this and that. The garden in many ways personified Martha and, even more, the love she bore Horatio. The garden was part of her expression of that love, a permanent and public declaration. That's what I felt—still feel—in this garden.

"I said I was puzzled to find it here. I knew Horatio left the house at Lake Windemere because he couldn't bear the memories of Martha all around him. It was too painful. Yet here was Martha's garden, now Horatio's garden. Why?

"It took a while to work it out, but there's only one explanation that fits." His lips twisted wryly; he looked into Phyllida's eyes. "And I now know what Martha was trying to metaphysically jog my elbow about that first day."

"What?"

"You. Not just you, but the possibility of what we could share. Martha was trying to tell me to open my eyes so I wouldn't miss it."

He glanced around again; his arms tightened as he brought his gaze back to her face. "Horatio re-created Martha's garden because he realized, as I now do, that you can't turn aside from love. You can't choose to love—it doesn't work like that—but once you do love, you love forever. You can't move counties and leave it behind; it stays with you, in your heart, your mind—it becomes a part of your soul. Horatio re-created the garden for the same reason Martha created it in the first place—as an expression of his love for her and recognition of her love for him. Martha was still with Horatio when he died— I know that as definitely as I stand here with you. They're still here, both of them, memories living within this garden. Their love, shared love, created it; while it lives, their love lives, too."

His lips twisted again, this time in self-deprecation. "For all that we—the men in my family—try to avoid love, for the best and most logical of reasons, when it strikes, there's not one of us, not through all the generations, who has turned his back and walked away. For us, not walking away is harder, more frightening, than fighting any battle, but if there's one thing I've learned from my family, it's that surrendering to love, to the demands of love, is the only road to real happiness.

"While I've seen love in action in my family, I've learned a great deal from Horatio and Martha. Love simply is—it asks no permissions. Acceptance is all love asks, the only demand it makes, but it is an absolute one. You can either admit it to your heart or refuse it, but there's no other option."

For a long moment, he studied her dark eyes, wide and lustrous. "You wondered what love was, what it was like—it's surrounded you for the past week. Have you felt it?"

"Yes." Her lips softened; her eyes searched his. "It's a frightening, sometimes scarifying reality, but so wonderful and glowing, so vital." She drew a shaky breath.

He bent his head and drew it from her. "Have you made your decision— whether to accept love or not?"

He whispered the question against her lips. They curved gently. "You know I have."

He kissed her again, gentle and easy. "When the time comes, I'll ask and you can tell me."

"Why not now?"

"It's not the right time."

When Phyllida surfaced from the next kiss, she managed to breathe, "When will be the right time?"

"Soon."

The next kiss made it clear that that was all the answer she would get that night. But he'd told her enough, shown her enough; she was content.

Content to let him awaken her, slowly, expertly, until she floated, languid, on a sea of anticipation. They drew back, turned; arms around each other, her head on his shoulder, they strolled through the garden—redolent with perfumes, burgeoning growth, and the never-ending promise of love—back to the house, to the bed, to the love they already shared.

Day followed day and the tension mounted. Jonas spent most of his time at the Manor; Sir Jasper called at least twice a day. Even Sweetie seemed more highly strung, although Lucifer wasn't sure how much she understood. She was the sweetest ditherer he'd ever met, and he knew quite a few; the idea of introducing her to his great-aunt Clara grew to an obsession.

The only thing that, however transiently, broke the tedium and, temporarily, the escalating tension was the replies that arrived from other collectors. The responses distracted Phyllida, and for that Lucifer was grateful. Unfortunately, although all of them expressed horror over Horatio's demise, none had any light to shed on the twin mysteries surrounding Horatio's collection.

Doggedly, Lucifer and Phyllida plowed through it, searching for … something. Some hint as to why Horatio had been killed, some hint as to what he had wanted Lucifer to appraise. Although no one stated it aloud, they were aware they had no idea what they were looking for. That put a definite dampener on their enthusiasm.

By Wednesday afternoon, Lucifer started to wonder why he'd received no further communication from Devil. His cousin was never one to drag his boots. The answer to his question arrived late that evening, just as he, Phyllida, and Sweetie were rising from the dining table.

The rattle of wheels on the drive was followed by the heavy thud of stamping hooves. Lucifer looked at Phyllida. "That, I believe, will be Devil's messenger."

It was—but it was a vision with guinea-gold curls and a neat figure encased in cerulean blue that first reached the front door.

"Felicity!" Lucifer went forward, hands outstretched. He should, of course, have expected it, but he hadn't thought things through.

"Hello!" Demon's youthful wife took his hands and raised her face for a cousinly kiss, but her gaze had already traveled past him. "And you must be Phyllida." Releasing Lucifer, Felicity stepped past him and descended on Phyllida. "Honoria wrote and told me. I'm Felicity. We've come to help."

Phyllida smiled—impossible not to when faced with Felicity's charm. She could see no point in dissembling, so she touched cheeks and clasped hands as if they were already related.

"Good God! You're almost at Land's End."

Phyllida looked up to see a tall, broad-shouldered, fair-haired Cynster shake Lucifer's hand.

"Not quite—it's a few miles farther on." Lucifer grinned and clapped Demon's shoulder. "It's good to see you." He glanced at Felicity. "Are you sure you can spare the time?"

Turning from greeting Sweetie, Felicity shot a warning glance at her husband, tilted her chin at Lucifer, and slipped her arm into Phyllida's. "We were with Vane and Patience when Devil's and Honoria's letters arrived."

Demon came forward. Taking the hand Phyllida held out, he calmly kissed her on both cheeks. "Welcome to the family, my dear. We did tell him running into the country wouldn't help—and here he is, right enough. Captivated."

Phyllida looked into a pair of blue eyes many shades lighter than Lucifer's. They did, however, contain a familiar devil-may-care gleam. She ignored it. "Welcome to the Manor and to Colyton, too."

"Perhaps ...?" Lucifer cocked an eyebrow at Phyllida.

He was asking her to act as his hostess—as his wife. With a calm smile, she gestured to the drawing room. "Why don't we sit comfortably and you can tell us the family news. You must be parched. Have you dined?"

"At Yeovil," Felicity replied. "We weren't sure how much further Colyton was. Demon didn't want to take any chances."

Lucifer blinked, but said nothing. He ushered Felicity and Demon into the drawing room. Phyllida gave orders to Bristleford to prepare rooms and bring the tea trolley in, then joined them.

"Well," Felicity said as Phyllida joined her on the *chaise*, "you two seem to be having all the excitement in the family at present, so we came to share. Honoria would have come, but in her condition Devil refuses to let her as far as the front door. And Vane's much the same—he seems to imagine Patience is made of bone china. Scandal was tempted, but Catriona agreed he could come if he brought her, so they're still at Somersham. And no one has any idea where Gabriel and Alathea are." She smiled at Lucifer. "So it's just us, I'm afraid."

The ingenuous speech had made Lucifer blanch—its conclusion revived him. "Thank God!" He glanced at Demon. "I didn't expect the whole troop to descend."

Demon shrugged. "It's summer—what else have we to do?"

Bristleford entered with the tea trolley and plates of cakes. They broke off to partake; Phyllida and Felicity sipped and nibbled delicately while they chatted; Demon and Lucifer settled for brandy and demolishing the cakes.

"So," Lucifer said as Demon finished the last cake. "Cut line—what have you learned?"

Demon didn't glance his way; his gaze was fixed on the *chaise*. Following it, Lucifer was just in time to see Felicity try to smother, then hide, a yawn.

"On the other hand," Lucifer said, "it's getting late and you'll need to get settled. Is there anything that won't wait until morning?"

Demon threw him a grateful look. "No." He considered, then shook his head and stood. "There's nothing that'll make any difference tonight, and I'd rather you told us what's been happening here before I fill you in on my discoveries, minor though they are. Knowing the details will help me set what I found in better perspective."

Phyllida stood, drawing Felicity with her. She'd seen the yawn and caught the earlier, fleeting reference, too. "Indeed. A good night's sleep all around, then we can start first thing in the morning." She smiled at Felicity. "Come, I'll introduce you to Mrs. Hemmings and show you your room."

They all met the next morning at the breakfast table. Rested and refreshed, Flick—she insisted everyone call her that—was agog to hear their tale. Demon, relieved of his own anxiety, was similarly eager. Lucifer and Phyllida started their story over the teacups, then continued when they adjourned to the library. Concisely, they described incident after incident; Demon interrupted with a question here and there. Flick sat and simply stared.

"How atrocious!" she declared when they'd concluded their tale. "That's monstrous—leaving you to die in a burning cottage!"

Phyllida agreed.

Lucifer looked at Demon. "So what's the news from London?"

"First of all, your neighbors are exceedingly law-abiding souls—Montague gave them all a clean bill of health. No debts, no peculiar past histories, nothing. All he found on Appleby was that he's the illegitimate son of a minor peer—old Croxton, now deceased. His papa was not fond, but did educate him and pave the way into the army. Infantry—you were right about that."

"So," Lucifer concluded, "Appleby is an impoverished ex-infantryman with an education sufficient to allow him to serve as a gentleman's amanuensis."

"Yes, but there's more. Appleby was the only one on your list who'd served in any capacity, so I had a relatively easy time. I tracked down his regiment— he saw action at Waterloo." Demon glanced at Lucifer. "He was with the Ninth. I managed to locate his immediate superior, a Captain Hastings. That's where things got interesting. I had to all but drink Hastings under the table to wring the nightmare from him, but it transpires that Hastings suspects that Appleby committed murder on the battlefield."

"Murder during a battle?" Flick frowned. "Can that happen?"

Lucifer nodded. "If you shoot someone on your own side deliberately."

Phyllida shivered. "How horrible."

"Indeed," Demon concurred. "During one particular cavalry charge—" He glanced at Phyllida and Flick. "The cavalry often charge from the flank, across the infantry's line of sight—the infantry usually put up their pieces during the charge. Most would use the time to clean and reload. Well, during this one charge, Hastings was standing almost directly behind Appleby. He swears Appleby drew a line on one of our own. He believes he saw Appleby shoot and one of the guardsmen fall, but ...it was midmorning, and that was a hellish day. By the end of it, so many were dead and we all had our own nightmares. Hastings wasn't sure enough to make any immediate charge, but he'd seen enough to check who the fallen man was.

"It turned out to be Appleby's best friend. They'd even shared a tent the previous night. Although wounded himself, Appleby had gone out and retrieved the body and was, to all appearances, deeply cut up. Hastings concluded that Appleby had merely been using his sight to keep a steadier eye on his friend through the charge. That's what he told himself. That's what he still tells himself, but when his tongue is loosened by good brandy, the truth tumbles out. Hastings still believes in his heart that he saw Appleby kill his best friend, Corporal Sherring." Demon looked at Lucifer. "Incidentally, Hastings said Appleby was an excellent shot with a musket."

"So"—Lucifer looked at Phyllida—"it *could* be Appleby."

"But is it?" Demon asked. "All we have is an unprovable possibility that Appleby has killed in cold blood before. We haven't anything to tie him to Horatio or his collection."

"And that," Lucifer acknowledged, "is the rub."

The entire matter hinged on the mysterious volume the murderer thought was buried in Horatio's collection. Demon and Flick joined the party searching through Horatio's tomes.

After an hour, Flick stepped back from the bookcase she was working through. "Why are we doing this?" She turned to Lucifer. "Whoever it is, they've presumably been searching every Sunday for months. But if they knew which book they were searching for, and presumably they must, then it wouldn't take that long to find it."

"Unfortunately, it would." Lucifer strolled along the shelves, then stopped and pulled out an innocuous-looking volume. He showed it to Flick. "Brent's *Roman Legions*. Nice binding, worth a few guineas, but nothing to get excited over." Then he slid the entire cover free. "In reality, however, this is a first edition of Cruickshank's *Treatise of the Powers*, worth a small fortune."

"Oh." Flick studied the cover and the book it had concealed. "Are there many like that in here?"

"Every few shelves and sometimes more often." Phyllida reached for the next book on her shelf.

"Many collectors use fake covers to hide their most precious works." Lucifer returned the priceless volume to its protective cover. "So in order to search Horatio's collection, every book would need to be checked."

They went back to checking.

After lunch, Lucifer and Demon, at their ladies' behest, walked up to the forge to confer with Thompson. No horse with a loose shoe had yet been brought in. As they ambled back down the lane, Lucifer slid a glance at Demon. "I have to say I'm surprised you agreed to bring Flick into this—I assume she's in an interesting condition?"

"Yes." Demon's proud grin was exceedingly brief. "But the damned woman wouldn't be left behind. She insists she's perfectly well and refuses to be cosseted. It's as much as a warm bed's worth to argue too hard. And, of course, Honoria supported her."

"Honoria?"

"Honoria, who is so damned pregnant, Devil has all but lost his ducal authority. He bowed to her decree that Flick was perfectly well enough to travel down here—he even urged me to bring her! Not, of course, because he thought it was a good idea, but because he didn't want Honoria upset!"

"Good God! Is that what I've got to look forward to?"

"Unless you're thinking of a platonic relationship—and I can't believe you are—yes, and that's the least of what's in store. Judging by the state Vane's presently in, it only gets worse."

Lucifer shook his head. "Why do we do this?"

"God only knows."

They exchanged glances, then smiled and lengthened their strides.

It was Flick who, late in the afternoon, put what they were all independently thinking into words. She waved her arms at the library's bookshelves. "If the murderer's after something here, why don't we just let him come and get it?"

She faced the rest of the room. "I don't mean let him get away with it, of course, but what if we organized a household picnic or some such affair, made sure the whole village heard of it so everyone would know there would be no one left at home, and then we'd go, but circle back and keep watch?" She looked at them. "What do you think?"

Demon looked at Lucifer. "I think there's some merit in the idea. We need to accept that there's a definite possibility that the murderer's taken care of that loose shoe in some way other than bringing the horse to Thompson."

"The village fete is two days from now."

They all looked at Phyllida.

"It's on Saturday," she said. "Everyone for miles around attends. It's virtually compulsory." Standing, she crossed to the window; Flick joined her as she waved. "It's held in the field just behind the church."

Both Lucifer and Demon joined them at the window, looking up the slope of the common to the church. Demon narrowed his eyes. "That's a very attractive proposition."

"Easy enough to arrange for a watch to be kept on the house—and on the possible suspects, too." Lucifer slowly nodded. "And the doors here, while locked at night, are never locked during the day, even now."

"On the morning of the fete, we'll all be coming and going, taking food and trestles up." Phyllida faced the others. "It should be easy for anyone to watch unobtrusively and note when we're all out of the house."

They considered, exchanging glances, then Lucifer nodded. "Right. Let's do it. But we'll need to work out all the details first."

They spent the whole evening planning, and were still arguing over the details of who should watch whom, when and from where, the next morning when the mail arrived. Bristleford brought the letters into the library on a salver and placed them on the big desk by Lucifer's elbow.

When they paused in their deliberations to consume tea and a plate of Mrs. Hemmings's butter cakes, Lucifer sifted through the pile. He tossed some to Phyllida and started opening the rest. "More replies from other collectors."

He'd finished opening and perusing those he'd kept and laid them aside with a shake of his head when Phyllida sat bolt upright, staring at the sheet she was holding in her hand. "*Good gracious!* Listen to this! It's from a solicitor in Huddersfield. He writes that our recent letter to one of his late clients was brought to his attention. In the circumstances, he felt he should bring to our notice the fact that his late client, an associate of Horatio's, died at the hands of an unknown assailant some eighteen months ago."

"*Heavens!*"

They all rose and went to read over Phyllida's shoulder. She held the letter out so they could see. "It says the other collector was strangled late one night and his records were ransacked."

Lucifer reached out to steady the sheet. "Shelby. I wonder ..." He returned to the desk and sat. From a bottom drawer, he retrieved a stack of cards. "Horatio always noted on his name-cards what sort of items he'd most recently traded with each person. The notes refer back to his ledgers." He flipped through the cards. "Shelby, Shelby ... *hullo!*"

The shock in his voice had the other three looking up at him. Lucifer sat, frozen, a card in his hand. "Well, well." He glanced at Demon. "Sherring."

"*Sherring?*" Demon came to look over his shoulder. "The Sherring Corporal Hastings thinks Appleby shot?"

"More likely his father." Lucifer laid the card down, then checked the stack further. "There's entries for Shelby, but they're more than three years ago and it looks like they were only trading furniture."

He restacked the other cards and put them back in the drawer, then returned his attention to the card for Sherring. "Books. One buy, just over five years ago."

"Almost immediately after Waterloo," Demon added.

Lucifer nodded. "Where are those ledgers?"

Demon laid a hand on his shoulder. "Before you do that, write a letter to this solicitor. Give him Appleby's name—see if he recognizes it."

Lucifer hesitated, then pulled out a sheet of paper. "We won't hear in time, presuming that horseshoe falls, but if all else fails ... I'll include a description of Appleby as well. If it was him, he might not have used his real name."

The letter was quickly written. Dodswell was dispatched to race it into Chard to catch the night mail.

Then Lucifer unearthed Horatio's ledgers—this time, they had a date and quickly found the entry. It listed nine books. They wrote the list on four scraps of paper, then they each took one and started along the shelves.

Jonas arrived. Amazed at the news, he joined in the hunt. Covey did, too. He checked the inventory they'd made thus far, which cut down the bookshelves they needed to search.

Lucifer told them to scan the titles on the grounds that none of the books appeared valuable enough to warrant a false cover. Even with six of them scanning, it still took most of the day, but finally they located all nine books. Along the way, they found three fake covers of *Dr. Johnson's Sermons*, six fake covers of *Gulliver's Travels*, and a staggering eight of *Aesop's Fables*.

"Enough to confuse anyone," Demon remarked.

"No wonder the murderer has had to search so carefully." Phyllida glanced along the ranks of bookshelves. "And there's no telling if Horatio, for whatever reason, concealed one of the Sherring volumes."

Lucifer shook his head. Carrying Horatio's card, he was checking the nine books. "No—these are the Sherring volumes. Horatio noted all the details, and he never doubled up on specific volumes."

"Only to use for fake covers," Demon replied.

At Lucifer's instructions, they'd pulled the books forward in the shelves, but left them where they found them.

At five o'clock, Lucifer went around the nine books for the third time, paying special attention to the *Sermons*, the *Travels*, and the *Fables*. He noted the location of each book on his list, then pushed them back to stand unobtrusively with their fellows.

He, Phyllida, Flick, Demon, Jonas, and Covey had all studied each book. There was absolutely nothing to explain why anyone would commit murder for any of them.

Demon sank onto the *chaise* beside Flick. "We must be missing something."

"Presumably." Lucifer settled into an armchair and considered the list. "Let's assume our man started searching in the library."

"Why?" Jonas asked.

"Because if I'd wanted to search for a valuable book in this house, I'd assume Horatio would keep it in his inner sanctum," Demon supplied.

Lucifer nodded. "So he finished in the library, tripping over heaps of fake covers in the process, and had started in here"—he paused to glance at the bookcases covering almost every foot of wall space in the drawing room— "when Horatio disturbed him. The night Phyllida and I saw him, he was still trying to search in here."

"Most of the Sherring books are in the library or in here," Phyllida said. "Only the real *Travels* and *Fables* are in the dining room." She looked at Lucifer. "Is that why you studied the books here and those two books especially?"

He nodded. "Four books, and while it's not my area of expertise, I would happily swear there's not a thing that makes any of them valuable. The *Aesop's Fables* has been used to hide something—the front cover's been hollowed out, but that's not unusual. The front of such books was a popular place to hide wills and such at one time. There's nothing there now except some canvas padding—I peeled away a corner of the covering paper and checked."

They all sat, digesting the information. In the end, Demon sighed. "This could, of course, all be some remarkable coincidence and the murderer is in fact someone else."

Lucifer grimaced. "Very true, which is why we need to give even more thought to how we approach tomorrow."

They returned to their plans, to the arguments, the suggestions—the possibilities of how to trap a murderer.

CHAPTER

Twenty

The day of the fete dawned still and clear. Throughout the morning, men and boys lugged boards and trestles up the common and over the rise. Thompson and Oscar helped Juggs roll two heavy barrels slowly up from the lych-gate, then down the slope behind the church. By nine o'clock a steady stream of women, gaily dressed in bright gowns and aprons, were ferrying all manner of foods up in baskets.

By eleven o'clock, when the Manor household climbed the common, a heat haze had formed—there was not a breath of wind to blow it away. The air lay heavy against the skin, almost cloying. Pausing beside the church on the highest point of the rise, Phyllida looked toward the horizon. "We'll have a storm tonight."

Lucifer followed her gaze. The horizon was smudged charcoal gray. "Looks like a big one."

Jonas nodded. "Our storms are something to experience. They sweep in from the Channel with a magnificent rush."

In the dip behind the church, the villagers and all the surrounding families were gathering. The Manor folk descended, exchanging greetings, introducing Demon and Flick; they merged with the throng and, as they naturally would, parted. They each had their roles to play.

Only those involved were privy to their plans. The more people who knew, the more likely someone would inadvertently do or say something to tip the murderer the wink. They'd agreed not to assume that Appleby was the murderer; their net was designed to cover all eventualities.

They'd decided on a simple scheme. Phyllida would be safe while surrounded by the entire village, yet Lucifer and Demon had been adamant that she and Flick should at all times stay together, and that both should wear their wide-brimmed villager hats, one tied with a lavender scarf, the other with a blue one—easy to spot in the crowd.

Lucifer and Demon shared the watch on their ladies and on Appleby. In the latter case, they were careful to do nothing overt. Lucifer introduced Demon and left him chatting. Subsequently, they passed Appleby in the crowd, exchanged a word if appropriate, but gave no indication that he remained always under observation. They were the only ones they trusted to do the job right.

Jonas had been assigned to idly wander about, keeping his eyes peeled for any unusual behavior in any of the other men, however unlikely. He conscripted a number of young ladies to aid him in disguising his intent, but behind his easygoing facade, he remained watchful and alert.

The others had the hardest task. Dodswell, Demon's groom Gillies, Covey, and Hemmings rotated the watch on the house, two of them watching at all times, one at the back, one at the front. They lay concealed in the shrubbery and the wood, but they had to change the guard frequently so that each appeared often among the crowds at the fete.

As the day wore on, the heat became oppressive. Phyllida introduced Flick to the local ladies; moving about the field, they chatted easily. Again and again, by a look, a veiled reference, the thoughts behind a pleased smile, it was borne in on Phyllida that the change Lucifer had wrought was complete.

She might not have answered any question or spoken any vow, yet she was, by her actions and her thoughts—her very desires—already his wife. The little changes in her station, the adjustments in the ways the other ladies related to her, were already made. The consensus seemed to be that her recent brush with death, combined with the lingering presence of her would-be murderer, more than excused a period of waiting before any banns were read. None doubted the wedding would come shortly.

Yet what had changed most was herself. She felt it inside her as she smiled and listened to the continuation of stories she'd heard developing all her life. She'd drawn back from them, not shutting them out, but they were no longer the central focus of her life; they'd moved to the periphery, where they rightly belonged. Her life was no longer an accumulation of theirs—their joys and sorrows, their problems, their needs. She'd started making a new life, one for herself and Lucifer at the Manor.

For the first time in her twenty-four years, she felt truly at one with the role that was hers to play—no regrets, no unfulfilled wishes, no nebulous yearnings.

After lunching on delicate sandwiches washed down, courtesy of Ballyclose Manor, with glasses of champagne, she and Flick helped Mr. Filing with the children's races, then, nothing loath, they supervised some games.

"I'm melting." Flick tipped her hat back from her face. "Even though I know why they wanted us to wear these hats, I'm quite glad we did."

"Easier to manage than a parasol." Phyllida saw Jonas cruising past with one of the local misses hanging on his arm. She caught his eye and raised a brow—he returned her look with his usual benign expression.

"What's the word?" Flick asked, looking the other way.

"Jonas knows nothing." Phyllida turned to look in the same direction and sighed. Heavily. Through clenched teeth. "If nothing happens today, I swear I'll scream. At the very least, I'll have hysterics."

Flick chuckled. "You'll shock everyone to their toes if you do."

Phyllida humphed. She saw Mary Anne and Robert through the crowd. They'd stopped and spoken with her earlier. Although they'd inquired about the letters, they'd accepted her lack of progress without panic. It was almost as if they'd finally realized that the letters were only a minor matter—nothing to get hysterical about.

Nothing to compare with a possibly multiple murderer.

The day wore on.

Then Appleby stopped beside the Ballyclose butler, said a few words, then strode off, openly making for Ballyclose Manor. Lucifer and Demon watched him go.

"To circle around, perhaps?" Demon suggested.

Lucifer nodded. "Most likely."

They parted and moved through the crowd. They visually checked their respective ladies but didn't approach. They worked steadily back through the throng, heading to where, standing by the church's side and concealed in its shadow, they could look down on the Manor.

That was their aim, but before they gained the graveyard, Oscar pushed through the crowd and caught Lucifer's sleeve. "Some'at you need to know."

Lucifer collected Demon with a glance and stepped back, a little away from all the others. "What is it?"

"Well—" Oscar stopped as Demon joined them.

"My cousin," Lucifer said. "You can speak freely."

Having taken stock of Demon, Oscar nodded. "Right. Well, I've just received this message, and it's left me in a quandary, like. I don't know as whether Miss Phyllida has explained about the gang that works out of Beer?"

"She said they were all but legendary in the annals of local smuggling."

"Aye, well, they're the real thing, no doubt whatsoever. Hardnosed lot, but we've always rubbed along well enough, and now they've sent me a message. Says a person contacted 'em about a passage 'cross the Channel—'parently it *has* to be tonight. Beer hasn't got a cargo lined up for tonight, but they knew we generally would, so they told this cargo where to meet up with us on the cliffs. All straight enough, but as you know, the vessel we'll be meeting is a legitimate trader, not a smuggler's boat. The Cap'n won't want no truck with any suspicious passenger."

Oscar glanced to where Phyllida and Flick stood talking to three young girls. "Didn't rightly want to bother Miss Phyllida with such a matter, and I don't know as how Mr. Filing would be much help, neither."

Lucifer frowned. "Quite. Are you running a cargo tonight?"

"We should've been." Oscar looked at the ever-darkening horizon. "But I'm doubting we will. That bugger's going to sweep right over us. Ain't none of us going to be putting out in the teeth of that."

"In that case, let's see what happens—" Lucifer broke off as Thompson pushed through and joined them.

Winded, Thompson struggled for breath. Excitement rippled through him. "Got 'im! M'boy just told me a horse was brought in with a loose rear left shoe this morning. The lad forgot, what with the fair. I just ducked back to check—it's the same horse. I'll take my oath on it."

"Who owns it?"

"Ballyclose Manor. Not one of Sir Cedric's—one of the general hacks. I collared the groom who brought it in. He says no one's been riding this one much that he knew of. Just Mr. Appleby now and then."

Demon glanced at Lucifer. "Is that enough?"

Lucifer's smile was all teeth. "I think so. Let's find Sir Jasper—"

"*Cynster*! Where the devil are you, man?"

Both Lucifer and Demon turned. Cedric came barreling through the crowd. He saw them, waved, and plowed toward them. Jocasta Smollet hurried after him. Others, anticipating some sensation, quickly gathered.

"It's Appleby, man—*Appleby*!" Cedric halted, puffing, before them. "Just got the word from Burton, m'butler. Appleby told him he's off home—touch of the sun. Silly blighter came with no hat. *That's* when I remembered. The hat! The hat Phyllida said was the murderer's hat. It's *Appleby's*. Seen it in his hands times without number, but I rarely saw it on his head. Just put it together. He hasn't been wearing a hat since Horatio was killed."

"That's correct, sir," Burton, the Ballyclose butler, stated. "While I cannot vouch for the particular hat in question, Mr. Appleby has not worn a hat for some time."

"I'm fairly certain Cedric's right," Jocasta put in. "I didn't get a good look at the hat that day, but I do know Appleby was forever doffing his—quite the gentleman in his way. He hasn't worn a hat for the past several weeks."

"We're going after him." Cedric straightened and looked around. "Hue and cry—that's what we need! We'll round him up and haul him back here to Sir Jasper."

"Excellent idea!" Basil surprised everyone with his vehement agreement. "We've plenty of men here—he won't escape this time."

Cedric blinked, but nodded. "Right, then! Finn, Mullens—come along, lads."

Basil was already collecting his workers. Grisby, too, was gathering his forces to join the swelling throng. The crowd was awash with exclamations and gabbling.

Sir Jasper strode through. "Cedric! What's this? There's to be no summary justice, you hear?"

"I know, I know—we'll truss him up and bring him back to you, and then we can hang him."

A rousing cheer rose. Before anything more could be said, the assembled congregation was off, streaming like a tide after Cedric, Basil, and Grisby, cresting the lip of the field, then pouring over, heading for Ballyclose Manor.

"He won't be there," Demon muttered.

"Assuredly not." Lucifer turned as Phyllida and Flick, having been deserted by the children, came up. Other than their small group and the older ladies and village women, the fete field was bare.

Sir Jasper eyed Lucifer, shrewd suspicion and certainty in his gaze. "Now, what's afoot?"

"We believe," Lucifer said, waving their group toward the church, farther from the remaining ladies, "that Appleby, if, as now seems likely, he's our murderer, will make another attempt to get at Horatio's books. That's what he's been after all along. To that end, we've purposely left the Manor vacant and the doors unlocked."

"A trap, heh?"

"Oh, *no!*"

They all turned. Mrs. Hemmings was staring round-eyed at Lucifer. "What is it?" he asked.

"Did you say that that murdering Mr. Appleby will be going to the Manor?"

"So we believe. But it's empty—"

Mrs. Hemmings was shaking her head. " 'Tisn't. Amelia went back a while ago—too hot for her, it was."

Lucifer frowned. "Amelia?"

"Oh, God!" Phyllida grabbed his arm. "Sweetie!"

Lucifer looked at Phyllida. "She went back?"

"Apparently. I had no idea."

"She left nearly an hour ago," Lady Huddlesford put in. "Quite wilting, she was, but she didn't want to cause any fuss, so she just slipped away."

Lucifer cursed beneath his breath. Grim-faced, Demon waved them up the rise. "We'd better get a move on."

They started up the slope. Before they reached the church, Jonas came pelting around it. He skidded to a halt. "Filing. He just went into the Manor. I saw him come up this way, then I realized he hadn't come back, so I went to check—I just glimpsed him going through the front door."

"*Filing?*" Demon said. "Where the hell does he fit in?"

"God knows, I'm sure," Lucifer muttered, "but I suggest we'd better go and find out. In case you haven't noticed, our simple plan has got holes shot through it."

"Never did trust plans." Demon locked his fingers about Flick's elbow as they rounded the church.

"Oi!"

They halted again. Dodswell came lumbering up from the Rectory. "Where're you off to?" He scrambled up the path to join them. "I just came to tell you that Appleby arrived and went in the back. He came through the wood. He's been inside for a good fifteen minutes or more. I had to come round by the shrubbery to stay out of sight."

Lucifer and Demon exchanged glances. "Right." Lucifer looked down the slope. "Only one thing for it—we go in and invent as we go."

He considered their assembled company. As well as himself, Phyllida, Demon and Flick, Jonas, Sir Jasper, and Dodswell, they had Lady Huddlesford, Frederick, and the Hemmingses.

"All of us go in—there's enough of us to make him feel too pressured to try anything clever, but not enough, if we all keep calm, to make him panic." He looked at Frederick and Lady Huddlesford, then at Jonas and Sir Jasper. "One thing—if you're coming down there with us, you must do nothing except what I tell you to do. At this stage, we just want to get Appleby out of the Manor and get Sweetie back without her, or anyone else, being harmed. No heroics. Agreed?"

Everyone nodded.

At the last, Lucifer met Phyllida's gaze.

"I'd never do anything to risk Sweetie."

Lucifer grasped her hand. "Naturally not." He looked at the others. "Let's go."

They reached the duck pond and saw Covey dodging through the trees. Dodswell waved him over.

"Miss Sweet came home," Covey gasped. "Before I could come to warn you, I saw Mr. Filing up by the church looking down. Then he came down, and I couldn't get out. He's gone in, too."

Lucifer nodded. "Join the crowd. We're going in to sort this out."

It wasn't quite the same as leading a charge, but with Demon at his shoulder and Phyllida and Flick at their backs, it had much the same momentum. Lucifer pushed open the Manor gate, uncaring of its squeak. He strode up the main path and rounded the fountain—"Stop right there!"

He halted. All the others formed up behind him.

The figure of Lucius Appleby was just visible in the shadows of the front hall. Locked before him, held captive in one arm, Sweetie in her pale gown was more easily seen. Light glinted off the blade of a knife.

"Can you see it?" Appleby asked.

"Yes." Lucifer didn't need to say anything else; his tone was enough.

"If you do exactly as I say, she won't be harmed."

"We're prepared to do that." Lucifer spoke calmly. "What do you want us to do?"

"File in, single file, slowly."

Phyllida grabbed the back of Lucifer's coat and refused to let go; Demon shot her a scowl and stepped behind her. They all followed Lucifer over the front step and into the cool of the Manor's front hall.

"Stop."

They did, blinking as their eyes adjusted. Phyllida focused on Sweetie. Her old governess's eyes were so wide she looked goggle-eyed, her face so pale it was the same bone-ivory hue as her fussy, frilly summer gown. Appleby had one arm about Sweetie's shoulders, trapping her against him; as he pulled her back down the hall, she moved stiffly. In his other hand, Appleby held a wicked-looking knife.

A groan drew all eyes deeper into the hall. By the stairs, Mr. Filing lay prone; as they watched, he struggled onto one elbow. A trickle of blood ran down his chin.

Some of them started forward—

"Stop!"

They all froze at Appleby's shout. He looked down the line. "You. Covey. Help the meddling curate."

Covey hurried down the hall; he bent and struggled to help Mr. Filing to his feet. Jonas snorted. With an unimpressed glance at Appleby, he strolled out of the line toward Filing. "Covey can't manage alone."

Appleby glared at him. Jonas returned the glare with his best blank expression. Appleby's lips tightened. "Very well. Just get him to his feet and keep up with the rest."

Appleby pulled back to stand almost against the wall to the right of the drawing room door. "Inside." He gestured with his head. "But stay in line and move slowly." He raised the knife and laid it against Sweetie's exposed throat. "You don't want to make me nervous."

"No," Lucifer said. "We don't."

Appleby looked into his face. "Line up along the wall of bookshelves opposite the windows."

They did. Jonas and Covey helped Mr. Filing into the room. Appleby followed with Sweetie. "Perfect." He scanned their number. "There's two of you to a bookcase. I want you to search for a particular book—*Aesop's Fables*. You'll need to pull out each book and look inside the cover—some of the covers are fakes. Look at every book."

They all stared at him.

"Get to it," he ordered. "Now! I haven't got all day—Miss Sweet hasn't got all day."

They all turned to the bookshelves. Phyllida lifted a hand to a tome and caught Lucifer's eye. She raised a brow—they, Demon and Flick, Jonas and Covey, all knew *Aesop's Fables* was in the dining room. With a nod, Lucifer indicated the books. He pulled out the first volume on the top shelf.

Phyllida started on the middle shelf. Beside her, Flick and Demon also started pulling tomes.

After a few minutes of silence, Lucifer glanced over his shoulder. "Why don't you let Miss Sweet sit down?" He waved at a straight-backed chair closer to the windows. "You're far enough away from us to still use her as your shield. And if she doesn't sit down soon, she might faint, which none of us would want." His gaze had fastened on Sweetie's wide eyes; he'd emphasized the word "none."

Appleby heard it. "Indeed. That wouldn't be at all helpful—not to any of us." He gauged the distance to the chair, then shuffled Miss Sweet to it. Before he released her, he looked at them. "Keep searching!"

They all turned back to the shelves.

Lucifer continued to pull books out and study them, then return them to the shelf. Phyllida pulled books out and shoved them in; her gaze lingered on Lucifer's face. She saw him exchange glances with Demon. She followed the exchange back and forth. It was as if they were communicating without words—as if their thoughts in such a situation were obvious, at least to each other.

Phyllida looked at Flick. She, too, had noted the silent communion. She met Phyllida's gaze and gave a helpless shrug—she didn't know what they were thinking, either. Flick went back to removing books; Phyllida did the same.

A minute later, Lucifer murmured, "Was this volume of *Aesop's Fables* the reason you killed Corporal Sherring?"

Despite the fact that he'd murmured, his voice carried through the room. He turned to glance at Appleby; Phyllida did the same.

Appleby's face was a mask of blank astonishment. His mouth opened, then shut, then opened again. "How did—" He broke off. "It hardly matters now." He paused, but couldn't stop himself. "How did you learn of it?"

"Hastings saw you do it." Demon glanced around, then looked back at the shelves.

"He never said anything."

"Hastings is a decent man." Again Demon glanced at Appleby. "He couldn't conceive of the sort of man who would kill his closest friend."

Appleby stiffened. "Sherring was a *fool*. A provincial nobody with a father rich from trade. They'd bought their way into a title and an estate—and all the luxuries that went with it. I was born better than him, but I would never have had half of what would have been his."

"So you arranged to even the score?" Like Demon, Lucifer continued to methodically search. The others glanced at them and followed suit.

Having everyone so steadily occupied calmed Appleby. "Yes, in a way. But they showed me how—he and his father. The night before the last battle, letters were brought around. I never had any, of course, so, thinking to be kind, Jerry Sherring read his aloud. His father had filled his library with expensive books and his gallery with valuable paintings.

"His heir, Jerry's older brother, cared not a fig for anything but hard coin. The old man was in failing health, but, almost on his deathbed, he'd made a fantastic discovery. He'd stumbled on a miniature by an old master. He was sure it was genuine, but wasn't strong enough to follow it up. He didn't want his heir to know of it and sell it off cheaply, so he hid it until Jerry, who felt as he did, could return from the war and help him."

"So he hid the painting in the book?" Lucifer glanced around briefly.

"Yes." Appleby stood directly behind Sweetie. Although clearly swept back into the past, he was too close to the chair for Lucifer to attempt to overpower him. "It was all there in the letter. The old man even warned Jerry to tell no one of it. Jerry didn't consider that he'd read the letter to me."

"He trusted you."

"He was a fool—he trusted everyone."

"So he died."

"On the battlefield. He would most likely have died there anyway. I just made sure of it."

"And then you accompanied his body back to his family, playing the grieving friend." Lucifer glanced along the shelves. The others remained facing the books, but their searching had slowed; all were following the tale. "So what went wrong?"

"*Everything*—everything that could." Appleby's tone turned bitter. "It took two weeks to get free of the army and across the Channel, then all the way up to Scunthorpe. The Sherrings lived beyond that. I arrived to discover the father dead and the brother already in possession."

"I'm surprised that was a problem."

"It wasn't in itself, but the brother's wife was an unexpected complication."

"Women often are."

"Not in that way." Appleby's tone was contemptuous. "The damned female was a tightfist, just like the brother. They'd known Jerry would kick up a fuss over selling the father's collections, so they'd had the dealers around before the old man was cold in his grave. They'd sold the *Aesop's Fables*."

Lucifer looked at Appleby. "You're not going to tell me you've been searching through all the collections in England?"

Appleby laughed, but the sound wasn't humorous. "If necessary, I might even have done that. Nevertheless, as has happened repeatedly in my search for this treasure, hope gleamed in the darkest hour. The brother's wife had a list of those she'd invited to the sale of the library. Fifteen collectors and dealers. I spun her a tale of wanting to buy some book of Jerry's as a memento and she gave me the list." He laughed again, bitterly. "Like everything in my life, that list was a boon and a burden rolled into one."

Lucifer turned back to the shelves. "The list was alphabetical?"

"Yes!" Appleby's temper exploded in a threatening hiss. "If I'd started working on it in reverse, I would be a hugely wealthy man today. Instead, I followed the list."

"That, I assume, accounts for the unexpected demise of Mr. Shelby of Swanscote, near Huddersfield."

Silence held sway for a long moment, then Appleby said, "You have been busy." Lucifer said nothing, nor did he turn around. Eventually Appleby continued. "Shelby would have lived if he hadn't been such a suspicious old coot. He caught me in his library one night. If he'd simply walked in, I'd have been able to slide away—I had an excuse ready. But he stood there and watched me search for some time. After that, I had to kill him.

"I could never let any of them suspect I was searching for anything—that's why it's taken me five long years to reach Welham's library. In every one of the fourteen other cases, I had to find a job, sometimes with the collector, which made life easier, but often in the neighborhood, then learn enough about the collector's household to know when I could search. I've become an expert on reading dealers' disposal ledgers. That was always the first thing I checked. But none of them has sold that book and the painting hidden in it has never surfaced—you may be sure I kept my ear to the ground over that. I know the book's here, and the painting's still inside. You're going to find it for me—I'm going to have it in my hands tonight."

There was a feverish intensity in Appleby's last words that had everyone

exchanging glances. With a sigh, Lucifer turned. "If that's the way it is, then
... we've already finished cataloguing this room. And the library. There's no
copy of *Aesop's Fables* in either room. False covers, yes, but not the book."

Appleby considered him through narrowed eyes.

Lucifer waved toward the library. "If you'd like to look at the inventory ..."

"No, that won't be necessary, will it?" Appleby's eyes were slits, but his
tone was more confident. "You just want me out of here, don't you? You're so
damned rich you don't give a damn about any painting, old master or not."

"I wouldn't go quite that far, but the painting certainly doesn't rate against
Miss Sweet's life, which brings us to much the same point."

Appleby studied Lucifer's face, then nodded. "Very well. Which room do
you suggest we search next?"

"I'd take the dining room next. The back parlor seems to run more to
garden, household, and recipe books."

They'd all stopped searching and turned; Appleby ran his eye along the
line. He drew a tight breath. "We'll move in reverse. I'm going to back out of
the door, then I'll wait in the front hall. I want you to file out, single file still,
cross the hall, and go into the dining room."

Pulling Miss Sweet to her feet, he held her to him and backed out of the
door. Everyone followed, trooping silently along. Toward the rear of the line,
Phyllida stared at the door, then glanced at the shadowy space behind it and
the huge halberd standing there.

"No," Lucifer whispered. "We don't need it—all we need to get Sweetie
free is that volume of *Aesop's Fables*."

Phyllida frowned, but shuffled past the halberd and out of the room.

As they filed into the dining room with the big table in the center and
bookcases all around, Appleby waved the ladies to one side and the men to the
other. Phyllida hesitated; Lucifer squeezed her fingers, then let her go. His last
words ringing in her mind, she made for the bookcase by the corner window.
Ironic that in this house of bookcases, the one that housed the vital volume
was the one Appleby had passed most often, the one by the window with the
faulty latch. Phyllida started searching along the shelves; Flick searched the
bookcase beside her.

Appleby retreated to a corner of the room, pulling a chair from the table
and pushing Sweetie onto it. He had a wall of bookcases at his back, the door
at some distance, and Mrs. Hemmings was the closest person—no threat.

Once they were all settled, Lucifer asked, in a mildly conversational tone,
"How did Horatio die?"

"It was an accident. I never meant to kill him. I didn't even know he was in
the house. I didn't hear him come downstairs and along the hall—his feet were
bare, so there was no sound. He was suddenly there, in the doorway, asking
what the devil I was doing. He'd seen me searching. I rose and walked toward
him. He was a fair size and in reasonable health—I didn't think I could
strangle him. He stood there and watched me come. Then I saw the letter knife
on the table." He paused, then said, "It's surprisingly easy if you know how."

"Why did you try to kill Phyllida?" Sir Jasper turned, frowning, then forced himself to continue searching.

"Miss Tallent?" There was laughter in Appleby's voice. "That was such a farce, with her stumbling on the body and then Cynster coming in and the halberd falling. I was so strung up I nearly laughed aloud. I saw her notice the hat, but then she bolted. When I left the house, hat and identity still concealed, I knew that no matter what happened, no matter what hurdles appeared, I was meant, in the end, to have that painting. I'd be able to live like I was meant to live—in reasonable comfort, like a gentleman."

"So why go after Phyllida?" Jonas asked.

"She came back for the hat."

Phyllida turned to stare at Appleby. He smiled, tightly. "I was in the hall when you asked Bristleford about the hat. You hadn't forgotten it—you weren't going to forget it."

"But I didn't know whose it was."

"I could hardly rely on your faulty memory continuing faulty. You'd seen me often enough wearing the wretched thing—it was the only hat I had. Of course, with Cynster here to fill your eyes and your mind, you were distracted enough not to remember, but you might have at any time."

Lucifer caught Phyllida's eye and frowned—she shut her lips on the information that she'd never noticed Appleby enough to remember his hat. She turned back to the bookshelves.

"I'd got rid of the hat immediately, of course. I stuffed it in a hedge at the back of Ballyclose. Later, I got to thinking, so I went back to find it and burn it, but it was gone. I assumed some tramp had taken it. I thought I was safe, or would be once I ensured Miss Tallent didn't remember whose hat it was."

"So you tried to shoot her."

"Yes." Appleby's voice tensed. "Then I tried to strangle her. All that did was make Cynster keep a closer watch on her, but I hoped it was also frightening her enough to keep her from remembering me. I tried to get at her again during the Ballyclose ball—I suspected she might search Cedric's hats. My plan didn't work, but then ... she got me to walk out onto the terrace and around the corner with her, asking after Cedric ... I could hardly believe my luck. I almost strangled her and hid the body in the bushes, but people might have seen us leave the ballroom together. Then Cynster arrived. I had to watch her walk away again."

Phyllida glanced, briefly, at Lucifer.

"Then she found the hat. Worse, she took it to Cedric. If I didn't act immediately, I'd be found out. So I wrote the note from Molly, knocked Phyllida out, and set the fire.

"The hat burned, Phyllida didn't." Appleby's tone was terse. "I gave up trying to kill her. At least the hat was gone—she had no proof to connect me with anything. But you'd put locks on this house, and there was still the possibility that suspicion would turn my way. I obviously had to act boldly and decisively to bring my search to a rapid and successful conclusion. The fete gave me the perfect opportunity. So here we are."

After a moment, Lucifer said, "You meant to take a hostage."

"Of course. It was the only way to get the job done—too risky to search a shelf or two at a time. I want that volume of *Aesop's Fables* in my hands before nightfall."

Phyllida's tongue burned with the need to ask why. She glanced at Flick, and saw the identical thought in her eyes. They both drew breath, then turned their attention back to the shelves and continued pretending to search.

Silence fell, broken only by the steady shuffle and thump as books were hauled out, then returned to their places. After some minutes, Phyllida glanced across the room. Lucifer caught her eye; he nodded.

Phyllida moved across the bookcase as if starting on the next shelf, and slid out the brown, buckram-covered tome whose spine bore the title *Aesop's Fables* in simple gold lettering. She weighed the book in her hand, then opened the cover—she could see where Lucifer had lifted a corner of the front cover paper. She pressed her fingers into the thick cover; there was a softness behind the paper. Lucifer had said he'd checked; she trusted he'd known what he'd been doing.

Shutting the book, she marveled that such an innocent-looking thing could be responsible for three deaths. For depriving Lucius Appleby of his sanity. Certainly his humanity. It had nearly accounted for her, too.

Straightening her shoulders, she lifted her head and looked across the room at Appleby. "I believe this"—she held out the book—"is the volume you seek."

Appleby nearly stepped forward, nearly stepped away from Sweetie, but at the last he pulled back. He couldn't read the title. He stared at the book hungrily, then licked his lips. He flicked a glance at Lucifer and Demon. "Everyone stay still." Appleby tugged Sweetie to her feet, then locked his arm about her shoulders as before, the knife in his right hand. He nodded at Phyllida. "Hand the book to Mrs. Hemmings, then retreat to where you are now. Everyone else, stay where you are."

Phyllida did as he asked. Mrs. Hemmings turned to Appleby. He beckoned her forward with the knife. "Give the book to Miss Sweet."

Mrs. Hemmings approached cautiously, then pressed the book into her old friend's trembling hands. "There, now."

Mrs. Hemmings stepped back.

"Good." Appleby glanced briefly down at the book. He was shaking. "Open the front cover."

Sweetie fumbled but did so. His gaze on Lucifer, Demon, and the other men, Appleby grasped the cover, not looking but pressing his fingertips into the concealed pocket. A fleeting expression of unutterable relief, of flaring victory, traversed his face, then his expression blanked.

He closed the book. "I want all of you to move to the end of the room, up against the bookcases."

Lucifer hesitated, then moved down the room. The others followed. All except Lady Huddlesford. She stood her ground.

"Miss Sweet is nearly done in." Lady Huddlesford lifted her chin; she had never looked so imperious. "If you want a hostage, take me."

Miss Sweet blinked. Trapped against Appleby like some poor, innocent bird, she peered at Lady Huddlesford and visibly rallied. "Why, thank you, Margaret. That's a very kind offer, but ..." Despite Appleby's arm, Sweetie straightened her spine. "I believe I'll manage. It's quite all right, really."

Lady Huddlesford considered, then inclined her head. "If you're sure, Amelia." With that, she swung majestically around and joined the others.

"If that's settled"—Appleby's voice sounded strained, wild excitement mingling with something closer to panic—"we'll leave you. I'll take Miss Sweet as far as the wood. I'll hear any footsteps long before you reach us. If I do, things will not go well for Miss Sweet. However, if you remain precisely where you are until she returns to you, you have my word she will not be harmed." He paused, his gaze flicking over Lucifer, Demon, Jonas, Sir Jasper—if he was searching for understanding, there was none to be had. "I never meant to kill anyone, not even Jerry. If there'd been some other way ..." He blinked, then straightened. Pulling Sweetie with him, he shuffled sideways to the door. "I will kill anyone who gets in my way."

"We'll wait here." Lucifer kept his voice calm and steady, as he had throughout.

Appleby nodded. "In that case, I'll bid you farewell."

Under his breath, Lucifer murmured, *"Au revoir."*

They waited. With a raised hand, Lucifer stopped anyone from moving. "He's on the edge—we're not going to give him any reason to panic."

Minutes crawled past. They heard the scrunch of gravel, the sound dying away as Appleby dragged Sweetie through the kitchen garden toward the wood. They exchanged glances but no words. They were all thinking of Sweetie.

Then came a patter on the gravel, drawing closer to the house. It was so light a sound, they were too afraid to imagine it was footsteps. Then the baize door at the back of the hall banged the wall; in a rush of pitter-patter steps, Sweetie appeared in the dining room doorway.

"He's gone!" She fluttered her hands furiously. "Away through the woods he ran!" She flung out an arm in the general direction of the wood—then fainted.

Lucifer caught her before she hit the floor. He carried her into the drawing room and laid her on the *chaise*.

Later, when she recovered and told her story to the assembled ladies of the village, Miss Sweet was, for the first time in her life, the heroine of the hour.

CHAPTER

Twenty-one

A s afternoon edged into evening, Lucifer, Phyllida, Demon, and Flick, with Jonas, Sir Jasper, Mr. Filing, and Cedric, gathered in the library to make a new plan.

"I've sent Dodswell to fetch Thompson and Oscar," Lucifer told them.

"Aha!" Demon said. "So *that's* what you meant by *'au revoir.'*"

Phyllida and Flick and everyone else looked their silent question; Lucifer explained. "Someone approached the Beer smuggling gang to arrange passage to France. It had to be tonight. The Beer gang told the man to meet with Oscar's band, who would normally run a cargo tonight."

Jonas looked out the window. The wind had come up as the sun had gone down; the storm was moving steadily in. "No one will be running anything tonight."

"I know that, you know that, most of us know that. The question is, will Appleby know that?"

"He was born and raised and lived most of his life in Stafford," Demon put in. "Stafford's about as far from the coast as it's possible to get, so chances are he won't immediately recognize the implications of the weather."

"Then he'll go to the meeting place expecting to meet smugglers." Phyllida was sitting beside Lucifer's desk.

"Men who have as much to hide as he does," Lucifer observed. "That's the only sort he'll feel safe approaching. He intended today to be a last and successful effort. He came to the Manor with his plans made, his arrangements in place—he never intended to return to Ballyclose."

Cedric snorted. "The horse he rode here came back a few hours ago. No other horses are missing."

Lucifer glanced at Demon. "With us here, both with strong teams, escaping on horseback would have been risky."

"He's a cautious sort, yet ..." Demon shook his head. "Fancy spending five years searching for something you'd only heard of from someone else's letter. And then it turns out the thing's not even still there to be found."

"He didn't know that. He's obsessed." Phyllida hugged herself. "That's the only explanation. He's mad."

"This picture that Appleby thought was in the book—he said it hadn't surfaced." Sir Jasper glanced at Lucifer. "That seem reasonable to you?"

Lucifer nodded. "The fanfare surrounding the discovery of a lost miniature by an old master would not be easy to miss. He's correct on that. I haven't heard anything."

"But if it's not in the book and hasn't been rediscovered, where is it?"

Lucifer looked at Phyllida. "You remember the item Horatio asked me to appraise—the item that brought me here?"

Phyllida stared. "You think it might be that?"

"It's the sort of thing Horatio would ask my opinion on. I'm familiar with the private collections of old masters held by various members of the aristocracy as well as the Crown. Even more to the point, it's an item he would guard very closely and tell no one else about."

"So where is it?"

"Hidden." Lucifer looked up at the sound of the front-door knocker. "We'll have to turn the house inside out, but first we must deal with Appleby."

Bristleford ushered Thompson and Oscar in, then approached Lucifer. As the others pulled up chairs to join the council, Bristleford murmured, "With your permission, sir, Covey, Hemmings, and I would respectfully ask to be included in any little excursion you might be planning."

Lucifer glanced into Bristleford's earnest face, then nodded. "Yes, of course. In fact, if Mrs. Hemmings can manage out there, perhaps you, Covey, and Hemmings could join us."

"Thank you, sir. I'll fetch Covey and Hemmings."

Bristleford retreated. Phyllida caught Lucifer's eye; she closed her hand over his on the desk. "They haven't yet gotten over the fact that they let someone kill Horatio."

Lucifer nodded, then turned to the others. Briskly, he outlined the situation. Oscar described the area where the smugglers met, the knoll to which the Beer gang had directed the impatient human cargo. They made their plans quickly, then they rose.

"Remember," Sir Jasper warned, "no heroics and no unnecessary violence. I don't want to have to take anyone else up for murder."

"There should be no need for any real action. There's too many of us for him to escape, and other than that knife, he'll be unarmed." Lucifer scanned the men's faces. "We'll meet at the knoll as soon as darkness falls—no one be late."

With the words "Aye" and "We'll be there—" the men departed.

Following them into the hall, Flick caught Phyllida's eye. "I wonder if I could have a word." Linking her arm in Phyllida's, Flick turned to the stairs.

Lucifer and Demon, reaching the library door, saw the loves of their lives, heads together, disappear upstairs.

"That doesn't look good," Demon said.

Lucifer grimaced. "I suppose we'd better face this like men."

His expression hardening, Demon headed for the stairs. "We can but try."

Twenty minutes later, Lucifer and Demon met at the head of the stairs. Their ladies were with them. Lucifer stared at Flick. Demon stared, equally surprised, at Phyllida. Then the cousins looked at each other.

"I won't ask if you don't," Demon offered.

Grim-faced, Lucifer nodded. "Agreed."

Neither Flick nor Phyllida appeared to hear; they led the way down the stairs, stepping easily in breeches and boots.

With Lucifer, Demon followed, his gaze shifting from his beloved's neat rear to Phyllida's shapely thighs. As they descended the last flight, he shook his head. "I'll be damned if any of our forebears ever had to deal with this."

Dodswell and Gillies were waiting, mounted, at the side of the house, both holding a pair of horses saddled—no sidesaddles, Lucifer noted. There was quite a little party gathered in the twilight, none of whom seemed to find anything remarkable in Flick's or Phyllida's attire. As they lifted their respective ladies to their saddles, then mounted alongside them, both Cynsters' hackles subsided—a little.

They set out. Lucifer kept a close eye on Phyllida; she sent him a sidelong glance. After she soared over the first fence and left him pushing to regain his position beside her, he stopped watching her and paid attention to their direction.

Crossing field after field, they headed south to the coast. Phyllida led the way—she was the only one who knew where they were going. The breeze strengthened, the salty tang increasing. A cottage appeared through the gloom, dwarfed by the huge barn behind it. Phyllida turned up the rutted track; she led them to the barn. They'd agreed to leave the horses there so as not to risk alerting Appleby.

The old farmer and his wife greeted Phyllida, clearly old friends. Dodswell returned from tethering their mounts. "Quite a few already in there—looks like Thompson with Sir Jasper and the others."

"Good." Lucifer looked around. "Oscar will walk in with the gang and ponies as usual."

Demon, too, had been scanning the woods. "How do you want to do this?"

"Strung out, single file, slowly. The meeting's not until full dark—we have time to be careful."

They were. With Phyllida in the lead, Lucifer at her shoulder, they walked quietly through the woods, silently skirted two fields, then entered the last stand of stunted trees close by the cliff's edge.

The others were there, waiting. Without words, the party from the Manor spread out, clinging to the deepening shadows under the trees almost encircling the grassy knoll. The land sloped up from the tree line to the cliff's edge and up from either side; beyond the knoll, the cliff fell away.

They settled, crouching in the shadows, the sounds of their shuffling subsumed beneath the relentless pounding of the surf on the rocks far below. The wind was strong, blowing cold in their faces. No ship would dare approach this treacherous coast with such a wind behind it.

An hour later, the storm had taken possession of the skies; darkness had fallen like a shroud across the land. Muscles had stiffened, joints were aching, yet still they waited patiently.

Then the tramp of feet reached them. Minutes later, the night shift of the Colyton Import Company arrived on the scene. They were all there—Oscar, Hugey, Marsh, and the rest. They milled about on the lower slope of the knoll, huddling against the wind.

"How long do we have to wait for this blighter?" Hugey asked for them all.

"He'd better make it soon," Oscar growled. "We got better things to do."

"I'm here," said a voice. "If it's me you're waiting for."

They all turned, peering through the darkness. Lucius Appleby staggered up from a hollow off to the side of the knoll. His clothes were disheveled. He clutched the volume of *Aesop's Fables* to his chest. His hair ruffled wildly in the wind. For a moment he appeared drunk, uncoordinated, then, with a visible effort, he pulled himself together. "About time you got here. I want nothing more than to leave this wretched place."

Every word stung, bitter as gall. He swayed, his gaze fixed on the supposed smugglers. He spared not a glance toward the trees. "Well?" he grumbled, voice rising. "What're we waiting for? Let's go."

He took an unsteady step toward them.

The smugglers, all except Oscar, backed away. They fanned out as they went, eyes never leaving Appleby. Then they joined with those moving forward, out from under the trees.

Appleby's eyes widened. Even in the poor light, the shock on his face as he took in the solid cordon and realized its meaning was evident. *"No!"*

Whirling, he scrambled up the knoll.

"Here!" Oscar remained on the knoll's lower slope. "Don't go near the edge."

Sir Jasper stepped forward. He regarded Appleby sternly. "In my capacity as magistrate, I charge you, Lucius Appleby, with three counts of murder and three of attempted murder, to all of which you stand self-confessed." He waited for a moment, then beckoned. "Come down, man—you can see there's no escape. No sense making it worse."

Book clutched to his chest, Appleby stared at him, then threw back his head and laughed maniacally. *"Make it worse?"* He caught his breath on a gasp and stared at Sir Jasper. "You have no idea.

"You see this?" Appleby thrust out the book, staggering back as he did so. "I killed three men to get my hands on this. Bartered my immortal soul and worse. Five long years I patiently searched, and for what? What do you think my life, my soul, would be worth?"

He wrenched open the front cover, holding it for all to see. The cover paper had been ripped away, the padding, too, exposing the blank board of the inner face. "Nothing." Appleby's voice dropped to a sobbing whisper, then abruptly rose to a shriek. *"There's nothing there!"* He yelled it to the skies. "Some bastard got there before me!"

Eyes wild, he flung the book at Sir Jasper, then whirled and raced onto the knoll.

"No! Don't—!" Oscar scrabbled up the slope. Thompson moved up behind his brother; Lucifer and Demon stepped forward.

Lips drawn back, Appleby turned on them. "Come and get me, then." He brandished his knife. "Who'll be first?"

He staggered wildly as he backed, grotesquely outlined against the roiling sky.

Thompson reached forward and locked a huge hand on Oscar's shoulder. "You don't understand—"

"It's *you* who don't understand. I'm not going to pay—not when there's *nothing there.*" Appleby laughed wildly. "I've already paid with the last five years of my life."

"You took the lives of three others." Lucifer pitched his voice over the rising wind.

"They got in my way!" Appleby yelled. He edged back, eyes darting this way, then that. "If they hadn't, they'd still be alive—it was *their fault.*"

The last word was swallowed by a thunderous, murmurous *shusssh.*

Everyone froze.

Then Thompson pulled Oscar back. In the trees, Phyllida clutched Flick's arm. "Oh, no."

Appleby didn't understand. He stood on the cliff's edge, staring wildly from one shocked face to the next.

"What?" he asked. *"Wha—"*

The ground beneath him disappeared; one instant he was there, then he was gone.

Lightning flashed, but it was tons of earth hitting rocks, crashing into the sea, that provided the thunder. The wind gusted hard, forcing them to hide their faces until the buffeting eased.

They looked up the slope. The new cliff edge cut through the middle of the knoll's top.

Both Lucifer and Demon turned and walked back into the trees. Phyllida went wordlessly into Lucifer's arms, hugging him tight, inexpressibly thankful for his warmth, for the solidity of the arms that locked about her, for the feel of his jaw against her hair. "Will he be dead?" she finally whispered.

"That cliff's at least six hundred feet high. I don't think there's any alternative."

Others wanted to be certain. They started off through the trees, Sir Jasper and Oscar bringing up the rear.

"The cliff path Oscar's band uses is safe," Phyllida explained. Together with Flick and Demon, she and Lucifer trailed the band. They reached the windswept outcrop where the path started. Most of the group were strung out below, heading down.

A series of lightning flashes out over the Channel provided sudden illumination. Everyone stopped and searched. Then there were shouts of "There!" Arms pointed.

From within the protection of Lucifer's arms, Phyllida looked down. The body of Lucius Appleby lay spread-eagled, facedown on the black water. There was no sign of movement, of life. Distance hid the damage undoubtedly inflicted by the rocks and the waves. As they watched, the body lifted on the swell, then whirled and was drawn out, toward the dark sea.

The light faded. Night closed in, blacker than before.

Lucifer's arms tightened around her. He bent his head and pressed a kiss to her temple. "It's over," he murmured. "Come, let's go home."

To her surprise, he took her back to the Grange. Demon and Flick didn't come in; at Lucifer's request, they took his and Phyllida's horses with them when they rode on to the Manor.

Everyone gathered in the drawing room. Phyllida, still in breeches, organized drinks and sustenance to chase away the lingering chills, both of the elements and of the evil that had been Lucius Appleby.

There were many exclamations and much shaking of heads, but a sense of ending, of relief, of rightness, prevailed. The threat that had disturbed the peace of Colyton was gone.

In the instant Phyllida fully realized that truth, she sought Lucifer's eye and smiled; she was no longer surprised they were here. At last she had her peaceful life back—the serenity and security of the village were restored. She was safe again. The only thing they'd lost was Horatio. And in his place, they had Lucifer.

Her eyes followed him as he moved through the room, exchanging words— the right words, she was sure—with Oscar, Thompson, and the other men. Life turned, changed, and moved on. Fate sometimes moved in mysterious ways.

Gradually, the crowd departed, at peace again. By tomorrow morning, the tidings would be spread throughout the village, the great houses, the farms and cottages.

Phyllida stopped beside Lucifer. Gazing out at the darkness of the back lawn, he drained his glass, then looked down at her. His gaze roved her face, then returned to her eyes. "There's a question I've been wanting to ask you, but it can wait until tomorrow." He hesitated, then handed her his glass. "I'll call in the morning."

Phyllida opened her eyes wide. "Does that mean you're going to leave me to walk back through the wood alone in the dark?" When he frowned at her, she smiled and patted his arm. "I'm coming home—to the Manor."

He blinked, then cast a glance at Sir Jasper, shaking hands with Cedric, the last of the others to leave. "Much as I might wish that—"

"It's got nothing to do with your wishes," she informed him. "You forget— all my things are there."

"All?"

"When you told Sweetie to pack my things, she did—all of them. She's an incurable romantic, so, for better or for worse, I'm afraid *all* my things are at the Manor."

Lucifer looked down at her, his dark eyes very blue. Then he brushed a thumb over her lower lip. "For better or for worse?"

Phyllida smiled; she pushed him toward the French doors. "Wait for me on the terrace—I must speak with Papa."

Lucifer glanced back at Sir Jasper, but Phyllida shook her head and pushed, so he went. She watched as he stepped over the threshold, drank in the broad shoulders, the strength cloaked in that effortless grace, then she smiled serenely and returned to her father.

Sir Jasper met her in the middle of the room. He took her hands in his. "Well, m'dear—a great relief, having this settled. Can't say I'm sorry Appleby's gone—a bad egg he was, no doubt of that."

"Indeed, Papa."

"Well, then." Sir Jasper stole a glance at Lucifer, waiting on the terrace looking out at the night. "I suppose, now there's no more danger, you'll be moving back, heh?"

His tone was neither insistent nor expectant; it was curious. He peered at her from under his shaggy brows, a light very like hope in his eyes.

"No, Papa." Smiling, Phyllida stretched up and placed a kiss on his cheek. "My place now is elsewhere."

"Oh?" Sir Jasper brightened; he all but grinned and rubbed his hands in delight. "Right, then—well, I daresay I'll see you tomorrow …?"

Phyllida chuckled and patted his arm. "I daresay. And now I'll bid you a good night."

Leaving her father, she walked to the French doors. Stepping outside, she slid a hand into Lucifer's arm. Just as he had been doing, she looked up at the sky, at the racing clouds streaming, fleeing before the thunderheads.

Lucifer glanced back, then she felt his gaze on her face. After a moment, she met his eyes. In the poor light, she couldn't see their expression, but possessiveness, protectiveness, fell about her like a cloak.

He closed his hand over hers. "Let's go home."

She let him lead her there, through the wood, now a-flurry with the storm. As the wind rose and the branches lashed more furiously, they walked faster and faster; eventually, he pulled her along at a run. She was laughing when he dragged her from the trees, down the drive, and around the house. She imagined he was heading for the front door, but once they gained the front of the house, she realized that wasn't his goal.

He tugged her across Horatio's garden—it was screened from the wind by the wood, the house, the village, and its own stand of trees. In the dark of the humid night, it was a paradise of evocative scents, of lush growth and mysterious shapes. Lucifer hurried her to the honeysuckle-draped, peony-backed arbor where they'd once before paused of an evening and discussed the realities of love.

Halting, he faced her. His dark hair was tousled, as if she'd already run her fingers through it; his face was hard-edged, his mobile lips straight. He studied her as she was studying him, then, her hands in his, he went down on one knee.

"Phyllida Tallent, will you marry me? Will you help me tend this garden over all the years to come?"

He'd pitched his voice above the roar of the wind, above the wild threshing of the leaves.

Phyllida looked down, into his face. He'd spun her world around, then steadied it; he'd taught her so much, answered so many questions. She had only one left. "This garden needs constant love to keep it blooming. Do you love me that much?"

He held her gaze. "More." He kissed the backs of her hands, first one, then the other. "I'll love you forever."

Phyllida pulled him to his feet. "Just as well, for I'll love you for even longer." She went into his arms, forever safe where she belonged. "I'll love you for longer than forever."

His arms closed around her. Their lips met, melded; their bodies eased against each other, seeking remembered delights.

Lucifer broke the kiss to ask, "When can we marry?"

Phyllida drew back. "It's Saturday. If we speak to Mr. Filing tonight, he could read the banns tomorrow. Then we could marry in just over two weeks."

They looked up the common at the Rectory. The small house lay in darkness. "I really don't think," Lucifer said, "that Filing will mind being woken—not for this."

He didn't; the curate was delighted when he heard their reason for hauling him from his bed. He assured them that the banns would be called in the morning. Declining his offer of a celebratory sherry on the grounds of the imminent downpour, they left the Rectory and raced down the common— anticipating a celebration of a different sort.

They reached the duck pond and the skies opened. They were soaked, dripping and bedraggled by the time they reached the Manor's front porch. The smell of rain-washed greenery and the ever-present perfume of the garden—their garden now—swept over them as they stood catching their breath while Lucifer hunted for his key.

He unlocked the door and swung it wide. Phyllida entered; Lucifer followed and reset the lock. Turning, he saw Phyllida standing just outside the open drawing room. He joined her as she stepped into the doorway. Slipping an arm around her waist, he held her back against him.

Phyllida crossed her arms over his and leaned back to whisper, "It's peaceful here now—can you sense it?"

He could. He rubbed his chin over the wet silk of her hair. "Horatio's gone to talk to Martha about her pansies."

Phyllida turned her head and smiled. Sliding around in his arms, she touched his cheek. "You're the most fanciful man."

He kissed her, then murmured, "I know what I fancy at the moment."

So did she. Her sigh was just a little skittery, just a touch breathless. "We'd better get upstairs."

"If you insist."

Phyllida led the way with him padding at her heels like some obedient jungle cat. She detoured via the linen press to fetch two large towels, then led him, not to her room, but to his. He made no demur but went past her to light the lamp that sat atop one tallboy.

It was pouring outside. Lightning still flickered and thunder rolled, but the storm front had already swept past. Rubbing her hair with the towel, Phyllida pushed the door shut, then turned—just as Lucifer adjusted the wick so the lamp shed a golden glow through the room.

"Great heavens!" She stared. "That's *it!*"

She walked toward Lucifer, her gaze fixed beyond him. He glanced around to see what had so excited her. "It, what?" Then the penny dropped and he stared, too.

"Don't tell me it's always been here." Phyllida reached up to lift the traveling writing desk from its perch on the corner of the tallboy.

"All right, I won't tell you," Lucifer replied. "But you didn't say *traveling* writing desk—I've been looking for something with four legs."

With the polished wooden box in her hands, Phyllida turned. "I *must* have said …" She caught his eye and grimaced. "Well, maybe I didn't. But I *meant* a traveling writing desk—*I* knew what I was looking for."

"Anyway, I thought you'd searched the whole house."

"I didn't search in here. I didn't imagine you'd miss a traveling writing desk if it was sitting in your room. The only other time I've been in here was at night in the dark."

"I didn't miss it—I knew it was there. It just never occurred to me that *that's* the sort of desk you meant." He studied the box. "Where's this secret drawer? It doesn't look big enough to have one."

"That's why it's such a good hiding place." Phyllida sat on the bed and placed the desk on her thighs; Lucifer sat beside her. "It's here—see?" Running her fingers along one of the back side panels, she found the catch and pressed it. The panel swung outward. Sliding her fingers in, she felt around, then gripped and pulled a sheaf of papers into the light.

She stared at them. "Good Lord!" She dropped the bundle between them on the bedspread.

They both sat, transfixed, not by the bundle of letters predictably tied with a pink ribbon, but by the small rolled canvas that had been tucked in with them.

It had unrolled just a little. Just enough to show the deep browns and rich reds of oils, and part of a hand.

Lucifer recovered first. "Careful—we're both dripping."

Phyllida wriggled off the bed. Lucifer stood and grabbed the second towel. While he rubbed at his hair and mopped his face, Phyllida shut the secret drawer and put the writing desk back on the tallboy. Returning to the bed, she swiped up her towel and dried her hands and reblotted her face, then twisted her hair up in the towel. Then she gingerly picked up Mary Anne's and Robert's letters and deposited them beside the writing desk. "Don't want to get them wet and have the ink run, not after all this."

Lucifer humphed. He joined her as she went back to the bed.

Phyllida eyed the rolled painting, then gestured. "You do it."

Lucifer picked up the canvas; touching only the unpainted edges, he unrolled it.

Even in the lamplight, the jeweled tones glowed. A woman—a lady by the richness of her dress—sat smiling at the painter. Her gown of wine-dark velvet had a square, heavily embroidered neckline; her headdress was a form of wimple, artfully folded. Her forehead was high, plucked, as had been the fashion centuries before.

Phyllida drew in a breath. "This is what was in *Aesop's Fables*, isn't it? This is the item Horatio invited you down here to appraise. The miniature—the old masterpiece—that Appleby killed three men for."

Lucifer nodded. "I wouldn't be surprised if he wasn't the first to have killed for this lady."

Phyllida looked from the miniature to his face, then back again. "It's genuine?"

"It's too perfect not to be. Too much like his other works."

"Whose work? Who painted it?"

"Holbein the Younger, court-portraitist for Henry the Eighth."

They spent the next hour talking, speculating, deciding that the miniature belonged in a museum. That resolved, Lucifer returned the painting to the secret drawer, then fetched the lamp and placed it on the table beside the bed.

He'd pulled off his wet boots and stripped off his coat and shirt long before; Phyllida was still in her damp shirt and breeches. She regarded him speculatively, fascinated by the way the flickering lamplight played over the muscles of his chest. She let her gaze drift downward, to where the wet fabric of his breeches molded lovingly to his form, then languidly brought her gaze back to his face—to his eyes, smoldering blue.

She raised a haughty brow.

He smiled. Intently. His fingers closed on the buttons on his waistband. He held her gaze as if daring her to watch as he peeled the wet breeches from him. Phyllida raised her brow higher—and did. His breeches hit the floor with a splat. He came onto the bed in a prowling crawl. With an ease that still shocked her—tantalized her and left her breath stuck in her throat—he picked her up and rearranged her so she was kneeling, sitting back on her ankles, her back to him as he knelt behind her, his naked thighs outside hers. She was facing the end of the four-poster bed. With the curtains tied back, she looked out at her reflection in the long, wide mirror hanging on the opposite wall.

The sight was mesmerizing. His shoulders showed above and beyond hers; she looked fragile and vulnerable all but surrounded by him. Female and male, one dressed, one naked; the contrasts were dramatic. His hands looked very large clamped about her waist. He checked the vision he was creating, then glanced down. Phyllida watched as his hands rose and his fingers busied themselves with the buttons of her shirt. At least, this time she wouldn't have to sew them back on.

"I'm going to strip these wet clothes from you, then I'm going to dry you, then warm you up—we wouldn't want you to catch a chill."

Phyllida had no wish to argue. She leaned her turbaned head back on his shoulder and, watching from under half closed lids, let him get on with it.

Let him peel the wet shirt from her, then unwind her sodden bands. Watched him grab a towel and apply it to her breasts in a slow, circular motion. When her breasts were not only dry but swollen and warm, peaked and firm, he dropped the towel and started on her breeches. Removing them required a little more cooperation; giggling at the curses and inventive suggestions he murmured between laying kisses along the back of her bare shoulders and licking errant drops from her skin, she helped him ease the cold, clinging fabric from her hips and down her thighs.

Without warning, he lifted her, whisking the wet garment over her knees and calves; it went flying to join the pile on the floor. He picked up the towel as he set her down before him, still on her knees, still facing the mirror. Fragile, vulnerable, and naked, surrounded by his strength.

He wielded the towel to telling effect, using the lightly abrasive pile to tease and tantalize until all of her body was flushed and heated, until every inch of her skin was sensitized and aching, until she was awash with a wanton desire that only he could slake.

Then he dropped the towel.

She was dry. He set his clever fingers, strong hands, wicked lips, and even wickeder tongue to the task of warming her up. Until she was gasping, heated to the point where her skin felt afire and molten need had spread through every vein. Through her lashes she saw her body flushed with desire, a glow unlike any other. She needed him, wanted him—she arched in his arms, sank her fingers into his thighs, and dropped her head back to his shoulder.

He shifted her, urging her on, molding her as he wished, showing her how to be as wanton as she dared.

Then he joined with her. So easily, so perfectly, so completely. He closed his arms around her and rocked her, rocked into her; she closed her eyes and savored the feel of him buried so deep within her.

He was as hot as the sun, burning up all around her, muscles flexing like hot steel all about her. He showed her what could be, then let her choose, let her turn and clasp her long legs about his hips and take him deep, let her wrap her arms about him and find his lips with hers, let her take him with her into oblivion.

Together. Forever.

They were married on a Monday, the day after Mr. Filing read the banns for the third time. Mr. Filing officiated before a church packed to the rafters. Everyone from the village, everyone from the surrounding farms and houses, was there, as were numerous Cynsters who had moved heaven and earth to be present.

Gabriel stood beside his brother and happily handed him the ring. Flick and Mary Anne were bridesmaids. Demon was the second groomsman.

In the body of the church sat Gabriel's wife, Alathea, smiling fondly, and Celia Cynster, Lucifer's mother, who cried happily throughout the short service. Beside her, Martin, Lucifer's father, looked smugly satisfied as he handed clean handkerchiefs to his spouse. Lucifer's three sisters, Heather, Eliza, and Angelica, all beamed.

Then it was done, and the last member of the Bar Cynster was wed.

Lucifer bent to kiss Phyllida; the sun broke from the wispy clouds to pour through the oriel window, enclosing the bride and groom in a nimbus of jeweled light. Then they smiled and turned, man and wife, to greet their family and friends.

At the bride and groom's insistence, the wedding breakfast was held at the Manor. The guests spread through the house, spilled onto the lawns, and strolled the wonderful garden. Standing at one side of the lawn with his father, Gabriel, and Demon, Lucifer watched as Celia all but paraded her new daughter-in-law, her delight in her second son's choice plain to see. Phyllida had, to the last, remained nervous of her reception into the ducal dynasty; it had taken Celia only three minutes to lay such trepidations to rest. In doing so, she'd earned her second son's enduring gratitude, but that wasn't something he intended to tell her. As a Cynster wife, Celia had weapons enough.

Beside him, Martin chuckled, the sound fond but wary. Lucifer, Demon, and Gabriel glanced at him, then followed his gaze to where Celia and Phyllida had met up with Alathea and Flick. They had their heads together.

Lucifer straightened. Demon sighed. Gabriel shook his head. It was left to Martin to put their thoughts into words. "Why we bother fighting it, the Lord only knows. Inevitability, thy name is woman."

Lucifer's lips lifted. "Actually, for us, I believe that should go: Inevitability, thy name is *wife*."

"Too true," Gabriel murmured.

"Indeed." Demon watched as their four ladies broke from their huddle and headed their way. "What now?"

"Whatever it is, we can't escape," Martin replied. "Take my advice— surrender with good grace." He strolled forward to intercept Celia.

Gabriel grimaced. "I wish he hadn't used that word."

" 'Surrender'?" Demon asked.

"Hmm. It might be the truth, but I don't want to hear it." So saying, Gabriel gracefully deflected Alathea, turning her toward the shrubbery.

"There's a secluded little folly down by the lake," Lucifer murmured to Demon.

"Where are you headed?" Demon murmured back.

"There's this arbor in the garden I'm working on filling with pleasant memories."

Demon grinned. "Good luck."

Lucifer saluted as they parted, each to his own special lady. "Good luck to us all."

And with that, the Bar Cynster surrendered gladly, each to his own, very special, fate.

Epilogue

August 1820 Somersham,
Cambridgeshire

It was nearly two years to the day that she'd first sighted this house, first strolled the wide lawns. Honoria, Duchess of St. Ives, stood on the front porch of her home, Somersham Place, and looked about her, marveling at the changes, and at how much, despite all, remained the same.

The side lawn was filled with family and connections, the froth of summer gowns scattered like confetti over the green. Many had taken advantage of the shade offered by the ancient trees to lounge at ease; others strolled, stopping by the various groups to chat, to learn the latest news, and, most of all, to greet the new family members.

There were many of those. That fact infused the gathering with an untempered joy, an effervescent sense of burgeoning life that was tangible.

Two years ago, many of those present had gathered here to mourn. Although Tolly, and even Charles, had not been forgotten, the family, like all great families, had moved on. They'd prospered, they'd conquered—now they were enjoying the fruits of their labors.

Cradling one such apple in one arm, Honoria raised her skirts and descended to the lawn. Before she'd taken three steps, her husband detached himself from one group and strode, fiendishly handsome and arrogantly confident as ever, to join her.

"How is he?" Devil bent his dark head to peek at his second son.

Michael blinked, yawned, then grabbed his sire's finger.

"He's fed and dry and therefore content. And I believe it's your turn to play nursemaid." Honoria divested herself of the shawl-wrapped bundle. Devil accepted the charge with alacrity. Honoria hid her grin; she knew he'd been waiting to play the proud father. It never ceased to amaze her that he—indeed, all the males of his family—while so strong and powerful and so arrogantly assured, so totally dominant, could and would, at the wave of a tiny hand, readily devote himself so completely to his offspring.

"Where's Sebastian?" She scanned the lawns for sign of their firstborn. He'd recently started to walk; running could not be far behind.

"He's with the twins." Devil lifted his head and located the girls. "They're on the steps of the summerhouse."

There was a frown in his eyes; Honoria knew it wasn't because he doubted the twins' ability to watch over Sebastian. She patted his arm; when he transfered his pale green gaze to her face, she smiled up at him. "Consider this. Better they dream of having children of their own, therefore accepting all the steps that come before, than that they don't."

It took him a moment to follow her reasoning, then his eyes hardened. "I'd rather they didn't think about any of that at all."

"You've as much chance of achieving that as of holding back the sun." She squeezed his arm, then waved imperiously toward the guests. "Now go and play host and show off our son, while I go and admire the others."

Majestically established in a wrought-iron seat placed at the center of the lawn, the Dowager and Horatia held court. Between them, they lovingly juggled three tiny, shawl-wrapped bundles, exclaiming fondly, displaying their grandchildren for the edification of the surrounding crowd that, for the past thirty minutes, had constantly changed but not diminished in the least.

In a lounger to one side of the seat, Catriona, Lady of the Vale, lay resting, still pale, her hair a fiery halo around her head. The glow in her face as she watched Helena cradle her babies rendered her nothing less than radiant. She looked precisely what she was, a madonna who'd been blessed.

Richard stood beside the lounger, his fingers entwined with hers. His gaze constantly switched from his wife to his children and back again. The expression in his dark eyes, on his lean, harsh-featured face, spoke louder than words of his pride and his joy.

Twins—one boy, one girl. If Catriona had guessed, she hadn't said a word, knowing how important it had been for Richard to travel south for this summer gathering of his clan. But twins rarely obeyed the typical schedules; they'd arrived a month early, small but hale and whole. So the next Lady of the Vale, Lucilla, had been the first ever born outside that mystical Scottish valley. She'd been born here, at Somersham Place, the ancestral home of her Sassenach forebears. Catriona had accepted that without a blink—she'd merely smiled and reminded Richard that the Lady knew what she was about.

And to keep him busy, there was Marcus—a son to train in all the complex management of the Vale lands and the people they supported. That was no longer a job that could be done by just one, so now they had two.

While much attention centered on the twins' red heads, there was just as much lavished on the fair-haired bundle Horatia rocked and jiggled. Christopher Reginald Cynster, Patience and Vane's son, had been born four weeks before, two weeks after Michael had made his orderly appearance. Thus, in common with Michael, Christopher was now an old hand at family gatherings; he yawned hugely, then batted aside his blankets, trying to latch onto a trailing lock of his grandmother's hair.

Everyone watching cooed and smiled delightedly; Christopher took it as nothing more than his due.

Noting his detachment, Lady Osbaldestone snorted. "A Cynster to his toes—already! Always knew it was inherited. Looks to have passed on undiluted." She shook her head, then paused, then she cackled as she turned away. "Heaven help the ladies of 1850."

Honoria checked that Helena and Horatia weren't tiring, exchanged a soft word and an understanding smile with Catriona, pressed Richard's hand, then moved on, looking over the throng, checking all was as it should be.

Having been delivered four weeks before, Patience was fully recovered, up and about. However, since it was his first time, Vane had yet to reconcile himself to allowing his wife out of his sight, indeed, very far from the protective circle of his arm. Honoria found them chatting with the General, Flick's erstwhile guardian, and his son, Dillon; they'd driven across for the day from Newmarket. In that circle, horses reigned supreme. Honoria exchanged speaking glances with Patience, then strolled on.

Flick and Demon were standing with a group surrounding Great-aunt Clara and little Miss Sweet, whom Lucifer and Phyllida had brought with them from Devon. Clara had already asked Miss Sweet to visit her in Cheshire; arrangements were being discussed and plans made.

Elsewhere, Gabriel and Alathea, and Lucifer and Phyllida, like Flick and Demon, were making the rounds, ensuring they met and spoke with all the relatives, all the connections and close acquaintances, who had eagerly traveled to Cambridgeshire for the express purpose of meeting the new wives, and welcoming them and the latest crop of infants into the wider family.

Satisfied that all was well, Honoria spent a few minutes quietly slipping through the shade, noting, as a matriarch should, just where and with whom, and in what manner, the younger members of the family were employed.

Simon was there, growing taller by the hour, or so it seemed. His fair hair shone guinea-gold in the sun, as bright as Flick's. His face was finer boned than those of his older cousins, not as overtly aggressive. But the same strength was there, behind a countenance that was so like an angel's that it would undoubtedly, in time, make women weep. He was not of the Bar Cynster, but he was a Cynster nonetheless—the one who would bridge the gap between Honoria's sons' generation and their fathers'.

In the same group, spread upon the grass like so many tulips, so many blossoms just waiting to fully flower, were Heather, Eliza, Angelica, Henrietta, and Mary. Some younger, some older, but all with the same eagerness for life, an enthusiasm for living, in their faces.

Honoria smiled and strolled on. She turned her steps toward the summerhouse.

The twins greeted her with joy in their faces; the cause of their happiness was not far to seek.

"We're free!" Amanda flung her arms wide, just missing Sebastian as he clambered into Honoria's lap as she sat on the steps in the sun.

Settling him, Honoria leaned back against the archway and smiled at the girls. "True, but now Lucifer's fixed in Devon, and between you and me, I can't see either him or Gabriel or even Demon back in town next Season—I rather think they'll have other things on their minds, if you take my meaning—then what, my dears, are your plans?"

"We're going to go through the ton's gentlemen," Amelia answered.

"Systematically and methodically," Amanda qualified.

"We're not going to rush, and we're not going to be rushed."

"We'll be nineteen next Season, so we have years yet, if we chose to be picky."

"And there's no reason we shouldn't be—picky, I mean. After all, we are talking about the rest of our lives."

"Indeed." Honoria inclined her head in approval. There was so much she wanted to tell them, to warn them of, to guide them, but how could she explain when, for all that they had had two Seasons, they were still so inexperienced, so unaware? "One thing," she said, and knew she had their complete attention. "If you seek love, don't expect it to be simple, don't expect it to be easy. If one thing is certain, it's that it'll be neither.

"If you want love, then by all means seek it out—search for it high and low. You know you'll always have us—all of us—here to help you, but when it comes down to it, love is a matter for each individual heart. No one can tell you, no one can warn you, no one can prepare you for what it will be like. When it comes, if it comes, you'll know it—and then you'll have to decide just how much you want it, how much you're willing to give to let it live."

They heard her in silence; in silence, they digested her wisdom. Honoria looked across the lawn to where her disgustingly handsome husband, he who now stood at the very center of her life, cradled their younger son. Their elder son lay, a warm, heavy weight in her lap.

"Is it worth it?"

She couldn't be sure which of them had voiced the question—Amanda or Amelia; it didn't matter. The answer was the same, now and forever.

"Yes. Many times over, it's worth it, but only if you have the courage to give, and let it live."

After a moment, Honoria stirred. Gathering sleepy Sebastian in her arms, she hefted him and stood, then strolled across the lawn to where she belonged, at his sire's side.

Devil had been watching her; one part of his mind and most of his soul was always with her. Who could have known? Who would have guessed? Not even the joys of twitting his archenemy, not an enemy at all but they so enjoyed butting horns, was enough to interfere with that ephemeral connection between himself and his wife.

"Just whose idea was it," Chillingworth asked, "to elect me an honorary Cynster?"

At the accusatory tone, Devil turned a mild smile his way. "Gabriel suggested it, and as you've been so remarkably helpful in assisting us in securing our futures, I seconded the motion, as did Demon, and the others were happy to support it. That's all it took. You are now, by election, a member of the clan."

Chillingworth met his gaze. "In *ceremonial* name only."

Devil grinned. "That will do."

"It won't. I can assure you with absolutely no risk of contradiction that *electing* me to the clan will not make me susceptible to your particular curse." After a moment of consideration, Chillingworth snorted. "Anyway, what sort of thanks is that to bestow, even on your worst enemy?"

"In your case, it's the most useful of all—consider it as giving you a secret map to some treasure. Follow the instructions and you, too, could be rich. Take it from us—we did, and see where it's got us."

What Chillingworth said in reply made Devil's lips twitch. "Anyway," he returned, "you can't escape, so why not take the bull by the horns and make a virtue of necessity? You do, after all, need an heir, or that vacuous cousin of yours from Hampstead will inherit the title. Have I got that right?"

"You have, damn you—don't remind me. My mother's actually started holding you up as a pattern card of virtue. I'm tempted to invite you and Honoria to the Castle simply so experience can set her straight."

"Do invite us down," Devil murmured. "We'll bring the family."

"That's precisely why I haven't—I'm not that daft." Chillingworth nodded at Michael, asleep in Devil's arm. "Deposit that in my mother's lap and my life will be hell."

"You're going to need one someday."

"Ah, but I'm altogether adamant on the price I'm willing to pay." Chillingworth watched as Honoria, Devil's heir asleep on her shoulder, stepped away from a group of guests and continued on her way toward them. One glance at Devil's face and Chillingworth shook his head. "A simple marriage will achieve the necessary result. I see absolutely no reason to indulge in the extremes you Cynsters seem to find so unavoidable."

Devil chuckled. "I'm going to seriously enjoy dancing at your wedding."

"The pertinent question is"—Chillingworth lowered his voice as Honoria neared—"will I?" He smiled and sketched a bow to Honoria. "If you'll excuse me, my dear, I must get back to London tonight. I'll leave your husband to your tender mercies."

He nodded at Devil, a smug glint in his eye.

Devil grinned back, unrepentant, undeterred.

"What was that about?" Honoria asked as Chillingworth strolled off.

"Vain hope." Devil watched his old friend stride away, then he looked at his wife. He jiggled the sleeping baby. "He's getting heavy. And Sebastian's sound asleep. Perhaps we should take them up to the nursery."

Honoria was too busy checking Sebastian's sleeping face to notice the unreliable gleam that had appeared in her husband's green eyes. "I'll find their nannies and have them take them up."

"Let the nannies enjoy the last of the afternoon. We can take them up. There's plenty of people indoors to keep an ear open for them."

"Well ..." The motherly need to tuck her darlings in herself warred with Honoria's hostessly instincts. "All right. We'll take them up, and I'll send the nannies up when we come down."

They strolled into the house and up the stairs, the sleeping children their obvious excuse. No one thought anything of their departure.

No one noticed when they didn't immediately reappear.

Indeed, only those with sharp eyes and suspicious minds noticed that when the duke and duchess eventually rejoined their guests, the duchess's ivory skin was delicately flushed and her eyes held the dreamy look of a woman well loved, and that a certain male pride—a wholly Cynster expression—glowed in her husband's green eyes.

Times may change; Cynsters never do.

NEW YORK TIMES BESTSELLING AUTHOR

STEPHANIE LAURENS

On a Stormy Night

TWO CLASSIC CYNSTER NOVELS

'Regency romance plus!' *Woman's Day*

AUSTRALIA'S PREMIER
Historical Romance
★ AUTHOR ★

On A Stormy Night

Two classic Cynster novels

Devil's Bride

STEPHANIE LAURENS

When Devil, the most infamous member of the Cynster family, is caught in a compromising position with plucky governess Honoria Wetherby, he astonishes the entire town by offering her his hand in marriage. As society's mamas swoon at the loss of England's most eligible bachelor, Devil's infamous Cynster cousins begin to place wagers on the wedding date.

But Honoria isn't about to bend to society's demands and marry a man just because they've been found together unchaperoned. She craves adventure. But could her passion for Devil cause her to embrace the enchanting peril of a lifelong adventure of the heart?

A Rake's Vow

STEPHANIE LAURENS

He vowed he'd never marry ...

To Vane Cynster, Bellamy Hall seems like the perfect place to temporarily hide from London's husband hunters. But when he encounters irresistible Patience Debbington, Vane realises he's met his match.

She vowed no man would catch her ...

Patience isn't about to succumb to Vane's sensuous propositions. Yes, his kisses leave her dizzy and his caresses make her melt; but Patience has promised herself she'll never become vulnerable to a broken heart.

Is this one vow that was meant to be broken?

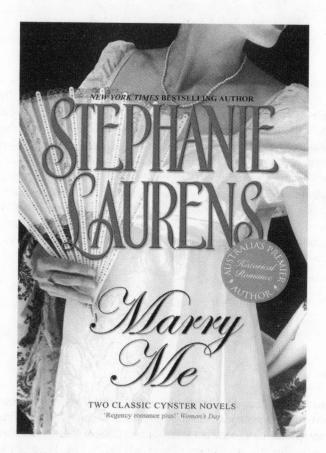

NEW YORK TIMES BESTSELLING AUTHOR

STEPHANIE LAURENS

Marry Me

TWO CLASSIC CYNSTER NOVELS

'Regency romance plus!' *Woman's Day*

Marry Me

'Get ready to have your heart stolen by another Cynster'
Romantic Times

Scandal's Bride

STEPHANIE LAURENS

Catriona Hennessy, honourable Lady of the Vale, has dreamt of a man with piercing blue eyes who is destined to father her children. She is appalled when she discovers he is Richard Cynster, a masterful rake with a scandalous reputation. More shocking still is her guardian's will that decrees she and Richard must wed within a week! Though charmed by his commanding presence, and wooed by his heated kisses, she will not — can not — give up her independence.

Richard is just as stunned by the will's command. Marriage had not previously been on his agenda, but lately he'd been feeling rather … restless. Perhaps taming the lady is just the challenge he needs. But can he have the rights of the marriage bed without making any revealing promises of love?

A Rogue's Proposal

STEPHANIE LAURENS

Demon Cynster has seen love bring other men to their knees, and he's vowed that he will not share their fate … until he spies Felicity Parteger sneaking about his racing stable. Demon remembers Felicity as a mere slip of a girl, but now she stands before him, begging for his help — all lush curves and sparkling eyes.

Felicity knows Demon is one of the ton's most eligible bachelors and a rogue of the worst sort, but he is the only person to whom she can turn. While she realises the power lurking just beneath his devil-may-care facade and the desire that flares when he takes her in his arms, Felicity believes Demon will never give her the love she desperately seeks. But can a marriage of passion alone — even with a man like Demon — be enough?

NEW YORK TIMES BESTSELLING AUTHOR

STEPHANIE LAURENS

To Distraction

A BASTION CLUB NOVEL

To Distraction

STEPHANIE LAURENS

The fifth bachelor of the Bastion Club has proved his courage while fighting England's enemies, but nothing has prepared him for that most formidable of challenges: the opposite sex.

Deverell, Viscount Paignton, is in desperate need of a wife. Unmoved by the matchmaking herd, he seeks help from his eccentric aunt Audrey. She directs him to her goddaughter, Miss Phoebe Malleson — and attraction instantly sparks between them.

But Phoebe has turned her back deliberately on matrimony, to pursue a secret crusade to save young girls from danger. Which means Deverell has to embark on a campaign to change one very stubborn lady's mind. Meanwhile, a powerful figure has targeted Phoebe's cause for destruction — and has Phoebe in their sights. Phoebe must accept Deverell's help, though the cost to them both might be dear … or even deadly.

'plenty of heat and loads of suspense … no one will be disappointed with such a witty foray into love and sensuality'
Romantic Times

'[Stephanie Laurens'] heroines are marvellous … feisty and strong'
Cathy Kelly, bestselling author of *Past Secrets*

AVON

ROMANCE CLUB

Become a member today ♥ Enjoy the benefits

♥ What is the Avon Romance Club?

The Avon Romance Club is a club designed for anyone who loves to read quality romance. Membership is FREE and it entitles you to a range of exclusive offers, benefits and prizes.

♥ Why should I join?

- Avon Loyalty program
- Quarterly newsletter
- Giveaways, competitions, sneak previews & reviews

♥ How do I become a member?

It's easy and it's free. Simply complete the details below, detach stub and post to:

The Avon Romance Club
HarperCollins*Publishers*
25 Ryde Road, Pymble
NSW 2073
or register online at www.harpercollins.com.au/avon

Join today and you will receive a free copy of a bestselling Avon title as our gift to you!

Please return completed portion to: Avon Romance Club, HarperCollins*Publishers*
25 Ryde Road, Pymble NSW 2073

Name: _____

Address: _____

State: _____ Postcode: _____

Phone No: _____

Email: _____

Sex: Female ☐   Male ☐   Age: _____ (optional)

How many romance novels do you purchase each month? _____ (optional)